The

House on

Salt Hay Road

The

House on

Salt Hay Road

CARIN CLEVIDENCE

Farrar, Straus and Giroux   New York

Farrar, Straus and Giroux
18 West 18th Street, New York 10011

Distributed in Canada by D&M Publishers, Inc.
Printed in the United States of America
First edition, 2010

Library of Congress Cataloging-in-Publication Data
Clevidence, Carin, 1967–
    The house on Salt Hay Road / Carin Clevidence. — 1st ed.
      p. cm.
    ISBN 978-0-374-17314-2 (alk. paper)
    1. Long Island (N.Y.)—History—20th century—Fiction.   2. Domestic fiction.
I. Title.
    PS3603.L497H68 2010
    813'.6—dc22

                                              2009043087

Designed by Abby Kagan

www.fsgbooks.com

10 9 8 7 6 5 4 3 2 1

For Jemma and Clement

Contents

PART ONE

A Floating House

The sound was the loudest Clayton Poole had ever heard, the noise he imagined a bomb would make if the Huns attacked Long Island. Twelve years old, a sturdy boy with freckles and a blunt boxer's jaw, he'd been sketching a line of sandpipers on the bottom margin of his Elson Reader. Pretty Miss Collier, in a brown-checked dress, stood with her back to the fifth- and sixth-grade children, writing a list of spelling words on the blackboard. The sound crashed around them like a breaking wave and the windows rattled in their casements. The chalk in Miss Collier's hand skipped across the slate like a stone on pond water.

Clayton was the first one to reach the window. To the west of Fire Neck, white smoke billowed against the sky. Maybe it *had* been a bomb. Where was his sister? What if she'd been hurt? At the front of the classroom, a girl in pigtails started to blubber. Clayton thought of the birds at Washington Lodge, where he worked every morning before school. The cockatoos were inside, he reminded himself, because of the man from Boston. "Sit down, children! Sit down!" cried Miss Collier. She slapped the desk with her ruler. But they stayed clustered at the window with their faces up against the glass like the turtles in the class terrarium.

Seeing his chance, Clayton edged toward the door.

Clayton's sister, Nancy, nineteen years old, was riding bareback down Old Purchase Road when the thunderous noise spooked her horse. She felt the animal contort beneath her, then surge forward like water through a broken dam. She hung on to the mane as they careered across the road, narrowly swerving around a child on a tricycle. Nancy saw a red cap and the round O of a mouth. Gripping with her knees, she hauled on the reins. The horse galloped into the woods that bordered the marsh. A flock of black ducks rose from Scheibel's Creek. Leaves and vines whipped against her, and Nancy crouched lower and tried to shield her face with her elbow. Then a branch loomed and she was scraped off the horse's back like mud from the heel of a boot. She landed on the damp ground among the skunk cabbage, rattled and indignant. It had been years since she'd fallen off a horse. In the distance she heard the sound of Buckshot crashing through the blueberry and the shadbushes.

In Fire Neck, just east of Southease, Clayton's grandfather woke with a start. In his dream a ship had run aground with all sails set and was breaking up on the sandbar. August Scudder had worked for most of his life in the United States Life Saving Service across the Great South Bay on Fire Island; his dreams were full of maritime disasters. Scudder jerked upright, surprised to find himself not in a lifeboat but in a chair on the front porch of his house. Out in the yard he saw his son, Roy, standing open-mouthed.

"What the hell?" Scudder demanded. Roy was staring over the trees at a ragged cloud smudging the blue sky. He wondered aloud if this might be war, if the town of Southease had been bombed by the Germans.

Scudder's thoughts leaped to his granddaughter, out riding her horse. The girl was his favorite, like her late mother before her, and he wanted her home. He distrusted horses at the best of times, skittish beasts, prone to shying. "Where was Nancy headed?"

Roy shrugged. Behind the house his hunting dogs barked and whined.

"And Mavis," said Scudder, thinking of his youngest child, "up at the lodge."

Washington Lodge, where Roy's sister Mavis worked, lay on a small rise between Southease and Fire Neck, much closer to the confusion. The two men exchanged a look. "Pigs," Roy said. "I'd better go and bring her home."

In the kitchen of Washington Lodge, Clayton's Aunt Mavis prepared to meet her maker. She'd scalded a goose and had just started to pluck it. There were two loaves of bread in the oven, and she'd opened the window above the sink to let out some of the heat. Then the room shuddered around her and a stack of dishes lurched to the floor. The goose slipped from her fingers. From the pantry came the tinkling sound of wineglasses breaking. Mavis, stout and ungainly, fell heavily to her knees and pressed her feather-covered hands together. Out the window an ugly gray cloud was rising above the trees. "Our Father who art in Heaven . . ." The cloud seemed to take on a shape. She could see it moving toward her. The fist of God, she thought, breathing in the smell of brimstone. She squeezed her eyes shut and prayed as fire whistles went off and dogs all over town began to howl. She prayed as flakes of ash as big as hands drifted in through the open window and brushed her face.

Rushing home, Clayton saw ashes dancing in the wind along the string of lanes that ran south toward the bay off Beaver Dam Road. They settled on the grass and on a half-empty laundry basket at the corner of Hawkins Lane, where a clothesline had been abandoned. The last shirt on the line fluttered a damp arm. Clayton rounded the corner onto Salt Hay Road, his shoes kicking up dust.

The Scudder house stood at the end of the lane, facing the uninterrupted marsh. Across the field, the Barto River flowed toward the Great South Bay. As Clayton turned into the yard, he could see the masts of the sailboats at Starke's Boatyard poking up over the far hedge. His grandfather stood at the door to the house, a sinewy man with a crest of white hair. His sharp nose protruded like a beak. "What happened?" Scudder asked.

Clayton struggled to catch his breath. "Where's Nancy?" Flakes of ash and charred paper drifted down around them. The stain in the sky had faded and spread toward them on an easterly wind that blew the sharp smell of gunpowder with it. Ash settled on the grass and on the yellow daffodils by the gate.

"Riding," Scudder told him. "Roy's gone to fetch your aunt. Why aren't you at school?"

"Riding where?" Clayton insisted. He had slipped out of school in the confusion, something he didn't care to explain, because his sister wouldn't like it. Now she wasn't home. What had started as a small uneasiness unfurled inside him, billowing like a sail in a gust of wind.

Scudder shrugged his bony shoulders. "Who knows where she goes on that animal. Run over to the Captain's house. See if he's all right."

Captain Kelley lived alone in a cottage across the field. He was an old man, almost as old as Scudder, and they had known each other since their days in the Life Saving Service. Clayton knocked on the door for form's sake before opening it. The small, dim house was overrun with cats. Two of them rubbed against his legs as he stepped inside. It took Clayton's eyes a moment to adjust to the darkness. In the front parlor, portraits of the Captain's mother and father hung on the wall, draped in dusty black lace. The shades were always drawn; Captain Kelley had once explained to Clayton that he hated looking out of dirty windows. From the sofa came the sound of snoring. Clayton tiptoed across the rug. The Captain was stretched out, with his head on a pillow and his mouth open. His white mustache rose and fell. The room smelled of fish and cats and standing water. Clayton closed the door softly behind him and stepped back into the sunlight.

Instead of going home, he skirted the field and headed into Southease. He knew his sister sometimes rode down to the Southease dock to watch the sailboats on the bay. Until he saw her, the jittery feeling in his gut would only get worse. At Hawkins Nursery, glass lay smashed at the base of the greenhouse like drifts of ice. A little girl stood barefoot on the porch next door and cried halfheartedly, rubbing her eyes with her fists. Across the street a man in a gray suit was stamping out a fire on an otherwise immaculate lawn. "What happened, mister?" Clayton called.

"The fireworks factory," the man said glumly. "Look at all this garbage!" Scraps of singed paper hung in the green privet.

Clayton asked if anyone had been hurt.

"I wouldn't be surprised," said the man in gray. "The blast nearly took my roof off!"

A policeman had blocked off Main Street with a sawhorse, forcing the traffic to turn back. On a lawn nearby, bits of orange and silver shone in the sunlight where a window had shattered and blown outward, along with an aquarium. Half a dozen goldfish lay strewn like bright fruit on the grass.

Clayton planted himself in front of the policeman. "Mister, have you seen a girl on a black horse?"

Intent and self-important, the policeman shook his head. He had a whistle between his teeth and blew it sharply, gesturing at a Buick convertible that had come to a stop and was now blocking traffic.

Clayton hurried on, past the fish market and the stationery store. A woman in curlers ran by, nearly knocking into him, a scarf clutched to her head. Clayton joined a cluster of people on the sidewalk. They stood watching as, across the street, firemen from the Southease Hook and Ladder hosed the smoldering debris that had once been the fireworks factory. Blackened and twisted shapes protruded randomly from the rubble. "I knew it the minute I heard it," a man in a houndstooth hat was saying. He had the stub of a cigarette in his mouth, unlit, and talked around it. "They were always testing something."

"Not like that," said another man, with a snort of derision or disbelief. "Not that loud. I thought it was gunshots."

A woman in the front of the group shook her head. "I knew it was fireworks. All that popping before the bang, and the colors. Red and yellow and green. Like a Christmas tree."

"Excuse me," Clayton said, pushing himself forward. "I'm looking for my sister. On a black horse?" An older woman with a shopping bag turned to look at him and tutted, sympathetic. No, no one had seen a horse.

The man with the cigarette stub spat it onto the ground. "Would have bolted," he muttered. "Miles from here by now."

Clayton felt their interest in his small problem ebb. The crowd turned back to the smoking wreckage across the street.

The fireworks at the Lights of Long Island were made by hand, packed one by one with a brief and particular glory, from penny snaps to aerial shells to set pieces that took weeks to construct. What had set them off was a rogue spark, a scrap of electricity. One squib shot up, then a few more. Then came the rolling explosion as the rest fired off together—the beehives and the Niagara Falls, the willow tree rockets and flying pigeons, the pinwheels, the crimson stars, the white-and-gold flitter, the revolving suns and the Saxon crosses—each carefully planned artifice of light reduced to smoke and noise.

Out on the Great South Bay, fishermen on their boats heard the loud report and saw smoke like a sudden thunderhead rise above the trees. In Southease windows shattered in houses and storefronts from Main Street to Oyster Lane. Burning debris hurtled through the air. A man on Ketchum Road later swore that the face of the Shah of Persia had appeared in lights above his vegetable garden. The stained-glass window in the Presbyterian church, the one showing Christ as a fisher of souls, fell in pieces. Greenhouses echoed with the sound of breaking glass. When the ground shook, people feared their homes were collapsing around them; a terrified mother tossed her baby out an open window. Wrapped in a blanket, he landed unharmed in the yellow branches of a forsythia.

While people panicked and dogs howled, the cloud of burned powder rose over the fireworks compound and the maple trees on the sidewalk. It broke up slowly, catching in the spokes of the windmills and the leafy tips of trees, curling south in wisps down Main Street. It drifted out over the tops of sailboats moored at the Southease dock, east over a stretch of oak and scrub pine, down Fire Neck Road, along the grasses and cattails of Scheibel's Creek. It spooled over the salt marsh, sifting powder and ash onto the spartina and high-tide bush. Beyond the marsh lay the Great South Bay, and beyond the bay stretched Fire Island, a long and narrow strip of sand clumped into dunes, where, days later, Clayton and his friend Perry would collect piles of blackened cotton and singed balsa wood that washed up along the beach.

Nancy stood and brushed herself off. The terrifying boom had come from Southease, nowhere near the elementary school where her brother was. The house on Salt Hay Road lay nearly a mile away; she had no doubt the horse Buckshot would be halfway there already. Much closer, just up the low hill toward Southease, stood Washington Lodge, where her aunt Mavis worked. Better to go there first, Nancy thought. Someone might know what was happening. Sirens sounded in the distance as she picked her way back through the woods to Old Purchase Road. The air had an acrid smell Nancy could taste in her mouth. With an uneasy feeling, she began to run, taking the shortcut that led to the back of the lodge.

Rounding the last of the trees, she saw the reassuring outline of Washington Lodge on the hill above her. A figure stood at the kitchen door, and Nancy put on a burst of speed. She was halfway up the hill when she realized the person in the doorway was a stranger. She slowed to a walk, surprised. He was a young man with a pale, freckled face and reddish-brown hair. The sleeves of his white shirt were rolled up. The way he stood facing her with his hand on the door it seemed, in the confusion of the moment, as if he were expecting her.

"I'm looking for my aunt," Nancy faltered, catching her breath. "She works here." There was a stitch in her side and her hip still smarted from her humiliating fall. The man opened the door wide, and she peered into the kitchen. The air smelled of burning bread, and also, faintly, of wet feathers. A stack of white china plates had fallen off the counter and lay broken in a gleaming line across the floor. Her aunt was kneeling under the open window with her back to them, head bowed over her clasped hands. Ashes sifted through the window. "Mavis," Nancy called gently. "Mavis, are you hurt?"

Her aunt did not turn. Nancy guessed the mumbling she heard was prayer.

She made a wry face at the stranger. "What happened?"

"I don't know." His voice was low and dry, and although he wasn't whispering, Nancy felt keenly that he was speaking to her alone. "It sounded like the Last Judgment."

Nancy's heart still pounded. She watched the stranger's face as he spoke. The noise had come out of nowhere, he said. "Like Armageddon. Without the trumpets." His name was Robert Landgraf, he told her, and he was visiting from Boston. Nancy thought his fair, freckled skin looked as if it would burn easily. She noticed ink stains on his fingers and the cuff of his white shirt. He'd heard glass shattering downstairs, he went on, and had searched the house in vain for other people. "I was starting to think the place had been evacuated without me. I found someone finally. Your aunt, I guess." He gestured toward the kitchen. "Then I opened the door and saw you." He smiled at her, and Nancy found herself smiling back.

The sound of a car on the pebble drive made them turn. Roy was behind the wheel. "She's in the kitchen," Nancy called as her uncle came toward them, looking concerned. She felt guilty for not venturing in before him. But Roy would do a better job of calming his sister, she told herself.

Roy paused at the door. "What the devil happened?"

"We think it's the Last Judgment," Nancy said with a nervous laugh, unable to restrain herself. Her uncle frowned. He glanced quickly from her to the man from Boston and back again before turning and stepping into the kitchen. Nancy knew she shouldn't make light of her aunt's religious fervor. She glanced down at her feet, abashed.

Nancy and Robert Landgraf stood in the doorway; like reprimanded children, she thought. Inside, Roy could be heard reasoning with Mavis. Glancing in, Nancy saw him helping her to her feet. He bent down to retrieve the half-plucked carcass of a goose and stood holding it for a moment, like a bachelor with a baby, before angling it into the gleaming white refrigerator.

"Let's all go home," Roy said firmly. He held his sister under the elbow and steered her toward the door. Mavis, pale with shock, blinked her wide eyes in the sunlight.

Nancy glanced at the stranger. It seemed unkind to abandon him. "Maybe Mr. Landgraf should come with us."

"Yes!" cried Mavis unexpectedly. "I'm supposed to cook his dinner. Mr. Washington won't be back till late." Roy nodded, shepherding them forward.

Robert Landgraf seemed grateful not to be left behind. Together they walked toward the car. A fresh wind brought another flurry of grit and the smell of burning. Mavis stopped to pull a handkerchief from her pocket and hold it over her nose. Roy handed her into the passenger seat of the Ford and opened the back door for the others.

Nancy hesitated. She couldn't bear the thought of riding back to Salt Hay Road with her aunt, who would pester Robert Landgraf with questions about his spiritual beliefs, embarrassing her. "I think we'll walk," she told her uncle. "Buckshot'll be back by now. But I lost my crop somewhere along the road."

Roy didn't protest. "Be careful!" Mavis called, waving her handkerchief from the window. The car sputtered down the white pebble driveway, leaving Nancy alone with the man from Boston.

She set off briskly. It seemed clear that while something had happened in Southease, maybe at the gas station, the ground would stay solid under their feet. Her brother was safely in school. Nancy's fear converted to nervous excitement, a sense of possibility. She felt acutely conscious of the man keeping pace beside her.

"Lively spot, Long Island," he said after they'd walked a few yards. "Ear-splitting booms, clouds of smoke. You locals must have nerves of steel."

Nancy laughed. "I grew up in Connecticut." She didn't want him to think she'd lived in the little town of Fire Neck all her life. "We're going to move back there in a few years. My brother and I. Once he finishes school."

"Still, I take it you're familiar with the local customs," Robert said. "You can translate the lingo, make sure I don't end up with my head on a stake." Nancy smiled again, trying to imagine what dinner on Salt Hay Road would be like with this stranger at their table. She could picture Clayton's pinched expression, sizing Robert Landgraf up, holding his white shirt and city shoes against him.

It had rained steadily for the past week and now the sun shone brilliantly. In the silence and the sunlight it was hard to credit the violence of the noise they'd heard before. The leaves on the trees were a bright acid green. Nancy left the road for a narrow trail that ran along Scheibel's Creek.

"You're in business with Mr. Washington?" she asked.

Robert explained that he was an assistant curator from the Museum of Comparative Zoology in Boston. "We heard a rumor there might be a rare bird here, a Carolina parakeet. Parrots are my specialty, so I'm the one they sent."

Nancy felt surprised that something as familiar as the birds at Washington Lodge should have caught the attention of a museum in Boston. "Did you find it?"

He shook his head, rueful. "No. They're similar, but it's not a *Conuropsis* at all. Something South American, in the genus *Aratinga*."

Nancy said, "You must be disappointed."

"Oh no. My hopes weren't high. And the collection is amazing." Robert whistled. "He's got African finches Peters would kill for. And a little psittacine I can't even identify. Maybe one of the New Guinea species . . ." His voice had become almost dreamy.

It still seemed incredible that the birds her brother fed and watered every morning were that remarkable. She asked, "But where does he get them?"

"He knows every ship's captain in New York Harbor, and he pays well. They bring him specimens from all over the world." Walking in front, unable to see him, Nancy listened to his disembodied voice listing the exotic names of the birds, *honeycreepers*, *jacamars*, *bee-eaters*; it was a strangely intimate arrangement, like talking in the dark. They were nearing the creek, and the air smelled damp and earthy. The brown spikes of cinnamon fern poked up from the undergrowth. She lifted a thorny strand of catbrier aside and held it. Robert took it from her, ducking his head.

"Where are you leading me, Miss Poole? Not into more danger, I hope."

Nancy had an image of him materializing out of the explosion, as if from an alchemical reaction. He had stood at the door of the lodge, she thought, waiting for her. A shiver rippled down her back. She said, "Call me Nancy."

It was late when Clayton got home from Southease. From the door on the front porch he could hear the clink of forks and knives on china, snatches of conversation: *train from Boston*; *brushfires*; *can't rebuild there, that's for sure.* Stepping in quietly, he saw that the family was sitting at the long table in the rarely used dining room, instead of in the kitchen: His grandfather Scudder sat at the head, with Roy to his left, then Mavis. Beside Mavis sat his sister, unharmed, holding out a bowl. At the sight of her he felt the worry that had drummed through him all afternoon subside, like the vibrations of a cymbal quieted by the pressure of a finger. And then he noticed the stranger beside her. A man with reddish hair and a foxlike face. As he watched, the man leaned toward Nancy and whispered something. A quick pink stain spread across her cheeks and throat.

"*Here* he is," cried his aunt, catching sight of Clayton. She gestured him toward the remaining chair and began to ladle stew into a bowl. "Now we're all together." She passed the bowl to Clayton and solemnly lowered her chin. "Let's say a prayer of thanks for keeping our family safe." Nancy made a face at him from across the stew pot.

Clayton sat and surreptitiously looked around him. The presence of the stranger at their table made him study the familiar faces as if he were seeing them for the first time. His plump aunt's mouth was moving faintly in her wide, soft face as she murmured grace. Beside her, his uncle Roy sighed with impatience, his dark hair falling onto his forehead. Tall and rangy, he shared only his coloring with his sister. His eyes closed, Roy seemed more solidly there among them. Often, Clayton felt, his uncle's gaze was held by something just out of view. Nancy, eyes shut but still irreverent, seemed to be smiling at some private joke. At the head of the table, his grandfather Scudder hadn't closed his eyes at all. White-haired, gaunt, his beaky nose protruding from his weathered face, he studied the stranger sitting next to Nancy with a severe expression.

Clayton and Nancy had moved to the house on Salt Hay Road five years before the fireworks factory turned itself inside out. He'd been seven then, Nancy fourteen. Before their mother's death they'd lived in a big house in Stonington, Connecticut, overlooking Long Island Sound. Confined to a daybed downstairs as the cancer whittled her away, their mother had liked to watch the sailboat races on fine days with a pair of opera glasses. Clayton didn't remember his father at all. He'd died of a heart attack the year Nancy was ten, Clayton barely three. "He used to swing you onto his shoulders when he came home from work," Nancy had told him. "You'd grab at his mustache to keep from falling. Don't you remember?"

What Clayton did remember was their arrival on Salt Hay Road. This would have been after their mother's funeral, though he recalled the two events separately, as though they'd occurred on different continents. First there'd been a church thronged with well-dressed strangers, where the collar of his shirt scratched him and his neck grew stiff from keeping still while perfumed women murmured into the air above him and stroked his hair. He'd realized with relief that he could hold his sister's hand without censure; he kept close to Nancy and stared down at the floor. In his mind he could still see the tops of her slightly too-large shoes, the little gap between the stockings and the black patent leather.

Later they were on the ferry. It was night. His grandfather and aunt and uncle must have been there, but he did not remember them, only his sister standing at the rail. Clayton clutched her hand. The wind tangled her hair, long then, and whipped it across her face as she cried. He shivered in the cold and wished she would notice him and go back inside the cabin. But the minutes passed and she stayed at the rail, and he could not imagine going anywhere without her. The wind came at them off the water and his eyes teared. He wiped his nose on his sleeve. In front of them the lights of distant houses trembled on the black horizon.

Then they were riding in a car, and the warm, close air smelled of leather and dogs and his aunt's flowery perfume. He fell asleep leaning on his sister's shoulder. After what felt like hours, he half woke as the car slowed and began a series of turns. Clayton found his muscles anticipating the route, waiting for the turn off Beaver Dam, the long bumpy stretch of Salt Hay Road, as though it had been mapped into his growing bones from the time he was a baby in his mother's arms. He felt the car turn and slow down, the tires laboring over the potholes where he'd watched flocks of sparrows bathing in the puddles after a rain. The ruts on the east side were deeper than those on the west; his grandfather Scudder said the car listed to starboard on the outbound tack and port on the homeward. Clayton was jostled against his aunt as the car pulled into the pebble driveway with a crunching sound.

The doors opened, letting in the chirping of crickets and the brackish, peaty scent of the marsh. The night was very still. Clayton, fully awake, kept his eyes half closed as his uncle picked him up off the backseat of the car and carried him into the house, ducking through the door and into the kitchen, where his aunt was already lighting the burner on the white enamel stove. Everything was just as he remembered it from summer visits: the smell of bread dough and potato peelings; the red-and-white-checked curtains at the window above the sink; the poster with the curled edges on the pantry door, showing different breeds of horses; the lampshade stippled with the outline of a square-rigged sailing ship. Clayton felt as if he were waking finally from a long nightmare. A knot loosened in his throat. His face tingled painfully, and he clenched his eyes to keep back the tears. Roy was still holding him, slung with careless affection over one shoulder. "Take him upstairs," he heard his aunt say. "The sewing room's his now, poor thing."

On that first night in his grandfather's house, after his mother's funeral, seven-year-old Clayton woke in the dark, confused by the smell of apple pie. In the morning, coming downstairs, he saw his uncle eating fresh pie for breakfast with a cup of black coffee and knew he hadn't dreamed it. Over the next few days he discovered that his aunt often baked at night, after the rest of the household had gone to bed. The old sewing room was just above the kitchen, and on nights when his aunt baked, he would lie in bed and breathe in the scent of ginger cake, cinnamon rolls, corn muffins, black walnut pie. Sometimes he heard her singing to herself while she rolled out the dough. Then he would slip out of bed and sit on the dark stairs, out of sight, but close enough to hear her. The songs she sang were the ones she'd learned at the piano with his mother when they were girls: "Annie Laurie," "My Darling Clementine," "My Sweetheart's the Man in the Moon." With his eyes closed, he could almost believe it was his mother singing.

His sister also noticed that their aunt had trouble sleeping, especially on moonlit nights. "Probably because she's so fat," Nancy remarked, unfeelingly. Clayton imagined the full moon tugging at his aunt's large body like a boat on the tide, dragging her awake and down the stairs. Over time, moonlight and the smell of baking linked themselves in his mind, and the full moon stirred in him a craving for fresh bread and cream.

The explosion of the Lights of Long Island fireworks factory killed four workers who were in the building at the time, and set over fifty homes alight in Southease and Fire Neck. What people talked about more than anything was the suddenness of the devastation, its unexpected force. "No warning at all," friends and neighbors repeated to one another, shaken. "Out of a clear blue sky."

In the house on Salt Hay Road, one of the matched pair of upstairs windows had been cracked by the blast. The windows were shaped like fans and set on either side of the chimney. According to Scudder, it had been the charm of those same windows, like winking eyes, that had tempted his father to bid on the house in an auction he attended in East Moriches by chance nearly seventy years earlier. After the auction he learned that the house was all he had bought; not a foot of land around it was included in the price. The house sat on the bank of the

Terrell River and the owner wanted the price of the house again for the waterfront lot.

Scudder's father said he'd be damned if he gave the land shark another penny. He took careful measurements and waited for the next high tide. Then he and a group of relatives and friends jacked the house up off the ground and rolled it on logs to a flat-topped barge they borrowed from Starke's Boatyard. They floated the house down the Terrell River to Moriches Bay and then southwest along the shore, past Forge River and Pattersquash Creek to the Barto River.

Scudder had not been allowed on the barge with the house, being only ten at the time. He'd waited on shore with the others as it came up the river from Taffy Point. Scudder remembered watching the house appear in the distance and how strange the silhouette of it seemed, like a boat built by someone with no understanding of water or wind. "She had an awkward look," he told Clayton nearly a lifetime later. He struggled to describe the odd sensation that had come over him as he watched the house float toward them, the water splashing up the white walls and around the door, a yellow curtain swaying in one of the windows. It had seemed almost spooky, he told his grandson; not the house itself, but its limping, stubborn progress across the waves.

This was where Scudder had lived ever since, in this solid, narrow house of two and a half white clapboard stories. Later, after his parents died and his brothers married and moved out, Scudder stayed on alone. For years he worked at the Smith Point Station across the bay on Fire Island. Then the house would stand empty for most of the year, while he bunked at the station with the rest of the Life Savers. The worst storms struck in the fall and winter, but the crew remained on duty through the spring. Patrolling the beach, Scudder collected flotsam: the name board from a ship called the *Heron*; a blue-and-orange pennant; planks of yellow pine; a music box, its gears clogged with sand. Every summer the crew disbanded for the season and Scudder returned to the house on Salt Hay Road.

Scudder used the salvaged lumber to build a storage room off the side of the house. When a branch came down on the kitchen roof, he sawed it into usable pieces and patched the hole with it. The house absorbed the smells of salt marsh and mud and waterlogged pine. Scudder hung the name board from the *Heron* on the porch and flew the pennant from the weather vane. When the *Water Lily* wrecked on a sandbar in a bitter sou'wester, his future wife fell out of the breeches buoy into his arms. Scudder told his grandson that everything he had came out of the sea.

Genevieve Chaffey had grown up on a cattle ranch in Arizona. She and her mother and two cousins had been returning on the *Water Lily* from a tour of Europe. Though she accepted her relative poverty as a fair price for marrying for love, there were times, hanging diapers out to dry in air heavy with the dampness of the marsh, or lying in bed at night listening to the whine of mosquitoes, that she missed her childhood home in Arizona, the bone-dry air, the soft-spoken servants. During the first years of her marriage, she tried to coax a line of weeping willows to grow along the southern edge of the property. The salt water proved too much for them. She had more success with the wisteria and the climbing pink roses she planted on either side of the kitchen door, and with the blue hydrangeas along the front walk.

Later, when she inherited some money, she suggested they look for a house in tonier Southease. Scudder refused to consider it. So Genevieve improved Salt Cottage, as she called it. She hired a good architect to enlarge the kitchen, add a porch to the east and a large, sunny room to the south, which she filled with potted plants. From the outside, the two parts of the house looked entirely harmonious. Inside, despite fresh plaster and coats of paint, the original rooms still exuded the faint but unmistakable odor of the sea. At night the posts and beams of the old house would creak, like the timbers of a ship under sail.

The morning after the explosion, Clayton peered into Nancy's room and saw an empty bed. He was often out of the house before she even got up; now, in his confusion, he feared she'd been kidnapped like the Lindbergh baby. He glanced wildly about, looking for clues. Beside the disordered bed, on the bureau, stood a photograph of himself on his mother's lap, a boy of two or three. His mother smiled calmly, her hair in neat waves, her eyes tired but still beautiful as a movie star's. The boy, in a neat-fitting sailor suit, stared back at him, chin thrust forward. Clayton felt angered by the photograph, as though it were a fake. He could not remember ever sitting on his mother's lap or wearing such ridiculous clothes. Since her death, he'd tried without success to imagine his mother watching over him. But it was Nancy who did that, Nancy who mattered most. He turned and clattered down the stairs.

Clayton had known his sister to be seriously ill only once. Not long after they'd moved to Salt Hay Road, when she was only fourteen, she'd had a fever for three days. He had watched her anxiously as she slept, her cheeks flushed, her hair dark with sweat. Mavis told him to go play outside, but as soon as she wasn't looking, he crept back in. When Nancy woke for brief stretches, her eyes glittered. Finally the fever broke. She slept for a day and a half, and Clayton realized she wasn't going to die.

That was when he'd formed the habit of checking on her first thing in the morning, before he went downstairs. He would have been embarrassed if anyone had seen him, but he found himself doing it nonetheless. If he could verify from the doorway that she was breathing, if she stirred a little in her sleep or if he caught the movement of the blanket as her chest rose and fell, he could almost pretend he hadn't needed to check on her but merely wanted to see if she was awake. If she lay with her face to the wall, or obscured by one of her many pillows, he felt compelled to tiptoe into the room until he could satisfy himself that she had emerged safely on the other side of the night, that dark tunnel. Once, she'd startled him by opening her eyes just as he leaned over her. She sat up, annoyed, and demanded to know why he'd woken her. Clayton had stammered an excuse and retreated as fast as he could, his heart pounding.

Now he found her downstairs at the kitchen table, leafing idly through the morning paper with a cup in one hand. Clayton hid his relief by humming "At the Codfish Ball." She glanced up, and he caught the feverish sheen in her eyes. It looked as if a reflection of the fireworks had somehow lodged there.

Nancy put her cup in the sink and stepped over to the little mirror in the hallway. "Do you think I'm beautiful?" she asked. She brushed the glass with her hand. It was an old mirror, the surface more gray than silver.

"I don't know," Clayton muttered. She wore a green puckered blouse and the brown riding pants that Mavis didn't like. Her short, dark hair had been brushed back away from her face and tucked carefully behind her ears. As he watched, she bit her bottom lip and rubbed her cheeks. Her skin reddened under the tips of her fingers. She seemed to expect him to say more.

"Perry's brothers think so," he admitted finally. He'd heard Charlie Gilpin whistle from the yard as Nancy rode by on Buckshot, and then say something about horses and luck. When he asked what that meant, Fred told him, "Your sister's a looker." Clayton felt annoyed by this, though he understood Fred meant it as a compliment.

"Oh, the Gilpin boys." Nancy dismissed them with a toss of her head. "What do they know?" She straightened her shoulders and gave the mirror a bright, intense look, as if she meant to stare it down.

Clayton loved all the Gilpins, and Perry's older brothers particularly. They worked on the bay every summer, and Clayton longed more than anything to have a job like theirs someday. "They know everything about clamming," he told Nancy loyally.

His sister laughed and turned away from the mirror. "Exactly," she said. Clayton was relieved to see her look more like herself.

In the aviary at Washington Lodge, Clayton was halfway through his morning work. He'd opened the heavy drapes and the sun streamed in through the many windows, thick as honey, and lighted the bits of down that floated in the air like the fluff from sea myrtle in the fall. He had changed the lining on the cages that hung against the wall and distributed fruit to the parrots, the cockatoos, and the trogons, neatly avoiding the quick beak of the African gray. He marked his progress through the maze of cages by species: he was in the smaller bird section now, moving slowly to avoid startling a pair of green lorikeets. Clayton refilled the lorikeets' water and placed a spray of millet on the tray. Over the screeches and the rustling of the birds he heard the rattle of the door.

A steaming cup in his hand, George B. Washington skirted the cages in a red brocade dressing gown and leather slippers. Washington had made his fortune during the Great War with his invention of instant coffee. When the U.S. Patent Office refused to let him sell George Washington Powdered Products, he'd simply added the initial *B*. His real name was unknown, though he was clearly a foreigner. Some believed he came from Eastern Europe, others South America. His manners were faultless and his English excellent, but he betrayed himself in small eccentricities: a fondness for yellow silk scarves, a disinterest in sailing, his huge collection of rare and exotic birds.

Mr. Washington stood near the open window and tipped his head, sniffing the air. Over the smells of the aviary, Clayton caught the harsh, lingering scent of gunpowder. "I sold firecrackers once," Mr. Washington murmured, almost to himself. He was staring out the window, and the steam from his coffee fogged the pane. "With my brother on the street corner. Many years ago." Mr. Washington was not given to conversation and usually spoke to Clayton only with instructions about the birds. "My first job," he added, surprising Clayton further by turning and addressing him directly. "I wanted the money for a pair of shoes. My mother took it to buy a pig." Clayton, standing with the tray of fruit and millet in his hands, glanced down at his employer's immaculate leather slippers. Then he caught Mr. Washington's wry smile. "Yes." The older man nodded. "But the boy I was then"—he pressed the fingers of one hand together and then opened his palm with a little snapping motion—"still shoeless." Clayton tried to imagine Mr. Washington, with his elegant black mustache, his dressing gown with the tasseled belt, as a barefoot boy with firecrackers spread out on a cloth. He opened his mouth to ask where that had been, then thought better of it, suddenly shy. Mr. Washington had turned back to the window and was studying the temperature gauge. "Warm enough for the cockatoos today," he said. The moment had passed.

On sunny mornings in the spring and summer, the sulphur-crested cockatoos were allowed into the branches of one of the copper beeches that lined the white pebble drive. A short chain tethered each bird by one foot to its own metal hoop. Clayton carried the birds out one by one, riding like pashas on his shoulder, the hoop clutched in his fist. The cockatoos' sharp claws dug into his skin, but even so, it was his favorite part of the job; they understood exactly where they were going and shrieked and whistled with excitement, making his ears ring.

Carrying the birds, Clayton considered how Mr. Washington had come from somewhere else and made his home here too. It seemed funny that Clayton had never looked at it that way before. He would save his own wages, like Mr. Washington had. Not for something dull, like a pair of shoes or a pig. Not even for an aviary full of birds. He would save up for a boat. He pictured it in his mind, a cockpit runabout with a six-cylinder engine.

He used a long wooden pole with a hook at the end to hoist the birds into the air. One by one, he fitted the hoops onto hooks in the branches of the tree. Secured among the leaves, the cockatoos stretched their wings and cocked their heads, gazing down at Clayton with smug benevolence. The sun glinted on their white feathers. They blinked their gray, hooded eyes. When the last bird was aloft, it looked like the copper beech had blossomed with enormous gardenias.

Mavis had walked to the lodge with Clayton to prepare Mr. Washington's breakfast and then his large lunch. Because he ate his main meal at two in the afternoon, she was usually able to go straight from Washington Lodge to Salt Hay Road in the late afternoon, leaving something light for Mr. Washington's dinner. All this changed when he had guests. The afternoon after the explosion, Mavis was preparing partridge in the kitchen. The partridge was in honor of the visitor from Boston, and it meant that she would not get home until after eight.

Mavis cut the fat salt pork into strips. Now and then she glanced out the window, remembering the cloud of smoke in the shape of a fist. The housekeeper had removed all evidence of ash and broken plates, and scrubbed the kitchen floor, but Mavis still felt nervous here and wished she were home on Salt Hay Road. If only she were certain what the explosion presaged. Danger, she thought, but from where, from whom?

A knock on the kitchen door startled Mavis badly. She jumped, nearly slicing her thumb, as her niece stepped in. Nancy's cheeks were pink from riding. "Hello," she said brightly, pulling off a pair of brown kid gloves. "I was out on Buckshot and thought I'd drop by."

The girl wore her riding breeches, something Mavis did not approve of, and a cropped, boyish jacket. Mavis was sorry Roy had allowed her to take up riding after Helen died, giving her free use of the two horses. Mavis loved her late sister's daughter, of course she loved her; she had welcomed her into her home. But the girl never reciprocated her affection, pulling away stiffly, even after her mother died, if Mavis tried to hug her. She was indifferent even to Mavis's cooking. Mavis had made an orange sponge cake for her eighteenth birthday, as a special treat, and her niece had poked at it with the tines of her fork, unimpressed, as if oranges were as common as apples.

There was a small mirror on the wall by the door. Mavis watched Nancy peer into it with a quick, critical look and tuck a loose strand of hair behind her ear. The girl knew she was pretty, Mavis thought with a flash of old bitterness, though she would never match Helen's cool and perfect beauty.

"Clay around?" Nancy asked.

"No," said Mavis. She resented being interrupted in her work. "I haven't seen him since this morning. He's probably just getting out of school." She rummaged in a drawer for the larding needle, found it, and threaded a strip of salt pork through the wide eye. "If you hurry, you'll be able to catch him."

Instead of leaving, her niece leaned indolently against the counter. "What is that?"

"Partridge," said Mavis, in the tone of someone stating the obvious. She took a long, shallow stitch with the needle, drawing the salt pork at a right angle to the narrow breastbone.

"Why are you poking it like that?"

Mavis sighed. Larding a partridge was a tricky job, requiring all her concentration. She picked up a second strip of salt pork and fitted it through the eye of the needle. "I'm larding it, of course. To keep the meat from drying out."

Nancy sat down at the table and toyed with a paring knife. Her thick, bobbed hair fell around her face, hair as glossy and dark as her mother's. *She'd* never had to work for a living, Mavis thought as she leaned over the puckered flesh of the partridge, her hands slippery with grease. No one had ever called *Helen* a dumb broad, or taken all her money, or walked out on her. Helen had been treated to a Grand Tour of Europe by Granny Chaffey when she turned seventeen, and a Venetian count had kissed her hand and called her a flower of America. Mavis, six years younger, had not been taken anywhere. Europe had gone to war, and Granny Chaffey broke her hip in a fall and never fully recovered.

The clock in the dining room chimed and Mavis realized she'd forgotten to take in the tea. She glanced at her niece, who did not look especially presentable in her breeches and cropped jacket. Mavis felt glad Mr. Washington wasn't home; the fellow from Boston wouldn't notice the irregularity. "Run the tea in, would you? You made me forget all about it. To the aviary. The farthest door on the right."

Nancy surprised her by jumping up and grabbing the tray before she'd even finished talking. Flighty, Mavis thought with irritation. She called down the hall, "Careful with the china."

"Guess who?" Nancy said lightly, brandishing the tea tray so that the cup and saucer rattled. Robert Landgraf was standing at the window beside a cage of bright green birds, a camera in one hand. She'd intended to say something funny about moonlighting as a parlor maid, but the look of pleasure on his face as he turned drew her up short. She felt her cheeks flush. Behind her the swinging door creaked to a close.

"I'm just helping my aunt," she told him. "I'll set this down here." She moved toward a table strewn with papers, rulers, and calipers of different sizes in the middle of the room.

Robert bumped against two birdcages, causing a screech and a panic of flapping wings in his attempt to reach the table before Nancy did. He flipped the sketchpad closed and pushed the charcoal pencils aside, too late to keep her from glimpsing the drawings of a girl in a riding jacket. She recognized her own short, dark hair, the set of her mouth.

"I didn't expect to see you," Robert said.

"I stopped by to check on my brother." Together they looked down at the tea tray. This was where he'd been when the fireworks factory exploded, Nancy thought. She remembered the way the sound had lurched through her, flattening her heart against her rib cage. Robert Landgraf would have felt that too. Nancy glanced back toward the sketches he'd covered up and a wave of giddiness surged inside her. "My aunt asked me to bring the tea in. She's busy darning your partridge."

"Darning my partridge?"

"With a needle. There must have been a hole in its heel."

"A specialty of the region?" Robert asked. "I can't wait to try it. In the meantime, can I offer you some tea?"

Nancy smiled. "There's only one cup."

"You drink from the cup? That's handy. In Boston, we prefer the saucer."

When Clayton arrived at Washington Lodge, he was surprised to see Nancy's horse cropping the grass at the base of the bird feeder by the kitchen door. He gave Buckshot's neck a tentative pat. Inside, the kitchen was empty. "Hello?" Clayton called, throwing down his schoolbag. When no one answered, he climbed quickly onto a stool and reached into the shelf of baking supplies. He didn't think his aunt would begrudge him a handful of raisins, but he'd never risked asking.

The raisins were a way to befriend the peacock, or at least conquer his fear of it. The bird menaced Clayton when he tried to collect the peahen's eggs. Once, it had attacked him from behind, pecking hard with its sharp beak and leaving a bruise on his calf that Clayton watched with interest over the following days as it turned from deep to lighter purple, blue, green, and finally yellow, not unlike the colors of the peacock itself. After that, Clayton entered the pen with a stick and held the peacock's gaze until he'd backed out again. Now he tossed the raisins into the cage and watched, fascinated, as it gobbled them up, its neck snaking out as if the raisin were prey that might escape.

Engrossed, Clayton didn't notice his aunt coming around the corner. Her voice made him jump. "Have you found your sister? She's looking for you." Clayton shook his head, turning toward the beech trees as if to check on the cockatoos. "What are you feeding that bird?" his aunt demanded. Clayton glanced down. The peacock, moving with ferocity, had swallowed the last raisin.

"Crickets," he lied. As soon as he'd said it, he felt ashamed of his mistake: it was spring, and the crickets wouldn't be out till summer.

Nancy rode back down Old Purchase Road from Washington Lodge. The sun shone through the green maple leaves. Here and there along the road lay bits of ash and charcoal-edged debris among the daffodils. Now that it was in the past, the fireworks factory explosion struck her as proof that anything might happen, even here in Fire Neck. Nancy nudged Buckshot into a trot and then, almost immediately, a gallop. They hurtled along the side of the road, the green trees blurring. Happiness bobbed inside her like a silver bubble.

At the intersection of Old Purchase and Beaver Dam, Nancy reined in, slowing to a trot. They turned onto Beaver Dam, and the horse tossed his head and snorted. Nancy was conscious of the figure she cut, up on Buckshot's dark back, and she thought of the charcoal sketches she'd glimpsed in the bird-filled room at Washington Lodge. The bubble expanded inside her. Laughing, she leaned forward and dug her heels into the horse's sides. They charged off again down Beaver Dam Road. From behind them she could hear the squawking of the Scheibels' chickens.

As they turned onto Salt Hay Road, Nancy's exhilaration faded. The familiar ground with its potholes and dandelions seemed disappointing, as if, riding so breathlessly, she'd almost expected to arrive somewhere else, somewhere new and different. At the barn, Buckshot breathed gustily as she dismounted. Standing on her two legs again, she felt puny, diminished. Already the conversation with Robert Landgraf in the aviary at Washington Lodge seemed like it had happened to someone else. Steam rose from the horse's back as she lifted the saddle and then began to brush him with the curry comb. She measured out extra oats and pulled off a clump of hay, scattering the fragrant dust.

Nancy was nearly twenty; her best friend from high school, Enid Snow, had already married the year before and moved to Brooklyn. Nancy didn't think much of Enid's husband, an X-ray technician with a nasal voice and strong views on politics and the economy. Enid sensed this, and a coolness rose between them. In high school Enid had daydreamed about studying architecture like her father. Nancy admired her for this, picturing Enid one day at work over a desk strewn with blueprints. She tried to imagine herself with a job as well, supporting her brother, and remembered the self-assured secretaries in her father's gleaming office and the way they could look her in the eye and type at the same time, their fingers rattling the black keys while they chatted. Instead, Enid had fallen in love, and soon afterward she left Fire Neck for Brooklyn. Nancy wondered what Enid's new, married life was like and whether she still made sketches on graph paper of mansions with glass domes and balconied windows.

Inside, the house was dark and cool, the rooms hushed. Nothing seemed to change here. The upholstery on the chairs in the sunroom had faded, the yellow flowers bleached nearly white, and the sewing room where her grandmother had made dresses for Nancy's dolls had been turned into Clayton's bedroom. But the rugs with the sand worked deep into the nap of the wool were the same, frayed a bit more around the edges. To Nancy, the house felt suddenly like something that had been given up on. While her grandmother was alive, it had been well kept, with fresh flowers on the dining-room table all spring and summer. Now the table was cluttered with her uncle's tools, with bits of string and scraps of cloth, and her aunt's books and pamphlets with titles like *Startling Facts in Modern Spiritualism*, *Psychic Science and Philosophy*. Everything felt worn thin, from the sheets on the beds to the chipped green-and-brown plates in the cupboards. The kitchen was the worst. It was a dark room with an ancient and temperamental cookstove and a low ceiling, made darker by the overhang of the porch outside. The pockmarked counter, though always clean of crumbs, had a stickiness to its wooden surface that seemed to resist soap and water. When Nancy asked once about replacing it, Mavis acted scandalized; she told Nancy there wasn't money for fripperies.

Nancy thought of her aunt, bent over the partridge in the kitchen at Washington Lodge. When she and Clayton first came to live on Salt Hay Road, Mavis had made a clumsy little speech. "Welcome to this house," she'd told them, as if they hadn't come to visit every summer since Nancy was a baby. "This is your home now. We're your family." Mavis tripped a little over the words, twisting a napkin in her hands. "You'll always have us." She sat down and patted her eyes with the napkin. Fourteen-year-old Nancy felt a spasm of rage, like a charley horse in her chest. She and Clayton had each other; that was enough family for them. No one could replace their mother. She glanced angrily at her little brother, who stared at their aunt and uncle with a devoted look that reminded her uncomfortably of one of the dogs. She cleared her throat loudly, so that he turned toward her instead, and the torturous moment was over.

Nancy watched Mavis closely after that, waiting for her to try to insinuate herself, to play at being a stand-in for their mother. She made it clear that her brother was her responsibility. When he wet the bed, she was the one who washed the sheets the next morning. When he broke his leg, she was the one who sat by his bed and read Sherlock Holmes stories, who bought him fat books of Buck Rogers and Tailspin Tommy comics with her carefully managed allowance. She rebuffed her aunt's offers of help and advice, until Mavis learned to stop making them. Working at Washington Lodge most of the day, she was easy for Nancy to avoid. Roy showed no interest in interfering, though he was kind to both her and Clayton in his distracted way. Her grandfather was the strongest presence in the house, and Nancy had always known she could wrap him around her finger. Within the walls of the house on Salt Hay Road, Nancy made a separate space for herself and Clayton. "She's very *independent*," she heard Mavis remark to Roy in an aggrieved tone, soon after they'd arrived. She'd carried the word like a talisman ever since.

Nancy went upstairs, to the small room that had once been her mother's. On the desk by the window stood her father's old black Remington portable, with her typing booklets beside it. Nancy picked up *Tips for Typists*. Squaring her shoulders, back straight, she started with a sample business letter: *Dear Sirs, We are pleased to inform you that in the matter of . . .* The *e* key, sticky with age or humidity, needed to be struck especially hard. Nancy had been practicing for three weeks now, after hearing that Enid Snow's older sister had found a typing job at an office in Patchogue. In spite of her improving speed, Nancy still made six or more mistakes per page. The problem, she thought, was the tediousness of it. She looked through the pamphlet of suggestions by Albert Tangora, the World Typing Champion, but it was evidently not a subject he felt the need to address.

In a fit of dissatisfaction, she stripped her bed and remade it with fresh sheets from the linen closet. Spring cleaning, she told herself. The typewriter could wait. She hauled up the green braided rug off the floor and dragged it down the stairs. Out in the yard, she draped it over the clothesline and beat it with a broom. Dust rose in satisfying clouds, and she had to move upwind. The rug had belonged to her mother. As she worked to beat it clean, she thought of the furniture from the house in Connecticut, nearly all of which had been sold at auction after her mother died. It had not occurred to anyone that she and Clayton might one day have a use for it in a place of their own, and this was something Nancy resented. Mavis or Roy, someone should have thought of that. But her aunt and uncle were entrenched in the day-to-day, as worn and unchanging as the house itself. There was nothing they were moving toward, no beckoning future. She felt an unfamiliar pity for her aunt, abandoned by her unfaithful, gambler husband, living in her childhood home and working as a domestic. Her own life would be different, the way her mother's had been.

As a typist, Nancy thought, she could find work anywhere big enough to have office buildings. She pictured herself in a busy office, like her mother's friend Georgia Spencer, a buyer for a furniture company in New Haven. Mrs. Spencer wore beautifully tailored clothes and exuded a confidence that Nancy attributed to working all day with clever men in suits.

The rug was still releasing dust, but Nancy's arm was tired. She dragged it back upstairs and rolled it out on the floor of her room. If they lived in Connecticut, they could still visit Fire Neck in the summers, she thought, as they'd done with their mother. Some of her earliest memories were of walking on the boardwalk that led to the beach at Old Inlet, her bare feet on the warm gray planks, the men around her carrying picnic baskets and a ukulele, and her mother scandalizing the local women with a swimsuit they would copy as best they could the following season. The rest of the year, Nancy decided, she and her brother would live in an apartment on the top floor of a tall building. She wanted Clayton to have a wider view of the world, a sense of greater possibilities than the ones that existed here. He'd have a job himself, she supposed, though this was something she could never actually picture. When she thought of the future, Clayton was the same little brother she'd been watching over from the time she was seven years old.

When the letter from the lawyer arrived, less than a week later, it confirmed Mavis's fear that the fireworks factory explosion had been a warning. She picked up the mail, as usual, at the post office by the Fire Neck station on the way home from Washington Lodge in Roy's Ford. It was raining lightly, a thin spring drizzle that made the air smell like grass and leaves, and Roy waited in the car while Mavis went into the post office. Leafing through the bills and circulars, she was surprised to see her name on a heavy cream envelope. The return address was a law firm in Fresno, California.

Mavis had put her failed marriage from her mind as much as she could. When she thought of her husband during the day, she threw a pinch of salt over her shoulder to ward off bad luck. She had come back to Fire Neck a few years before her niece and nephew, when only Roy and Scudder were living in the house on Salt Hay Road. Mavis had written to them from Ohio, saying simply that she was coming home alone, and for good.

On the afternoon of her return, it occurred to Roy at the last minute that the kitchen was not entirely clean. He spent twenty minutes swiping halfheartedly with a damp sponge, and then, on his way to the station, the Ford ran out of gasoline. Roy had to walk all the way to Southease with the gas can.

So Mavis stepped off the train at Fire Neck to a deserted platform. The ticket collector helped her with her luggage. Then the train pulled away in a flurry of dust. There were six barrels lined up along the track waiting for a westbound train, and as Mavis sat down on one of them, she felt the purpose and activity that had sustained her across three states drain out of her like blood. Her husband, Ramsay White, had abandoned her in Cleveland, taking with him the last of the money she'd inherited from her mother. Mavis knew he would not be back. She had felt relieved, even as failure settled on her heart like a hen on an egg.

She sat on the barrel and twisted the ring on her left hand. When her brother arrived, more than half an hour late, she almost resented being interrupted in her vacancy. She came back to Salt Hay Road in a listless daze. And it was only the extreme and unexpected squalor of the kitchen, with its smell of dogs and its strangely streaked windows, that roused her.

It took two weeks, cleaning from morning till night, to restore the kitchen to order. After their mother died, Roy had taken to feeding his dogs there. The pantry had been abandoned to the squirrels. In the bird's-eye corner cabinet that had been part of her mother's dowry, she found a desiccated sparrow in a soup tureen, its clawed feet gripping at nothing.

Mavis had always been a fitful sleeper. When she woke at night, she felt grateful each time to find herself in her own narrow bed in the house where she'd grown up. She kept the top curtains open so that she could look out her window and be sure of where she was. The moonlight often woke her. After she'd lain awake for an hour, she'd pull a flannel robe over her nightgown and go downstairs. She moved as quietly as she could in her stocking feet, her thin hair loosening from its braid. Some nights she could go back to sleep after cooking a pan of cornbread. Other nights she baked till dawn. Once, Roy found her asleep at the table when he came downstairs at six, with two loaves of bread, a nut cake, and a blueberry pie cooling beside her.

It was baking that drove Mavis to employment. Her father wasn't mean, but he was thrifty, and Mavis felt guilty spending his money on butter and sugar, let alone the poppy seed and candied ginger she craved. One day after she had surreptitiously given away an apple pie and a loaf of soda bread, she overheard the fish man tell her brother that George B. Washington had advertised for a cook. "I wonder what he eats, anyway, with all his money," the fish man grumbled. "Not what I'd call overfond of fish, I can tell you."

She knew her mother would have been ashamed to see her working. Part of Mavis was grateful that her mother had died while she was still in Ohio, before her marriage had come apart at the seams. Genevieve Scudder had been old-fashioned in her views and thought a wife's role was to ornament the home. Her father and brother accepted Mavis's job at Washington Lodge without complaint. She saved half of her earnings and put the rest into housekeeping. With Mavis away most of the day, Roy could enter the house without removing his boots, and if his dogs slipped into the kitchen, no one raised a fuss.

Now Mavis got back into the car mechanically, the mail clutched damply on her lap. She had no reason to correspond with lawyers. Unless it had to do with a will. Her mind sprang like a trap: maybe Ramsay was dead. The idea brought a rush of feeling so strong it shook her. She had never wished him harm, she reminded herself quickly. Even when he was at his worst, when she realized he was penniless and had courted her on the slim hope of her Chaffey inheritance, the most she'd ever hoped for was only that he would leave her alone. But now for the first time she saw how cramped the world felt with him at large in it. All these years she'd felt him lurking in the shadows. If he were dead . . . She would finally be safe from him, from the menace he represented and that she was certain he would exert over her until he died. She'd be a widow instead of a discarded wife. Dead, he could never reappear, never make any further claims or threats. She hoped, virtuously, that his end had been painless. Knowing him, it seemed unlikely.

"All right there?" Roy asked. Mavis didn't trust herself to speak. She nodded, keeping her eyes on the road.

Back at the house, Mavis took the envelope upstairs and opened it in the privacy of her room. Unused to the stiff, official language, she read for a full minute before she realized that her husband was not dead after all. He was missing. The lawyer was attempting to contact him on behalf of a client.

Stricken, Mavis leaned against the door. The bitterness of her disappointment brought tears to her eyes. She told herself she was an evil woman for jumping to such a conclusion, for entertaining such a hope. Taking the letter downstairs, she felt that she deserved whatever trouble it foretold. Roy was mixing up a salve for his dogs, and the kitchen smelled of turpentine, something Mavis would usually have complained about. Instead, she handed him the envelope. "I don't know what to do," she said, dropping heavily onto one of the kitchen chairs.

Roy scanned the cream-colored page with its perfect knife's-edge creases. "Do you know where he is?"

She shook her head.

Roy shrugged. "Why don't you write back to tell them that?" He tossed the letter on the table, and Mavis saw a smudged thumbprint where he'd held it. The smudge seemed to strip the letter of some of its power. It was only a piece of paper, she reminded herself. "He probably owes someone money," Roy went on. "Write back and explain that you haven't seen him in however many years. I imagine that'll be the end of it."

"Do you think so?"

"Sure," Roy said easily, stirring the salve with a wooden spoon. The smell of turpentine was very strong. "I wouldn't worry."

Mavis watched her brother lift the pot and pour the mixture into an empty jelly jar. Part of her longed to confess her deepest fear: that her husband was trailing her, like a fox tracking a rabbit. That any day he might show up here on Salt Hay Road. She avoided saying his name, afraid of conjuring him inadvertently. Since the day of the explosion, she had not slept well. In her dreams she saw the ugly gray cloud moving toward her, and then she knew that her husband was here in Fire Neck, on Salt Hay Road, he had opened the kitchen door, he was mounting the stairs. She would wake up with her heart hammering like a sparrow's. As close as she was to her brother, as dearly as she loved him, she had never told him much about her marriage.

She felt instinctively that her fears were better left unstated, as if putting them into words could somehow bring them about.

Roy had finished wiping the jelly jar with one of her dish towels. Whistling for his dogs, he made his way out of the kitchen. Mavis stood for a moment by the counter and silently prayed: *Please, Lord, keep my husband away from here.* Then she remembered her evil hope of a few moments before and despaired. She didn't deserve God's protection. And yet, she thought miserably, she needed it so badly. She took the letter and carried it back upstairs, grateful for the smear Roy's thumb had made. If her husband did track her, her brother would be here. She would not have to face him alone. That thought, more than any other, calmed her.

It was impossible for Nancy to pretend she'd arrived at the train station by chance. She sat waiting by the platform on Buckshot as Washington's car pulled in. Robert Landgraf, emerging from the backseat, spotted her immediately. He started toward her, smiling. Nancy slid off Buckshot's back and gripped the reins.

"Hold on," the driver called. Nancy heard him explain that Robert would have to buy his ticket on the train. "In Boston you probably have a big station. Here we just have this." The driver gestured at the little wooden platform.

"Thank you," Robert said, picking up the bag. "I'll wait by the tracks."

"Not too close," the driver admonished. From down the track they heard the whistle of the train. "Be careful in New York," the driver added, getting into the car. Robert turned at last toward Nancy with a mocking, secret wink. The train, throbbing down the tracks, stirred up clouds of dust. Robert stood holding the handle of his suitcase, tipped slightly to the side by the weight, as if some force inside the tracks were drawing him toward them. He was heading into New York City to see colleagues at the Museum of Natural History before continuing back to Boston.

Nancy wished suddenly that he would ask her to go with him to the city, just for the day. She wouldn't, of course, it was out of the question. But she wanted to be asked.

"Would it be all right," Robert said over the noise of the approaching train, and for a moment she thought he was thinking the same thing, "if I wrote to you?"

"Oh, of course," Nancy told him. "Sure. Box 17." She tried to act breezy, as if men wrote to her all the time and one more or less was not of much consequence. But she had to raise her voice as the train pulled in, and it sounded thin and childish to her ears. She felt angry at herself for not staying away. Buckshot whinnied, pulling against the reins as the train squealed to a stop. The conductor was opening the door at the top of the steps. "Goodbye," said Nancy, trying to smile. "It was nice to meet you."

"Westbound!" shouted the conductor. Robert was gazing at her with a fixed expression, as if he had just asked a momentous question and was waiting for her answer. Buckshot shuffled and snorted behind her. She gave the reins a yank, exasperated and close to tears.

The conductor shouted again. Robert turned. With a little wave in Nancy's direction, he stepped onto the train. He hadn't kissed her, Nancy thought bitterly, he hadn't even held her hand. Now it was too late. She would probably never see him again. Above her on the train, she saw Robert struggling to lower the window. It was stuck in place. He reappeared in the next row. The train pulled away, gathering speed. The window flew down and Nancy saw Robert's face protrude, his expression earnest. He called something down to her, but the noise of the engine drowned him out. Nancy stood and watched the train grow smaller before it rounded the corner and hurtled out of sight. The unheard words seemed to hang suspended in the smoke and dust.

Scudder was of two minds about the haircut. He sensed, in his granddaughter's offer, an urge to make him more presentable, something he naturally resented. On the other hand, and although he claimed to feel like a prize pig at a county fair, he secretly enjoyed being fussed over by Nancy. It was rare that he had her full attention lately. At first he'd been relieved when her typewriter went quiet and she stopped talking about secretarial jobs in Patchogue. He hadn't liked the idea of her in an office full of men, most of them undoubtedly married, though of course he hadn't been able to tell her so. But she seemed distracted, even sulky. She'd turned down his offer of going sailing twice in the last two days. He suspected the haircut was her way of making amends.

With a show of reluctance, he allowed her to set a kitchen chair in a patch of sunny lawn and submitted to a towel thrown around his shoulders and fastened with a clothespin. It was a still morning, the spring air warm and heavy with the promise of summer. A kingfisher flashed above the pond, making its cheerful racket.

Scudder leaned back in his chair. White hair drifted onto his lap and onto the green grass. "Mattress stuffing," he said, poking a tuft with his boot. What it reminded him of more than anything was the ash that had fallen from the sky after the fireworks factory explosion. Scudder wondered if it was the explosion that had affected Nancy's moods, or the weedy-looking guest from Washington Lodge who'd come to dinner that night; first she'd been so agitated, now she seemed inclined to mope. He closed his eyes, feeling the sun on his face and the movement of Nancy's hands as they tugged and snipped. Well, the man had gone, he knew because he'd asked Mavis, and it seemed unlikely that the explosion would have shaken someone with nerves like Nancy's. The girl thought nothing of danger, you could tell by the way she rode. Scudder had tolerated horses on the property ever since his marriage; his late wife had grown up around the animals on her family's ranch, and she'd insisted the children learn to ride. But the sheer bulk of the beasts had always bothered him. His granddaughter seemed so slight, so precariously perched.

He remembered how once when Nancy was still in diapers they'd found her at the top of a ladder set against one of Roy's greenhouses. She was bobbing happily above their heads, directly over the bright expanse of glass. Scudder had felt his heart seize like a clogged bilge pump. His daughter Helen stifled a scream.

"Boat-th!" shouted tiny Nancy, pointing out over the greenhouse roof. "I thee boat-th!"

"Ahoy," Scudder called, forcing himself to speak. "Can I have a look?" He'd moved up the ladder slowly. In the Life Saving Service he had climbed masts after sailors who'd taken refuge there on listing ships and then grown too cold or too terrified to get down. Once a man toppled just before Scudder reached him; Scudder grabbed for him as he fell and caught him by the jacket, the dead weight nearly dislocating his arm. The ladder shifted as Nancy bounced on her small bare feet. Below, Scudder could see roses through the clear roof of the greenhouse, a mass of yellow, a mass of pink, a mass of red. "Easy, missy," he said when he reached her, wrapping his arm around her waist. His hands were shaking. "Why don't I whittle you a boat out of wood?" She let him carry her down the ladder. Her skin smelled pleasantly of soured milk. Helen had wanted to beat her with a hairbrush, but he wouldn't allow it.

Sitting in the warm sun, he felt a chill as he remembered her at the top of that ladder, oblivious to the danger beneath her rosy feet. "You ought to be more careful on that horse," he said. He felt her fingers pause for a moment. Then the scissors resumed their snipping.

"Of course I'm careful."

"I knew a man, one of the Life Savers. His wife was thrown by a horse and died."

"Maybe she wasn't a very good rider," said Nancy bluntly.

"And don't forget Kelley's brother," Scudder added. The Captain's brother, dead now, used to visit him from Pennsylvania every summer. He'd been kicked in the throat and spoke in a rough whisper, fascinating the children so much that they kept up a long string of questions simply for the thrill of hearing his raspy voice, which made anything he said seem fraught with peril and romance, even if it was only "Get out of here, you wretched whelps! Can't a man rest his head a moment?"

"It was a mule that kicked the Captain's brother." Nancy moved his head to the side, and he felt her begin to cut around his left ear. "Mules are different from horses."

"They're unpredictable," Scudder said. "Either one."

"Oh, I could live on horseback." Nancy's tone was cheerfully emphatic. "Like they do in Mongolia."

Scudder sighed. How ridiculous, he thought, that one of the things he loved most about his granddaughter was her disdain for his advice. Why should that be? He demanded obedience from his own children, but Nancy had a spark of mischief he couldn't help but admire. He felt the comb rake through the hair on the top of his head, and then a tug as the girl snipped without hesitation. He had watched her throw herself into the saddle of that monstrous horse and handle the reins with the same assurance with which she now wielded the scissors. Mavis, poor thing, was nothing like that. Not her fault, of course, Scudder admonished himself, just a woman built along different lines. Mavis put her faith in God and good-luck charms, and a lot of spiritualist hooey that had started when her mother died and worsened since her husband left her.

From the direction of the driveway he heard the engine of the car start and then sputter. Roy was tinkering with it again. He remembered his late wife worrying before she died that Roy would never marry. He'd been surprised by how agitated the thought made her; their own marriage had been happy, in the main, but they'd had their share of difficulties, especially early on, and his own advice, had he and Roy ever spoken of such things, would have been against making a hasty decision.

"Almost done," Nancy said. "I'm just trying to even this out."

Scudder closed his eyes, happy to feel her fingers in his hair. He would look like a shorn ram, he thought; it didn't matter.

Since she and Enid Snow had fallen out of touch, Nancy rarely took an interest in the mail. Her aunt usually stopped for it on the way home from working at the lodge. But after Robert Landgraf returned to Boston, Nancy found herself riding past the post office every afternoon. It was around the corner from the train platform in a small shop that sold candy, pens, boxes of envelopes, powdered milk. Inside, Nancy studied the dusty pencils, the postcards showing sailboats at the mouth of the Barto River. She could feel Miss Reese, the postmistress, watching her from behind the counter. Miss Reese was past seventy and devoted to her job: she read every postcard and held each envelope up to the light to glean what she could of the contents. She was a small woman with a large head, and her gray hair sat on top of it in a tight bun, like a rock cairn on a mountain.

Now her small, sharp eyes glittered at Nancy. Robert had been gone less than a week, and Nancy told herself again that he probably hadn't written, probably never would. But she refused to let herself be intimidated by a gargoyle like Miss Reese. She sauntered to the counter and asked if there was anything for Box 17, then waited, forcing herself not to fidget, while the postmistress checked the cubbyholes of mail. For five days she had tried without success to put the possibility of a letter from her mind.

Miss Reese turned back with an envelope in her hand, and Nancy saw her own name in an unfamiliar, masculine hand. Her heart stuttered. "Thank you," she said, smiling in spite of herself. Miss Reese pursed her ancient lips.

Outside in the sunlight, Nancy sat for a moment holding the envelope. She felt almost frightened to have an actual letter from him in her hands. She opened it carefully and smoothed the folded paper. *Dear Miss Poole,* she read. *Do you, by some miracle, actually exist? Here in my familiar rooms, surrounded by the objects of my prosaic days, I find myself thinking about you and the strange circumstances of our meeting. I remember standing at the back door of Mr. Washington's house, and the way you ran toward me across the lawn. I have a hard time concentrating on the lifeless specimens here in the museum. Will you take pity on me and write? I would be grateful for some proof that I did not imagine you.*

Nancy got up from the bench outside the post office and walked quickly around the building, and then sat down and read the letter nine more times. She'd had admirers, shy local boys who worked on the bay and boys from Southease eager to show off their fathers' cars. But they seemed now to belong to a different category altogether. With her finger she traced the letters that formed her name in Robert's large, orderly script, and the silver bubble bobbed wildly inside her.

Summer 1937

Roy Scudder was a gentleman farmer, which meant he dabbled in agriculture. He liked horses and would have been a rancher, he used to say, if only he had a hundred more acres. For a few years, after he'd come back from college, he threw himself into growing flowers. With money from the Chaffey side, he built two long glass greenhouses and filled one with roses and the other with carnations. Later he added sweet peas and violets, but never turned much of a profit. Then he became interested in duck farming and had blueprints drawn up for a duck barn that would empty into the pond. By then the money had dwindled, and when he learned he'd have to pay pluckers up to five dollars a day, he got discouraged and abandoned the plans. For a while he raised quail in large wire pens set off the ground and sold their tiny, speckled eggs to restaurants in Southease and Moriches. There was a pigeon loft, for squab. He'd kept pigs, both Durocs and Chester Whites. For several years he'd raised hunting dogs to sell, adding a series of pens along the edge of the horse barn and building a long, narrow barn for goats, which he kept to produce extra milk for the puppies. Roy cooked the dog food, a mixture of meat scraps and cornmeal, in kettles on the big stove just inside the kitchen, waiting till after Mavis had left for work at the lodge.

Though they never spoke of it, Roy suspected his father looked askance at his efforts to make a living; Scudder seemed to think the Chaffey money had softened him. By the mid-1930s, when Clayton and Nancy came there to live, the outbuildings behind the house on Salt Hay Road were already falling into disrepair. Roy had gradually lost interest in everything but the hunting dogs he kept for his own use and his horses, Buckshot and Hardscrabble. He spent his days on the marsh and his weekends with friends from the boatyard and the Pattersquash Hunting Club.

Roy was fond of his niece and nephew, and glad to have them join the household after Helen died. And yet they left him somewhat at a loss. They cleaved together, naturally. He worried that he should be doing more for them, especially Clayton, without knowing exactly what. He wished he could somehow make up for the loss not only of their parents but of their once-considerable inheritance. Roy knew the details of this, because he had traveled to Connecticut after his brother-in-law died of a heart attack, with the idea that he might be of some use to his older sister.

He had found Helen pale but perfectly composed. Black suited her; in her simple dress she looked like a model in a magazine, and Roy felt slightly chilled by this, as if she should be unkempt, somehow; unmoored. Helen had never been demonstrative. Mavis, nervous and uncertain, relied on him, and so he tended to know what she was thinking. Helen kept her feelings to herself. Bertrand Poole had fallen in love with her at a beach party on Fire Island, after she'd won the Women's Sailboat Regatta for the third year in a row. Roy remembered her raising the gleaming cup in triumph, laughing, her teeth white in her tanned face, her hair tousled with wind and salt. The next day Bertrand had three hundred roses delivered to the house on Salt Hay Road. Their mother ran out of vases, and there'd been roses in canning jars, red, pink, and white, in buckets and tin cans. The house smelled like a perfumery. Helen accepted them without surprise, as if roses were her due, and Roy found himself wondering if her beauty had spoiled her, the way she'd been spoiled by Granny Chaffey and her trip to Europe. Later, after her marriage, it was Roy's private theory that she hadn't taken her adoring husband seriously because, for all his success in the world of business, he didn't know how to handle a boat. "He's so clever," Roy overheard Mavis tell her at the wedding, with a touch of awe.

"In his way," Helen said carelessly. "But he's *helpless* on the water."

In Stonington, after the funeral, Roy worked to shake the feeling that Helen should be more distraught. Together they met with her late husband's business partner. Bertrand Poole had left a generous legacy. His partner, Mr. Connell, went over the details. There was a certain amount in a savings account, he explained, addressing himself to Roy, man to man. The rest was in a carefully chosen portfolio of stocks and bonds.

"Why do I need those?" Helen asked. She pulled a white handkerchief from her purse and patted her nose. "I'd rather have it all in one place."

Mr. Connell explained that stocks were shares in a company, almost like loans to that company, and that bonds were like loans too. Having them in different places helped to balance the risk. Hers were doing very well, he assured Roy. Returns on some were over 10 percent.

"*Loans?*" Helen looked at Mr. Connell sharply. "I don't

think we want *that*." Turning, she addressed Roy, "Remember how Grandfather kept all his savings in a canning jar in the cellar? And Grandpa Chaffey only invested in land. Good and solid."

"Ha-ha," said Mr. Connell, and then, as Helen regarded him stonily, "Should we discuss this another time?"

Helen shook her head. She was taking the children down to Long Island the next day for a visit, she explained, and she'd like all the money now, in a nice lump sum.

"My dear Mrs. Poole, I don't think you understand. We're talking about hundreds of thousands of dollars."

It was the wrong approach to take with Helen. Roy could see her elegant shoulders squaring ever so slightly in the black silk dress. "If I don't understand," she told Mr. Connell briskly, "it's because the money seems to be spread all over the place. Naturally I want it all together, where I can see it."

"I'll arrange for you to have as much as you need, my dear. The rest is doing very well in the stock market." Here he suggested a number, holding up a slip of paper. It sounded like a great deal of money to Roy. Helen shook her head firmly, giving Mr. Connell a withering look.

Mr. Connell doubled the number, holding up another piece of paper with a sigh that indicated he was being more than reasonable. Now Helen hesitated, turning to Roy. He couldn't remember another time that she had asked for his advice. But what did he know about stocks and bonds? Mr. Connell appealed to her wifely feeling. "Your late husband was a man of business. I'm sure he'd want you to leave everything just the way it is."

Helen clutched her purse, and Roy knew she was tightening her grip on an imaginary tiller. "Bertie couldn't even sail a catboat," she began.

Roy felt compelled to step in. "Helen, please. Leave it alone for now. You can get the rest when you need it." She sighed and closed her eyes, and Roy saw the grief in the lines of her face. The handkerchief in her hand drooped like a small white flag. Roy and Mr. Connell shared a brief but relieved glance over the top of her head.

A year later, when the stock market crashed, Bertrand Poole's legacy vanished overnight. Roy had wished many times since then that he'd backed his sister up that day in Mr. Connell's office. But how could he have known that she was right and Connell wrong? At least the money she had insisted on taking with her had made her last years comfortable. What was left for the children came from the sale of the big house in Stonington after she died.

Clayton loved the outbuildings just as they were—the barn with its hayloft and smell of horses, the empty pigsty, where the rich, dense odor of pig manure still lingered, especially after a heavy summer rain. He and Perry liked to scramble up the side of the A-frame pig house, their fingers gouging the moss-slicked shingles, and sit on the ridge of the low roof beneath the chokecherry branches. The small red cherries were tart on Clayton's tongue. He and Perry spat the pits high into the air and watched them skitter down the slanted roof.

Closer to the road, a lush abundance of oversized weeds and saplings thrived in the abandoned greenhouses. Inside, it was always several degrees warmer, the air moist with the smell of damp soil and rot. Clayton and Perry played long games of Jungle Hunter, taking turns as the Wily Beast, games fraught with real danger due to the broken glass on the dirt floor and the weakness of the remaining frames. In the tangle of vegetation they sometimes came across a splash of white carnations or yellow roses. Every so often Roy would decide to fix the greenhouses up, this time to grow tomatoes or lettuces to ship to New York City. He might spend a whole day reviewing the necessary repairs and scribbling with a thick pencil on the back of a brown paper bag. Once, he had a glazier come by, and the two of them walked in and out of the greenhouses, pointing and discussing prices and materials. In a box in his room Clayton kept the red and yellow stubs of Roy's discarded builder's pencils. It took some time for him to realize that nothing came of Roy's bursts of initiative, that the greenhouses, like the pigsty and the pigeon loft, were safe from improvement.

As soon as school let out in June, Clayton spent much of his free time at the boatyard. *Playing,* Nancy called it, as if he were six years old and he and Perry were shooting marbles. She had taken a morning off from typing practice to get a list of recommended titles from his teacher, Miss Collier—*All Set Sail, The Good Master, Young Fu of the Upper Yangtze*—and now she plagued him to start one, ignoring the fact that September was two and a half months away. "Don't play too long at the boatyard," she said. "There are books you should be reading."

Clayton and Perry knew every boat docked at Starke's, from the smallest leaky rowboat to the 42-foot cabin cruiser with the plum stem grandly called the *Coronet.* Perry's favorite was a long, sleek motorboat with an open cockpit that belonged to a lawyer from the city who used it only once or twice a month. Clayton liked the sturdy clamming boats with the wide, flat decks and rounded bows. He would have at least three boats when he grew up, he told Perry: a work boat, a sailboat, and a cruiser.

Today Clayton sat in the shade of the boat shed alone. Perry had been made to stay home with his little sister, Pearl, who had a toothache, while their mother went into town. Sam Burnett and George Rowley were mending eel pots and discussing a racing schooner being built in Patchogue. Clayton listened to the men, hoping to pick up a new phrase or technical term to impress his friend.

Theron Greaves came around the corner of the boat shed with a bucket in one hand, a flat blue cap low on his forehead. He was an older bayman with a face like leather. Clayton knew his boat, a 21-foot cat skiff called *Leda*. In the winter Theron coated his cotton jacket with fish oil to keep out the cold, and all year his clothes smelled of rancid fish and tobacco. A little black dog with a spotted face followed behind him and sat with an air of resignation as Theron joined Sam Burnett and George Rowley at the eel pots. Clayton, listening intently, heard him say he needed a scapper for the season.

Clayton was on his feet almost before he knew what he was doing. "I'll do it!" The three men turned, surprised, and he realized he had shouted. "I can scap," he said, forcing himself to lower his voice. "I'm good with a net. I can do it. I'll show you."

Theron Greaves gave him a long, appraising stare. Clayton felt like an eel on a slab of ice. He stood up straighter, trying to appear taller, and wished with all his heart that he looked more like one of Perry's muscular brothers.

Theron did not seem particularly impressed. He turned toward the other men and jerked his head in Clayton's direction. "Sober fellow?"

Sam Burnett grinned. "Sure. That's Scudder's grandson. Roy's nephew."

"Got all his fingers?"

"I suppose he does," said Sam. The three men looked back at Clayton. Confused, he held up his hands to show them his digits.

"Scap good?" asked Theron. He glanced around the boatyard, as if hoping for other, more likely, candidates.

"Could do," said Sam. "You give him a try with the net."

"Two o'clock tomorrow, then," Theron said, addressing Clayton for the first time. "*Leda*." He nodded to the other two and walked off in the direction of the canals with his bucket, the black dog trotting after him.

Clayton punched the shingled wall of the boat shed in his excitement. A job on the bay! A job with Theron Greaves! If only he didn't mess up. He'd crabbed off the docks plenty of times with Perry: they'd put a fish head or a piece of chicken neck on a string and lower it into the water. When a crab went for the bait, the string tightened and began to move. Then one of them pulled the string in slowly while the other stood by with the net. When the crab came into view, clutching the bait, the scapper scooped it out of the water. The trick was in the timing. If he scooped too soon, the crab would scuttle away before the net reached it. If he waited too long, the crab grew nervous and abandoned the bait. Clayton went over the procedure in his mind step-by-step, more anxious than he'd ever felt before a test at school.

Nancy sat on the porch, working on a letter to Robert Landgraf on her portable typewriter. His were playful, asking what had spontaneously combusted lately while lamenting the dreariness of his days spent roughing out specimens in the museum basement, "in grave danger of forgetting what a live bird looks like, always excepting the pigeons." Nancy, trying to respond with something clever, gave up in despair after half a stilted page. Far in the distance she could hear the drone of an airplane. The smell of the lilacs outside the door hung sweet and heavy in the air. She tried to imagine Robert in Boston, but she couldn't picture where he lived, or the museum where he worked, or where he ate his dinner, or with whom. "I have never been to Boston," she wrote finally, stopping to unjam the keys. "Can you tell me more about it? My uncle swears someone once drowned there in a flood of molasses."

What Robert liked about Boston, he'd written, was the press of people, the sense that he was in the thick of something. He lived in an apartment "smaller than a bread box, but with much the same charm." He'd grown up in Winslow, Maine, where his father and older brothers ran the family dairy farm. Sometimes he still missed the bobolinks, he told her, the way they flung themselves from the branches in the spring when the air was full of cottonwood fluff. Reading this, Nancy thought of Clayton and the fascination with birds' nests and turtle shells he'd developed since they'd come to Fire Neck. It pleased her to draw that little parallel between them.

In his latest letter, Robert asked what she liked most about Long Island, "besides the clouds of smoke, of course." Nancy tapped at the shift key. Since Robert left, she'd felt more dissatisfied with Fire Neck than ever.

She thought of her mother growing up in this same house, and wondered if she had felt a similar impatience with the unchanging rooms, with her family. Nancy's father had fallen in love with her in the course of a single evening on the beach. Nancy had heard the story so often she could see it in her mind: her mother with her sailing trophy on her lap, her face lit by the flames of the campfire. Six months later, they were married and living in Stonington, another sailing town. Nancy allowed herself to wonder for a moment how it would feel, not the move from the house on Salt Hay Road so much as the leap of faith, the trading of one life for a different one. Of course, her mother would have taken it in stride fairly easily, Nancy thought. She was a woman unsurprised by her own successes.

Glancing up from the Remington, Nancy caught sight of Clayton coming across the field. He'd been hanging around at the boatyard, she guessed. At the fence he stopped and she saw him make a series of odd, scooping motions in the air with his arms. His face, pinched in concentration, made Nancy remember the way he used to frown, biting his tongue, back when he was learning to read. "What are you catching out there?" she called merrily, and Clayton jumped. Nancy thought again how much he'd changed in the last year. He had grown gangly and secretive. Sometimes she found herself missing him, though of course he was right there. "Come sit with me a minute," she called. Her brother paused and then walked over, hands in his pockets, his shirt in need of a wash.

"Do you ever think about what kind of job you might want?" Nancy asked. She worried that he didn't apply himself at school. His teacher had told her that Clayton often scribbled pictures in his workbooks and that he needed to pay closer attention. He'd been caught playing hooky. "Later, after you're through with school?"

Clayton looked startled. He moved his head in a noncommittal gesture.

"It's just that you know so much about birds and insects. You might be able to work in a museum someday."

He shot her a suspicious look. "I like being outside."

"Of course," Nancy said. "Of course you do now. I meant later, when you're older."

"I won't want to be inside then, either."

"It was just a thought." Nancy didn't want to argue about it. She knew how stubborn he could get. But now Clayton was looking at her with a shy smile.

"I might get a job tomorrow," he confided. "Maybe. A job on the *bay*!" He sat back, pleased with himself. Nancy realized that the fierce concentration she'd seen on his face earlier had been connected to this, and she felt a twinge of disappointment; clamming or crabbing would never translate into a job at a museum, a career. "I'm not sure, though," Clayton added, suddenly sounding anxious. "I don't know if I'll be good enough."

Nancy reached over and squeezed his hand. "Sure you will." He smiled at her again, grateful, and she seized her chance. "Now promise me you won't skip school anymore."

Clayton glanced at his lap. He shrugged elaborately. "It's the *summer*," he pointed out.

Nancy held his hand tight as he tried to withdraw it. "Promise me, Clay. It's important."

He rolled his eyes. "Fine, I promise!" He pulled his hand away, but not unkindly, and trotted off in the direction of the barn. He was just a kid, Nancy thought, half sorry she'd been so stern.

Clayton arrived at the *Leda* ten minutes early. Across the canal, red-winged blackbirds burbled in the reeds. He waited nervously, worried the job had been a joke on him, until Theron Greaves appeared, carrying his bucket. The old bayman nodded to Clayton. The bucket was half full of pieces of pungent salted eel. From underneath the bow of the *Leda*, Theron passed Clayton a huge spool of line, tied with lumps of old eel skin that looked like black gristle. They sat down on the dock with the spool and the bucket beside them. Wordlessly, Theron showed Clayton how to take a chunk of eel, score it with a knife, then tie it onto the line with a clove hitch. He left a space of about six feet between the pieces of bait. The dog had jumped into the boat and stretched out in the shade under the bow. From time to time Theron threw her a scrap of eel skin, which she chewed steadily with half-closed eyes.

When the trotline had been baited from one end to the other, Theron loaded it back onto the *Leda* and they got aboard. A light breeze had come up. Clayton cast off from the dock and the canvas sail bellied out. Theron steered the *Leda* along the canal, past the boats at their docks and the men working on eel pots, mending nets, and fixing rudders. At the river he nosed up into the wind and tightened the main sheet. The *Leda* shivered, listed, and picked up speed. Clayton sat on the windward side and leaned out over the water. He breathed in deeply, loving the smell of marsh and mud, the spray on his face. He felt a wild spasm of affection for Perry's little sister; without her toothache, his friend would have been at the boatyard the day before and might have been chosen instead.

They sailed toward the mouth of the river, to a small indentation in the bank called Rose's Cove. Clayton had been there once before in a rowboat, looking for marsh wren nests. Theron came up into the wind, and they anchored one end of the trotline and marked it with a yellow buoy. Then he worked slowly back across the river under sail, and Clayton played out the trotline as they went. Near Long Point they anchored the other end. The sun had come out from behind the clouds and the water shone. Out on the bay a white powerboat touched its reflection as it bounced along. The hull and its image met and parted, met and parted, cutting the water like a pair of shears.

They sailed back to Rose's Cove, giving the crabs time to find the bait. There they picked up the line on a shiver attached to the gunwale; the shiver lifted the line and dropped it back down, bringing the bait close to the surface. Theron pointed with his chin toward the flat net, a skimmer made of chicken wire. Clayton took it and stood in the bow. Below him on the trotline a piece of black eel swam into view. He breathed in, to steady himself. No crab on that bait. The boat sailed slowly, almost drifting. It was quiet except for the lapping of waves along the hull and the barking of the gulls. Clayton stared down into his own distorted reflection. A crab appeared briefly, then faded into the murk. Clayton plunged the net, far too late. "Look lively," Theron said sharply from the stern, and Clayton jumped, almost dropping the net. He felt his eyes sting with shame. In another instant a second crab rose toward the surface, and this time Clayton plunged the net into the water. Up came the crab, gripping the chicken wire. Clayton flicked it into the basket in the bow, waking the dog. He turned back in time to see another crab hanging on the line. Down went the net, breaking the undulant gloss of the water. Twice he missed the basket and the crabs scuttled into the bilge, brandishing their pincers.

When the bait gave out and the yellow buoy appeared, Clayton looked up, surprised by the blue sky. He felt like a swimmer coming up for air. His eyes hurt from staring into the bright water, and he realized he'd been grasping the pole of the net so tightly his fingers ached. "Ready about," Theron said, and the *Leda* pivoted neatly in the water.

By the end of the fourth run, the basket was full and Clayton's technique had improved. A few of the crabs looked too small to keep. Clayton gripped them one by one with the tongs and glanced back at Theron. When he shook his head, Clayton flung the crab in question out over the water. Next he retrieved the two from the bilge and added them to the basket. Now that he'd acquitted himself well, he felt filled with happiness and relief. Beyond Long Point the salt marsh stretched, a haze of yellow green bordered by the darker green of high-tide bush and mallow. A marsh hawk flew low over the spartina. On the bank toward the boatyard a heron stood without moving. In the boat, the crabs clicked and bubbled, pinching at each other. The tide had begun to turn. They hauled in the trotline and returned for the other end, winding the line back on the spool as they went. The line would be stored in a barrel and covered with salt to keep it from rotting; they could use the same bait for several days.

Back at the boatyard Clayton learned how to pack the crabs in seaweed in small barrels, using a pair of tongs to keep from getting pinched. With a hatchet, Theron chopped out pieces of the barrel stays for air. They covered the barrels with burlap tops and tagged them. Theron did not own a car, so Jimmy Starke drove them down to the Fire Neck train station in his truck. Clayton rode in the back with the crabs. In his mind he played over the afternoon, the net gripped in his hands as he waited for the bait to come into view. At the station, he and Theron loaded the barrels onto the platform, where others already sat, waiting for the next New York train. The price for crabs was three dollars a barrel.

Theron held out his hand, and Clayton, confused, started to shake it. Then he felt the coins jingle into his palm. "Tomorrow at three," Theron Greaves told him. He turned and whistled for the dog. Clayton clambered onto the truck for the ride back to the boatyard. He stood up against the window, clinging to the roof. The wind whipped around him as if he were flying. It had been, he felt, the best day of his life.

Waiting at the train station, Nancy fought a rising panic. Over the last month and a half she had collected a small pile of envelopes with Boston postmarks. On days when there was nothing for her at the post office she affected nonchalance and bought a bag of Red Hots for Clayton. One day a letter came that was only a page: *I've convinced our director that the New Guinea psittacine in the Washington aviary demands closer study. I'm packing my calipers and my camera and will be returning to your exotic island in two weeks. I look forward to seeing you again.*

At the end of the platform a friend of Roy's whose name she couldn't remember picked at his teeth with a toothpick, a folded newspaper under one arm. Washington's driver was waiting with the car. Nancy tried to keep from pacing. She was making a fool of herself for a man she hardly knew. Maybe she'd misjudged his interest, she thought, maybe he was amusing himself at her expense. She remembered reading the letter on the bench beside the post office, and how, when she'd finished, she'd raced Buckshot down Old Stump Road at a reckless gallop. She worried now that Robert would think she was too forward, meeting the train like this. At the side of the building Buckshot stood tied to a post, flicking his tail at the flies. The train whistled in the distance. She glanced back at the horse, calculating the time it would take to unhitch him and mount. If she left now, she thought, Robert wouldn't see her. The whistle sounded again. Nancy imagined riding home. In the house on Salt Hay Road, her grandfather would be dozing over his cards while Mavis and Captain Kelley carried on another endless discussion about the nature of the divine.

The train pulled in, brakes squealing, and there was Robert stepping out of it three cars down from where she stood. He looked younger than she remembered, his hair sticking up in the back, his gray suit rumpled from the trip. She felt a momentary uncertainty, as if this might not be the man she'd been writing to for all these weeks. He blinked, dust in his eyes, and scanned the platform. Nancy stepped out from the shadow of the station wall and their eyes met. The happiness on his face was unmistakable. She felt herself smiling.

"Mr. Landgraf!" Washington's driver was hurrying over. Robert turned toward him with a groggy look, like someone torn from a deep sleep. "Mr. Landgraf, the car's over here."

"You can take the luggage on ahead," Nancy said boldly. "I'll bring Mr. Landgraf myself."

"Yes," Robert said. "Thank you. I need to stretch my legs." The driver looked unsure. Robert fumbled in his pocket and handed over a tip. The driver pocketed it, then picked up Robert's bags and turned in the direction of the car.

The train was pulling out again, and they moved away, toward Buckshot. Nancy unhitched the horse. "Where are you leading me this time?" Robert asked.

"To the lodge, like I said." She grinned at him. "On horseback."

Robert took a step backward. "Better not. I fell off one of those as a boy. Never learned to work the brakes."

"You'll be fine," Nancy said. She saw the hesitation beneath his mock alarm. "Leave it to me." For weeks she had wondered what it would be like when she saw him again, haunting the post office while she waited for his letters. Now she understood that it would be hard for him to refuse her. She felt a burst of reckless pleasure.

The station had emptied except for a small gang of boys playing marbles. She led Buckshot to the horse block at the edge of the road.

"Observe," Nancy said. She held the reins and put her hands on the horse's neck. Grasping the mane in one hand, she swung herself onto Buckshot's back, aware of her own easy grace. She looked down at Robert, who was watching her with a gratifying expression. "Your turn," she told him. "Put your left hand here." The horse whinnied and shuffled his back legs.

"Why don't I walk beside you instead?" Robert asked without moving from where he stood. "I have a lovely view of you from here."

"But you'd never keep up with me." Nancy reached toward him. "Hold on with this hand and raise yourself on your arms." Robert looked up at her, shaking his head. He was wearing black leather shoes, city shoes. After a long moment he moved forward. Nancy watched his foot step onto the whitewashed horse block. He put his hand on the edge of the saddle and lurched toward her. Buckshot tossed his head and began to sidle away, and Robert stumbled back, his face flushed.

"I'm going to break my neck," he said. Nancy considered taking pity on him. But he had already grasped the saddle again. Buckshot sidestepped, head bobbing, as Robert swung himself up in a single desperate assault, nearly unseating Nancy. She felt his body pressed abruptly against hers, his legs on either side of her own. Goose bumps broke out along her arms.

Robert laughed in surprise. "I'm a cowboy!"

Nancy felt him shift behind her in the saddle as he tried to give her more room. "Sorry," he murmured. She lifted her hands, and without being told, Robert put his arms around her to grasp the horse's mane. He smelled faintly of camphor. The ride had been an idle impulse, a way to tease him. Now his man's hands lay in front of her, his fingers stained with black ink, the veins and muscles showing under the reddish hair. What had she done? What was she doing? She could feel him breathing behind her. She had crossed a border into foreign territory.

"Here we go," Nancy cried, clacking her tongue and giving a jab with her heel. The horse started with a little jump, and Robert's arms tightened around her. Buckshot, unused to the extra weight, stepped with a nervous prancing motion. They turned off the road, taking a path through Kozlowski's back field. The air was thick with pollen and the smell of honeysuckle.

Nancy wondered what would happen when they reached the lodge, how they would act toward each other with their feet on the ground. She thought of Danny Traphagen; how childishly flattered she'd felt when he asked her to dance at a party the summer before, how clumsy he was in his car afterward as he pulled at the strap of her dress. Her curiosity had given way to annoyance, and she told him she had to get home. He drove sullenly, without speaking, and Nancy was glad to reach Salt Hay Road and get out of his car. When she saw him again, at the beach four days later, he'd made a point of ignoring her.

"All right back there?" Nancy tried to keep her voice light.

"Never better," Robert said, his mouth close to her ear.

There was a soft explosion ahead of them as half a dozen bobwhite quail shot out of the grass and scattered, wings whirring. Nancy's hands tightened on the reins and Buckshot drew up, ears pricked forward. She felt Robert's breath on the back of her neck. The birds disappeared, leaving a swirl of dust in the air, and after a moment the horse wheezed and reached down to crop the grass at the edge of the path. Robert's hands still gripped the mane in front of her. Nancy watched his ink-stained fingers disengage from the coarse black hair. Slowly he opened one hand and lifted it over hers. With the smallest movement of her foot, Nancy thought, the horse would start forward. Robert's warm fingers laced around her own. She held completely still, barely breathing. Through the fabric of her blouse she felt his beating heart.

Clayton's friend Perry lived with his family on Carman Street. Like most of the roads south of Old Purchase, Carman deadended in the Great South Bay. At low tide Clayton and Perry were sent to the little margin of beach to collect eelgrass to mulch Mrs. Gilpin's garden. "Don't forget your sister!" Mrs. Gilpin called from where she stood beside the henhouse with a scrap of chicken wire. Perry rolled his eyes. His sister was nine. She was the youngest Gilpin and the only girl out of seven children. Mrs. Gilpin had named her Pearl, she said, after the pearl of great price. Her brothers called her Pearl the Girl.

Clayton studied the Gilpins furtively, like a field biologist. He was fascinated by the way Perry and his brothers spoke to their mother and how she answered them, exasperated and affectionate, and by Pearl, who was so little like his own sister. She had no authority over her brothers at all.

"Mo-ther!" Perry complained now, kicking the side of the wheelbarrow. "She'll get her shoes wet!"

"See that she doesn't! Stay out of the water, all three of you!" Hearing Mrs. Gilpin include him in her order, Clayton felt a flush of gratitude.

Perry and Clayton each took a handle of the wheelbarrow. The rakes rattled against the side. "Come *on*, Pearl," said Perry.

On the way to the water, on the other side of the street, was the Fleming Tree Nursery. Because Pearl was with them, they had to stop at the nursery to look for Molly and Dolly, the two big mares that pulled the nursery wagon. Pearl called to them across the field and they lumbered over and breathed heavily into the children's hands, searching for lumps of sugar.

Farther along lived Chicken Jackson. It was rumored among the neighborhood children that he was one hundred and one years old. Chicken Jackson raised white leghorns and Rhode Island Reds and sold eggs and pullets from a shed in the back of his house. In the spring he went around town in a goat cart and caponized roosters at ten cents apiece. The goat was a billy with yellow eyes and a heavy, musky smell that clung to the cart and also to Chicken Jackson.

At the end of the road the seaweed had washed up along the narrow beach in dark snaking ridges. Fire Island shimmered in the distance, looking as if it had broken into pieces that floated on the horizon. "Come on," said Perry. He lifted a huge armful of black eelgrass into the wheelbarrow.

Pearl sat down on a high ridge and waved a cattail like a scepter. "I am the queen!" she announced. Her brother pitched a clump of seaweed at her and she screamed.

That night on Salt Hay Road Nancy came in half an hour late for dinner. Her cheeks were pink and her eyes shone. She looked feverish again, Clayton thought in alarm. Roy and Scudder stared up at her, their forks poised in midair. "Your plate's on the stove," said Mavis shortly. "I'm afraid the potatoes are cold."

"I'm engaged!" Nancy burst out. "I'm going to be Mrs. Robert Landgraf!" She threw her arms around Clayton's shoulders and gazed out at the others with a brilliant smile.

No one spoke. Clayton sat as stiff as a rabbit under his sister's embrace. *Mrs. Robert Landgraf*: it was the name of a different person, someone he didn't know. She was marrying the man from Boston. *Boston.* The syllables brought to mind a cold grayness. A city crammed with buildings and concrete and strangers. It seemed at that moment farther than Peking, a world away from the landscape he knew. *Boston, Boston, Boston.*

At the head of the table Scudder frowned down at his plate, the announcement a wave of icy water down the neck. What was the girl thinking? Marriage, at her age, and to a stranger from another state! She would take herself off, after all they'd done for her. Did the girl have no family feeling? He couldn't bring himself to look at her. She was shameless, he thought angrily, like a cat in heat.

Roy turned from his niece's gaze. He had been that age once; how long ago it suddenly seemed. For the first time in years, he recalled the despair that had led him to that unconfessed moment of folly on the bay. Had he really loved a girl so badly he'd believed he couldn't live without her? He felt a grudging admiration, as if, in the extremity of that youthful grief, he'd elevated himself above the mere unhappiness of the rest of the population. Plenty of people suffered in love, but how many went out of their heads like he had? What surprised him most, looking back on it, more even than the astonishing fact that she'd loved him, was the ferocity of his own emotion. It seemed hard to credit. Now he barely remembered what she'd looked like. She had faded in his mind, like the Cheshire Cat, leaving only her gap-toothed smile.

Mavis was remembering the view from Madame Sonya's dress shop on Old Purchase Road. As her mother and Madame Sonya discussed adding a panel to the train of her wedding gown, Mavis stood idly looking out the window. A large black fly crawled back and forth along the bottom of the pane. Outside, a Liberty truck loaded with pine caskets rumbled past along the road. It was 1918, and the soldiers at Camp Upton were dying of the Spanish flu. Behind her Mavis heard her mother's voice: "Our last girl . . . I want it to be perfect . . ." A second truck passed. It seemed to Mavis now that there had been an omen in the casket-laden trucks; she had sensed it at the time, but had ignored it.

Nancy let go of her brother's shoulders and stood up, her face cramped. "Can't anyone say something? What's the matter with you all?"

Mavis cleared her throat. "It's very sudden. And right in the middle of dinner . . ."

"Doesn't anyone care that I'm happy?" Tears glittered in Nancy's eyes.

Boston, Boston, Boston. In the hush punctuated by Nancy's choked breathing, Clayton stood and pushed back his chair. With a vague nod he made for the door. He walked deliberately, like someone who has received a blow to the head that he is unwilling to acknowledge, or of which he is not yet fully aware.

An hour later Nancy tapped on Clayton's door. Inside his room, the floor was littered with glass specimen jars. Nancy remembered how, the summer before, he'd collected over one hundred beetles and insects. First he sketched them, and then he stored them in jam jars in the barn, each one wrapped in tissue paper and carefully labeled. At the end of the summer he stayed up past midnight arranging them on a corkboard with pins. Under each specimen he wrote the Latin name and the date it had been found. That night while he slept the barn mice found the board, and by morning the beetles and insects had been eaten. All that was left were the pins in the corkboard, each with a scrap of white paper beneath it, and, along the floor, a jumble of brittle legs and wings.

"Clayton," Nancy said. He sat on the rug by the bed with a glossy black beetle in one hand. She disliked his fascination with dead animals and insects, the way he would crouch for an hour beside a chipmunk covered in ants, drawing it from different angles. Sometimes she wondered if it had something to do with their parents, if her brother was trying to understand the meaning of that loss by studying the mechanics of decay. At other times she thought perhaps it might be a kind of strange comfort to him to feel that death was all around them, though on a manageable scale. Either way, she found his interest macabre and wished he would grow out of it.

Nancy moved aside a sketchbook and sat down beside him on the floor. Another wave of impatience with the others downstairs coursed through her, the way they'd all stared at her when she told her news. They couldn't bear change. But Clayton would see her side of it. Trying to meet his eye, she realized that she wasn't sure what he was thinking. He was closed off like a turtle in its shell. He used to follow her around, after their mother died, unwilling to let her out of his sight; now he disappeared all day with Perry Gilpin and came home smelling of mud and bait fish. He had his own spending money from his job at Washington Lodge and used it on books of natural history and collection jars that arrived in the mail from a supply company in South Carolina that he'd found who knows how. Nancy remembered when his greatest pleasure had been the sticks of black licorice she brought him from a candy store in Drowned Meadow.

"I should have told you first," she said at last. "I planned to, but then I came in and everyone looked up at me and I couldn't keep it in. I'm so happy!"

Clayton said nothing. He fiddled with the top to one of his jars.

"I told Robert I couldn't go anywhere without you too," Nancy said. "Of course he understands. He likes you already, Clay. And you two have so much in common."

Clayton picked up another jar and moved it from hand to hand, as if judging its weight. "Why do you want to get married?"

Nancy laughed. "We love each other! Come on, Clay. Most people get married."

He lifted his head and met her eyes. His face seemed leaner, less rounded, his stubborn jaw more pronounced. "No, they don't. Roy never did."

"The point is," said Nancy, "I'd never, ever leave you. You're my brother, Clay."

Clayton looked back down at the beetle. Nancy stood. "I know you're going to like it." She bent down quickly, before he could shift away, and kissed him above the ear. His hair smelled brackish, unwashed. She remembered how, as a child, he'd presented his bumps and scratches to her for kisses. It had been easy to reassure him then. Now he seemed almost sullen in his self-possession. Sometimes she looked up and saw him watching her from the doorway. Yet he would hardly let her pat his shoulder.

"And Robert works in a museum," she added, at the door. "He'll be able to show you how they mount the exhibits. Think of all the specimens you'll get to see."

Clayton frowned down at another label, his pen in his hand. "I don't want to go to Boston."

Nancy shook her head at him fondly. "Wait till you see it."

He would come around, she reassured herself in the hall. He would get used to the idea. But she felt an uneasiness about the way they'd all reacted, staring at her in that awkward silence, the dinner congealing on the plates. Why should it be so surprising? She was old enough to know her own mind. Was she supposed to put off falling in love until her brother finished school? Did they expect her to stay here forever? Didn't she deserve her happiness, after everything she'd been through?

She and Robert had been in the aviary, among the cages and his instruments and reference books. Robert held a little brown-and-white bird with bright, seedlike eyes, its pink, scaly legs tucked firmly between his middle and forefinger. As he tried to measure it with a pair of calipers, it jabbed its small beak fiercely and repeatedly at his gloved hand. Robert laughed, rueful, glancing up at her. "The stuffed ones are easier to handle." Finished, he slipped the bird back into a cage near the table and pulled off his leather work gloves. The light in the room, tumbling through the large windows with sudden brilliance, illuminated the bits of fluff that hung in the still, guano-scented air like dust motes. Turning to her, Robert's face grew serious. Around them the bright, darting birds trilled and screeched and sang. "That's how I feel about you, Nancy." She leaned forward so she could hear him above the din, distracted by a white spot on his right eyebrow. A piece of down, she realized, caught like an unmelting snowflake. Without thinking, she moved her hand to brush it away, and then stopped herself, afraid it was too intimate a gesture. Robert misunderstood and fumbled for her hand. "Being with you, and being apart. It's like the difference between these birds and the dead ones I work with." Nancy caught, at last, the change in his manner. She stared hard at his eyebrow, uncertain and confused. How was she supposed to respond? The asymmetry of the white fluff gave Robert a startled look, and it struck her that he was as unsure of what to do next as she was. And then he said, "I don't suppose you'd ever want to marry a man like me?"

Of course that was what she wanted. Of course. There was no need to feel confused. How easy it would be, after all. She raised her hand and gently brushed the fleck from above his eye.

In her room, Nancy opened the window and leaned out into the warm, dark air. They would all be happy in Boston, she told herself. She felt her future billow out before her like a kite on a string, pulling the three of them forward.

The day after Nancy announced the move to Boston, Clayton sneaked onto the roof, using the remnants of his grandmother's wisteria trellis for a footing. From the yard he was screened by the pine tree. No one knew where he was, and this was what he valued most about the spot, even more than the view. On hot days in the summer he and Perry climbed up here often. Looking south over the marsh to the bay, they could see the flat ribbon of Fire Island in the distance. They'd try to guess which boats were docked by the position of the masts at Starke's Boatyard, whether the one with the blue-and-white pennant belonged to the *Comet* or the *Foam*. Sometimes they brought the thick heads of cattails from the marsh and smoked them like cigars; they'd hold the stem between their teeth and light the other end with a match filched from the kitchen, cupping their hands against the wind. The cattails smoldered, giving off just the right amount of smoke. Below them the world seemed to shimmer. When they tired of their cattail cigars, they'd pick at gobs of tar along the seams and chew them. The tar tasted like something that was probably good for you, like Malt and Iron, or the castor oil mixed with orange juice Perry got a nickel a week for drinking.

To the north, between the house and Starke's Boatyard, stood Captain Kelley's squat, one-story cottage. At five o'clock in the evening, Clayton saw the Captain step out of the door with his brown cap and his bow tie, ready for his constitutional. He took off briskly around the perimeter of his house, trailed by six or seven cats. At intervals he stopped to do his exercises. The air was still and Clayton heard his reedy, old-man's voice carried up on the evening air: "Arms in! Arms out! Arms in! Arms out!" After a few circles, the cats grew bored and wandered away, except for a gray one, which stopped when the Captain stopped and sat beside him, delicately scratching its neck with a back leg, until he resumed his walking.

At six the fish wagon made a delivery. Clayton saw the fish man in his white apron knocking at the cottage door. Then the Captain stood outside his little kitchen, gutting and scaling the fish on a plank of wood. When he finished, he threw the remains to the cats, which rushed with them into the overgrown garden, dragging the entrails in the dust.

Later Mavis came out and called Clayton's name, close enough so that he could hear her mutter "my best East India salad too" in the silence after he didn't answer. She and Nancy had been airing out the house; the clothesline was hung with wash and the lawn littered with linens and bedding. As Clayton watched, they were gathered in, sheets and blankets, lawn-chair pillows and tablecloths, and then the doors and windows were shut, the house like an enormous flower furling itself for the night. The darkness seemed to seep upward as if from the ground. Fireflies blinked in the field. Clayton smelled the warm, rotten scent of the pond, where low tide had exposed the peaty mud.

He thought of the birds at Washington Lodge, his scapping job with Theron Greaves. It made him angry that Nancy expected him to leave this all behind because of her. She wasn't his mother; she couldn't force him to go anywhere. Tears prickled his eyes and he wiped them roughly with his sleeve. Let her go to Boston if she wanted, he thought fiercely. She could move to China for all he cared. He sat looking out toward the dark marsh with his arms around his knees. The first stars came out and the moon hoisted itself over the river, lopsided and bruised.

Even now, as angry as he'd ever been at her, it was hard to imagine his sister going so far away. It was like trying to convince himself that he could walk with only one leg. Perched on the dark roof of the house, he felt a coldness seep into him. His biggest fear had always been that Nancy might die, like their parents had, and leave him alone. He remembered waiting up for her in secret when she went out to dances in Southease, unable to sleep until he knew she was safely home. It hadn't occurred to him then that there were other ways to lose someone.

But it was her fault, he thought. She was the one who'd decided to get married. His chin poked forward in the dusk. He had other family besides his sister. Why should he have to go to Boston? He would live in Fire Neck, in this house, for the rest of his life.

The morning after his granddaughter announced her engagement, Scudder woke with an ache in his left knee. Over the course of the day the pain lessened, but he couldn't shake a morbid fascination with it. He found himself probing the spot with his fingers, the way once, after a tooth extraction, his tongue had sought the pulpy hole in his mouth. Seventy-nine years old, he'd never allowed himself to dwell on minor aches and pains before, convinced that cosseting would only encourage them. And sure enough, within days of the first pain in his knee, other troubles followed: his shoulder felt sore, his hip made a sound like a squeaky boom, he grew short of breath after climbing the stairs. Acknowledged at last, his body clamored for attention.

He realized bitterly that he had wasted his last good season of sailing, like a sentimental fool. That spring he and Clayton had found a nest on the mast of the boat, on one of the spreaders. Scudder borrowed a boathook to knock it down, but as he returned, a swallow darted overhead. He couldn't bring himself to destroy the nest, not with the boy watching. "I don't think there's enough wind, after all," he muttered. Clayton nodded, looking relieved.

After that, every time Scudder wanted to go sailing, he looked up at the nest and the swallow peered back down at him. He'd turn around and leave the dock, cursing swallows and birds in general. George Rowley began to call the boat *The Incubator*. Ten years, even five years ago, he would have cleared the nest off the spreaders without a thought. Now he couldn't help but think of his daughter Helen, dead in her prime. He was going soft in his old age, he berated himself, as maudlin as his late wife. But he'd spared the nest once, and after that, it seemed ungentlemanly to change his mind.

Finally, one afternoon, there was no bird on the nest. A lively southeast wind was blowing and Scudder stepped on board and uncleated the lines. He'd reached the channel marker at the mouth of the canal when he noticed two birds darting frantically after him. The eggs had hatched, he realized, and the chicks were in the nest above him, hungry and cold. Scudder sighed, came about, and sailed back to the dock, the swallows fluttering around the mast.

Now, sitting on the porch nursing his sore shoulder, he remembered how hard it had been even then to move around the deck, the way his arms had ached from holding both the tiller and the mainsheet even that short distance. He would never sail alone again. The realization pierced him.

As soon as Roy came back from dropping Mavis at the lodge, Scudder told him he wanted to haul the boat. Roy pointed out in surprise that it was early in the season. Scudder declared he was through with sailing. Saying this, he thought of his granddaughter, who seemed hell-bent on throwing her life away, moony female that she was. He'd expected more from her. Now it pained him to have her around. "I'm swallowing the anchor," Scudder told Roy. Then he added unkindly, "It's not as if you have any use for a boat." There was nothing Roy could say to this. He went down to the boatyard after feeding the dogs to make arrangements with Sam Burnett.

By afternoon the boat lay upside down on blocks along the privet hedge. Clusters of dirty-white barnacles and rot showed on the faded red hull. Scudder wanted everything properly stowed, and had dismayed Mavis by putting two cans of varnish in the icebox, insisting that it had to be applied cold. Mavis felt sure it would affect the taste of the butter, but something in her father's manner kept her from objecting. Scudder and Captain Kelley took over the yard in front of the porch, littering it with tackle, rags, spars, red and yellow cans of turpentine and polish, scraps of sandpaper worn supple as chamois.

Nancy sat on the porch behind them, writing a letter to her friend in Brooklyn on her portable typewriter. Scudder, his back turned toward her, could hear the clacking of the keys. In the pauses he imagined her playing with the envelope, tapping it against her chin while she thought of new ways to express her happiness in prose. He pressed hard against the spar in his hand, smoothing the rough bumps and making a cloud of dust that hung in the air and sifted onto his trousers, fine as flour.

"Remember the body Randall found in the bay?" he asked the Captain suddenly. Behind him the typewriter keys clattered.

"A sad affair," muttered the Captain. "I wish I remembered that sight less clearly."

"Such a young girl," Scudder said. "Only nineteen or twenty." He spoke a bit loudly, telling himself the Captain had grown hard of hearing. "Beached in the reeds without a stitch on her."

The Captain shook his head and reached for another scrap of sandpaper. "It doesn't bear thinking about."

"They held a gentleman friend for questioning," Scudder went on, ignoring this last remark. "But they couldn't prove he'd done it." Behind him a chair squeaked against the floor, and a moment later the porch door slammed.

"I heard he moved out West," the Captain said. "That always seemed a bit suspicious."

But Scudder had lost interest in the drowned girl. The spar was nearly smooth now, and he needed to find a clean brush for the varnish.

Nancy began mucking out Buckshot's stall in the horse barn in the early evening, giving her a clear excuse for missing dinner. She knew her brother was avoiding her and understood he needed time to get used to the thought of moving to Boston. But no one else in the house seemed willing to look her in the eye either. She shoveled violently away at the manure-heavy straw, frustrated with all of them. She wondered about her friend Enid's engagement and thought uncomfortably about her own coolness on the subject. Even though Robert was completely different from her friend's pompous husband, she wished now that she'd been less critical. The horse rubbed his head against her shoulder as she finished shaking fresh straw onto the floor.

It was nearly dark when Nancy stepped into the kitchen. Roy and Scudder sat at the table, an empty dish before them. The eggy smell of bread pudding hung in the air. Mavis was at the sink, washing up, and Clayton stood beside her with a tea towel in his hand. Like a boy helping his mother, Nancy thought resentfully. The room was strangely hushed, and Nancy felt sure they'd just been talking about her. "You're going to need help packing all your odds and ends," she told Clayton briskly. "You won't be able to bring every specimen jar; I hope you realize that."

Her brother looked away from her. The room seemed very quiet. "I can help you sort your things," Nancy added, sorry already for the way she'd sounded. She wished the others were somewhere else, that she'd waited to talk to her brother alone. "Those glass jars should be wrapped in newspaper."

"I don't want to go." Clayton spoke softly but clearly.

For a moment she saw him as a toddler again, a boy in blue flannel pajamas jutting out his little chin at bedtime as he announced that he wasn't tired. She almost had to bite back a smile. "Don't be silly. You're going to love it. You'll see."

"I want to stay here," her brother said. Nancy was dismayed to hear tears in his voice. She stepped closer to him, but he held up the dish he was drying, as if to ward her off, as if she were going to haul him north to Boston this very moment. "I'm right in the middle of school."

"There are schools in Boston." As if school mattered to him. "Robert's job is there. We have to go. I've already told you."

Clayton was no longer looking at her. She was surprised to see him glance beseechingly at Roy, who sat at the table with the paper in his hands as if there were no sound in the kitchen but the radio news. Scudder, beside him, polished a spot on the table with the frayed sleeve of his shirt. Nancy felt sure he was enjoying her discomfort.

Clayton looked at their aunt. "*Please* could I stay?" He was asking Mavis, not Nancy, as if Mavis were in charge.

Mavis straightened up with a sigh and turned, a soapy wooden spoon in one hand. The suds ran onto her wrist and dripped to the floor. "You know there's always a place for you here." Her eyes met Nancy's. "I don't see why he needs to go, just because you want to."

Nancy felt a sudden heat, as if she were standing in front of a furnace, the door to which had been wrenched open. Her dislike of her aunt flared, white hot.

"We're all family," Mavis added blandly. She turned back to the sink to rinse the spoon she'd been holding, as if to indicate that it was all the same to her.

"He's *my* brother!" Nancy said, more loudly than she meant to.

Roy put down the paper, rustling the pages. He looked up for the first time in the conversation. "It's his choice, don't you think?" He said it reasonably, as if he were merely pointing out something they would all agree was obvious.

"But *I'll* be in Boston, Clay," Nancy said. It had happened so quickly. How had she come to be pleading with him? "Please, darling, you want to be with me, don't you?"

Carefully, Clayton set down the dish he'd dried and picked up the next one. Only then did he look up at her, apologetic and pained. But his face was set in that way she knew. Shocked, Nancy saw that he had already decided. He'd only been waiting to make sure Mavis and Roy would allow it.

"Think about it first," she cried. "There's no need to hurry! We can talk about it later, after we've all calmed down!" Her voice rang in the low-ceilinged room. Her heart pounded. The others stared, taken aback.

"I'm staying here," her brother said.

"But why shouldn't he?" Robert asked. They were in the aviary at Washington Lodge, surrounded by the chirping, rustling birds. Robert had set down his camera. He was looking at her with concern and a little confusion.

Nancy struggled to control her tears. She'd been up most of the night, veering between fury at her brother, at Mavis and Roy for being party to his decision, and her own horrible uncertainty. She thought of how much easier it must have been for her mother at her age, with no one to take care of but herself.

"He's happy here, isn't he?" Robert went on. "Your aunt and uncle will take care of him."

They don't know him the way I do, Nancy wanted to say. They'll let him run wild. He'll play hooky, neglect his homework, and no one will notice. "It's not the same," she said, after a moment. She tried to put her feelings into words, but nothing sounded reasonable. Clayton should be with her because he was her brother and she loved him. She'd take care of him. Why was everyone making it so hard for her? She supposed Clayton would be safe with Mavis and Roy. But she didn't want him to end up trapped on Salt Hay Road, like they were. Clayton didn't see it this way, he was too young to understand, but she did. Leaving Clayton behind felt like consigning him to something dreary. She wanted to pull him with her into her own bright future, and he was making it so difficult; she felt as if she were trying to heft him bodily, the way she'd done when he was a child throwing a tantrum, unwilling to leave the park or the beach, and he was making himself into a dead weight in her arms.

Robert was still gazing at her, his forehead creased. Nancy chewed her lip. "My mother expected me to take care of him," she said desperately. "Mavis is his legal guardian, but *I'm* his sister . . ."

"It's not like you won't see him, sweetheart. He can visit us anytime. He might decide to stay, once he's been there and seen it."

Nancy felt the lump in her throat swell like a sponge. She wanted to believe Robert was right. She knew Clayton was mulish and she couldn't bully him into changing his mind. Maybe if she let him think he was getting his way, he'd like it when he visited.

The moment of her defeat in the kitchen came back to her with its smell of eggs. The family had united against her. She gripped Robert's hands. His green eyes, flecked with brown, stared into hers, and she remembered the bit of white fluff caught in his eyebrow on the day he'd proposed. Around them in the aviary the birds warbled in their cages. Could she marry Robert and move to Boston if it meant leaving her brother here? She felt suddenly afraid. Clayton seemed determined to stay behind, and this made everything tenuous. She and Robert had to marry soon, she thought, before the summer was over. In that moment, there seemed only two possible fates for her: to marry and move away, like her mother had, or to end up on Salt Hay Road forever. She wouldn't let her chance for happiness slip away. In a flash, she saw how she would seal this decision. Today, before her courage failed her.

"I've never seen the rest of this house," she cried suddenly. "Would you show me around?"

Robert looked surprised. "If you'd like . . ."

Agitated, Nancy glanced out the window. Clayton stood under the copper beeches, his back to her. He was bringing the cockatoos in for the evening. Above him, the hook on the end of the pole swayed and fumbled before it caught against a metal hoop. The cockatoo flashed its white wings and squawked, lunging at the pole as Clayton lowered it to the ground, where others already rested, the hoops obscured by the grass, the birds preening themselves or prancing, bowlegged, at the end of their chain tethers.

She stepped to the open window. *"Clay!"* Nancy called. Beyond him she could see the figure of the gardener, bent over a clump of greenery. Mavis had already gone home. "Clay!" she called again, as loud as she dared. He turned, and Nancy waved him over, staying just inside the doorway, where she hoped the gardener would not be able to see her.

"Do me a favor when you're finished and take Buckshot home. You can ride him if you like. It'll save you some time. Just don't let him go faster than a trot."

"Why?" Clayton asked.

"Because we're walking into town soon." The lie came out smoothly, if a little fast. "I don't want him to be spooked by the traffic, and besides, he's been out all day. Put some hay in his stall and make sure he has plenty of water, would you? I owe you one."

"I mean, why shouldn't he go faster than a trot?"

Nancy felt her cheeks flush. "I don't want you falling off. If he gives you any trouble, slap him on the neck with the reins."

"I guess," said Clayton.

Nancy studied his face for signs that he believed her. Since he'd told her he wasn't moving to Boston, they had treated each other carefully, with a certain distance. "You don't mind? It's not too much of a bother?"

But Clayton had already lost whatever interest he'd had in her plans and was turning back to the beeches and the few birds still in the branches. He shrugged. "I can do it."

The absence of the horse did not commit her to anything, Nancy thought. She swallowed. "Thanks. Make sure Mavis doesn't hold dinner. I'll be home later."

Robert stood waiting for her on the landing with a bemused look. "Clay's taking Buckshot back," Nancy said as casually as she could. She thought again of how Robert had proposed, the way his eyes had widened when she'd said yes. She would marry him and live with him in Boston. She clung to her resolve, like a tow rope.

Down a long corridor hung with prints of birds and flowers, they came to the room where Robert was staying. He opened the door with a little smile. "This isn't my natural habitat." The room was nearly the size of the entire upstairs of the house on Salt Hay Road. There were three arched windows through which the late-afternoon sun streamed, warm and buttery, like the light that fell in churches. Nancy was aware, without looking directly at it, of the canopy bed, its pale, glossy coverlet gleaming like icing on a cake. The carpet was thick under her feet, and she wished she had on pumps instead of her riding boots. She stared at the walls, covered halfway up in a light green brocade, and at the white marble fireplace. Beside the fireplace was a dark leather armchair. A mahogany desk stood under the window. Robert's sketch pads and charcoal pencils were jumbled on one side. A wardrobe carved with a pattern of leaves sat against the far wall, opposite a matching dresser.

"I keep expecting to hear someone coming up the stairs," Nancy said, trying to account for her jumpiness.

"We could stow you in the wardrobe," Robert offered. "Until the coast was clear. Or else in here." He opened a door on the other side of the fireplace, revealing a closet the size of a small bedroom. It smelled of cedar. Three or four of Robert's shirts hung close together near the door, as if for comfort. The back wall was mirrored, and Nancy stared at the reflected image of herself, dwarfed by the room behind her, her face small and pale.

"There's a nice view from the window," Robert told her, closing the closet door. Nancy was relieved to leave the mirror behind. There was no reason for the opulence of the room to cow her, she thought. She had grown up in a house that, if not quite as grand, had not been so very different from this one. Her chin rose, ever so slightly, at the thought of being intimidated by a brocade wall. Out the window the flat surface of the pond shone in the late-afternoon light. They stood in silence, peering down. The gardener was pushing an empty wheelbarrow along one of the gravel paths toward the white gardening shed.

Nancy wished that it were dark. Why hadn't she foreseen the difference this would make? Robert was still staring down at the lawn. She realized that she could comment on the loveliness of the room and then ask him to show her something downstairs, the library or the dining room, and he would escort her down the hall politely. It was probably what he expected. She wondered in a sudden panic what he had attempted before and with whom. Someone should have prepared her better for what she was about to do. She thought of her mother telling her after Clayton was born that they'd found him at a florist's shop in New York City, beside the potted gardenias. Nancy, seven years old, had understood that this was both absurd and not to be questioned. She studied the freckles on Robert's neck. He glanced toward her, his eyes patient and amused. Nancy felt her determination ebbing. Taking his hand quickly, she spread it open and pressed his palm to her cheek. His fingers smelled faintly of charcoal.

They kissed on the edge of the gleaming bed, and Nancy waited for the breathless urgency she'd felt before, kissing Robert on horseback, but it was different here, in the stately, impersonal bedroom, prearranged. She felt anxious to get it over with. Robert seemed to sense this and to hesitate. Nancy worried again that she would lose her nerve. She lay back and flung out her arms. The glossy bedspread was slippery under her fingers. Robert watched her. "Nancy," he began. She turned toward him and kissed him hard on the mouth, aware that she was close to tears. He began to unbutton her blouse, his fingers cold. She felt his hand on her stomach and shivered. His belt buckle pressed against her hip and he stopped to unfasten it. It seemed to take a long time for him to disengage from his pants. Nancy glimpsed his legs, pale and unprotected, and his undershorts tenting out above them. She squeezed her eyes shut. After a moment she felt him fumble with the zipper of her riding breeches. Blindly, she helped him peel them down her legs.

Approaching the bird feeder where Nancy had tethered the horse, Clayton was careful to stay clear of Buckshot's enormous hooves. He had nothing against Buckshot particularly, but he found horses unsettling, a fact he tried to conceal from his sister. The animal snorted. His huge head bobbed up and down, reminding Clayton of Captain Kelley nodding at Mavis. He wonders where Nancy is, Clayton thought. He remembered Roy saying that poker cards and horses could both sense fear, and forced himself to pat Buckshot's side. His hand seemed insubstantial against the muscle heaving beneath Buckshot's sleek coat. It would feel, to the horse, like a fly landing. He patted harder, and Buckshot's black tail swished around and whisked him in the face.

He felt bad for the way he'd told his sister he was staying; he should have done it in private, he realized now. But he'd needed the rest of the family there in order to say it. She wanted to boss him around, and this time she couldn't. He was sorry for her, but she was the one who'd decided to go. A part of him hoped she'd give up the whole idea, but last night she'd sat for hours at the kitchen table with a map of Boston in front of her, measuring distances with a ruler. He hid his unhappiness, more determined than ever to stay on without her now that he understood he was one of the things she was prepared to leave behind.

He wondered if the horse would miss her. There wouldn't be a place for Buckshot in Boston. It had always impressed Clayton how fearlessly Nancy handled him, pushing him aside to load hay in the feed bin or prying a hoof off the ground to check for stones, as if Buckshot were an oversized dog, a good-natured Labrador. Clayton untied the reins from the base of the bird feeder and pulled. He was gratified when Buckshot lurched forward. Clayton held the reins under the horse's chin, like he'd seen Nancy do, and Buckshot's head bobbed beside him, one enormous eye visible. Clayton could feel the gusty breathing in his ear and on his face. Buckshot's black, rubbery lips moved, showing teeth as long and yellowed as piano keys. The black lips reminded Clayton of the movement of a caterpillar's back feet, but a caterpillar of monstrous size. Bristly hairs stuck up from the soft flesh of Buckshot's nose. The horse heaved a noisy sigh and, swinging his head toward Clayton, nudged him hard on the shoulder. "Whoa," Clayton said, side-stepping quickly. "Easy."

In the upstairs bedroom back at Washington Lodge, Nancy opened her eyes. She was surprised to feel the pain diminishing, the sharpness of it giving way to something more like an ache. Robert rocked awkwardly on top of her. She felt the muscles of his chest straining. He made a gasping sound, his face pressed against the side of her head. Above her the white canopy arched. Nancy tried to think about the wedding, tried to imagine the flowers and the dress, but she couldn't escape the ebbing pain and the weight of Robert's body pressing and pushing. All his habitual self-possession had been stripped away. He seemed to have disappeared, leaving her alone in her awareness of this interminable moment. It had never occurred to her that it would take so long.

She felt a warmth on her neck. Robert kissed her jaw, the lobe of her ear, his mouth moving with a wet, steady urgency. The ache intensified. Suspended inside it, she felt it shift to a glimpse of something almost familiar. It was like approaching a jump on horseback, anticipating that surge of muscle and then the effortless feeling of being airborne. Nancy moved toward it. A feral noise escaped her throat.

Immediately Robert stopped. Nancy stiffened as he pulled away, his weight on his hand, until he was looking into her eyes. For a moment they stared at each other like frightened strangers. Nancy felt the blood pound in her head. "Did I hurt you?" he asked hoarsely. His cheeks were flushed, his eyes anxious. Nancy shook her head and pulled him closer, until he couldn't see her face.

Five weeks later, Nancy Poole married Robert Landgraf in a small ceremony at the brown-shingled Presbyterian church in Southease, overlooking the bay. Robert's oldest brother, attending from Maine as his best man, nearly fumbled the ring at the crucial moment; Nancy tried to hide her alarm, but Robert noticed it, and apologized later on his brother's behalf, explaining that he grew flustered around beautiful women. Nancy flashed him a smile and bent her head over her bouquet of yellow roses. She wore a simple cream-colored dress in a halter style, cut on the bias, without a train, so that she could dye it for later use. Stepping out of the darkened church, the bride and groom were pelted with rice by Clayton and Perry. Nancy held the roses up to shield herself, laughing. Beyond the sloping church lawn, the water of the bay shone in the August light, so bright they had to avert their eyes.

On Salt Hay Road, the house had been scrubbed from top to bottom and hung with white and pink streamers for the reception. Mavis served a fruit punch and a molded Kentucky salad, and a wedding cake layered with figs and citron. Enid Snow had come from Brooklyn with her husband; marriage had softened him, Nancy felt, and Enid herself looked plump and happy. Nancy made a point of charming Robert's brother, forgiving him his moment of clumsiness with the wedding ring and his cheap suit, and the fact that he had none of his brother's easy banter. Like Robert's, his hands seemed slightly too large for his wrists. He stood by the end of the dining-room table, placing molded salad on his flowered china plate. Robert glanced over at them, and she felt his worry; perhaps his brother embarrassed him, the way she sometimes felt about her aunt. "Thank you again for being here," she told him, putting a hand on his brown wool sleeve. She felt a fresh admiration for Robert, who'd grown up in the same household and yet forged a different life. "It means so much to both of us."

"None of us get away much," Robert's brother said. "Because of the farm." He glanced down at the salad and seemed to remember something. "We hope you'll be very happy together," he added gruffly, and it was clear to Nancy that he was speaking for the entire somber Landgraf clan, and that they had their doubts. She nodded, a little shaken, and moved on to attend to the other guests.

A hush hung over the house when Nancy came for her things. She and Robert had spent a rainy weekend on Shelter Island for their honeymoon. Inside the house on Salt Hay Road the rooms were dark except where a ray of sunlight shone on the stairs and illuminated a pair of muddy shoes. Clayton had set them neatly on the stairs with the laces folded in. Now he would be crabbing barefoot on the river. Roy had gone out after rabbits with his gun and his dogs; Mavis was working at the lodge. Only her grandfather was home. He sat on the porch, feigning sleep in his chair, as if she would believe he'd fallen asleep with a pipe in his hand. She had never guessed before her engagement that he could be so childish. She'd expected that it would be sad to leave, but now she couldn't wait to be gone. The air itself seemed to strangle her. If only Clayton's shoes weren't perched like that on the stairs, so muddy and so precisely arranged. For a moment she imagined snatching them up and bringing them with her. She dashed back up for another look at her room. The white walls were bare, the bed stripped down to the mattress. The typewriter sat on the table, its black keys furred with dust. She had no use for it now. Out the window the leaves of the pepperidge trees shook in the wind. Her husband called her name. Nancy clattered down the stairs, past Clayton's shoes, and grabbed at the handle of her suitcase. There came Robert, smiling at her as he strode across the lawn. She turned, but the porch was empty. Even the smell of pipe smoke was gone.

"Goodbye!" she cried to the empty house, hefting her suitcase behind her.

In all the years Captain Kelley had lived across the field, Scudder had visited him only half a dozen times. He knew the Captain enjoyed seeing Mavis, and the light at his own house was better for cards. Besides, Scudder was not fond of cats. Now, as the Captain opened the door, blinking, several of them thrust themselves forward as if attempting to trip Scudder up.

"Come in, come in," the Captain exclaimed. He pulled the door open, and more cats emerged and twined themselves around Scudder's legs. Inside, Scudder could barely see. The light outside had been blinding, and here the shades were all drawn. Scudder stood just inside the door, hobbled by cats. He felt the Captain's hand on his elbow. "What a pleasant surprise. Will you have some tea? A drop of brandy?"

"Brandy," Scudder said. His own voice sounded odd to him, a croak. He let himself be led to a small table cluttered with books and dishes, feeling suddenly feeble: an old, broken man. A cat hopped up beside him and rubbed against his shoulder. Something rose in his throat. It threatened to choke him. He coughed hard, smothering what might have been a sob.

The Captain placed a jelly jar in his hand. "Good for the heart."

Scudder drank it down, and the reassuring warmth of it spread over his chest. The Captain began to shuffle a deck of cards, and he found the sound soothing, like the lapping of waves against the hull of a boat. The Captain dealt. Scudder reached across the table almost without thinking. He picked up the cards and fanned out his hand.

Later Scudder thought he heard the rumble of a car pulling away down Salt Hay Road. But he had drunk several jars of brandy by this point, and perhaps, he told himself, it was only the purring of Kelley's cats on the crowded table.

PART TWO

Honey in the Walls

The August that Nancy married Robert Landgraf and moved to Boston, Clayton was invited to stay with Perry Gilpin's family for a week at their house on Fire Island. There Mrs. Gilpin and the children lived each summer. Clayton walked through the boatyard with his knapsack to the ferry dock, nodding to Sam at the boat shed. There were two ferries to choose from, the *Okalee* and the *Westaway*, their schedules posted at the landing. Clayton waited for the former; the captain, an old bayman and friend of Theron Greaves's, sailed instead of using the engine whenever possible. Clayton and Nancy had always preferred the *Okalee*.

Clayton made his way quickly to the bow and found a seat. Around him crowded families with picnic hampers, a boy with a melting ice cream, a man in a straw hat carrying only a mandolin. The *Okalee* motored past Rose's Creek out to the mouth of the river, and then the captain hoisted the sail. In the quiet after the motor was cut, Clayton heard an osprey's high-pitched call. They were retracing the route, Clayton thought, of his great-grandfather's house, from the Terrell River all the way to

Starke's Boatyard along this same stretch of shore. He stared out at the green spartina, the pepperidge trees, and high-tide bush, wondering how much it had changed since the house had floated past.

In the distance, Clayton could see the bridge where the bay narrowed and the contours of the barrier beach dipped toward Long Island at Taffy Point. There were nearly a dozen houses along the shore to the west. Most were summer houses for people from the city. A few of the smaller ones belonged to local families like the Gilpins who'd bought the cheaper land on the bay side and done some of the work themselves. As they drew closer to Fire Island, Clayton could make out the figure of his friend, barefoot on the dock. Perry waved his arms in mock semaphore. Clayton signaled back.

The Gilpins' beach house was yellow, with a wide front porch that faced across the bay toward the Barto River. Perry's mother had named it Beach Plum, he told Clayton, after the tart little fruits that grew wild nearby; the others called it Off Plumb, because of the way the front porch had settled in the sand, listing toward the west. There were three low-ceilinged bedrooms upstairs, one with bunks for the boys, one for Mr. and Mrs. Gilpin, one for Pearl the Girl, and a kitchen and living room downstairs, all with plain wood floors worn by the sand. The outhouse had a water tank on top for outdoor showers.

Every Friday after work, Mr. Gilpin joined his family at the beach, bringing the mail and fresh supplies. The evening of Clayton's arrival, he lit a bonfire on the shore and they roasted potatoes in the embers. In the past Clayton had sometimes seen bonfires on the beach from his upstairs room on Salt Hay Road and the sight had made him feel like a sailor on a ship at sea, glimpsing the lights of a port along the horizon.

Charlie, Perry's oldest brother, who worked for the Southease Hook and Ladder, was there on a rare visit. He claimed to have been knocked low by the news of Nancy's marriage. "We flew the station flag at half mast," he teased. Clayton sat on the sand, holding his steaming potato, and stared into the glowing ashes. Since his sister had left Fire Neck, he himself had felt off-plumb, a three-legged dog.

It was easier, at the Gilpins' house, for Clayton to put Nancy out of his thoughts. Here at least he didn't half expect to see her every time he entered a room. Sometimes he pretended to himself that he and Perry were brothers and that he'd always lived in the noisy, affectionate Gilpin household. Lewis and Fred had finished high school and now worked on the bay, saving up for their own boat and clamming gear. They were brown and freckled, the skin on their noses eternally peeling, and their arms and shoulders bulged with enviable muscle. Donald, two years older than Perry, was obsessed with bicycles. He considered Fire Island a form of exile, a wasteland of boardwalks and sandy trails, and spent as much time as he could on the porch poring over bicycling advertisements and dreaming of macadam.

Clayton slept in a sleeping bag on the floor of the room Perry shared with his brothers. Long after they'd finished talking about boats and fishing and plans for the following day, and after the breathing of the others had deepened and grown regular, Clayton lay awake. He listened to the unfamiliar roar of the breakers out the window and felt a sharp stab of homesickness, not only for his room on Salt Hay Road, but also for the house with his sister in it. He thought of reasons that would make her return, and drifted off to sleep imagining himself in the hospital with rheumatic fever and Nancy hovering over him, full of self-reproach.

In the morning the mood had passed completely, like a fall of rain that evaporates within the hour. He woke to someone stepping on his foot. The house smelled like sausages and coffee. "Hurry up," Perry hollered. Clayton pulled on his clothes and followed the other boys as they trooped loudly down the hall. On the way they passed the small room Pearl had to herself. Darting in, Perry and Donald pulled the blankets off her bed. Pearl shrieked and threw her pillow at them.

"You leave that girl alone!" Mrs. Gilpin bellowed from the kitchen. "You'll spoil her disposition!"

After breakfast Clayton chased Perry along a path through the beach plum and bayberry, swatting at the mosquitoes. They crested the low hill of dunes and there was the ocean, hurling itself at the sand. The warm air felt damp and salty on Clayton's face. With a whooping cry, Perry hurtled down the face of the dune, ignoring the wooden steps. Clayton followed. Down on the wet margin of the shore, sand fleas exploded around their bare feet, as if the beach itself were effervescent.

They plunged into the surf and porpoised through the breakers. When the water finally became too cold, Clayton flopped on the sand, rolling over until the sand grains covered him. Perry and his brothers called this "breading" themselves, after their mother's manner of dredging fish. As the sun heated their skin, the sand grains dried and could be brushed away. The sand worked itself everywhere. Before dinner they rinsed off quickly outside the kitchen door, taking turns holding the hose, and still their sheets and pillows were always dusted with a layer of sand.

One afternoon, splashing out of the surf, they heard a familiar voice call their names. Blinded by the sun, it took Clayton a moment to realize it was their teacher, Miss Collier. She stood before them in a bathing suit, her hair around her shoulders. Clayton felt a deep, reflexive panic. Miss Collier usually wore her thick blond hair pulled back and loosely pinned. When she turned to the blackboard, the nape of her neck was exposed, and he had relished the view of that patch of bare skin. Now most of Miss Collier was bare. Clayton had dreamed of her many times since school let out, in much the same state. "Enjoying yourselves?" she asked. Perry said something about the beach house while Clayton stared at Miss Collier's bare shoulders and bare arms and bare thighs and knees and legs. Roy had told him once that when he was a boy it had been considered a thrill to catch a glimpse of a woman's ankles as she stepped up to board a train; at the time, Clayton had wondered at anyone having the slightest interest in an ankle. Now the sight of Miss Collier's bare feet in the sand made his head pound. Instinctively, he put his hands down to cover his wet shorts. But he had nothing to hold in front of himself, no towel, no chair to hide behind. Miss Collier, listening to Perry, had turned to look in the direction of the Gilpins' beach house. In a moment she would turn back and see Clayton with his thin, clinging shorts angled toward her. His face hot, he turned and flung himself into the surf. The cold water surged mercifully over him. He waved in the direction of the beach and dove below the surface, his entire body tingling.

At dinner, Clayton sat next to Perry at the Gilpins' crowded table. Mr. Gilpin was a short, energetic man who spoke loudly from the constant need to make himself heard over the noise of his household. He had grown up in Fire Neck and remembered the beach twenty years earlier, when the soldiers from Camp Upton used to arrive on their days off. The soldiers, he told them over dinner, were huge, strapping boys from the Midwest who'd never seen the ocean. They yelled to each other all the way across the boardwalk. "You could hear them a mile away," said Mr. Gilpin. "They swarmed over the top of the dunes, making war cries, shucking off their clothes. They'd tear down the beach in their undershorts and charge at the water as if it were Lake Michigan. The surf just scattered them like ninepins. We'd sit on the dunes and laugh. They'd come up spluttering and coughing. Didn't know what hit them."

Mrs. Gilpin was passing a plate of bluefish. "You know," she said, her voice unusually quiet, "some of them never made it home."

"Well, you're right," Mr. Gilpin answered, chastened. He was silent a moment. "I guess the war surprised some of those boys worse than the Atlantic."

Clayton, reaching for another ear of corn, caught the glance that Mrs. Gilpin cast around the table at her own boys, while Perry licked his fingers and Donald and Lewis kicked each other under the table. It was a maternal look, full of love and worry.

That night, in his sleeping bag on the floor, he found himself thinking of his mother. Toward the end she had lost interest even in the sailboats on the Sound. She had rested during the day in a downstairs room with tall windows where a white-clad nurse admonished him to lower his voice. The light seeped in around the edges of the curtains, and when he thought of his mother now, he saw in his mind those dark curtains edged with light. He remembered the softness of her palm on his cheek and the dry, floral smell of talcum powder as he inclined his face to receive her kisses. He'd felt oppressed, not only by the silence and the still, close sweetness of the air, but by the understanding that no matter how long he stayed, it would never be long enough. Lying in the dark in the Gilpins' beach house, he wondered for the first time what his mother had thought about during those slow, hushed mornings and afternoons. He wished now he'd asked about the polished sailing trophies lined up along her bureau, or about his father, or her childhood on Salt Hay Road. But he had not been interested. Or rather, it had been hard for him to believe that she'd once existed outside the heavy silence of the room with the velvet curtains. He had visited her mostly for the butterscotch candies she kept in a glass jar with a fluted lid, each wrapped in a square of waxy paper, and he wondered now if she had kept them for precisely this reason. It hurt him to think how clearly she must have seen into his greedy little heart.

At the house on Salt Hay Road, Scudder and Captain Kelley had been playing cribbage since nine o'clock. Scudder, distracted, had lost almost every game. It was past midnight, warm and still. The tide would be ebbing, he thought. He could smell the salt marsh and the mud. June bugs and moths bumped against the screen door, drawn to the electric light. The rest of the house was dark and silent, as if he and the Captain were the only ones left, marooned in the kitchen with a deck of cards. At the table the Captain finished shuffling. He licked his thumb and began to deal.

"Remember the *Margaret Harte*?" the Captain asked, pushing the cards across the table. This was another game they played, quizzing each other out of nostalgia and the need to prove they still remembered. Seven surfmen and the keeper lived at the Smith Point Station back when they'd worked together on Fire Island. They had a wreck pole near the station to simulate a mast and practiced rescues on it, trying to get someone off in the breeches buoy, a life ring run on a pulley, in under five minutes. They learned the international signal code and the colors of the Coston flares: Red, *You are seen*; blue, *Do not attempt to land.*

Scudder leaned back in his chair, fanning his cards in front of him. "The *Margaret Harte*? Eighteen eighty-nine. Her cargo was whiskey and peanuts."

The Captain's bow tie bobbed as he nodded. "Every fisherman from here to Moriches was trawling for bottles."

Scudder remembered crowds of barefoot children, their pockets stuffed with waterlogged peanuts. "Remember the *Chippewa*?"

"She was the one with the ostriches—1908. Ostriches, watermelons, yellow pine."

"What about the *Clementine*?" Scudder asked.

The Captain grinned. "Still got my fork." The *Clementine*, bound for Boston from Jacksonville, Florida, had struck an outlying rock one morning in a thick fog. The sea was calm and they reached her easily in the lifeboat. The ship seemed safe enough, and when the captain, profusely apologetic, invited them into his cabin for breakfast, they accepted. Kelley had just speared a piece of ham when a wave smashed through the cabin door and swirled around them. He fought his way on deck and into the dory. There, reaching for an oar, he'd found the fork still clutched in his hand.

"And the cargo of shoes?"

"The *Geoffrey Manning*," said Scudder, and he recited:

"There were shoes galore along the shore
In assorted styles of leather,
But the undertow had scattered them so
There wasn't a pair together."

"Bravo," said the Captain. "You always had a head for verse." Scudder snorted, though it was true. At night, patrolling the beach, he used to keep himself awake with poems he'd learned as a schoolboy, "The Highwayman," "Gunga Din," and another called "The Bell Buoy."

The Captain played an eight on Scudder's seven and advanced his ivory peg with a flourish, winning the game. Scudder shuffled while the Captain took out his tobacco pouch and filled his pipe. "I remember one night," the Captain said, pausing with his fingers in the tobacco. The aroma drifted across the table. "The sea was full of phosphorus. You've seen it like that. Pitch black, and the waves glowing as they break on the bar. Spooky." The Captain bobbed his head again. "I don't mind admitting it. And about halfway to the hut, near the hulk of the *Bethany D.*, I heard a clapping noise. It sounded like two flat sticks slapped together. My hair fairly stood on end. I kept going and met up with the other patrol, Jeb Scheibel, I think it was. I didn't say anything. I was hoping I'd imagined it. But on the way back I heard it again. And you know what?"

Scudder had filled his own pipe. Now he struck a match and lit it, leaning back in his chair. "Your hip flask was dry?"

"No, you old sinner." The Captain lowered his voice. "The next day it blew from the north and the *Sun Dog* went aground."

"The *Sun Dog*," repeated Scudder. "That was 1903. Turpentine, cotton, and tobacco. We got everyone off just fine."

"It was a warning," the Captain insisted.

There was a noise on the stairs and they broke off talking. Scudder looked up as Mavis appeared in the hallway wrapped in a blue flannel robe. His heart flooded with a ridiculous gratitude; since Nancy had left them, he'd realized that he was an old man, and it comforted him now to have what remained of his family around him.

"Oh," Mavis said, startled to see them at the table. She rubbed her eyes. "The moon's so bright, I couldn't sleep." She bustled into the pantry.

Scudder watched as the Captain stared fondly after her, ignoring his cards. He and Mavis shared an interest in spiritualism and religion. They traded books on mesmerism and had attempted to contact the departed Mrs. Scudder through the use of a Ouija board. Mavis lifted down the flour and the sugar and began to measure them into a bowl. The smell of cinnamon drifted from the counter. Molasses cake, Scudder thought. He had long since finished dealing and was regarding his hand with a severe look, because it was a good hand finally, kings and fives, and he didn't want the pleasure to show in his face. The Captain chatted with Mavis while she mixed the batter with a wooden spoon.

With a clatter, Mavis set the cake in the oven. She stood by the table and looked down at the cribbage board. Her face was pink and her dimpled hands dusted with flour. She pushed a strand of hair from her forehead. Scudder sat with his cards fanned out, waiting to resume the game. "Your turn, I believe."

The Captain fingered a card, considered it, examined another. "Oh, I meant to thank you," he said, addressing Mavis again. "That was an interesting pamphlet you loaned me."

Mavis brightened. "Do *you* think of God as a righteous will? Or more as absolute energy?"

Scudder cleared his throat, a bit loudly, but the other two

didn't take any notice. The smell of molasses filled the room. One o'clock struck on the hall clock. He heard Mavis telling the Captain, "It's so important to be scientific."

The Captain nodded. "Yes, by all means. By all means." Scudder watched with disappointment as his friend absently laid his cards face up on the table in order to fiddle with his tie. "Although," the Captain added, "there's also faith to consider." He rose and, with a stilted gallantry, picked up a dish towel and offered to dry the dishes.

Scudder rested his cards on the table. In the same way that his body had finally mutinied, revealing its aches and pains and demanding his attention, his mind had also grown peevish and fitful. He found himself returning to memories that pained him. Now, as the others talked about belief at the sink, he remembered with harrowing precision exactly how he had lost his own faith half a century earlier. This was something he'd carefully hidden, from his wife, Genevieve, when she was alive, and now from his grown children and his friends. He lived with it like a secret illness that was fatal but not contagious. It had happened during a rescue, one that neither he nor the Captain ever spoke of, though Scudder was sure they both remembered it more clearly than any of the others.

In 1890, a storm had hit during the worst winter any of the Life Savers had seen. William Bryden, patrolling the beach, sighted a three-masted schooner aground on the outer bar. It was late afternoon and bitterly cold. Scudder and Mapes had been playing gin in the station house when Bryden came in with the news. They dropped their cards and pulled on boots and oilskins.

Outside, the wind howled around them, tearing at their caps. The sand was frozen in hardened mounds beneath their feet. They followed Bryden to the shore, where a strong surf was running. Ice clogged the waves and the spray froze as it fell, stinging Scudder's face as he stared out at the ship. The schooner had hit a sandbar about four hundred yards out and was being pummeled by breakers. White water frothed over the listing deck. Scudder could see the forms of sailors who had climbed into the rigging. He counted eight. "Mother of God," Mapes said beside him. Randall and the others arrived with the cart, hauling the Lyle gun and the surfboat.

They got the Lyle gun pointed at the schooner and King fired it off, an incredible shot. The wind cleared the smoke, and the men's eyes followed the line as it looped over the pounding waves. Randall slapped King on the back. "I think that took." They'd all seen lines fall short, especially in high winds, but King was one of the best.

Now they waited for someone on board to climb out of the rigging and make the line fast to a mast or a spar; with the line secured, the surfmen could send out a breeches buoy and bring the sailors off one at a time. They watched from the beach, straining their eyes. But the line was either too far out of reach or the men too weak to climb to it. King shot another line aboard. "Come on, boys," he muttered, willing the sailors to move. "Come on, haul her in." Finally, there was a movement in the stern. Scudder caught his breath. The figure swayed for a moment, like a drunkard about to break into song. Then it dropped from the rigging and vanished in the surge.

"Sweet Jesus," said Mapes. "Sweet Mary and Joseph."

"Man the boat!" Randall bellowed. In seas that rough, the surfboat was a last resort. Scudder scrambled into the dory and took his place with Bryden, Miller, and King. Mapes and Kelley waded into the icy wash, holding on to the gunwales and trying to point the bow directly out from the beach. The boat pitched and pulled. The men in the water waited for a receding wave, then pushed the boat through the surf. The oars iced over in Scudder's hands; he could barely grasp them. He felt the blades skitter on the water. A wave broke over the bow and knocked him sideways. He came up, wiping his eyes, and heard Miller yelling over the roar of the breakers. Looking down, he saw water gushing through a hole punched by the ice. The next wave hammered the surfboat against the sand. Randall and the others grabbed it before the water could suck the boat away. The hull was bashed in like the shell of a hard-boiled egg.

Kelley was sent west to the Southease station, Bryden east toward Lone Hill for more men and another surfboat; this was before each station had a telephone. The others stood on the beach beside the ruined dory. A crack appeared in the clouds and lit the figures caught in the rigging like flies in a web. Scudder thought he saw the shape of a woman, her dark skirts whipped by the wind, her arms wrapped around the aftermast. The light began to drain from the sky. King shot four more lines out onto the ship, until all they could see was the dirty white on the crests of the breaking waves. Driftwood littered the upper beach and they built a fire to warm themselves. Sometime during Scudder's watch the wind shifted. For two hours, he listened to the crash of the waves against the ship and the grinding thump of the hull on the bar. It was brutally cold. He tried to pray. All night, over the shriek of the wind, he kept hearing human cries.

In the first dawn light they made out six figures still clinging on. It was a miracle, Kelley said. The stays of the mainmast had snapped in the night, and now the mast swayed out in a broad arc each time a wave pounded the hull. Randall paced along the shore. The fire had died down to embers. Mapes came up, dragging flotsam, and started it blazing again.

That morning Scudder watched helplessly as another figure

pitched forward and was swallowed by the waves. Volunteers from the Southease and Lone Hill stations arrived soon after dawn with a horse dragging another surfboat, but it was only after the wind had dropped a notch that they were able to launch it. Scudder sat in the bow, waves breaking over him, as they maneuvered through the floating ice. When they came up under the lee of the tilting hull, it grew strangely quiet. Scudder was the first into the heaving rigging and made for the closest figure, on the jibboom. He saw with shock that it was a boy. He was hunched down, very quiet, but he was still there, he hadn't fallen. Scudder spoke to him, cupping his hand against the wind. The boy did not stir. Scudder thrust out his hand and touched the boy's cheek, but his fingers were too numb to feel. He grasped a halyard and leaned forward, pressing his mouth to the child's forehead. A slick film of ice melted under his lips. The boy's eyes stared past him, frozen open.

The word that Kelley had used that morning caught in Scudder's throat. A *miracle*. He fought the urge to retch over the side. His belief in God he'd carried unthinkingly, a smooth white stone in his pocket; only now, when he felt how completely it gave under the pressure of his fingers, did he see that it had been hollow, like an egg, all along.

The woman was dead as well. He helped Randall wrench her arms free of the mast. Her black hair had frozen wildly to her face. On the mizzenmast, sheltered slightly by the topsail, two men were unconscious but still alive. The surfmen got them into the dory with the bodies of the boy, the woman, and a thin sailor found frozen in the stern. One of the survivors was a bearded giant it took three of them to lift. He wore seaboots that had filled with water; the water had frozen solid. He died a few days later at the Marine Hospital on Staten Island after the doctors amputated both his legs. The other survivor was a

Swede named Magnus Carlsson. When he came to, warmed by the fire in the station house, he narrowed his pale blue eyes. "I'm a tough one," he rasped. "It'd take more than that to do me in." Scudder, who was piling him with blankets, bent closer to hear, and the Swede fixed him with a malevolent stare. "I could have hung on all night," Carlsson said, raising his voice. "With a can of beans. And my pipe." Later that week he was taken to Amityville to an asylum for the insane.

"I told you," Mavis said to Captain Kelley. She stood at the kitchen counter, lifting a square of molasses cake out of the tin. She set pieces on three plates, careful of crumbs, and the Captain helped her carry them to the table. "He's not interested in the divine." Mavis bent forward and Scudder smelled her lilac perfume. "You'd rather talk about shipwrecks, wouldn't you?" She set a piece of cake before her father and smiled. A large dark moth, more shape than substance, fumbled against the screen. Steam rose from their plates, molasses-scented. The Captain stood and held out a chair. Mavis settled into it, and the three of them began to eat.

The house with Nancy gone was not, outwardly, so different. Clayton, back from his visit with the Gilpins on Fire Island, still sneaked onto the roof and smoked the odd cattail cigar. Without Perry, or the possibility of being caught by his sister, it was not as much fun as it had been. Mavis complained to Roy about the dogs in the kitchen, and Scudder and the Captain played cribbage on the porch and discussed the many ways the world was going to hell, starting with the ill-advised merging of the Life Savers with the Revenue Cutter Service a dozen years earlier and ending with the Italian invasion of Ethiopia.

In the evening, Mavis cooked blue claw crabs Clayton caught with Theron Greaves, and Clayton felt a satisfaction in seeing the family sit down to eat food that he'd provided. It made him feel a little like his uncle, who brought home ducks and rabbits and the occasional squirrel for dinner. Maybe this year, he thought, Roy would take him hunting when duck season started.

It was at night, long after the dishes had been washed and the downstairs lights turned out, that Clayton felt that the house with Nancy gone was irrevocably changed. Lying in bed, kept awake by the insistent mosquitoes, he listened to its muffled creakings. The house seemed less substantial, as if a flaw in its construction had been revealed by his sister's departure. Down the hall the door to Nancy's room yawned open, and its emptiness merged with the darkness until the house around him seemed hollow, even flimsy, little more than a skiff or a raft. In those moments of loneliness he imagined he could feel it bumping slightly against the ground beneath them, like a beached dinghy on an incoming tide, and it seemed to him that the house was in danger of floating away.

From below him, faint but distinct, came the pinging sound of a spoon against a bowl and then the creak of a cupboard door. His aunt was also awake, moving quietly in the kitchen with its solid chairs and table, the stippled lampshade, the white enamel stove. Reassured, Clayton felt the house settle firmly around him once again. In another moment he had fallen asleep.

On the marsh, the pepperidge trees were the first to redden, bright against the tawny reeds and the green high-tide bush. In September, Clayton and Perry went back to school. On afternoons when the tide was right, Clayton continued to scap for

Theron Greaves. Once a week Mavis made him sit down at the kitchen table and write a letter to Nancy in Boston. His letters were short: *Today me and Perry caught three toads near the pond. Thank you for the sweater.*

Nancy wrote long letters poking fun at herself in Boston. She'd taken a wrong turn coming back from the market, "like the rube I am," and found herself in a narrow street where a throng of people waited in line for food. "Some had their shoes tied on with rags." She'd asked a short-tempered policeman for directions. She wanted to know if Clayton was keeping up with his schoolwork. Did he remember the promise he'd made her not to play hooky? Reading this, Clayton felt annoyed; she was still trying to tell him what to do. And she wanted Boston to sound important. He thought of the far-off places Washington's birds arrived from, the Solomon Islands, the coast of Madagascar. If he ever left Fire Neck, it would be for somewhere halfway around the world.

Scudder spent more time at Captain Kelley's. When he wasn't playing cribbage with the Captain, he liked to sit in his chair on the porch, smoking his pipe or dozing. He never mentioned Nancy, nor did he show an interest in her letters, but when he said to Roy, "The winters are much colder up north, you know. I bet they get plenty of snow," Roy guessed that he was thinking about her. Her marriage still felt to Scudder like a personal affront. It would probably fail, he told himself, with a certain grim satisfaction. *Marry in haste, repent at leisure.* She'd come home again eventually, just as Mavis had. At the thought of Nancy suffering, he felt a thawing in his chest, and had to remind himself that she was still married and, as far as any of them knew, entirely happy.

————

Nancy stood at the counter of the small kitchen that was now hers, breaking eggs into a blue glass bowl. Beside her Robert measured coffee with a spoon. They had stayed in bed too long, and now he had to hurry to get to the museum on time. She felt shy and a little clumsy, bumping his elbow as she handed him a plate of scrambled eggs. He ate them in a few bites, then laced up his shoes as she packed a cheese sandwich for his lunch. At the door he kissed her tenderly on the mouth, and she smelled the camphor and naphthalene under his aftershave, stronger here in Boston because he used them every day at the museum to protect specimens from the dermestid beetles. Then he hastened out into the street. From the window she watched him until he disappeared around the corner.

Nancy turned, feeling slightly at a loss. The smell of the coffee, rich and bitter, hung in the air. From the street came the squealing of a trolley and the shouts of children playing ball. The apartment itself was hushed. In the narrow kitchen, she washed and dried the breakfast dishes. Arranging the blue-and-white teacups on the shelf above the stove, she smiled at the memory of Robert saying he drank from a saucer. Their apartment was on the first floor and overlooked a small yard that might once have been a garden, now hung with clothes and linens from the laundry next door. The incongruous smell of soap permeated the rooms and the dingy yard, as if they were actually squeaky clean. Empty stockings dangled side by side, like the shed skins of snakes. The oddness of the image made her think of her brother, and she wondered what he was doing at that moment.

She glanced at the clock. It was only nine forty-five. A few months ago she would have been practicing her typing. Of course, she had left her typewriter behind. She imagined Buck-shot, grazing idly in the field beyond the barn, then pushed the thought away. There were stables in the city and she'd hoped to ride here from time to time, but hiring a horse turned out to be far too expensive. From a few doors down she heard the muffled barking of a dog.

Walking into the small sitting room, she surveyed the faded brown curtains. The apartment was rented furnished, a euphemism, Nancy thought, for cluttered with hand-me-downs. She would stitch up some pretty ones to replace the curtains, she decided, and fresh pillow covers for the mole-colored sofa.

Beating the pillows in the small backyard, she raised a cloud of dust and earned a nasty look from a red-faced laundry woman in a white blouse flecked with suds. "Sorry," Nancy murmured, abashed. She didn't know what rights, if any, she had to the space where the laundry hung. But she could hardly beat the pillows on the front steps. She felt the city suddenly pressed tight on either side of her, block after block of crowded buildings where tenants squabbled over cramped and weedy yards. She threw the pillows on the couch, amid a puff of remaining dust, grabbed her handbag, and went out to look for material for curtains.

In October the director of the Museum of Comparative Zoology threw a party for the benefactors and the board of trustees. Nancy took pains deciding what to wear, wanting to make Robert proud. She was afraid that the nicest dress she had, an A-line in rose-colored silk, looked girlish, and besides, it was too late in the year. In the end she decided on a navy crepe gown that felt more sophisticated. She put on red lipstick and a pearl necklace that had been her mother's, and scanned the mirror in their little black-and-white-tiled bathroom, pleased with the result.

Entering the wide front doors of the museum with her husband, she felt the first flutter of uncertainty. Ahead of them, a blond woman in a calf-length white fur coat leaned on the arm of a man who carried himself like a film star. Smiling to keep her anxiety from showing, Nancy moved closer to Robert. She'd visited him at the museum before, down in the basement room smelling of sawdust and tobacco where he painstakingly removed the flesh from dead birds to make study skins at a table overflowing with cotton batting and cornmeal. She realized now that she had expected to see the same white-haired men in moth-eaten jackets and earnest, flat-chested secretaries in dark skirts and white blouses she'd come to associate with his work. This was another world altogether.

They made their way inside, moving within a throng of well-dressed people. Nancy noticed a woman in black velvet, draped in diamonds. Flocks of bright, motionless birds behind glass lined the long hallway. "From the Pennand collection," Robert said. He hurried her along, nodding to people he knew, unconcerned by the finery around them. She wished he'd thought to warn her.

In a high-ceilinged room hung with chandeliers, the diamond-draped woman gazed reverentially at the paintings on the walls. "Audubons," Nancy heard someone murmur. "Originals."

A moment later Robert exclaimed, "There's Dr. Peters!" Nancy caught sight of a tanned, scruffy gentleman across the hall, mobbed by admirers. "He's just back from Mexico. Let me see if I can get a quick word with him, darling."

Nancy found herself wedged between two lepidopterists who were discussing South American moths. Snatches of other conversations reached her: *When we were last in Greece . . . Not with the market what it is . . . German submarines, they told us . . .*

The lepidopterist on her left had eyebrows that poked out in front of his face like the feelers of an insect, and she wished she had someone to share this observation with. She imagined Clayton on the floor of his bedroom, his vials and specimen jars spread out around him, his inexplicable urge to collect the dried husks of beetles and give each one its proper Latin name. He'd always been a quirky kid. She remembered how, as a toddler, he had been scared of sneezes. She'd never found out why. It wasn't the noise alone, because even a picture of a sneezing frog in a book had frightened him. She'd completely forgotten that. It had lasted only a month or two, at most. And now he was thirteen years old. He probably wouldn't believe this if she told him. She wished suddenly that he were with her, and scanned the room as if he might somehow be spotted among the crowd of sophisticated strangers.

Beside her, the lepidopterists waved to someone they recognized and moved away. Nancy stood by the display case, hemmed in by a paunchy man with a beard who was telling a small group about an expedition to Argentina. "Twelve hundred specimens in a single year," he announced triumphantly. "Peters is already planning the next one."

She glanced down, into the yellow glass eyes of a stuffed crocodile. The room bustled around her. *Caiman crocodilus, El Salvador*, the sign beside the crocodile read. *New Bride*, she thought, *Long Island*. Robert had told her how the museum organized research and collecting parties to places across the globe. She knew he hoped he'd be asked to take part in one. But wives weren't invited along, she was sure of that, and she hadn't thought to ask how long these expeditions lasted. A month in Florida would be one thing. But what if it was somewhere far away? Would Robert abandon her for a year to shoot birds in Tibet? She realized that given the opportunity he probably would, and a panicky feeling gripped her at the thought of being left behind in a city where she had no one.

Across the crowded hall she caught sight of Robert, now standing beside a tweedy gentleman who gestured excitedly as he spoke. Robert was looking directly at her, and she realized he'd been watching her. He would be concerned that she was bored. Quickly, so that he wouldn't worry, she waved her hand and smiled. He smiled back, over the heads of the crowd. Then the tweedy gentleman pulled a passerby forward and Robert turned as he began to introduce them. Nancy stood beside the crocodile and wondered how long they were expected to stay.

On Long Island, the pokeweed had turned from green to red, and duck hunting season had started. Clayton, home from school, lingered in the kitchen. He knew Roy would be out on the marsh with his gun and the dogs, and was hoping he'd return before Mavis came home from Washington Lodge. He missed his sister, though without her here he was free to sketch the dead bat he'd propped against a bowl on the kitchen table. Clayton had found it in the hayloft, and now he was sketching the delicate bones and the webbing of its wings, putting off the more difficult job of drawing its wrinkled, inscrutable face.

He heard his uncle whistling first, then the snuffling of the dogs. Roy came through the door sideways, bearing a cluster of ducks, their limp heads strung together, their orange feet dangling. Seeing Clayton with the dead bat at the table, he gave a conspiratorial wink: Mavis wouldn't want undressed game in her kitchen, either. Clayton, who longed to hunt with Roy, knew the names of all the local waterfowl: canvasback, scaup, black duck, brant, bufflehead, and goldeneye, the mergansers that tasted of low tide no matter how long Mavis soaked them in milk. Now he admired the blue-winged teal while Roy patted his face dry with a striped dishcloth. Outside, a light rain had begun to fall, and Roy smelled of marsh mud and wet dog. "Ugly out," he said, lighting a burner on the stove for coffee.

Clayton wondered for a moment if he should save up for a gun instead of a boat. No, a gun wouldn't be as good. The boat changed frequently in his mind, sometimes a runabout, sometimes a clinker, most recently a flat-bottomed scow, built for the Great South Bay. It struck him as odd that his uncle didn't keep a boat at Starke's. Scudder had practically given the family sailboat away to a friend of Dr. Thayer's, which broke Clayton's heart, though he hadn't let it show. Roy didn't have a boat at all. Clayton glanced up at his uncle, leafing through the paper. Tall and deliberate, with the same spare build as Scudder, Roy hunched his shoulders slightly. Standing motionless, lost in thought, he reminded Clayton of a heron. The rain drummed on the roof, making the kitchen somehow more private.

"Wouldn't you like a boat?" Clayton's voice sounded squeaky. He cleared his throat. "I mean, a boat of your own."

Roy looked startled, as if he'd forgotten Clayton was there. His eyes took a moment to focus. "No." He shook his head. "I don't really care for the bay."

Clayton felt taken aback. Not care for the bay? It was like claiming not to eat strawberries and cream. But when he thought about it, he realized Roy never came sailing; it was always Scudder who took them. Roy seemed to sense his amazement. "Your mother loved it, of course. She was the sailor in the family. You've got it in your blood."

But she was your sister, Clayton nearly said, and then thought of Nancy trying to interest him in riding, his schoolwork. Still, he wished he could prove his uncle wrong, or talk him into changing his mind.

"You know all about engines," he protested. "What about a motorboat?"

Roy shook his head, folding up the paper and finishing his coffee. He filled a large pot with water and set it on the stove. The ducks lolled on the drain board, giving off the heavy smell of damp feathers and blood.

Sailing, Roy thought: he'd rather sit under a clothesline strung with bedding and have cold water splashed in his eyes. His nephew sat at the table with a crestfallen look. The water was boiling on the stove. Roy picked up the first of the ducks by its limp feet and scalded it. Steam rose from the pot, and the smell of wet feathers overwhelmed the kitchen. The boy seemed to be waiting for something. So after a moment Roy said, "I've never been much of a swimmer."

The boy stared at him, then glanced down at the floor as if embarrassed on Roy's behalf. Roy felt again that he disappointed the kid, who clearly wanted something more from him. He tried to imagine how he would appear through a boy's eyes: lonely, middle-aged. A man with the stuffing knocked out of him. He was gripped by a spasm of self-disgust.

He pulled a clump of wet feathers loose with a practiced jerk. An urge came over him to prove he hadn't always been like this, and he thought of how wildly he'd once gone out of his head, the day he had sought the water out. "There was a girl I knew," Roy said, "when I was younger." His back to the boy, eyes on the folded feet of the duck in his hand, he began the story he'd never told before.

He'd come downstairs late for breakfast. It was a Sunday. His mother and Mavis were at church, his father at the boatyard. Helen was married by that time and living in Connecticut. Roy had picked up the paper idly, a slab of bread and butter in the other hand. And there was the headline, DEBUTANTE KILLED IN TRAGIC ACCIDENT, and there was her name, Grace Elizabeth Perdue, underneath her picture. It was a posed photograph, done in a studio, and though she looked beautiful, her mouth was closed, hiding the little gap between her teeth.

When he looked down, he'd been surprised that the table was still there, as if nothing had happened. The walls stood, the ceiling held. He forced himself to read on: *rain and fog, Merritt Parkway, family inconsolable.* He had a sudden image of her father, red-faced in a white linen suit, leaping to his feet with a roar at the sailboat races, and then Grace glancing over at Roy. She hadn't liked sailing either; that was how they'd met, bored at the Southease dock watching the races. He had been staring abstractedly at her pale straight hair, so unlike the carefully scalloped curls the other girls favored, unable to help himself. When the race ended and her father launched himself off his seat, their eyes met and she smiled with a little shake of her head.

He looked back down at her photograph. *The victim had recently broken off her engagement to the son of Mr. and Mrs. Alfred Kehlenbeck of Albany, New York . . .*

Her family had come out from Manhattan for the summer and were staying at the Pattersquash Inn. Her fiancé was up in Albany until September, she said. He was the son of family friends, Roy gathered. He didn't care. The next day he borrowed a horse for her and they rode together all the way to Drowned Meadow and back. Her father nearly had a seizure.

The poor girl, Roy found himself thinking now, so many years later. He hadn't given her a moment's peace. One morning, when he knew her parents had planned a trip to Fire Island, he walked all the way from Taffy Point to the Southease beach as the sun came up and wrote her name in clamshells across the highest dune. Recklessly, he played his ukulele outside her hotel window until the lights went on in the downstairs office. He brought her to Salt Hay Road and walked with her through the humid, rose-scented greenhouse to the quail pen. Into her soft cupped hands he slipped a single brown-speckled chick, no bigger than the first joint of his thumb. How could her fiancé not seem a cold fish in comparison? The night before she went back to New York City, Grace whispered that she would end her engagement. That had been the last he heard from her. He'd been afraid that she had changed her mind.

Roy left the note on the white enamel stove, where his family would find it when they came home from church. He didn't remember walking, though it was nearly a mile to the end of Carman Street, only the light on the water as he moved toward it, the way it seared his eyes. He could see Fire Island, shimmering and broken by the distance into a string of islands floating within the meniscus of the horizon. His mind was entirely clear.

The road ended, and Roy kicked off his shoes. The Great South Bay lay flat and calm under the undulating light. Far out, a single black cormorant flew low over the water. It was late September, but the water hardly felt cold. The light on the bay was so bright it was like walking into fire. He felt a stern exultation: he was going to drown himself in the brightness of the water.

He walked and walked and walked. His foot came down on something that scuttled away, and he jumped instinctively before continuing on, more gingerly. The exultation faded. He walked some more. He looked back, and the sand at the end of the road was a smear of white in the distance. The water reached only to his thighs.

He stood in his wet socks in the middle of the Great South Bay, dry from the waist up and entirely alive. Of course he knew the bay was shallow, everyone knew the bay was shallow. But *this* shallow? What a joke! Even now, more than twenty years later, the memory of that moment made him wince. He'd let out an inarticulate howl of misery. A flock of gulls rose from the surface of the water and flew off toward the Southease dock. He dropped to his knees. The salty water soaked his shirt and filled his mouth with the taste of tears. Now he was kneeling in the bay with his head protruding like a turtle's. He should have stayed home and slit his goddamn wrists.

Roy had taken engines apart and put them back together, and later he felt as if something similar had happened to him in the still middle of the Great South Bay. In that moment of personal disassembly, a small part of him went missing; he almost believed he'd heard the muffled plunk of it hitting the water. It was something almost insignificant, like the washer off a bolt, not observable from the outside at all. But he had never worked the same again.

He stood and, after a moment, turned around and began the long walk back. Emerging gradually, the water coursing down his legs, he saw his black shoes on the white sand at the end of Carman Street. They seemed to be waiting for him, with the patience of the inanimate, as if they had known all along that he wouldn't actually go through with it.

His wet clothes stuck against his skin as he limped home with his shoes in one hand. The gravel bit into his feet. In the kitchen he was relieved to see the note still on the stove. He tore it up and threw it on the coals. When the family came home, they found him in bed, listless with an illness he didn't specify.

Roy felt the boy's eyes on him after he finished, but did not turn. The ducks lay on the drain board, stripped of their feathers. He was here at this moment, he thought, as the result of his own ridiculousness.

Mavis woke from a dream in which she'd been screaming. She struggled in the tangled sheet. Any moment she expected to hear her husband's tread on the stairs, his voice thickly singing, *"Fare thee well, Polly m'dear, I must be on me way."* She fumbled for the electric light beside the bed, and her own room on Salt Hay Road sprang up around her. Breathing as steadily as she could, she tried to calm herself. It had been years since she'd dreamed about Ramsay. Her nightgown clung to her skin, damp with sweat, and she went to the window and opened it to the cool air. Outside, nothing stirred. The full moon showed the tide at dead low. Mavis, still rattled by her nightmare, had a vision of the entire field molded under aspic.

She had received two more letters from the lawyer in California. The last one threatened her with "legal action" if she failed to respond. She had meant to write back, and went so far as to purchase an envelope and two sheets of writing paper at the post office. But she couldn't match the formal language the awful lawyer used. Standing at the counter at Washington Lodge, brushing her teeth before bed, she tried to find the words that would explain how little she knew and how none of it was her fault. In the end, she'd given up, ignoring the letters in the hope that they'd stop coming.

Now, standing at the window, the menacing dream came back to her. It hadn't been the fist-shaped cloud this time.

There had been something tightening around her. It was the ring she still wore on her right hand, an opal ring her husband had given her before they were married, claiming it had once belonged to the French grandmother who'd been a childhood friend of her own Granny Chaffey. They'd been on the porch alone after dinner. The ring was in a little blue velvet box, slightly worn around the edges. He held it out, and she'd exclaimed over it, surprised and flattered. She remembered how he had put his two hands out and drawn hers toward him. And then he took the ring and slid it onto her finger, working it over the knuckle.

In a flash of rare and perfect clarity Mavis saw that the ring itself was cursed. She had to steady herself against the windowsill. For all this time she'd been carrying the curse on her right hand. Before he'd given her the opal ring, her life had been innocent and good. After the ring had come her unhappy marriage, the death of her mother, her childlessness, her sister's cancer. Even the explosion of the fireworks factory, and her niece decamping with a man nobody knew! She stared down at the thin band and the opal like a blind eye on her finger. It seemed to be poisoning her bloodstream. She pulled at it. But her hand had grown plump; she couldn't get it over her knuckle. In a frenzy she gouged her skin, drawing a bead of blood. The pain made her pull herself together. She found the washbasin. The soap stung the cut, but she worked the ring up and down in the lather until she could wrench it off.

Holding it in her palm, she marveled at its smallness. It looked so malignant to her now that she couldn't believe how long it had taken her to realize the truth.

Mavis grabbed her robe and her shoes. Carrying the ring in one hand and the shoes in the other, she made her way quietly down the hall. Anyone hearing her would assume she was just going downstairs to bake. In the kitchen she lit a kerosene lamp and laced up her shoes. Again she forced herself to breathe deeply and steadily. She opened the kitchen door. The night air was chilly. The moon outlined the trees still heavy with leaves, the spiky reeds along the edge of the pond. Mavis walked down the path toward the road, studying the ground. Where the gravel ended there were flagstones. She placed the ring on the flat slate and stamped on it hard, over and over, nearly losing her balance. When she was through, she bent down. The ring was flattened, the metal crumpled like a ribbon found between the pages of a book. The opal had turned to fine grit that sparkled in the moonlight. Mavis gathered it into her palm, using the flat of her thumb to pick up the last of the opal powder. Cupping the ruined ring in her hand, she flung both metal and dust over the low fence. Then she turned back to the house, exhausted and relieved.

In the kitchen she took off her shoes, carefully wiping clear the place where the opal had left a dusting as of flour. Blowing out the kerosene lantern, she made her way upstairs by feel. She climbed back into her narrow bed and fell into a sleep so sound that Clayton had to wake her in the morning by tugging at her arm. She had prepared a story about losing the ring in the sink at Washington Lodge. But as it was, no one noticed it was gone.

Three days later Mavis received another letter from the lawyer in Fresno, California. This one stated that unless her husband could be located she would be held responsible for his debts. How could that be true? She hadn't seen him in over nine years. Even when they were together she had had no control over their finances.

Dear Sir, she wrote back. *Believe me, I am not responsible for my husband's debts. You have to understand that my husband can be unreasonable. In fact, I will tell you frankly, he is a difficult man.* The rest of the page yawned whitely before her. But she felt there was nothing more to say. When she showed the letter to Roy, he was silent for some time. He tapped the paper against the table.

"I tell you what," he said finally. "Let's talk to Al Donner. He's a lawyer. He'll know what to do."

The next afternoon, Mavis changed into her black wool dress and put on her best hat. She had not slept well. In her hand she carried a loaf of potato bread as a gift for the lawyer. Roy escorted her into the small office. He looked ill at ease in a stiff white shirt and brown jacket and stood behind Mavis's chair, fiddling with a button on his cuff.

Mr. Donner did not seem, to Mavis, particularly sympathetic. He read the letters and turned to face her across the polished oak of his desk. "Mrs. White," he said, "I understand you and your husband are separated." Mavis nodded. "Has your husband attempted any communication with you since you last saw him?"

Mavis felt goose flesh stand up along her arms. It occurred to her that maybe Ramsay *was* dead. Maybe, she thought, he had been sending her messages from beyond the grave. She gaped at Mr. Donner. "Communication?"

The lawyer leaned forward to indicate that he was being patient. "Has he sent you any letters, Mrs. White? Any telegrams? Has he contacted you by telephone?"

"Oh no," said Mavis. "No, he hasn't."

Mr. Donner asked a few more questions and promised to look into the situation further. He would take over all correspondence with the lawyer in California. But he cautioned her that he was not optimistic. "In the eyes of the law," he explained to Mavis, "you and Mr. White are still man and wife."

Mavis feared for a moment that he meant the law could force her back to him. "How do you mean?"

"If your husband has failed to honor his financial obligations, the injured party or parties will look to you for restitution."

"Restitution?"

"You will have to pay his debts."

Mavis turned her wide, pained eyes to her brother. Roy shuffled his feet. "Hold on now, Al," he said. "I don't see how that could be right. The man deserted her."

Mr. Donner rose. "I'll see what I can do, of course. But you should be prepared for that eventuality."

Back on Salt Hay Road, Scudder headed across the field to Captain Kelley's for a game of cribbage. The November wind had turned sharp, and the yellow leaves of the locusts fluttered like fish in the net of the bittersweet vines. Scudder knocked. When no one answered, he pushed open the door. Inside, he was surprised by the cold. The fire in the woodstove had gone out. Cats seethed across the kitchen table and across the floor. Scudder called for the Captain. The dark house was silent.

He stepped through the tiny kitchen into the sitting room. The couch with its threadbare arms was empty. Scudder called again, "Kelley? You home?" The cats mewled and pressed against his legs.

Scudder looked in the small back bedroom only as a last resort. It felt strange to open the narrow door; he'd never been through it. A pale rectangle of sunlight fell from the one high window onto the brown bedspread, and in the light a gray cat slept. The Captain lay in the bed staring fixedly at the ceiling.

Scudder knew in an instant that his friend was dead; he had seen eyes open like that before. The Captain lay flat, with his arms at his sides. He must have died in his sleep, Scudder realized. He swallowed, his mouth dry. He thought of the men he'd found dead in the masts of wrecked ships, their hair stiff with ice, and of the bodies washed up on the beach after winter storms.

Once, as a boy, Scudder had misjudged a breaker at Old Inlet while playing in the waves. Instead of cutting through the water as it broke, he'd been snatched and pummeled by it. The wave came down on top of him like a train. He had tumbled for what seemed like hours between water and sand. When he finally fought himself free and had finished retching up salt water, he sat for a long time staring at the crashing waves. He mastered the trick of riding them that summer, but he never forgot the raw strength of the water or its colossal indifference. It was as if the sea were pure brawn, muscle with no reason behind it. He didn't believe, then or later, that there was anything malicious in the sea. Shells, pebbles, ships, men; it was all one to the flexing waves.

Now he felt that same dizziness, the sting of salt in his eyes. He sat down on the only chair, displacing a heap of socks and sweaters. The walls of the room were hung with fly-specked maps and magazine illustrations of sailboats and the insides of cathedrals. To the left of Scudder, above the chair, was a curled photograph of the men of the Smith Point Life Saving Service. They stood in their uniforms, the station house behind them. Scudder remembered the year Kelley joined the station. He himself must have been twenty-six or -seven then. Kelley had seemed younger than he actually was, gawky and painfully shy. A few days after he'd first arrived, somebody's sister, maybe it was King's, had brought a cake out to the station house. Kelley came in from patrol and got halfway across the room before he noticed her. The sight of the girl so flustered him he walked into a chair. It crashed over with his foot caught in it, and he'd gone down hard on the floor. Kelley had simply lain there, and they feared for a moment he'd knocked himself out. But he was too embarrassed to move. The men laughed hard, Scudder with them. Mapes nearly choked with laughter. King's sister told them all to let the poor man alone, but it did no good. For the rest of the season they threw the word "girl" into every other sentence, just to watch Kelley's ears turn red.

Scudder studied the grainy black-and-white faces. They stared back at him, young and serious in their white uniforms, their bristling mustaches. He thought of the unofficial Life Saver's motto: *You have to go out, but you don't have to come back.* In the photo only Mapes was smiling, his head tossed back. Kelley stood very straight, as if being measured for a suit. In the middle sat Randall on a chair, his hands on his knees, not knowing that one day he'd be lost over the side of the lifeboat, his body never recovered. And Bryden, who died not long after that of stomach cancer. Miller outlived his wife and two of his children. Scudder heard it was pneumonia that finished him. And Oates had hanged himself, years before Miller's death, from a rafter in his father-in-law's barn. Scudder sat on the chair by Kelley's bed with his hands over his face and cried for all of them. And for himself, an old man whose last friend was dead, whose wife and daughter were dead, whose granddaughter had left to throw in her lot with a stranger up in Boston.

Mavis and Roy drove back from the lawyer's in silence. Once or twice Roy shook his head and patted his sister on the knee. Mavis sat slumped beside him. She was too stunned to cry. She wished now that she knew where her husband was. Before, she had felt better not knowing, as if it somehow made him less real, less menacing. Now it occurred to her that as long as she had anything he would find a way to take it from her.

She remembered that her father had once complained of Ramsay's boots. This was after he'd first been invited to dinner at the house on Salt Hay Road. They'd had a woman who came in to help then, who drank too much but made perfect, airy soufflés. Mavis came back into the sitting room after wishing Ramsay good night in time to hear her father say ". . . boots like that."

"What could you possibly mean?" her mother asked.

"They're too tight," Scudder said. "You can tell by the way he walks. I never trust a man who doesn't know his own shoe size."

At the time, Mavis had been affronted, though she pretended not to have heard. She took it as an example of her father's lack of breeding.

Lost in thought, Mavis didn't see the crowd gathered in the field beyond Salt Hay Road until Roy gestured toward it. A figure, seeing their car, broke free of the group and ran toward them. It was Clayton. He waved his arms, and Roy brought the car to a crunching stop in the driveway. "It's the Captain," Clayton stammered. His face shone with importance and horror at the news he was delivering. "He's dead."

Roy wrote the letter to Nancy as plainly as possible, telling her the Captain had died in his sleep of a weak heart. *He was a good friend to all the family*, he wrote, *and will be deeply missed here.* This was the first letter Roy had ever written to his niece, and he found it difficult to compose. He was not a man to elaborate, but he felt bound to acknowledge his sister's strange behavior. In the end he added, *His death has hit your aunt especially hard.*

Roy found himself wishing that Nancy were home; not that she and Mavis had ever been chatty, but maybe another female could have somehow reasoned with her. Because Mavis had completely astonished him by running into the house and locking herself in her room as soon as she'd heard the news. Roy had to talk to her through the keyhole.

"Open the door, there's my dear girl." There was a strange gasping, as though she was having trouble breathing. Then he heard her voice, but she didn't seem to be speaking to him. It sounded like some dreadful chant.

Roy tried again. "Please, Mavis, come down to the kitchen with me. Come have a cup of coffee."

"Oh God, ohgodohgodohgod." Her voice sounded muffled, as if she had buried her face in a pillow.

"Pigs!" muttered Roy, under his breath.

He had to drive up to Washington Lodge that evening and tell them she'd been taken ill. He couldn't say when she might be back to work. A sudden onset, he explained. Roy concluded privately that the shock of Captain Kelley's death, on top of her anxiety about her husband's debts, had unhinged her. The sound of her weeping kept him awake that night. Lying in bed and listening to her strangled sobs, he wondered, embarrassed, if perhaps the Captain had meant more to his sister than he'd previously thought.

The Captain's funeral was held at the sprawling Catholic church in Southease on a day of driving rain. Afterward, Scudder developed a bad cold. For three days, he stayed in bed, and when he was strong enough to come downstairs, he seemed to have aged ten years. His eyes were hollowed out and his face had sunk, leaving his nose protruding more than ever, like a rooster's beak. Clayton, helping him down the stairs, was surprised by the skin of his hands, as brittle and dry as the yellowed paper he found wrapped around the pears Mavis saved for the winter in a dresser in the attic. Scudder had never been a large man; now he seemed puny. Clayton was sure he could have carried him down the stairs himself, though he would never have offended the old man's dignity by suggesting it.

Downstairs Scudder sat in an armchair close to the living-room fire, a red-and-black-checked blanket wrapped around his legs. His illness had left him with a harsh cough. Mavis made him nettle tea with honey to ease it, and the smell of the tea lingered in the kitchen and hall. Roy tried to interest him in patience, since no one in the house played cribbage and it was a game he could play alone. But before the round was half over, Scudder had fallen asleep with the cards tumbled in his lap.

Scudder's cough eventually faded, and Mavis stopped brewing nettle tea. But even after he recovered, he spent most of his time in the chair by the fire. Some days he never left the house. He kept *The Collected Poems of Rudyard Kipling* on the table by his chair and read it methodically, from start to finish, and over again. Many of the poems he already knew by heart. Roy brought him other books as well, Edgar Allan Poe and the detective stories of Arthur Conan Doyle. Scudder leafed through them disdainfully, and then returned to Kipling.

Captain Kelley's death had aged Mavis too. She spoke infrequently and her face looked worn. She baked more and ate less, and donated food to the Relief Center in Patchogue. On Sunday she went to church in Southease, wearing her black wool dress and her hat with the feather. On the way to the car she shocked Clayton by suggesting he come with her. When he shook his head, she crushed him painfully against her and he heard her whisper above her choke hold: *"Take pity, Lord!"* Skittish afterward, he tried to avoid her unless her arms were full.

The following week, Clayton was in the kitchen, where the bread was still warm from the oven, when his aunt mentioned Kelley's cats. "We should take the poor creatures in, Roy."

Clayton watched his aunt's dimpled hand on the handle of the knife, cutting into the smooth crust. The heel pulled slowly away, steaming, exposing the pale inside of the loaf.

"No," Roy said. "You know the old man hates them."

"We can't leave them to starve!" His aunt's chin trembled. "I think one's died already." Clayton wondered if he should leave. He stared hard at the loaf of bread. "It's un-Christian not to help them."

"*People* are starving. All over the country!" Roy sounded exasperated. There was a charged pause. Then he said, more kindly, "They're half wild, you know they are. The dogs would only chase them out again."

"*Please*, Roy." His aunt sounded so desperate, Clayton almost hoped his uncle would give in. He glanced up quickly. Roy's expression was set. In that moment he reminded Clayton of Scudder.

"Do you want our house smelling like that cottage? Leave them where they are, Mavis. I don't even want you feeding them."

Mavis sniffled as she passed Clayton a slice of bread. He

smeared it with cream lifted from the top of the milk jug with the flat of the butter knife. The cream was yellow with fat, thick as leather. Clayton sprinkled sugar over it and then crammed the slice into his mouth. The grains of sugar pressed against his tongue.

Later he saw Mavis taking dishes of milk across the field when she knew Roy had gone out. "I'm not *feeding* the cats," she told Clayton sternly. "I'm giving them something to drink."

November continued, cold and windy. From the end of Carman Street, where he and Perry had collected eelgrass, Clayton saw a flock of broadbills in a dark line like a false horizon. Staring out at the gray, metallic surface of the bay, he tried to imagine his uncle wading into it. Disturbed by the story itself, Clayton was still awed that his uncle had confided in him. "And damned if that water wasn't too shallow to wash a dog in!" Roy had said. Clayton hadn't known how to answer. He wondered now if Roy had meant it as a lesson, making a joke out of something that pained him.

He walked home along the edge of the marsh. Surely his uncle hadn't really wanted to drown himself, he thought. On the pond, the last of the maple leaves were tumbling onto the choppy water and capsizing like flimsy boats. Clayton was surprised to see, beyond the maples, a figure in front of the Captain's cottage. A tall woman stood surrounded by a haphazard collection of bags and boxes. She wore a frayed gray coat that whipped in the wind. There was no indication of how she and her meager belongings had arrived, and Clayton let himself believe for a moment that she had parachuted into the field. One of Kelley's cats sat on top of a cardboard box and yowled pitifully.

When he told Mavis that someone was moving into the Captain's house, his aunt put her black hat on her head and took Clayton with her across the field. She brought a fresh loaf of bread and made Clayton carry a pie. The pathway worn by the Captain's feet had begun to grow over with grass. Clayton hadn't been into the cottage since the day the old man died. Once or twice Perry had tried to interest him in a dare, but he'd refused to rise to the bait.

The door opened and a smell assailed them, the smell of cats and the stale, ammoniac urine of cats. The tall woman greeted them cheerfully. She had dark, untidy hair and an angular face. "I'm trying to air it out," she told them, "but as soon as I open a window, they come back in." She glanced over her shoulder, into the room, where a thin cat scratched at the kitchen floor. "I suppose I'll have to drown them," she said distractedly. "The poor things."

"We live in the house across the field," Mavis explained, and they introduced themselves. The woman, Judith Purlowe, was a widowed niece of Captain Kelley's. At the time of his death she'd been living with her sister-in-law's family in Pennsylvania. She seemed delighted to have inherited the house, the cat problem aside. "I'd love to have you in," she said, waving toward the dark, low-ceilinged room. The small living room and the smaller kitchen were piled with bags and makeshift luggage. They continued to stand in the doorway. "I could brew some tea . . ." Judith Purlowe began to riffle through a brown paper bag, producing a shoe with a broken heel and a scrap of cloth that might have been a pillowcase.

"Another time," said Mavis. "Once you've settled in."

"I'm sure I have tea *somewhere*." Judith Purlowe squinted toward the sink.

Clayton had stood through this conversation with the pie grasped firmly in his two hands. Now Mavis set the loaf of bread carefully on top of it. "I'll leave my nephew here," she said. "He can help you unpack your things."

Judith Purlowe turned from her search and smiled a quick, wide smile that illuminated her face, making her suddenly pretty. "Thank you for the things to eat, Mrs. White. I'll bet you were a blessing to my uncle."

Clayton was mortified to see tears appear in Mavis's eyes. But Judith Purlowe had turned toward the kitchen, loaf in hand, and was looking in vain for a bread knife. "Make yourself useful," Mavis told Clayton on her way out.

Clayton set the pie gingerly on the counter. Judith Purlowe had abandoned her search for a knife and stood in the center of the kitchen, holding the loaf of bread. "I'm not sure where to begin," she confessed. "I guess I'd better clear out the cupboards." She handed Clayton a paper bag. "You can start in there." She pointed to the small living room with the sway-backed sofa. "Once we empty out the cabinets, we'll sort through it all."

The dresser was covered with a layer of gray dust and cat hair. The top drawer squealed as Clayton pulled it open. Compacted inside lay pieces of string and twine and colored yarn, rolled into balls and knotted, crinkled sheets of cellophane and shiny paper, tinfoil carefully peeled from packs of cigarettes, lengths of bent wire, jars of buttons, and others of screws and nails. One corner of the drawer was heavy with bottle caps. Clayton began to extract objects in groups to arrange on the floor. It was like taking apart a mouse's nest; pressed together for so many years, the cellophane maintained the drawer's rectangular shape as if molded.

The third drawer stuck. Reaching his hand inside, Clayton felt the sharp corner of a box and bore down with his fingers until the drawer popped open. Mixed in with odd shoelaces were backgammon boards, cribbage sets, and playing cards. Clayton had cleared nearly all of them when he found, beneath a chess set with a broken hinge, a deck of playing cards with worn edges. The deck was held together with a rubber band the color of putty that fell to pieces in his hand. The card on top showed a dark-haired woman with her back to the viewer, looking over her shoulder, her pale, dimpled buttocks exposed. Clayton felt his heartbeat quicken. He glanced toward the kitchen. The tips of the widow's shoes were visible on one of the rickety kitchen chairs. Quickly he fumbled through the deck. Every card showed a half-naked woman. Sirens in old-fashioned hairstyles reclined on sofas, half dressed, or lifted their skirts, smiling coyly. The Ace of Diamonds rode a rocking horse, pitched forward, her heavy bosom grazing its mane. The Four of Hearts winked at him, a hand propped behind her head.

From the kitchen came the thump of a cabinet door. Guiltily, Clayton crushed the cards into his pocket. He couldn't let the widow see them. What if she'd been the one to find those pictures? The thought appalled him. He imagined her gasping for breath, collapsing in a faint. He kept the deck in the front pocket of his pants, where it pressed uncomfortably, distracting him as he sorted through more piles of frayed papers, books on mesmerism and the spirit world, empty tobacco tins. Against his thigh it seemed to generate a faint, illicit heat.

An hour and a half later, lifting a pile of yellowed handkerchiefs from a dresser in the Captain's bedroom, Clayton felt something between the layers of worn cotton. He shook the handkerchiefs onto the bed and out fell a wad of paper money.

Clayton peered quickly through the small bedroom window. Judith Purlowe was outside, beating the striped kitchen rug with a broom. Clouds of dirt and dust swirled around her. Clayton sat on the bed and counted the crumpled bills. It was a small fortune, thirty-two dollars in all. Who would know if he kept it for himself? he thought. His aunt and uncle did not keep track of how much he earned, though Mavis told him every payday at Washington Lodge that he should "put something away." His sister would have noticed if he suddenly had more spending money. She might even have sensed something just by looking at him. But Nancy was in Boston. He felt that it would somehow serve his sister right if he took money that wasn't his.

He stood and pressed the bills into a pile. Trying to stuff them into his pocket, his hand was brought up short by the indecent playing cards. There wasn't room for both. Outside, the dull thump of the broom on the rug had stopped. He could see the widow set the broom down on the grass. He pushed the bills into the other pocket. Now both pockets bulged, like the face of a chipmunk with acorns in either cheek. It seemed clear to him in that moment that he would have to choose between the money and the deck of filth and pleasure. He felt a rush of shame.

Judith Purlowe came back into the house with the kitchen rug draped over her arm just as Clayton dashed out of the dark back bedroom. The cards hidden in his pocket thumped against his leg. He held out the creased and folded dollars. "Look!" he called. "Look what I found for you!"

Mavis knew she was responsible for the Captain's death: she had thrown the remains of the opal ring over the fence onto his property, and four days later he was dead. That she had done this unwittingly, that she would never have wished him any harm, that he was one of her oldest and dearest friends, only worsened the horror of it. She knew that curses do not take into account.

There was no one she could talk to. Roy would never believe what she knew was the truth. She considered her brother's understanding of these things limited, at best; he would fall back on scientific fact. No one at her church would be able to see past what they'd call superstition. The only one who would have listened to her and sympathized was the Captain himself.

Mavis took an instant dislike to his slatternly widowed niece. But this in no way lessened her acts of charity. She returned the following afternoon with a pot of soup and found Judith Purlowe washing her hair. The house was in the same wild disarray and the smell still overpowering. Nothing seemed to have been cleaned or organized. Back at home Mavis asked Clayton what he'd done to help the day before. He told her Mrs. Purlowe had had him emptying drawers. "And I found money. A heap of it."

"Money?!" said Mavis. It seemed obscurely unfair that a strange woman, especially such an untidy one, should come into a windfall. Though it was clear, thought Mavis, that she had need of it, judging by the state of her coat and shoes.

"Thirty-two dollars." Already it seemed to Clayton that he'd never hesitated to hand the bills over. The cards he'd needed to keep to protect Mrs. Purlowe. He would throw them away, he told himself, or burn them, but he had to wait until he was sure his aunt wouldn't see them. In the meantime, he'd found a hiding place under the mattress in his room.

———

Guilty over the Captain's death, Mavis tried to interest Roy in helping the widow. "We need to be neighborly. She'll never get that gutter back up on her own." A gutter over the kitchen window had collapsed months before. Now it listed across the window itself, giving the small house a drunken look. Roy complained that he had enough to do maintaining their own property. The greenhouses were becoming unsafe, the barn roof leaked, he needed more oats for the horses.

The next day, while Mavis was at work at the lodge and Clayton at school, Roy noticed the widow hauling a ladder around to the front of the house. He stood and watched her from the porch as she climbed the rungs. At the top, bracing herself with her feet, she tapped at something with a hammer. Then she pulled a piece of wire from her coat pocket. It took her several tries to hook the wire around the gutter. Roy felt a prick of conscience. But he stayed on the porch. Not out of laziness or unkindness; he simply wanted to keep watching her. She was going about the repair entirely wrong, wrapping wire around the gutter and attaching it to a hook instead of nailing the gutter itself directly to the wall. He wanted to see how she would manage. After about ten minutes, she climbed down from the ladder and surveyed her work. The gutter hung straight above the window, bisected by a line of wire. Judith Purlowe picked up the ladder and disappeared around the back of the house. Roy found himself grinning. When Mavis came home, he pointed out that the gutter on the cottage across the field had been fixed without his interference.

One morning in early December, Scudder didn't come downstairs for breakfast. Mavis was getting ready to leave for the lodge when she realized he hadn't appeared. "Run up to your grandfather's room," she told Clayton. "He must have overslept."

Clayton found the old man collapsed on the floor of his bedroom in his nightshirt. Terrified, he stood frozen in the doorway. His grandfather had always seemed invulnerable. Now Clayton saw the spindliness of his bare, old-man's legs, one thin, ropy arm spread out across the rug. Scudder's eyes were closed, his stern face half pressed against the floor. Clayton made sure that he was breathing, then ran for his uncle.

Together they got Scudder back into bed and made him comfortable. He seemed more affronted than injured and pretended not to understand why they were fussing over him. Dr. Thayer was summoned, at Mavis's insistence. "Nothing's broken," he reassured them. "He's bruised his hip, that's all. But he's an old man and his bones are fragile. A break at his age could lead to complications."

That evening Roy and Mavis decided it would be safest to move Scudder from his upstairs bedroom to a corner of the living room. Out in the barn Roy put a rough daybed together out of spare lumber, finishing by the light of the kerosene lamps that Clayton helped carry out. Back inside the house they made space downstairs for Scudder's bureau and his bookshelf.

"We've set up a bed for you downstairs," Roy told Scudder. It sounded like an apology. "So we can keep an eye on you."

Scudder fixed his son with a clear, fierce gaze. Clayton, standing in the doorway, was reminded of an injured hawk. In a hoarse voice, not addressing them but rather a point on the far wall, Scudder spoke: *"And he risks his life for others in the quicksands and the breakers. / And a thousand wives and mothers bless his name."* It was a poem about surfmen that Clayton had heard once or twice before. No one moved for a moment after Scudder broke off. Finally, Roy stepped forward and put his arm carefully under his father's back. Clayton hurried to help him. "It's warmer downstairs," Mavis said with false cheeriness. "You'll be right near the stove." Scudder didn't answer. He held himself stiffly between Roy and Clayton and did not in any way assist them, allowing his feet to brush the floor without supporting his weight. His bones under Clayton's arm felt brittle, a bundle of dry sticks. Tentatively they made their way down the stairs.

Once in place, Scudder made no complaints. The daybed was near the fire, and from it he could look out the window onto the marsh. Soon the entire downstairs smelled of pipe tobacco. He was often asleep, and to keep from disturbing him, the rest of the family spent more and more time in the kitchen.

Clayton watched with fascination as his grandfather turned slowly into a bird. Not the rooster or hawk he had at times resembled, but the hatchling of some altricial species, a blue jay or a mourning dove. Scudder's eyes were often shut, so that the closed lids veined with blue seemed not to have opened yet. His white hair stuck up from his head like tufts of down. His nose looked more than ever like a beak, but a fragile one that had only recently pecked its way out of a shell.

It was Clayton who asked Mavis if they should bathe him, when the sour, rotten smell began to permeate the room. He used a sponge and a basin of water while Mavis held her father under the arms and primly averted her face. Seeing his grandfather's spindly legs and soft, extended belly made Clayton think of a hatchling again. When the wet sponge hit Scudder's groin, the old man's eyes opened in alarm and he struggled. Mavis kept him from falling as she tried to reassure him, but the bath was considered a failure and they did not attempt it again.

And it was Clayton who most often remembered to feed him. Mavis alternated between furious bouts of baking and trancelike states during which she sat at the kitchen table and stared up at the ceiling as if attempting to read something in the cracks in the plaster. Clayton fed the old man oatmeal, because it was easy to chew.

Standing over his grandfather with the oatmeal bowl, Clayton thought of the shipwrecks the old man had told him about: the *Lucy Norton*, the dark-eyed figurehead of which stood at the entrance to the Southease town hall; the rescue divers who worked for weeks to salvage bolts of cloth and bags of mail off the *Belle of the Isles*. Since before he could read, Clayton had known the names of ships that sank fifty years before he was born. He imagined those lost cargoes strewn across the shores of Fire Island, buried like treasure in the sand.

"Time to eat." He rattled the spoon in the bowl. His grandfather's eyes were closed. Clayton watched his chest, relieved when it rose with the old man's shallow breathing. "Time to eat," he said again.

His grandfather couldn't just die, he told himself. Not a man who had lived through so much. Scudder knew more about Fire Neck than anyone. He loved the history of the roads they walked on and had told Clayton the stories behind the names. Fire Neck, for the signal fires the Indians burned on the banks of the river to guide whaling parties through the inlet and back across the bay. And he had mapped in his mind the shifting cartography of the south shore. It was not as solid as it looked, he'd told Clayton. Back in the 1700s the ocean burst through narrow Fire Island and made an inlet across the Great South Bay from Southease. With a single storm, the town became an ocean port. Scudder had described the shipyards, the wharves that reached into the bay, the mansions with cupolas and widow's walks that went up along the shore. Then, in another storm, a ship loaded with grindstones sank in the channel. Underwater, sand swept and settled around the wreck. The next ship that foundered there carried a load of salt. Together the two wrecks closed the inlet.

Clayton remembered how, as a little boy, he'd believed what his grandfather told him: that this second ship was the reason the Great South Bay was salty. Out east, Scudder had explained with a poker face, out near Shinnecock, the water tasted sweet: that was where a ship bound to Boston from Havana went down with a cargo of molasses.

Reaching out with the tip of the spoon, Clayton tapped his grandfather gently on the lower lip. Please eat, he thought fervently, *please*. The old man's eyes stayed closed. But at the pressure of the spoon his mouth opened, like the mouth of a baby bird.

Roy was up on the roof of the horse barn patching a leak when he noticed Judith Purlowe heading across the field. She carried a burlap bag at arm's length and moved slowly but grimly, her neck bowed. It was not yet six-thirty in the morning and the gray sky sagged with clouds. Roy was anxious to mend the roof before the rain or snow hit, and had come out before he'd had his coffee. At the edge of the pond Judith Purlowe hesitated. She set the bag on the grass, where it began to writhe. Roy watched her run a hand through her hair. Standing by the pond in her ancient overcoat, the dark clouds massing in the sky behind her, she looked forlorn beyond bearing. Roy abandoned the roof and set off to intercept her.

She slowed down when she saw him and waited till he reached her before she began to explain: "I can't keep them out. The whole house smells. I tried taking them to Southease one night, but they were back before morning. You have no idea what it's like. They're all over me every time I sit down to eat. I can't possibly feed them through the winter." As she talked, she kept up a steady, resigned shaking of her head. "It's taken me days to get them all together. You should see the scratches on my arms."

The thought of scratches on her skin offended Roy. "Do you have a brick in there?"

The widow shook her head again. "I've never done this before." She said it like a confession. Her bottom lip was chapped, and Roy found himself wondering if she chewed it. "Is the brick required?"

"I understand it speeds things along."

They regarded the bag beside them on the grass. It had gone strangely still, as if the cats inside were listening. The silence stretched on. Even the clouds seemed to be waiting.

"Why don't you let me take care of this," Roy found himself telling her. It seemed the obvious thing to say. It was, he realized, why he'd left the roof in the first place.

Judith beamed at him. She had a bright, surprising smile. Roy smiled back, to lessen her embarrassment. They stood grinning at each other. "Thank you," Judith said. "You have no idea . . . I appreciate it . . . You're so kind." Her brown eyes glistened. She reached forward quickly and pressed his hand with a warm, strong grip.

Roy felt the blood rush to his face. Before he could speak she'd moved away, walking back across the field toward the Captain's cottage. It had begun to rain, a cold, spattering rain. The burlap bag struggled blindly at his feet. He picked it up, feeling light-headed but purposeful. He looked toward the marsh. Could he really let it drop into the river, knowing it would float for some time? He was a man famous for his squeamishness, a man who had failed at his own self-destruction. Should he fight against his essential nature? His hand tingled where Judith Purlowe had touched it.

Roy carried the wriggling bag to his car and spent the

morning driving to Wading River. There he opened the bag in the woods outside of town. He backed away quickly as the cats tumbled out, their fur matted, scratching and spitting. Roy watched as they disbanded, hightailing it into the bushes. It was a cowardly act on his part, and he knew it. The cats would slowly starve, or attack a stranger's chickens. He could not defend himself. He drove home in great spirits, singing loudly out the window into the freezing rain.

One Saturday morning Perry arrived with the news that the canals had frozen at Starke's Boatyard. He carried his older brother's eel spears. Clayton borrowed a hatchet from Roy's toolbox, and the two boys walked down to the boatyard with a bucket on the end of the long-handled spears. Out on one of the frozen canals they smashed the surface with the hatchet and cleared the broken ice away to make a hole. Clayton's fingers smarted in his wool mittens. Into the hole they thrust the eel spears, each with its row of barbed hooks. Somewhere in the mud below them the eels lay curled against the cold. At the first hole the boys plunged and plunged without any luck. "Pigs," said Clayton, feeling grown-up.

They moved the gear farther out on the ice, toward the opening at the mouth of the river, then used the hatchet to smash another hole. "One, two, *three,*" called Perry. Standing at the edge of the hole, they poked into the dark water. "Got one!" Perry yelled, in the same instant that Clayton felt the handle jerk in his own hand. They hauled their spears to the surface. Caught between them like a thick black rope writhed a single eel. The boys shouted with triumph. Working their spears free, they pushed the huge, dripping eel into the bucket.

Then they watched, transfixed, as it thrashed its sinewy bulk against the sides.

They caught three more, adding them to the black tangle in the bucket, but none could match the first. "Go on and take the big one," Clayton told Perry when, hands stiff with cold, ears stinging, they'd finally decided to head back. "There are only four of us." Around them the canal was pocked with the rough holes they'd made in the ice, as if a rain of meteors had fallen. Along the shore the docks rose at odd angles like enormous insects, the pilings pushed up out of the mud by the grip of the shifting ice. Perry dared him to climb the tallest dock and Clayton ran to it, sliding on the ice. He clambered out on the gray planks as if the dock were a ladder, egged on by the urge to impress his friend and by his own agility. At the top he felt the dock sway under his weight like a pair of stilts. He could see over the wild privet hedge to the field beyond and the roof of the Captain's cottage and the house on Salt Hay Road. By their woodpile, his uncle was chopping wood. Clayton suddenly wished he hadn't offered the monstrous eel to Perry.

"Come on," he told Perry, jumping down off the dock so that the planks clattered. "I've got to get home."

They carried the bucket between them. Clayton, trying to get back before his uncle finished with the wood, sloshed frigid water onto their legs in his hurry. They clambered over the fence, the eel spears tangling in the privet, and Clayton was relieved to see Roy still by the woodpile. Intent on his task, Roy didn't notice them until they were nearly beside him. They set the bucket down on the brown grass, and he looked up, startled. Clayton, abashed by his own eagerness, couldn't think of anything to say.

"We caught the great-grandfather of all eels," Perry announced. He pointed into the bucket. "Clay said I could take it." He glanced up at his friend, to make sure the agreement still held. Clayton was watching his uncle from the corner of his eye.

Roy stepped forward and peered into the bucket. He let out a low whistle. "That's the biggest eel in Christendom," he said solemnly.

Clayton felt his chest expand with pride. "We speared it at the same time," he explained.

That night he sat at the kitchen table under his aunt's stern eye to work on his weekly letter. *Dear Nancy*, Clayton wrote, *Today me and Perry caught the biggest eel and Roy said* . . . He knew even as he wrote the sentence that it wasn't something that would impress her.

In Boston, Nancy shopped for Christmas presents alone. Robert was working extra hours at the museum to catalogue the new birds from the Mexico expedition and often didn't come home until after eight. They had agreed to stay in town over the holiday in order to save money, and it had seemed to Nancy at first like a romantic idea. But in the days leading up to Christmas, as she returned with bags and boxes to a dark and empty apartment, she often thought of the house on Salt Hay Road. Robert had asked if she wanted a tree, and she'd stoically said no, thinking of the cost, and instead bought a few pine boughs and put them behind picture frames to bring a little greenery inside. On Long Island, Clayton and Roy would have gone onto the marsh and brought back a small red cedar, and Mavis would tell them not to get sap on the rugs. In the past, she and Clayton had decorated the tree with white paper stars and red paper flowers, and popcorn strung on thread, and with the two dozen green and red glass ornaments from their grandmother Genevieve, stored in tissue paper in a box in the attic. It would be warm in the kitchen, and it would smell of the rum cake Mavis made each year especially for Scudder and the ginger-bread Clayton loved to eat with cream.

On Christmas morning, Robert brought her coffee and toast in bed. "I blackened it specially," he said.

She sat up, smoothing her hair. "Is this a Landgraf Christmas tradition?"

He laughed, and the coffee sloshed onto the tray. "Hardly. I spared you the sweet onion sandwich."

"No!"

Robert nodded, climbing back into bed beside her. "My father eats one every morning. Christmas, Easter, Fourth of July. He says it's good for the teeth."

Robert didn't speak much about his family. Nancy knew they hadn't approved of his going away to college, and that his mother had died during his freshman year, so that he'd never had a chance to convince her he'd made the right decision. "Do you miss them?"

He was quiet for a moment, and she worried her question had pained him. But when he spoke, he sounded merely thoughtful. "Only my uncle. He used to let us ride with him on the snow roller. That was a treat. You probably don't have those on Long Island. They're for packing down the roads after a snowstorm, some planks bolted to a frame like a drum. He's a potato farmer. The black sheep of the family, till I came along. If you ask him what he grows on his farm, he says *rocks*."

Nancy raised herself on her elbows and looked down into Robert's face. He smiled at her, ink smudges on his chin. She thought happily that he would be home with her the whole day. "You don't wish we were there?"

"Good God, no," he said with feeling. "All they'll talk about is cows, and the diseases of cows, and which is better, Holsteins or Dutch Belted, and silage, and who's joined the Dairymen's Association." A bitterness she'd never heard before crept into his voice. "If I hadn't gotten my scholarship, I'd have gone to work canning corn. Anything else."

Nancy, her head on his shoulder, thought of how much she appreciated her own family since moving away. "I'm sure they miss you, though."

"They'll manage." He put his arm around her. "I forbid our sons to be dairymen," he said solemnly. "Dogcatchers, sure."

The thought of a son seemed oddly disloyal to her brother. "I'm only having daughters," Nancy declared. "We can name the first one Helen, after my mother. Or maybe Helena."

"Helena," Robert murmured, kissing her shoulder. "Helena handbasket."

They opened their presents on the sofa, under the largest of the evergreen branches. Nancy had found him an illustrated book of parrots of the world in a bookstore on Washington Street and was gratified by his awed whistle as he unwrapped the brown paper. Heavy, gilt-edged, with tissue paper between each of the exquisite plates, it had cost quite a bit more than she should have spent. The money would have to come out of her housekeeping allowance, and the thought of the gifts she'd sent to Long Island as well made her nervous.

"My mother loved Christmas," Nancy said, remembering a time when money hadn't mattered. "We always had a big tree in the front hall, and she'd decorate it in blue and silver, and there'd be candles in all the windows. The cook made marzipan farm animals every year, they looked just like toys. One time when Clay was little, he tried to eat a painted lead pig in the nursery because he thought it would taste the same."

Robert was silent. When she picked up the small box with her name on it, he grimaced. "I don't know, Nancy." He put his hand out to stop her. "I'd rather get you something else, something better."

"Don't be silly." She laughed, opening the box. Inside was an olive-green bracelet of large square beads. They looked to Nancy like Bakelite. The ugliness of it took her aback. Recovering quickly, she thanked him and put the bracelet on her wrist, where it gave her skin a sallow cast. It didn't matter at all. She thought of the thin blond girl with dirty hands and a baby in her arms who'd asked her for money on the street just the other day, avoiding her eyes. She didn't care a fig about a bracelet. Only it surprised her that he could misjudge her taste so completely.

She glanced up, smiling, but Robert didn't meet her gaze. He took the discarded wrapping paper and stood with it balled in his hand, as if judging its weight. Outside, it had begun to sleet. Later, it seemed to Nancy that in that moment she felt the day veer off its course with a lurch, like a horse that stumbles mid-stride on a stone. Without the normal workaday bustle of the street the apartment seemed eerily quiet. Even the neighbors with the terrier were gone. A musty dampness hung in the air; the laundry had closed for the holiday week, revealing the apartment's underlying smell. Robert turned and walked into the kitchen, and Nancy sat on the couch, confused and hurt. Was it her fault that her gift had been perfect and his hadn't? Was it fair of him to blame her for that? She had spent too much on the book, but only out of love for him. Going over it in her mind later, in the house on Salt Hay Road, she would wonder what she could have done differently.

Down on Long Island, Roy accompanied Mavis to church in Patchogue, while Clayton stayed home to look after Scudder. For dinner, Mavis served ham with potatoes and leeks, and rice pudding for dessert. They unpacked the box from Nancy, full of oranges and chocolates for Scudder, socks for Roy, real vanilla in bourbon for Mavis, and a new jacket for Clayton. It was blue with brass buttons, and it reminded him, in its color and its vaguely military cut, of the little sailor suit he wore as a child in the photo Nancy had of him. After trying it on, he hung it carefully at the back of his closet. When Mavis asked later where it was, he claimed it was too nice for everyday. In his heart he felt that it was the jacket of a city boy, a boy who could never catch an eel or smoke a cattail cigar, someone he would despise instantly, should he ever come across him.

One morning in January, after three days of rain, Clayton woke to find the world dismantled in the night and replaced with a reproduction in ice. The sun gleamed on ice fields and ice trees, and there across the field stood a small ice cottage. At a fair in Riverhead he and Nancy had once seen a life-size statue of a cow, sculpted in butter. This was a thousand times better. Maybe the bay itself had frozen, he thought; he would find Perry and see. They couldn't possibly waste a day like this at school, no matter what he'd told his sister. Downstairs, he heard Mavis talking gently to Scudder in the sitting room. Stealthily, he grabbed a biscuit from the kitchen table and crept outside. The light stung his eyes.

It took him an eternity to walk to the end of Salt Hay Road; it was so bright it was hard to see, and he slipped and fell, slipped and fell. No one else was out. On Beaver Dam he passed a car abandoned along the side of the road. It had swerved into a low stand of bushes. The branches, encased in ice, clacked in the light wind against the windshield. All around him he heard a sharp cracking and clattering. There were no other sounds.

At the Presbyterian church he turned onto Carman Street. Here the trees that lined the road staggered under the weight of their ice-slicked limbs; they bent nearly double, the branches of each tree entangled with those of the tree across the road. It was like entering a long, glittering tunnel. He walked slowly, to keep from falling. Distorted images of trees and sky shifted on the gleaming surface beneath his feet. The cold air seemed to burn his nose and throat. By the Watsons', he heard a tearing crack and then, ahead of him, a large branch tumbled down and shattered like a crystal chandelier.

He had nearly reached the Gilpins' house when he heard a new sound, a steady scraping. Behind him, incongruous beneath the trees, sailed an ice scooter. The west wind blew behind it. It sailed on a reach, and the white canvas billowed out over the road, just clearing a gray mailbox. Clayton stepped back and it glided past, silent except for the scrape of the runners against the ice. The bundled figure at the tiller nodded to him with polite formality as the scooter swept by. Clayton stood staring after it as it sailed down the road, headed for the bay. It must have been the Coles' boat, he told himself, rigged at their house at the head of Carman Street. The lone scooter dwindled soundlessly in the bright distance. He thought of the ghost ships that his grandfather and Captain Kelley used to speak of in low voices, late at night when he was supposed to be asleep.

At the Gilpins' he learned that school had been canceled. Mrs. Gilpin made him sit down at the table and eat a plate of eggs with Perry before she'd let them out of the house. Slithering and laughing, the boys made their way down the ice-encrusted road to the bay. It shone like an enormous mirror. They walked out onto it, glancing back at the shore as it receded behind them. By the Southease dock scooters gathered on the ice, their sails like white wings, darting and settling like a flock of skittish birds.

Exposed on the frozen bay, they felt the wind scrape at their hands and faces. They pressed on, past the humped shape of John Boyle's Island to the east, toward the low dunes of Fire Island and the dock at Old Inlet. Here too the ice had pushed the poles up out of the mud. Planks hung like broken teeth. The boardwalk was silent, the landscape brown and bare. It felt, Clayton thought, as though they had returned many years later to a place that had been abandoned. Trying to shake the eerie feeling, he ran to the top of the dune and stood looking out over the beach where the waves had cut away the shore. There was no sign of another living soul. The ocean pounded against the sand, and it seemed unbelievable to Clayton that they were looking down on the same stretch of land where he and Perry had dug trenches and splashed in the water less than six months before.

They walked back down the slope of the boardwalk and returned across the bay in silence, feeling as if they were coming back from the moon. Already the light had changed. The sun had gone behind a bank of clouds and the ice seemed to emit a cold radiance.

At the end of Carman Street, a man in a red knit hat was skating. He moved, intent and graceful, in a series of turns and flourishes, as if through the steps of an archaic dance. Clayton and Perry passed him with their eyes averted, unsure what to make of him.

Later that week Clayton spotted the man in the red knit hat again, near the mouth of the river at twilight. He mentioned the skater to Roy, and his uncle nodded. "He likes to skate the Lord's Prayer on the ice."

Mavis had grown accustomed to scanning the mail for the lawyer's embossed return address. When a thick brown envelope came from Canada, she carried it out of the post office and rode all the way home with it on her lap, unaware of what she held. Only after she set the mail on the kitchen table at Salt Hay Road did Mavis notice the familiar handwriting with a feeling of vertigo. She sat down abruptly with the envelope in her hands. She hadn't heard from her husband since the day he left her. The blue stamps showed a picture of a steamer and a seaplane, the return address a post office box in Manitoba. He was not close by, Mavis thought, and he was not dead. He could pay his own debts.

Heartened by the thought of the distance between them, Mavis ripped the flap of the envelope. There was a sheaf of folded papers and a four-page letter on thin airmail stationery in Ramsay's rough, impatient hand. In places words and even whole lines had been crossed out, tearing the paper. *Mavis . . .* The letter began as an apology and veered almost immediately into a confession. He had been a bad husband, he wrote. He'd made a joke of the state of matrimony. Mavis realized she was holding her breath and stopped reading to steady herself. A miracle had been worked on her husband, she thought, awed by the power of God. And she felt a pinch of fear. She was still his wife, and he might expect a reconciliation. With a certainty like a stone inside her, Mavis knew that she would never go back to him. Not if he became a deacon, she thought fiercely, or even the Pope himself. Not if he were canonized.

She picked up the letter again and read the details of his unfaithfulness. He had been a drunkard and a fornicator. Debts from playing dice led him to clean out their bank account and disappear. First he'd gone to Michigan to stay with a lady friend, then to California, to Washington state, and from there to Canada. *I drifted like a bum*, he wrote, *stooping lower and lower*. And then, at a church supper in Manitoba three years ago, he had been saved by an angel. Mavis, a literalist, read several sentences describing her before it dawned that the angel Ramsay meant was the daughter of a potato farmer. Ramsay had found a job and rented a house. He married Gretchen Holgersson without anyone guessing that he already had a wife back in the States. Four months ago, he wrote, they had been blessed with a son. Here Ramsay had taped a photograph to the paper. It was barely larger than a postage stamp and showed a baby with a head like a turnip, its mouth open in surprise. *He's smart as a whip*, Ramsay wrote. *I can see it in his eyes when I talk to him. Also, he squeezes my thumb.* Holding his son, he'd realized how deeply he'd wronged the boy's mother. He was writing to ask Mavis to grant him a divorce, so that he and the mother of his child could be properly married. The enclosed papers had been drawn up by a lawyer in Canada. *I imagine you'll be happy to be quit of me for good*, he wrote. *I'm sorry for the things I did. I truly am.*

Mavis sat in the kitchen while a numbness spread out from her chest and radiated down her arms. There had been some mistake, she thought. She turned the letter over in her hands; a few scraps of paper with the ink bleeding through it. She picked up the envelope. The writing was familiar, and the name, but the man she thought she knew had been someone else. There was so much she didn't understand. Her head throbbed. The numbness revealed itself as pain.

For as long as she could remember, Mavis had lived with the fear that something important eluded her, like an object hovering just outside her peripheral vision. At times she resented the certainty and purpose other people seemed to possess. Life seemed to her like one of those French examinations that had caused her such misery at school; she could never be sure she understood the questions she was trying to answer. She remembered a small, dark-haired girl who'd sat at the desk in front of her in French class, how easily she seemed to rattle off verb conjugations, like a bird singing. Mavis felt her own tongue awkward in her mouth, the taste of bitterness like a rotten tooth. How could Ramsay be living happily in Canada, with a wife named Gretchen and a baby who pulled at his finger, when all this time she'd lived in terror of him showing up on Long Island? How could God allow good men like Captain Kelley to die and men like Ramsay to be saved by fertile angels? She gripped the packet of papers and felt the stiff envelope first resist and then crumple in her hands. She'd write back to the lawyer, but not to Ramsay. Let him wonder what had become of her for a change, she thought. He needed something from her now. He could go on needing it. She looked at the tiny photograph again. The baby stared back at her, homely and astonished. "You little *bastard*," Mavis said out loud. The vehemence in her own voice shocked her.

Nancy woke to the clinking sound of a spoon. She was alone in bed. The clock showed it was ten minutes to seven. Confused, she pulled herself up and threw on a robe. In the kitchen there were black coffee grounds on the counter and scattered across the floor. "Are we out of bread again?" Robert looked up from the bread box.

"What are you doing?" Nancy asked.

"Peters is coming in early. Didn't I mention that last night?" He drank the last of his coffee, standing at the sink. Nancy could tell by his face that his thoughts were already on the possibility of a collecting expedition, the endless cataloguing and correspondence that waited for him at the museum. Putting down his cup, he moved toward the hallway. Nancy followed.

She watched her husband putting on his coat and hat, and he looked different to her, as if the angle from which she observed him had changed. The feeling of remove unnerved her. She put out her hand and touched his shoulder. Robert patted it with one hand while rummaging in his pocket with the other. He seemed, in his ignorance of her condition and the obliviousness with which he jangled his keys, to be a thousand miles away.

"Don't forget to pick up some bread." He kissed her on the side of her head and stepped outside.

For twelve days now Nancy had suspected she might be pregnant. She hadn't said anything to Robert yet, because she didn't know for sure. She wanted to wait until her instinct was confirmed. The possibility both excited and scared her. Everything around her seemed to recede to make room for it.

Nancy sat down on the sofa. Outside, she could hear the yapping of the terrier. She had been dreaming something when the sound of the coffee spoon had woken her; the dream itself had melted away, but it left a bitterness behind, a residue of ashes. Her secret felt suddenly too big to bear alone.

She wouldn't wait to see the doctor, after all, she decided.

She'd tell Robert that evening. Resolved on this, she felt a pressure lift from her shoulders. She went back into the bedroom and lay down. She thought of the day the fireworks factory had exploded, the day she and Robert first met. They'd walked to Salt Hay Road from Washington Lodge, and she'd led him on the shortcut that ran past Scheibel's Creek. On the marsh they found a solitary tree. From a distance it had looked at first like a flock of strange birds had perched on the branches. As they drew nearer, they saw it was peppered from the explosion with scraps of yellow bunting and tiny American flags. What she remembered now, more than the strange sight of the tree festooned with flags, was the way Robert had gazed at her in amazement, as if she were somehow responsible. "I think we've discovered a new species," he'd teased. She hoped, when she told him about the baby, that he would look at her with that same wonder on his face.

It was nearly ten o'clock when she woke again, disoriented and queasy. The dog was still barking next door. She stood up quickly and pulled on her clothes. The relief she'd felt after deciding to tell Robert had vanished. She remembered something he'd said in passing about a colleague at work, a man with seven children. "Poor Aldrich! His wife won't stop producing them." What was that supposed to mean, Nancy wondered, indignant.

She went into the kitchen and made herself boil and eat an egg. Trying to picture Robert with a baby in his arms, she felt an unease that reminded her of being seasick. Now she wondered what would happen if she needed bed rest during the last months, like her mother had with Clay. How would she manage to cook dinner and do the shopping and keep the apartment clean? Her mother hadn't needed to bother with any of this. Nancy remembered Clayton as a red-faced baby, crying inconsolably, and the matronly nurse in her blue uniform whisking him away.

Now it seemed stupid to tell Robert anything before she knew for sure. She would find a doctor and make an appointment, so that there could be no uncertainty. Then she would present the fact to Robert. It was too late to ask him now whether or not he was ready for a child or if they could afford one. She had to trust that he'd be pleased. Maybe, she thought, a baby would ease the tension she'd felt between them since Christmas.

Nancy finished her late breakfast. As she washed the plate, she wondered what she would look like in a few months' time. She had a memory of her pregnant mother, surrounded by pillows, in her silk bed jacket, flexing one bare foot and then the other and grimacing. "My ankles have turned into sausages," she'd said in a tone of resigned disgust. Nancy dried her hands and went to the mirror in the hall. Her hair hung limp, and there were shadows under her eyes. She smiled bravely, tipping up her chin, and the prettiness flashed back into her face and then faded as she held the smile too long.

On the apartment steps she ran into her neighbor, Mrs. Pelagias, a broad, stately woman with a dark mustache and twin sons who fought each other constantly, whom Robert referred to, privately, as Cain and Abel. Nancy asked if she could recommend a good doctor with an office nearby. "Not for anything serious," she said quickly, flustered. Mrs. Pelagias beamed. She knew just the doctor, a grand man with women and children, she said. Nancy felt her face redden. Mrs. Pelagias drew a map on a slip of paper, marking the streets and the route to the doctor's office in great detail. Giving it to Nancy, she patted her on the cheek with a rough, warm hand.

All afternoon Nancy was conscious of shielding her secret, cupping it like a flame. The small errands she had to run, mailing a letter to her brother, buying a loaf of bread and carrots and onions for the soup she'd planned for dinner, seemed to take hours. By the time she got back to the apartment it was already dark. She switched on the light and looked around for what felt like the first time, struck by the illuminated shabbiness. The paint had begun to peel in a section of the ceiling and on the radiator against the wall. All the little improvements she had dreamed up in her newlywed excitement seemed pathetic to her now; the flowered pillows she'd been so pleased with only emphasized the sofa's threadbare arms. She pulled the curtains shut with a feeling almost of shame.

In the kitchen she studied the recipe for vegetable soup in the Fannie Farmer cookbook her aunt had given her for a wedding present. She was determined to cook a good and economical meal. While the onion sizzled in the pan, she set the table, using the pretty calico tablecloth they'd gotten from her friend Enid. She took the candlesticks off the mantel and set them in the center of the table.

Robert came home half an hour later, his hat and coat damp with melted snow. He was whistling. "I talked to Peters," he called, unwinding the scarf from around his neck. "He says Greenland's out, but Peru's still possible."

Nancy felt something burst inside her, like a balloon. He came into the kitchen and put his hand on her shoulder. She shrugged it off, like a horse shaking away a fly. "What's the matter?" he asked in surprise.

"Nothing."

Robert looked unconvinced. Nancy stood very still and stared at the carrots on the cutting board. If he would just go away for five minutes, she'd be able to master herself. She felt like running into the bedroom and closing the door.

She saw for the first time that Robert had planned his life in a way that had never occurred to her. He'd gone against his father to go to college, and he was determined to succeed. The expedition meant more to him than a chance to travel. He longed to impress his boss, become a full curator, to discover a new species and claim it with his name. Falling in love had been an unforeseen departure, unscripted. She wondered with a flash of bitterness if he regretted it.

"What is it?" Robert asked finally, his voice concerned. "What happened?" Nancy turned away, clutching the knife. She'd reduced the carrots to orange matchsticks.

Robert stood watching her, waiting uncertainly, and she felt a burst of fury like a flame. He would consider the baby an inconvenience. She was not going to be tricked into confiding in him. "Nothing," she repeated.

She'd left behind her brother and everything she knew, she thought. An overwhelming homesickness washed over her. If only she could dig her heels into Buckshot's flank and ride away. She remembered trying to explain to Robert why she felt her brother belonged in Boston with them, and how he hadn't been able to see what she meant. Alone in a strange place, she felt unable to make herself understood.

Robert's equilibrium seemed maddening, suddenly. "You have no idea what it's like for me all day!" she cried.

"How do you mean?" Robert sounded startled. "You seem happy . . ."

"Here? Without any friends? Without my family?"

He glanced around the cramped kitchen, looking defeated. "You have me," he pointed out, trying to put an arm around her. Nancy moved away from him, biting her lip to keep from crying. Her arms were folded tight against her chest. She should tell him she was pregnant, she needed to tell him, but nothing had gone as she'd planned. The dinner wasn't finished. The onions sat shriveled in the pan.

A pained silence followed. Nancy could hear the drip drip drip of the kitchen faucet. Robert stepped back. He looked unsure of what to do with his farmer's hands. We can't stop here, she thought desperately, we can't go on like this! She moved unsteadily toward the bedroom. He couldn't wait to go off without her, she thought, and it made her long to hurt him. "When I was a girl," she found herself saying before she shut the door, "my room was the size of this entire place."

Two days later a telegram arrived from Long Island. Robert had already left for work. With a sense of the world collapsing around her, Nancy read that her grandfather was dying. "Not expected last week," Roy had written somewhat confusedly. Nancy began to snatch up clothing and stuff it into her suitcase as if she could save her grandfather if only she got to Salt Hay Road in time. The idea of talking to the switchboard operator and then waiting for someone to track Robert down in the basement of the museum was too much to bear. She didn't even know if she wanted to hear his voice. Writing him a short note, she could not help feeling, even in her anxiety and confusion, a sense of relief that she was going.

It was on the train between Boston and Providence, after a two-hour wait at the station, that she first felt the cramping pain. In the dirty, lurching bathroom of the train she cleaned the blood away as best she could. She didn't know now if she'd been pregnant or only a few weeks late. Back at her seat she hugged her suitcase to her chest and cried, pulling her bobbed hair in front of her face like a curtain.

She did not allow herself to think about her grandfather dying. She held him in her mind, suspended, as if she could somehow make him wait for her. Instead, she thought about her brother, the miracle baby who'd beaten the odds after all their mother's years of struggle. She remembered how, as a toddler, he'd liked to talk to strangers. At the beach, at parks and restaurants, he would approach unknown women in large hats and declare, "My daddy died." Nancy had an image frozen like a photograph in her mind of Clayton in his blue jacket with the white trim, his brow creased in a considering stare. She would smile and give his arm a little tug as the stranger asked Clayton how old he was. At the end of the conversation he'd announce, using his pet name for her, "Nennie loves me." As if he felt the need, before parting, to reassure the unknown woman in the hat that he would fare just fine in the world. As if the death of his father and the love of his sister were the chief facts of his existence.

Ashamed, Nancy thought of the small part of her that had been glad when Clayton decided to stay, the small part that had felt freed. The day the fireworks factory exploded, instead of hurrying home to check for him, she'd walked back so she could flirt with Robert. She had grabbed at her first chance to leave, even when it meant abandoning her brother. Remembering that moment in the kitchen when he'd told her he was staying, she stared down at her hands. There had been no soap in the little bathroom, and the skin under her nails was dirty with her blood. The bare landscape flung itself past the window. In the seat ahead of her, a couple argued interminably about the broken buckle of a shoe.

Clayton rode in the Ford with Roy to Drowned Meadow on the north shore, in a manly and companionable silence. A part of him worried that Nancy's visit would change the new camaraderie he felt with his uncle. Roy might go back to deferring to Nancy on anything that had to do with him. And yet he found himself bouncing a little on the seat of the car. As they turned into the dirt parking lot by the dock, he craned his neck to catch a glimpse of the boat that was bringing her home.

Together they watched Nancy step off the ferry in a neat, dark hat, carrying her little suitcase. The first thing Clayton thought was how much smaller she seemed. He had worked hard to put her from his mind in the months since she had left Long Island. Seeing her, he felt a painful dislocation. It was a cold, windy day in early March and her dress blew around her legs. She looked uncertain, out of place, like an arrival from another country. When she saw them, she hurried over, waving. She was thinner. Clayton felt it when she embraced him. For once he let her squeeze him close without pulling away. At first he was measuring himself against her to see how much he'd grown; in the months they'd been apart he had shot out of most of his clothes and he was now as tall as she was. Then he felt her breathing catch and he realized she was crying. He stood, clumsily shielding her. She seemed to have gotten younger while he'd grown up.

After a moment Nancy patted her face with her handkerchief and stepped back. "Look how big you are," she said. "Those pants are appalling."

At the car Nancy pushed Clayton into the front seat with her, so that he was crammed between her and Roy. She asked about Scudder. Roy assured her that he didn't seem to be in any pain. He was merely fading away, his hold weakening. "Don't expect him to know you," Roy warned. "He's not aware of much. A week ago he said something about a breeches buoy. He hasn't spoken since then." Nancy sniffled into her handkerchief. Her hand found Clayton's, and she held it.

Pressed beside his sister, listening to her voice as she talked with Roy, Clayton felt a spreading ache in his chest. It was like the feeling in his fingers when he washed them in hot water after being out in the snow, the tingling pain of the blood moving back into the veins as the feeling returned, and they began to seem like hands again and not like blocks of ice.

Stepping into the living room of the house on Salt Hay Road, Nancy thought at first that her grandfather had died before she could get home. He lay still under the red-and-black blanket, his face waxen. She turned to Clayton, her eyes filling with tears. "He's sleeping," Clayton said quickly, understanding her look. "He sleeps most of the time."

Nancy sat down and gingerly picked up Scudder's hand. The nails were long and yellowed with tobacco, though it had been over a month since Scudder had smoked his pipe. She remembered that they'd once collected black walnuts from under the trees at the end of the road and how their hands had been stained yellow by the juice after they worked to pry them open. Nancy put her other hand on Clayton's arm, gripping it. "What does he say about me? Tell me the truth."

"He doesn't talk much," Clayton told her, glancing toward the stairs. In fact, Scudder hadn't mentioned Nancy after she left them to move to Boston. Quickly he offered to carry her suitcase up to her old room.

Nancy stayed in the chair beside her grandfather, holding

his cool, limp hand. Looking over the familiar walls, the worn rug on the floor, she thought of her hurry to leave this all behind. Now she tried to take some reassurance from the faded red chair and the braided rugs, the painting of the lighthouse in a storm, as if nothing would change so long as the room remained just as it always had been. She leaned her head against the wall, exhausted. Her lower back still ached. Though she'd scrubbed her hands again on the ferry, she needed a proper bath, a change of clothing. When she closed her eyes, she had a vision of the close, swaying bathroom on the train, the blood on her underthings and thighs.

After a while, she heard the car in the pebbled driveway and then the familiar squeak and bang of the kitchen door. Her aunt, back from work, surprised her by rushing in and pressing her tightly against her bosom. Mavis's polka-dot dress smelled pleasantly of cream sauce. "You poor girl," she exclaimed. "You're skin and bones! Let me get you something to eat."

The unexpected kindness in her voice made Nancy's eyes prickle with tears. "I had eggs with Clay and Roy," she stammered. Her instinct had always been to refuse any solicitude from Mavis.

Her aunt waved her hand dismissively. "Is that all? After your long trip?" Mavis hurried into the kitchen. "I'll fix you a bowl of stew and some pudding."

The girl had obviously had a bad scare, Mavis thought; Roy must not have prepared her, and she had always been the old man's favorite. Her niece looked skinny as a wet cat, with smudges under her eyes like bruises; Mavis doubted the girl had learned to cook so much as an omelet. She heated up a big bowl of stew and buttered three biscuits. When she carried the tray into the living room Nancy's eyes were closed, as if she had drifted off to sleep in the chair. Mavis set the dishes down on the little table beside the bed and Nancy started. "Oh, thank you," she said. The steam rose from the bowl. Nancy put it in her lap, lifted a spoonful to her mouth and blew.

"Eat that all," Mavis told her. "I'll be back with the pudding."

It took Mavis longer to reheat the bread pudding because she decided to add some raisins softened in a bit of warm brandy. She piled the pudding with brown sugar and then filled the bowl with cream. Mavis had to step carefully to keep from spilling it. Just before the open doorway to the living room she glanced up. The small electric light was on beside the bed, the rest of the room in shadow. Mavis stood in the dark hallway and looked in. Her niece was eating, not nibbling the way Mavis remembered, but ravenously, like one of the Captain's half-starved cats. Her face shone with tears. She tore a biscuit in half, weeping, and wiped the bowl with it. The tears dropped off her chin onto the biscuit and the bowl. There was something utterly unguarded about the girl. Mavis backed away very slowly and returned in silence to the kitchen.

Mavis sat at the table with the cooling pudding, giving Nancy time to finish her meal in private. The girl had always seemed so jaunty in her youth and her confidence. Now she reminded Mavis of herself, many years earlier, married and deeply unhappy. She thought of Ramsay's letter, hidden upstairs in the top drawer of her bureau, and the familiar bitterness rose in her like nausea.

She put the bread pudding in the oven to keep it warm. After a quarter of an hour, she took it out and carried it back into the living room. She brought a clean dish towel from the cupboard. Nancy's eyes were closed again. The bowl and plate sat empty even of crumbs. Mavis set the pudding down, and Nancy opened her eyes.

Without thinking, Mavis reached out and brushed a strand of hair from Nancy's cheek. The girl didn't seem to mind. Her face was streaked and puffy from crying. "Here," Mavis said, and her niece thanked her, raising her hands greedily for the bowl.

The cats had not come back. Judith Purlowe thanked Roy every time she saw him. If she caught a glimpse of him across the field, she waved her arms exuberantly. Roy told himself it was best to keep his distance, but he found himself worrying about her. The money Clayton had found in the Captain's drawer would be running out, and she hadn't yet been able to start a garden. Roy wondered how much of a pension she got. Unbidden, an idea for a business scheme flickered in the back of his mind. Remembering the quail chick he'd placed in Grace Perdue's hands, he imagined raising game birds again. Maybe ring-necked pheasant that he could sell to gun clubs and hunting lodges. He thought of the wire pens and dusty incubators stored in the barn and wondered what pheasant eggs cost.

The next morning on the way back from the marsh he stopped at Kelley's old cottage to offer Judith one of the black ducks he'd shot. She beamed when she saw him. "Come in! I'm just making coffee."

"I won't intrude," he started to say, but Judith laughed and took him by the elbow. Roy stepped into the small kitchen. It was dark inside and he stood still for a moment, his eyes adjusting. He could see the orange glow of the flames through the chinks on the top of the cookstove. The room was warm. He slipped his jacket off and hung it over a chair, then felt self-conscious. Removing his jacket seemed too familiar. But he felt stifled by the heat even without it. "I love duck," Judith was saying as she poured the water from the kettle into the battered coffeepot on the counter. "Especially in a stew."

Roy's arms prickled. "Duck is good," he said stupidly. "Good for stew."

Judith turned toward him. "Milk?" She held a chipped white creamer in one hand.

Roy watched her mouth as it formed the word. Her bottom lip was still chapped, as if she bit it without thinking. He sat down. "Yes. I mean no. No milk. Please."

"Sugar's on the table. Would you like a slice of bread?" She moved toward him, holding a steaming cup. He felt as though he could measure out the distance from his body to hers to a fraction of an inch. The smell of the coffee rose toward him.

Roy shook his head, unable to speak. He took the cup from her, bumping against her hand and spilling hot coffee on his fingers. Gulping at it, he scalded his tongue. Judith had moved back to the counter and was pouring a second cup. Roy watched her body shift as she tipped the coffee from the pot. She wore an orange sweater and a dark gray skirt that hung past her calves. Roy found himself staring at her ankles, bisected by the strap of her shoes, and at the back of her stockinged legs.

He saw too late what a mistake it had been to come. "Thanks," he said. He grabbed his jacket. "For the coffee!"

"Wait!" Judith laughed. "You've barely touched it."

"I need to go." He rushed for the door like a sailor in a flooded ship making for the hatchway. But the latch was stuck. He rattled it helplessly.

"It's tricky," Judith told him. "I'll get it." He stepped back and Judith reached for the latch. Roy had a glimpse of the pale skin of her neck as she bent forward, before the door swung open and the daylight shone in his eyes.

"Come back for some stew," Judith said. He waved blindly and hurried across the field. The throbbing pain had spread throughout his body. He stumbled like a man on fire.

Spring and Summer 1938

A bird was singing. Nancy opened her eyes, surprised; in her dream, she'd been in the apartment in Boston. Her suitcase sat on a chair under the window, looking temporary. The bird sang again, and the fluid, warbling notes seemed to pierce her. She got out of bed, and the floor was cold on her bare feet. Out the window the early light shone on the brown field and the muddy pond and on the roof of the Captain's dark cottage. Nancy had never thought much about Captain Kelley; his bow tie and his obvious crush on her much younger aunt had struck her as faintly ridiculous. Now his life in that small house seemed unbearably sad. She imagined him waking up alone every morning and going to bed alone every night, with only his cats for company. She thought of her husband. He'd be asleep right now in the creaky bed in the small room at the back of their apartment, and she wanted to be lying beside him, under the gray wool blanket, listening to his breathing and planning what to make for breakfast while the trolley passed in the street outside, squealing as it made the turn. Tears rose in Nancy's eyes. Her married life seemed like an island on the horizon, and she felt herself carried farther and farther from it. The feeling was more than she could stand. Grabbing her dressing gown, she ran downstairs.

In the living room her grandfather lay in the same condition. Nancy held his hand again, relieved that it was warm. She kissed his forehead. He smelled sweet with decay. She sat and stared at his face; the skin seemed heavy, congealed with age. Unsettled, she tiptoed into the kitchen and called softly for her brother, as if, by speaking too loudly, she might disturb the still form of her grandfather in the living room. There was no answer.

She was making a pot of coffee when she heard Roy on the porch, singing a song she'd never heard: *"I'm something of a sporting man, I'll always take a bet, 'cause I stand a chance of winning, though I haven't done it yet."* The door opened. He seemed startled to see her. "Up in the barn," he said. "Sorting through some old equipment." His face shone with the cold. He pulled off his boots, whistling the same tune under his breath, and Nancy poured him a cup of coffee. Roy sat at the table, sipping it. The clock ticked behind the stove.

Her uncle looked different, Nancy thought, but she couldn't decide how; he seemed more fully awake, perhaps. For the first time she wondered why he'd never married. Of the three siblings, only her mother had been happy in love. At least, she thought, as far as she knew. "Never tempted to get married, Uncle Roy?" she asked lightly.

Roy amazed her by flushing red from his throat to his ears. Nancy had never seen a grown man blush so deeply. She looked quickly down at her plate and began to press crumbs up with the tips of her fingers.

He finished his coffee and stood up. Nancy had not expected him to answer, but he said abruptly, "Not cut out for it, I guess." She glanced back at him and was relieved to see the blush had passed. He made a wry, pained face. "Too risky now, at my age. Like chicken pox. I leave it to youngsters like yourself."

Nancy spent the day in the living room with her grandfather. He didn't seem to know her, though she fed him oatmeal and later some broth. Worried that the spring air was too chilly, she got the fire going again. Bored, she picked up the volume of Kipling. The book fell open on her lap to a poem called "The Bell Buoy," and she remembered hearing her grandfather recite it:

> *I dip and I surge and I swing*
> *In the rip of the racing tide,*
> *By the gates of doom I sing,*
> *On the horns of death I ride.*

Nancy cleared her throat. There was no one else in the house. Clayton was still at school and Mavis was at the lodge. Roy had gone back to the barn. Nancy began to read out loud, hesitantly at first and then falling into the rhythm of the lines:

> *"They christened my brother of old—*
> *And a saintly name he bears—"*

The telephone rang and Nancy jumped. Who would be calling now, in the middle of the day? She felt a tremor in her stomach as she walked toward the hall and lifted the receiver.

"Nancy?" Her husband's voice, scratchy with distance, sucked the air from her lungs. She pictured him in the basement of the museum, a bird turned inside out like a mitten on the table before him. He cleared his throat, and when he spoke again, he sounded guarded. "How's your grandfather?"

She glanced at the still form on the daybed as her heart beat against her ribs. "Not well. About the same."

There was a pause. Did he miss her? she wondered. Was he hoping she was no longer needed? She listened to the clicking echo of the phone line. "How long are you going to stay there?" Robert asked.

"I don't know." Why didn't he tell her what *he* wanted? Why didn't he ask her to come home? "Until he's better, I guess. Or until . . ." She couldn't say it. "Until we know more."

"Well, they're sending me to the Smithsonian." It came out abruptly, harshly. "In Washington, D.C. For a month or two. A new species account . . ."

The floor of the hall seemed to open beneath her feet like a trap door. She felt herself falling and put a hand against the wall.

". . . with the U.S. Biological Survey," he was saying. "Mayr wants a holotype." She couldn't go back to Boston, Nancy thought. He wouldn't be there.

A crackling emptiness hung between them on the line. Then he added, "And you're busy with your family. You weren't happy here. I don't flatter myself you'll miss me."

You're leaving me behind! While my grandfather's dying! A buzzing like cicadas filled her head. She opened her mouth. Her throat felt clogged, as if with sand.

"If you need to get in touch," he said, "you can contact the museum."

Stunned, she put the receiver back in the cradle and stood in the shadowed hall with her hands slack at her side. The house seemed empty, hollowed out like her chest. After a moment she went back to her seat beside the daybed. She studied her grandfather's face. He lay as unmoving as before.

Scudder was sleeping when Mavis came home from Washington Lodge. Nancy left the chair where she'd spent most of the day and sat with her aunt at the kitchen table, waiting for the water to boil for tea. Mavis slipped her feet out of her shoes with a sigh. Her husband had left her in Ohio, Nancy knew, but she had never thought much about Mavis's marriage. She wondered now how Mavis had learned he was leaving her. Had he told her as he was walking out the door? Had he written her a note? Or maybe he had simply not come back.

Years before, when Nancy was a child and used to visit Fire Neck with her mother, a couple named Waldron had lived on Oyster Lane, near Starke's Boatyard. The husband raised chickens, breeds like Orpingtons and Black Minorcas, and a flock of guinea hens. The guinea hens were loud and shrieked at night when it was windy, and the halyards on the boats slapped against the masts. One night the Waldrons had a terrible fight. The wife marched out to the hen yard in her nightgown and rubber boots and shot the whole flock with her husband's shotgun. Nancy remembered the adults talking about it in scandalized, delighted whispers. The noise! The feathers! The gun! Until now, Nancy had never stopped to wonder what the husband had said afterward, back inside the house, and how the wife, in her blood-splattered nightgown, had answered him. Because the Waldrons continued to live there for several more years, before they moved somewhere out East. She hadn't left him, and he hadn't left her. People said they were always fighting about something. They had three children, younger than Nancy, with ash-blond hair, who played cheerfully at the boatyard among the wood shavings.

And there were the Whitneys, on Koos Neck Road, who supposedly hadn't spoken a word to each other in twenty years. They were rumored to eat every meal together at the dining-room table and to communicate through their housemaid.

Nancy hadn't paid much attention to her own parents' marriage. Expansive, good-humored, older than her mother, her father was often away on business trips. Nancy remembered sensing early on that her mother treated him a bit like a child. What had surprised Nancy most, the first time he took her to the big, gleaming office where he worked, was the deference everyone showed him. His secretary made a fuss over Nancy, giving her a pencil to draw with and a lollipop, while an important-looking man in a dark suit tried to interest her father in a sheaf of papers, bending toward him earnestly while her father laughed, not unkindly, and shook his head. At home, around her mother, he always spoke in slightly hushed tones, ceding to her wishes about the fountain she wanted built in the side garden, a trip she didn't care to take. Nancy realized now that he must have been concerned about her miscarriages, maybe even felt guilty. She'd seen him watch her mother brush her hair in front of the mirrored dresser; he had followed the sweeping motion of her hand with fond and anxious eyes.

Why hadn't anyone counseled her to wait? But she was the one who'd wanted to rush, she thought miserably. "Why is it so hard to be married?" she said out loud.

Mavis looked up with a shocked expression, and tea splashed from the flowered pot in her hands. Nancy wished at once she could take the words back. How stupid of her to say something like that, given her aunt's unhappy experience. Flustered, she rose from the table. "I'll check on the woodstove," she called over her shoulder.

Mavis sat holding the teapot. So that was it, she thought. The poor, poor girl. She remembered her own husband, the wet tips of his mustache, his drunken mouth, his predatory nocturnal advances. There had been no one for her to confide in, no one to protect her. She thought of her niece's husband, who'd seemed so mild-mannered. But Mavis had learned that you could never tell, from the surface.

Roy found himself watching Judith Purlowe's house. He noticed when she opened the curtains in the morning and when the lights went out in the kitchen at night. From the house on Salt Hay Road he couldn't see the window of the back bedroom where he imagined she slept. For that he'd have needed to walk down to the pond, something he wouldn't allow himself to do. He had not been inside the cottage since he'd dropped off the duck and scalded his hand with coffee. When he saw that the woodpile along the side of her house was dwindling, he brought over a wheelbarrow full of split logs, first waiting until he knew she'd left for town. The next day she came across the field to thank him, and they stood looking at the barn together while he explained how he had a hundred pheasant eggs in two incubators and wanted to get chicken wire around the old dog runs before they hatched. Pheasants panicked easily, he told her, and he'd need to shade the pens with branches and matting to keep them from getting spooked. He rambled on too long, half afraid that she would ask him over for coffee. But she merely thanked him again for the wood and said she'd come back to see the chicks, before turning toward the cottage alone. Roy watched her ambling walk. She had on the same gray overcoat and long skirt. Her dark hair snaked in the wind, and he saw her hand go up to her face and brush it away. When she reached her door, he turned back to the barn so that she wouldn't see him staring after her.

The next evening, setting the table for dinner, Mavis said, "I see our neighbor has an admirer."

Roy's face grew hot. He turned away, toward the pantry, as if looking for more napkins. Was he so transparent? he wondered. He would have to give Mavis more credit. "I don't know what you're talking about," he muttered, stalling for time.

"Oh, Roy, of course you know Mrs. Purlowe. The Captain's niece. The widow. She has an admirer. Someone from the boatyard. They were chatting over the fence for nearly an hour yesterday."

Roy's chest tightened. He felt a coldness spread along the back of his neck.

"I don't see the appeal, myself," Mavis went on, setting down the salad bowl with a thump, "considering the way she wears her hair. But a man who guts fish all day can't be choosy."

All through the meal Roy found it difficult to concentrate. The food tasted dry and chalky in his mouth. "Pass the *salt*, Roy," Mavis asked him for the third time. After dinner he tried to read the paper without succeeding. Finally, he gave up.

Upstairs, he changed into a pressed blue shirt. Before leaving the house, he ducked into the pantry and scanned the shelves, looking for something that might serve as a pretext for visiting Judith Purlowe. The shelves were dusty, with wide spaces between the jars of preserves that Mavis had put up the summer before. Roy grabbed one at random.

It was dark as he started across the field, a night with no moon, and the stars seemed closer than he'd ever seen them. Behind him the clatter of dishes in the kitchen died away. He hadn't said where he was going, letting Mavis assume he was checking on the incubators before turning in. He felt ridiculous, sneaking across the field under cover of darkness. The smell of daffodils reached him as he neared the cottage. The glass jar was cool and heavy in his hands.

He knocked, and Judith opened the door. She did not seem surprised to see him so late at night. "Come in," she said, and Roy ducked into the cramped, familiar kitchen. The same mess of bags and papers was strewn across the table. The air smelled of strong coffee and faintly, still, of cats. He held out the jar.

Judith reached to accept it, and Roy felt the same prickling awareness of her hand almost touching his. " 'Chokecherry jelly,' " she read. "Thank you. I've never tried that." Roy remembered the flavor of the jam suddenly and why there was still so much of it. Mavis had scorched it slightly and it had a burned aftertaste that lingered in the mouth.

"I hope you like it," he said. "A bit of an acquired taste."

"Shall I make some toast to put it on?"

Roy nodded, determined not to run this time. Judith moved to the counter and began to slice a loaf of bread. He took off his jacket and placed it deliberately on the back of his chair.

"Are you settling in here?" His voice was scratchy. He cleared his throat. "Making friends?"

"Oh sure," Judith said. "Now that the cats are gone." She turned and smiled her wide, generous smile, and Roy's heart rolled over in his chest, a dog doing tricks.

They ate the jelly on toast, sitting at the kitchen table. Roy finished two slices very quickly, hardly tasting them. He stopped himself reaching for a third and looked instead at Judith, buttering a slice of bread from a butter dish covered in crumbs. Her fine-boned, narrow face was etched with thin lines. He realized he knew nothing about where she'd come from or what her life had been like before she arrived at the Captain's cottage in the dead of winter. He wondered most about her husband.

"You must miss the people you knew," he ventured.

She nodded. Roy's heart sank. He thought of Grace Perdue and his own insane grief.

"And your husband." It was a question. Roy felt it pulled out of him. He was hardly sure, for a moment, where the words had come from.

Judith tilted her head. "Yes. I was living at his sister's when I got the letter about this place. I don't miss that." She looked up and gave a small smile.

"What did he do?" Roy persisted. "I mean, what line of work?"

Judith sat back in her chair and sighed. "He wanted to be a sailor. But he ended up working in the mines, like his brothers. He wasn't lucky, that's how he saw it. He always drew the short straw." She looked down at her hands. "Six of them were trapped the day the tunnel caved in. Four made it out."

She glanced up, and her eyes caught his and held them, calmly but without smiling. Roy felt the room fold around them like a tent.

"I'm sorry," he said. He leaned forward as he spoke, and it was unclear whether he meant he was sorry about the loss of her husband or the fact that he was kissing her in spite of it.

In the house on Salt Hay Road Nancy sat by Scudder's bed in the living room, stoking the fire and reading aloud from his volume of Kipling. She wanted him to eat another bite of rice pudding, but he kept his mouth closed when she prodded him gently with the spoon. Nancy thought his face looked firmer than when she'd arrived. Perhaps, she cautioned herself, she'd only grown used to his changed appearance.

Packing for Long Island in a hurry, Nancy hadn't brought much besides her black wool dress and black shoes. No one at that point had expected Scudder to last more than a few days. That had been nearly six weeks ago, and now the snow had melted and water dripped from the eaves. For two days she hadn't been outside; it had been too wet and muddy. Nancy thought of her rubber boots and, more wistfully, of her riding clothes, unused in the closet of the apartment in Boston since the cost of hiring a horse had turned out to be so great. Now there was no one to ask to mail them. Robert had sent a brief note to let her know he'd arrived in D.C. Reading it in her up-stairs room, she thought of the letters he'd sent before they were married. She remembered the thrill she'd felt the first time she saw her name scrawled in his handwriting, how she'd hung around the post office, the drafts she'd gone through, per-fecting her replies. And this was what it had all been leading up to, she thought miserably. In her mind she studied their courtship, looking for the flaw.

As a child, she'd loved to watch her father light the fire in the big living-room fireplace. There would be a layer of crum-pled newspaper, one of kindling, and then the logs balanced on top. Her father always rearranged them once or twice, as if to align them in precisely the right configuration. Then he knelt down with the box of matches in his hand. It looked like a magic trick: her father held the match and flicked his wrist and the flame burst out, like a scarf from a magician's throat. One afternoon when she was supposed to be napping, she slipped out of bed and found the matches she'd seen her nanny hide in the bathroom. She crumpled a few pages of her drawing paper and set them in the middle of the rug. Two small chairs taken from her dollhouse approximated the kindling. Kneeling, she dragged the red head of the match across the scratchy side of the box. Nothing happened. She tried again, this time mimicking the flourish of her father's wrist. A tiny orange flame appeared, a genie conjured out of a lamp. Delighted, she watched the flame creep down the matchstick until it singed her fingers and she had to drop it. The next match she held close to the paper. She watched, immensely proud of herself, as the flame climbed the edge of one crumpled sheet and jumped to the next. The doll's chair blazed and blackened. Then the rug began to smolder. The smoke made her cough. A moment later the bed skirt blazed. Nancy backed toward the door. As her pillow began to burn, she left the room, careful to close the door behind her. In the hallway she stood still for a moment, wondering what to do next. She was playing on the swing set when the fire trucks arrived.

What struck her now was neither her irresponsibility nor her fascination with the sight of her bed in flames, but her certainty that, by shutting the door, she had solved her part of the problem.

Nancy remembered getting off the ferry at Drowned Meadow and catching sight of Clayton in his outgrown pants and Roy, smiling as they strode toward her, calling her name. Returning to Fire Neck had been an escape, a way to turn her back on the mess she'd left in Boston. As a child she had set the fire in her room deliberately before walking out and closing the door. Now her marriage felt like a burning house, but she couldn't understand how it had happened.

She felt angry with herself, restless. The kitchen was quiet; Mavis had finished putting away the dishes and gone upstairs to bed. Clayton would be asleep already, no doubt dreaming about beetles or the salt marsh. The clock ticked in the hall. The portable typewriter she'd brought downstairs sat on the little side table. Nancy aligned a fresh piece of paper along the back edge and cranked it into place. She glanced at her grandfather, motionless under the wool blanket; the sound had not disturbed him. She sat up straight and pushed back her shoulders. *Dear Sirs*, she typed briskly, *We are happy to inform you that in the matter of . . . Robert, in my dreams you stare out the window, missing me, and you eat your lunch sad that I am gone . . .*

She backed the carriage up and x'd out the words one by one.

The last day she'd spent in Boston the city itself had seemed hostile because of their stupid quarrel. There were people everywhere she turned and not one familiar face. The strangers looked through her, as if she were made of vapor, and she'd felt again, acutely, the loss of nerve she'd experienced at the museum party in October, the sense of not belonging. It was dark by the time Robert came home from work. She sat at the window, looking out at the streetlights and the dark figures hurrying past. When she recognized him, the way he held his face up to the night air, his stride, she ducked into the kitchen. She didn't want him to know she had been waiting.

She hammered on the keys again. *I'm sorry I told you I wasn't happy. I don't care about the apartment at all. I love you and I know we can make a better go of it. I thought we were going to have a baby but now we aren't and Robert I wish it hadn't all gone wrong . . .* Nancy pulled the paper from the typewriter and crumpled it into a ball smaller than her fist. She felt a perverse satisfaction in the waste of paper.

She threaded a fresh sheet into the typewriter. *Dear Robert, Thank you for your letter. I hope you can appreciate how needed I am here. My grandfather is about the same.*

But Scudder was not the same. She hadn't said this to anyone, in case she was mistaken. He had been eating more and his grip had grown stronger. Several times she thought she felt him squeeze her hand. That afternoon his eyes had opened and rested on her. And then they had widened, ever so slightly. Nancy was sure that he'd known who she was.

Nancy folded the letter and put it in an envelope. It was nearly midnight. She leaned over and gripped her grandfather's knobby shoulder. "Good night," she whispered into his still face. "I'm going upstairs, but don't worry. I'm here."

Roy woke in the dark. For a moment he did not know where he was. A woman's warm, bare hip was pressed against his thigh. It felt so strange he could hardly credit it.

Lying in Judith's bed, he thought of a night in his wild youth when he had gotten drunk with his friend Wes Hart and Wes's brother Garrett. The three of them had made twenty dollars each unloading boxes down by Indian Landing under cover of darkness. No one said anything about the contents, but they all knew there was booze inside. It must have been two in the morning by the time they were through, and the man in charge—they never learned his name—slipped them each a bottle of bad whiskey. They'd gone to a house Garrett knew about over in Moriches. Roy didn't remember the girl he'd gone upstairs with, only that the laces of his boot had snarled and he'd sawed through them with a pocketknife to the sound of her high-pitched laughter. He woke up wet and cold in the bottom of a rowboat, his temples throbbing. A strange, persistent barking rang in his brain. Overhead, the dawn sky loomed fresh and pink. He reached for the oarlocks and gingerly pulled himself up till he could peer over the gunwale. White ducks surrounded him as far as he could see; thousands upon thousands of ducks, all of them quacking from their orange bills. He was adrift in a rowboat at Epher Brown's duck farm, on the east side of the river.

Judith Purlowe shifted in her sleep, and Roy felt her hair brush against his shoulder. In the barn, the pheasant chicks would be pressed together under the low brooding lights. He remembered the little bolt he'd convinced himself had gone missing from the engine of his being, that day in the middle of the Great South Bay. It seemed to him now that the problem might just as easily be something different. A little dirt in the carburetor, he thought to himself, and grinned in the dark, like an idiot.

Clayton pulled open the thick curtains, and the yellow morning light streamed into the aviary at Washington Lodge. The birds rustled and squawked in their cages. He was giving the last piece of sliced apple to the gray parrot when the gardener stopped by outside, leaning on the open window. Stooped and wizened, his hands seamed with dirt, he cared for the grounds with a jealous tenderness and waged constant war on crabgrass, beetles, and the moles he killed in steel traps and whose perforated bodies Clayton sometimes found on the compost heap, their gray fur like ripped velvet. The gardener usually kept to the grounds, but today Mr. Washington was away on business and he had felt like chatting. He and his cousin had gone up the Barto River in a rowboat and found a mass of watercress, he told Clayton. "I could grow it in the pond here, but the ducks would foul it." Mr. Washington kept a flock of fulvous tree ducks that had the run of the grounds and roosted at night in the orchard.

Walking home with the sun on his face, Clayton wondered if Roy would take him upriver for watercress. His uncle was different lately, and it seemed to Clayton in his innermost heart that he himself might somehow have effected the change. Roy had confided in him. He noticed him more. When he'd started up the pheasant business, before he even ordered the eggs, he'd asked for Clayton's help. Maybe Roy would take him upriver. He started to run, hoping his uncle was home.

Clayton burst into the kitchen of the house on Salt Hay Road, his chest heaving. Roy sat at the table with the newspaper. "There's watercress upriver!" Clayton cried. Mavis looked up from the sink in surprise, and Roy put down his paper. Embarrassed, Clayton felt his neck flush.

Then Roy said, "Well, don't just sit there, woman!" Winking at Clayton, he stood and drained his coffee with a show of haste. "Organize the provisions." He put his cup in the sink. "There's watercress to hunt."

Roy headed for the boatyard to ask Sam Burnett if they could borrow a boat. Mavis, grumbling, began to pack a picnic lunch. "What have you done to your uncle?" she asked Clayton. "You know he's not a man for the water." Clayton shrugged, grinning, and ran out to the shed for buckets and pails. It wasn't his imagination, he thought; even his aunt had noticed that Roy had changed. Clayton moved quickly, knocking over a can of nails in his haste.

He was in the kitchen helping Mavis with the hamper when Nancy came downstairs looking sleepy. "We're hunting watercress. In the boat," Clayton told her. "Hurry up."

Roy whistled from across the field and waved for them to join him.

"Shouldn't someone stay here?" Nancy nodded toward the living room.

Clayton shook his head. He grabbed at her hand and pulled her, expansive in his happiness. "He's sleeping. Come on. We need you."

They made their way through the boatyard to the dock where Sam's boat was tied, and Clayton jumped in and held out his hand to help his sister. A group of ducks swam over and eyed them meaningfully, hoping for bread. "Shoo," said Mavis, to no effect. She waved her hands at them. The ducks, thinking she was throwing something, swam closer, and Nancy caught Clayton's eye and grinned.

Roy and Clayton took turns rowing while Nancy sat in the bow and shaded her eyes against the sunlight. In the stern, Mavis clutched the hamper that held their lunch. The single glossy feather in her black hat jerked in the air above her head to the motion of the oars. She faced straight ahead; like her brother, she disliked boats.

They passed Big Fish Creek, Runny Nose Creek, an osprey nest high in a dead tree. Roy pulled on the oars, leaning forward, and Clayton watched the water swirl around them, making a pattern on the surface of the river.

The tide was high, and when they came to the narrow railroad bridge, it looked at first to Clayton as if they wouldn't fit under it. "Heads down," Roy called. They bent low in the boat as Roy guided them underneath the trestles. Between the wooden beams Clayton saw the mud nests of barn swallows. As the rowboat floated by, stirring the air, the hatchlings rose in their nests and flung open their yellow beaks like clusters of blooming flowers.

Clayton spotted the watercress past the bridge on the east side, in a stretch of shallow water near the bank. They collected it by hand, filling buckets and wicker baskets with dripping green leaves and stems. Roy and Clayton chewed it while they worked. Mavis stayed in the boat, unwilling to take off her shoes. In less than twenty minutes they had enough for both their house and Washington Lodge, as well as a basket for Sam Burnett and one for Judith Purlowe.

"That's enough," said Mavis. "Unless you want watercress soup for a month."

On the way back downriver they stopped at Indian Landing for lunch. Clayton jumped off first, still barefoot, and pulled the rowboat up onto the sand. Roy helped Mavis off, and she spread the picnic blanket on a grassy spot under the cherry tree, with a view of the river.

Mavis unpacked the hamper while Nancy poured lemonade. It felt to Clayton as though his sister had never really left them, her marriage a brief folly for which they could now forgive her. They ate cold venison with yellow tomato preserves and Spanish pickles, spring salad, cornbread, and molasses cookies. The sun fell through the trees in dappled shades of green. Clayton finished the last of the cookies and sat back, watching a great blue heron on the opposite bank unfold its wings and launch itself into the air. Roy got up and disappeared into the woods. Mavis began to sing, almost under her breath, and Clayton was surprised to hear Nancy join in. It was a song he remembered their mother singing, "My Darling Clementine."

Roy came back and sat beside the hamper on the flattened grass. He put his fist to his mouth and coughed into it, loudly clearing his throat. Mavis and Nancy had finished the song and were packing up the lunch things. Roy coughed again, and Clayton looked up at him, his daydreams pierced by a sudden concern.

"Can you breathe?" asked Mavis sharply. Roy shook his head, red in the face. He gave another long hacking cough, covering his mouth, and the next moment a small brown bird shot out of his hand. Clayton let out a strangled yelp. Mavis dropped the jar of pickles. They stared in astonishment as the bird flew into the bushes.

"There," Roy said. "I *thought* I had something caught in my throat." He collapsed forward onto his elbows, shaking with laughter. A joke, Clayton realized, more amazed by this revelation than by the sight of the bird issuing from Roy's mouth. His uncle had played a joke on them!

"What in the world . . ." said Nancy. Mavis stared at her brother, then at the bushes where the bird had flown, then back at Roy. Tears streamed down his cheeks.

"Marsh wren," Roy said, wiping his eyes. "I found a nest." His cheeks and ears were red from laughing. He doubled over again. "If you could see your faces!"

In the still, hot afternoon, trapped in the living room, Scudder was thinking about clams: the salty flavor of the raw flesh in his mouth, like eating gobbets of the sea itself. Back when his children were young, he'd treaded for clams on the bay on summer afternoons. Waist-deep in water, he felt along the bottom of the bay with his bare feet for the smooth shapes of cherrystones and little necks while his wife fixed lunch and the children played on the deck of the catboat and splashed along the side. Laughing, he held up a rock he'd mistaken for a clam and showed it to Roy, who frowned and turned it over in his little hand.

In his daybed by the cold woodstove, fear started with a ripple, like a cat's-paw on the surface of a bay: What if he never left this bed in the downstairs parlor? He could feel himself settling, a ship on a sandbar, another hulk destined for the breaker's yard. He thought of the motto they'd joked about in the

Life Saver's station house: *You have to go out, but you don't have to come back*. Setting his jaw, he pushed himself out into the fear like a lifeboat into the running surf.

The family ate a late crab dinner in the kitchen that night. The windows were open. Clayton could hear the katydids, the moths bumbling against the screen. Out in the field the fireflies were beginning to appear. The family ate without speaking, cracking the shells between their teeth and picking out the flesh. It was a messy meal, and the table was spread with newspaper. Near Clayton's plate a headline read NOTES FOR A GEOGRAPHY OF MORALS, and he wondered at the strangeness of the phrase. The table was quiet except for the snapping of crab claws and the clattering of discarded shells into the bucket on the floor. When Clayton heard a muffled bumping from the living room, he thought at first that it was one of Roy's dogs trying to get through the side door. He looked up from his plate. There stood his grandfather, gripping the frame of the doorway with his bony hands. The old man braced himself against the wall. His white hair was stiff and uneven, his face tight with effort. His eyes blinked in the soft light of the kitchen. Clayton dropped the crab he had been holding, and it banged against his plate. The others looked up. There was a moment of complete silence before Nancy cried out and Mavis staggered from her seat, upsetting the bucket of discarded crab shells. Roy bent to help her pick them up. Nancy threw her arms around Scudder just as his knees gave out. In that moment of chaos a look passed between Clayton and the old man. He caught the triumph in Scudder's ancient eyes.

That night as he lay in his bed Clayton thought to himself that he had watched his grandfather rise from the dead.

———

Nancy wrote to Robert first thing the next morning. The typewriter seemed too formal, so she used a pen and told him the good news in sloppy haste. Buoyant with happiness, she realized how much her grandfather's coldness about her marriage had weighed on her. Now he was better. She'd stayed in Fire Neck far longer than she'd meant to, but it had been worth it. And maybe Robert had missed her, she thought; maybe the time apart had been good for both of them and everything would seem easy once they saw each other again. She remembered the dark bedroom of their apartment in Boston, and the time she'd shaken Robert awake, convinced she could hear a rooster crowing in the street; he'd taken her in his arms and explained in a sleep-slurred whisper that Boston was plagued by roosters, it was a terrible epidemic, and no one could stop it because the mayor himself was a famous chicken fancier. He began to shake, and she realized he was laughing and hit him with her pillow. They had not gone back to sleep.

Robert's brief reply arrived two days later. Home from the Smithsonian, he offered to come down to Long Island from Boston and escort her back. He wrote that he was happy to hear of her grandfather's *remarkable recovery*. What did he mean by putting it that way? Nancy thought. Flat on the page, the uninflected phrase conjured up a vision of Robert's sardonic face, one eyebrow slightly raised. It seemed to mock not only her former anxiety but also her present relief. She wondered suddenly if he had doubted Scudder's decline in the first place. Did her husband actually suspect her of fabricating it?

From the kitchen came the sound of Roy and Scudder talking. Nancy left the porch, the screen door slapping behind her, and strode blindly across the yard. As a girl she'd once walked into a glass door at a birthday party. Distracted by the balloons on the lawn, she'd turned toward the porch with her paper cup of lemonade and smacked right into it. The lemonade spilled down the front of her red party dress and soaked her white socks. Worse than the pain was the shock of finding glass where she'd expected air. Someone's sympathetic mother patted her with a napkin as the other children stared. Nancy, dazed, felt obscurely wronged. The helpful mother tried to press a cold towel to the bump on her forehead, but Nancy pushed away, humiliated by her mistake and by the lemonade on her socks and the way it looked as if she'd wet herself. In her distress everything around her seemed unjust, from the door to the woman with the cold towel, even the clown out the window on the lawn surrounded by pink and white balloons.

Still holding Robert's letter, she passed the woodpile and skirted the edge of the pond. She was too shocked even to cry. All her shame about her own behavior evaporated in a blaze of indignation. When she most needed his sympathy, her husband had not even believed her. She couldn't imagine telling him now how she'd thought she was pregnant, how she had suffered on the train. He might think she'd made that up as well.

Her feet were wet. Looking around, she realized she'd walked out onto the marsh, following one of the trails made by the deer. She supposed her brother would be familiar with the place, but she herself had never come this way. Around her on all sides stretched the thick marsh grass. It grew lush and coarse, springy under her feet, pushed by the tide and the wind into clumps like cowlicks. Standing on it, Nancy imagined the hide of an enormous animal that had been licking its vivid fur. The warm breeze carried the smell of brine. In the distance the sun flashed on the river. Still and green, the marsh seemed, to Nancy, as far from the apartment in Boston as she could get.

Maybe she wouldn't go back at all, she thought angrily. Maybe she'd stay here on Salt Hay Road.

Just like Mavis, a small voice whispered. At that, Nancy rallied. Of course she had to return. She wouldn't hide any longer. She would go back to Boston and make the best of it. She thought, melodramatically, of soldiers returning to the front after their leave was over. But she would not allow her husband to treat her like a package that needed to be delivered; she could make her own travel arrangements.

Nancy walked back across the marsh and along the pond to the house. Upstairs she typed a quick, stiff note, telling Robert she would return by herself on the following Tuesday. She chose the date at random, wanting the certainty of something specific. *Your assistance*, she wrote, banging on the keys, *is not required.*

She might as well go riding, she reasoned, having given herself so little time left on Salt Hay Road. Going into the barn for Buckshot's saddle, she found Clayton wrestling a long roll of wire down the stairs from the hayloft. He was helping Roy mend a hole in the dog kennel. Looking up, he grinned at her, straw in his hair. Nancy, anxious to get it over with, said quickly, "I'm going back to Boston." She held up the letter she'd just written to her husband. "On Tuesday."

Clayton rested the wire on the cement floor of the barn. His gaze seemed to flatten.

"I can't stay here forever!" Nancy snapped. "Grandfather's better now." She hadn't expected any sympathy from her brother, and yet she wished he would say something. "And I'm married, Clay. Everyone seems to forget that."

Clayton didn't answer. He picked the wire back up and began to drag it toward the corner of the barn, as if she had already gone.

The next day, Clayton decided to show Nancy one of his best-kept secrets, something they didn't have inside a museum. When she asked where they were going, he told her it was a surprise. They walked together across the field with the sun on their faces. The warm air smelled of dry grass and, as they neared the boatyard, hot tar. At the boat shed, Clayton asked Sam for the loan of a rowboat, "to go to Knowles Point." Sam motioned with his chin toward a fish carcass discarded beneath the cleaning table, and Clayton seized it by the tail, disturbing a cloud of flies. Nancy made a face. "What do you want that for?" She would see, he told her, clutching the fish, an ace up his sleeve.

The fish carcass lay in the dirty water on the bottom of the rowboat, its tail moving slightly with the motion of the oars. On the other side of Knowles Point the remains of a sunken boat stuck above the water. Clayton brought the rowboat up alongside the gunwale. It was one of his and Perry's favorite places, and today the tide was just right. The half-submerged boat was slick with green-black algae. It listed forward, the stern protruding. In the dark water of the cockpit, beneath the overhang of the remaining deck, half a dozen snapping turtles craned their thick necks toward them. "There!" Clayton exclaimed. A snapping turtle could bite a broomstick handle clear through, even take a man's hand off at the wrist. "Aren't they beauties?" Black and gleaming, the turtles sat nearly motionless in the bilge of the ruined boat. "Watch this." Clayton picked the fish carcass up from the bottom of the rowboat by the tail and flung it over the side of the wreck. It fell among the snapping turtles, and there was a thrashing of thick limbs as they churned around it. The turtles lashed and snapped, and a shiver ran up Clayton's arms. Nancy stared. In a moment every shred of fish had disappeared. Clayton sat back, his hands on the oars, and glanced at his sister.

She stared back at him, perplexed. The look on her face was one of confusion, touched with distaste. It was clear that the turtles did not interest her. Clayton lifted the oars. In silence he rowed his sister back across the river.

Over the next few days Nancy tried to broach the subject of her departure with Scudder. He grew stronger by the day and would sit on the porch overlooking the marsh for hours, as long as Nancy sat with him. One warm day she helped him outside to a chair she'd set in a shady patch of the lawn and trimmed his still thick white hair. "I felt myself going under," he told her gruffly. "Like a derelict ship. But I knew you'd come home. I couldn't do it."

She laughed nervously. "I think it was all the Kipling."

Now they sat on the porch drinking lemonade. The thick, humid air smelled sweetly of overgrown privet. Neither of them had made any mention of her marriage or the fact that she was expected back in Boston. He'd taught her to play cribbage, and as she won yet again, it dawned on her that he'd been throwing the games in her favor.

"I'd better get back to my husband soon," she told him, trying to make it into a little joke. "Before he forgets all about me!"

"Your turn to shuffle," Scudder said.

Nancy tried again. "I'll write to you from Boston. Will you promise to write back, to tell me how you're doing?"

Scudder picked up his cards and fanned them out. "You don't know how much your brother missed you." He stared at his hand as if disappointed with it. "Poor motherless kid."

On Tuesday the ferry to Drowned Meadow came and went without Nancy. In the house on Salt Hay Road, no one asked about her plans. Mavis set her place at the table as usual, and afterward she and Clayton washed the dishes. Nancy wrote to Robert, explaining that she'd been delayed. He would have to wait a little longer, she told herself. She imagined him coming home from the museum to an empty apartment, whistling as he took off his hat in the hall. He'd fry himself an egg for dinner and eat it standing at the counter, and then he'd sit by the window, because he liked the evening air, and read the *Journal of Field Ornithology*, not thinking about her at all.

Three weeks later a telegram arrived for Nancy. She read it in the kitchen, where Clayton was eating a bowl of Grape-Nuts with cream. "Robert's coming down tomorrow," she said, half to herself. Clayton stopped chewing. He sat still, braced for the inevitable. "Why don't you come back to Boston with me?" Nancy asked brightly, as if the idea had just occurred to her. "You could come for a visit, just a few weeks. You wouldn't be missing any school." She sat down next to Clayton and put her arm around his shoulder. "I'll take you to the park and we can ride the swan boats."

Clayton shook his head. "I have to help with the pheasants. And I'm working for Mr. Greaves and Mr. Washington."

Nancy sighed. She tilted her head until it was just brushing his. "I'll miss you."

Clayton, relieved that she was not going to insist, patted her stiffly on the hand. But a familiar tightness gripped his lungs. He felt the way he had on his first day of school at Fire Neck Elementary, standing by the doorway of the strange classroom as Nancy spoke with a formidable-looking teacher in a black suit that reminded him of the men at their mother's funeral. He'd known she had her own school to go to, and that she would be late herself, but all the time she talked, he kept his eyes fastened on her, ignoring the whispers of the unknown children at their desks, half believing he could will her not to leave him.

It did not take Nancy long to pack. She carried her small suitcase down the stairs and set it on the floor in the living room, where it was visible from Scudder's bed. His eyes lingered on it, but neither of them said anything. After dinner they played cribbage and ate the orange charlotte that Mavis made in honor of Nancy's departure.

That night, asleep in her single bed, Nancy dreamed of carrying her brother in her arms. In the dream he was very small again, a baby as light as a laundry basket.

Clayton was on the roof, smoking a cattail cigar and looking through the Captain's deck of pornographic playing cards, when his brother-in-law arrived. Mavis had left for the lodge already, after saying a tearful goodbye and packing a large picnic lunch for Nancy and Robert to share on the ferry. Clayton ducked his head and shoved the deck of cards into his pocket. In a minute he would come down to say goodbye to Nancy. In the meantime, he didn't want to reveal his hiding place. He heard Robert knock on the side door, the one that led into the kitchen, and then call Nancy's name. No one answered. From where Clayton sat on the roof, he could just see the top of Robert's head. He remembered hearing that soldiers in besieged castles had dumped boiling oil on the enemy from above.

"Hello?" he heard Robert call again. "Nancy?" The silence stretched on. Clayton shifted his elbow. He wondered what was taking his sister so long. There was another, louder knock. "Nancy?" he heard Robert say. "Anyone home?" After a moment Clayton heard the squeak of the kitchen door opening. "Nancy?" came Robert's voice again, sounding hollow. The door slammed shut. Moving quickly, Clayton slipped down the wisteria trellis and into the yard.

Just as he straightened up, Robert came back out of the house. "Clayton!" he cried, his face brightening. "I was getting worried. It's like a ghost town here." He looked smaller than Clayton remembered him, his face young and tired. Since he'd seen him last, at the wedding, Robert had slowly changed in Clayton's mind into a comic-book villain, with heavy brows and a thick neck. Confronted with the real person, Clayton found himself disarmed. Robert had brought him a present. "It's in here somewhere," he said, fumbling in his bag and pulling out a dented cardboard box. Inside was a yellow model airplane with red silk wings. Clayton stared at it in surprise. He had never been particularly interested in model planes, but this one was undeniably beautiful. Framed in wire, it was twice the length of his palm and looked like it could really fly. He pulled it through the air above his head, testing the wings.

"How's your grandfather?" Robert asked Clayton. "I hear he's better?"

"*Now* he is," Clayton said. "You should have seen him a few weeks ago." He felt grown-up, having witnessed his grandfather's brush with death firsthand. Lowering his voice slightly,

Clayton used an expression he'd recently learned. "He almost *bought the farm*." He was gratified to see Robert's eyes widen.

"I didn't realize it was that serious," Robert said, after a moment. He seemed suddenly impatient. "Where's your sister?"

"Inside."

"I didn't see her."

"I'll get her." Clayton ducked into the house, still holding the plane. The kitchen was empty. In the living room Scudder lay on the daybed, sleeping or pretending to sleep. Nancy's suitcase stood at the foot of the stairs. Clayton called for her. There was no answer. Upstairs, her room was empty, the sheets stripped from the bed. Clayton peered into the other rooms, one by one. They were all empty. He felt a prickling on his arms; supposing she had vanished, he thought.

Standing in his own room, Clayton heard a faint movement above him, like the darting of a squirrel. Very quietly, his heart pounding, he climbed the narrow stairs to the attic. Outside the door he stood and listened. There was a rustling sound and a tap, as of a finger resting against a windowpane. Clayton reached forward to open the door. The lock caught, holding it closed. In a moment there was a thud and the door thumped in its frame and he realized that Nancy had thrown herself against it. They stood on either side of the door. Clayton could hear his sister's breathing. "Robert's here," he said. He felt frightened without understanding why. It seemed important to act as if everything was normal.

There was a long pause. "I'll be down in just a minute," Nancy said at last. Clayton felt his lungs empty with relief. "Go tell him that."

Coming downstairs, Clayton could see his brother-in-law in the kitchen, fiddling with the brim of his hat. He looked up at the sound of Clayton's footsteps, his face creased. Clayton hardened his heart. As far as he was concerned, it was Robert's fault that Nancy had left them and moved to Boston. They had been happy until Robert came along, uninvited, and broke the family up. "She's in the attic," he said.

Robert's expression tightened. "What's she doing there?"

Clayton shrugged his shoulders. "She wouldn't tell me." This was not a lie, exactly.

Robert stepped toward the stairs. "Don't go up," Clayton told him quickly. "She's locked herself in. She said she'd come down when she was ready."

Robert hesitated. He looked toward the stairs and moved from one foot to the other. Clayton had the momentary fear that the man might cry, though he felt sure this was ridiculous.

"If you bother her," Clayton added, "it'll just make things worse."

It was lunchtime, and Clayton felt hungry. He wasn't used to playing host. "There's bread in here," he said, "if you want some." Robert stopped toying with his hat and put it on the counter. He stood in the doorway leading into the living room while Clayton got out a plate of cold venison and the pot of mustard and made them each a sandwich. They ate in silence. Every few minutes Robert glanced at his watch.

After they'd eaten, Robert paced around the kitchen, looking toward the stairs. Clayton cleared up the food. He was confused by his sister's behavior. But if she'd locked herself in, it stood to reason that she didn't actually want to leave.

Robert stopped his pacing and turned toward the stairs, where Nancy's suitcase sat like something in a lost and found.

"I'll go see if she needs any help," Clayton offered.

"Tell her . . . tell her I'm sorry," Robert said. "I might have offended her. I didn't mean to. I just want to see her, to explain."

Clayton ran up to the attic. He could hear rustling on the other side of the door. "I'll be there in just a moment," his sister called. Her voice sounded thick, as if she had a cold.

"Take your time," Clayton told her. There was no answer. He turned back toward the stairs, wondering how to get his brother-in-law out of the house before she came down.

In the attic, Nancy listened for the sound of footsteps. She needed a moment of privacy with Robert before she had to brave her grandfather and Clayton. She wanted to be sure of where things stood between them. If Robert would just come up the stairs, she thought, and say her name, she'd open the door and he'd realize how real her suffering had been. She imagined his arms wrapping around her, the things she would then be able to say.

The attic smelled of pears and old, dried paint and the wax Mavis used for canning. Motes of dust hung in the air. Nancy turned her head from the door and glanced out the high, small window. Far below her, she was surprised to see two figures walking away across the field. She would recognize Robert's stride anywhere, the way he tipped his head and swung his arms. The sight of him made her rush forward. She leaned against the dusty glass. Where were they going? Watching Robert turn the corner of the woodpile and disappear, Nancy felt a terrible panic. She wanted to fling herself after them.

But what would she say when she caught up to him? She thought again of the letter he'd written and the reference he'd made to Scudder's *remarkable recovery*. It *had* been remarkable, almost miraculous, she thought. Maybe Robert had meant what he wrote, maybe she'd been wrong to take offense. That was what came of being sarcastic too often, she thought in frustration. How could it be her fault if she couldn't tell what he meant? Would she know when she saw him? Or would they just stand there, stiff and unfriendly, eyeing each other like roosters in the spring? A claustrophobic feeling seized her. It could go wrong in so many ways, she thought in despair.

She would have to go down to the kitchen and wait, she decided. She didn't know which trail they might have taken. They'd come back from the marsh and find her on the porch with her suitcase beside her. But why had Robert left the house at all? Why hadn't he just come upstairs? She remembered his brother suddenly, and the stiff way he'd wished them happiness at their wedding reception, making her feel that he thought them ill suited for each other. Had he sensed an incompatibility she hadn't seen? Maybe she and Robert had simply been mistaken about each other, the way the Carolina parakeet he'd hoped to find at Washington Lodge turned out to be another bird entirely.

A memory came back to her of walking between her father and her grandfather. They must have been in Southease, she thought, on their way to the dock to watch a sailboat race. She'd have been about seven, in a new white dress, with ribbons in her hair, and people had smiled at them on the street and remarked on how pretty she looked. What she remembered most was her awareness of the two men beside her. She was proud to be allowed out with them, not left in the care of her nanny. Flanked by their masculine presence, she'd felt the world spread out like a picnic before her.

Clayton and Robert walked in silence. It was hot and bright. They made their way through the far field and along the edge of the pond. Outside the Captain's squat cottage Judith Purlowe was hanging laundry on the line. She stopped to wave at them, smiling with her mouth full of clothespins. From the distance it looked as if she were about to light three cigars at the same time.

Clayton led Robert through the high-tide bush and cattails along a trail he and Perry had made. The falling tide had left the ground wet. Clayton considered his brother-in-law's shoes, which were shiny leather and entirely unsuitable for the marsh. They made a gratifying squelching noise. "We might see a diamondback terrapin," Clayton explained, deviously thinking of a reason to be taking this muddy path. He stopped to point out a red-winged blackbird on a reed. But Robert merely nodded, his eyes unfocused. Clayton glanced down at the inappropriate shoes. They must be getting wet inside. Unfortunately, Robert didn't seem to notice. Clayton led him out onto the yellow-green salt hay. It was wetter here, and his own canvas shoes were soon soaked through.

Down at the bank of the river stood a pole dock where Scudder had once kept his sailboat. Approaching it through the low screen of high-tide bush, Robert tripped on a stump. He went over with a muffled thud. Clayton stared openly, awed by how well his plan was working. Robert's pants were wet from the knees down with marsh water that had also splattered up the front of his shirt and jacket. There was a smear of mud on Robert's cheek. His hands dripped with brown water the color of weak coffee. He straightened up and began to brush ineffectually at his soggy knees.

There was another place to look for turtles at low tide, Clayton told him quickly. But they'd need to borrow a rowboat. "Come on." He turned and sped back over the salt hay before his brother-in-law could complain. Behind him came the squelching sound of Robert's unsuitable shoes.

At the dock, Clayton told Robert to sit in the stern of the borrowed boat. He would wait until they were out in the river, he decided, and then capsize in a way that would look like an accident. He imagined Robert swimming back to the bank in a drenched suit, returning to Boston alone.

Clayton shoved off from the dock and jumped in, taking the seat in the middle and hurriedly extending the oars. To row he had to sit directly in front of Robert, facing him in the small boat. Robert's face was pale. He looked seasick, and so harmless that Clayton felt his resolve weakening. He thought of the beautiful little airplane that Robert had surprised him with. But then he remembered how empty the house felt with his sister gone. A dunking in the river wouldn't hurt anyone, he thought, steeling himself for the moment when it would be time to capsize. The wind had picked up. As they came out of the canal into the river, Clayton felt the spray on his face.

He rowed along the east side of the river. Robert gazed off in the direction of the marsh. Clayton wanted to wait until the boat would be shielded from sight by the riverbank before he made his move. "I bet she's ready now," Robert said suddenly. Clayton, his eyes on the shoreline, wondered at first if he was talking about the boat. "Let's get back," Robert urged. "She'll wonder where we are."

Clayton was trying to judge how much force he'd need to apply to the gunwale in order to tip the boat when he remembered the playing cards. He'd been admiring them on the roof when Robert knocked, and they were still in his pocket. Distracted by the plane and by Nancy's refusal to come downstairs, he'd forgotten to hide them back in his room. Clayton couldn't bear to think of the cards exposed to the brackish water; the colors might run. Angry at himself for planning this so badly, he nodded to Robert and brought the boat around.

Halfway to the mouth of the canal, they heard a clap of thunder. A moment later it began to rain, big, pelting drops that dimpled the surface of the river. Clayton hunched his shoulders and kept rowing. In the stern, Robert seemed indifferent to the rain, so lost in thought that a dunking in the river would have been wasted on him anyway. The sun shone through the rain and each splash glistened. Just as they reached the boatyard it stopped. Sam Burnett poked his head out from the boat shed as first Robert and then Clayton stepped onto the dock, the water coursing from their clothes and hair. Around them in the cattails the perching swallows preened their wet feathers.

Up at the house, Clayton glimpsed his aunt through the screen door. She was unloading the shopping onto the kitchen counter. He put a warning hand on Robert's arm. "Nancy?" Robert called, oblivious. He had opened the door and was making the grave mistake of stepping inside.

"Out of those clothes!" Mavis looked scandalized. She rushed to the closet. "You're dripping onto my clean floor."

She came back to the door and passed them each a flannel rag. "I thought she'd be with you." She gave Robert a pointed look, as if to suggest he had been out on the marsh in the rain on some sort of boyish lark.

"I suppose you'd better dry off in the parlor." Slowly, as if with reluctance, Mavis stepped aside. "Don't put your wet things on the table. That's mahogany." She turned back to the counter and picked up a bag of onions.

Clayton had wriggled out of his sodden pants with the strip of flannel wrapped around his waist. "I'll run up to the attic," he said. He darted toward the stairs with his wet shirt and pants jumbled in his arms.

Behind him, he heard his aunt demand, "The attic? What would she be doing there?" Clayton glanced back, one hand on the newel post. Robert stood hunched and shivering with a rag around his waist and his socks and pants in his arms. He tried to shrug, but in his wet clothes the movement became an awkward hunching, and it looked to Clayton more as if he were fending off a blow. His shirt, dark with water, was plastered to his back; his legs were white and bare under the skirtlike flannel.

Then Clayton heard a cluck of displeasure from his aunt. She was swooping down toward something on the floor. With a feeling of horror, he recognized the blue-patterned back of one of the Captain's playing cards. Without waiting, he ran up the stairs. At the top he paused, his heart pounding. It was utterly silent below, the silence of two people staring at each other. Moving very slowly, Clayton ducked his head just enough to peer down into the room. His aunt must have seen the picture on the card. She was holding it out to Robert, with a look of condemnation and disgust. Clayton shrank farther into the shadows.

From where he sat he couldn't see Robert's face, only the shaking of his head. Mavis looked him over with utter scorn. Holding the card like a dead mouse, she turned and flicked it neatly into the cookstove. Clayton saw Robert glance helplessly toward the stairs, as if in the hope that either he or Nancy might appear. Moving stealthily, Clayton pulled his head back out of the line of sight. He tiptoed to his room.

Later, he heard the sound of the front door slamming.

That night Clayton overheard his aunt tell his uncle that Nancy would be staying on Salt Hay Road.

"What about her husband?" Roy asked.

Mavis made a clucking sound. "That awful man . . ." His aunt's voice dropped, and Clayton didn't hear any more.

The next morning Clayton was in the kitchen making scrambled eggs when Nancy came downstairs. Her eyes were puffy and swollen. "Where's Robert?" she asked.

Clayton stared at her. "He left. Last night."

"Yes, I know," Nancy snapped. "*Where* did he go?"

Clayton shrugged. "I guess he went back to Boston."

"Just like that?"

Clayton paused before answering. He wondered if she could suspect him of trying to make Robert leave. "You were in the attic," he pointed out, defensive.

"So he just went? Didn't he leave a letter or a message?"

Clayton shook his head. He picked his plate off the table and carried it to the sink, worried she would ask him more questions. But Nancy was silent. She sat at the table with her chin thrust out. Her eyes shone with fresh tears.

Clayton left for school before he had to and waited at the Gilpins' house while Perry finished his Cream of Wheat. His brother-in-law had been driven away, just as Clayton had intended, but instead of feeling happy, he was ill at ease. Had Robert told Mavis the playing card wasn't his? If he had, would she have believed him? Clayton almost wished that Robert had stormed and yelled, proclaiming his innocence. The thought of him guessing the truth and keeping silent about it made Clayton squirm.

He would bury the cards by the pond, Clayton decided.

That way they could never be traced to him. This conviction soothed him a little.

In the wake of Robert's departure, a charged silence fell over the house on Salt Hay Road and the subject of Nancy's continued presence within it. Only Scudder seemed to treat the matter as permanently settled, dismissing her lapse in judgment now that she was back among them. For the others, it was a relief to have a straightforward problem to talk about when, nearly a week later, Clayton first noticed the bees.

He'd found one crawling across the window at the top of the stairs and trapped it in a specimen jar so that he could sketch it before releasing it outside. On the floor below the window lay the dry bodies of several more. Later in the day he was up in Scudder's unused bedroom looking for a clean shirt for the old man. Checking the bottom drawer of the dresser, he happened to put his hand on the wall. The plaster felt strangely warm against his palm. He touched the wall by the door for comparison; it was cool as wood. At the same moment he became aware for the first time of a low background humming, a sound he could almost feel. The hair stood up on the back of his neck. He thought of the ghosts that Mavis and Captain Kelley had tried to contact by Ouija board. Then his rational mind reasserted itself; he remembered the bee at the window and realized there must be a hive inside the wall. Clayton ran downstairs and out the door, forgetting the clean shirt he'd been sent for. Standing in the grass, he stared up at the east side of the house. He watched for some time before a bee drew near, bumbled onto the white clapboard beneath the window frame, and disappeared.

He remembered his sister taking a yellow jacket out of his

hair. They'd been somewhere he could envision only dimly, a party at the neighbor's house perhaps, one late summer afternoon. He'd been four or five years old, and had wandered off behind the fence to look for a tree to climb. The nest must have been under a log he tripped on. The yellow jackets flew up at him like embers stirred in a fire. He ran toward the house, screaming and swatting the air. On the lawn the grown-ups in their linen suits and summer dresses rose and turned, their conversations broken off. "What is it, darling?" His mother stretched out her arms. But Clayton ran past her, swinging his head from side to side like a bull, toward his sister. He could feel the buzzing just above his ear.

Somehow Nancy understood. "Keep still," she told him. "I'll get it." She worked through his thick curls while he blubbered with relief. She held his head with one hand and used the other to slip off her shoe. One moment the buzzing seemed nearly deafening. Then he heard a faint crunching sound just above his ear. "There," she said, with a mix of satisfaction and disgust. Their mother came over and led him into the house to wash his face and smear the stings with a paste of baking soda and water. Over his shoulder he'd seen Nancy wipe the heel of her party shoe briskly on the grass.

Clayton announced his discovery to the others at dinner. Roy suggested leaving the bees alone. They hadn't stung anyone, and it would be difficult to remove them. Mavis put down her knife and fork. "I don't intend to live in a beehive, Roy. I can't stand the thought of them crawling inside the walls." She shuddered and rolled her heavy shoulders. "Let's get rid of them before they spread." Clayton imagined what the house would look like filled with bees. Not content with the hive they'd built, they'd crawl on the walls and ceilings, clog the kitchen sink with honey. He looked over at Nancy, trying to catch her eye. But she was staring out the window as if the beehive in the wall didn't interest her at all.

The next day Roy examined the wall in Scudder's upstairs room, shadowed by Clayton. Then he set up the ladder and studied the outside wall. Nancy helped Scudder to a chair on the lawn, and the two of them played cribbage and watched. Roy sent Clayton and Perry down to the pond for cattails. While they were gone, he wound a piece of wire around his ankles, bunching his trousers against the skin and then around his sleeves at the wrist. The boys came back, and he took out two smokers, like tin lanterns, filled the bases with the cattail punk, and lit them. Clayton and Perry each held a smoker, reverently, as if in church, while Roy rigged himself into a brimmed hat that he'd covered in mosquito netting. Veiled like a bride, he climbed the ladder with one gloved hand, clutching a smoker in the other. At the top of the ladder he took a hammer and nail from his belt and made a hook on which to hang the smoker. He felt along the clapboards with his hands, occasionally pressing his ear against the wood. When he'd mapped the contours of the hive by feel, he braced himself against the wall and cut a hole into one of the white clapboards with a small saw. From below, Clayton could see bees emerging, sluggish from the smoke. Roy worked quickly and deliberately. With a pry bar he pulled up first one board and then another. Underneath, the comb showed dirty white with the black bodies of bees crawling over it. Roy took the smoker off the nail and waved it over the exposed hive like a censer. Clayton smelled the rich sweetness of honey mixed with the scent of burning cattail. Above him, Roy pulled up another board. The nails squealed against the wood.

Roy managed to trap the queen and most of the drones using half a cardboard cereal box like a scoop. The air around the swarm as he lowered it into the bucket, following the queen, felt heavy with electricity, like the humid pressure that comes before a storm. The bees flowed into the bucket in a liquid swarm. Roy clapped a glass pie dish over the top. Clayton and Perry stared through it as if it were a window, hypnotized by the dark, crawling mass. More bees buzzed around their heads, and Clayton brushed a few from Perry's back with the sleeve of his shirt.

The comb broke apart in jagged, dripping clumps. Clay and Perry chewed on the broken fragments, and the bits of wax crumbled in their mouths and stuck in flecks to their teeth. Roy collected the comb in a second bucket, using the smoker to fend off the bees and setting a piece of oilcloth over it to keep them out. When Judith Purlowe came from across the field to watch, she stood beside Roy while the others gazed up at the rough hole in the wall of the house and the confusion of bees around it. Out of the corner of his eye, Clayton glimpsed Roy handing her a clump of honeycomb; the widow took it from his fingers with her lips, like a horse accepting a lump of sugar.

When the last of the hive had been fished from between the walls, Roy went to his car and unloaded the extractor he'd borrowed from George Rowley's brother. This was a metal drum with a spigot at the bottom, fitted inside with chicken wire and turned with a crank. He carried it into the cool barn, away from the agitated bees, while the others followed, Clayton carrying the second bucket. The boys watched him shear off the outer layer of wax from a piece of honeycomb using a knife warmed first in boiling water. Then he placed the comb inside the wire and turned the crank; the honey spun out of its wax pockets and collected on the bottom of the drum. It took the rest of the afternoon for Clayton and Perry to extract the honey while Roy mended the hole in the wall. They weighed the honey, jar by jar, on Mavis's kitchen scale. There was over seventy pounds of it.

PART THREE

Falling Houses

Clayton walked down Salt Hay Road with his schoolbag over his shoulder, wishing he were on the beach at Fire Island. The day before, in the aviary at Washington Lodge, Mr. Washington mentioned that a whale had washed up near Old Inlet, about three miles away across the bay. Clayton badly wanted to see it. Mr. Washington hadn't been able to tell him what kind of whale it was, only that a hobby pilot he knew had spotted the carcass while flying over the dunes. At the end of Salt Hay Road, Clayton paused. Perry wouldn't be ready for another few minutes, he told himself. Maybe he'd just dash to the boatyard to see if Sam Burnett knew anything about it.

By this time of year, most of the summer people had gone back to New York City. Beside the long shed at Starke's Boatyard, vessels hauled out for the season lay upside down, exposing the wear on their black-and-red hulls. Sam Burnett sat on his high stool by the boat shed, mending an eel pot and smoking his pipe. He hadn't heard anything about a whale on the beach. "It's getting ready to blow, though," he told Clayton.

Clayton wondered what a storm would do to the whale. It was only Wednesday, he thought desperately. The whale might be washed away before the weekend dragged around, or covered in sand. Clayton ran down to the canal and scanned the docks on the off chance a boat might be headed across the bay. After Labor Day, the ferries ran only on weekends.

The promise he'd made to his sister not to skip school came back to him, but he pushed the thought away. The morning was hot and humid, and now it began to drizzle. The canal that led out to the river looked gray and choppy. Clayton wondered if the whale had teeth or baleen plates; could it be a humpback? A fin? Mr. Washington knew only that it was bigger than a pilot whale.

The honk of a horn made him turn. Back near the boat shed a blue truck idled by the door. Sam Burnett waved Clayton over. Did he want a ride across the bridge? The plumber who owned the truck was on his way to Taffy Point.

He had made a promise to his sister, a small voice insisted. But she had never understood, Clayton thought. She didn't love it here the way he did. He remembered the day he'd shown her the snapping turtles at Knowles Point, his stupidity in thinking she'd be impressed by them. He was skipping school today as a point of honor, he thought hotly. Not because of the whale at all, but because he loved Fire Neck. *He* loved it, and he would go to the beach in spite of the weather, and in spite of the assurance that had been forced out of him.

Clayton hauled on the door and hopped up into the cab. "Thanks, mister," he told the driver.

"Regards to Moby Dick," said Sam.

As the truck crossed the bridge, Clayton noticed whitecaps in the bay. To the east of the Gilpins' cottage, two more beach houses were going up. The scaffolding jutted above the sand like the hollow husks of giant insects. At the construction site, he jumped down and thanked the plumber, who waved and wished him luck. Clayton put his shoes in his schoolbag and wound his way through the sandy hillocks of beach grass and the hollows where the beach plums and rugosa roses grew. He climbed over the dunes. At the crest he stopped and looked down with the thrill he always felt gazing out on the Atlantic. Along the beach, breakers hurled against the sand. Mixed with the salt spray flew orange-and-black butterflies; the monarchs were migrating south along the coast. Clayton walked down toward the surf, breathing in the smell of the sea. He could hardly believe he had almost gone to school, and he spared a thought for Perry, stuck indoors. Tumbling over the sand were bright scraps of butterflies that had been ripped apart in the wind. Others struggled through the spray and the drizzle. The air felt warm and heavy, in spite of the breeze and the pounding surf. Clayton strained his eyes, looking for a shape on the expanse of sand. But on either side the distant beach dissolved into fog. He felt gloriously alone as he started west toward Old Inlet, an explorer on an unmapped shore.

Clayton smelled the whale before he saw it. The warm air carried the oily, rotten stench, and then the whale itself came into view, dark against the pale beach, a mound that seemed to expand as he trudged toward it across the damp sand. It lay on its side. A black-backed gull stood on its huge cheek like a child playing king of the castle and hammered its yellow beak at the whale's sunken eye. Clayton had hoped to see it while it was still impressive, still whalelike. But the carcass was already a ruin. The enormous hulk lay before him like a collapsed dirigible. He guessed it was over fifty feet in length. Its arched mouth gaped open, and he could see the baleen plates, longer than Roy was tall, and the bristly gray baleen. Maybe a right whale, he thought. The gull had savaged the paler flesh of the enormous tongue. He stepped closer and waved his arms, and the bird lifted itself and flew a few feet off to wait him out. Clayton ran his hand along the cold, colossal face; the whale's skin felt like a massive punctured tire. There were thick black hairs on the tip of its lower jaw. He concentrated on breathing through his mouth. The water had scooped out the sand beneath the whale's weight, so that it was half buried already.

Around the other side Clayton counted two blowholes. *Mysticete*, he scribbled in the back of his math notebook; *two blowholes and baleen plates*. He began to sketch the whale's head, struggling to capture the wartlike patches on its face and snout; in his drawing they bore a frustrating resemblance to mushrooms. Crouched on the wet sand, the book balanced on his knee, he tried to shelter the paper from the drops of rain as best he could. He went through a handful of pages, growing more and more dissatisfied. Every sketch he made looked flat and lifeless.

The tide was rising. With each wave the water hurtled farther up the sand, frothing around the massive tail, beating against the limp black form. The dull sunken eye of the whale appeared through the foam and disappeared, as if winking. The rain had picked up. Reluctantly, Clayton closed his book and tucked it into his schoolbag. For the first time, he considered the problem of getting back to Fire Neck. He chased the gull off again, in a token gesture, and then turned from the forlorn and monumental body. Trudging east along the beach into the wind, he wondered where he was in relation to the mainland.

He wanted to come back with Perry this weekend to see what would be left of the whale. One day, after the flesh rotted, they might be able to salvage some of the bones. He imagined an arch made of massive ribs in front of the house on Salt Hay Road.

The waves grew wilder and it became hard to walk on the shifting edge of the sand. Clayton climbed over the dunes. The wind was quieter in the hollow of land between the ocean and the bay. From the lee of the dunes he could look across Fire Island at the whitecapped bay and Fire Neck in the distance. He picked his way slowly through the beach plum and stands of bayberry. The leaves of the poison ivy had begun to turn, brilliant smears of red and orange among the yellow of the goldenrod. Clayton tried to gauge how far he still had to go. He hoped there'd be someone at the construction site where the plumber had dropped him off. Otherwise he would have to walk the seven or eight miles home. Ahead of him a bright flash of spray rose above the top of a dune.

At the house on Salt Hay Road, Nancy glanced up from her cards. Rain was pelting the windows. A large, pale leaf, carried by the wind, flattened itself against the glass like a hand. She went into the kitchen and found the floor wet where the wind had forced rainwater under the doorsill. Scudder sat over his cards with the expression of muted disgust with which he tried to hide his satisfaction in a good hand. Nancy hadn't noticed. She found it hard to concentrate on the game and was playing haphazardly. She tried not to think about Robert, who had written a week before to say he wanted to see her. "We need to come to an understanding," he'd said.

"It's getting worse out there," she remarked.

Scudder nodded. "A line storm. It'll take a while to blow itself out. Where's your brother?"

"It's Wednesday," Nancy reminded him. "He's at school."

Behind the dunes, Clayton strained his eyes. His clothes were damp and thickly caked with sand. They pulled at him, slowing him down. The heavy, salty air made him thirsty, and he realized how stupid he'd been to come without an apple or a canteen of water. He felt sure he'd walked for over a mile already and was wondering if he had somehow missed Taffy Point completely when he saw the shape of a house ahead and to his left. He trudged toward it. It was the Everitts' cottage, the westernmost of those on the bay, still a mile from the point. The Gilpins' beach house was only a few yards farther. Clayton pushed on through the beach plum bushes and the sand. His fingers were puckered, as if he'd been in the bath too long. The sight of the Gilpins' blue door and the listing porch cheered him. He imagined drinking a glass of water, borrowing dry clothes from Perry's upstairs room. He found the key on the little hook under the steps and let himself in.

Inside, it was dark and unfamiliar. The walls creaked in the wind. With a sharp sense of disappointment, Clayton saw that the house had already been packed up for the winter, probably when school had started again. The chairs were stacked along the wall, the rugs rolled up. At the kitchen sink he turned the tap, but nothing happened. The pipes had all been drained, of course, and there was nothing for him to drink. At least he was sheltered, he thought. Clayton found rags in the hall closet. He stripped down and dried himself off, hanging his wet clothes over a chair in the kitchen, where they dripped onto the or-

ange linoleum. Wrapped in an old towel, he made his way upstairs to look in the boys' room for a change of clothes. The
dresser was bare, its drawers stacked upside down on the floor.
The stripped mattresses rested on their sides. Back downstairs,
Clayton pulled his wet and sandy clothes back on. The cloth
caught on his skin. Outside, the wind seemed to be rising.
Clayton realized that anyone working at the construction site
to the east would have left the beach already. He thought of
Perry, warm and dry at school, and decided stubbornly that he
was still glad he'd come.

Roy came into the kitchen on Salt Hay Road in a rainy gust of
wind that rattled the cupboard doors. His hat dripped water
onto the floor. "Nasty out," he said. He'd been on the marsh
with his dogs when he noticed the sky turn the dirty yellow of
an old bruise. Nancy started a pot of coffee while her uncle
went upstairs to change his clothes. When he came down, he
drank his coffee hurriedly, pacing back and forth in the
kitchen. He should have stopped at Judith's first, he thought.
She wasn't used to this kind of weather, and he remembered
that the Captain had complained just before he died about a
leak above the kitchen window. He put his cup in the sink.
Nancy was writing what looked like a letter, and Scudder had
fallen asleep in his chair. "I'd better go down to the boatyard,"
Roy told his niece. "See if Sam needs help doubling lines." He
took a slice of bread smeared with butter and glanced out the
window. Squalls swept over the field and flattened the grass.
The thorny branches of the rosebush on the fence whipped
in the wind. "I'll stop in across the field," he added, heading
for the door. "See how the roof is holding up."

At the cottage Judith had buckets and pans arranged across the kitchen floor to catch the drips. "I don't like the sound the wind's making," she told him.

"We get these storms every fall," Roy said, "when the sun goes over the equator. Wait and see. It'll blow for three days and then clear." Judith was crouched at the kitchen door, mopping up rainwater with an old bedspread. Her hair stuck to her forehead. If he married her, Roy thought, where would they live? Not in the house on Salt Hay Road with Mavis; his sister would never take to that arrangement. The Captain's cottage was simply too small. His head practically scraped the ceilings. He wondered what Gus Hart wanted for the house on Carman Street his mother had lived in. It would need to be fixed up, of course. The prospect excited him. It was on a nice stretch of land, with a path down to Scheibel's Creek.

"I'm making soup for lunch," Judith said, startling him from a vision of her on the porch of a house that was not yet theirs. "Can you stay?"

He shook his head and told her he was going down to the boatyard.

"Come back soon, before I'm swimming in my own kitchen."

Safe inside the Gilpins' house, Clayton quickly grew bored. Outside, the wind howled. Rain and flinging sand stuck to the windows. Clayton wished the house faced the beach, so that he could watch the ocean. From the upstairs window all he could see was the spray off the waves.

As he stared out toward the dunes, hoping for a glimpse of the ocean, he was startled to see a hunched figure moving slowly across the inner meadow. He noted it with a twinge of disappointment; he had been sure he was the only one left on the beach. Then the figure broke apart and he saw it was a woman carrying a child. The child slid to the ground, holding on to her dress, and the woman rested a moment and then lifted it up again. He wondered what they were doing out in the rain. Maybe, he thought, she needed to use the telephone. He went downstairs and unlatched the back door. It jerked out of his hands and flew open, thumping against the wall. Sand stung his face. He waved his arms and shouted uselessly into the wind. Seeing him, the woman moved with renewed purpose in his direction. Clayton saw that she wore a loose pink dress and a pair of incongruous rubber boots. Summer people, he thought.

The woman struggled in and sat abruptly on the linoleum as Clayton fought to close the door. She was pretty in the brittle way city women often were, her glossy brown hair disheveled by the wind. The child clung to her without speaking, a boy of three or four who watched him with wide-set eyes. ". . . *hours* ago . . ." the woman was saying. Clayton handed her a towel, and as she reached out, he saw her hands were shaking. She took it and patted the boy's wet hair. "He told me he'd be back soon . . ."

"Who are you talking about?" Clayton asked. He was not entirely sure she was right in the head.

"Our handyman. We're packing up the house for the season. I sent him into town for boxes. Late this morning. I kept waiting for him to come back with the car. Then the water started coming in. We managed to crawl over the dune. I looked back, and I saw the bathhouse blow away."

Clayton stared out the window again. Salt spray blurred the glass. The sky was darker and the wind seemed to be shifting to the east. "Where's your house?"

She pointed. "On the dunes. It's the white one called Sea-crest. There was a bathhouse, like I said. It's gone now." She be-gan to shake again, harder this time, like a dog getting out of the water. "We'd just passed it. If we'd been a moment later, when the gust came . . ." She pulled the little boy against her and he buried his head in her neck.

"We're safe here," Clayton said. "We'll call someone in town to come pick you up."

The woman stared at him. "The phones aren't working."

Clayton picked up the Gilpins' phone. The line was dead.

"We're on the bay side," Clayton reassured her. "We can wait it out." At that moment there was a popping noise and then a crash. In the living room the east window had blown in and the storm entered the house with a roar of noise. Wind rat-tled the windows. The sashes pinged against the wall. Shards of glass glittered on the floor. Clayton grabbed the broom from the kitchen to sweep up the glass and sand. But rain and wind were howling through the screen. Even moving, the air was strangely warm and heavy. The wind seemed almost due east now. He realized he would have to patch the hole with some-thing and was wondering how he could hold anything big enough in place when beyond the window a flash of white caught his eye. A wave crashed high above the dune in a froth of white water. As it fell, the sand beneath it dissolved like sugar.

Clayton did not own a watch and the woman wasn't wear-ing one. The clock in the Gilpins' kitchen had stopped at ten to twelve on an unknown day in the past. Clayton generally had a good sense of time, but now, with his long walk to see the whale and the strange darkness of the sky, he was unsure if it was one in the afternoon or as late as three. Either way, he knew high tide was scheduled for somewhere around six; it would keep rising for several more hours.

They stood and watched, with spellbound horror, as the waves battered the dunes. It was like seeing a sand castle give way. One moment the line of dunes stood between them and the ocean, and then the line was gone. White water surged through the break, churning with debris. Before their eyes, the break widened, like a sheet of cloth ripping apart. The Gilpins' house stood on a slight rise about two hundred yards from the newly formed inlet. Below them, to the west, the ocean surged around the Everitts' house, sweeping flowerpots and driftwood off the porch, foaming up the windows. Clayton saw how wrong he'd been to think that they could wait it out. Fire Island itself was washing away.

He thought of the bridge, a mile to the east. "Do you think you could make it to the point?" He had to yell to make himself heard, even inside the house.

She gripped the back of the chair. Her knuckles whitened. "We barely made it here." Even if they reached the bridge, Clayton realized, it might already be impassable. He imagined looking down at Fire Island from above, the bay, the thin spit of sand, and then the ravenous ocean.

At the boatyard Roy took care of George Rowley's sailboat first, doubling the spring line and the painter and putting an extra fender on the port side. Sam Burnett came out of the boathouse, his arms full of rope and his pipe clenched tight in his mouth. They started along the edge of the river, where the larger sailboats were, adding lines and checking knots. The halyards slapped in the wind above them, a frenzied twanging. For the most part they worked without speaking. About half the slips were empty, where boats had already been hauled out for the season. Roy noticed that Theron Greaves's boat, the *Leda*, was gone. "Theron's not crabbing in this dirty weather?"

Sam shook his head. "He's out at John Boyle's Island with George. Seining for shiners." The little silver shiners were good bait for snapper fishing. Sam glanced toward the mouth of the river. "They'll be headed in now, at any rate. Probably reefing the main." He paused, remembering something. "Your nephew back?"

"Clayton?" Roy looked at him in surprise. "He's at school."

Sam straightened up. He took the pipe out of his mouth. "He went over to the beach, Roy. Looking for a whale. About nine this morning."

Roy stared out toward the marsh in the direction of Fire Island. Even as he and Sam had been working, the wind had gotten stronger. What would the boy do now? he wondered. How would he get home? "Pigs," he said.

"I suppose he could be anywhere now," Sam said quickly. "He probably left the beach hours ago."

Roy understood that he was being dissuaded. Clayton would have stayed to watch the surf, he was sure of that. He thought of his father and all the times he had ventured into the ocean, risking his life for strangers. When he was six or seven years old, Scudder had taught him how to swim at the end of the pole dock on the river by tossing him in over his head and expecting him to make it back. Panic overtook him as he'd flailed his arms, gulping and choking. His eyes stung and he squeezed them closed. He had been sure he was going to die. When he finally touched the bottom, the mud sucked at his feet, as if trying to pull him under. "That wasn't so bad, was it?" his father demanded when Roy struggled out at last and stood on the bank, shaking in his wet cotton underwear, his teeth chattering in spite of the sun. Roy hadn't answered. Though they never spoke of it, his father had gradually stopped trying to interest him in boats and the water. He'd concentrated on Helen instead, and Roy had been relieved, in spite of a vague but persistent sense of shame.

Roy glanced once in the direction of the cottage. Judith would wonder what was taking him so long, but it couldn't be helped. "Sam," he said, "I'm going to need a boat."

Clayton stood at the upstairs window and watched the Everitts' house wobble on its foundation. It came loose with a popping motion, like a limpet pried from a rock. The waves lifted it for a moment as if it were nearly weightless. Then the walls seemed to stagger and roll, and the water swallowed it. Clayton saw the roof heading toward the bay like a flat-bottomed scow. He turned to where the woman and the boy clung to each other on the bedroom floor. The child's eyes were squeezed closed, and his grubby hands gripped the fabric of his mother's pink dress. They'd come upstairs when the first floor flooded and the surf began running through the kitchen. "We have to go," he said.

"Can't we stay here?" the woman pleaded. "Eddie's scared."

"The house next door just broke up. It's floating away. This one might be next."

The woman began to shake again. Tears welled in her eyes. "Eddie can't swim," she said. The boy opened his eyes at the sound of his name.

"I want Bunny," he cried. "I don't like it here! I want to go home."

Clayton turned away from them and went down the stairs.

Water surged across the kitchen floor and splashed up the sides of the stacked chairs. He could feel the floorboards undulate beneath his feet, a movement that traveled up his legs to his stomach. The straps of his schoolbag flapped on the counter as if attempting to fly. He thought of stowing it upstairs, perhaps under a mattress, but the sight of the Everitts' house had shaken him. The door facing the bay had been forced open. Gripping the door frame, Clayton stepped out into the storm. The sound of the wind vibrated through him; it was as if the power of the wind lay not in its velocity but in that insistent, penetrating sound. Sand cut into his face like slivers of glass. Looking toward the bay, he saw white water. Swirling in it, like twigs in a puddle, were enormous pieces of broken boats and scaffolding. Around the side of the house was the boat locker; he pried open the hinged door and found the life jackets in a tangle of paddles and ropes. Clayton grabbed three cork jackets and a length of line and made his way back upstairs.

He knew very well that it would only get worse as the tide continued to rise. They had to make it to Taffy Point, he thought, and hope the bridge was passable. If not, the mainland was closest there, and they'd have a shorter distance to cross if they had to swim for it. He ran up the stairs, relieved to be moving, to have a plan. In the bedroom the woman was huddled on the floor with her mouth moving in a whisper over her son's hair. She looked up at Clayton in astonishment, as if at a ghost. He thrust two of the life jackets at her. "Get these on," he yelled. "Hurry!"

The woman scrambled up, wiping her eyes with the sleeve of her pink dress. "I thought you'd left without us."

They stepped outside, and the wind howled around them with a sound like that of a train going past. Off the porch, to the west, the surf ran in a wide torrent, awash with wreckage from the houses on the dunes. Crouching low to the sand, they set off east, away from the new inlet. Clayton walked in the lead. The woman followed haltingly, carrying the boy on her back. As they scrambled over the hillocks of sand, Clayton saw a flock of small birds, chipping sparrows, he thought, huddled in the lee. The birds squatted close to the ground in a wedge-shaped formation, their beaks facing into the wind. As Clayton and the woman drew near, the birds rose in alarm, and the wind whisked them away like specks of dust.

The woman, burdened with the boy, began to lag behind. Clayton forced himself to wait. He was anxious to get to the bay's edge and angry with himself for not insisting they leave the house earlier. The woman was struggling through the beach plum, which caught at her boots. Clayton went back and signaled that he could take the boy. But the child clung to his mother, his arms clamped around her neck. "Just for a minute, Eddie," the woman pleaded, raising her voice. "So Mama can rest." The child closed his eyes and held on with a death grip, shaking his head so violently it looked as if he were having convulsions. The woman lowered her head and struggled on with the boy on her back.

As they neared the bay, the bridge came fully into view. It was standing, Clayton saw with relief, though the span seemed to sway in the wind. But it looked farther away than he'd imagined. Beside him, the woman had collapsed on her knees and was holding the boy in her arms now, sheltering him from the wind. Clayton looked back along the bay toward the Gilpins' house. It was still there, though part of the porch had disappeared. Behind it, where the Everitts' house had been, the ocean was running headlong into the bay. Between the inlet and where they stood, Clayton saw the Pastorizas' dock. The Pastorizas had a big house on the dunes and kept their cabin cruiser on the bay, along with several other vessels. These had all ripped free in the wind, except for a small white rowboat tied on the leeward side. It would just fit the three of them, Clayton thought. He pulled at the woman's shoulder and shouted, "This way."

As they approached the dock, Clayton saw it shudder. The rowboat was tied fore and aft, stretched out like a man on the rack. Clayton strained to pull the boat in by the painter and cleat it closer to the dock. "Get in," he yelled to the woman. He helped her free herself from her son's arms. The boy screamed and writhed. "Hold on," Clayton shouted uselessly. "Just a minute." The woman jumped down into the boat. The instant her feet touched the seat, the painter snapped like a guitar string. The boat whipped around in the wind, pivoting on the stern line. With a scream that Clayton felt against his arms, the boy catapulted out of his grasp and flung himself after his mother. He hit the water with a noiseless splash. Buoyed by the life jacket, the child swept toward the rowboat like a bit of flotsam. The woman lunged out, nearly capsizing the boat, and grabbed him by the strap of his cork jacket. She hauled him over the side and into her lap. At the same moment the stern line parted. The boat with its two passengers shot into the bay like a horse from the starting gate at a racetrack. Standing on the dock, Clayton stared after it. It moved as fast as a car on Old Purchase Road. He was utterly alone. The boat dwindled before his eyes. Already he could hardly see their faces.

Beneath his feet the planks began to ripple. Clayton moved to the locust pole that secured the dock to the shore. Boards and logs swept past him, pulled from the dunes through the new inlet to the bay. An icebox floated past, and then a bathtub, carried upright at a jaunty angle. Above him, high in the air, sailed a green door with a brightly polished handle. Every few seconds another wave hit, and white water and debris surged around the dock. Turning toward the inlet, Clayton saw the bulky shape of a house moving in silent slow motion through the shallow chop like a clamshell tumbled in the surf. As he watched, the front crumpled inward like a wad of paper. The gabled roof peeled off and sailed into the air toward the bay. It landed on top of the water with a bounce and spun toward him. Clayton threw his arms around the pole. With a crunch he could feel but not hear, the roof lodged itself against the Pastorizas' dock. Clayton jumped onto it and scrambled over the wet shingles to the peak. In the next instant the dock gave way beneath its weight, and the unmoored roof set sail.

In the kitchen at Washington Lodge Mavis was having trouble with the pilot light. The huge house seemed oddly still, though outside, the branches of the copper beeches flailed. It had grown darker. She walked to the kitchen door and opened it. The wind made a sound she'd never heard, a keening cry. Mavis felt a creeping sensation travel up her back. The yard was deserted, the gardener's bicycle gone. She stepped back into the house. Mr. Washington was due back that afternoon from his factory in New Jersey. She had to cook the chicken for the salad mold she'd planned. She knelt on the kitchen floor and fumbled in the dark interior of the stove. Standing up heavily, she bumped a round metal tray off the table. It hit the floor and rolled into a cabinet with a thunderous clang. The sound echoed off the walls. Mavis picked up the tray. Still holding it, she stepped out into the hall with the superstitious fear that the noise had summoned something. The house was quiet. Mavis walked softly down the hall. Outside the aviary she realized why it seemed so still: the room full of birds was eerily silent.

She clutched the tray and rushed back down the hall, mumbling a prayer under her breath. In the kitchen she felt safer. She sat beside the cold stove and listened to the wind become a deep thrumming, like a low note played on a cello. The sound seemed to leach into her spine.

At the house on Salt Hay Road the rain leaked in even through the tightly closed windows. The drops hit the double-hung sashes so hard the water was forced up between them, until a moving sheet of water obscured the lower half of the glass. Rainwater coursed down the pane on the inside and streamed onto the floor. Nancy ran between the windows and the kitchen door, mopping the floor with rags and towels and wringing out the water into a bucket. "They've never leaked," Scudder began to say, then stopped himself. He didn't want to frighten her further. But he could tell that the wind was still rising, and he'd seen, while she was busy with the streaming windows, a cherry tree in the field below them lurch over onto its side and tumble along the ground. The pond had overflown its banks and now lapped against the woodpile.

"Clayton should have been home already," Nancy was saying anxiously. "Maybe they're keeping them at school." As she spoke, there was a sharp bursting smash against the outside wall. She and Scudder stood perfectly still. The sound repeated itself. They peered out the rain-smeared window. The wind was whipping panes of glass from Roy's greenhouse against the wall of the house like a boy pitching pennies.

Scudder hobbled to the opposite side of the room and began to open the windows. "What are you doing?" Nancy cried.

"It stops the pressure building inside." With the windows on the leeward side of the house open, Nancy and Scudder looked out toward the driveway. The telephone pole bent at a thirty-degree angle. Nancy glanced back toward the green-house and saw the shingles on the roof of the barn ruffle like the feathers of a hen in a dust bath. Then the shingles began to lift off and spiral upward.

Nancy picked up the phone; there was only silence. Angrily she hit the receiver. It was probable, she thought, that Clayton had taken shelter with the Gilpins on Carman Street. Walking into the kitchen, she found water pushing under the door around the sodden bathmats and towels. She got out the mop and moved what she could off the floor, but the water surged in again a moment later. Back in the living room, she tugged Scudder gently by the elbow. "We'd better get to higher ground. The kitchen's flooding." He nodded, unprotesting, and she thought of how much he had already lived through.

Upstairs, the windows were clearer and they saw that the pond had risen until it surrounded the house. Logs from the woodpile drifted by in water thick with leaves and branches. "I'll be damned," Scudder said softly. It looked as if the house were floating once again.

Nancy settled Scudder into his old room. Then she sat at the top of the stairs and stared down at the water rising below her. At the foot of the stairs, a saucepan set loose from one of the kitchen cupboards bumped against the wall. She felt marooned. If only Roy or Clayton would come back, she thought. Even Mavis. Lonely, she missed her husband. She imagined describing the scene to Robert in one of the letters she typed meticulously but did not mail.

A splashing noise came from downstairs. Clayton! "Hello?" called a woman's voice. Judith Purlowe appeared in the living room, dressed in her ancient overcoat and a fisherman's sloped rain hat. The water foamed around her legs.

"Up here," Nancy called, trying to hide her disappointment. She had so badly wanted it to be her brother.

Judith looked up. Her eyes under the rain hat were wide with fear. "Is your uncle here?"

"I think he's waiting it out at the boatyard," Nancy said. "Come join us."

Judith looked as if she might burst into tears. She sloshed toward the stairs and gripped the banister. "What's happening?" she cried. "The field's completely flooded. There's water at my windowsills."

Judith began to climb the stairs, and Nancy saw with surprise that she was barefoot. "My boots filled with water. I had to take them off," Judith explained. Nancy thought of the horses. They would be huddled at the far edge of the field where the land was highest. The biggest danger for them would be falling trees.

"I'll get you some dry clothes," she told Judith. Mavis might be stranded at the lodge, Nancy realized; Roy and Clayton would come in hungry, and she had no idea what to make for dinner.

At Washington Lodge Mavis returned to the relative safety of the kitchen. From time to time she ventured out into the hall and tried to reach Roy on the telephone, but the line wasn't working. After nearly twenty minutes, she managed to relight the pilot by herself, and this small accomplishment reassured her. Everyone else had disappeared, but she'd bravely stayed on, in spite of the storm, and done her job as Mr. Washington would have expected. Mavis boiled the chicken, and then she shredded the meat and placed it in the mold. She garnished it with celery tips, making sure each one was the same size.

Looking up as she finished, she was surprised by how much lighter the kitchen had become. The terrible noise of the wind was gone and a hush like that of an empty church hung over the rooms. She opened the kitchen door. Outside, the sky was clear and blue and the sun shone on a lawn strewn with wet leaves and branches. Furrows of dirt had been gouged by the rain and the air smelled heavily of damp soil. Several trees were down and a telephone pole listed by the road, wires dangling like vines. Mavis went inside and put the plate of chicken on the lacquered tray and covered it with a sheet of waxed paper. Mr. Washington would be delayed by the storm; there was no point in her staying, now that his dinner had been prepared. She put her hat on in front of the little mirror by the kitchen door.

Outside, the ground was soft and muddy. Mavis picked her way down the long white pebble drive, realizing sadly that the walk home would ruin her shoes. At the end of the drive she turned onto Old Purchase Road. There was not a human figure in sight. Mavis had the uncanny feeling that everyone else in the world was gone; she knew it was absurd, and yet she couldn't shake it. She thought of the Rapture that Captain Kelley had spoken of, how everyone was supposed to ascend to Heaven. It would be just her luck, Mavis felt, to be left behind.

She walked down Old Purchase Road toward Fire Neck, stepping carefully around the fallen limbs and tangled wires. At the foot of the hill a huge puddle had formed like a muddy lake. On either side the water gave way to washed-out earth and sodden grass. Mavis was trying to decide between skirting along the edge and walking through it with her shoes off when the sky darkened. It seemed to happen in an instant. The sun disappeared and the wind picked up again, blowing even harder than before. The surface of the puddle broke into chop. Mavis grabbed at her hat and held it down. She was only a fraction of the way home. As she stood staring across the puddle, a tree lurched over on the far side of the road. She turned, fighting against the strengthening wind, and struggled up the hill down which she had just come.

Back in the lodge, Mavis paced the length of the hall. It was hard to see out of the ground-floor windows, and she didn't dare go inside the aviary, where the birds, unnaturally quiet, would fix her with their small, bright eyes from inside the hundred cages. At the end loomed the wide stairs that led to the second floor. Mavis hesitated. Her heart thudded in her chest as if she were about to break the law. But she forced herself to ascend the stairs to the landing, so that she could get a better view of what was happening outside. Below her, the copper beeches whipped in the wind. A flock of pigeons flew past in a gray blur. Mavis stood and stared as the small gazebo by the pond backed itself across the grass and lodged with a shudder in a stand of white pine. More shapes flew by the window, and Mavis saw that what she'd thought were pigeons were actually shingles. The wind flung them off the mansard roof like a pack of playing cards. Mavis crossed herself. It seemed to her that God intended to peel the earth back like a scab. As if, beneath its hardness, something tender and new had been forming all this time.

Roy headed out the mouth of the Barto River in a borrowed powerboat. The wind came straight at him. The bow of the boat rose and fell into every wave with a motion like a bucking horse. Roy wished he were riding one. Anything but this, he thought. He gripped the throttle in one hand and shielded his face as best he could with the other. The rain drove into his skin like needles. Sam had insisted he borrow an oilskin, and he was grateful for it now.

At the mouth of the river the waves became steeper. Roy held the throttle with two hands, fighting to keep the boat faced into the wind. The bay was unrecognizable. Squinting into the rain, Roy couldn't see anything beyond the whitecaps, no glimpse of the familiar shoreline or houses or trees. The sky was a greenish black. It was as if he had somehow found his way onto the open ocean. He knew that John Boyle's Island should be to one side and the tip of Long Point to the other. But he couldn't find a single landmark. He felt lost in a hostile, foreign landscape.

Roy couldn't tell how far he'd gotten when he first felt the motor skip. It would be the ignition wires, he thought. Water must have leaked in with the spray. There was no escape from the water. Even worse than the pelting rain was the air itself, full of spray so fine it seemed to smother him. The motor sputtered, and Roy hit it hard with the flat of his hand. "Pigs," he said out loud.

In the moments before the motor failed completely, Roy understood that he would not make it to Fire Island. He would not save his nephew. He saw the stupidity of coming out on the water, a novice like himself. He hoped the boy had had the sense to make for the bridge in time. He thought of Judith, stirring soup while the rain leaked into pots on the floor. And he remembered, with a sense of incredulousness, how he'd wanted to drown himself nearly twenty years before.

Without the engine to hold it into the wind, the boat swung like a wide door opening. In the next instant a wave hit it broadside, swamping the boat with swirling water. Roy felt his feet slip out from under him. He managed to grab the gunwale. Then the boat was hit again and he found himself pitched overboard. The water exploded into his mouth and eyes. He fought against it like a cat in a bag.

Clinging to the floating roof, Clayton felt a wild exhilaration. He was glad to be alone, unencumbered by the woman and her clinging child. The rest of the world fell away, like meat from a bone; there was only the storm, and he and the storm merged together, so that the wind throbbed through him, pounding in his blood. His body moved without hesitation, independent of conscious thought. One minute the roof had crashed against the dock, and in the next he felt the grooved shingles, rimed with salt, under his scrabbling hands. Each instant was charged with a shimmering physicality. He felt entirely sure of what he needed, moment by moment, to do. The possibility of death did not occur to him.

Looking up from his makeshift raft, he saw the Taffy Point bridge in the distance. As he watched, it broke apart, silently, as in a Buster Keaton movie. It seemed to be happening in the past, as if he already knew that the bridge was gone. The minutes were both condensing and expanding. It might have taken a second for the bridge to break apart, or half an hour, or four hours, a lifetime. He looked for the woman and her little boy without really expecting to see them, remembering them only vaguely, as if they were people he had met a long time ago or had heard about in one of his grandfather's stories. Sheets of water blocked his view. Clayton clutched the peak of the roof and wondered for the first time what it had been like to be born. He felt thrust into the headlong fury of the world, and at the same time it seemed clear that the world was ending, that it was coming apart before his eyes. The storm was like time intensified, exposing the inevitable ruin of every earthly thing: houses, trees, people, the land itself, which broke apart, ripped like old fabric, and was crumpled and tossed aside.

The sky cleared a little, and Clayton tried to get his bearings. He saw that he was still on the Great South Bay, though it was nothing like the bay he had known. A massive migration was under way; every stick of wood, every plank of lumber, every broken piece of flotsam seemed to struggle in the same direction. With each blast of wind, bits of debris lifted off the surface of the water like flocks of misshapen birds. A black dog passed close by, riding on the red hull of an overturned boat. When it saw Clayton, it raised its black hackles and barked without sound.

A shoreline appeared, flattened in the wind. Beyond the grasses, trees were writhing. The roof grounded with a shudder on a sandbar near what Clayton guessed must be the mouth of the river. Stretching his cramped legs, he crawled to the edge. He dropped into the water and found that it reached only to his knees. The bay felt warm as a bath. Clayton picked his way carefully to shore. The wind still howled like a train. Doors and chunks of flooring flew by. He crept to a rise in the grasses near where the trees started. The trees themselves bent and flailed in the wind. Clayton fell exhausted in the marsh grass, his face pressed against the rough spartina. His mouth was parched with salt. From where he lay he could look out at the Great South Bay, and he watched as the wind scooped the water out of the basin like a child cupping sand to make drip castles. The water rose into the air. Revealed beneath it were dark patches of seaweed, gullies and troughs, and the black, straight lines of ancient shipyards. The air smelled of the ocean and the bay together and, mixed with the two, a charge like the one he had felt in the air around the swarm of bees.

———

It was dark at Washington Lodge when Mavis heard the sound of a car on the drive. Roy, she thought, coming to take her home. For hours she had been sitting in the kitchen, trying to read her pocket Bible by the light of the candles. She ran to the door. The car's headlights sliced through the dark. They stopped at the front entrance and Mavis hesitated. It was not Roy's Ford. And Roy would come to the kitchen, never to the front. A moment later the lights were cut and the engine coughed and went silent. The car door swung open and a figure stepped out. Mavis darted back inside the kitchen and hurried down the hall just as Mr. Washington came through the front door. He had left his factory in New Jersey that morning as planned and had driven through a labyrinth of impassable roads and scenes of increasing devastation. Now he stood in the hall before Mavis, his eyes glassy, his dark hair plastered to his skull. His silk scarf clung to his neck like a limp rag. Staring at him, Mavis was overcome by a deep uneasiness. The sight of Mr. Washington so disheveled disturbed her more than all the uprooted trees on Old Purchase Road.

Mavis turned to the sideboard and poured him a glass of brandy. He drank it down, and spots of color appeared on his cheeks. "How are my birds?" His voice was thick. Mavis assured him they were safe. "I'll change for dinner," he announced. He seemed unsteady on his feet, and Mavis wondered if she should follow him. But she didn't want to overstep her place. She went back to the kitchen and took his dinner out of the refrigerator. She removed the wax paper and set the plate on the black lacquer tray. The celery garnish had wilted somewhat. Mavis pulled at the limp tips of the leaves. She found more candles and set them on the dining-room table. They shone in the long gilt-edged mirror. The sight of the chicken salad, so pretty in its mold, pleased her. After a moment's hesitation, she poured Mr. Washington a second glass of brandy and set it by his plate. Then she stood in the doorway and waited for him to reappear.

He never did. She found him in the bathroom twenty minutes later, dressed in a dinner jacket, his hair neatly combed. He had collapsed with a bottle of cologne in his hand; heart failure, the doctor would determine later. The cologne had emptied out onto the white tile floor and shrouded his body with a smell of musk and cloves.

Theron Greaves and George Rowley made it back up the river on a reefed jib, in a feat of seamanship the men of the boatyard would speak of for years afterward. At times, the strength of the wind pushed the bow completely underwater; "more like plowing than sailing," Theron said later, rendered almost loquacious by the memory. George had bailed without stopping while Theron steered and the dog with the spotted face whimpered in the bow. Sam Burnett saw the *Leda*'s sail and watched them approach, waves breaking over the gunwale and the wind forcing them nearly sideways. He helped them ashore, and they fought to secure the *Leda* to the dock. "We saw a fellow go over," George told him. "Not far from Rose's Point. It looked like the Marchands' boat."

Sam, a lapsed Catholic, crossed himself. "Roy. His nephew's on the beach," he said. "Any chance he made it to the point?" Theron and George glanced at each other. They shook their heads. The three men stood for a moment and stared toward the mouth of the river, where water rose off the surface in twisting sheets of vapor.

"Someone should go up to the house," Sam said finally. He gestured across the field toward the house on Salt Hay Road.

From the top of the stairs, Nancy and Judith watched the lapping water recede. The wind had shifted direction, and the water that had been blown out of the pond and over the field was now being swept back and forced into the river. From where they sat they could see the high-water mark, just past the third step, grow dark against the lighter wood. The cooking pot had long since capsized and sunk. After a time the tread below the high-water mark emerged. Then the next. They were standing on the stairs, curious to see the state of the kitchen, when they heard a hammering from outside. Nancy sloshed across the floor. She opened the door and saw George Rowley standing with his hat in his hands.

It was nearly ten o'clock when Mavis made it back to Salt Hay Road in Dr. Thayer's car. The house glowed with the lights of kerosene lamps. As she stepped into the kitchen, a terrible stink assaulted her. The floor was thick with mud and silt. Junk lay jumbled in the corners and along the edges of the room. At the kitchen table her niece and Judith Purlowe sat motionless in front of a pot of coffee. Nancy rose without speaking and came forward. It seemed to Mavis that the girl had a shifty look on her face. Nancy put her arms around her shoulders, pressing a cheek against her neck. In the back of Mavis's mind an uneasiness grew. She looked at Judith, whose eyes were red and swollen. Even as she watched, the widow's face crumpled. Mavis pushed Nancy away. "What happened? Where is everyone?"

"We don't know," said Nancy. "We're worried about two things." She spoke slowly and quietly, as if to a child. "One is Roy, Mavis. His boat went over."

"Don't be stupid," Mavis snapped. She had sat alone for hours in a dead man's house and her nerves were frayed to the breaking point. "Roy doesn't have a boat." Nancy had guided her to a chair and pressed her into it.

"He borrowed one from Sam." Nancy's face twisted, and her dark eyes teared. "He was trying . . . He wanted to get Clayton off the beach."

Mavis stared at her. "Clayton . . . ?"

Nancy nodded, and Mavis recognized the raw fear in her face. "He was on the beach. We don't know any more. Whole houses got swept out to sea . . ." She paused, and Mavis saw her swallow. "George Rowley came by to tell us. He saw Roy's boat go over."

"That doesn't mean anything," Mavis cried. Already her mind bloomed with possibilities: Her brother had clung to a piece of wreckage; he had made it to the beach but had been knocked unconscious; he was safe in a house across the river, suffering from amnesia.

A snuffling sound intruded on her thinking. At the table, the widow's hair hung messily over her shaking shoulders. Through her shock and disbelief, Mavis felt a bracing flare of anger. "Stop that!" she yelled at the other woman. "Pull yourself together!"

Nancy had gripped her by the shoulders and was repeating something into Mavis's face. Mavis heard the words "high school." What was the girl talking about? Nothing made sense. In a swift motion, Mavis shoved her hard. The girl staggered back, catching herself from falling. She stood on the other side of the table, and Mavis watched impassively as her eyes closed for a moment before reopening.

"Someone needs to go to the high school," Nancy repeated slowly. "To look for them."

"The high school? Clayton goes to the elementary . . ."

Nancy stood very still. "That's where they're taking the bodies."

Mavis glanced away from her, down toward her feet. A layer of green-black mud was spread over the kitchen floor like badly applied icing. There was something in the dark corner that looked like a sodden loaf of bread. She had a sudden memory of coming home to Fire Neck from Ohio after Ramsay left her and how filthy the kitchen had been. This was a hundred times, a thousand times worse. Nothing would bring the room back to rights. The smell in the air was thick and oppressive, the stench of marsh dredge and manure. Unbearable. She stood up too quickly and bumped against the door frame on her way into the other room.

Her father sat on the daybed in the living room. The light of the kerosene lamp made his skin look sallow; his eyelids drooped, too heavy for his eyes. He seemed ancient, mummified. "What was he doing out on the water?" he asked, looking up at her. His voice, often so stern, sounded weak and querulous. "I don't understand it. It isn't like Roy at all."

Roy. Mavis dropped into the chair beside the daybed. Her head pounded, as though the storm that had blown itself out had found its way inside her skull. What did it all mean? What did Roy have to do with bodies at the high school? She remembered the fist-shaped cloud that had appeared in the sky the day the fireworks factory exploded, bringing with it the smell of destruction, the ring with the curse inside its opal setting. She'd tried to understand these things, but she'd misread the warnings. All this time, she'd feared her husband, imagining him coming after her when he was really two thousand miles away, remarried. She'd been so sure that she was the one in danger. Now Mr. Washington was dead in his own house and Roy was out on the water, unguarded, unprotected.

A blasphemous frustration seized her: Why couldn't God make Himself clearer? Would it be so hard for Him to tell her plainly what He meant?

In the kitchen, Nancy pulled on a pair of boots that Clayton had outgrown. They were too big for her; she felt her mind catch on this fact, unable to go any farther, as she tightened the laces until the leather buckled. "I'll come with you," Judith said suddenly, and Nancy jumped. Thinking about Clayton, she'd forgotten for a moment where she needed to go.

She glanced up at Judith, grateful.

Nancy found a jacket of Roy's for Judith and grabbed Scudder's brown wool coat for herself. The familiar smell of hair oil and tobacco did something to comfort her. She found the big flashlight Roy kept in a drawer for checking on the dogs at night. Before leaving, she peered into the living room. Scudder lay on the daybed with his eyes closed, the red-and-black-checked blanket over his legs. Mavis sat on the sofa as if carved from rock. "We're going now," Nancy told her quietly. Her aunt did not look up.

It was nearly a mile to the high school. The night was clear and the stars shone bright and cold. Nancy and Judith walked without talking. It was very dark. Nancy carried the flashlight, and its faltering beam made the surrounding night seem vast, their passage through it temporary and uncertain. The only other lights were the soft circles of yellow thrown by kerosene lanterns through the windows of houses and then, as they drew nearer to the crossroad, the headlights of a turning car.

A group of lanterns had been set at the front entrance. As they came closer, Nancy saw a flashlight click on as a huddled group stepped off the sidewalk and passed them. Someone sobbed while another voice murmured something kind and ineffectual.

The squat brick high school seemed to Nancy to crouch against the ground. Inside, it was dark, the air close and infused with that smell of frustrated youth peculiar to buildings of public education. She and Judith followed the ray of light to the gym, where Nancy had only a few years ago played basketball with Enid Snow and danced at school dances. Lit by kerosene lamps, the room looked dark and cavernous. On the polished hardwood floor, half a dozen dark shapes lay awkward and unmoving. Nancy averted her eyes. A balding man with a short grizzled beard sat at a small desk by the door with a pad of paper. He looked like a bayman, weathered and capable.

"We're looking for my little brother and my uncle." Nancy kept her eyes on the man's lined face, blocking out the half-lit room around her, and spoke softly, as if the still figures on the floor were sleeping and shouldn't be disturbed. "He's thirteen. He should have been at school."

"And Roy," Judith prompted, beside her. "In a green canvas shirt . . ."

"And my uncle too. Dark hair . . ." Nancy stopped, because the man with the pad of paper was nodding gravely, without surprise, as if he'd been expecting them.

"They brought a boy in less than an hour ago," he said. "I'm sorry. A terrible business." Nancy was aware of Judith reaching for her hand and gripping it hard. The man stood up, flashlight in hand, and led them toward the middle of the room. The few bodies rested against the backs of upturned chairs taken from the school cafeteria. They were tilted upright, each in the posture of someone reading the paper in bed. Nancy saw that some of the chairs were empty; they seemed to wait in mute anticipation. She looked quickly away.

"Here." The man shone his light on a small figure. It was a boy of seven or eight, with a pale, puffy face that was nothing like her brother's. There were freckles on the dead boy's nose. His mouth was open slightly, the way Clayton's sometimes was when she checked on him before she went to bed. A savage joy tore through Nancy, as if the death of this unknown child meant somehow that Clayton had been spared. Tears flooded her eyes. "He's not ours," she said hoarsely, turning away, ashamed of her relief. The beam of her flashlight fell on a woman's white legs and then on a bare elbow. Her hand began to shake and the light bounced, creating a ghoulish effect; a face appeared in the beam and seemed to move. Nancy dropped her hand, and the light burned into the shiny floor. She thought of her mother in her coffin in a blue satin dress, her forehead smooth, and Clayton gripping her hand as he repeated stubbornly and with complete assurance, "*That* isn't her. *That* isn't Mama."

"Over here, miss," the man directed them. "There's more." Nancy switched her flashlight off and allowed their guide to light, one by one, the faces of the assembled dead.

After Nancy and Judith left, Scudder fell into a heavy sleep and Mavis returned to the kitchen. Even filled with muck, it was the room in which she felt most at home. She sat at the table and rested her head on her arms. The house was utterly silent, as if the normal noises drowned by the roar of the hurricane had been obliterated and would never come back.

Mavis felt her eyelids drooping. At the sound of the kitchen door, she raised her head. A man stood in the doorway. She could hear him breathing, a raspy, labored sound. The man stepped forward, and the light of the lamp shone on his face; haggard and broken, it was still the face in all the world that she most wished to see. He was barefoot and his clothes were torn, and a dark bruise showed like stubble along his chin. She understood what had happened without his speaking a word. He'd washed ashore by Taffy Point, clinging to a piece of wreckage. He'd twisted his ankle. All night he had struggled home.

"Roy!" she cried, relief choking her throat. He reached out his arms.

She lurched toward him, and her chair tipped over onto the floor with a crash. It was this sound that woke her from the dream. Standing, shaken, Mavis looked around. The kitchen was empty. The door was closed.

Walking home on the east shore of the river, Clayton counted more than twenty boats stranded on the marsh or caught in the trees. He took the shortcut over the railroad bridge. The track was strewn with branches. Once, he had to clamber around a large, waterlogged sofa. Seaweed hung from the limbs of the pitch pines. It was very quiet. It got darker as he left the track for a path through the woods. After a while he sat down to rest and felt himself falling asleep, lowered abruptly into it as if on a bosun's chair. He woke up stiff and so thirsty he could hardly swallow. The air had turned colder, all the strange warmth gone. Shivering, he stood and tried to find the path again. His hands ached where he had scraped them on the roof, and his legs were sore. It was completely dark. After a long time, he emerged from the trees.

He found the split-rail fence and followed it down the length of the field, past the dark silhouette of the Captain's cottage. In the house on Salt Hay Road, a yellow light gleamed through the kitchen windows. He stepped inside and saw his aunt at the table. "I'm back!" Clayton cried. "I walked the whole way home!"

Mavis stared at him. The light from the lantern etched her face severely. There were shadows under her eyes, and he had the odd sense that she was older than he'd thought, her bones fragile under the mass of her flesh, her hair on the brink of turning gray. Clayton faltered. It seemed, in the dim light, that there were tears in her eyes.

"Your sister's looking for you," Mavis said after a moment. There was a catch in her voice.

His first thought was how angry Nancy would be at him for skipping school. He had forgotten everything but the storm and his own heroic progress through it. "Looking for me where? Did she go to the beach?"

"The beach? They said that washed away. No, she's up at the morgue. Looking for you and your uncle."

Exhausted, he did not fully understand what she meant. And yet something began to shake inside him. His sense of exhilaration, of triumph, shifted to uncertainty. He stared around the kitchen for reassurance. It smelled of low tide and the mud that covered the floor, but there was the stippled lampshade, dark now, the poster of the horses. There was the same table where, years before, his aunt had said in her voice so like his mother's that this would always be his home. He thought of the houses he'd just seen caving in upon themselves, collapsing soundlessly before his eyes, and the dark, familiar kitchen seemed to tremble around him. He didn't know how he could keep it from falling.

"For Roy?" he faltered. The dread hardened into a tight ball and lodged itself deep in his throat.

She nodded, still watching him with her strangely shining eyes. "He went out on the bay." Clayton was aware of a shuddering that seemed to be coming from outside him.

"But why?" he said. "He doesn't like the bay." He still didn't understand.

"Sam told him you were on the beach." His aunt's face glistened in the yellow lantern light. "He went to bring you home."

Roy's body was found by a search party two days later. He had washed up among the wreckage on the east side of the Barto River, among the planks of lumber, the disjecta membra of walls and roofs, the odd appliances, screen doors, masts and booms, wire crab traps, buoys, dead gulls and terns. One of the search party, a girl Nancy's age, stepped on something yielding as she climbed around a baby carriage with its wheels in the air. Looking down, she saw a pale, protruding hand. The body was battered but identifiable. Along the same shore many of the boats from Starke's Boatyard had stranded, and strewn among them were the carcasses of hundreds upon hundreds of white Peking ducks. They'd been washed out of Brown's Duck Farm in the storm and swept in again on the next day's tide. The white feathers shone in the bright sun against the brilliant green spartina and the brown drifts of mud and debris.

Nancy was carrying a basket of wet towels to the clothesline when she saw a figure in the driveway. She and Judith had spent the morning scraping sour mud off the downstairs floors. A thick crust of salt still covered everything, like an early frost. She'd taken a break to hang out the washing. The lawn was littered with detritus: an icebox, an armchair, the front half of a sailboat, scraps of wood that bristled with nails, and dozens of pale, bloated fish. The man in the driveway stood with his back to the house, staring at Roy's car, apparently arrested by the sight of the maple limb that had pierced the windshield like a javelin. He held his head tipped slightly to the side in a way Nancy knew. Her hand went involuntarily to her hair, covered with a red bandanna. She had on a faded blue skirt and a pair of oversized rubber boots to protect her feet from all the broken greenhouse glass. Her arms were flecked with soap. "Robert?" she said.

He turned. She saw her husband's familiar face. His mouth, tight with worry, fell open. He stretched out his arms. The clean, damp towels tumbled behind her as she dropped the basket and flung herself toward him.

Behind the barn, Clayton pulled at the fallen branch that had ripped a hole in the wire pheasant pens and allowed the whole flock to escape during the storm. He heard his sister's voice from the other side of the house as it rose with breathless, unexpected happiness. Without thinking, he dashed around the corner, and for a sliver of an instant the figure beside her looked like his uncle. The man glanced up, and Clayton stopped short.

"Look, Clay!" Nancy cried. "Robert's here!"

———

Inside the house, Mavis was cutting large rectangles from a piece of Scudder's old sailcloth. Two windows needed to be patched, as well as one at Judith's cottage, and there was no glass to be bought in Southease or anywhere else. When Nancy came in with Robert Landgraf, he looked at Mavis questioningly, unsure of his reception. Mavis nodded flatly and went back to cutting sailcloth.

She could hear them talking about a telegraph office, a train that had been derailed, a ferry that lost power on the Sound and floated aimlessly for a day and a half. She gathered he had walked a long way. It was not knowing what he would find here that had been the hardest, he was saying, his voice husky.

"We'll stay as long as you need, Mavis," Nancy said. "Help get the house in order, things working again." She raised her voice slightly. "Clayton, you'll come to Boston. I want you there with me." Nancy said this calmly and firmly. Mavis glanced up, surprised out of her grief for a moment. She searched for the flighty girl who had teased her about partridges and wept into a bowl of pudding. Already, her niece looked years older.

By the door, Clayton made no sound. Mavis was aware, without looking at him, that he was standing very still, with one hand on the latch. She felt the mute appeal of his bright, anguished eyes. Nancy and Robert had stopped talking. They watched him also, waiting.

In her mind, Mavis saw the dark empty kitchen lit by the kerosene lamp, the sodden loaf of bread in the corner. She told herself again that it was not the boy's fault. It wasn't his fault, and she must forgive him. And yet, she thought, if he'd been at school where he was supposed to be, Roy would have come home from the boatyard instead of going out into the storm—she could feel the litany spooling out inside her like thread from a bobbin, tangling in its hurry—and Roy would be home right now, he would be standing in this kitchen pretending not to notice that she was blinking back tears. He would still be alive, if only the boy hadn't gone.

Mechanically, Mavis raised the sailcloth. The opal ring that she had ground to powder on the flagstone all those months before had not been the cause of her unhappiness, nor had it killed the Captain. She'd imagined a curse, needing a reason, wanting to put the blame on something she could touch. The scissors flashed in her hand. The only sound in the room was the snip of the blades through the cloth. The boy would go with his sister, as he should. But she couldn't bring herself to look at him, and she kept her eyes on the line she was cutting and the cloth that fell on either side in stiff, uneven folds.

After a moment, Clayton turned his gaze from her and darted out the door like a swallow. Nancy and Robert left a moment later, murmuring together and holding hands. It was a relief to Mavis to have them gone, out of her kitchen, her house. She felt betrayed by the disorder of the world. All she could imagine wanting now was silence.

When Mavis, going through the mail a week later, saw the word *Esquire* on the heavy vellum envelope, she opened her mouth to call for Roy, then shut it again. For the first time since the hurricane she remembered the letter from the man to whom she was still legally married. Her bitterness toward him had broken, like a fever. The papers from Canada sat upstairs in her room, unsigned. Without stopping to reconsider, she hurried up the stairs and pulled the brown envelope from the drawer. She took it back to the kitchen and signed the documents on the lines indicated. Not even the photograph of the baby disturbed her. They were people she didn't know, and now they were out of her life for good. She picked up the fresh letter, the one from the lawyer in New Jersey, with a feeling of being put-upon, as if now that she had washed her hands of this business it was inconsiderate of them to keep harassing her. But the letter had nothing to do with Ramsay White. It was a notice concerning George B. Washington's estate.

It was a warm morning in early October when they gathered at Washington Lodge for the reading of the will. Clayton arrived early and sat waiting on the kitchen steps. Since Mr. Washington's death, he had taken it upon himself to feed and water the birds. Along the white pebble drive, copper beeches lay where they had fallen in the hurricane, leaving gaps in the row like missing teeth. There were bare patches among the shingles on the mansard roof, and the grass had grown in the pathways and around the kitchen door.

The housekeeper and the gardener arrived, nodding to Clayton, and stood talking in low tones. Mavis came last, puffing up the long driveway in her worn black shoes. At five minutes past nine, a sleek DeSoto pulled up. They watched as a man in a dark suit stepped out. He walked around to the other side of the car and opened the door with a stiff little bow. A girl emerged, her skin the color of milky coffee. She wore a simple green dress, and her straight black hair hung nearly to her waist. Clayton thought her the most beautiful girl he'd ever seen; she made the women on the playing cards look coarse in comparison. The lawyer gave her his arm, and they went in through the front hall, followed by Clayton and Mavis and the others. In the dining room, the lawyer took a long time reading the will and even longer explaining it in terms no one could understand.

Mavis received five hundred dollars; Clayton received one hundred. He did not know how he would spend it, now that he was moving to Boston and had no use for either a boat or a hunting rifle.

After the will had been read, Washington's niece indicated that she would like to see the house. She admired the kitchen, with its wide windows and shining tile floor, and nodded to Mavis when it was explained that she had been the cook.

The lawyer motioned toward the door, and they walked down the hallway and turned into the aviary. The air inside smelled of droppings and old apples and damp newspaper. The curtains over the floor-length windows were closed, and the group stood still for a moment, blinking in the darkness. Clayton slipped through the crowd and pulled aside the curtains, as he had done for Mr. Washington countless times before. The morning light streamed into the room in honeyed shafts. Clayton heard the girl catch her breath, and he felt a rush of pride, as if the aviary were his to give her. Around them the waking birds seemed to come to life, stretching and hopping. They began to call, hesitantly at first, then loudly, a ringing cacophony. The girl darted toward one of the enormous windows. Clayton, standing nearby, saw that she was trying to open it and hurried to help her. She gave him a grateful smile. Then she turned toward the cages and began to fumble with the latch of the biggest, an ornate white one that housed a flock of striped finches. Agitated, they hammered themselves against the bars. The girl flung the door open with a metallic clang. There was a moment of stillness. And then the first finch shot out of the cage. The girl laughed. Moving quickly, she pulled open the door to a cage of conures, then of lorikeets. Loose in the room, the birds flew tentatively, testing the air with their unaccustomed wings. A white cockatoo landed heavily on the floor, panting in alarm. A parrot beat its green wings against the windowpane. The lawyer retreated toward the doorway. The housekeeper flapped her hands. A parakeet brushed the gardener's shoulder and swooped through the open window and out of sight. There were over a hundred cages in the room, and the girl opened them one by one, shooing the birds toward freedom.

Clayton stood helplessly in the corner. Tears of frustration welled in his eyes. He knew the birds belonged to the foreign girl. Even if he could speak her language, he had no right to stop her.

Walking into Southease along Old Purchase Road, Nancy and Robert were surprised to see three green birds burst out of the trees ahead of them. "Honeycreepers?" Robert exclaimed. A moment later an antshrike and a trogon flew across the road. "From the lodge," said Robert. They stopped to stare. Lovebirds, motmots, jacamars, manakins, jays; the trees rustled with bright, exotic wings. Robert put his arms around Nancy's waist. "I never know what to expect with you around." In a shrub by the side of the road a green bird with a brilliant blue tail perched like a Christmas ornament. A pair of yellow-headed parrots chased each other above the maples, screeching. Pressed against each other, Nancy and Robert craned their necks toward the sky as birds exploded from the branches around them. A white cockatoo landed in the road and looked around, confused, before taking off again in the direction of the Great South Bay. Watching it dip from sight, Nancy shivered with a sudden realization, and Robert pulled her closer. It was October. The birds were tropical, gathered from rain forests and sunny islands close to the equator. Even if the winter was exceptionally mild, the birds could never survive here. She glanced at her husband and saw from his eyes that he had understood this from the start. Above the trees rose a macaw with a head the color of fire, beating its blue-green wings. They watched without speaking as the last of the birds disappeared and the screeching and the chatter died away.

In their last days in Fire Neck, Nancy pleaded with Mavis to keep Roy's horses. "They need too much care," her aunt said flatly. "What would I want them for now?"

Nancy felt a thickening in her throat. "Just Buckshot, then?" Mavis shook her head. Nancy opened her mouth in the stubborn hope that she could wear her aunt down. But then she saw how petty her concern for a horse must seem to Mavis. Two days later, heavyhearted, she took them to a riding stable in Manorville owned by a friend of Sam Burnett's. Judith Purlowe took Roy's hunting dogs, to keep her company, she said.

Scudder sat in the living room with a book on his lap and listlessly turned the pages. He was entirely lucid. But something about him now filled Clayton with a superstitious fear. Clayton didn't like to be alone in the same room with him. There was an absence, a vacancy, that he could feel, like a cold spot in an otherwise warm room. The force of his grandfather's tremendous will had finally gone. A replica seemed to have been substituted for the man Clayton had known, the way goblins were said to replace human babies with their own.

Nancy had dreaded speaking to her grandfather about their departure. She hadn't even told him she was taking Clayton with her. The night before they left, she brought Scudder a cup of tea. She sat beside him on the daybed and put her head gently on his shoulder. "We leave for Boston tomorrow," she said, as if making conversation. "Clayton's going with me. We're taking the ferry, and then the train." There was no answer. She pulled her head back so she could see Scudder and make sure he wasn't feigning sleep. His eyes were open, though they seemed to be looking at something far away from her. He reached out and patted her hand. Nancy's throat tightened. "I love you very much," she said. "I promise I'll write, and visit when I can. I miss you when I'm away."

Scudder patted her again. He didn't speak. But he rested his hand on hers for a long moment, dry and warm, his fingers stained with tobacco.

Clayton stood at the railing in the stern as the ferry pulled away from the pilings with a grinding shudder. The dock receded, slowly at first, then gathering speed. The crowd grew smaller and less distinct, and he lost sight of Mr. Gilpin, who'd given them a ride, and then of Perry in his red shirt. It felt to Clayton as if he himself were being pulled, stretched thinner and thinner, like saltwater taffy. Now the throng had begun to disperse. Only a single figure remained—he thought it must be Perry—waving a white handkerchief in a wide arc. The wake grew behind them like a furrow cut in the water. At the house on Salt Hay Road, his aunt and grandfather would sit down to dinner tonight in a kitchen emptied out. The ferry's wake stretched like a path that would lead him home, and he imagined diving off the stern rail into it and swimming back. The ferry swung out through Pine Gut. The houses of Drowned Meadow were a cluster of white and brown surrounded by the patchy green of the storm-damaged trees. Clayton felt his sister's hand on his arm. He kept his gaze on the churning wake. Out of the corner of his eye he thought he saw his brother-in-law take in his tear-stained cheeks. A part of Clayton longed to bury his face against Nancy's shoulder. But Robert's hand was around her waist with an easy possessiveness, and she was leaning against him. Clayton's eyes stung. The wake blurred before him. Long Island became a low dark shape on the horizon. He watched as it flattened and broke, into a line like a raft of scoters, into a smudge like smoke, until there was nothing left behind them but the water and the sky.

In the house on Salt Hay Road, Scudder sat in the living room by the cold woodstove. After a time, Mavis came in and sank into the chair beside the daybed. Scudder noticed for the first time that her face had lost much of its roundness. She had never looked old to him before. Closing her eyes, she let out a little whimper, almost inaudible.

Scudder felt as if he were watching her at a terrible remove, impotent and helpless. The feeling was eerily familiar. He tried to trace it back to its origin in his past, but his mind moved with arthritic slowness. He leafed through his many years like pages in a book that had gripped him at the time but that he could now only imperfectly recall. At last he realized what the feeling reminded him of: that awful night he'd spent on the beach in 1890 as the three-masted schooner he and Kelley never spoke about was gradually wrecked on the bar. He saw again the distant figures falling without sound into the wash of the indifferent water. He had buried his wife and two of his children, he thought. Here was Mavis, the last of them. He was overwhelmed with a tenderness he had no way to express.

"Can I teach you cribbage?" Scudder asked at last. It was a

question that took all the meager brightness he could muster. Mavis turned her wide, dark eyes to him, and he felt that he would do anything in his power to comfort her. He'd been too hard on her all this time. He had teased her about the one real consolation with which she tried to ease her many heartaches.

Scudder tried for a moment to give God the benefit of the doubt. For Mavis's sake, he tried to imagine Him. And what came to his mind, forgive an old sinner, was not a God who was omnipotent at all but an ancient God, all-seeing but deeply tired, a God who watched the people on the earth He had created the way Scudder had watched those doomed figures in the rigging of the wrecked ship. God heard their cries in the darkness; He loved them and He wished he could reach them. But He was very, very tired, and He was so far away. He could not save any of them, in the end.

Clayton was not as miserable in Boston as he'd intended to be. In the spring of 1939, he discovered the Navy Yard. He was sorry Perry Gilpin couldn't see it lit up at night, the giant shapes of the grain and coal terminals on the skyline, the workers hurrying by as the shifts changed, the blue flame of the welding torches. There he was able to find odd jobs at the dry docks and the Ropewalk, and watch the construction of Gleaves-class destroyers, of destroyer escorts, and high-bridge and low-bridge Fletchers. He kept a list of the ships he'd seen built: *Mayrant, Trippe, O'Brien, Walke, Madison, Landsdale, Gwin.*

But at night, in the small room off the front hall of the apartment he never thought of as home, he dreamed repeatedly of searching for something along one of the faint, narrow paths made by the deer as they crisscrossed the marsh through the spartina. Or he would dream of houses collapsing in silence while he watched but could not move. Sometimes he imagined running away and returning to Fire Neck. Once, when he was fifteen, he saved enough money for a train ticket, and even went to South Station and waited on line. At the ticket window he faltered, imagining his aunt's expression when she opened the door and saw him. Nancy kept in touch with Mavis and Scudder, writing frequent letters and talking on the phone. But he'd been back only twice since the hurricane, preferring to exile himself in Boston when Nancy went to visit. He didn't mind staying with Robert, who sometimes listened to Fibber McGee with him on the radio and never questioned him about where he went after school: "Just no juvenile delinquency, or it'll be my head on a stake." Clayton couldn't imagine facing Mavis again, couldn't think of any way he'd ever make amends.

"Where to, then, son?" asked the white-haired man at the ticket window.

"Nowhere," he murmured, ducking away. "Sorry."

August Scudder lived just long enough to see the country join the war, dying of pneumonia in February 1942. Clayton traveled from Boston with Robert and Nancy, who was six months pregnant. They arrived at the house on Salt Hay Road after dark. Clayton felt his chest tighten as he got out of the car and saw the lights from the kitchen windows shining on the snow. Mavis met them at the door, and Clayton was taken aback by how small she seemed. As he stepped inside, the kitchen closed around him, as if in his absence it had diminished as well. The warm air smelled of streusel and the fresh loaf of bread steaming on the counter. He hung back as Mavis embraced the others, patting Nancy's belly and leaving a dusting of flour on the green fabric of her dress. When she turned toward him, Clayton found he couldn't meet her eye. He glanced down in the direction of her shoulder. "You're scraping my ceiling," she exclaimed, giving him a brisk hug. Feeling her arms pressed around his chest, he remembered how, after Captain Kelley died, she used to snatch him close and whisper a prayer above his ear. He'd hated it at the time. Now he caught the faint smell of yeasty dough and lilacs in her thinning hair, and wished she would hold him a moment longer.

At the funeral, Clayton stood in the cemetery with his sister and brother-in-law, hemmed in by drifts of dirty snow. Mavis swayed for a moment beside the grave, and Clayton wanted to put a hand under her elbow; she seemed frailer out of doors, exposed in the raw air. But he kept back, afraid of imposing.

The minister who gave the eulogy praised Scudder's heroism and spoke of how he'd risked his life to save the lives of strangers. He quoted from the Bible: *Although he had done no violence, and there was no deceit in his mouth* . . . Clayton shifted uncomfortably in his stiff, cold shoes and kept his mind on his grandfather, how he'd stood in the kitchen doorway on that summer night, alive through sheer will. *He poured out his soul to death* . . . Clay pictured him sitting on the porch wreathed in tobacco smoke, frowning over the cribbage board with a look of cunning on his weathered face.

The last time he'd spoken with Scudder on the telephone, at Nancy's insistence, Clayton had been on his way out the door to meet some friends. Impatient, he'd half listened to his grandfather's querulous voice talking about Pearl Harbor while wondering if the girl with the short red hair who liked Tommy Dorsey would dance with him if he got up the nerve to ask. "Armor-piercing bombs," Scudder cried at the other end of the line. "Think of the poor bastards in the hold . . ." What agitated the old man more than anything was the thought of the sailors trapped on the capsized *Oklahoma*.

Back in Boston after the funeral, Clayton took the day off from high school and enlisted in the Navy. He was nearly eighteen years old. He told himself he owed it to his grandfather, though in his heart he'd never planned to stay in Massachusetts. Walking back from the recruiting office, he wondered if he'd be assigned to one of the ships he'd watched being built at the Navy Yard. They'd finished the *Matagorda*, a Barnegat-class seaplane tender, in December.

It was dark when he got back to the apartment, and he paused for a moment before opening the door. His sister lay on the sofa, her belly cradled in her arm. She started guiltily at the sound of the door, then saw it was him. "I'm so tired today," she said, apologetic. "It'll have to be eggs for dinner again." She shifted on the sofa, making room for him.

He remained standing. "I joined the Navy," he told her baldly. "I'm waiting for my boot camp assignment."

He watched her mouth open, as if she'd been hit. Her face was puffy already from the weight she'd put on; he had the strange sense that he was catching a glimpse of her in some unhappy future. Of course, he'd expected her to make a scene, hardening himself to the thought of it as he walked back from the recruiting office, a swagger in his step.

Nancy didn't speak. Clayton watched her eyes fill with tears. He was a block of ice, a stone. He wanted her to suffer. Since she'd made him leave Fire Neck, he'd lived in their apartment like a lodger, out of it as much as he could be, returning to sleep in the little room off the front hall that they would soon need, he knew, though no one had yet said it, for the baby.

He waited for her to catch at his hand and beg him not to go. He wanted to tell her how he had to do his part, that he wasn't a boy anymore, that she couldn't stop him. What did school matter? The country was at war! A reckless certainty filled him that his ship would be torpedoed by German subs. He saw Nancy standing in the doorway with a telegram that announced his death in the line of duty somewhere off the coast of France.

Turning toward the wall, Nancy wiped her face with her sleeve. Clayton swallowed, waiting for her to say something. After a moment, she reached out and ran her fingers over the silver paint on the tall metal radiator against the wall. The paint, thickly applied, was flaking in places. Clayton watched as she pried at a daub with her fingernail, revealing a patch of dark brown beneath it.

"So I won't be here to see your baby," he found himself saying. And then, superstitious because he'd just imagined his own death, he added quickly, "I mean, I'll be at sea."

She looked up from the radiator's peeling paint. Her eyes were wet, her gaze pained but steady. "That was the biggest scare of my life," she said. "The hurricane. I didn't know if you were dead or alive, Clay. Now you want to scare me like that again."

He didn't know how to answer this. It wasn't his fault, he wanted to shout. Frozen in the hallway, his swagger gone, he tried to break free of her eyes. In his mind he could see the kitchen of the house on Salt Hay Road and his aunt's face in the lamplight as she looked up at him.

Nancy moved her hand from the radiator, and for a moment he thought she was reaching toward him. Instead, she rubbed her large belly, her hand moving with an unthinking, abstracted tenderness. "You used to climb into my bed at night and cry, you know." Her voice had softened. "After Mother died. You've probably forgotten that." Clayton looked away from her. She'd always lord it over him, he thought, that she remembered things about his childhood that he couldn't. He felt trapped in the narrow hallway, like a cave of the past, his sister immobile on the sofa. The smell of the soap from the laundry next door oppressed him. "You were so small then," Nancy said. "I remember the feel of your little ribs, like a rabbit's."

Two weeks later he left for boot camp in Newport, Rhode Island. It was raining, and Nancy refused to merely drop him off at the bus station but waited with him for the bus while the rain flattened her hair. When it was his turn to board, she held him too long, sniffling into his shoulder. He felt embarrassed by the lump in his own throat, and by her obvious, pregnant bulk. Suddenly he realized that the other recruits might mistake their relationship, and he disengaged himself more firmly than he meant to, just as she was telling him she loved him. She stepped back, hurt and confusion in her face. "I have to go," he mumbled. Grabbing up his bag, he hurried onto the bus. From his seat on the aisle he could feel her eyes on him. His face burned with something like anger, and he did not turn, although he saw her faintly from the corner of his eye, a pale blur like one of the ghostly apparitions supposedly captured by photography in the pamphlets his aunt and Captain Kelley used to read. Finally, the last recruit took a seat and the bus pulled away, rain streaking the windshield.

After her father's death, Mavis sat every night in the kitchen on Salt Hay Road alone. Across the field, the lights shone in Captain Kelley's old cottage, but she had never gotten over her dislike of Judith Purlowe. Since the hurricane, the house smelled more than ever of the marsh, as if the mud had seeped into the plaster. At night as she lay in bed the walls creaked around her as if threatening to come down.

One morning she walked over to the boatyard and asked Sam Burnett if he could recommend a builder, just to look it over for her. "It sounds silly," she confessed, "but I'm worried it's going to fall in on me."

Sam's gnarled fingers worked on an eel pot as he nodded, his pipe clenched in his teeth. "Nothing's sturdy like it used to be," he muttered. "The whole world's coming down around our ears."

The builder, when he came, walked through the house with a stern, critical eye. Silently, he sighted along the outside walls, heaved himself against the frames of doors, while Mavis followed behind, trying to guess what he was seeing in the mundane contours of each room. "Solid," he announced at the end of half an hour. He slapped the kitchen wall for emphasis. "No need to worry. This one's built to last."

Mavis paid him and the next day put a hand-lettered FOR SALE sign in the front. The house might be safe, but she didn't want to live there anymore.

With the money from the sale and from Mr. Washington's bequest, she bought a one-story cottage inland in Ronkonkoma, away from the Great South Bay and the ocean. Through a friend from church, she found work at a bakery. It was the first job she'd held since Mr. Washington died, and she enjoyed earning her own money again. She knew exactly what needed to be done, and she was good at it. Six mornings a week, she got up in the dark to make pastries and to punch and mold the bread dough into loaves before the owner came in to work the counter.

The bakery stood near the train station, and Mavis sometimes noticed a gaunt signalman pass on his way to work while she was setting the rolls and buns in the window before opening. One morning in February she could see his breath in the cold air, a tiny ghost cloud of vapor. He trudged into the light from the bakery window, and she glimpsed a black bow tie at his neck. Mavis found herself smiling, reminded of Captain Kelley and the kitchen on Salt Hay Road. Outside on the cold street, the signalman stopped, confused by her sudden stillness in the window and her expression. Their eyes met for a moment. The rolls steamed in the basket in Mavis's hand. On impulse she thrust a handful into a brown paper bag.

The signalman in his black jacket had continued on his way. He was walking toward the station, his back to her, his narrow shoulders hunched, when Mavis opened the door. The bitter cold made her breathless. "Wait," she managed to call, "wait!" He turned in surprise, and she held out the paper bag.

His name was Stanley Hoose, and he was a widower with three children. He courted Mavis all winter and all spring, and they were married on the first Sunday in June. Nancy and Robert came down from Boston for the wedding with little Helena, who was teething and wailed loudly at the start of the service, until one of the Hoose children slipped her a whip of black licorice. Mavis, stately in lavender crepe as she walked down the aisle, felt a momentary panic as she realized that this marriage, like her first, was starting during a war. Then the minister addressed them, *Dearly beloved*, and she looked into Stanley's calm blue eyes. When her turn came, she answered with a steady voice.

One night, a few weeks later, Mavis lay awake beside her sleeping husband. The full moon shone in through the bedroom window and made a great bright square on the opposite wall like a door into another world. Outside, a lone bird trilled, hesitated, trilled again. Mavis was afraid that if she got out of bed and went to the kitchen, she might wake her husband, who had to get up early for work. So she lay as still as she could and watched the square of moonlight inch slowly across the wall. Had there been a sign in the caskets she'd seen from the dress shop window before her first marriage? Did God hide messages in the shapes of clouds? The image of Ramsay's turnip-headed baby came back to her, without pain, like a photo in a newspaper story. In the next room her three stepchildren slept; that night at bedtime, the youngest had shyly kissed her. And then she remembered Clayton as a boy, watching reverently as she rolled out pie dough. She felt with a shock how far away he was at that moment, on a ship halfway around the world, and it made her afraid. Mavis murmured a prayer for his safe return.

She tried to keep her eyes open, but her lids were growing heavy. Maybe the signs she'd looked for didn't matter. Maybe no one ever knew for sure, and she could only pray and hope God heard her. She felt her husband stir in his sleep and pull her toward him. The door on the wall slanted into a diamond that wanted to tell her a secret in the language of diamonds. Mavis leaned forward, amazed, because she understood what it was saying, and found herself slipping into a dream. The bird warbled in the tree outside the window, fooled into song by the brilliance of the moon.

In Boston, Nancy woke to the rattle of an early-morning delivery truck passing on the street. Robert's side of the bed was empty, his pillow cold. A cat mewled in the backyard, where the laundry lines hung, but the apartment was quiet. Confused, she slipped out of bed. In the semidarkness of the kitchen, she could make out the counter clean of coffee grounds, the dishes neatly stacked; if Robert had left for work early, he hadn't eaten breakfast first. On her way to Helena's room, she glanced into the front parlor. And there was the still form of her husband, stretched on the gray sofa, with his feet tucked under a pillow and the baby asleep on his chest. Mesmerized, Nancy sank quietly into the armchair and watched them as they slept.

Slowly, the morning light brightened. It shone on Helena's rounded cheeks and her small pink mouth, which moved as she dreamed. Objects emerged from the dimness, and Nancy saw the dust she'd missed on the surface of the oak sideboard, the painted wooden rattle Mavis had sent, on the floor. The light fell on the fine lines around her husband's mouth and on the gray hairs mixed with brown on the patch of chest between his pajama buttons. He seemed, in that moment, heartbreakingly mortal. One of Helena's chubby legs kicked free of the flannel blanket, and Robert opened his eyes.

Nancy leaned forward and kissed him. "Why didn't you wake me?" she whispered.

He smiled sleepily at her. "I tried. You might as well have been hibernating." Stretching, he sat up, gingerly cradling Helena, and Nancy moved next to him on the sofa. She leaned against his sleep-warmed side and looked down at Helena's perfect half-open mouth, the curl of her dark lashes against her cheek. A frown passed across her face, momentarily creasing her blunt, dimpled chin.

"What woke her up?"

"Those Boston roosters," he answered, yawning. "She has her mother's ears."

Clayton's ship was preparing to leave Hawaii when he got Nancy's first letter. *I imagine this will be hard to learn, but Mavis has decided to sell the house.* Reading this on deck, the smell of tar and decay in the tropical air, Clayton felt the shock like a blow to his gut. *She says it's too big for her now,* Nancy's letter went on. *I think, perhaps, it holds too many memories.*

There was only one place on a ship with a crew of over a hundred men where Clayton knew he'd have some privacy. At the door that led to the engine room, he snapped on a pair of headphones and hurtled down the ladder into the stifling heat. The farther south they'd gone, the more unbearable it had become. Now the 6-cylinder Cooper Bessemers throbbed around him, drowning out all other sound. The sweat started on his face. He felt it soak his uniform with a feeling almost of relief. The noise, the staggering heat, the sense that the rivets might pop at any moment from the walls, all of this helped to ease the pain spinning through him like the sparks of a Catherine wheel.

Closing his eyes, he imagined himself back on Salt Hay Road. In his mind, he moved through his grandfather's house room by room, as though he could clutch it to him and hold it through his faithfulness alone. He stayed until the deckhand on watch, coming down to check the engine gauges, jumped, and nearly dropped his clipboard at the sight of him.

Clayton came to love the ship, the USS *Remorseless.* On deck, surrounded by the vast Pacific, he thought how big the Great South Bay had once seemed. It was like comparing Starke's Boatyard with the Boston Navy Yard. Some of his shipmates spoke longingly of home and complained about the endless stretch of ocean, the quarters, the food. Clayton welcomed it all. He felt older day by day, as if the ship were bearing him away from the vestiges of his childhood and his sister's apron strings.

Three Samoans worked as mess cooks on board, big, bronze-skinned men with dark hair. They were held in awe for

their massive arms and their easy familiarity with both the officers and the landscape. They'd joined, Clayton learned later, as
part of the Fita Fita Guard, and it was a mark of their status on
board that no one ever teased them about the grass skirts of
their dress uniform. One morning, as Clayton tied a stiff new
pair of dungarees to a heaving line to soften in the ship's wake,
one of the Samoans approached him, a sleek blue flying fish on
his platelike palm. He reached out with meaty fingers and
gently extended one delicate silver "wing" like a fan before
handing the fish to Clayton almost formally, in silence. Clayton
took it aft to his cabin like contraband and spent his free time
sketching it until his bunkmate complained about the smell. It
was the first thing he'd sketched since the whale on Fire Island
on the day his uncle died.

Anchored in the lagoon of an atoll one afternoon, a couple
of the men succeeded in catching a hammerhead shark, using
heaving lines and homemade hooks. Clayton hurried to watch
it being hauled out of the water on the boat davits. Huge and
gray, its bizarre eyes staring from fleshy stalks, it thrashed a long
time slung over the side while members of the crew took
swipes at it with boat hooks. Finally, the second mate came
down from the bridge and shot it once in the head. The huge
body went still, and after a moment the crowd dispersed, considering the show now finished. Clayton stayed, saddened but
fascinated. Now that it was safely dead, the fishermen winched
it nearer, until it hung close enough to touch on the other side
of the rail. It was well over ten feet long. Blood flowed from the
gunshot in the blunt head and from its mouth, bristling with
teeth. Probably a greater hammerhead, Clayton thought, though
he didn't know for sure. Welch, the boldest of the shark fishermen, lashed his Bowie knife to a pole and hung over the
bulwark. "All kinds of stuff inside a shark," he called over his

shoulder, cutting roughly into the great belly, the way you'd gut a bluefish or a bass. "My buddy on the *Ontario* found a can of yellow paint!" An instant later they were astonished as half a dozen sleek gray forms with misshapen heads plummeted from the jagged opening in the shark's gut. They splashed into the water like a series of small bombs and swam away. Clayton stared after the flicking of their tails. "It's a cannibal!" shouted Welch, who'd nearly dropped his knife overboard in surprise and now tried to cover his confusion. Clayton didn't correct him. The dead one was a female, of course, and the smaller sharks her viviparous young.

Later the Samoans showed them how to cut out the jawbone of the shark and remove the perfect, jagged teeth. There were hundreds of them, and Welch let him keep a handful.

One evening, anchored at Ulithi, Clayton jostled with the rest of the crew on their way to the fantail to watch a movie. They'd joined a convoy of nearly a thousand ships, and the ocean, usually so empty, seemed as crowded as a city street. It struck him, as he stepped out of the hatchway and onto the deck, that around them in either direction every other ship's company would be congregating in the twilight for their movies too. To the west lay a small atoll, studded with palms like a desert island in a cartoon strip. An Essex-class carrier was anchored astern, the USS *Barnaby*. Out of the corner of his eye, Clayton caught a blur of movement. In the next instant the *Barnaby*'s flight deck exploded. A black cloud burst over it. General quarters sounded on the *Remorseless*, and Clayton began running forward toward his station in the engine room. Above him lunged a Japanese plane, so low he could see lines of rivets on its aluminum belly. He followed it with his eyes, powerless, the way he'd felt in his dreams of falling houses. The plane passed low above them, dove directly into the island, and exploded in a ball of fire.

Later, the general speculation was that the Japanese pilot had mistaken the atoll for another carrier. Darkness came fast on the Pacific. It would have been hard to see anything clearly at twilight and they would have been flying low for a long time to make it that far undetected, with so many ships at anchor. Clayton wondered. Part of him wanted to believe the pilot had passed over their ship deliberately. A weakness on his part, he knew, and thought of his grandfather and the nest of swallows on the mast.

He did not write to Nancy often. He felt a resentment toward her that he couldn't put into words and remembered the stilted weekly letters he'd been made to compose at the kitchen table under his aunt's stern eye after his sister first left Fire Neck for Boston. But when mail arrived onboard, he hoped for her letters in spite of himself. In one, Nancy told him the war had already changed things at the museum. Instead of expanding the collection, Robert was now assisting on a huge book called *A Check-list of Birds of the World*. In another, that Clayton was now uncle to a little girl named Helena, after their mother, the loveliest and most stubborn baby in the world. *She has her father wrapped around her tiny finger. When she cries, her chin wrinkles, and she reminds me of you.*

Mavis sent a short, dutiful note to tell him she was remarrying. Reading it, Clayton felt an echo of the pain the loss of the house had caused him. He would be missed at the small ceremony in Ronkonkoma, the letter said. Later, Nancy wrote to describe the wedding, and added that while they were on Long Island they'd stopped in at Fire Neck. The grounds at Washington Lodge were being used for Victory Gardens. Clayton imagined lines of staked tomatoes and peas where the manicured lawn had been, and beyond them the copper beeches where the cockatoos used to perch on sunny days. To please her, Nancy continued, Robert had driven down Salt Hay Road. She knocked at the old house, but no one had answered the door. The greenhouses were all gone, of course, along with the old wisteria trellis and the climbing roses. The house had been painted yellow, and the windows were different, the panes larger and without mullions. *It was like seeing a stranger's eyes looking out at you from a familiar face.* Reading this, Clayton had a sudden, vivid memory of his uncle on the ladder set against the house, pulling a slab of dripping honeycomb from between the walls like a magician. He stuffed the letter on the bottom of his seabag and did not read it again.

A few nights later, he dreamed he was on his way to the mess room when he noticed a small hatchway he'd never seen before. Behind it, a set of worn stairs led to the kitchen of his grandfather's house, and when he sat down, no longer in his uniform but in a pair of flannel pajamas, he heard his aunt's soft, uneven singing: *Everybody has a sweetheart underneath the rose, Everybody loves a body, so the old song goes . . .*

He woke on the fantail, the ship at anchor. Above him hung the bright southern stars for which he'd invented his own constellations: the Nine of Hearts, the Queen of Spades. A cool breeze blew off the water. He could hear the soft splash of something swimming nearby, the slap of waves against the hull. His dream of the house came back to him, and he felt the habitual paralysis of his guilt, and how it had followed him doggedly, mile after oceanic mile. He had never spoken to Mavis about Roy, or the night he'd returned home to Salt Hay Road through the aftermath of the hurricane. And he never blamed her for wanting to wash her hands of him. Standing in the kitchen that night, he'd felt their makeshift family pull apart like a house in a storm, like an island made of sand.

It was only after something broke into its individual parts that you saw how miraculous the whole had been, how fragile. He should have known this from all the sketches he'd made of dead things that had once been living.

On the train Clayton heaves his seabag onto the luggage rack above him. The war is over. Already he has traveled halfway across the Pacific. Now he's on the *Empire Builder* from Portland, through Spokane and Minneapolis, all the way to Chicago. And from there to Boston, on the far side of the continent.

Turning toward the sunny window, he takes out the much-crumpled paper and reads it again, holding it close, so that no one in the surrounding seats can see it. It's a citation from the Commander of Amphibious Forces, United States Pacific Fleet: "For excellent service in the line of his duty . . ." He knows it by heart but needs to see it written on the official letterhead to fully believe it. "Through outstanding effort and determination, displayed in the face of extremely hazardous conditions . . ." The destroyer ablaze, the smell of hot metal and melting rubber, the heat rippling as he ran toward it, tripping over the hoses. "By his utter disregard for personal safety, his coolness and promptness in action, he was an inspiration to all." Behind him, someone coughs. He folds the letter quickly and tucks it away.

Two days earlier, he'd been on deck as they neared the mouth of the Columbia River, an hour or so before dawn. The wind off the coast carried the smell of damp earth and greenery. Even in the dark, he felt the land pressing in on the ship from either side as they left the open water and moved upriver. Blurred and glittering, the lights of houses on the shoreline stirred his memory: a ferry, and his sister at the railing. After his years in the Pacific, surrounded by the ocean's tang and brine, the night air seemed thick with half-forgotten scents. As they passed Astoria, there was a rank oily smell from the salmon cannery. Later, the scent of sawdust and pine as they drew close to the dark shore to avoid a tug and log boom.

And then, astonishingly, he caught the brackish rot of marshland. He'd closed his eyes, breathing it in. Something moved in his chest then, like a fish flicking back into water.

Out the window of the train, a beaming man on a sunlit billboard lathers his pink face with Lifebuoy shaving cream. With sickening clarity, Clayton remembers the Japanese sailor with his chin sheared off, eyes widened in surprise, on the enemy freighter they'd cleared from Apra Harbor, how wading through the half-charred bodies floating in the rank, blood-warm water he'd felt compelled to roll them over, one by one, searching for a face he knew he wouldn't find. Across the wide Pacific, Clayton has pulled men from burning ships, from sinking ships and ships aground on coral reefs, and it was never his uncle he pulled out of the waves. If he lives for all eternity, he knows it will never be Roy.

He thinks of the USS *Barnaby* exploding before his eyes in a billowing black cloud, the screams of her sailors as they tried to swim through water slick with burning oil. He risked his life to save them, to salvage what he could. It is not his fault that he survived when so many didn't. It is not his fault. The shame he has carried halfway around the world weighs on him, a small but infinitely heavy burden he longs to set down.

He imagines the railroad track already behind him, cutting across the country like the wake of a ship, and fingers the letter again.

The landscape is in shadow now, and lights glow in the houses they fly past. Clayton thinks of the man in the red knit hat who used to skate the Lord's Prayer on the frozen surface of the Great South Bay. The skater must have liked the challenge of it, having competed, Roy told him, in Canada and Europe. Or perhaps, thinks Clayton, it was a private form of worship, etching the words with the stylus of the skate blades while the shadows lengthened and the cold air rose off the ice where the scooters had raced all afternoon. A wistful, ironic prayer, as if anyone watching from on high could read the looped cursive letters in the fading light.

The train pulls out of the darkness into a station. Beneath a lamppost, a woman stands alone, smoking a cigarette. Living on a ship, surrounded by other sailors, Clayton finds women as foreign as dry land, civilian clothes, peace itself. Around him, passengers bustle toward the doors, hauling luggage and parcels. Outside, the woman takes a last drag and flicks the glowing butt of her cigarette away. It arcs into the darkness like a shooting star. Clayton follows it with his eyes as it hits the platform floor and skitters away, throwing off its tiny sparks of light.

The train moves on, carrying him toward what is left of his

family: his sister, his niece, his aunt. He is a war hero, he reminds himself, with a handful of shark's teeth in his pocket. But he feels afraid. Coming ashore has shaken him, like a bottle in which some sediment has rested undisturbed at the bottom by means of a studied immobility.

A longing, a homesickness, grips him like a cramp, and he remembers waking in the spring in the house on Salt Hay Road to the call of the bobwhite quail. He feels, like the phantom pain of an amputated limb, the loss of the house. The train lurches, picking up speed. He is moving toward the Atlantic now, away from Leyte Gulf, from Mindanao, Tawara, Ulithi. He thinks of his little niece, safe in Boston in the room that had been his. Someday, when she's older, he can take her to Fire Neck. He is beginning to doze. He will show her the swallows along the Barto River in September. His eyes are closing, and now he sees the sky along the riverbank, thick with the migrating birds that have congregated every year in enormous flocks since before there was an America, a Germany, a Japan. The birds dart and weave over the darkening marsh. Swirling, they mass into something fluid and distinct, like a transparent bead of mercury, like smoke. The cloud rises and falls in twisting paisley shapes, the movement hypnotic, like the licking flames of a campfire on the beach. Then a rip appears in the belly of the cloud and the swallows begin to tumble through the hole, slowly at first, and then faster and faster, pouring like sand through a clear funnel. The cloud empties like a balloon losing air. The last birds vanish for the night to their roosts in the cattails and the high-tide bush, and the dark sky is a blackboard, wiped clean.

All this time, he thinks, he has held it against Nancy that she took him away from Fire Neck. It was easier to blame her for his misery than himself. He should have told her the day he left that he loved her. His eyes open on a dark window, where, for an instant, a boy in a sailor suit stares back at him. Something rattles in his chest. He is twenty-one years old, but he understands what it is. His heart, in its cage of bones.

He imagines knocking on the green door of the narrow apartment in Boston, his sister's eyes widening in relief and surprise. "I missed you," he'll say, lifting her off her feet. "I want to meet my niece."

The compartment has grown stuffy, overheated. Outside, he sees nothing but scattered lights. The rhythmic movement lulls him. Eyes heavy, he feels himself drifting like a small boat in a current. He's going to see his sister, he reminds himself, he will finally tell her he is sorry. For a moment he can't remember why. And then it comes back to him how he went out to the beach that morning when he should have been at school. He shouldn't have gone. But his sister loves him, he remembers now. She will forgive him. His hands are tightening on the smooth wooden handle of the crab net as it rises above the water, and drops scatter, painfully bright. A flock of gulls wheels in the air. He is on a ferry, leaving the dock behind, leaving a white blur that swings back and forth like a handkerchief waved in a wide arc. He is riding in a dark car down a potholed lane, a boy pressed half asleep against his sister's shoulder as they travel together down a bumpy road toward a room that smells of bread dough and potato peelings.

Acknowledgments

I am deeply grateful to the following for their help with this book: Sarah Burnes, Jennifer and Peter Clement, Gary Clevidence, the Fine Arts Work Center in Provincetown, Peg Hart, Courtney Hodell, John Kuegel, Jhumpa Lahiri, Celia Pastoriza, the late Dennis and Betty Puleston, the Rona Jaffe Foundation, Tom and Kathleen Scheibel, the late Bob Starke Senior, and Jill Shulman. Thank you also to John Starke for the ducks, and to Jay Watson for the wren.

Of the many books I consulted in my research, I am particularly indebted to *Bellport and Brookhaven: A Saga of the Sibling Hamlets at Old Purchase South*, compiled by Stephanie S. Bigelow for the Bellport-Brookhaven Historical Society; *A Wind to Shake the World: The Story of the 1938 Hurricane*, by Everett S. Allen; *Wrecks and Rescues on Long Island*, by Van R. Field; *Shipwrecks in New York Waters: A Chronology of Ship Disasters from Montauk Point to Barnegat Inlet, from the 1880's to the 1930's*, by Paul C. Morris and William P. Quinn; and *The Boston Cooking-School Cook Book*, by Fannie Merritt Farmer.

ACCLAIM FOR AMAZON JOURNAL:

"Analyzes the variables of greed, racism, hunger, sentimentality, adventure, idealism, violence, and corruption that confuse how the Amazon is perceived."
—*New York Times Book Review*

"A wrenching inside account of the social and environmental chaos wrought by modern civilization."
—*Details*

"A superb memoir . . . [told] with great critical penetration and sometimes biting humor. Compelling. A heartfelt and acute book."
—*Providence Sunday Journal*

"A comprehensive and candid view of Brazil's well-hyped but quickly forgotten attempt to save its forests and Indians. O'Connor provides a unique insider's perspective."
—*High Times*

"Reveals the true complexities of the region's environmental crisis."
—*Condé Nast Traveler*

"A sad and revealing tale of one of the most tragic and complex stories of our time."
—Mark J. Plotkin, Ph.D., author of *Tales of a Shaman's Apprentice*

"Engrossing . . . a riveting description of a cross-section of all varieties of interlopers and natives in the Amazon."
—*Publishers Weekly*

"O'Connor's portraits of Indians, settlers, government officials, and environmental activists alike are right on the mark. A literate, unexpectedly funny, and ultimately alarming book."
—*Kirkus Reviews*

GEOFFREY O'CONNOR is a documentary filmmaker whose 1993 film *At the Edge of Conquest* was nominated for an Academy Award. His recent film, *Amazaon Journal,* is a companion to this book. O'Connor has also produced segments of Michael Moore's Emmy award–winning *TV Nation*. *Amazon Journal* is his first book.

BRAZILIAN AMAZON

AMAZON JOURNAL

Dispatches from a Vanishing Frontier

Geoffrey O'Connor

A PLUME BOOK

PLUME
Published by the Penguin Group
Penguin Putnam Inc., 375 Hudson Street, New York, New York 10014, U.S.A.
Penguin Books Ltd, 27 Wrights Lane, London W8 5TZ, England
Penguin Books Australia Ltd, Ringwood, Victoria, Australia
Penguin Books Canada Ltd, 10 Alcorn Avenue, Toronto, Ontario, Canada M4V 3B2
Penguin Books (N.Z.) Ltd, 182–190 Wairau Road, Auckland 10, New Zealand

Penguin Books Ltd, Registered Offices:
Harmondsworth, Middlesex, England

Plublished by Plume, an imprint of Dutton NAL,
a member of Penguin Putnam Inc.
Previously published in a Dutton edition

First Plume Printing, September, 1998
10 9 8 7 6 5 4 3 2

 REGISTERED TRADEMARK — MARCA REGISTRADA

The Library of Congress catalogued the Dutton edition as follows:
O'Connor, Geoffrey.
    Amazon journal : dispatches from a vanishing frontier / Geoffrey O'Connor.
        p.   cm.
    Includes index.
    ISBN 0-525-94113-4 (hc.)
        0-452-27610-1 (pbk.)
    1. Environmental degradation—Amazon River Region.
2. Environmental degradation—Brazil.
GE160.A685026   1997
333.75'137'09811—dc21   97-23611
                                                                      CIP

Original hardcover design by Eve L. Kirch
Printed in the United States of America

BOOKS ARE AVAILABLE AT QUANTITY DISCOUNTS WHEN USED TO PROMOTE PRODUCTS OR
SERVICES. FOR INFORMATION PLEASE WRITE TO PREMUIM MARKETING DIVISION, PENGUIN
PUTNAM, INC., 375 HUDSON STREET, NEW YORK, NY 10014

*For my mother and late father
for their love and their courage,
and for the people of Amazonia
who trusted me with their stories.*

A question is like a knife that slices through
the stage backdrop and gives us a look at what
lies hidden behind it.
—Milan Kundera

fron•tier (frun-**teer**). 1. the land border of a
country. 2. the edge of settled territory, facing
the wilderness. 3. the limit of what is known
in a subject.
—*Oxford American Dictionary*

1

"*Aqui*," says the miner Sebastião, motioning with his hand to the jungle off to our left. He is directing us towards a small opening in the trees just a few yards from the airstrip. We descend into dense tropical forest, a chopper passes overhead, the dirt path becomes narrow and slippery, still wet from last night's rain. I look to my right, where I see a wall of vines twisting around trees the size of high-rise buildings. They stretch upward into the sky, their leaves creating a lush green ceiling made translucent by the bright sunlight. As we follow the path, it veers sharply to the left. Then twenty yards in front of us there is a clearing where I can see a maloca, a massive thatched hut, conical, open at the center to release smoke. The communal house of the Yanomami Indians, it can hold up to one hundred people—families living together in a circle, husbands and wives and children sleeping in hammocks, each nuclear unit with its own fireplace but sharing the game brought in from the day's hunt, the fish caught in a local stream, the fruit and vegetables gathered from a nearby garden.

As we walk towards the maloca a young Yanomami man stumbles from the dark interior and vomits just outside the entrance. Upon seeing us approach, a younger Indian woman, terrified, runs off around the side of the communal house and disappears.

More helicopters are now passing above us, swirling dust

that sweeps through our clothes and hair. I am walking directly behind the mining entrepreneur Sebastião, carrying my video camera, which I'm beginning to think is probably indistinguishable from a gun as far as most of the Yanomami Indians are concerned. And guns are a problem here, or so some human rights activists have been saying. Rumors of conflicts between Indians and miners have been getting back to the cities: four dead and mutilated Indian bodies left here on this jungle airstrip just a year ago, two miners murdered in a retaliatory attack, another six Indians shot and killed at Homosxhi village. And diseases, that's the other rumor, contagious epidemics passing from village to village, brought in by the miners and left to take their fatal toll on the native population. If the rumors are true, then another nightmare page has been written in the history of Indian societies in the Americas, isolated indigenous populations succumbing to disease and armed conflict resulting from the rapid expansion of a lawless frontier. Gold, again, is the catalyst turning this world upside down: nature overwhelmed by technology, faces and bodies contorted by panic and culture shock, rules and logic thrown to the wayside. This is the Amazon's frontier in 1989.

Amidst all this *confusão*, as the Brazilians call it, Sebastião is trying to maintain the pretense of a formal press junket. As the right-hand man of a powerful gold miner, his job is to watch over us during our stay in the forest. This whole trip is part of an elaborate scheme concocted by his boss, José Altino Machado, to convince Brazil and, in my case, the international press that the illegal presence of forty-five thousand miners in Yanomami territory can be justified—that the Yanomami "like" the miners and want them to stay. And Sebastião is determined to prove it even if these initial reactions of the Yanomami provide evidence to the contrary. He is, he says, going to introduce us to some Yanomami who will support what the miners have been saying all along: that their presence is improving the Indians' lives.

Sebastião is a hawk-eyed man in his mid-thirties with a pencil-thin mustache and coiffed brown hair. Even in the forest he continues to wear his city attire: shiny brown patent leather shoes, gray synthetic pants, a matching shirt in pale gray and brown paisley. These clothes cling to his body like a disco outfit from the 1970s. There is something comic about him, but sinister as well. Walking up the landing strip en route to this village, he told my Brazilian soundman, Mario "the Wolf" Salgado, that he would kill a Brazilian TV crew accompanying us if they made a "bad" report about the situation here. This crew was flown in on a separate plane to do a documentary for Rede Manchete, Brazil's second largest television network. Mario is now relating the story, whispering to me in English, as we walk along the side of the maloca. *Would he really kill them?* I think. *Would he kill me? He's got to be joking.* But as I look at Mario I can tell he is concerned. That severe crease in his forehead is now reappearing, a dead giveaway that the Wolf is worried. We have both heard the stories about the criminal elements that make up the miners' population. Perhaps my cultural distance allows me to take it a little more lightly. Perhaps this is one of the pluses of what I call the "gringo factor"—the naivete that got me here in the first place.

We continue walking around the maloca, the young Yanomami man still throwing up in the vegetation adjacent to the communal house. I go through my checklist of the diseases most commonly contracted by isolated indigenous populations. Measles, malaria, smallpox, influenza. Which ones have vomiting as a symptom? Then too, I have heard that the rivers are polluted by mercury used in mining. The miners aren't drinking the water but has anyone told the Indians? Or perhaps it's the alcohol. Some Catholic missionaries are claiming that several Yanomami have died from overdoses of *cachaça*, a sugarcane drink, given to them by the miners in exchange for food and, in some cases, Indian women.

Sebastião is now looking anxious. We've been stopped at the entrance to the maloca by João Davi, a young Yanomami man who looks to be in his twenties, wearing shorts and a T-shirt with an image of Charlie Chaplin on the front. Clothing is often the most obvious sign of contact with our world. The shorts traditionally used to come from the missionaries, but the practice has been appropriated by the miners. They are offered as part of what the Brazilian Indian agency, FUNAI,* calls the "attraction" process: a way of gaining favor with the Indians, getting them to come out of the forest and into contact with "white" society. (This can take bizarre forms. As we stand outside the entrance to the maloca, two Yanomami women, bare chested and with long thin pieces of wood extending from their chins, approach wearing men's underwear on backwards. As they pass by us, they quicken their pace, ushering their children into the dark entrance of the communal house.) These "gifts" of clothing are just one part of what anthropologists call the "middle ground," the relationship of reciprocity that is established between our world and theirs. The attraction is often initiated through gifts, but eventually—once there is a period of sustained contact—this relationship becomes based on exchange or barter as we attempt to integrate them into the ways of our world. And that is when things can get complicated, where misunderstandings can take place. If there is a breach of trust and honesty, the middle ground can quickly degenerate into a tangled relationship clouded in deceit and deception. Violence very often becomes the final arbitrator. A lack of shared cultural cues and of a thorough understanding of each other's languages diminishes the potential for negotiation. That's the scary part. It's what makes the middle ground a precarious environment, a sociological terrain where human behavior is often seen in its rawest form, a place where anything can happen.

The Yanomami man standing before us and confronting Sebastião, this João Davi, is one of his society's middlemen, an ad hoc cultural diplomat called on by local leaders to negotiate their people's relationship with the invading army of gold miners. He was not randomly selected but chosen because he has certain skills that facilitate his encounters with Brazilian society. He knows how to wear the white man's clothes. He

---

*FUNAI is the acronym for the Fundacão National do Indio. This government agency provides medical and educational services to the Indians and oversees their relations with the national society.

also speaks broken Portuguese. His hair is styled more like the miners' than the traditional Yanomami bowl cut depicted in various anthropology texts. And he is not afraid to take on Sebastião.

"No one can enter with cameras," he says.

But this is part of Sebastião's tour and he doesn't want "his" journalists to miss it. We were brought here to see that the Yanomami still lead their traditional life. And that they are happy that the gold miners are here. And, as he and other miners have said on numerous occasions, that it is the Indians who invited the miners into the area.

At Sebastião's suggestion I hand my camera to Mario and enter the maloca with the woman reporter from TV Manchete. It is pitch black. One hole in the center of this vast cone-shaped structure supplies the light, a beam of sun that cuts directly through the darkness to illuminate a spot approximately three feet in diameter. A little dust adds texture to the beam, which falls on a square but indistinguishable object about twenty yards away. Various people are now screaming in the Yanomami language from the far reaches of this large circular room. Yanoman, as it is called, is a language I don't understand and one that perhaps only a dozen people outside their culture speak. I pass a man in a hammock, emaciated and coughing, his eyes watery and lifeless. I start to run another mental check—malaria, influenza—but my mind is fixated on this object under the light.

Sebastião lingers at the entrance, trying to convince João Davi that he should speak in front of the cameras. Looking back, I see their silhouettes in the doorway gesticulating passionately, probably working out the parameters of their troubled middle ground.

Now I am getting closer to this object in the center of the room. Crossing the dirt floor, I concentrate on trying to make my presence unthreatening, thinking that I can somehow distinguish myself from the gold miners. *Will they understand the word* jornalista? *Where do I go from there? How do smiles translate in their culture?* A small naked child, wobbly legged and disoriented, appears before me. Here, I tell myself, is an opportunity for a "baby friendly moment," a chance to ingratiate myself with the locals, a ploy borrowed from politicians but one I've used extensively in my documentary work with different cultures across the planet. The basic message: *I like children too. Trust me. I'm human.* I smile at the child and extend my hand but he is quickly snatched away by a young mother who disappears into the cool darkness to join dozens of others who have sought solace from the scorching heat of the equator's midday sun.

The village chatter level reaches a loud, intolerable pitch. Now I have done it, I've probably reconfirmed what these Indians have always thought: that the white man is a babysnatching monster sent down by evil spirits in giant birdlike helicopters to wreak havoc on their population. If someone were to suddenly plant an ax in the back of my head, I wouldn't be surprised. "Not a very smart move," I mumble to myself as I proceed through the darkness. Then, just five feet in front of me is the object that has drawn me into the depths of their communal house.

It is a gas stove—the type you would have in a small economy-size apartment—with torn metal hoses protruding from the back, somehow left abandoned in this fantastic structure, a strange anomaly in this traditional village. Was it traded for a piece of land? Or perhaps given by the gold miners as a joke? None of what has happened today seems to make any sense, each event just another absurd piece of what is quickly becoming an indecipherable puzzle.

"*Oi, Jefferson!*" Sebastião screams from across the room, inciting more clamor from the surrounding Indians. "*Volta.*" Come on back, he is saying, standing at the entrance and waving his arm in a gesture intended to lure me from the darkness.

Jefferson is the name I have come to use in the Amazon—a suggestion of the Wolf, who usually does the introductions. Geoff or Geoffrey doesn't translate well in Portuguese but Jefferson is a gringo name familiar to Brazilians. It seems that there were quite a few Confederate Jeffersons who opted to travel to Brazil rather than accept rule by the Yankees after the Civil War. They carved out their niche in the south of the country. There's even a town in the state of São Paulo called Americana where they settled.

Gringos were more readily accepted back then. We weren't considered a serious threat. It was only later that the U.S. Congress debated occupying the Amazon as part of their effort to promote the Monroe Doctrine. The Portuguese monarchy still dominated the Amazon Basin in the nineteenth century. That was before the United States became a global power, before gunboat diplomacy brought American troops to Nicaragua, Panama, and the Dominican Republic, before clandestine quasi-government operations helped to undermine governments in Guatamala and Chile and, some say, Brazil. Now attitudes have changed. Gringos buying property anywhere in Brazil are looked on with suspicion. Gringos with an interest in the Amazon come under even closer scrutiny. Anyone could be a CIA agent or a representative of American multinationals. The disinformation campaigns are effective. One's reputation is fragile. Since I did my first documentary here in 1987 I have worked hard to keep a low profile: I'm always accompanied by a Brazilian soundman and never open my mouth unless it's absolutely necessary. But inevitably the gringo stands out and can easily get caught in the complex North-South dynamic that has been building between Brazil and the United States for the past two centuries, one that is tainted not just by superpower politics but also by the economic inequities and cultural confusions existing between our two countries. American banks currently hold the Brazilian economy hostage to a longstanding debt while our television culture for years has been exported into their living rooms. Generations of young Brazilians have been raised watching dubbed versions of American television fantasies like *Bewitched* and *I Dream of Jeannie*. American music, magazines, and products increasingly dominate the life of youth in Brazil, creating an uneasy balance with their own vibrant tropical culture.

And now the Brazilians are being told by the world that the Amazon must be protected because it is a critical component of the earth's environment. More conspiracy rhetoric, say the miners. Just another way for foreigners to take control of our country.

journal entry
Paapiú Airstrip
2/23/89

Here are some facts from initial conversations I've had with the miners. Cokes cost five dollars apiece and many of the men are buying them with gold dust. Planes are flying constantly with estimates at two hundred and fifty landings and takeoffs per day.

Over lunch a group of angry pilots confronted the Wolf and me with a copy of Time Magazine. They wanted to know why Americans were getting involved in the affairs of their country. I explained I was here to listen to both sides, that I wasn't Time Magazine. The Wolf—once again the lifesaver—diluted the tension with some jokes.

It must be 105 degrees in the sun. I'm just hoping my camera holds up in this insane tropical heat.

As I step back into the light of day it becomes clear that the interview has been denied. Sebastião has failed in his first task as a part-time press agent. The problem is, as Mario explains to me, that none of the Yanomami will talk to him. Not a soul. But he is prepared. He has brought Marcelo from the city, an orphaned Yanomami boy of eighteen years who traveled with us in the back of the cargo plane. He's someone who spent his first year in a Yanomami village before being whisked away to the Brazilian capital by an Indian Agency employee. Just before we flew in to the jungle, a woman with a pair of sixties bee-eyed sunglasses and bleached blond hair—possibly the wife of a miner—stood on the airstrip in Boa Vista instructing Marcelo on how he has to tell Brazilian people the "truth" about the Yanomami situation. That "the Indians like the miners." This is a phrase I have already heard a half dozen times in the last twenty-four hours: *Os indios adoram os garimpeiros*. This was not a conversation but a lecture, each word a further assertion of the power that this white woman felt she could exert over an Indian. Whether it is true or not that "the Indians adore the miners," it is becoming part of the focus of my story and the hurdle I will have to overcome if I want to accurately document this collision of cultures.

How the miners found Marcelo I do not know. What I do know is that they give him free rides into the jungle and that he is one of a number of Indians that they are grooming as part of their campaign. He is someone who could serve as a spokesperson to the outside world, who can speak Portuguese but understands very little Yanoman. He could tell the media what the gold miners want the Indians to say. Someone they could manipulate. Someone they could control. A token Indian. An invaluable instrument in their campaign to stay in the forest and tap one of the world's last unexplored regions of mineral wealth.

Sebastião grabs Marcelo by the shoulder and sits him in front of the maloca, telling him to speak to the press, which in this case is the crew from TV Manchete. The director from Manchete, like myself, has been promised exclusive access to gold mining sites by the mining leaders. We are the first television cameras to be allowed into Yanomami territory since the gold rush began two and half years ago. Their camera starts rolling. Mine doesn't. I've tried to be a diplomat, but I refuse to be manipulated by the miners. I sit watching this clumsy photo opportunity unfold—the way the miners have orchestrated the event for the cameras and the way the Manchete crew is complying with Sebastião. Are they being diplomatic? Is this the story they are going to tell? Is this the story I came here to document?

The director tells the cameraman to pan down from the top of the maloca to Marcelo. Connection: traditional house, Indian face. If you had seen this whole thing set up you'd know the pieces don't fit but, properly executed, the puzzle comes together. The journalists have their story ("Yes," Marcelo tells them, "it would be good if the Indians could work with the miners") and the gold miner has controlled the situation.

Mythmaking in action. Reality relegated to another dimension, an obstacle that need not interfere with meeting the deadline of a breaking news story.

Happy with his work, Sebastião retreats several yards away to a small makeshift hut. I sit crouched with Mario behind the Machete crew wondering if I should waste tape and precious battery power on this ridiculous scene. Instead I wander over to the hut, where our press agent is in the middle of an argument with his local Indian contact João Davi. They are having a heated discussion about landing rights, something the miners have told me about in the city—one of the ways they say they are helping the Indians, introducing them to the white man's economy, providing them with a little surplus cash, getting them used to the "civilized" way of doing things.

The shack is tiny and the light inadequate. But I have found what I came here to cover: interaction. The meeting of two worlds, the coming together of these wildcat miners and the Indians, the establishment of a middle ground. This is an encounter that has been played out throughout this part of the world since the Portuguese explorer Pedro Cabral first stepped on the shores of Brazil's eastern coast in the year 1500 and convinced the coastal Indians to cut down brazilwood trees for export back to Portugal.

I hit two small switches and the camera is up, the little gray screen of my eyepiece quickly snapping into focus. I am behind Sebastião, who sits with his back to me. The Wolf steps into the shack and positions his shotgun microphone dangerously close to the ceiling, which is a tangled mesh of branches and large leaves now faded brown by the equatorial sun. Seated opposite Sebastião on a plank is João Davi. He is agitated, bouncing nervously on the flimsy board. I'm having difficulty getting a frame because the camera keeps knocking against the roof. But I am rolling. My grasp of Portuguese is limited but I am able to understand the general drift of the argument.

"After, after, they always say they will pay after," says João Davi. "When the planes land here in Paapiú, they have to pay. The planes land, they pay. But all they are doing is talking and lying to the Indians."

Sebastião is now aware that we have entered the shack and looks over his shoulder. I play the stupid gringo and keep rolling, trying to ignore the unnerving sensation caused by his penetrating glance. Sebastião turns back to João Davi. Reverting to the role of press agent, he makes another attempt at asserting his position, hoping to establish once and for all that the miners have been welcomed here as if they were heroes from a liberating army, saviors who come in the name of progress and civilization.

"It is good, no? You want the gold miners to continue to work here," he says.

"Let's just take care of this situation first, okay?" responds João Davi.

"Okay, okay," says Sebastião.

João Davi stares at Sebastião angrily, tired of being manipulated, tired of being "talked at" rather than conversed with. The conversation falls into a momentary lull. Sebastião sits slump-shouldered, probably contemplating his next move. This is undoubtedly not the type of scene he had in mind when he brought these TV crews into the forest. He needs to change tacks and make one last attempt at burnishing the image of the gold miners.

"If our chief was here," says João Davi, "I could ask him what he thinks. But I am alone here, what can I do?"

"You don't have the authority to speak?"

"No, I don't. Our chief is in Boa Vista being treated for a sickness."

"Is he sick? What does he have?"

"He has malaria."

"When you lived here *by yourselves*, you used to get malaria, didn't you?"

Here it is, the moment of truth, the critical point in the debate being waged in the cities: whether the presence of the gold prospectors has had an impact on the health of the Yanomami. Small bouts of violence can be explained away as an inevitable consequence of frontier expansion. But proof that a malaria epidemic is under way—one introduced by the miners—would have terrible consequences for their efforts to whitewash this gold rush.

"No, we *never* had malaria before," says João Davi.

Sebastião turns and stares back at me with a vicious look, an evil eye meant to intimidate. It does. I turn off the camera and the scene dissolves. João Davi disappears through an opening in the back of the hut, leaving Sebastião staring at his shiny shoes and bouncing alone on the plank of wood. No one moves. Not a word is spoken. There is just the piercing squeak of the wobbling wood. Sebastião has made a fool of himself and I have found a critical hook for my story. Faits accomplis. I'm not about to erase the tape. That part I don't think needs explaining.

"*Então?*" I say with a gringo smile: "So what now?"

Sebastião stands, glances at Mario, and walks past us. I look at Mario, who looks right back, his head shaking, his eyes still and tense. This is the first time I have seen the Wolf at a loss for words. I walk outside and he follows. As we head back towards the airstrip, Sebastião, no longer sulking, ignores us. He spends his time joking with the crew from TV Manchete. The message is obvious: we have not played by the rules of the game, therefore he is going to make us pay for it.

Mario walks head down, chin to his chest, kicking the dirt. At times like this I feel sorry for the Wolf, a born fatalist who somehow manages to muster the motivation to go on these trips with me. I wonder if he knew what he was getting into. I did try to explain the nature of this story, but then again I didn't really know what to expect. He's probably asking himself why he let this stupid gringo talk him into coming out to this corner of the Amazon's frontier. He's also probably calculating the extra days he'll now be away from his girlfriend in Rio. But I have been with him in these kinds of situations before. I know he'll come out with it.

"We now have *confusão*," says the Wolf as we walk alone.

"Confusion?" I ask.

"Yes. Mixed up. You call it a meese."

"You mean a mess."

"Yes, that is what I said."

"You think we will also have trouble."

"Yes. Trouble also."

"Will Sebastião kill us?"

"No. He will kill *you*," he says. "You are the gringo."

The Wolf spits on the ground and takes a drink from one of our water bottles. He shoots me a blank stare, then lets forth a lunatic chuckle. I get the joke and begin to lose it myself, my body suddenly convulsed with belly laughs. I laugh so hard that it hurts, but there is also a sense of relief that comes with the laughter. Humor is a great facilitator in places like this, different from naivete but equally effective. It smooths the rough edges of tense and tricky situations. It allows you to forget for a moment the obstacles being faced. It gives you time to consider the next step in your plan. I just wish I had a plan.

2

I've always been a bit of a wanderer, but this trip into the Brazilian Amazon looks to be pushing things to the edge: two degrees from the equator, a malaria epidemic possibly under way, precarious air travel, a story no television news agency seems interested in running, and a population of gold miners whose criminal past is common knowledge to everyone including the local branch of the federal police. It is late February of 1989. I think the date is the twenty-third. I am beginning to loose track. We were held up in Boa Vista for several days before we got permission to fly in here. I arrived just this morning hoping to make a documentary on what is happening to the Yanomami Indians, the largest unacculturated indigenous society in this hemisphere. This was a gamble but one that I had convinced myself was worth taking. I read the appropriate books, consulted other journalists and anthropologists, persuaded the gold miners to take me in, then bought my plane tickets. But now the whole scheme seems to have backfired, so I can add self-deception to that list of great facilitators that got me into this mess in the first place.

In truth I am beginning to think that my decision to document this gold rush is just another stage in the mind game I've been playing most of my life: put myself out on the limb, use impulse rather than logic as the compass by which to chart my course, then let the story unfold. In years past this let-it-happen-as-it-may philosophy cloaked itself in various guises. When I was nineteen it took the form of the Rastafarian credo Positive Vibrations which I picked up as a college dropout living with dreadlocked hill dwellers in Jamaica's Blue Mountains just outside Port Antonio. A few years later in Europe I was swept up by Sartre's "self-surpassing" existentialism as the justifying philosophical wellspring for reckless romances, bar brawls, and many a lonely roadside hour spent trying to put together the unresolved chapters of my young life. Traveling through a dozen countries over a two-year period I tried to escape the soft confines of my middle-class upbringing, hoping that the experience of the tougher side of life would bring spiritual salvation. To drop headfirst into any unknown adventure was the inevitable course my life took during that period of cathartic soul-searching. On various trips to Carcassonne, Killarney, Istanbul, or Marrakesh, I would pass my time trying to decipher the cultures I encountered, seizing on images that seemed to define the place and my experience in it. In the south of France it was those old women dressed in black with their strong, knobby hands wrinkled and weathered from years of hard work in the fields. Or outside Izmir it was those village cafes patronized only by burly Turkish men with dark sandpaper beards, an enclave unto its own which informed you immediately about the sex roles of that culture. In each country I became obsessed by these details and the way they reveal the dynamics of the larger culture. My visual take on the world was actually defining itself, but I was too caught up in the moment to realize what was going on.

I remember sleeping one night in the park in Belgrade and waking to the sound of folk dancing in the morning. To my left was a young man in his late teens, his black hair disheveled and his clothes dirty and unkempt. He was standing next to a bedroll and peering through the same bushes I had used as my shelter the night before. He spoke neither French nor English, the only two languages in which I had any fluency. But we shared bread and chocolate and found a few words in common, enough to have a rudimentary conversation. The cluster of low-lying brush where we had awoken separated us from the spectacle of Yugoslavians dancing before us. I was an outsider. I had a reason to be sequestered on the periphery. But I couldn't understand why he too felt the need to stay hidden behind these bushes. As we searched for other ways to exchange our thoughts he pointed to himself and said "Croat." He then pointed to the people dancing in the distance and uttered the word "Serb." The image of Yugoslavia that had been exported to the West, as a controlled and orderly society, was suddenly broken by this dynamic of ethnicity; our ready acceptance of their government propaganda had overshadowed the complex underpinnings of culture and ethnic identity as determinant forces in the rise and fall of nation-states. When the Croats and Serbs went to war two decades later, this brief encounter, this personal and specific incident, became for me the defining image for understanding the conflict. I knew then that in the future I would depend on moments like these to interpret the world.

During those years in Europe I visited with relatives and started to piece together the stories from my parents' past. My mother, born to an American father and French mother, had come as a young woman to the United States from France after World War II. My father likewise had immigrated to America, from Ireland, with his parents as a young boy. For my two brothers, my sister, and myself, our childhood tales were of the Nazis taking over my mother's house outside Paris, of her and her sister and my grandmother living in a kitchen for three years. She told us stories of German soldiers committing suicide in the backyard rather than face the prospect of being sent to the Russian front, and of girlhood friends arrested for participation in the Resistance. The accounts on the Irish side were filled with family lore about my radical grandfather who made two trips to the United States with his wife and son, each time barely escaping the grasp of the British military. On their second journey they decided to stay, and my father grew up in an enclave of immigrants in Manhattan's Yorkville. This was a time when the Irish and Italians were the exploited immigrant class. It was they who filled the prisons, panhandled on the streets, and ran illegal liquor franchises during Prohibition. But the lucky ones—like my grandfather—were able to find jobs. He became a bus driver in Manhattan and later a union organizer. Over the years, through sheer will and determination, he and a generation of his countrymen made Irish ethnicity a force to be reckoned with in New York City politics. My father, in turn, carried out the dream of his immigrant father. He became a doctor and set out to define a place for himself in an Anglo-Saxon Protestant world that had, up until then, excluded the Irish.

These family stories with their repeating theme of cultural conflict were the prism through which I came to look at life. When I returned to the United States in the late 1970s, I got a degree in anthropology and set out over the next two decades on a journey of shooting and directing documentaries. After those years of intently watching encounters between people, looking through the lens was second nature; my obsessive interest in the details of human behavior had become focused and transformed in the manipulation of moving pictures.

The stories I was drawn to were those of cultures and societies at a breaking point: Puerto Rican street gangs in the decaying South Bronx, West Virginia steelworkers trying to save their hometown factory from bottom-line Wall Street economics, Vietnamese immigrants seeking refuge in Middle America, the Soviet Union during perestroika, Panama before the fall of Noriega, and Japanese society amidst its explosive economic boom of the mid-1980s.

However, in 1987 my work took a sudden geographic shift when I did a story about a priest under death threat who lived on the perimeter of the Amazon's frontier. It was there that I first heard about a gold rush taking place on Indian lands deep in the interior of the rain forest. This was a part of the world I had always wanted to travel to, a blank space on the map that seemed to fulfill my continuing need to immerse myself in exotic cultures in foreign terrains. If you wanted to "get lost" there seemed to be no better place than that giant green expanse called the heart of the Amazon, a region where roadways had failed to penetrate, and towns and cities were still the distant dreams of urban planners.

But there was also a more focused and serious side to my interest in this part of the world. The more I researched the story, the more unbelievable it appeared to be: one billion dollars worth of gold was leaving Yanomami territory every year, yet the Brazilian government was not intervening nor, it seemed, was anyone reporting on it. When I contacted various international news agencies, I was told that the story was not newsworthy enough to warrant an assignment: "Nobody cares about Indians in the Amazon," one executive producer said to me as he stood up abruptly, signaling the end of our meeting. "But thanks for coming by." So I did what any self-respecting freelance journalist would do: I ignored the opinions of colleagues and set off at my own expense to cover the story.

I remembered enough from my college history courses to know that a gold rush of this magnitude on Indian lands was going to have devastating consequences. It was a sociological time bomb waiting to explode. So I spent the next year and a half researching the story, immersing myself in the history of the region and the cultures that inhabit the forests. I picked up another freelance assignment, as a cameraman shooting a documentary in a small frontier town about a union leader named Chico Mendes. My grasp of the language was improving, and I was beginning to understand Brazilian culture. Then I set off for Yanomami territory, where I have quickly learned that no research could have prepared me for the clash of cultures I have encountered. Hopefully in the coming week I will be able to gather enough material to document this gold rush, yet I already know that there is a larger story unfolding here, a story I find myself drawn to in ways that are difficult to explain. Amidst all the chaos and insanity of this strange, edgy world, I feel a rush of excitement that I have never experienced anywhere else. *Predictable* is the last word that anyone would apply to the Amazon's frontier. Yet it's precisely its unpredictability that I find most seductive.

3

The Wolf walks up the steps of a ramshackle plywood house sitting under a high canopy of trees. He pushes his way through the screen door without introducing himself. I follow, my television camera dangling from a shoulder strap, exhausted from Sebastião's lunatic press tour at the Yanomami village near the airstrip. This house is just one of a number of makeshift structures bordering the Paapiú runway, which has become the center of operations for five hundred gold miners occupying an area of forest that until recently had been the exclusive domain of three hundred Yanomami Indians.

The wobbly structure we've just entered is known among the miners as the Goldmazon house, the home and headquarters of a wildcat mining entrepreneur by the name of Elton Kronholt. Elton is a large, amiable guy with a striking resemblance to Jackie Gleason. He is also known to be one of the richest gold miners in the Amazon. We met him at a press conference in Boa Vista several days ago, and he immediately extended an invitation to stay at his house in Yanomami territory. Such a gesture of hospitality took me by surprise, in light of his posturing as a militant renegade and die-hard xenophobe. In countless press reports Elton has spoken vehemently about the international environmentalist conspiracy to take over the Amazon. To back up his outspoken opinions he carries a gun made of gold, a weapon he has threatened to use against foreign intruders, particularly those who don't agree with his opinions. Recently his photo appeared in the well-known Brazilian newsmagazine *Veja*. He is pictured standing on top of a cluster of logs at night, wearing a trenchcoat and a weird Sherlock Holmes hat, his eyes fixed on some distant point in the darkness and his precious pistol extended before him. The caption quotes him: "I am not going to be a zookeeper for the Americans."

As we step into the front room of this little house with its low, crooked ceiling, I have the impression we've walked into the middle of a Sam Shepard play. Everyone is hyped up, a little on edge. The floorboards bend and creak under our feet. Helicopters whirl above us every few minutes as they take off from a nearby launch pad, transporting equipment and prospectors farther into the jungle. Each time the screen door slams, it announces the entrance of yet another quirky character in this strange little stage play, more misfits from Brazil's interior seeking fortune and salvation in this expansive green hell. There is Ana, a big-boned woman in her late teens who is constantly teased by the others for being an Indian. Her features resemble those of the Macuxi, a local indigenous group contacted by Brazilian society more than a century ago, but she denies any kinship. She is the housekeeper. Then there is Artur, a plump gay man in his mid-twenties who is the cook. He walks about in an open short-sleeved shirt and bikini bathing suit talking incessantly about his crushes on various miners who have appeared that day at the encampment, just some of the two hundred men said to be arriving daily in Yanomami territory. A few minutes after our arrival Artur pulls me outside and insists that I take a photo of him so that *gatos americanos*, sexy American men, "can see what a real Brazilian man looks like." He jumps into an open-air shower a few yards from the house and wets down his flabby frame. The yard surrounding me is a mess of wood shards and jagged tree stumps that have been haphazardly cleared by miners with chain saws and axes. I stand outside checking the exposure of my little Olympus and looking around for an appropriate background. Artur emerges from the shower, hair slicked back, soaking wet,

glistening in the afternoon sun. He suddenly strikes a body-
builder pose amidst the severed stumps and shredded wood.
The shot is both pathetic and comic but I take it anyway. This
little photo opportunity is simply an innocent, fleeting moment
in the fantasy of sexual prowess and promiscuity that seems to
dominate Artur's life here in the forest. Besides, I like Artur.
His vulnerability and sense of humor provide a relief from the
rugged macho culture of gold prospectors and frontier entrepreneurs. To Artur's credit, there is nothing mercenary or cruel
about what he is doing. If anything, the joke is on him and he
knows it.

This shot is very different from the other, more troubling,
photographic encounters I have had today when the miners
would grab an Indian and force him or her to strike a pose in
front of my camera. Normally I shut the camera down during
such scenes, but today I made certain to grab the images
because they are a part of this story, posed moments that have
as much validity as my documentary coverage of the airstrips
and the few interviews I have conducted so far. This environment is unlike any I have ever worked in. This gold rush is not
simply about the assertion of power by one group over another.
That story I have documented before in New York and Central
America and elsewhere when the police, the military, and the
paramilitary used force and intimidation to control and subjugate a population whose actions challenged the status quo.
That story is one-dimensional. There is a clear delineation
between good and evil. But here there is something more complicated taking place, a game of manipulation being acted out
that remains hidden behind the layers of cultural differences
separating the Indians' world from my own. To not film con-
trived moments would limit my understanding of the story
unfolding here. In this story it is not just what people do and
say that is important but how they consciously choose to act in
front of the camera. I look for messages in their performances,
hoping that in the process I might discover some answers.

"Is it good?" Artur asks through his teeth without breaking
his smile. Then suddenly he twists his torso to the right and
thrusts his curled arms above his shoulders in a vain attempt at

a more seductive pose. I can hear him gasping for breath as he sucks his stomach in.

"It's perfect," I tell him. "The *gatos* are going to love it back in the States."

The shutter clicks. Artur remains frozen for a moment, then breaks his stance with an ecstatic little cry. As he returns to the shower to towel down, I go back into the house, where I find the Wolf chatting up Ana. In the background an intense young man with short, curly dark hair sits listening to the blaring garble of a ham radio spewing out directions to incoming pilots and ad hoc news reports of murders and accidents from various airstrips in the forest. The Wolf introduces him. His name is Martins and he is the person responsible for supervising Elton's operation at Paapiú. Artur comes in and brushes by me, bestowing a lingering, lascivious glance. "Ciao, Jefferson," he says. He walks into a small room at the back of the house and slams the crooked door of rough wood planks.

As I look about the little abode I am struck by a quality this crazy group of people seem to share. They are all very nice, but there is a sadness about them, as if they are all a little lost. Perhaps this characteristic provides a cohesive bond for their eclectic community of misfits. That and the likelihood that there is nothing left for them back home. Money, or lack of it, I have come to learn, is not the only force that propels people to the Amazon's frontier. These are individuals attracted to life on the edge. So far in my conversations with many of the miners on this airstrip I have found that living in the dense tropical forest is a preferred choice over a more civilized existence in the interior country's towns and cities. It provides an escape from broken marriages, bad romances, perhaps even the complications of a criminal past. "The Amazon," an anthropologist friend of mine once said, "is like a psychiatrist's couch. It attracts a lot of people from a lot of different places, trying to work things out." I can see it in their eyes and those of my colleagues as well, other anthropologists and journalists with whom I have worked over the years. On this trip and the others I have caught a glimpse of it in my own reflection in a mirror, a piece of glass, the window of a beat-up Cessna. A little bit of that intensity. A desire to immerse myself in some new unexplored corner of the earth, hoping that perhaps here I will find the answer, the experience that will finally soothe my soul, allowing me to return to the norm of existence with a family, a fixed schedule, a pattern to life. Maybe after I've done my time I will be able to give up the harried journalist's existence that has provided a seemingly worthy excuse for not coming to terms with my own life. But for now there is the task of completing this documentary and dealing with the inhabitants of this airstrip. Their unpredictable nature has made this part of the stay amusing at the very least.

"*Artur sai*"—Artur is leaving—I hear announced from behind me in a whisper as Artur comes back into the front room in a flowered shirt and matching shorts, reeking of cologne. He picks up a bag from the counter and sashays out of the house, slamming the front door for added effect.

"I'm like the old shoe that fits anywhere," the Wolf says about himself. He is a man who often gets his clichés mixed up, an endearing characteristic that also manages to add an extra layer of truth to the observations he makes. But what I appreciate most about him is that he's adaptable and comfortable in almost any environment. In situations like these he is at his best: drinking, playing cards, flirting with the plump Macuxi girl, swapping recipes with Artur, putting everyone at ease in the wisecracking manner of the *carioca*, the native son of Rio de Janeiro, that seductive coastal city whose inhabitants are known throughout Brazil as disarming charmers and incorrigible womanizers. Thanks to the Wolf we have quickly settled into relaxed relations with the various occupants of the house: Artur, Ana, Martins, and a fourth person named Guilherme, a scruffy middle-aged mechanic with curly brown hair, small dark eyes, and a beer barrel of a belly. Guilherme worked the oil fields of the Middle East in the early 1980s and was brought here by gold mine owners to service the hydraulic pumps that power their jungle mining operation. We are accepted into this circle at the Goldmazon house in part because we help to break the monotony that has descended on them after six continuous months in the forest. But there is a second, perhaps more significant, factor facilitating our entry into the group. We have brought with us food that is hard to come by in this corner of the world: large cans of tuna fish and sardines, pasta, canned meat, cookies, and coffee.

Sharing—whether you are with Indians, missionaries, or miners—is the key code of conduct in the forest. The underlying message is simple: if you don't share or participate in an equitable exchange of what you have, then you will inevitably fight over it. And if you fight over things on the frontier, chances are you will lose everything or kill somebody or be killed yourself. If you do kill, it is understood that you are submitting yourself not to the hands of formal justice but to vendetta, the code that rules in most of the towns, cities, and miners' encampments in the Amazon—the uneasy glue that holds together the rickety social structure of the frontier. The circumstances in which these scenarios unfold start simply but can quickly erupt in chaos and violence.

One such scenario: a group of Yanomami give bananas to a miner who promises to give them a dozen machetes. The miner then ignores the Indians' persistent requests for compensation. After several weeks the Indians, frustrated, decide to raid the miners' encampments and take what is owed to them. Undetected, they steal pots, pans, machetes, and mirrors and retreat to their village. To exact revenge—to maintain their control of the forest—the miners wait outside the village and kill two Indians who have set off on a hunt. The Indians in turn exact revenge by killing three miners. There are no intermediaries, no institutions of justice to negotiate differences. This is the undiluted power of vendetta invoked as the result of a mismanaged exchange.

Here in Yanomami territory the miners say that, among themselves, there are two to three killings a week in the hundred or so mining airstrips scattered throughout Indian lands. Most of those murders stem from disputes over the division of profits. In other parts of the frontier, however, violence is most commonly the result of conflicts over land. In the last twenty years sixteen hundred nuns, priests, lawyers, union leaders, and local politicians have been assassinated in the Amazon with only twenty-six trials and fourteen convictions. The majority of those murdered died defending the rights of desperate Amazon migrants who for decades have come to this region seeking arable parcels of rain forest for subsistence farming. Some of the poor—there are an estimated 12 million people without land in Brazil—manage to claim small plots for themselves, but others have chosen to follow the perilous life of squatters rather than subject themselves as peons to the medieval conditions that await them as laborers on large estates. Ironically, miners and missionaries both affirm that the gold camps are filled with former gunslingers known as *pistoleiros* who were hired by large ranchers to exact vengeance in disputes over land. I am sure that is true (no one denies there is a significant criminal element here), but these camps are predominantly inhabited by the impoverished of Amazonia—part of an army of three hundred thousand miners—many of whom would prefer to be working the land rather than toiling in the forest. Out of frustration they have given up the dream of owning their own plots of land and come here to pursue *a droga*, the term used by many to describe the crazed and intoxicated state that overcomes people in pursuit of gold.

Earlier today at the landing strip, a local Indian Agency employee described to me an incident that brought violence to this community of Yanomami. Almost a year ago a Yanomami man shot and killed two gold prospectors in a drunken dispute near the airstrip. The miners retaliated by abducting and killing four Indians. They chopped their bodies to pieces and left them on the runway not far from one of the Yanomami villages. More than revenge on behalf of the dead, this was an act calculated to terrorize the living, adding to the Yanomamis' long-standing fear of outsiders abducting their women. And it has been effective. The Indians, particularly the women, seem paralyzed by fright each time they must cross the landing strip. Their faces contract in horrific grimaces whenever I, or anyone from outside their culture, try to approach them. The Indian Agency official also told me that after the murders the governor of this territory (the region has yet to become a state) sent in a federal policeman to supervise the area. The policeman, however, spent most of his time searching for gold in mining pits rather than trying to maintain order in this reckless frontier community.

After dinner I retire to my hammock strung up on the front porch next to the room of the mechanic Guilherme. As I secure the knots and prepare to sleep, Guilherme sits near a small kerosene lamp talking to his dog and touching it gently on its back and sides. Much of his day was spent being choppered in to various mining sites to repair the hydraulic pumps that run constantly in the pits. In the evenings Guilherme hangs around the house sipping coffee and trying to seduce the housekeeper Ana. I can tell that he has spent a lot of time in foreign countries: he is more comfortable than the others in my presence. To him I am not so much an item of curiosity as a potential source of entertainment.

"Are you going to go out there to piss in the night?" he says to me as I begin to undress.

"Maybe."

"Make sure you bring a lighter."

"You mean a flashlight, a *lanterna*, not an *acendedor*, a lighter," I say as I mime the action of striking a Bic lighter. (I'm once again succumbing to the tourist ritual of acting out what I am trying to say, something I always promised myself I wouldn't do.)

"No, no." He laughs. "A lighter."

"Why a lighter?"

"Because of the vampire bats." He pauses a moment to let this sink in. "It's the only way to get them off. You have to put the flame right up next to them." He lights his Bic. The dog, startled, makes a sudden movement.

"*Sério*. You are serious, yes?"

"Sure," he says. "Look at what happened to him last night."

Guilherme now turns on a *lanterna*, a flashlight, and shows me the dozen deep, bloody scars on the back and sides of his dog. There is a pained and terrified look on the animal's face and a sick grin on the face of his owner.

"If you don't scare them away with the flame," he warns me, "they will just sit there sucking into you, drawing out the blood."

I'm speechless. "Thanks," I say finally.

As Guilherme pats his dog, he stares at me for a moment. He then breaks out in a big smile—a sign of contentment, I take it, that he has managed to sufficiently upset his gringo visitor. I say good night and settle into my hammock.

Looking up above the tree line of the forest I can see the vampire bats as they crisscross the sky in sharp, rapid semicircles, a strange web of violent and chaotic silhouettes, disturbingly reminiscent of the way life unfolds in this corner of the world.

4

The Yanomami didn't always inhabit these forests. Some historians believe they are descendants of the first Asiatic populations that traveled across the Bering Straits during the Ice Age and headed down into the Americas twenty thousand years ago. The theory is that for generation after generation these peoples moved closer and closer to the lower, flatter parts of what is now the Brazilian Amazon. Anthropologists call them lowland Indians. Highland Indians can be found in the mountains of Peru, Colombia, and Ecuador. In North America we had the Plains Indians, the Pueblos, and Coastal societies. Separate cultures, economies, and belief systems. These were worlds unto themselves. In the land now known as Brazil, entire societies have lived for centuries sequestered in the forest, occasionally bumping up against each other, sometimes in conflict, sometimes with a mutual sense of awe that there are others out there sharing the forest, surviving in this plentiful but hostile environment. The specific climate, geographic location, and ecosystem of each of these groups in the Americas has necessitated a different cultural development. Today an estimated one hundred seventy different Indian societies live throughout the Amazon Basin in Brazil. And many of these societies, not just the Yanomami, continue to be threatened by the encroachment of the civilized world on their once isolated communities.

Indian populations in the Amazon can be roughly classified into five linguistic subgroups: the Ge-speaking people, the Tupi, the Panoan, the Carib, and the Arawak. Although sharing similar language bases, Amazonian societies have developed in relative isolation, giving each a specific culture, language, and genetic makeup. The Yanomami, like many of the lowland populations in the Amazon, have developed extremely efficient forms of ecological adaptation. A mix of hunting, slash-and-burn agriculture, and the gathering of products from the forest kept them completely self-sufficient for centuries—until their first contacts with white explorers. Then the big picture began to change, and with it their ancient worldview. The start of the gold rush in 1987 forced the Yanomami to come to terms with the sheer numbers of the white man, a strange people who by the tens of thousands descend to earth in giant metal birds and who employ noisy machines to carry them everywhere, to bring light to their houses, to give energy to the orange hoses and hydraulic pumps tearing apart the once pristine riverbanks of this part of the forest. (The Yanomami refer to the miners as "wild pigs snorting in the mud" because of the way they press their bodies into the sides of rivers as they search the embankments for gold.)

When white missionaries, anthropologists, and Indian Agency employees first began to live among the Yanomami in the early 1960s, the Indians believed that these strangers communicated with each other by utilizing the same supernatural songs that their shamans used to communicate with the spirit world during ritual chants. They would watch the white men talk all day into boxes called radios: a man would sit there speaking, then a voice would come out of the radio. It only made sense that these strange white men were employing a form of communication that the Yanomami were familiar with. But with time the high-tech logic of Western European societies started to become incorporated into the worldview of the Yanomami and radios are now understood to be devices of communication. Still there are vast dimensions of reality and experience that the Yanomami could not share with us and we cannot share with them. And to assume we can is a dangerous proposition. Because the moment we presume that there are no differences between their world and ours, that twenty thousand years' separation has no lasting import and is only a minor obstacle to social interaction, at that moment misunderstandings take place.

In Yanomami territory and throughout the Brazilian Amazon, differences of culture and language exacerbate problems: a miner might believe that a young Indian girl has been promised to him by a village elder, or an Indian man may assume that he is to get ten times more in an exchange than was actually offered. Such misunderstandings often have brutal, even fatal, consequences because there are no shared cultural or institutional means of mediating conflict. In the case of the murders at Paapiú, no one knows what prompted all the violence. Perhaps it was a fight about a woman or an argument over the runway landing fees that had been promised to the Indians.

Each time I hear such stories I think how many similar misunderstandings must have been reenacted in the history of contact between Indians and Western European explorers in this hemisphere. And I wonder, can we ever hope to really comprehend a society so different from our own? To do so we must make a giant leap into another cultural landscape, must completely immerse ourselves over a period of years in the logic of a separate world dependent not on the high-tech functioning of cities and towns but on an intimate relation with the plants, the animals, and the rivers of an untouched tropical forest. It is unfortunately a leap few of us are willing to make, and so we go along, as we have for centuries, blindly interacting with a people whom we don't really understand, creating that intermediate but tenuous space called the middle ground. There are some anthropologists who have referred to societies such as the Yanomami as our contemporary ancestors. I think it is best to simply recognize these people as our equals operating on a separate plane. It's safer that way for everyone involved: miners, environmentalists, journalists, and all the rest of us who have decided to enter this forest, a land where the predominant logic and rhetoric of our Western world suddenly become ineffective—at times an obstacle—in our efforts to relate to the indigenous inhabitants.

So when did we outsiders come into the picture? That is still a debate in anthropology circles. Some Yanomami have not yet seen—despite the gold mining invasion—the face of an outsider, the mythical "white man." Yet the influences of the Western European world more than a century ago penetrated even the most isolated areas. Machetes, knives, fishhooks, pots, pans, mirrors, and even guns have reached distant areas through an elaborate trade network joining approximately 350 villages. While anthropologists working with the Yanomami have their theoretical differences, all seem to agree that these Indians are fanatical traders, looking to exchange almost anything for valued objects from the outside world. Like most cultures, including my own, these are a people always on the lookout for a good deal.

The first documented cases of contact with the Yanomami were by Portuguese explorers in the late eighteenth century. But it was not until the 1910s that the Yanomami experienced a period of sustained contact with rubber tappers, the Indian Protection Service (FUNAI's predecessor), and missionaries who had navigated small, lightweight boats up the intricate waterways of Yanomami territory, carrying them over waterfalls so that they could penetrate this remote part of the northwest Amazon. It was these natural barriers (*cachoeiras* the waterfalls are called in Portuguese) that protected the Yanomami from the large boats that over the past three centuries had already penetrated most points of the lower Amazonian river systems. But the most persistent explorers were getting through in smaller boats, and the goods they were carrying attracted some Yanomami communities closer to the rivers. These Indians were seeking trade items that could be bartered back in the forest, machetes to clear gardens or to be presented as gifts in the elaborate seasonal visits that take place between villages. However, in spite of these points of contact, the Yanomami have historically enjoyed only brief periods of limited interaction with small numbers of outsiders. They eluded the

Portuguese slave raids of the seventeenth and eighteenth centuries which depopulated villages bordering the Amazon, leaving behind epidemic disease that killed off the majority of the remaining inhabitants. The Yanomami also escaped the attentions of Jesuit priests in the sixteenth century who, with the help of the Portuguese government, tried to "civilize" the Indians of Amazonia by luring them into regimented evangelical communities organized like jungle communes. The work was done collectively but the land and the assignation of labor tasks was strictly controlled by the clergy. Although considered a liberal alternative to slavery, these disciplined Catholic compounds—at one time the Jesuits had set up over sixty of them along the Amazon's riverbanks—were responsible for the obliteration of native languages, customs, and traditional shamanistic practices.

But miraculously over a period of five centuries the Yanomami managed to maintain their indigenous worldview—including a dimension embraced by many other lowland Indian societies before contact with Portuguese colonizers or Brazilian nationals. These Indians believed they were the first people, the center of the universe. The creation myths of most lowland Amerindian societies are constructed in such a way as to position their own culture at the point of origin of the world. The particular manner in which a society's creation takes place changes with the mythology of each culture. But what didn't change was that the first people were *their* people, and that the world—or what they knew to be the world—evolved from them.

By the 1950s, however, the increasing presence of outsiders could no longer be ignored. It was obvious that there were more types of people in the world than just the other Amerindian societies—"the real foreigners" the Yanomami call them—who had been their neighbors and, at times, enemies in the past. These new people were a type of *napë*, or non-Yanomami, who had entered their universe: these were called *kraiwa*, the white people. The exact size of their population and their intentions were still unclear. Contact was limited and controlled by certain intermediaries: missionaries, anthropologists, an occasional group of rubber tappers, and the country's Indian

Protection Service. They arrived by canoes and planes and, in most cases, seemed to be friendly. Slowly they started to be incorporated into the Indians' belief system. Today the Yanomami shamans give a simple explanation for the appearance of these people: the *kraiwa* are descendants of the Yanomami. Their arrival on earth is ascribed to a breach of the ritual seclusion of a young couple in a menstruation hut, a common practice in Yanomami villages. Couples often marry very young. When the girl has her first menstruation, she and her husband are secluded in a small temporary hut just outside the village, where they are required to remain over the course of a week. Food is brought to them by relatives. Instead of using their hands to eat, they must use a stick. They may speak only in a whisper and then only to their closest relatives. In the eyes of the Yanomami this form of ritual seclusion protects the village from the dangerous effects of menstrual blood, which, if exposed to members of the community, has the power to make the world collapse.

"A very long time ago" a fight broke out during a village festival. Two Yanomami shamans who had passed the morning taking the ritual drug yakuana now stood facing each other, reeling back and forth on their heels, overcome by the yakuana's powers. They had spent the preceding hour blowing small bits of the hallucinogenic substance into each other's nostrils with a long thin reed resembling a blowgun. Somehow an argument had broken out between them, and they were now in the village center, a crowd of neighbors and relatives forming as they prepared to face off in a bout of chest pounding.

On this day one of the sisters of the two combatants was sequestered with her husband in a menstruation hut located just outside the village. As the pounding match began, it soon became clear that the young woman's brother was to receive a terrible beating, yet he stubbornly refused to surrender. Quickly his mother came to the hut and pleaded with her son-in-law to intervene in her son's defense. With each blow that landed, the old mother wailed and begged her son-in-law to leave the ritual seclusion and defend his suffering relative. Each time he refused. But eventually the hysterical pleas of both his wife and his mother-in-law became unbearable. With great hesitation the young husband emerged from the menstruation hut and intervened in his brother-in-law's defense.

Suddenly the sky turned dark and a tidal wave surged up from the foot of a nearby hill. A wall of water swept through the forest, knocking down villagers and carrying off their bodies. Those Yanomami who escaped by fleeing to the forest were transformed into deer and jaguars. Those who tried to climb to safety in trees were turned into termite nests and sloths. Still others were overpowered and eaten by giant otters and caimans. The bloody remnants of the carnage mixed with the water and created a red foam that traveled through the forest and became the river Catrimani. This bloody foam was carried downstream to that place on the distant horizon where the sky meets the earth, the land that is home to Remori, the immortal hero of the Yanomami people.

There at the edge of the earth Remori stepped in front of the waters and directed them into the underworld beneath the earth's surface. Leaning over the bloody river, he gathered the red foam into his hands and molded it into the form of human beings. He then placed his mouth against it and spoke into the foam a sound like "Rerererere," a sound similar to that which the white men make when they speak into their radios. These words of Remori suddenly brought life to the foam, creating human figures which he placed down on the side of the riverbank. When these figures began to speak they uttered the language of the white people and this is how Remori brought white people into the world.

Until this time Remori had been the only "foreigner" the Yanomami had known, a spirit-being able to fly through the air as the white people do today. It was he who gave the white people radios, machetes, pots, and pans and told them to return to the Yanomami lands carrying these objects as gifts. "These things you will give away among the people there," Remori said to the white people as he set them down on the riverbank. "You shall go then where you came from and take gifts back to your people who remained there."

Ever since this time, white people created by Remori have continued to visit the Yanomami, the people from whom they were originally created.

This mythic tale of the arrival of white people has been told in different versions throughout Yanomami territory. Each time, the shaman recounting it will transform it slightly so as to incorporate the specific geographic and cultural details of the region in which it is told. Where one shaman will refer to the Caltrimani River another might refer to the Pacu or the Jundia. In one version the whites return in canoes, in another in airplanes. To this degree myth is active, not static; it tracks the changes taking place in the larger society and incorporates them into the telling of the tales. It is their historical record.

Our history works the same way. It is also steeped in its own mythology, particularly those histories that recount our contact with indigenous populations. The one being told at present by gold miners in Brazil extols the rugged frontier explorer advancing steadily into an untamed forest with the aid of new technological breakthroughs. The Indians' myths and our own are struck from different molds, but they have a common impetus: each attempts to explain the place of the other in the forest.

In Brazil in the 1980s Yanomami territory became an area of renewed interest for wildcat gold miners as a result of recent advances in satellite photography and the availability of affordable lightweight aircraft. The first photographs of Amazonia were made by the Brazilian Radar Institute (RADAM) in the 1960s. On Yanomami lands they detected large deposits of gold and cassiterite, the latter an extremely valuable mineral substance which is the prime source of tin. During this time frontier entrepreneurs like José Altino Machado were anxious to lay claim to the mineral deposits before corporations had tied up all the exploration contracts with the military government.

In fact a cat and mouse game between mineral extraction companies and freelance gold prospectors had been going on in the Amazon for some time, and Machado was an expert gamesman. He was considered by many to be the quintessential Brazilian pioneer of this new era of exploration. He was a pilot who had made a small fortune working other gold sites in Amazonia and had now focused on the last unexplored regions of the rain forest as a new challenge. Not only was he a shrewd frontier explorer but he was also an articulate, charismatic man in his mid-forties whose weathered good looks helped to make him a favorite of the Brazilian press. Although he was often in front of the cameras, the tall, dark-haired José Altino dressed simply; jeans, lightweight shirts, and green aviator glasses were the staples of his attire. He stayed regularly at the Hotel Tropical in Boa Vista but also maintained homes in Manaus and Brasília. As one of the region's most successful pilots and mine owners, he was easily elected president of a loose confederation of 300,000 gold miners known as the Syndicate of Gold Miners in the Legal Amazon or, in its Portuguese acronym, USAGAL. Although he had recently vacated this post, he continued to be quoted regularly in the press as the region's most influential mining leader.

In his comments to the media Machado, like the Yanomami shamans, practiced his own particular version of mythmaking. He always depicted the Brazilian prospector as the "little man" or the "real Brazilian" who had been denied a role in a society that had become increasingly dominated by big government and uncaring corporate interests. In various meetings I had with José Altino he referred to himself as antimilitary, antigovernment, and a free market "anarchist" who did not want anyone telling him how he and his fellow miners should conduct explorations in Amazonia. "You can't have laws created by a civilization that occupies the south of the country applied to those who live in Amazonia, because these laws are incompatible and even impossible of being carried out," he told an audience of businessmen in São Paulo when I first met him. For José Altino the Indians were merely an obstacle to his efforts, a people who existed "on the periphery of the white man's economy." During one meeting in Rio de Janeiro he told me he considered himself a disciple of Aristotle, adding that in the Amazon traditional concepts of authority don't exist because "nature itself determines the course of society." I can only assume he was referring to the Aristotelian concept of "mutatis mutandis" where the acquisition of goods from the environment is categorized as "natural" and therefore not to be altered by society. Aristotle went so far as to include piracy in this category because pirates, like hunters, "simply live the life that their needs compel them to." In this sense some of Aristotle's writings provided a perfect model for José Altino to create his own myth justifying the occupation of Yanomami lands by Brazilian miners—an act of piracy in its own right. But perhaps the part of Aristotle that José Altino forgot to read was the chapter recounting the story of the King of Phrygia known as Midas, who found that "because of the inordinate greed of his prayer everything that was set before him turned to gold." Midas eventually starved to death, unable to eat any food set before him. The sad king is now a relic of Western European history. The fate of José Altino and his forty-five thousand miners is still to be determined.

———

During the 1970s and early 1980s Machado and several other mining entrepreneurs began to position themselves at the forefront of efforts to establish wildcat gold mining operations on Yanomami lands. Slowly and carefully they made periodic incursions into Yanomami territory, testing the reactions of the region's inhabitants as well as the local branches of the federal police.

In October of 1980 Ottomar Pinto da Souza, then governor of Roraima, sent in planeloads of prospectors to Yanomami lands just fifty kilometers from a large Indian community in the area known as the Serra dos Surucucus. Very quickly a measles epidemic broke out and twenty-seven Indians died. The Catholic Church and an alliance of anthropologists protested the invasion. Medical teams were sent in and three thousand miners were expelled. For a few years the situation was under control.

Then in 1984 a presidential decree gave mining companies the right to prospect on Indians lands. José Altino, fearful that freelance Brazilian miners were going to be excluded from reaping profits, went into action. In February of 1985 he flew dozens of gold miners in his own planes to a semiabandoned airstrip near the Venezuelan border. Once on the ground, he led an expedition of prospectors back to the Serra dos Surucucus, one of the areas the recently released radar photographs had confirmed as being rich in gold and cassiterite. It was also one of the most densely populated parts of Yanomami territory and the same area that Ottomar Pinto da Souza had invaded five years earlier. José Altino's strategy was to start a de facto gold rush before the mining companies could have their contracts approved by the military government. According to a Yanomami leader by the name of Davi Kopenawa, José Altino and his fellow miners took the extra precaution of wearing military fatigues and describing their group to local villagers as being part of an army expedition. But the Brazilian armed forces, tipped off by Kopenawa and local missionaries, soon arrived on the scene. They apprehended José Altino and his group, though not before the miners had hacked their way through the bush and discovered for themselves extensive mineral deposits. Although José Altino was never charged with impersonating a military official, he was arrested on February 13, 1985, for illegally entering Indian lands. He claims he was arrested not because he was breaking the law but simply because he and his men represented a threat to large mining concerns like the Paranapanema Group. His sentence was twenty-six days in jail, a ritual baptism for a frontier renegade determined to continue penetrating Indian lands, drawing on the mineral wealth that he claimed belonged to the Brazilian people.

These invasions by José Altino and Ottomar Pinto confirmed the worst fears of Brazilian human rights activists: there was an untapped fast-buck El Dorado just sitting out there in the rain forest.

But during this period new obstacles emerged to threaten José Altino's campaign for wildcat mineral exploration in Yanomami territory. Democracy, after two decades of military rule, was returning to Brazil. Frustrated by their own reckless economic mismanagement, the generals had decided to give the government back to the people. A new constitution was in the process of being established and, for the first time, institutions of justice were slowly gaining a foothold in the previously lawless terrain of Brazil's frontier. Nongovernmental organizations throughout the country—seizing the momentum of activism that arrived with this new period of democracy—were publicly protesting on behalf of the poor as well as the nation's indigenous populations. José Altino and his fellow miners found themselves working against a clock: the country's new constitution was to take effect in 1988 and the pro-Indian lobby had entered into preliminary negotiations extremely well organized. Machado's response was to continue to use the press to promulgate his vision of the rain forest as "a separate universe, accountable to the laws of nature but not to politics." Looked at in the context of Brazilian history, José Altino Machado's political maneuvering simply followed a formula for success that had been established in the nineteenth century by Brazilian pioneers known as *bandeirantes*: stay ahead of the institutions of the state, make your own laws, and get out with the profits before the state holds you accountable for your actions. This strategy (now repackaged by José Altino with an Aristotelian slant) had always worked along the Amazon's frontier. He wasn't about to change his ways nor was he willing to tolerate growing international protests—particularly by celebrities—about the burning of the rain forest and the displacement of the region's indigenous people. "If Sting shows up here," he once told me, "I will personally cut off his ponytail and send him on the first plane back to England."

By the time I entered Yanomami territory in 1989, the miners' occupation of Indian land had become an established fact and José Altino was moving forward with his agenda for frontier expansion. Recently he had won the support of the newest local governor, Romero Juca, who now backed the miners. He was simultaneously proposing in the press that the Yanomami "be put onto a reservation instead of taking out the forty-five thousand miners who are already there." He seemed unstoppable and the plight of the Indians a lost cause.

"What is the biggest obstacle you face now?" I asked him outside the Hotel Tropical in Boa Vista one afternoon. As I finished my question I focused my attention on trying to see behind the dark green lenses of his aviator glasses. A glint of golden sunlight just barely exposed the pupils of his eyes.

"My biggest obstacle now?" He paused to take a drag on his cigarette. A small smile creased his leathery face. I knew from our various encounters that this was the kind of moment he enjoyed. "The international press," he responded as smoke billowed from his mouth. He then slapped my back to accentuate the joke's-on-me tone of this little power-play riposte.

As I watched him walk into the hotel, I thought how brilliantly he had manipulated both the press and the government to create a smoke screen around those forty-five thousand miners out there in the forest, an army of peons toiling away in the shadow of sad King Midas. And I wondered if, or how much, he was also manipulating me.

5

"*Peixes e arroz à troca por as bananas.*" Fish and rice in exchange for bananas, says a man called Vivi who is standing inside a makeshift cafe and supply store constructed from cast-off pieces of wood and covered by a blue tarp. This establishment is just one of a half dozen rickety enterprises that hug the periphery of the landing strip. They supply miners and pilots with food, fuel, and radio transmissions either back to Boa Vista or to one of the other encampments in the forest. Farther on behind this shack, another twenty yards or so, the edge of the rain forest starts to creep in—a fifty-foot wall of green tropical trees and entangled vines which have to be beaten back each month with machetes and chain saws.

As we step off the runway, a small Cessna jostles past us, the rear section waggling precariously as the plane makes its way down the muddy track, the pilot revving the engine and testing the propellers prior to takeoff. When the sound of the plane drifts into the distance I lift the camera to my shoulder and nod to the Wolf to start recording sound.

It feels good to enter the shade after a brutal morning in the equatorial sun. We've been sprinting up and down the landing strip getting images of the details that make up the miners' operation in the forest: a Brazilian flag mounted on a makeshift pole; miners, laden with supplies, trekking off to the forest; dozens of planes and helicopters coming and going. Now here, just outside the store and shaded by the trees, I can get a closer look at Vivi. His powerful arms bulge out from his polyester short-sleeved shirt, the buttons opened halfway down to expose the black mass of hair sprouting from his bearlike chest. He has a large head and dark, deep-socketed eyes. At approximately forty years of age, Vivi has succumbed to considerable baldness. He compensates for it by obsessively pasting his errant hair onto the top of his shiny round head.

I focus the camera on Vivi standing at the entrance of his makeshift store looking at three Yanomami women shuffling about nervously in front of him. *"O que você quer?"*—So what is it you want?—he asks in a tone of voice that seems more like a command than a question.

The women's clothes are dirty and torn, the once colorful patterns of their dresses are now undistinguishable under the layer of grime that covers them. They are probably hand-me-downs given by missionaries who used to occupy this airstrip, or maybe they were gained in a trade for bananas or corn with some local miners. The women, small in stature like most of the Yanomami, all appear to be in their twenties. They have strong arms, large muscular shoulders, and sturdy legs. According to what I have read, they can deftly handle an ax or trek twenty miles through the forest in a single day. Their lives are spent cultivating the gardens, fetching hefty baskets of firewood, and toting water jugs from nearby rivers and streams. All of this work is done while they tend to their children, very often carrying infants in tree-bark slings as they go about their tasks. Among these three women a few young boys, no older than six or seven, hover with tiny bows and arrows clasped tightly in their hands. The eyes of the women—probably the boys' mothers—shift about as if they expect to be struck at any moment. Occasionally they reposition their young children in their slings in what I am assuming is a more protective position.

A miner seated at a table at the back of the cafe starts cackling hysterically. He then cries out: *"Elas têm medo!"*—These women are scared!

Vivi goes to the rear of the store and I move a little closer, ducking under the thick blue tarp that serves as a roof, turning the camera around on the Indian women. "What is it that you want?" Vivi says again to them from behind me. The women shout Portuguese words—*peixe, arroz*—as their children group around them in what may be a circle of defense.

I turn the camera back on Vivi who, now aware of the photographic eye, quickly fixes a few dangling strands of hair. He gives the women a plastic bag of rice with some pieces of fish thrown in.

Begging has now become part of life for these women, a chore that they have learned to incorporate into their daily routines. With the rivers polluted and increasing numbers of hunters getting sick, the prospect of getting enough fish or game by traditional means has become remote. The scenes of begging I've witnessed over the last two days confirm the worst fears of health officials in the cities: malnutrition will go hand in hand with malaria in decimating this once healthy Indian population.

I pull my eye away from the camera to check the larger scene, then enter back into the black-and-white images of my viewfinder, panning the camera from Vivi to the Yanomami women still standing at the entrance. I focus in on a young boy about five years old who is being carried in a bark sling on the back of his mother. His drab brown hair is thinning and falling out, his legs look like sticks: common indicators of a severely deficient diet. He stares at me as his mother turns to leave, his almond-shaped eyes fixed on the strange being with a bizarre metallic object attached to its shoulder. The boy's face has that deadpan look so commonly found in the adopt-a-poor-child ads in magazines in the United States and Europe. His mother continues walking, glancing behind her to see if anyone is following. I've now become accustomed to blank stares and phobic reactions, this last one mild in comparison to a woman yesterday who threatened me with an ax when I tried to take her picture on an isolated pathway. She scared the life out of me. She seemed to be hysterical with anger and rage. I have no idea what I would have done if she came after me with that ax. Fortunately, her husband appeared and calmed her down.

Lesson learned: in the last two days I've realized that my feeble attempts at introducing myself as a journalist—thereby distinguishing myself from the miners—have failed. That categorization means nothing to the Yanomami. I am a white man just like Vivi, and there is no way of getting around it. To these Indians the miners and I are simply a people to be kept at arm's length except for the occasional exchange of food and products. I can only assume that they see us as beings from another planet. We appear and disappear with a seemingly endless supply of metal objects, tearing away at the earth, taking pictures of them (do they even understand what that means?), sometimes giving them a token ax, knife, or piece of clothing. While working in the midst of their forest we kill and maim in pursuit of *ouro*, gold, a substance that for them has no value. We destroy their riverbeds and pollute their water. Then we return to the sky in our birdlike containers powered by strange loud rotating wings, scaring away the game animals on which they depend for food. This is as surreal an environment as I've ever seen. It makes me wonder if the Indians have a name for hell on earth.

I know now that negotiating this middle ground between their world and ours is the real challenge to documenting this story. I was naive to think that I could come in here with some rough phrases in Portuguese and a few icebreaker techniques that had passed the test in other cultures. This society is vastly different from any I have seen before. I had hoped to be here with an anthropologist, but the handful who know the Yanomami and speak their language feared breaking Brazilian law by entering the area. They were heeding the military's advisories that this "national security zone" should be off limits to all unauthorized personnel. I don't have authorization—but then again, neither do the forty-five thousand miners who now inhabit these forests. As much as I feel I am in over my head, I am still glad I made the trip. Someone needs to be documenting this gold rush and the havoc it is leaving in its wake.

I follow the women and the children with my camera as they climb up the the rocky slope leading to the runway. The little boys now stop and raise their bows and arrows, aiming at us as if they are about to shoot. In unison they let out a small war cry, a reminder that they too find this predicament intolerable: their mothers reduced to beggars, an army of men occupying their forest, a strange man here in front of them pointing provocatively with a long piece of glass attached to a metal box.

Vivi smiles at the children's gesture of defiance. He shakes his head, then turns towards me, waiting for his time on camera. His hair has managed to stay in place this time and there's a smile on his face.

I pan back to the women rushing off down the airstrip, hugging the periphery of the red dirt track, careful to avoid the path of another plane landing at a hundred and twenty miles per hour. As the aircraft buzzes by, I can see a group of miners huddled together in the back, another group brought in from the city to stake their claim to the untold riches lying below the floors of this forest.

"Why don't you go there at the Raimundo Nemen, man?" Vivi asks. "There is the right place for you to go and make a report. The Indians there are really wild ones. You will see lots of Indians if you go over there."

As he speaks, a clump of dirty unprocessed gold bounces about on his chest. It is suspended from a thick chain, also of gold. Its combined value is enough to make a down payment on a house. Such gaudy displays of wealth are de rigueur for those who have made it. Other varieties include Rolexes, gold bracelets, large diamond rings, new cars, and young blond girlfriends, dozens of whom can be found lounging at poolside in minuscule bikinis at Boa Vista's Hotel Tropical, awaiting the return of their jungle entrepreneurs. These ostentatious symbols—including the women—are meant to impress. Impact takes precedence over style, and gestures can be extreme. Recently in a crowded Boa Vista restaurant I asked Edem Barbosa, a wealthy mine owner, for his telephone number in São Paulo in order to do a follow-up interview. He wrote it out for me on a twenty-dollar bill, passing it across the table as if this were a common business practice. "Sorry I don't have a card," he said. He then turned his hand over and showed me a ring with a large sparkling diamond. "It's worth twenty thousand dollars," he said. "U.S. dollars. No joking." He then offered to lend me his condominium in Bahia if I wanted to use it for a vacation in the winter. I copied the number off the twenty-dollar bill and handed it back to him. I didn't like the suggestion implicit in his gesture: another act of seduction, this time the gold miner buying off the journalist. I found Edem amusing but I was also wary. He was part of what the Brazilians refer to as their mafiosi: a legion of loan sharks and wheeler-dealers who have made billions in Brazil's black market, an unbridled "parallel economy" said to be as strong as, if not stronger than, the legitimate national economy currently racked by hyperinflation and massive debt. The uncontrolled gold rush was just another opportunity to add to their riches and not pay taxes. A common sight at the airports here is mine owners with attaché cases chained to the wrists, cases filled with money heading off to the more "civilized" parts of the country.

"*Um momentinho, Vivi,*" I say, interrupting him to get a close-up of the nugget on his chest.

Vivi takes my interest in this symbol as his cue to give me a little background. "I not just a store owner," he says. "You see, I am also a pilot."

"Uh-huh." I struggle to say the bare minimum for fear that my speaking will shake the camera.

"I'm one of the first pilots to fly this area," he adds. "I've got a plane and a helicopter. I can show them to you if you want."

I am having trouble finding a focus point for these chunks of gold. Then, just when I have the image I want, Vivi hands me a slab of dried beef jerky, which he thrusts towards the camera, ruining my shot. I am forced to pan up to him. I assume that was his intention. He seems used to being in control.

"I can take you to see wild Indians," he says. "Don't worry. I am an expert pilot. No crashes. I promise."

Vivi is the classic unsolicited interview, a real character. I can just let the camera roll, interjecting a question here or there to keep him talking. Each phrase, gesture, and detail of his behavior provides me with further insights into what this man represents in the context of the gold rush.

"Those are real savage Indians they have over there," he offers again without any prompting. "It's about forty minutes' flying time from here. Those are the Indians who have never seen people before. They're angry, really angry. I flew over their village in my helicopter, and they all ran away. Do you understand? Angry like you can't believe. You have got to see it. There is no way to have contact with them. You come close and they run away."

I have heard rumors about such expeditions—miners in copters hovering above the Yanomami villages, the propellers acting like a high-tech tornado, blowing out the fires, sending the Indians' few possessions flying in all directions. An act of distraction for some bored prospectors but another instance of terror for these once isolated people. I never thought the rumors were true but, having met Vivi, I am beginning to change my mind.

Vivi takes another bite of beef jerky. When his mouth is sufficiently full, he repeats, "Wild ones, really wild. I'll take you. You got to see it."

"I appreciate your offer, Vivi, but we have enough to see here at Paapiú."

"Okay," he says and heads into the back of the store to talk to someone calling from Boa Vista on the radio.

After changing batteries we position Vivi by his white Cessna out on the runway. It is time to add a little variety to his backdrop. If I have too many shots in one locale, I'll never be able to cut together a sequence. Before we start Vivi fixes his hair, checks his collar, then adjusts his necklace of gold. The Wolf gives me a quick summary of what he was saying while I was off changing the batteries. I check my scribbled notes for the next question.

"What about the relationship between the Indians and the miners?" I ask from behind the camera.

"The Indians love the miners," Vivi says, glancing back to the store where some of his friends have congregated. "Before the miners arrived, the Indians lived their lives inside the jungle, they lived their normal life, but now they have more comfort, they have more food."

Within the close-up framing I'm using, I can see men milling about in the background sorting through orange hoses, blue tarps, and Yamaha generators, essential bits of equipment to be transported by helicopter to other mining sites. I slowly zoom back, opening up the lens, the background becoming less prominent as the gestures of Vivi's hands begin to play in the foreground. The slab of gold sits prominently displayed on his chest in the center of the frame.

Vivi is enjoying the attention. "And the gold miners bring them progress also; we bring plenty of food, clothing, all the things they need." Vivi pauses a beat, takes a quick breath, then continues as flawlessly as a late night talk-show host. "Here as you saw we try to give them whatever we can. We never leave them in a hard time. We always give them something so they don't hate us and, like that, we get along fine."

He has given me a perfect summation of the miners' position. I shut down the camera, making a mental note of how much battery power we will have for shots in the morning. A minute later we leave Vivi standing by his store and head off across the airstrip in the direction of the Goldmazon house. As we climb up on the runway I can hear him talking to his friends. "I'm going to be shown on television abroad," he says. "I'm going to be famous."

We cross the airstrip and grab another shot of a plane about to take off in the late afternoon light. *Two hundred and fifty planes passing through here daily*, I remind myself. I need these images to tell my story. I'll get them tomorrow.

From deep within the forest we can already hear the sounds of cicadas. Walking along the path, I watch the trees turn from green to blue to black as the day becomes night. By the time we return to the Goldmazon house a blanket of stars has risen up in the sky and the tree line of the forest has passed into silhouette. During the evenings here there is some movement on the runway and in the miners' encampments but no one in his right mind roams out there in the forest unarmed and alone. It is the unconquerable ones, the snakes and jaguars, who rule by night. And it is the jaguar who is the ultimate power, that mythic being that many Indian groups believe to be part man, part animal. It alone can instill fear in the people Vivi likes to refer to as "savages." Once I heard an entire Indian village shrieking in the early hours of the morning upon the arrival of a jaguar.

After a great deal of commotion, the unruly beast made its way back into the forest. The next day the village elders recounted for the awestruck younger generation the details of the animal's prowess: its ability to leap incredible distances, its razor-sharp teeth, its lightning-fast reflexes. On another occasion I saw a group of Indian hunters, armed with shotguns, stop dead in their tracks at the first sign of a jaguar's presence. Fresh pawprints on the side of an embankment showed where the animal had leaped approximately fifteen feet from a log that traversed the river. We stayed absolutely quiet for half an hour, careful not to attract the animal's attention. "We're in their house now," a gold miner once said to me when we ventured deep into the forest. "That is something you simply have to respect."

"Jefferson, vamos à pista!" a voice calls to me—Jefferson, let's go to the airstrip.

I awake to the sight of Artur standing at my side, his face grossly distorted by the mosquito netting of my military-issue hammock. It is night but somehow still bright, probably a full moon, judging by the strong burst of light hitting him from behind. Off in the distance, from the direction of the airstrip, I can hear music and men laughing.

"Não quero, Artur. Eu quero dormir agora."—I don't want to, Artur. I want to sleep now.

"Olha, Jefferson"—Look at this—and he proceeds to model his outfit for this night's adventures, tiptoeing in little half circles on the front porch of the Goldmazon house. His getup consists of a straw hat frayed at the edges, a pair of tight, low-cut white shorts, and a matching white T-shirt that has been slashed from top to bottom in a series of vertical slits exposing the soft, flabby flesh of Artur's chest and stomach.

Mario passes by, entering the house hand in hand with a female companion, one of two women who work as cooks in the miners' encampments. He stops momentarily to look. "Give the man a break, Artur," says the Wolf in Portuguese as he turns and walks into the house, his girlfriend giggling behind him.

Artur blows me a kiss, then disappears into the night. "Ciao, gringo," he says as the slapping sound of his flip-flops mixes with that of the cicadas.

6

Behind Vivi's jocular macho banter about the Indians is the prototypical Western European's struggle to figure out the degree of "Indianness" of the indigenous people he encounters. "Those are real savage Indians they have over there," he told me. Yet I wondered, if they were the "real savage Indians" over there, then what type of Indians were the women in rags standing before us?

In the days that followed I did learn more about these women: they put on dresses only when they expected to be in contact with the miners, and they had learned a few phrases of Portuguese so as to scrape together some food for their families. These were ad hoc changes made to adapt to the rapidly changing circumstances of their environment. Although their outward appearance had become dramatically transformed, they had not yet abandoned the culture and language base they shared with those "real savage Indians" Vivi was referring to. Vivi was confused about the Indians he was encountering. And it was a confusion I understood. Making a distinction between different types of Indians was one of the problems I first encountered when I started working in the Amazon.

Before I entered Yanomami territory I probably had a dozen meetings with anthropologists in Brazil who had worked among the Indians but were now banned from returning during the gold rush. By this time I had gotten the miners to agree to take me in, and I had decided to ignore the military's restrictions. I just needed to determine which part of Yanomami territory I wanted to visit.

During our discussions I would point to various villages on a map, asking my informants whether or not the native inhabitants were "wearing any clothing." The eyes of my academic sources would usually twitch and flicker as I pressed this question. Commonly there was a moment of hesitation as I watched them collect their thoughts. I had obviously hit a raw nerve. Yet they were kind enough to explain to me what I might expect to find in a particular region: whether the villagers wore clothes, how long they had been in contact with missionaries or Indian agencies officials, and what might happen if I showed up in a community without the traditional escort of an anthropologist or a native guide. They were accustomed to this line of questioning. They had made a career out of explaining the world of indigenous people (or what little they knew of it) to the outsiders. I was not the first person to inquire whether the Indians wore clothing and I would not be the last. Like Vivi I was simply approaching this trip from the frame of reference of my culture. I was only doing what outsiders have always done in their attempts to understand Indians. I was trying to determine the extent of their acculturation by relying on external indicators. Vivi and I are essentially occupying the same boat as we attempt to navigate the complicated waters of this middle-ground world. But there is one difference: he and I are paddling in opposite directions.

Vivi, following in the tradition of the conquistadores and frontier pioneers, is someone who is intent on civilizing the Indians by *bringing them progress*. I, on the other hand, am trying to understand these native peoples by *bringing them sympathy*. My goal is not to change them but, through my work, to help them preserve their culture. This dichotomy among "whites" is not unusual and, in fact, can be considered part of a process or phenomenon that has been acted out in many periods of contact between Western European explorers and indigenous populations in the Americas. Even Christopher Columbus was scourged by a conscientious Dominican cleric and biographer by the name of Bartolomé de Las Casas whose opinions and observations often ran counter to those of the great Italian navigator. Columbus wrote, just after he had made first contact with the people he mistakenly called Indians:

> I saw a kind of peninsula with six huts. It could be made into an island in two days, though I feel no need to do this, for these people are totally unskilled in arms, as your Majesties will learn from seven whom I had captured and taken aboard to learn our language and to take them to Spain. But, should your Majesties command it, all the inhabitants could be taken away to Castile, or made slaves on the island. With fifty men we could subjugate them all and make them do whatever we want.

These sentiments of Columbus were later criticized by Las Casas who, when writing about the explorer, went to great pains to point out

> how far the Admiral was from the proper observation of divine and natural law, and how little he understood the duty of the King and the Queen and himself toward these natives, as he so lightly could say that they might take all these Indians, the natural inhabitants of these lands, to Castile or make them slaves on their own island, etc. This was very far from the purpose of God and His Church, to whom his voyage and the discovery of all this world and everything in and about it should have been dedicated.

Although we were separated by five centuries, Vivi and I and Las Casas and Columbus were in fact on the same voyage; we were descendants of Western European cultures who had found ourselves swept up in a quest for gold bringing us into contact for the first time with isolated Indian societies and a culture vastly different from our own. What separated us as Western Europeans into two opposing groups was what Las Casas referred to as "the proper observation" or what I have come to call the vision of the Indian. He didn't think Columbus had an accurate understanding of who the Indians really were or how they should be treated. I have the same criticism of Vivi. I cannot understand how he is able look at the cultural degradation taking place before him not as an outcome of his actions but as the responsibility of the Indians themselves. I believe that, like Columbus, his way of observing the Indians allows him to proceed with his conquest of their forest. In his mind his actions are justified: he is doing them good, helping the Indians in his own way.

It is a refrain I have heard from countless miners as well as politicians and pundits in the frontier states and federal capitals. I once interviewed a Brazilian congressman named João Fagundes, who told me that if Indians were dying of malaria in Yanomami territory it was not because the miners were bringing it into the forest but because this was a society where "starvation and bad nutrition" were common factors of everyday life. On another occasion, at the height of the gold mining invasion in Yanomami territory, Brazil's Indian Agency released alarming statistics about the numbers of Indians dying daily as a result of diseases such as malaria. In response to this announcement, the mining leader Machado offered me his own theories on Yanomami society. Sitting in his modern high-rise apartment in Brasília, he gave his interpretation of their culture which led neatly into a scenario wherein the miner is once again the savior. He cited a litany of statistics about the low birth rate of the Yanomami, which he claimed was "the lowest in the world." He informed me that thirty-five to forty percent of the women die in childbirth, a figure that is refuted by anthropologists, one of whom told me that he had seen only two such deaths in the two decades he has worked among the Yanomami. When I brought up the matter of "white" diseases among the Indians as reported by the Indian Agency, José Altino went off into an angry tirade about how "the Yanomami man never works. . . . The persons who build the houses, carry the loads and the children are the women. So the loss of the women is a fundamental loss to the tribe."

Certainly these sentiments are in part a smoke screen of

rhetoric intended to hide the agenda of the miners. But I have come to believe that José Altino, his political allies, and other miners believe what they are saying. They are expressing their vision of the Indian based on their limited contact with these cultures and on what they want to see. That is, if a glass can be half empty or half full depending on how you look at it, so too can the Indian be portrayed as a depraved savage or an innocent victim, obstacle to progress or saviour of the rain forest. It all depends on the view an individual chooses to take.

Adding to the complicated vision of the Indian is the fact that, under Brazilian law, indigenous people are "wards of the state." This bizarre and seemingly condescending categorization ironically is defended by activist lawyers and indigenous leaders alike. It is the one legal device they have at hand to distinguish Indians from the "citizens" of the national society, who, for the most part, are descendants of Portuguese colonialists, European and Asian immigrants, and African slaves. Wards are not subject to the same laws, but they are also not allowed to vote and their rights have to be mediated through the government's Indian agency known as FUNAI. Because the state is their guardian, they are also guaranteed—at least on paper—medical care and education provided by the Brazilian government. And perhaps most important, they have certain inalienable rights to the land they have traditionally occupied. Brazil's 1988 constitution, established after twenty-four years of military rule, represented a major victory for a well-organized coalition of Brazilian human rights activists, liberal politicians, lawyers, and a significant number of indigenous leaders who had learned how to negotiate the labyrinthine, futuristic hallways of the nation's federal capitol in Brasília. They played on the mythology of the national connection to and responsibility for the Indian. And they won some major battles including guaranteeing—again, at least on paper—indigenous people's right to the lands they've inhabited since time immemorial.

What they were not able to control, however, were the "mineral or subsoil rights"—the extremely valuable gold, cassiterite, and titanium that sit below the surface of Indian territories and are, according to the constitution, owned by the national society of Brazil. True, only under special circumstances can these lands be mined, and only with the government's supervision. But men like José Altino, Sebastião, and Elton Kronholt have seized upon this reference to subsoil rights in the constitution to justify their illegal incursions into Yanomami territory. They claim that men like Vivi and the forty-five thousand other miners who have descended on Yanomami lands are entitled to this mineral wealth because it belongs to the citizens of Brazil. The result of the dispute is that, by the time of my arrival, Brazil has for two years been a messy political quagmire overseen by a hapless José Sarney, an octogenarian politician who inherited the presidency after the charismatic and popular Tancredo Neves died of a mysterious disease just two weeks after taking office. Neves had enjoyed a landslide victory in an indirect election presided over by an electoral college handpicked by the dictatorship. Yet he was still the first president since 1964 who was not directly appointed by the military junta. But he had also brought with him, as part of a package of political compromises he needed to get elected, Sarney—a man no one expected would ever rise to power, a compromise appointee who has found himself in the middle of a political minefield pitting the Brazilian government—which refuses to take action to stop the gold rush—against a handful of politicians, lawyers, and activists who are calling the invasion unconstitutional, inhumane, and potentially genocidal.

This classification of the Indian as having a separate status—living in the country but not a citizen—remains a highly politicized concept. In the two decades prior to the 1987 constitutional hearings, Brazil's interior ministry was pushing for the "emancipation" of the natives so that they could be "integrated" into Brazilian society. Free from the tutelage of the Indian Agency, it was argued, they could be incorporated at a faster pace into Brazilian society. But, as the pro-Indian lobby understood, once they entered the state of being "acculturated" they would lose the rights to their land

and be moved into Indian settlements. For this reason indigenous leaders and their sympathetic lobbyists have fought to maintain the classification of Indians as wards of the state, a legal status that highlights their unique cultural and historical legacies. But frontier politicians and pioneers see the distinction chiefly as an obstacle to their claims that the Amazon belongs to the citizens of Brazil. From their point of view, if they can establish that indigenous peoples are Brazilian citizens, then they can nullify the Indians' unique legal status and with it their claims to eighteen percent of the Amazon's land or eleven percent of the national territory of Brazil. No wonder many miners and frontier politicians take almost any opportunity to attack the Indian Agency's credibility. They would like nothing better than to see it abolished. I have frequently been told by miners in Yanomami territory that they, in fact, are the ones helping the Indians with food and medicine and not the Indian Agency. "The Indian Agency," José Altino says, "has the reputation in Brazil as knowing the Indians less than anyone else, particularly in the Amazon."

One of the core points of debate between these two groups is the degree of an indigenous person's "Indianness." The frontier congressman João Fagundes once gave me an elaborate version of his vision of the Brazilian Indian as someone who "already likes to watch TV, he already likes to go to the hospital, he already doesn't cure himself with the resources of biodiversity the jungle offers. He is not the primitive Indian." Fagundes's definition of the Indian fit conveniently into his plan to develop zones of economic activity inside Yanomami territory, thereby legalizing the presence of miners. He assured me that "there isn't this primitive Indian that the international press is concerned about. This primitive Indian doesn't exist."

The problem is that such assessments are based on external indicators: the way people dress, or dance, the houses they live in, whether they have a bank account or can drive a car. They don't take into consideration the worldview of a society, its customs, the way its members make their livelihood, or how they perceive themselves in relation to other cultures. All these things are the below-the-surface factors that are critical in determining the identity of an indigenous group—the difficult-to-discern cultural characteristics that have historically complicated the interactions between the white man, who assumes he knows what an Indian is, and the Indian populations themselves. This dynamic was probably at work when Columbus wrote in his journal:

> I gave them a thousand pretty things in order to get their affection and make them want to become Christians. I hope to win them to the love and service of your Highness and of the Spanish nation, and make them collect and give us the things which they possess in abundance and which we need. . . . They believe that power and goodness are housed in the sky and they are absolutely convinced that I come from the sky with these ships and men.

Today, as in Columbus's time, ideology and perception have become intertwined as convenient, flexible frames of reference for justifying the economic imperatives of the particular colonial or national societies ruling over the indigenous populations of this hemisphere. The Uruguayan writer Eduardo Galeano put it succinctly when he wrote in 1973 that "the Indians have suffered, and continue to suffer, the curse of their own wealth; that is the drama of all of Latin America." Undoubtedly it can be argued that there were very different social, political, and economic forces that drove Columbus to the Caribbean, Custer to the American West, and Brazilian miners into the Amazon. But what can't be denied is that gold was a key catalyst for their expeditions and that they shared a vision of themselves as superior beings motivated by a higher purpose, bringing progress and civilization to a backward and deprived people. That is the history, and the story we have told to our children and grandchildren, of the conquest of the Americas—a tale steeped in the mythology of the Western world with its people depicted as being swept up in a developmental trajectory that began in ancient Greece, continued through the Enlightenment, and blossomed in the Industrial Revolution. As the anthropologist Eric Wolf points out, this vision of the world is

> misleading, first, because it turns history into a moral success story, a race in time in which each runner of the race passes on the torch of liberty to the next relay. History is thus converted into a tale about the furtherance of virtue, about how the virtuous win out over the bad guys. Frequently, this turns into a story of how the winners prove that they are virtuous and good by winning. If history is the working out of a moral purpose in time, then those who lay claim to that purpose are by that fact the predilect agents of history.

Who are the predilect agents of history? The chosen ones, the righteous, the ones who "bring them progress" as Vivi says, those who convince themselves that they are part of a "manifest destiny," that they are carrying out their ventures in the name of a civilized Christian God. On an expedition into the Black Hills in 1873 a Lieutenant James Calhoun, serving under General George Armstrong Custer, wrote:

> the hives of industry will take the place of dirty wigwams. Civilization will ere long reign supreme and throw heathen barbarianism into oblivion. Seminaries of learning will raise their proud cupolas far above the canopy of Indian lodges, and Christian temples will elevate their lofty spires upward towards the azure sky while places of heathen mythology will sink to rise no more. This will be a period of true happiness.

Shortly after the discovery of gold in the Black Hills, with its attendant trumpeting of the arrival of an American El Dorado, an editorial in the Chicago newspaper *Inter Ocean* declared the "red man . . . is but an episode in the advance of the Caucasian. He must decrease that the new comers grow in wealth." In this same period the U.S. Congress in a report entitled "The Condition of the Indian Tribes" attempted to explain the destruction of Indian societies as simply "the irrepressible conflict between a superior and inferior race when brought in the presence of each other." The battle cry of that period was Manifest Destiny, which, as promulgated by Washington policy makers, portrayed Europeans and their descendants as being "willed by destiny" to expand westward. One of the many frontier groups to take up the call was a coalition of pioneers in Cheyenne, Wyoming, known as the Big Horn Association. They proclaimed that

> the rich and beautiful valleys of Wyoming are destined for
> the occupancy and sustenance of the Anglo-Saxon race. The
> wealth that for untold ages has lain hidden beneath the
> snow-capped mountains has been placed there by
> Providence to reward the brave spirits whose lot it is to
> compose the advance-guard of civilization. . . . The destiny
> of aborigines is written in characters not to be mistaken. The
> same inscrutable Arbitrator that decreed the downfall of
> Rome has pronounced the doom of extinction upon the red
> men of America.

But what are the consequences of the advance of civilization? It is estimated that at the time of the arrival of Columbus, the territory that now comprises the United States was inhabited by some two to ten million Indians. By 1865 that number had been reduced to only three hundred thousand.

The statistics on the conquest and colonization of Brazil were, and continue to be, equally startling. Since the Portuguese explorer Pedro Cabral arrived in Brazil in 1500 the population of indigenous groups has been reduced from four million to just over two hundred thousand. In this century alone eighty-seven Indian tribes have become extinct.

The extent to which warfare, slavery, and starvation contributed to these statistics varied in both Brazil and North America. The U.S. military did carry out extensive military campaigns against indigenous peoples in the nineteenth century and earlier but their impact, in comparison to other factors, has been grossly overplayed by the popular image of cowboys fighting Indians in Hollywood movies. The most devastating of all forces in the Western Hemisphere has been outside diseases transmitted by Europeans to indigenous societies. In North America such diseases were responsible for ninety percent of all deaths of native peoples between 1492 and 1900. As early as 1514 a smallpox epidemic swept through the native populations of Panama. In succeeding decades waves of cholera, tuberculosis, scarlet fever, measles, and influenza devastated indigenous societies throughout the Americas. A little-mentioned fact, substantiated in the 1867 Congressional Report on the Condition of the Indian Tribes, is that one of the biggest killers of indigenous societies in the nineteenth-century American West was "venereal disease, particularly secondary syphilis" transmitted by the white man to Indians of this hemisphere—a dirty secret of our legacy that popular historians have chosen to delete in their accounts.

But the last five centuries of conquest have not gone without condemnations by outraged witnesses from our world sympathetic to the plight of native peoples. There have always been clerics, journalists, and soldiers, people who came into sustained contact with indigenous societies and learned to look at them with a perspective different from that of the dominant society. I recounted earlier the scathing critiques of Columbus by his chronicler Las Casas, but there were others throughout the centuries who documented and objected to the abysmal treatment of indigenous societies by pioneers and conquerors. Among them was the mythic trapper, guide, and soldier of the American West, Colonel Kit Carson, who spent more than forty years living among North American Indians in both peacetime and war. In 1865 he delivered lengthy testimony before a U.S. congressional committee on what he perceived as the origin of the conflicts between whites and Indians. "As a general thing the difficulties arise from aggressions on the part of the whites," he stated. "The whites are always cursing the Indians, and are not willing to do them justice." He went on to detail how cultural misunderstandings are often the catalyst for violent conflicts. A journalist accompanying Carson on one of his final expeditions wrote for the New York *World* that "we are goading the Indians to madness by invading their hallowed grounds, and throwing open to them the avenues leading to a terrible revenge whose cost would far outweigh any scientific or political benefit possible to be extracted from such an expedition under the most favorable circumstances."

In Brazil in the twentieth century there has been an unprecedented outcry by individuals and associations working in support of indigenous peoples. The most famous of them all was Colonel Cândido Rondon, who in 1910 founded the Indian Protection Service and inspired generations of Brazilians after him to maintain some institutional form to mediate between their society and the indigenous populations of their country.

For me the most poignant of all of these sympathetic reactions was that of an anonymous sixteenth-century deserter from the French army. In the ruins of an abandoned outpost deep in the wilderness of the New World, he left behind an epigram carved into a plank of wood. It read: WE ARE ALL SAVAGES.

7

Bad news often comes when you least expect it.

We spent the early morning getting establishing shots of the runway under a clear blue sky. Each image was crisp and sharp in the brilliant light. The arrivals and takeoffs of the planes appeared to be perfectly choreographed for my camera. Everything has gone so well, we have covered the scene in half the time expected.

Ready to move on, we have gathered our equipment from the Goldmazon house and begun making our way to the airstrip to meet Sebastião. He agreed late yesterday to fly us to a mining site so that we could see the operations of one of the most profitable gold pits in the area. But now across the airfield he is walking briskly toward a prop plane with the crew from TV Manchete. He glances in our direction, then enters the aircraft and shuts the door. As the engine starts, the Wolf and I both stop in our tracks, struck by the realization that there is no point in going any further. There will be no goodbyes. No opportunity for discussion. No handclasps or pats on the shoulder. This is a de facto desertion. We've lost. He's won. I probably should have shut off the camera the other day.

As the plane jogs down the runway, I turn to the Wolf and watch his chin fall suddenly against his chest and his shoulders cave inwards. I ready myself to catch him before he falls, but I remember that he loves to indulge himself in theatrics at such moments.

Sebastião's plane lifts off with a mechanical roar, disappearing quickly over the jagged stretch of blue-green forest at the end of the runway. We catch a glimpse of him in the small side window of the Cessna as it soars above the empty shells of crashed planes littering this part of the airstrip. He stares down at us like some cruel Greek god on a quick jaunt back to the heavens. The message is clear: he has punished us for questioning his omnipotent powers.

I turn to the Wolf to gauge his mood. He begins kicking the dust, and making a clicking sound with his tongue. It is my cue to begin speaking. I suggest we splurge on a meal of meat, beans, and five-dollar Cokes. A small smile appears at the corner of his mouth. He doesn't speak but bobs his head up and down. I interpret this as some primal signal of affirmation. We head off to the lunch shack beside the runway.

After lunch, the Wolf's spirits restored, we begin negotiating our way out of here, aided by a few cartons of Hollywood cigarettes. A young man who runs a helicopter supply store allows us to use his radio to communicate back to Boa Vista. We contact the mining leader José Altino who originally arranged for our trip into the forest. We inform him that his people haven't kept their end of the bargain and we still need to be taken to the second mining site.

"I need shots of the gold pits to make my story work," I reiterate to the Wolf who translates for the kid at the radio who relays the message back to a guy in Boa Vista sitting at a radio receiver who, by phone, is passing the message to José Altino. I can barely understand any of the Portuguese spoken during these transmissions but, judging from the Wolf's upbeat appearance, the tide may be turning in our favor. Occasionally I make out the standard response of *"Positivo"* but that's about it. The rest is a strange garbled mess, as if I were listening to a chicken being slaughtered through a megaphone. *There's got to be a better way to do this*, I think to myself. *Something is going to get lost in translation. We're going to be here forever.* Then the kid at the radio turns to us. "You will have your answer tomorrow," he says. Mario gives him another carton of Hollywoods. I'm doubtful.

The next day I am cleaning the equipment when the Wolf comes back from the radio shack. We have gotten a message that José Altino has arranged for a pilot named Roberto to drop us at a mining site called Baiano Formiga or "The Little Ant from Bahia." The plane is supposed to be here within an hour. According to the message, once we arrive there we will be able to spend several hours filming before returning to the state capital. José Altino told me about Baiano Formiga when we were back in Boa Vista. It's one of the largest gold pits in the region. "A place where the Indians are working side by side with the miners. Actually sharing the profits. This you must see!" he said, all excited as if he were describing an interethnic Shangri-la rather than this era's El Dorado. I can't, however, shake the feeling that there is something odd about this part of our journey. Although I am pleased, I don't understand why José Altino is continuing to help us. Just yesterday our part of the press junket was ostentatiously terminated by Sebastião. Certainly José Altino spoke to him. He must know by now that their game of trying to control the truth hasn't been working, that I've been refusing to play by their rules. So why then is he facilitating this trip farther into the forest? Maybe there are in fact Indians and miners working collaboratively at Baiano Formiga? That could be true. I am willing to suspend judgment for now. The delays have hurt: I'm short on money and time and I can't leave without shots of a gold pit. Without those I can't tell the story of the gold rush.

Roberto flies us into Baiano Formiga as promised, unannounced, just past noon, banking in over an abandoned, partially destroyed Yanomami village and touching down on an earthen landing strip. As the little Cessna bounces along, a few miners emerge from the half dozen makeshift shacks. As in Paapiú these are men looking for distraction, hoping to find something to break the monotony of life in the forest. Most of them are bare chested, in soccer shorts, with scraggly beards and thick thighs made sturdy by long hikes through the mountains laden like pack mules with food and equipment.

I already know a little bit about this place and I can tell a lot from looking around. The landing strip and environs have been constructed more recently than those at Paapiú. There's less activity, less evidence of attempts to beat back the jungle. The tall trees of the forest loom over the airstrip: it's claustrophobic here. We're farther into the forest, farther away from the flights heading directly to and from the local capital, farther from any direct line of communication with a developed society.

As we get out of the plane, I am struck by the immediate impression that the forest is engulfing us. The humidity, oppressive as ever, is counterbalanced by a cool stream of air wafting in from the jungle, surrounding us and providing--for the moment—a sense of relief from the heat. An echo reverberates through the trees as our pilot Roberto revs his engine for takeoff. He has promised to come for us in two to three hours, cautioning us to be careful, not to ruffle any more feathers.

This last-minute warning adds to the ominous sense I already have of this place. There is no mistaking it: this is really the frontier. No missionaries, no restaurants, and no Indian Agency employees. In plain fact, the collection of mines surrounding Baiano Formiga have the worst reputation of all the gold pits in the region. No one talks about it much, but most miners say they don't want to work here. The bosses are considered ruthless and dictatorial. More than a few murders are reported to have taken place in and around this encampment. Roberto wouldn't answer any questions on the flight in. Yet he smiles now as he passes, safe in his Cessna. Happy, I guess, to get the hell out of here. Perhaps also amused at the dumbfounded expression on my face. *What next?* I have been asking myself since we touched down. Here I quickly realize my style of stumbling about the periphery of a story—searching for a way in—is not going to work. There's not enough time. I need to be more focused than at Paapiú. I can't leave as much to chance.

I pick up the camera and send the Wolf to find out who is in charge. Meanwhile I start with cover shots of the airstrip.

Through my lens the runway looks as if it had been ripped out of the rain forest. Half of a mountain in the background has been razed, leaving a hillside of felled trees lying in zigzag patterns in the distance. In the foreground solemn and weary miners wearing shorts, T-shirts, and hiking boots carry huge lengths of orange tubing as they pass en route to one of several mines in the area. These men are the *formigas* or ants, another generation of South American peons once again chasing a dream of riches in a remote unconquered terrain. With high-powered hoses they prospect the mineral-rich embankments of the region's innumerable waterways, snakelike tributaries that twist and turn through the rain forest as they descend towards the great and mighty Amazon. The fat orange hoses carried by the *formigas* are components of an elaborate procedure called hydraulic mining. It is all part of the age-old business of sifting through the earth in the hope of discovering precious metals. In this new era, though, Yamaha generators and filtration tanks and high-powered hoses have replaced the primitive process of panning by hand. Here it is as if the Medieval Age and the Industrial Age have suddenly become fused: paradise for those who own the mines but purgatory for those who are forced to work them. Most of these men have recently come from the gold rush at Serra Pelada in the southern part of the state of Pará. There a giant *garimpo* or mining pit became the center of activity for an army of eighty thousand fortune seekers. But in the mid-eighties Serra Pelada ran dry and in desperation more than half of those gold-seeking migrants set off for Yanomami territory. Here they have carved out their own place in Brazilian history, making this gold rush the largest ever to take place on Indian lands.

We start by interviewing the Colonel, one of the *donos* or mine bosses who share in the profits from several *garimpos* in the area. Just a few minutes ago, he pulled the Wolf aside to speak to him, Brazilian to Brazilian, as I went about getting cover shots of this lonely airstrip operation. I know enough to know that, at times like this, it's important to stay out of the way, to let go of my tendency to be the control freak and remember that the Wolf is brilliant when it comes to getting people to cooperate. After their brief tête-à-tête Mario returns with his interpretation of their little encounter: if we are going to film here at Baiano Formiga, then we had better respect the local hierarchy and start our filming with the Colonel.

"Do the right thing," he pleads. "Interview him. *Calmamente*," he adds for emphasis.

As I look at Mario's sorry face I can tell it is time to get out of here. These long days in the jungle have eroded his confidence in me and my dubious enterprise. My status is quickly plummeting: the dumb gringo has become the dangerous gringo, a liability in a place like this, a lot more than he bargained for. I don't blame Mario, though. Our life has not been easy recently. We have both passed our birthdays here, commemorated only with snapshots on the airstrip: sunburnt, bearded burnouts looking homesick and weary. He is now having severe *saudades*, heartaches, for his city of Rio and the girlfriend who awaits him. I am suffering less, perhaps because this is my project, perhaps because there is less for me to go back to. Sure, I keep telling myself I will settle down after the next assignment, straighten out my personal life, "get it all together." But already I sense a problem with that plan. The Amazon has the makings of an obsession: there are too many good stories to tell, too many fantastic vistas to take in, too many ways to get lost.

For the interview we position the Colonel with the airstrip in the background. He is a proud ex–military officer in his late forties, but the soft years of civilian life are starting to show around his midsection. When he speaks he pulls in his stomach, forcing his chest out in a pose that could be found at any Veterans of Foreign Wars function in any part of the U.S. But just as we are about to begin, the Wolf starts to have trouble with his equipment. There is static coming through one of the cables.

I smile at the Colonel, trying once again to smooth over one of those uncomfortable moments before an interview, that time when the subject wonders what he is going to say and you wonder what you are going to ask. Avoiding his eyes, I look across the runway at a group of miners standing outside a one-story shack watching us. The Colonel, however, doesn't pay them any attention. It's his hour of glory.

The Wolf has switched cables but now we must wait for an

aircraft to land, another small prop Cessna built for four but carrying ten miners. I wonder for a moment if the Aeronautics Association, or Brazil's equivalent, has checked out the over-crowding of these planes. Then I remind myself that no one has investigated anything out here. This is the frontier. People—Indians and miners alike—often disappear without question. "Anything can happen in the forest" is the common refrain.

"The gold miner is a common man just like any other Brazilian citizen. The gold miner is an anonymous hero. He is a struggler. Nothing stops him," says the Colonel, rattling off this litany as if reading from a Teleprompter.

"I consider the gold miner to be a frontiersman, a discoverer of new wealth, new heritage," he says. "The gold miner works with his heart and soul. Many times the gold miner gets sick but he doesn't go back home without meeting his objective."

I have seen only one Indian since we arrived, a young boy walking arm in arm with another miner, the first sign so far of a relaxed relationship between the two groups. Perhaps José Altino is right? Perhaps the miners are working side by side with the Indians? I ask the Colonel about this, but he tells me without hesitating that the "average Indian won't work more than two hours before he quits."

"What kind of future can the Indians have, working together with the miners?" I ask.

"We have to begin approaching more and more Indians. We have to colonize this area. We have to teach them how to work," he says, suddenly inspired by this line of questioning. "We have to do something with them. The Indians have to work as well for the success of the country."

The Colonel goes on to tell us that there have never been any Indians working in the mines as far as he knows.

His statements make me wonder what José Altino could have been talking about. Didn't he believe that I would ask this question when I arrived here? Perhaps he simply forgot to call ahead and arrange to have a few token Yanomami working the pits? Perhaps he thought a lone gringo with a video camera was nothing to worry about? Maybe I am just part of some larger scheme he has concocted, a pawn who has yet to meet his destiny. But there is no time to obsess over these details. I need to cover the story, get the facts, and get out. I'll worry about the details when I am back in New York.

"I don't have any more questions," I tell the Colonel as I look over at Mario, who is smiling and looking content for the first time in a while. The Colonel, for his part, also seems satisfied. I congratulate myself on being politic and we move on.

The Colonel escorts us down to the end of the airstrip where we can see several mining pits—great ugly holes in which a dozen men, dwarfed by their environs, do in fact resemble ants. Off in the distance a line of trees, two hundred feet tall, make up the forest's new perimeter. According to the Colonel, there are approximately twenty-five pits like this one in the area, producing a combined total of six kilos of gold per day, at a world market value of half a million dollars per week. He takes us to one of the largest and most productive mines. We pass a group of men with chain saws and torches, cutting and burning, clearing ground for more barracks to house the hundreds of new miners arriving daily, impoverished pilgrims who have substituted gold for God as the path to a more fortunate life.

Standing on the perimeter of one pit, I have the impression I am looking down into a football stadium that has sunk into the earth. We knock off a couple of wide shots to establish its size, then descend the slippery slope barefoot with a minimum of equipment—an extra tape, extra battery, that's it. As we search for footholds in the mud, our arms flail about, grabbing desperately for broken roots to check our slide. The camera bounces precariously at my hip, a constant reminder that a sudden tumble could put an end to the entire film. Our steps are short and precise, each one calculated to get a few feet ahead to the next position. I look back up at the Colonel, who smiles and waves. The Wolf curses in a low voice, just loud enough for me to get the joke. I now become aware of my own breath gasping for air in the humid midday heat. I think about the heart attack my father had when he was just a few years older than I am now, then assure myself his fate will not be mine. Halfway down I begin to wonder whether there might have been an easier way to do this. But after seventy-five feet, the terrain suddenly begins to level off. I can now stand upright.

Down here the dimensions and details are different. It resembles a devastated lunar crater. Everything is awash in the light brown mud splattered from the riverbanks by the high-powered hoses. Two large tree trunks, recently torn from the earth, sit lopsided in front of me. A miner, eyes vacant, covered in dirt from head to toe, slowly wades past through a pool of water, showing no recognition of our presence. This is the land of the walking wounded, a mud-caked hell on earth where men are so far beyond the point of exhaustion that a simple hello is visibly difficult. Most of them just blink at you as if a wave or gesture entails too much effort in this dreadful heat.

In the middle of the pit portable Yamaha generators sit vibrating continuously on wooden platforms. The tiny, powerful machines drive the hydraulic pumps and give off a deafening noise permeating every corner of this devastated landscape. The miners who control the hoses seem to be in a hypnotic trance as they twist and turn, their bodies wrestling the blast of the jet spray. Mud flies everywhere as other men, barefoot, walk up and down the sluiceways kicking free the debris that disrupts the murky effluence.

Up on top of the embankment the *donos* in clean clothes stalk the perimeter, clipboards in hand, overseeing operations. They are the ones who originally discovered the sites, purchased the equipment, then transported the miners into the forest at a cost of eight hundred dollars to be taken out of each man's share of profits. The take from the extracted gold is seventy percent for the owners and thirty percent for those working the pits. The workers buy food, supplies, and medicine at the company store at prices that are five times what they would be in Boa Vista. There are no unions out here, no police to resolve conflicts, only the owners who resemble nothing so much as modern-day feudal barons ruling over little forest fiefdoms.

We talk to one José Rodrigues, an old, gap-toothed worker with a sunken face and gray whiskers. He provides us with a little background on his fellow miners in the pits. I start to scribble a series of notes and questions, listening with one ear to Mario's rough translations. The men here are refugees from the poverty of Brazil's northeast, the dark-eyed sons of peasant farmers who worked as indentured servants at the turn of the century. Many of them have recently left jobs as field hands for patrons because they couldn't support their families on two-dollar-a-day wages. Most have several children whom they don't see for a year or two at a time. They have come here in the expectation of a better income, six times their normal wages as field hands. José is the oldest in the group, the one who seems to have the most experience in the mines. Seasoned men like him become de facto leaders who make the deals with the bosses and speak for the group as a whole. They also act as father figures and go-betweens for younger men—some as young as seventeen—who are spending their first time away from home, learning the ropes, and dealing with the boredom, fatigue, and loneliness of work shifts that can last for six months straight.

I flip on the camera as José continues to describe his life at Baiano Formiga. He pauses, a sudden sadness coming over him as he talks about his home.

"God knows that there is suffering back in our cities, in the streets. But here in the bush, there is always rain during the day and then the heat, dealing with the mud, the water, ninety days of working without stopping. It's difficult to tolerate this life."

José is standing in a muddy stream of runoff from the mining. As he speaks he makes small circles with his feet, breaking free the rocks and soil sediments and allowing the water to flow freely into filtration tanks. Every action here is directed towards sifting and cleaning, all of it part of the painstaking effort to uncover each and every ounce of gold.

"We tolerate it because of the money. If it wasn't for the money believe me we wouldn't be here." José stops for a moment and looks down at his feet as if he is mustering the strength for his next statement. "You can't imagine what it is like at night with the cold and the rain," he says. "Much of the time we go without sleep."

We pause for a minute to change tapes. I look around at José and the others. I try to grasp what he has said and what that means for his life and that of the others. I consider doing other interviews, but the Colonel is now motioning for us to meet him on the other side of the pit.

We say our goodbyes to José and the half-dozen lost souls moving aimlessly on this strange, ravaged landscape. "De nada," José says—It was nothing—turning back to his work, his bare feet wading through the small man-made river, his entire body caked in a thin layer of dried brown mud.

Climbing out of the pit is easier, the camera balancing steadily on my back, the footholds now simple to find in the incline. We reach the Colonel in a matter of minutes and he take us to the filtration tanks where the gold is separated from other soil sediments. He says that the miners here do not use mercury to separate the gold from soil sediments—a process that is illegal in Brazil—yet downriver at Paapiú the miners told me they are afraid to drink the water coming from this direction. It is common knowledge that everyone uses mercury to process the gold, though no one will admit to doing it. At the filtration tank a twenty-four-hour guard stands posted to prevent raids by neighboring miners.

A man comes up and speaks to the Colonel and then heads off to one of the pits. The Colonel quickens his pace, hurrying us along on our tour. A soft rain is beginning to fall. A little thunder rumbles in the distance. After a minute the Colonel informs us that one of the donos has asked to meet with us. It seems he wants to discuss the focus of our intended report. Mario turns and glances back at me. That telltale crease has reappeared on his forehead. The Colonel has stopped talking to us. A cool breeze arrives with the approaching rain. I check my watch. Roberto should be arriving in a half hour.

We approach a small wooden building adjacent to the airstrip and I tell the Wolf to go on in. I figure he will be able to smooth-talk this dono pretty easily. Meanwhile, the rain has let up and I want to knock off a few more shots.

I work quickly, trying to get the last material I need to make the sequence work. A helicopter passes overhead, and I pan and tilt as it speeds off into the forest. The pilot dips his chopper right at me as he passes by, intentionally ruining my shot. Now more men with more rubber hoses trot by and I grab other images that I missed before, these from a low angle and using a wider lens. Another plane lands and I zoom out, revealing the airstrip. I've got it covered, so I power down.

Moments later I step into an office with Mario standing in front of a desk and a man introduced to me as Mr. Mineiro sitting behind it. Mineiro translates as a man from the state of Minas Gerais—or simply as miner. Mr. Mineiro is a small man in his late thirties with curly blond hair, the obligatory gold chain hanging from his neck. Behind his desk an automatic rifle stands just out of reach. As I position myself against a side wall, I am immediately struck by the tension in Mario's eyes. Something is going wrong. I take it his standard jokes and small talk haven't broken the ice with this *dono*. I begin to think that I underestimated the seriousness of this request for a discussion. Mario fidgets nervously with his sound cables and explains that Mr. Mineiro is confused about what we are doing here. Mineiro now begins directing his comments to me. When a young and very pretty woman—his girlfriend, I assume—walks through the office with a young child following, he asks her to close the door, which I had deliberately left open. He rambles on incoherently about the ecologists' plot to stop the work of the gold miners. He talks at me but never looks me in the eye. His voice becomes tense, almost inaudible, as he starts talking about *Time* magazine and the North American press. "Regarding the ecology, the gold miners don't destroy, don't burn the forest," he says, raising his voice in order to be heard over the chain saws blaring across the way.

I check my watch and realize that if our pilot comes and doesn't see us on the airstrip, he will leave right away. Pilots here don't fly at night. There are no identifiable landmarks to stand out in the darkness, making aviation an impossible task.

Suddenly Mineiro slams his fist down on the desk, an action not called for by anything he is saying. He continues rambling but still doesn't look into anyone's eyes. "The gold miners' interest is gold. They get gold and leave the rest. The gold miners don't destroy anything." I consider asking him about those H-bomb craters we just walked through, but I don't want to get provocative. Besides, he is sitting too close to that rifle.

It is obvious to me that we have stumbled upon a psychopath. The longer we let him get worked up, the better the chance we will miss our flight back to Boa Vista. I interrupt Mineiro in midsentence. Mario turns and looks at me as if I too am crazy. His eyes, now bulging and imploring, are locked dead on mine.

"I think we should do an interview with Mr. Mineiro," I suggest to Mario in English as I open the door to the office. *"Quer fazer uma entrevista, Senhor Mineiro?"*—Do you want to be interviewed, Mr. Mineiro?—I say to him in my halting Portuguese. Mario pauses, then translates again just to be certain Mineiro has understood our request.

When I exit, the Wolf is right behind me. "Let's get out of here," he whispers in English as we shuffle our way across the dirt runway.

Mineiro follows us, thankfully leaving behind the rifle. With both his hands he adjusts the gold chain hanging from his neck as he catches up to us on the airstrip: even the insane can be vain.

We set Mineiro up in front of a plane, instructing him to simply say what is on his mind. I can see the tables turning slowly, the intimidating Mr. Mineiro somehow neutralized a little bit out here in the open, the electronic gaze of the camera helping to pacify his troubled soul. Perhaps this is part of what I've come to call "the Hi-Mom, phenomenon"—the need of anyone, including lunatics like Mineiro, to look good in front of the camera because maybe their mothers will see them. This is partly a joke, but at such times I begin to believe that this theory is true. Somehow television and its images have become more than a means of communication. They have established a presence in our consciousness: a strange mirror reflecting back to us our dreams and myths, and perhaps even the discerning eyes of our mothers and fathers. Maybe it is because we have all grown up with a television in our homes, and it has become like a relative you just don't want to offend. Whatever the case, I am grateful for its special power at times like this.

"*Tudo bem, Senhor Mineiro?*"—Is everything okay, Mr. Mineiro?—I say to him as I hit the start button on the camera.

He stares at the ground, then recommences his ranting. I do a slow dance from right to left, trying to catch his eyes in the perspective of the lens. The Wolf is recording sound, keeping one eye on the sky in expectation of our plane.

Five minutes into Mineiro's incoherent interview, a small Cessna bounces to a halt on the dusty runway; our pilot Roberto has returned. The camera clicks off, we say our good-byes to Mineiro and take off.

Once in the air I ask Roberto again about the *donos* and rumors of murder at Baiano Formiga. He just smiles, refusing to comment, abiding by another of the unspoken rules of this land: Don't make enemies of your clients, especially these characters. I glance down at a pint bottle filled with gold dust lodged near the landing gear. Silence is not without compensation. Roberto knows what he is doing.

I look out the window and see a Yanomami maloca, a little circular dot sitting almost imperceptible in the green forest. I think of the Indians' side of the story, the one I wasn't able to get on this trip, the one I will need to get if I want to have a complete understanding of what is really happening here. So far I've heard only the miners' side with its convoluted ideology of half-truths trumpeted by a battalion of men who, I believe, are obstinately refusing to see what is taking place around them. Certainly I have enough material to knock out a few news reports on the miners' gold rush. Those are plain facts. We can see them. That's journalism. But there are more complicated levels to this story. There is something going on here that has less to do with what we see and more to do with the way we are seeing it. It's as if there is an elusive truth that wavers between their world and ours—a truth that belongs to neither one of us but we each claim as our own.

8

journal entry
Conçeição do Araguaia
August 8, 1987

I arrived at 5:00 pm and was met at the airport by Father
Ricardo. He was accompanied by a tall tough-looking
theology student from Imperatriz. Ricardo immediately starts
telling me about the two peasants murdered in the last three
days. He expects that there will be more violence by the end
of the week.

We took a long road into town and fireworks broke out in
the background as we talked. A quick turn of my head had
both the priest and the student laughing.

Once in town Ricardo couldn't drop me at the hotel
because it is owned by one of the local ranchers, and he says
he is afraid of being shot. This information triggered
something in me. After I got to my room, I started feeling
flipped out and was talking to myself. It hit me that I had
spent the afternoon driving around with some guy on a death
list. I didn't sleep, but by daybreak I was settled down and
ready to cover this story.

* * *

"**D**on't go on that road to Trevo" is what João Moreira's godmother remembers telling him before he headed off into town and never came back.

João Moreira was an impoverished peasant and father of eight in a country where 120 million people live below the poverty line. He and his family were just a few of the estimated eight million people in Brazil who had migrated into the country's rain forest since 1966. These dirt-poor migrants began arriving in droves after the dictator General Castelo Branco initiated Operation Amazonia, the first of several ill-conceived plans under the military regime to "open up" and develop the Amazon. General Geisel's approach was essentially a military operation to "integrate" the Amazon with the more developed and heavily populated southern half of the country. A special branch of government known as the Superintendency for Amazonian Development, or SUDAM, was put in place to oversee the expansion of the frontier. It was during this period that liberal tax incentives were given to corporations and wealthy individuals to foster cattle ranching in the region. However, the real catalyst to migration came in 1970 when a newly appointed military dictator, General Emílio Garrastazú Médici, initiated a "penetration scheme" into the Amazon whereby an extensive highway system would be built as part of an official government policy to populate the region with economic refugees from the drought-stricken region of northeast Brazil. During this time the country's Indian Agency was put into the hands of a group of colonels who were mandated to begin turning indigenous populations into "normal" people. Over the next fifteen years 9,300 miles of railways lines, 1,850 miles of paved roads, 8,700 miles of dirt roads, and General Médici's dream scheme, the gigantic 2,700-mile Transamazon Highway, were constructed to create an infrastructure for immigration and economic development.

As part of their initiative for resettling the poor, Médici's government reserved a six-mile stretch of land on each side of the Transamazon Highway so that migrant families could start a new life. João Moreira, his wife, and his young children were part of a wave of landless people who—responding to the

General's well-publicized plan—took advantage of these new roads to settle in the southern part of the state of Pará. As with many of the peasants who were traveling to this region, the dreams of the Moreira family were modest: a small plot of land, some cattle, and enough cash from a season's crops to put meals on the table and pay for life's essentials.

But within their first decade these projects created a number of problems unforeseen by the military dictators and their functionaries who ran SUDAM. Hundreds of previously untouched Indian tribes were suddenly thrown into contact with Brazilian highway workers, and many of them soon died off from disease. The work of cutting through the forest was also much more difficult and labor-intensive than had originally been expected. Stronger and more powerful tractors and bulldozers were needed. The budget for the operation quickly doubled in size. Then as Brazil's dictators scrambled for international financing, a third serious problem began to emerge: open war between the ranchers, the *fazendeiros*, and the landless peasants who had come to claim their promised plots of land.

In part these violent disputes could be traced back to the land distribution strategies of SUDAM. While the military government had promised free plots to the nation's poor, it was simultaneously giving huge tax incentives for the creation of large-scale farms and cattle ranches. As thousands of immigrants poured into the region, the competition for available plots reached fever pitch. The problem was exacerbated by corruption and mismanagement on the part of SUDAM. Because of bribery, shoddy record keeping, and a generally disorganized settlement process, plots that had been settled for a number of years by peasants were also being assigned to large landowners and corporations. With the possibility of obtaining any land from the government diminishing, many of these desperate migrants became *posseiros*, peasant squatters who, in accordance with Brazilian law, were claiming areas of large estates that were not actively being cultivated. If the *posseiros* could prove that they had been working the land for five years, then they were legally entitled to claim it as their own. If they settled an untilled area of rain forest for a year and a day, they could also claim it as their own. But as land speculators continued to buy more and larger plots, there was a surge in the number of land-title conflicts between peasant populations and *fazendeiros*. With no effective justice system in place, the cattle ranchers and peasants resorted to violence and terrorism to settle their disputes. The region that had once been a dream land for João Moreira and his family was transformed in a few short years into a land rife with violence and terrorism—an area with the worst human rights record in all of rural Brazil.

To understand poverty in the Amazon, it is necessary to look at the larger picture of land ownership in all of Brazil. Two percent of the people control sixty percent of the land, while close to seventy percent of the poor families have no title to property. The estates of some of the large ranchers are so extensive that you can drive for hours and never leave their property. A survey of 340 of the largest ranches in the Amazon totaled 183,397 square miles—an area larger than the state of California. Slavery and debt servitude are also common. And for decades there has been almost no judicial infrastructure in most frontier communities.

The problems of social injustice and severe discrepancies in wealth, so evident in the Amazon, have led to organized attempts at revolution in other Latin American countries such as Chile, Argentina, Bolivia, Uruguay, and Paraguay. Yet in recent Brazilian history there has not been an armed insurgency movement with the exception of a Maoist campaign in the south of Pará in the early 1970s. This Guerrilha do Araguaia was a band of eighty revolutionaries who had split off from the Brazilian Communist Party in 1969 and fled into the backlands of Pará in hopes of fomenting an armed insurrection. Their model might have been Fidel Castro's Twenty-sixth of July Movement but their fate was closer to Che Guevara's disastrous peasant revolt in Bolivia. They had not foreseen two major obstacles: the weakness of their support among the peasantry and the severity of the government's opposition. General Médici responded to the news of the Guerrilha do Araguaia by transforming Operation Amazonia into a full-scale military endeavor. Twenty-five thousand troops were sent in to root out the ragtag revolutionaries. Roadblocks were everywhere. For three years the military controlled the region. Peasant houses were routinely searched and any arms—even the simplest hunting rifle—confiscated. At the end of the campaign two thousand people had been killed. When the armed forces finally abandoned the area, there was still no effective judicial infrastructure to carry out the law. As the decade progressed, land disputes began to increase and conflicts became more extreme. Impoverished farmers like João Moreira now found themselves increasingly pulled into small-scale wars pitting a loose alliance of landless *posseiros* against the big ranchers and their hired *pistoleiros*.

When he arrived in this region João had been one of the lucky people to be given a plot of land by SUDAM. He built a small wooden house and was able to raise his family on the meager yield of his cultivated fields and the revenue brought by a small herd of cattle. But as is common in the region, he encountered trouble when his two eldest sons were ready to marry. It is customary among Brazilian peasants for a father to subdivide his plots at the time of a son's marriage. But João had no land to spare, so he settled his children on some uncultivated acreage that, it turned out, was also being claimed by a cattle rancher referred to locally as Doctor Jundir. Who actually had the legal right to this land has never been settled, but the invocation of brutal violence to resolve the dispute has been well documented. Soon after João Moreira had settled his sons on the new plot, he began to hear rumors that *pistoleiros* were pursuing him. "Sometimes a car passed by," his godmother told me when I arrived at his house the day after his death, "and he would say, 'the man passed by but he didn't see me.' But that day he was caught." The killers—the family believes there were two of them—were waiting in some low scrub by the side of the road as night fell on this quiet peasant community. They had taken precautions. The area was populated; João Moreira was well liked; gunfire would have alarmed the community. They had armed themselves with thick pieces of wood.

The Wolf and I drove out to João's small settlement in a beat-up Chevy I had hired along with a driver named Amori.

This was August of 1987, the first time I had ever been in the Amazon. It was also right in the middle of "the burning season," the driest time of the year, when the forest was being torched by cattle ranchers to clear land for pasture. Small farmers also burned off their meager plots then as part of their slash-and-burn agriculture. There was smoke everywhere. Driving along, we could see huge trees in flame; occasionally they would burst and crumble, their limbs shooting out sparks as they hit the ground. I remember the forest floor as one long stretch of crisp black ash—a medieval vision of a desolate hell. The air in the car was too stifling if we rolled up the windows, so we wore bandanas around our mouths to cut down on the intake of dust and smoke. I draped my shirt over my camera, hoping to protect it from all the ashen fallout. I never thought about getting a shot of the fires. I didn't understand their significance. I had come here to focus on human rights.

When we knew we were close to João Moreira's home we stopped in the small town to ask directions. But the locals were hesitant to tell us where the Moreiras lived. It took them a while to believe that a journalist from North America would be interested in the story of a peasant killed in their little town. I remember a poster of Tina Turner hanging from the wall— bizarre juxtaposition, I thought.

The townspeople were typical of many frontier communities in that they didn't trust outsiders. *Pistoleiros* were most often strangers brought in from out of state, killers with no links to the towns in which they murdered. But the Wolf persisted. He answered their questions and gave lengthy explanations of our intentions. Eventually we gained the confidence of a shopkeeper who directed us to João Moreira's house not far from the cluster of stores that comprised the town's center. There we learned that the burial had taken place the day before. We found a family in a great deal of pain. The youngest daughter was catatonic with grief. As we introduced ourselves she stood in the front yard chewing on the base of her thumb. An old woman who identified herself as João's godmother was only able to muster a few barely comprehensible phrases before she would break down in tears. But one of the oldest sons, Clecio, had a different reaction to his father's death. He was outraged. He wanted to talk about it. So he took us to the site of his father's murder.

Clecio believed João Moreira was caught off guard as he came down the dusty road on his way to town. On each side barbed-wire fence enclosed a field of tall grass. "It was there," he said, pointing to the field. "It was there that they must have been hiding."

Clecio thought the first blow, to his father's head, knocked him down. Then, he explained, the killers must have cracked open his skull with the hard wooden planks. As we followed a trail of blood, Clecio described to us how the assassins probably dragged his father's body four hundred feet into a nearby field to finish the job. "They destroyed his whole face," he told us as we walked about filming the scene of the crime, the flies swirling frantically around the remnants of thick blood still stuck to the tall grass at the roadside.

I stopped to get a shot of a small wooden cross erected by his children. His name and the date of his murder were crudely inscribed on the wood with red and blue paint.

"They pierced his eyes so that no one would recognize him," Clecio said as I panned the camera from the cross to the blood still staining the dirt roadway. "He was identified by his boots, because by looking at the body no one could tell that it was my father."

I remember Clecio's phrases coming in short spurts as he tried hard to fight back the emotion of the loss of his father. "It was Jundir, the landowner of the Bela Vista estate, who sent the killer over here. He was the one who paid somebody to do the job," he said. "They picked on him because he was the biggest *posseiro* around here. They tortured him and they killed him. They tortured him a lot."

I had left Conceição do Araguaia early that morning in the hope of arriving before the burial. If you want to sell a violence story to television you need to have corpses. That's the way it works, or so I was told. "Don't come home without one," a news editor warned me over the phone before I left. "If you want me to run that story, I gotta have a body," he reiterated in the I've-seen-it-all tone common to assignment editors. So I made the effort to "get the body." But this was the Amazon. Corpses decompose quickly. João had been buried the same day that he had been found; not even Clecio had a chance to see his father before the funeral took place. By the time I arrived the police had done a cursory investigation which consisted of stopping by the house to ask the family a few questions. No one was holding the body for an autopsy. Besides, there wasn't a morgue.

After spending the day with João's family I returned to my base in Conceição do Araguaia where, over the next few days, another five peasants involved in land disputes were killed. They were all buried before we could get to them, though there was one whose burial had been substantially delayed, intentionally. In this case the *pistoleiros* were keeping watch over the victim's body so that it couldn't be recovered and properly laid to rest. They wanted it to rot in the tropical heat so that the victim's friends and family would eventually find only a decaying cadaver infested with maggots. This was part of their tactics of intimidation, and it was effective. His friends and family were obsessed with getting to the body. It was as if the continued abuse of the body of the victim had become a means of furthering the impact of the *pistoleiros*' violence. They were torturing the living. I've never seen anything like it. It made me understand how violence could become an art form.

Although I never did get my shot of João's disfigured body, a Catholic nun named Sister Tarcísia had taken a black-and-white photo of João in an open casket, his face bloody and punctured, his youngest daughter standing beside him, her hands placed delicately on the edge of the casket, her face registering shock. I eventually used this still shot in a news report I did back in the States. The news editor never complained. The testimony of Clecio and his family had been so powerful that no one seemed to notice. For all his I've-seen-it-all pretensions, my editor was actually moved by the story.

A report on the João Moreira murder case was filed with Amnesty International by Father Ricardo Rezende, a local Franciscan priest whose best friend, a fellow clergyman named

Father Josimo Tavares, had been killed the previous year by a *pistoleiro*. Rezende—as I had found out on my first day here—was on a *lista negra* or blacklist of those to be killed. Padre Ricardo, as he is referred to by the locals, is one of those handsome priests over whom old ladies swoon at parishes everywhere. He has long, curly black hair and a thick mustache that is stylish in this region of Brazil. He is also one of the hundreds of politicized priests inspired by liberation theology and working in the Amazon. He divides his time between ministering to the spiritual needs of the people and advising them on legal matters regarding land conflicts. His small office, cluttered with papers and folders, is located on one of the dusty back streets of Conçeição do Araguaia. The battered metal filing cabinets lining the walls are filled with reports on murders that have never been brought to trial. "Eighteen-year-old Leonilde Resplande was raped by eighteen *pistoleiros* and burned alive in front of her husband who was then also killed," he told me one afternoon as I filmed him behind his desk. "The group of *pistoleiros* who killed them were commanded by Sebastião da Teresona and included the three Guedes brothers who were in prison for three weeks and then set free."

In the few hours I spent with Rezende he pulled dozens of photographs out of his files: bodies burned, decapitated, and, almost always, beaten beyond recognition. It was clear that murder in the south of Pará had become part of a strange and terrifying ritual. And as Rezende put it, "The violence here has a pedagogical trait: to kill isn't enough, it also terrorizes those who remain alive."

A year later I took an assignment as a cameraman which brought me to another violent locale in the Brazilian Amazon. This was the state of Acre where a well-organized movement of *seringueiros* or rubber tappers was involved in conflicts with local cattle ranchers. I had been hired to shoot a documentary on sustainable development produced by an independent filmmaker named Miranda Smith. She had brought along her own soundman, an amiable, low-key fellow called Dudu. For ten days she and Dudu and I followed the daily life of one of the region's most popular union leaders, a man who had already escaped six assassination attempts. This was Francisco "Chico" Mendes, a forty-three-year-old self-educated union leader whose precarious life now necessitated the constant presence of two machine-gun-toting policemen. Unlike João Moreira's, however, Chico's death would not go unnoticed. It would dramatically change the face of politics in the Amazon.

———————

"We cannot tolerate the threats of the gunmen with all these police around," Chico said as he ate lunch with his two children, his wife, Ilzamar, and a half-dozen other rubber tappers at the long wooden table in his kitchen. He was a handsome man with wavy dark hair and hefty forearms. The pupils of his eyes were deep black. His face, although round and puffy, still maintained the exuberance of a young boy.

Chico had grown up in the forest outside the small backwater town of Xapuri. He was the son of rubber tappers, one of eighteen children. "There's not much to do in the forest," a rubber tapper had told me the day before when I asked him why families in this area were so big. He then informed me that he had sired twenty-five children of his own, all with the same woman. A big smile stretched across his face as he took in my awestruck reaction. "Have you thought about contacting the Guinness Book of World Records?" I asked as my soundman, Dudu, patiently translated. The man's face went blank. He had no idea what I was talking about. Dudu began to laugh. "It is time for you to realize, Jefferson, that you are in another world." That was November of 1988. I was still learning about life on the frontier.

The atmosphere in Chico's house that day had been lighthearted and celebratory. It was election day in Xapuri and Chico and his friends were anticipating a victory for the left-wing *Partido dos Trabalhadores*, or Workers' Party. The PT was started by a combative autoworker named Luís Inácio "Lula" da Silva who, earlier on, had been a supporter of the rubber tappers' movement in Acre. As I watched Chico that day, I found it hard to believe that this was a man who lived under the constant threat of assassination. He seemed relaxed and happy, as if he didn't have a care in the world. But as I came to learn, Chico was good at keeping up appearances. He needed to be. It was part of his job. He was the leader of Xapuri's local union of rubber tappers. If he showed fear the union would fall apart. The intimidation practiced by his enemies would have paid off.

Besides, he had a plan that, he told friends, was going to get him out of the corner that he had been backed into. He was going to get to the killers before they got to him—not with violence but with justice. He had found out that Darly Alves da Silva, the local cattle rancher threatening his life, was wanted for murder in the state of Paraná. Chico was determined to have justice exacted in a region little known for it. He intended to put away the man whose reputation for brutal violence posed a threat not just to his own person and livelihood but to the entire rubber tappers' movement. On learning of the outstanding indictment against Darly, Chico had contacted local prosecutors, the federal police, and even the governor, urging them to take action against Darly. "I believe in God," he told his uncle Amaro during this period. "And I'm going to take hold of God and drive these bad people away." He assured the friends and family who had been concerned about his welfare that it was just a matter of time before Darly was put away. He seemed to believe it, so we all did.

But this day, when someone at the table mentioned Darly's name, the entire mood changed. It was as if the spirit of Death had suddenly entered through an open window, lingering among the living, letting them know that it was close by. Through my camera I could see the fear working its way into Chico's face. I knew then that behind the upbeat facade was a man in fact frightened, not just by the threats of a sociopathic killer, but also by the impotence or indifference of the frontier judicial system. As I would find out later, Chico's pleas to the local prosecutor, the federal police, and the governor had gone unheeded. His fate was being left to the violent vicissitudes of life on the frontier.

Darly Alves da Silva owned a ten-thousand-acre estate known as Fazenda Paraná located on the outskirts of Xapuri. There he lived with his wife, three mistresses, thirty children, and a dozen ranch hands whom the locals considered to be part-time *pistoleiros*. Early in the year he had been involved in a bitter dispute with Chico and his union over a contested piece of forest known as the Seringal da Cachoeira. The government land agency, INCRA, had intervened and decided in favor of the rubber tappers. This was an unprecedented victory for the forest workers, one they hoped to build on in years to come. As part of the compromise agreement Darly was compensated for his disputed tracts of rain forest. Publicly Darly said he was satisfied with the settlement but, according to local rumor, he was privately set on vengeance. The protracted conflict between himself and Chico prior to the settlement had reached ever more unbridled levels of machismo, which carried over to related conflicts between the rubber tappers and other cattle ranchers. In the spring of 1988 two adolescents participating in a rubber tappers' demonstration were shot. Several weeks later another friend of the rubber tappers' union, a church monitor and Workers' Party candidate, was murdered outside his home. Chico was certain that Darly, and a son of his by the name of Darci, were behind the killings. The rubber tappers believed the actions were part of a campaign of intimidation intended to destabilize the union movement before it was able to capitalize on growing domestic support. Perhaps most important, the rubber tappers' victory at Seringal Cachoeira represented a serious setback to cattle ranchers intent on developing the same tracts of pristine forest that Chico and his men were working to preserve.

In the weeks before our arrival rumors of Chico's imminent death had been increasingly circulating on an elaborate grapevine of friends and relatives in Xapuri. According to the warnings trickling in, ten thousand dollars had been anted by a group of cattle ranchers as a reward to Chico's assassin. A deadline had also been set: Chico was to be killed by Christmas. That was just four weeks away. Friends of his had told us that *pistoleiros* and cattle ranchers had started appearing regularly at Chico's house at all hours of the day and night. These visits were part of their intimidation tactics and they soon spread to other locales—his union headquarters, his favorite little coffee stand—each time subjecting him to the evil eye. This is a look sociopaths specialize in, a look so venomous it manages to penetrate the very depths of one's soul.

I have been on the receiving end of such evil eyes in Brazil and elsewhere in Latin America on more than a few occasions. My first came courtesy of a goon in Guatemala City, one of the two-dollar-a-day killers hired by death squads to carry out their dirty deeds. He had been waiting for me outside my hotel as I loaded my equipment into a van one morning. He looked straight into my eyes with such intensity, it was as if he was trying to give me an intimation of my own death. Although it was my first experience with such looks, I knew what it was—and I knew why. It took me hours to recover. I was in Guatemala doing a human rights story on the atrocities perpetrated against that country's peasant populations, most of whom are descendants of Mayan Indians. Someone had reported our presence in the city paper the day before: we had filmed a body found on the roadside, the hands chopped off at the wrists and a scrawled message left that read, "More to come." Clearly, someone felt that we had gone too far in gathering the details of this story. A decision had been made to intimidate us, hence the visit from the goon. But there was more. That afternoon in a remote hilltop village we found ourselves suddenly surrounded by five jeeps with mirrored windows. The intimidation phase had intensified to terrorization. A dozen men emerged with sidearms and rifles. Once again they simply stared. No words. No threatening gestures. Then after a few minutes they climbed back in their jeeps and disappeared into the mountains. We left two days later, our story over. We were foreign journalists. We could do that.

Chico could also have left, yet he chose to stay. "I have a moral commitment to myself," he told us in an interview that morning. "I cannot leave this fight even if one sunny day I am struck by an assassin's bullet."

In these last weeks of Chico's life his family and friends became increasingly concerned. They wanted him to heed the warnings circulating through Xapuri, but he wouldn't listen. He was a hardened political animal. He had confronted and beaten more formidable opponents. He wasn't about to back down to Darly's threats. On two occasions Chico had taken on the military junta and won, once in the 1970s and then again in the 1980s. In both cases he had been accused of fomenting dissent against the government, an offense for which people could "disappear" or, if convicted, draw a jail term of up to thirty years. Chico was imprisoned and tortured but did receive a trial. "I was lucky to have some good lawyers," he told us. He won both cases and continued his organizing work with the rubber tappers. And now he assured us that "for the first time there has arrived here a military commander who has an interest in putting in prison the hired gunmen. The judge of the judicial district also has an interest in jailing the gunmen," he said. "Yet the higher levels of government neither permit nor provide the conditions for them to jail the gunmen. This is a grave problem."

"Were they all there including Darly?" Chico asked the man sitting next to him at lunch that day.

"Yes, they were all there," said the man.

Chico's wife, Ilzamar, an exotic beauty sixteen years younger than he, pulled her lush mane of dark hair back over her shoulder and looked up from her plate of rice, beans, and meat. The clatter of the dishes came to a halt. "When I was there I saw them," she said. "They were gathered together plotting something."

Chico's eyes went blank while his wife recounted the story of seeing Darly that morning. He stared off into the distance, past the wooden shutters of that cramped little room, lost in thought, perhaps imagining the unimaginable: how and when his life would come to an end. *Would it be a "sunny day"? Who would find him? What would become of his children?*

How, one asks, did Chico find himself in this predicament? The answer is rooted in the history of the forest reserves in his home state of Acre, a frontier region that shares a border with Bolivia.

Acre had seen a wave of settlement during the military government's "economic miracle" of the late 1970s. But before the peasants and cattle ranchers arrived there, the state had been populated by men like Chico's father, immigrants from the northeast who came to live among the Indians and tap the rubber trees for latex to be sold back in the cities. From the turn of the century until World War II latex collecting had enjoyed an economic boom, particularly for the rubber barons of the region who had profited enormously from contracts with the Ford Motor Company. But by the 1970s the world economy had changed drastically. Rubber was being produced more cheaply and abundantly in the Orient. The bottom had fallen out of the Brazilian market and rural land barons had abandoned the region, leaving the forests to the tappers.

Freed from the exploitive practices of these feudal patrons, the rubber tappers managed to support themselves by selling the latex and Brazil nuts they collected in the forest. But then the arrival of cattle ranchers, encouraged by government tax incentives to settle the area, threatened the reserves in which the rubber tappers made their living. By the late seventies, violent confrontations between the *seringeiros* and cattle ranchers were escalating. The military government intervened on occasion, but usually on behalf of the cattle ranchers.

During this period the rubber tappers developed a series of sophisticated techniques for combatting the destructive encroachments of cattle ranchers. They held *empates*, or pacifist demonstrations, in the rain forest. They would surround a group of workers sent in to clear the land, and try to show them the destructive implications of their action—how it was ruining not only the local economy but the forest on which they all depended. With time the *empates* became a powerful organizing tool, frustrating the attempts of cattle ranchers to cut down the forest. The Seringal had been the site of a decade-long struggle of the rubber tappers in which numerous *empates* had taken place. The success of the tappers began to gain wider recognition from national politicians and international environmentalists, journalists, and filmmakers.

"Without international support, without the international press, without the international environmentalist organizations," Chico said in our interview that morning, "we would still not have a single reserve."

Yet as the rubber tappers' tactics became more effective, attacks against their membership increased. By 1988, Chico's local union of a thousand men had lost ten of its leaders to assassination, three of them in the last year alone. Pressure by Amnesty International had forced the military police to provide bodyguards for Chico, but his friends and family were still worried. Xapuri was a remote backwater town. There was still no full-time prosecutor, and for a decade there had been no judge. This absence of a judicial infrastructure had, as in southern Pará, ensured a culture of lawlessness. Local cattle ranchers knew they ran little risk of prosecution for violent acts. Although Chico repeatedly requested the federal police to intervene on his behalf, nothing was done. Darly Alves da Silva remained free and the threats of death continued to circulate along the Xapuri grapevine.

"Either the police will have to take care of this problem or we will," he said that afternoon at the kitchen table. Chico was opposed to using violence for political change, but he was not against picking up a pistol to defend his own life.

After lunch that day I went to the front room of his modest three-room house to change the battery on my camera. The streets were still busy with people going to the polls. They were also rife with tension. Two truckloads of heavily armed soldiers had been brought in from a nearby post following rumors that a local candidate was trying to rig the elections; they blanketed the streets, guarding the voting booths and town hall, with bayonets mounted and machine guns at the ready. Ever since Darly's name had been uttered at lunch, Chico appeared distracted and nervous. He was now pacing around the house while his family cleared the table. As I pulled the used battery from my camera I looked up and saw Chico surveying the street through his front window. Suddenly he moved to the cupboard, pulled out a small pistol, checked its chamber, and returned to the window. Kneeling there in my dim corner, I could feel my adrenaline rushing, the senses of touch and sound disappearing as the world suddenly switched into slow motion. I stared at the old pistol by his side, my camera resting on my knees and my mind scanning for the next move. *What about the battery?* I asked myself. *I need to get the shot.* Yet I couldn't move. Chico stood perfectly still for a moment, his free hand signaling to me not to move. Here I was supposed to be the distant observer and not one of the victims, and he had broken the sacred space between journalist and subject and pulled me into his life: it all happened that fast. Then he simply turned back to the cupboard, replaced the gun behind some books, and walked quietly out of the room. Once again I became conscious of the camera on my lap, the sounds of his friends and family, the job I had been sent here to do. I looked out on the street. There was no one there. That morning Chico had said he was becoming increasingly worried by the thought that his "enemies will get one of my children, or kidnap someone in my family." He reiterated, however, that although he did not fear for his own life, he still didn't want to die. "After death we are useless," he had told some friends lately. "Living people achieve things—corpses nothing."

Contrary to what he thought, Chico wasn't killed on a "sunny day." It happened at night, just two days before the Christmas deadline. As he stepped into his backyard on a hot, muggy evening, two figures emerged from the bushes. The shots were fired at close range with a 20-gauge shotgun—eleven pieces of lead tearing through his lungs, sending him careening back into his kitchen, where his wife was making dinner. There he tumbled into the arms of one of his bodyguards and slowly bled to death in the cramped hallway of his tiny three-room house. "They've killed Chico!" his wife cried out as she ran into the streets in search of help. He was buried on Christmas Day.

In the weeks following his murder, Chico's name appeared on the front page of almost every major newspaper in the United States, France, England, Italy, Spain, Japan, and Germany. His international "friends" had made certain that the world would recognize his death. Hollywood producers and stars—spurred on by eco-conscious spouses, colleagues, and the mounting volume of this big-story reporting—quickly began vying for the rights to Chico's life. They courted his widow Ilzamar in the United States and sent development "execs" on jets to the jungle to meet other members of his family as well as his union. Robert Redford and Warner Brothers eventually spent over a million dollars in two separate deals purchasing the identity of a man who had left this earth with no more than a hundred dollars to his name.

The irony was that Chico's story was not much different from that of João Moreira or any of the thousands of other labor leaders, lawyers, and church workers who had been gunned down, tortured, threatened with death in towns and cities throughout the Amazon. What distinguished Chico's death from those others was the time and place. The world was ready for—indeed, desperately needed—a human face to attach to the rain forest cause. The international media lost no time in transforming him into a mythic being, a "Gandhi" of the rain forest, in the words of *Time* magazine. But what was left out of the postmortem eulogizing of Mendes was that he was—in essence and in his own eyes—a left-wing union organizer. He had been schooled as a child by a Communist political refugee who sought asylum in the forests of Acre after a military junta had put his life in jeopardy. When I filmed Chico on election day he was actively campaigning for the electorate's support of the left-wing Workers' Party. Just two years earlier he had named his son Sandino, after the Nicaraguan revolutionary who had led a successful peasant uprising against American marines in 1927. His daughter, Elenira, had been named after Elenira Rezende (no relation to Ricardo), the first woman to die among the Guerrilha do Araguaia in João Moreira's home state of Pará. Although Chico had a closer alliance to Marx than to Gandhi, the whitewashing of journalists and environmentalists and politicians had managed to eliminate that part of his persona from world consciousness, paving the way for global acceptance of a new type of hero. Hollywood deals were being closed. Book contracts were signed. Big-name casting choices were circulating in the popular press. Chico Mendes had become the world's first eco-martyr.

9

As I go to unlock the door to my room at Altamira's Hotel Americana, it suddenly swings open. Startled, I step back into the hallway and watch as two tall, scantily clad European women—English is my guess—emerge, their faces covered in circular black patterns vaguely resembling the traditional designs of the Kayapo Indians. The women both drop over-stuffed suitcases on the hallway carpet, raising a small cloud of dust which eventually settles against the light green baseboard of the shabby corridor.

My "trusted" companion the Wolf, here with me on another trip to the rain forest, approaches from the opposite end of the hallway. One look at these exotic beings and he stops short of the doorway, his shoulder bag of batteries and tapes and microphones hitting the floor with a deafening *clunk*. An old fluorescent fixture hanging above him flickers as if suddenly short-circuiting from errant electrical impulses emanating from his body. I watch his forehead crease spasmodically and his lips move frantically as he struggles to utter a coherent opening line in English.

The taller one, statuesque and stately in that British way, glances up at us and pauses for a moment, puzzled as she tries to figure out what we're doing there.

"Oh, sorry. We'll be out in a minute," she says as she and her friend turn and go back into the room, our room, the one the hotel manager just said was ready for us.

"Is there something or anything I can help you with?" says the Wolf, following them inside. I stand there, amused, but also a little startled by the presence of these strange creatures. No more than two months after the death of Chico Mendes, the Amazon appears to be a very different place.

Coming in from the airport a bald, ruddy-faced taxi driver with powerful, hairy arms held his steering wheel in a vise grip as he maneuvered around traffic and dodged potholes while giving us the breakdown of what was taking place in this depressed city of 38,000 inhabitants on the banks of the Xingú River. Six hundred Indians, one hundred international journalists, and a couple of hundred other *ambientalistas*, environmentalists, from Europe, the United States, and Brazil had descended on this backwater town for the Altamira Encounter, an event touted as the largest conference on the environment ever to take place in the Amazon.

"Brigitte Bardot will be here tomorrow," he added. "Sting, Prince Charles, and the King of Sweden are supposed to arrive today." The car swerved, he blasted the horn, and a man riding a mule cursed at us as we sped by.

After passing through the rocky streets of Altamira's outskirts, we came upon the smooth macadam boulevards leading to the center of town. They were crowded with the horse-drawn carts of peasants who had come to sell their produce in the central market. Down the side streets I could see groups of Indians in traditional dress from various Amazonian tribes. Some were carrying bows and arrows, other had only their mahogany war clubs. Most had their faces painted in traditional designs. Interspersed in the streets among the Indians were sunburnt North Americans and Europeans. These were wearing pieces of urban-hip lightweight jungle wear, carrying cameras and shoulder bags, their necks craning left and right as they tried to catch glimpses of the Indians while being careful not to tumble headfirst into the muddy trenches flanking the boulevards of this town known to most of Brazil as a strategic truck stop on the Transamazon Highway.

I wasn't surprised by what I saw coming in from the airport but these *turistas* in our hotel room are another story. The Wolf and I have arrived here a day late. I called ahead saying I would pay for the night but that the hotel should please hold on to our room. In the interim, the manager rented it to these women but forgot to tell us that they were still there. He did remember, however, to pocket their fee and ours, double payment for the night.

As I watch the two women—now accompanied by the Wolf—gather their remaining belongings, I begin to realize that I am not psychologically prepared for this type of "encounter," much less for Prince Charles, Brigitte Bardot, or the King of Sweden. I consider myself a serious journalist. My three trips to the Amazon were spent with small tribes, peasant squatters, or the men and women who extracted latex from the forest's trees. Those were stories with discernible issues that could be dissected in the black-and-white terms of statistics and legal precedents. But these young women (and the people I passed on the streets on the way in) represent a new social phenomenon: they are eco-activists from Europe and North America arriving in Brazil in support of the Indian cause. Perhaps what scares me most is that I could be considered one of them. I have entered a new realm, one that I am beginning to realize will necessitate a new perspective.

But the Wolf—suddenly transformed into Sir Walter Raleigh—has other concerns. "Where will you be staying now?" he asks the English women in his softest, most sincere tone as I pull him away by the back of his jacket. They break into smiles as they pick up their belongings. I can tell this little tug-of-war between us is only adding to his charm. As they walk away down the stairwell laughing, they bestow upon us a final "ciao" and disappear around the corner.

The Wolf throws himself against the wall. "There is no cure for my disease," he mutters. "I am a dead man."

"Patience," I tell him. "I think maybe you need more patience."

"Yes," he says. "Maybe I will try that." He then pauses to reflect on his words. "But I don't think it will work."

We enter the room and start organizing our equipment for a shoot. I test the camera while the Wolf stuffs day bags with tapes, batteries, cables, and some energy bars I brought from home. I check the schedule of events for the conference. We're already an hour late.

The cab driver lets us out a few hundred yards from Altamira's Civic Center. Working our way through the dense crowd, we pass some graffiti scribbled on the side of a building: CHICO MENDES DIED FOR OUR SINS. This crudely scrawled epitaph signals that Chico has joined the ranks of Che and Sandino; soon others will be naming their children after him. We continue dodging bystanders and vendors outside the Civic Center and soon we are inside a small arena of gray cinder block packed to the rafters with five thousand people. An aluminum ceiling soars a hundred yards above us. Television and still photographers blanket the perimeter of the stage area. Protest signs hang from rafters: STOP KILLING THE YANOMAMI and SAVE AMAZONIA and PEOPLE OF THE FOREST UNITE. I can hear bits of Italian, English, Japanese, and German being spoken all about me. The air is stifling but the atmosphere of the crowd is electrified by this incredible gathering of peoples. Groups of Indians—maybe six hundred—sit in tribal clusters in front of the makeshift podium and stage. The rest of the room is packed with journalists, environmentalists, politicians, and an odd assortment of observers. Some are academics, but there also appear to be representatives of the right-wing UDR, the Rural Democratic Union, a cattle ranchers' organization with questionable ties to incidents of rural violence in Amazonia. Many people have blamed them for Chico Mendes's assassination. I read in the paper this morning that yesterday they rode through town on horseback toting guns and placards in a show of support for the government's controversial dam scheme.

This proposed Kararaó hydroelectric station—a $5.8-billion project entailing the construction of forty-seven dams in the central Amazon—would flood an estimated 480 square miles of land. Even if only five of the proposed dams were built, the flooding would produce the largest artificially created body of water in the world. Environmentalists and Indian leaders are contending that the entire dam scheme would result in the displacement of nine thousand indigenous people in the surrounding area. The dam's supporters, however, claim its construction would be a critical catalyst to the local economy. Power is a major problem for this region: there is at least one blackout a day. And the infusion of capital would bring jobs to a marginalized frontier proletariat that feels it has been betrayed by the power brokers in Rio, São Paulo, and Brasília, the same ones who promised that the "opening" of the Amazon would solve their financial woes. The controversy surrounding the dam scheme has linked Altamira's impoverished classes with its local entrepreneurs. The Indians to them simply represent an obstacle to the region's economic advancement. Altamira has therefore become the focus of a showdown, a kind of Amazonian *High Noon* in which developers are facing off against activist Indians and their sympathetic eco-allies.

Seated at the table on the podium is a roundish Brazilian man in a green short-sleeved shirt, with a moon face and sleepy eyes. He is holding a microphone and explaining something in Portuguese to the audience. His words are almost incomprehensible to me, echo-chamber acoustics compounding the problem of a bad public address system. I check my watch and the schedule of speakers. He must be José Antônio Lopes, the engineer for the government's dam scheme. The Wolf gives me a rough translation of what he is saying, something about how the dams won't have a negative impact on the lives of the Indians. As he speaks I scan the auditorium looking for a place where we can cover the action.

Back at the podium a Kayapo woman steps towards Lopes from the crowd with a machete raised in her hand, screaming in the high-pitched wail of her native tongue. Senhor Lopes sits transfixed as the woman approaches, his arms resting on the wooden table, his hands folded delicately on his wrists. She is about five feet tall, heavy set, wearing black Jockey shorts, her breasts covered by two thick strands of red and blue beads. Her hair is long and dark, and there is a small rectangular shaved patch at the peak of her forehead. Unlike the gringa imposters this morning, this woman is the real thing, unmistakably

Kayapo. The machete in her right hand is a good two feet long. As she stands now in front of Senhor Lopes she continues screaming, punctuating her message by slamming the handle of the machete on the wooden table.

Things are off to a good start, I tell myself, half guilty at the exploitive nature of this thought. The problem is, I am still not in position for a shot.

Each time the woman hits the table it reverberates through the now silent auditorium as five thousand people hold their breath. Are they about to see a brutal beheading? Or maybe just a ritualized temper tantrum? The photojournalists below us twist away at their lenses, desperate to find the right focal length. They jostle, elbows extended, protecting their space, in anticipation of the perfect moment. The clicks of cameras are interspersed with curses in French, Portuguese, and English, as fists hit rib cages and hips swish left and right in a fight for steady ground.

The woman's machete lifts higher after her last gesture and then plunges down towards the man's neck. Several people gasp and turn away, but the majority of the crowd simply stare. With a sudden but slight twist of her wrist, the Kayapo woman flattens the blade and lays it flush against the side of Lopes's soft, blubbery face, delivering a little pat on the cheek, a harmless taste of hardened steel—ritual transformed into spectacle at a conference promising to be much more interesting than I could ever have imagined.

While the Wolf and I weave our way towards the podium, I do a quick breakdown of the crowd. There's an Indian with a boom box just in front of me taping the speeches; a Brazilian kid, maybe ten years old, works the audience selling ice cream; a couple of young U.S. print journalists scribble away in reporter notebooks as three local girls eye them from the periphery of the crowd. The rest of the room is reduced to a whirl of bodies and blurred faces as I try to get to the stage before I miss the next big moment in this surreal scene. My pangs of conscience have disappeared as the priorities of get-the-shot have taken all-consuming precedence. The crowd releases another burst of applause. The cluster of bodies packed near the podium eases, but the arms of photographers still fill the air, holding their cameras and clicking away, desperately snatching images.

A space opens before us. We push past a phalanx of Brazilian soldiers armed with pistols and dressed in baggy green fatigues. They stand like plastic toys against the cinder-block wall. It must be cooler there, I think to myself as I suck in the thick, acrid scent of the crowd: an unusual mix of ranch-hand sweat and European colognes with a hint of the ochre paste the Indians use to paint their bodies. I turn the camera on as we near the stage, stepping up onto a small space in a back corner. It is cramped, but I am close enough to get a shot. The "security man" stationed on the podium smiles at me and rolls his eyes, a signal that if I am crazy enough to attempt what I am doing, then he is just going to go ahead and let me do it. It is at times like this that I love working in Brazil, a land where bending the rules is a way of life: *o jeitinho brasileiro* they call it here—the Brazilian way.

Catching me off guard, the Kayapo woman returns to the podium. I am rolling now and zoom in on her face for a focus point as Lopes braces himself defiantly for another impassioned aria of contempt, her hatred for the whites spewing out unrestrained as the crowd watches in delight.

The dam scheme is yet another part of a continuing legacy of reckless development that has characterized large-scale projects in this region. But now, after two decades (and the setback of the Mendes assassination), the tables appear to be turning. In a powerful initial display of bravado, this young Kayapo woman has quickly confirmed the expectations of the international politicians and environmentalists assembled here: Chico was not a lone Amazonian phenomenon—the Indians of Brazil also have the requisite amount of savvy and courage to mount a campaign of resistence against the Brazilian government and the international lending institutions that threaten tropical forests and the people who inhabit them. And, if we can trust our taxi driver, there is more to come. The celebrities have yet to show.

The Kayapo woman begins again to shout and gesture with

the machete. I wonder whether this time she's going for his jugular. Suddenly she backs away and returns to the crowd as a young Kayapo man on the podium named Paulinho Payakan steps forward and grabs the microphone from the bemused Lopes. *"Obrigado"*—thank you—Payakan says to Lopes, who leans back looking relieved for the moment to be out of the spotlight. Payakan is wearing the traditional Kayapo headdress of blue and red parakeet feathers, a matching necklace of beads, no shirt, and a colorful pair of red and yellow surfer swim shorts. He smiles down at Lopes while simultaneously extending a hand to quiet the crowd.

At this point another Kayapo man leaps up from the audience, passing the woman with the machete as she takes a seat. This is "Colonel Pombo" (Colonel Pigeon), a powerful—some say Machiavellian—Kayapo leader who is also a consummate showman. He begins dancing about in front of the stage with a spear in his hand, gesturing violently with his weapon and derisively screaming out the name of the Kararáo Dam, one of the proposed dams that would flood his people's territory. A round of camera flashes goes off as he thrusts his spear into air and then back towards the ground as if he is single-handedly fighting off an onslaught of rival warriors. After thirty seconds of this traditional tirade he returns to his seat. The auditorium is silent. The audience members don't really know what they just saw.

"That was a war cry," Payakan says, simultaneously smiling with the ease of a trained orator. The crowd responds with applause. Each of Payakan's words and gestures now triggers a new flurry of camera flashes from local stringers for *Newsweek*, Reuters, *Time*, and dozens of other Brazilian and international news organizations. "It's the traditional war cry of the Kayapo people," Payakan adds, surveying the room, smiling and making eye contact with the audience even as he squints at the television lights. His words have given context to what would otherwise have remained an impressive but impenetrable display of native ritual. For an audience eager to understand the Indians' world, every little insight is appreciated. Payakan knows intuitively that this is true of a certain type of white people. He is a master at navigating the middle ground between their world and ours.

Paulinho Payakan organized Altamira with the help of several Brazilian nongovernmental organizations as part of the Indians' initiative in the new global movement to save the rain forest. In recent months he has emerged as the preeminent figure in a growing alliance of Indian societies in the Brazilian Amazon. His Portuguese is fluent. His manner among Brazilians is confident and, at times, self-consciously condescending. His years of contact with the whites have taught him how to play their game.

"And what about the Indian?" Payakan continues. "Is it in ten years that the Indian will be wiped out? Is it in ten years that the Indian will no longer have a place to live in Brazil?"

Payakan looks down accusingly on the dam scheme engineer as the audience obliges with more applause. Lopes stares off into the distance, his face a mix of sulkiness and confusion; he's probably wondering why he accepted the invitation to speak here in the first place. Perhaps he and his superiors never thought that the Indians could possibly pull off an event like this. That is understandable. Lopes and his colleagues gained power during the dictatorship, when pushing through such initiatives wasn't a problem. But this is a new democratic era, and they are being obliged to play by the rules of a participatory democracy.

Payakan, the son of an important chief from the village of A'ukre, was sent away as a young boy to be educated by Jesuit missionaries in a small town near Altamira. After school he didn't return to his village but went to work for the Brazilian Indian Agency as a guide and translator for *sertanistas*, those daring Indian Agency employees who were sent into the forest to make contact with and pacify isolated indigenous populations. After a few years with these groups, Payakan hired on with work teams in the construction of the Transamazon Highway. There too he worked as a guide and translator, literally paving the way for whites to enter the forest. Eventually he quit, reportedly dismayed by the negative impact the highway was having on the Indian communities. Recruited again by the

Indian Agency, he then became the first Kayapo to act as a government functionary at a village outpost. He was stationed in the village of Gorotire, a community that in centuries past had had hostile relations with his native village of A'ukre. As a government representative he began negotiations with local loggers and miners who had connived their way onto Kayapo lands. In an unprecedented agreement he forced them to pay a meaningful percentage of their profits to the Indians instead of the pittance that had been allotted on a sporadic basis. He also insisted that the Kayapo leaders divide the profits equally among the members of their community. To effect this he created a communal bank account. While his negotiations with the Brazilian entrepreneurs were appreciated, his attempt at redistributing wealth was received with bitter resentment by the traditional Kayapo hierarchy, who railed against his interference in their affairs. They wanted to do as they always had done: reserve the majority of the wealth for themselves and dispense the rest as they saw fit. Payakan was eventually forced out of Gorotire in an uncomfortable power struggle. However, his efforts had caught the attention of the regional director of the Brazilian Indian Agency. He was sent to the city of Belém, where he worked for the area supervisor, overseeing the relations of the Brazilian government with all the Kayapo villages scattered through a section of rain forest stretching from the state of Mato Grosso to the southern part of the state of Pará. He was the Agency's troubleshooter, responsible for four thousand Kayapo in fourteen villages. He made certain that medical supplies were delivered, that profits were returned for the sale of products, and that the children were being educated. These trips gave him regular access to all the Kayapo communities and their leaders. He made new alliances, patched up old conflicts, and served as a critical link between the Kayapo and the ever-encroaching outside world. He was a new Kayapo leader of a new era, politically savvy, in touch with a broad constituency but with no constricting allegiance to any one village—a factor that would both help him and hurt him in the years to come.

As Payakan confers in front of the podium with a few members of the Xavante tribe, I step off the stage and into a crowd of photographers. They are firing off shots at a dozen Kayapo warriors standing like stoics with war clubs and bows and arrows. The Indians pose compliantly at the direction of the photographers, who are eager to manipulate the Kayapo into the expected, sanctioned image of the native warrior—more evidence of the way reality is often jettisoned by my colleagues as they rush to collect archetypal images, images bearing a closer resemblance to museum displays than to the real people standing before us. This little bit of mise-en-scène is not simply about getting a good angle. My fellow image makers are not content with the Indians as they are; they want them to conform to the tired, unquestioned icons that haven't changed much since Columbus's time. Lost to these photos are the ambiguities and subtle possibilities of an unanticipated moment, the magic that can make a simple photograph into a work of art.

The Kayapo, for their part, seem inured to the barrage of camera flashes; they absorb them as if they are part of the price of admission. Their complicity (I am assuming) is part of a calculated dimension of the Altamira Encounter, an attempt to win over the media, and hence the Brazilian and international public, in their efforts to block the dam construction project.

Looking back into the center of the crowd, I spot amidst a group of Indians a young Kayapo man holding a video camera and focusing it on the podium. He is Kuben'i of Gorotire, the Kayapo videographer who, I've been told, has been given the job of documenting this event. As I am jostled about by my fellow photographers I wonder about the images he is taking, whether they differ from mine and those of my colleagues. Perhaps if I saw his images they might tell me something about the Indian's perspective on the world. Then maybe it would be easier to understand what is happening here at Altamira, an event that appears to be a fusion of indigenous ritual and Brazilian *carnaval*.

Behind Kuben'i I can see faces of dozens of different nationalities, all aglow in the energy of the moment. These people, most of them environmental and human rights activists, have seized upon the momentum of the death of Chico Mendes and embraced this new cast of heroes who have suddenly been thrust—or thrust themselves—center stage in the movement to save the rain forest. *Woodstock in Amazonia*, I think. *Indians as ecological saviors. Where is this all headed?* I make my way towards the exit for a breath of fresh air. Mulling over the confusing tidbits of today's events, I find myself at a loss to make sense of those strange *turistas* at the hotel and this ritualized beheading of an Electronorte representative. But by the time I reach the bright glare of the Amazon's midday I recognize that there is more going on here than can ever be grasped in a cursory journalistic survey, that only by looking back to the past can I hope to understand the perplexing pieces of this curious puzzle.

10

The Kayapo have arrived at this unique moment in history through a slow and difficult process of adaptation to the white man's world. Part of the linguistic group known as the Ge-speaking people, they live in the low forests and savannah of the south-central Amazon between the Araguaia and Iriri Rivers. For three centuries their reputation in Brazil has been similar to that of the Apache of the American West: fierce fighters with the potential for horrifying brutality. Their relations with Portuguese colonialists and, later, Brazilian citizens have been characterized by periods of warfare with occasional episodes of peaceful coexistence. Since the Kayapo were "pacified" or brought under the control of the Brazilian government in the 1950s, the murders and kidnappings of poachers, miners, loggers, and settlers have occurred less frequently. But unlike the Apache, the Kayapo have managed to survive until this day with most of their traditional culture intact.

The word *Kayapo* is derived from the language of the Tupi Indians and means *como macao*, monkeylike. In the eighteenth and nineteenth centuries, Portuguese colonialists used this epithet to encapsulate a broad cross section of indigenous groups who today are referred to as the southern and northern Kayapo. The former include the Paraná and the Kreen-Akrore peoples, who in the last two centuries inhabited the region that today geographically corresponds to the Brazilian state of Goais. Their societies bore the brunt of contacts with Portuguese colonialists, who through massacre and disease devastated the Kayapo numbers, leaving behind small pockets of populations who migrated to the protective reserves of the Xingú Park. They unwittingly acted as a human buffer zone for the northern Kayapo, who currently inhabit the region of northern Mato Grosso and southern Pará. By bearing the brunt of the first waves of colonial contact, the southern Kayapo permitted their neighbors to the north to live in relative isolation until well into the twentieth century.

It was Portuguese slave raiders who first contacted the southern Kayapo in the late eighteenth century, when they invaded the Indians' forest seeking bodies to work the sugarcane plantations and gold mines that formed the backbone of the colonial economy. During this time small groups of Kayapo were pacified with gifts of metal products and promises of transcendent miracles by the white man's Christian God. Indians who were enticed into the cities were often baptized en masse, delighting the colonial clerics who had been assigned the responsibility of tending the Indian flocks along the frontier. But by the middle of the eighteenth century Queen Maria I of Portugal began supporting a government plan to resettle the Southern Kayapo into "model villages" outside of the city of Goias. These settlements were to be overseen by her colonial administration. The role of the Church was being restricted. It had become too powerful in the view of the Portuguese crown, particularly as it related to Indian affairs. Government was now responsible for "civilizing the savages."

During this period colonial administrators had the good fortune to have the services of an extraordinary Kayapo woman by the name of Daiawa. In 1781 her father had been one of the first southern Kayapo leaders to accept the rule of the Portuguese colonialists when, with Daiawa in tow, he was persuaded to settle near Goias. Daiawa was baptized and then educated by the local authorities. She took the name da Cunha (which had been that of the local governor) and grew up to be a devout Christian and the willing subject of the local authorities. As a young woman she married a white soldier, and in 1808 she began a successful career luring hundreds of Kayapo from the forest with promises of gifts, Christian benevolence, and resettlement in model communities. In spite of Daiawa's success, the majority of the Kayapo—particularly those in the northern regions—resisted pacification. And as the numbers of the colonialists grew, the southern Kayapo fled westward across the Araguaia River into an area of savannah and low-level forest larger than the size of Scotland, an area that today comprises the territories of Mekragnoti, Rapôt, Kararaó, Cateté, and the Area Indigena Kayapo. Refusing to succumb to the rule of the white man, these Indians terrorized Portuguese settlers who encroached on their lands by staging daring assaults on local fortresses, roadways, and pioneer communities. Their combination of guerrilla warfare tactics and the skillful use of traditional weapons gave them a substantial edge over the colonialists with their clumsy armaments and scant knowledge of the forest.

In 1831 the colonial government's efforts to control the southern Kayapo suffered a serious blow when Daiawa died of hunger and exhaustion during an expedition to some uncontacted Indian villages. For the next several decades Kayapo encounters with white society were limited to raids on settlers and rubber tappers in order to obtain firearms and other manufactured products. For a time the Kayapo allied themselves with runaway African slaves, strengthening their numbers in their attacks on the Portuguese colonialists. Those southern Kayapo who had been lured into model villages over the last few decades were suffering from the neglect of their colonial administrators. Historical records of this period are filled with accounts of starvation, forced labor, and widespread death by disease among the southern Kayapo. While some of the Indians were lucky enough to flee back into the forest, those that remained intermarried with local whites or passed their last days living in small thatched huts—their former model villages having been usurped by Portuguese pioneers. In just a few decades Queen Maria's dream of an ideal Indian community had ended in complete failure. Once again, white society was at a loss for an alternative to armed conflict and enforced pacification. Yet as the frontier expanded, Portuguese colonialists were forced to contend with the region's indigenous populations. It was in this period that the northern Kayapo first began to come in contact with colonial society.

The failure of the government administrators opened the way once again for missionaries to try their hand at pacifying the Kayapo. At the turn of the twentieth century a French priest named Gil Vilanova established a mission for Indian children, which he called Conceição do Araguaia. Vilanova had conducted three different expeditions into the unexplored region of the northern Kayapo in the 1890s. Traveling by boat along the western banks of the Araguaia River, he had managed to establish ongoing contact with a group of Indians living in a village he called Pau d'Arco. Over the course of the decade he convinced the village elders to send their children to a missionary school that had been established by Vilanova and a fellow French cleric, Guillaume Vigneau. The Indians' parents were permitted to construct a modest village nearby and to visit the children on a regular basis. For almost a decade Vilanova and Vigneau were successful in slowly introducing Portuguese culture to small bands of the northern Kayapo still living east of the Araguaia River. But then both clerics succumbed to an epidemic of malaria. New Church administrators were unprepared and unqualified to carry on the work of these dedicated priests. The mission closed. Yet Vilanova and Vigneau's limited success helped to preserve a role for missionaries in the sphere of Indian affairs in Brazil. From the turn of the century onwards Protestant and Catholic emissaries would be allowed to establish small missions in remote corners of the rain forest. Proselytizing, educating, and administering medical care would become their sole mandates. More complicated questions of the Indians' relationship with the larger society of Brazil were, as of 1910, to be decided by the Indian Protection Service (SPI) under the direction of its founder, Colonel Cândido Rondon.

As a Brazilian military officer Colonel Rondon had supervised the exploration of the Amazon's frontier and other remote areas for a period of twenty years. In the course of his career he and teams of young military officers mapped more than fifty thousand square miles of rain forest, laid out some fourteen hundred miles of telegraph line, discovered twelve new rivers, and came into contact with hundreds of previously isolated Indian societies. During these decades of unprecedented exploration, Rondon began lobbying the Brazilian government to create an organization to protect such Indian societies.

Indeed, frontier violence was not the only threat to the Indians. In the cities of Rio de Janeiro and São Paulo academics and legislators were calling for the eradication of indigenous peoples in order to facilitate economic expansion. They often cited the precedent of U.S. government intervention in the American West as their model. Rondon, however, had been inspired by the writings of the French philosopher Auguste Comte and his guiding altruistic principle Live for One's Neighbor. He had developed his Indian Protection Service in direct opposition to those political and economic forces intent on genocide. The guiding motto of the SPI became "Die if necessary, but never kill." Working under the Ministry of Agriculture, the new agency's mandate as of 1910 was to protect the Indians from starvation, contact diseases, poverty, and exploitation by whites along the frontier. Its teams often spent months at a time in the forest before first contact was made. Rondon was determined to alter the tragic history of contacts between Western European explorers and indigenous populations.

By the time SPI teams approached the lands of the northern Kayapo, there were already dramatic changes taking place within their communities which set the stage for a new period of rapprochement between white society and indigenous villages in the states of Mato Grosso and Pará. Violent internecine battles had been breaking out between the Kayapo of Gorotire and the people of Mekragnoti, a group whose name translates as "people who paint their upper faces with red urucum." Then as the Mekragnoti moved westward fleeing the encroachment of outsiders, they came into conflict with the "people with shaved heads" or Kreen-Akrore and other southern Kayapo tribes as well as Brazilian rubber tappers who had been traveling the Araguaia River.

During this period the northern Kayapo stepped up their raids against Brazilian settlers, seizing as bounty high-powered Winchester rifles, which they used against their indigenous adversaries as well as Brazilian pioneers. The Indians' new arms combined with their fierce warrior traditions made them a major obstacle to government efforts at frontier expansion. The SPI stepped up their efforts to pacify the northern Kayapo by increasing the number and amount of gifts offered to the Indians. Peace eventually came about because the Indians found it easier to attain metal products, ammunition, and glass beads through sustained contacts with the Indian Protection Service than by plundering local pioneers. Throughout the 1930s and 1940s SPI teams were able to set up outposts in a number of Kayapo communities through the steady distribution of gifts to the Indians. But it was not until the 1950s that these ferocious warriors were officially pacified, setting the stage for a new era of dependency on Brazilian society.

But pacification was not without problems. Increased contact with white society brought new diseases. Violent internal schisms also continued to flare up between various Indian communities. The Indian population began to dwindle rapidly. One of the first villages contacted in the 1930s, Gorotire, saw its numbers decline from well over eight hundred inhabitants to barely one hundred in just a few years. During this era, missionaries and SPI officials worked to suppress the Indians' culture by giving them clothes, proselytizing among them, and moving their families into Brazilian-style houses. Throughout the country this official SPI policy of deculturation and the devastating impact of contact diseases led to population loss among Brazilian Indians, from one million in 1900 to less than 200,000 in 1957. In that time eighty-seven different Indian societies simply disappeared, either killed off by disease or assimilated into the mainstream of Brazilian society.

For the surviving communities, particularly the Kayapo, corruption within the SPI was becoming a major problem. SPI employees, drafted from the impoverished classes and paid a pittance, often acted as middlemen in the sale of the Kayapo's Brazil nuts to merchants in nearby towns and cities. They frequently pocketed large parts of the Indians' profits or made false claims that the harvest had been destroyed or lost in transport to urban areas. Even more scandalous activities on the part of SPI employees were exposed in 1968, when Brazil's attorney general Jader Figueiredo investigated the Agency's activities. In addition to widespread corruption Figueiredo charged SPI employees with acts of enslavement, sadism, and several different massacres carried out in collusion with frontier pioneers. Of 700 people in employment at the SPI at the time of the investigation, 134 were charged with crimes and 238 were dismissed from their jobs. One former head of the SPI, a Major Luís Neves, had amassed an astounding record of abuse and misconduct. He was accused of forty different crimes including several murders of indigenous people, the illegal sale of Indian lands, and the embezzlement of $300,000 of SPI funds. The northern Kayapo, like most indigenous groups contacted during this era, had little or no recourse against such crimes. They had almost no understanding of Portuguese, scant knowledge of the legal system, and few allies within the larger society of Brazil. Although the attorney general promised to clean up the SPI, the Indians found themselves caught in a double-edged predicament. To change the course of their destiny would mean rejecting Brazilian society, the very source of the food and medicines upon which they had become dependent for survival.

Meanwhile, in spite of persistent efforts at acculturation on the part of SPI employees and missionaries, the Kayapo managed to preserve many of their traditional customs. And their cultural resistance was to prove their salvation. Elaborate naming and initiation rituals continued to be performed with the changes in the seasons. Myths—"things that take a long time to tell"—were still passed down from generation to generation. Small wooden plates known as "lip plugs" were inserted into the lower lip, a tradition of ornamentation practiced exclusively by the men. Some groups maintained the Kayapo hair style of long hair with a shaved forehead. Many women still painted their bodies in traditional Kayapo designs but kept them hidden beneath their "Brazilian" clothes. These traditions and rituals retained by the Kayapo were not a self-conscious expression of their culture but remained in effect because "they had always been done that way." In fact, as with many Indian societies before contact, the Kayapo knew only one culture, their culture. That other societies had specific rituals and customs was not something they had been conscious of: their way of life was simply the way life was, the way it had always been.

Resilient as they were, however, even these age-old traditions were by the early 1960s succumbing to the powerful influences of contact and acculturation. The Kayapo had reached a crisis point. Their cultural foundation was slipping away, while it seemed unlikely that they would ever secure a foothold in Brazilian society. But then a new group of outsiders appeared, transforming the northern Kayapo's relationship with the larger world and with their own traditional culture.

The first of this new group of whites, sympathetic whites, had arrived in their villages in the 1950s. Decidedly different from the intolerant missionaries, miners, and corrupt Indian Agency employees who had dominated Kayapo encounters with outsiders in the past, the newcomers didn't seek to transform the Indians into supplicant subjects. These people—anthropologists, filmmakers, musicologists, botanists, and environmentally concerned individuals—were interested in Kayapo culture as a valid and valuable entity, as something to be appreciated, preserved, and reflected upon. By the 1960s they began arriving in the Indian villages in increasing numbers, rattling off endless questions, taking thousands of still and moving pictures, and recording the Indians' ceremonial chants. They accompanied hunters on week-long forays in the forest and permitted the Indian women to paint their white-skinned bodies with traditional designs. These whites were spending tremendous amounts of time and money documenting a way of life that, up until then, had been denigrated, abused, and rejected by previous generations of outsiders. All of which prompted the Kayapo to look at their own culture in a different context, to see their status in Brazilian society as separate rather than subordinate.

As the years passed, and the encounters and explorations continued, the impact on the Kayapo consciousness became indelible. Once the Indians started seeing their culture as a specific entity distinguishable from Brazilian society, they soon began to identify themselves not just as Kayapo but as "Indios"—people, whose worldview, history, and tradition lay in closer proximity to that of other Amerindian societies than to the lately dominant culture of Brazilians and their white predecessors, the Portuguese colonialists.

The Indians also came to understand that being Kayapo—practicing traditional dances or oratory, adorning themselves with body paints, participating in initiation rituals—was something that attracted these sympathetic whites and consequently would provide revenue for their communities. In the barter process, beads and manufactured goods and medicines could be obtained in exchange for the outsiders' access to life in their villages. The Kayapo had found a way to manipulate outsiders rather than be manipulated by them. They had uncovered the key to asserting power vis-à-vis the outside world.

In years to come, the northern Kayapo would learn to apply this new power dynamic in the larger field of Brazilian and international politics. And, as fate would have it, their efforts would coincide with the global movement that had taken off in the 1980s to save the rain forest. Suddenly they found themselves making common cause with hundreds of thousands of outsiders who in turn were being led by their own political, environmental, and media ideologues. This new generation of whites, like those who arrived in the 1960s, expressed a passionate interest in helping the Kayapo in their quest for cultural survival. They wanted to "save" the Indians.

However, the Kayapo were already defending their identity vigorously. In the 1970s a warrior and political leader named Raoni had emerged in the forefront of the society's new relationship with white society. He was from the generation before Payakan—someone who, according to Kayapo custom, is respectfully called Payakan's "uncle" to signify his status as an elder. Unlike the younger leader, Raoni did not have a childhood influenced by the teachings of Jesuit missionaries or an early career spent working for wages in various frontier enterprises and administrations. Raoni had grown up in the forest, living a life steeped in the traditions of Kayapo culture and indigenous community politics. Also unlike Payakan, whose negotiating strategy reflected a hybridization of white and Indian society, Raoni remained confrontational, acutely sensitive to the legacy of conflict with white society that had been passed down through the generations.

"My father told me it has already begun, the white man has come here to take our land," Raoni explained to me the first time I interviewed him at Altamira. "He said to me, 'They have come to take our land and then when they are finished with our land, they will destroy us also.' "

Raoni's emergence as one of the Kayapo's most powerful leaders came shortly after the disreputable Indian Protection Service was replaced by the new administrative branch of government known as the National Foundation for the Indian (FUNAI). On paper the new agency's mandate was more far-reaching than that of the SPI. It purported to be interested not just in protecting Indians but in preserving their traditional culture and lands, two elements only recently recognized as being essential for safeguarding indigenous peoples from the devastating consequences of the contact experience.

Then, just two years after FUNAI was created, General Emílio Médici was named president by the military junta that had seized power in 1964. As one of his initiatives to transform the country, General Médici introduced a grandiose scheme to open up the Amazon for development through the construction of extensive roadways. In furtherance of this plan the General appointed a new head of FUNAI, General Bandeira de Mello, to bring the mandate of the agency into conformity with the country's new economic imperatives. Almost overnight the emphasis of the Agency's work shifted from preservation to integration. "Ethnic minorities such as the Indian," General Bandeira de Mello said during this era, "must be oriented to a well-defined planning process, taking into account their participation in national progress and integration as producers of goods."

What this new regime of generals was not aware of was that their rise to power had been simultaneous with the emergence of a new generation of Kayapo leaders. Men like Payakan and Raoni, schooled in the ways of Westerners and embraced by a new generation of sympathethic whites, were now able, as their ancestors had not been, to confront the aggressions of outsiders.

This was a generation no longer interested in being pacified. They wanted contact with the whites on their own terms.

As a young adult Raoni became friends with Orlando and Cláudio Villas Bôas, two brothers whose exploits and calls to action captured the imagination of the Brazilian public in the same way that Colonel Rondon had done a generation earlier. They had first entered the territory of the northern Kayapo as part of a government survey team in the 1940s. Working outside the structure of the Indian Protection Service, these sympathetic whites successfully championed the cause of Amazonian Indians by convincing the country's government to develop protective legislation to assure the preservation of indigenous populations. The work of these fraternal *indigenistas* became the genesis of the creation of FUNAI two decades later. In their frequent encounters with Raoni they taught the young warrior Portuguese, instructed him in Brazilian politics, and helped to shepherd him through the complex web of the country's Indian Protection Service, and later FUNAI, and the state and national political machines. When in the 1950s the Villas Bôas brothers established the first protective reserve for Brazilian Indians in the Xingú Park, Raoni became one of its earliest administrators. By the 1960s these combined experiences had allowed Raoni to make a name for himself as a powerful political figure both within his community and in neighboring Kayapo villages. He had direct access to the Villas Bôas brothers, the Indians' closest and most supportive allies, and he had become recognized as someone who could be relied on to effectively assert the needs of his community within the larger world of Brazilian society. All through this time, however, Raoni continued to live in his native village of Porori, solidifying his role as a traditional leader in Kayapo society. His power was derived from a tradition of alliance building that starts within one's community and extends into neighboring villages through a web of kinship ties, historical allegiances, and intervillage exchanges.

Raoni's role as preeminent in the sphere of national politics was launched when a feeder road of General Médici's Trans-amazon Highway reached the territory of the northern Kayapo in 1971. The roadway, BR-080, cut dangerously close to his native

But it was also there that Payakan began to assert himself in the sphere of radical indigenous politics that Raoni had spearheaded throughout the late 1970s and 1980s. Suddenly two generations of Kayapo were coming together under the tutelage of individuals who exemplified two styles of leadership. Raoni personified the quintessential Kayapo warrior: aggressive, combative, and afraid of no one. Payakan by contrast was the harbinger of a new era. He was smooth-talking and diplomatic. Where Raoni didn't hesitate to phrase his arguments in confrontational rhetoric, Payakan would say, "Violence, guns, and threats didn't solve anyone's problems. What solves problems is making yourself seen and heard." In combination these two leaders furthered the Kayapo cause by fusing their distinctive leadership roles. Working in alliance with Brazilian human rights activists and politicians, they managed to successfully assert their political agenda in a new era of democratic rule.

No event in the twentieth century carried greater weight for the future of Brazil's indigenous people than the hearings surrounding the establishment of the new Brazilian constitution. The military dictatorship had ground to a halt just two years earlier, its aged leaders no longer interested in commandeering a country they had driven into bankruptcy. A "new Brazil" was now being established, and talks on the fine points of legislation regarding Indians began in 1987 and continued into February 1988. By June 1988 there was a pitched battle between conservative members of Congress (many from the Amazonian states) and their more liberal opponents concerning the decrees on Indian rights that were coming up for approval. Participating in this debate (though not in the actual voting) was an unprecedented alliance of Indian leaders and supporters who included, among others, human rights activists, ethnologists, academics, and church leaders. Although Payakan was actively a part of Kayapo actions surrounding the debate on this constitutional mandate known as Decree 266, it was Raoni who was still the principal spokesperson for his people.

In an event that has become part of Brazilian political folklore, Raoni—supported by dozens of Kayapo warriors—staged an occupation of a congressional caucus chamber and held court for an array of television and print reporters on the eve of the critical vote on Decree 266. This proposed provision of congressional legislation was intended to guarantee Indians living within Brazil an array of rights not available to them under prior constitutions. Raoni's daring move could easily have backfired. But with characteristic flair Raoni succeeded in dominating the discussion of indigenous rights and presenting his case in clearly identifiable but emotionally charged terms. "The president of the Indian Agency, he thinks we are stupid," he told reporters as he displayed a map of Kayapo territory. "Where are our children and grandchildren going to live? I am not going to tolerate the way things are today. The Kayapo have their own rights. [President] Sarney is stupid. I don't like stupid people. I like nice people."

The next day Decree 266 was approved. For the first time in Brazil's history the country's constitution protected the languages, beliefs, and customs of all indigenous people as well as their inalienable right to their traditional lands. Perhaps most important, the decree granted that "Indians, the communities and organizations are legitimate parties capable of suing in defense of their rights and interests." While still maintaining their status as wards of the state, this legal entitlement to sue on their own behalf meant that Indians were no longer dependent on the Indian Agency to defend them in the judicial system. They could even file claims against the Indian Agency if they chose to do so. For the Kayapo at least, the days of absolute dependency appeared to be part of the past.

It could be said that Raoni's storming of the Congress was merely symbolic, as it came weeks after the discussions in which the fine print of Decree 266 had been analyzed and debated. Yet it cannot be denied that his action sent a message to Congress and the public at large that Indians in Brazil would no longer remain in the forest as their fate was being decided in the cities. Although not recognized as citizens, the indigenous people of Brazil could participate in the decision-making process affecting their lives. The passage of Decree 266 set the stage for a new era wherein indigenous people could hold government administrations accountable for transgressions of the law. This would have been unheard of in the time of Colonel Rondon.

One of the first people to test the limits of Brazil's new democratic spirit was Paulinho Payakan who, shortly after the constitutional hearings, traveled to the United States to speak at a conference on tropical forest conservation at the University of Southern Florida. There he gave a rather perfunctory account of the importance of the rain forest from the indigenous perspective. But when he proceeded north to Washington, trouble began.

At a World Bank meeting Payakan, accompanied by a fellow Kayapo leader named Kubei and an American ethnobotanist named Daryl Posey, spoke out critically about Brazil's plan to create a massive hydroelectric scheme on Indian lands. Payakan for his part knew all too well the government's intentions. He had served as a guide and translator for survey teams that had traveled the entire region in exploratory stages of the project. His views represented an informed indigenous perspective on the negative impact of the dam scheme on the Indian peoples of Brazil.

World Bank officials, to their credit, were open to hearing it. Kubei and Payakan were fortunate in the timing of their visit. For a decade the Bank had been reevaluating its criteria for guaranteeing international loans. The officials assembled at this meeting were aware that prior Bank support of Operation Amazonia and subsequent Amazon development schemes had caused problems, to say the least. They couldn't overlook the fact that between 1964 and 1971 the U.S. government and its various lending institutions had provided Brazil with $3.5 billion in bilateral aid and international loans, many of them directed towards the Amazon—and that by 1972 Brazil had surpassed all other countries as the major debtor nation to the Bank. Nowhere was the role of the World Bank and the Inter-American Bank more apparent than in the $400 million provided for highway construction in the Amazon between 1968 and 1972. After several international scandals the World Bank had become uncomfortably aware that Brazil's military dictatorship and its local frontier governments had consistently ignored long-standing warnings regarding the lethal consequences of uncontrolled contact with isolated Indian societies. Several European newspapers had uncovered cases of brutal genocide against Brazil's Indians. The SPI scandal of the late 1960s and subsequent investigations by international journalists had tarnished the image of the World Bank. Even within Brazil the country's Indian Agency had been referred to by then–Attorney General Figueiredo as "a den of corruption and indiscriminate killings." To make matters worse, many journalists filing Amazon stories made a direct connection between World Bank funding and the roadways that had brought ruthless pioneers and corrupt administrators to the Brazilian frontier. Perhaps the most scathing of all critiques was Shelton Davis's landmark study *Victims of the Miracle*, which in 1977 systematically documented the relationship between cases of genocide against Indians and World Bank financing of frontier expansion projects. Subsequently, damage control had become a priority in Bank decision making, and hearing the testimony of affected forest dwellers fit conveniently into its new agenda for evaluating loans.

Although no final decision was reached during Payakan's visit to Washington, news of the unprecedented meeting sent shock waves throughout Brazil. When Kubei, Posey, and Payakan returned to Brazil they were charged by the attorney general with defaming the national image. This was big news and made all the major newspapers: the crime was punishable by one to three years in jail or expulsion from the country. Just a few months after Raoni's success at the constitutional hearings, his "nephew" was now in the nation's spotlight. And Payakan took to his role with the zeal of an ambitious understudy.

Posey, Payakan, and Kubei hired a local lawyer to defend them. Then, in what was fast becoming a Kayapo tradition, Payakan added another dimension to his defense strategy. On the day he was to appear in court, he and Kubei showed up in the port city of Belém accompanied by two hundred Kayapo warriors armed with war clubs and bows and arrows. They threatened and harassed military guards who surrounded the courthouse as the judge and his assistants barricaded themselves inside. Blocking off the street, the Indians then lined up in four rows of twenty, chanting in unison and performing a traditional Kayapo dance. The local press was mesmerized. Photojournalists and television crews fell over themselves attempting to capture these extraordinary images. During breaks between ceremonial dances and the ritualized berating of the military police, Payakan placed a map on an easel in the middle of the street and gave impromptu lectures to the tribesmen on the impact of the dam scheme and his motives for appearing before the World Bank. Adding to the array of photogenic images was Payakan in traditional face paint and dress documenting the event with his own video camera so that those villagers remaining in the forest could see what their fellow Kayapo were doing in the cities.

All in all, the event showed that the Kayapo's years of interacting with sympathetic whites had made them acutely aware of what types of images would work in their favor with the public at large. And it didn't hurt that Payakan—the event's master of ceremonies—exhibited a flair for public relations that surpassed even that of his uncle Raoni who, although in attendance, kept a very low profile during the course of the day's events.

In the months following the Belém demonstration there were no further hearings in the Brazilian courts regarding the charges against Payakan, Kubei, and Posey. During that period, Payakan was busy making plans for what became known as the Altamira Encounter. Once that event got started, the charges mysteriously disappeared in the Brazilian courts.

11

"Get us six *frangos* to go," squeaks the walkie-talkie as the production assistant steps up to the counter of a local Altamira restaurant. He's wearing Ray•Ban sunglasses, a green Benetton shirt, long khaki shorts, and a spotlessly clean pair of Nike Airs. "Roger that," he responds. To his mouth he raises a clear plastic container of Evian water—just one bottle, rumor has it, from several cases flown into Altamira from the States by a Hollywood film crew.

The Wolf and I are sitting here taking a break from Day Three of the Encounter. We're trying to restore our energy before we subject ourselves to another round of international camera jostling. Beside us lie the remnants of a small feast of meat, beans, and rice that was consumed in a matter of minutes. We stopped only to swat the flies or take sips from our Guarana sodas. Before pushing on to dessert and coffee, we are soaking in a little of the atmosphere, trying to get a feel for what this town is really like. Scattered about the restaurant taking their noontime meals are a cross section of indigenous leaders, some with traditional headdresses, others adorned only with ceremonial paint. They all wear the requisite bathing suit; this year's fashion leans towards brightly colored surfer shorts. Around wooden tables they sit huddled in distinct ethnic clusters—representatives of the Xavante, Kayapo, and Panara people. There doesn't seem to be much mixing among them, which is perhaps an indication of language differences and their own cultural barriers rather than any history of conflict between their societies. The intertribal battles of the past have dissipated in recent years as, one by one, these groups have come to recognize themselves as *Indios* and started to ally themselves in opposition to the national society of Brazil. Slowly they have begun referring to other Indians as their "relatives" while still characterizing most whites as a group not to be trusted.

Above us an old wooden ceiling fan spins, wobbling precariously, providing the vague semblance of a soothing little breeze. Tables and chairs screech against the concrete floor as other Indians arrive to join the groups already seated. From a transistor radio off in the kitchen we can hear the scratchy sounds of Brazilian country music mixed with the chatter of the restaurant staff; it's not exactly my favorite style of music but it provides a welcome relief from the endless conference speeches which, after two long days, seem to have blended together into an indistinguishable litany of ecological woes. So far in this Encounter I have been pummeled, threatened, and kicked at least two dozen times. I am not eager to get back to it, and this guy with the *frango* order is a sufficiently amusing distraction to justify lingering over our meal a few minutes longer. I get a lot from moments like these, incidents that don't make their way into the reports I file or the documentaries I knock out back in New York. They tell me a lot about the nature of this traffic jam involving Western and indigenous cultures. Certainly both groups share an avowed desire to "save the forest" but what I find puzzling is that, beyond this one factor, there is no reason these disparate groups should come together: no link, no ties, just a catchy idea that has swept up the world and me along with it. For now I am content not to figure it out but simply to soak it in. I sit here fascinated by the way the Indians stare blankly at the young man as he jokes with his colleagues on the walkie-talkie and, for his part, the way Mr. Frango-To-Go cannot separate himself from his techno-toy and settle into the atmosphere of the room. He uncomfortably surveys his surroundings as he rambles on into his portable squawk box about what he is seeing in the restaurant as if he's an astronaut, nervous but excited by his new discovery, reporting back to planet Earth after touching down on an alien terrain.

In the last two days there have been two or three people who have spoken out in support of the government's position on the hydroelectric project and the massive destruction it would entail. But, as would be expected, the majority of the speakers have condemned it. One of the project's proponents, Brazil's environmental secretary Fernando Mesquita, was booed off the podium this morning as he tried to lecture the Indians and the audience on how they should behave at their own conference. Mesquita appears to be an honest man in a difficult place: he has been asked to undo overnight the ecological crisis created by twenty years of trying to develop the Amazon. But he has made the classic mistake of the stereotypical bureaucrat: he preaches to his audience of indigenous leaders rather than conversing with them, conveying an assumption that the white man's words carry greater weight therefore the Indians should simply sit back and listen. What Mesquita obviously hasn't realized is that this is a new era. The balance of power has changed. The Indians are "empowered" (as one anthropologist said today) by their alliance with international environmentalists and their welcoming reception in institutions of power like the World Bank and the U.S. Congress. In fairness to Mesquita, his manner of speaking to the Indians is not exclusive to representatives of government. Even the most well-intentioned sympathetic whites—and there are plenty of them at this event—can be condescending and patronizing in their efforts to "help these people" as opposed to keeping them in their place. Each is an assertion of power and each can be dangerous. Here, however, no one seems to be concerned about such details. Everything is happening too fast. Everyone is swept up in the moment, and the "cause."

One interesting fact I noted today is that the number of representatives of various Indian societies attending the conference—the Kraho, the Xavante, the Kreen-Akrore—has suddenly dropped. They too must be getting bored. There were fewer men marching into the convention center this morning as they sung tribal chants. It was easier to get a shot. I wasn't spending as much time tripping over my camera-laden cohorts. One of my anthropologist sources told me that the Indians are spending more time at their makeshift village on the outskirts of town. He suggested rather surreptitiously over breakfast that I take a trip out there this afternoon. I assumed I was being passed a lead on something exclusive, which is a most welcome gesture considering that this conference appears to be grinding to a halt. I can tell by the nighttime banter in the bars that my journalist and filmmaker friends have the same concern: we are all searching for a new take on the old story, hoping to justify our presence in this pleasant backwater town for just a few more days.

Certainly, the arrival of a few celebrities would spice things up. Mr. Frango-To-Go standing before us does bear witness that at least one Hollywood contingent has graced us with its presence. But there is still no sign of a marketable celebrity. Those of us who are "capturing" the images here know that "celebs"— real ones—can provide the picture-perfect moments that will be the big sellers back on the home turf: Brigitte Bardot with a headdress, Prince Charles gesturing defiantly with a war club, the King of Sweden twostepping to the beat of the Kayapo Corn Dance. As freelancers we can sell such images to the entertainment shows and journals while hoping to slip in a few "artsy" shots or ethnographic sequences to market to the more "serious" broadcasters and publications. Most of us detest this approach, but that's the way it is if you are working without a contract: the glitz and glamour pay the way for the committed work of the freelancer interested in stories that are deemed too political or too offbeat. I have paid for a few of my trips down here already with magazine pieces about Brazilian music, the soap opera industry, and a profile of Xuxa, the platinum-haired former Playboy playmate and onetime girlfriend of the soccer player Pelé who wears micro-miniskirts and talks nonstop four hours a day as the hostess of Brazil's most popular children's show. That's an "easy sell," as they say in the entertainment industry. Tales of political violence are more problematic.

"No one cares about sixteen hundred people who have been

assassinated in the Amazon," a high-powered television executive told me just a few months ago. He was trying to usher me out of a producer's office as I was pitching a story on the deaths of rural leaders in the Amazon over a two-decade period. This was three months before Chico Mendes was killed. The 1,600 other nuns, priests, lawyers, and labor leaders who had been murdered in the rain forest were people this executive did not consider newsworthy. But Chico's story, and the way it crossed over into the international arena, had an unusual twist. After his death someone else bestowed upon him what I call "the aura of significance" by putting him in the news and thereby making him worthy of news coverage. He appeared in print before getting on television, a progression that is becoming increasingly prevalent. Marlise Simons from the *New York Times* wrote a front-page story on his assassination within forty-eight hours of his death, catapulting his story onto the desks of television news editors in this country and abroad. Only then did his story have credibility.

That's often the way television journalism functions these days. News bureaus around the world have closed down, so very few people are doing original reporting from the field. The length of foreign news stories is being cut in half with the explanation that "no one is interested." What replaces them are softer puff pieces, celebrity profiles, and voyeuristic tabloid violence that attempt to present themselves as "serious" news because there is a "serious" side to the stories, often involving rape, murder, child molestation, divorce, drugs, drinking, a celebrity, a politician, a prostitute, or any combination thereof. So America's view of the world is turning myopic as a new generation of media executives struggles frantically to "give the American public what they want" or perhaps, more accurately, what it perceives the American people want. The corporate heads are tired of losing dollars on the news business and are trying to turn a profit by adding some glitz, glamour, and, let's be honest, voyeurism. At the end of the day it's about money. Foreign news stories get the lowest priority.

And that's where freelancers come in. Increasingly, foreign coverage of obscure stories is brought in by stringers reporting from regions of the world where they have a special interest. But selling such a story is not an easy proposition. It's not just about convincing the news bureau that the issue you've documented is newsworthy in its own right. You usually have to do more. One ploy is to convince the prospective buyers that their competition wants it as well—that someone *else* considers it newsworthy and they risk getting scooped. Another option is to tip off your colleagues in the print world to the same story. You then wait for their coverage to appear in the *New York Times*, the *Washington Post*, or *Time* magazine. When you go in the next day and make your pitch, bingo, you've got your sale. Still, it's only the big foreign stories that are guaranteed coverage these days: the fall of the Berlin Wall, Tien-an-men Square, Mandela's release from prison. Those stories are safe. They are easily identifiable and they are on the agendas of the competition. What gets lost, and what we are losing as a nation, are the smaller stories that put us in touch with real people in remote regions.

But I shouldn't complain. The Amazon is now "hot" and I am lucky to have the exposure and access that I currently have. News editors will take my calls; I can even call collect from these little frontier towns. The fact that I delivered the Chico Mendes story has put me on the rosters of several news organizations. Even so, as a stringer, I am considered a good source of stories but not someone to be absolutely trusted. "Are you an environmentalist?" or "Did you set up that shot?" are questions I have been asked more than once. And for all the recent inroads I have made, no one in the United States seems interested in this unprecedented meeting of Indians in the Amazon. But I'm not going to be deterred by their reactions. One thing I have learned is that freelancers live and die by their instincts. You follow your hunches until one pays off. Then your access to the remote and exotic suddenly becomes marketable. You can then pay off your bills and have the satisfaction of seeing your once unnewsworthy story now in the spotlight. That is, until the next big story comes along.

Mr. Frango-To-Go exits with his order and we finish our

meal with a *cafezinho* or "little coffee," an Amazonian amphetamine version of espresso that does a little more than simply "recharge the batteries." I can feel it pumping its way through my system as the Wolf and I exit the tiny cinder-block restaurant, stepping out into one of Altamira's narrow back streets. Suddenly we are enveloped by a dense mass of soft, warm humidity. A light rain is blowing in from the west and, above us, the sky has turned gray. The rain and light have transformed the color of the dusty clay road into a dark, rich red. The Wolf has gone down the street in search of a taxi and I stand here guarding the equipment under a torn blue canopy flapping in the breeze. I watch the pattern of the rain as it hits the street, sweeping left and then right in tandem with the bursts of the wind. Above me the palm trees are bending sideways as their long green leaves twist and spin backwards. An emaciated old Indian man on a beat-up bicycle appears suddenly from around the corner wearing only a headdress, bathing suit, and flip-flops. He bounces by, flashing a crooked smile and giving me the thumbs-up sign, the universal salutation used throughout Brazil but particularly common in the Amazon. Another gust of wind arrives, sweeping away all sound except the *rickety-rack-rickety-rack* cadence of the bicycle's chain. Returning his attention to the road, the old man swerves to dodge a large puddle of brown water in the middle of the dirt roadway. His bike tips but then he steadies it miraculously with a quick jerk. Just as another burst of wind comes tumbling down the street, the old man disappears around the corner. There remains before me only a row of colorful one-story houses on a little back street totally abandoned by those who have sought protection from the oncoming storm and the heat and humidity of the Amazon's midday. I pull my poncho out of my camera bag and cover the equipment as another powerful burst of wind sweeps down, this time bringing with it a sheet of heavy rain. I stand with my feet on the corners of the poncho to hold it in place. For just a minute the manic insanity of the last few days disappears. There is only a pleasant calm. I search my camera bag for my journal, hoping to jot down a few impressions. But then the Wolf pulls around the corner in a little four-door taxi, the car stereo blasting out

Gilberto Gil's latest pop-funk-samba hit O *Eterno Deus Mudança*, "The Eternal God of Change." *"We feel what the people feel,"* sings Gil. *"The people want to scream."*

12

Driving out of town on a two-lane blacktop, our taxi finally clears the blinding sheets of thick gray rain that have swept over us since we left town. As the *motorista* Manoel clicks off the wipers and throws the car into high gear, the last rivulets of water disappear from the windshield to reveal a vista of blue sky and swirling white clouds. This view has an almost cinematic effect, as if it's part of a projected landscape, shifting ever so slightly in time with the beat of the car stereo. *"Terras, povos diferentes—outros sonhos pra sonhar."* "Different lands, different peoples—other dreams to be dreamed," Gil's voice cries out from the radio as Mario and Manoel exchange banter in the front seat and my mind drifts off into the surrounding countryside.

Where the road meets the horizon, a rainbow cuts a broad arch across the sky, slowly dissolving into one of the larger clouds. Zipping by on our left and right is the high green grass of a cattle ranch set back behind crudely constructed barbwire fences with crooked tree limbs serving as posts. I can see small groups of cows grazing in the fields a few hundred yards in the distance as our little Ford taxi picks up speed, the macadam highway now shiny from the recent shower. Scattered across the pastureland are the tall, thick charcoal shells of once massive Amazonian trees: this part of the state of Pará was the front line of Amazon development in the 1960s and 1970s, one of the first regions to get torched in the push to tame the forest.

Manoel taps his horn as we zoom by an old peasant walking barefoot, carrying a machete and wearing just a pair of torn and dirty pants. His body, or what's left of it, is an emaciated shell of sun-dried skin clinging uncomfortably close to the bony frame of his shoulders and rib cage. In the rearview mirror I catch a glimpse of him as his tired hand rises slowly, acknowledging the passing presence of our air-conditioned vehicle. This modest car is worth more money than he will ever make in a lifetime, just another of the mind-boggling discrepancies of wealth in this country, a nation that has the greatest division between rich and poor of any in the Western Hemisphere. The numbers of the indigent grow daily as the economy spirals downward, caught in a relentless cycle of hyperinflation and recession: more crime, more violence, more children on the street each day; more people losing their land, and those landless then crowding into the cities to take up residence in the shantytowns, the *favelas*, that spill across the hillsides of Rio or the outlying parts of São Paulo. Eventually the poverty of the cities becomes unbearable, forcing legions of the poor out into the Amazon in a last-chance crusade for economic salvation. Most of these Amazon migrants, like the old man now disappearing over the horizon, will die as they were born: destitute and desperate in a land of unrealized dreams.

"Está por aqui, gentes"—It's just near here, people—says the driver as we turn right off the highway and bounce down a dirt road heading in the direction of a Catholic mission where the Indians have established their temporary village during the Encounter. This area has, up until now, been spared our attention: off limits to anyone with a camera. But someone has decided to open it up to the media, and so we have come in search of more images to tell our stories. The driver lowers the music and we pull into the Church complex, where the atmosphere in the parking lot is much like that at a college stadium before the big game. Car doors open and close as people, mostly environmentalists and journalists, rush excitedly towards the large iron gates of the mission entrance. Our car inches forward; the people who swarm around the car appear decapitated in my partially obstructed view. They are dressed in an array

of bright-colored shorts and shirts and they tote cameras, tape recorders, and pocket-sized notebooks en route to their next assignment. In the front seat the Wolf and Manoel lower their windows and a wave of the Amazon's hot humid air sweeps into the car. They deliver to the bystanders a mix of heavily accented expletives and lighthearted jokes designed to negotiate our way through the crowd. But it's too dense. The Wolf and I get out and proceed on foot.

As we pass through the large iron gates, we enter what is best described as an Amazon theme park. The Indians are encamped in a large courtyard in which stand a dozen hastily constructed shacks like those put up by hunters for temporary shelter. There are no walls to these structures, just roofs of thatched leaves suspended on sticks for protection from the rain. Men, women, and children—mostly Kayapo, it seems—are scattered about the area occupying themselves in a variety of activities. They are carrying out what, under normal circumstances, would be the simple rituals of daily life: women cleaning the carcasses of animals brought in from the hunt and cooking them over a fire, a group of men in the midst of a discussion, a young child adding an extra layer of palm leaves to a rickety roof. Surrounding various clusters of Indians are groups of photojournalists fighting among themselves to get their best camera angles against the sharp rays of the afternoon light. They push and shove, struggling to frame out any hint of the modern world. These photos are designed to place the Indians in their "natural setting." They eliminate the cars in the background or the box radio sitting in the foreground, all the details that connect the Indians with our world.

The atmosphere is strange—weird and wired. It's as if an entire wax museum of lowland Indian peoples has suddenly come to life and the attendant tourists—cameras at the ready—are swooping down upon them in a vigilante act of anthropological documentation. I take a moment to check my battery. The Wolf and I then enter the throng.

We step past a cluster of television crews filming an old Kayapo man sitting and weaving a headdress. Beyond them I have a clear shot of the Englishwoman I met on my first day at the Hotel Americana. She's getting a touch-up to her face and long, thin black lines are being added to each arm. There is an air of serene contentment about her, as if I've caught her in the midst of a blissful conversion: Botticelli's Venus suddenly transformed into a New Age goddess. I can tell the Wolf is distracted because the boom pole has drifted into the shot. I clear my throat. He recovers and retrieves the pole just enough for me to get the shot. We then move on. As I look about the encampment I can see that there are more than just a few of these individuals caught up in the joyous frenzy of bonding with the Indians. Somehow, like mushrooms, dozens of them seem to have popped up spontaneously after the heavy rains. A few feet behind the New Age Botticelli is an American television producer who, judging from her face paint, also seems to be surrendering to the spirit of the moment. As she poses for a picture taken by her friend, I pivot to document this little scene: I pan from the picture taker to the subject posed, hands on hips, in front of a thatched hut. Slowly I zoom in, creating a frame that is the equivalent of a snapshot. "For my mother," the producer says as my lens homes in to a stop exactly timed to match the shutter click of her friend's Nikon. The sound of that still camera joins the cacophony of whirling gears and shutter snaps coming from the hundreds of other Canons and Leicas and Olympuses firing off around us.

I change my camera battery, but before I can move on to the next image the Wolf taps me on the shoulder, calls time-out by placing his hands in the shape of a T, and points down at the cables falling out of his mixer: he needs time to unravel this mess. Disengaging the cable that joins his mixer to the camera, the Wolf heads back to the equipment bags we have left sitting next to a tree a few feet away. I turn on the camera's automatic microphone so that I can work independently.

Looking up, I notice that near one of the larger thatched huts there are a half dozen television and film crews lining up their tripods in what looks like a preparation for a press conference. I ask an English colleague what's going on.

"Sting's coming, man," he says without looking up from his

camera. "You better get your spot or you'll be covering it from on top of one of these rickety huts."

I see that three more crews have arrived in the few seconds it has taken him to divulge this information. The buzz that has permeated this little village since we first entered is now getting frenzied in expectation of the arrival of a commodity more marketable than a forest dweller returning home with a day's catch. This is a rock star, an icon of our own.

The British are the ones who are really getting hysterical here. Sting, the pop-star-turned-activist, is a hometown boy. This means potentially big sales for freelancers and major career points for television producers who can work his image— perhaps even an interview—into their satellite newscasts. However, my British colleagues' unaccustomed exposure to equatorial sun has turned their cherubic white complexions to dark shades of crimson, adding a demonic aspect to their already questionable demeanor.

"Back off," shouts a burly Englishman as he pushes his assistant to the side and locks his camera into its safety plate, then in a violent thrust mounts it on top of the tripod. Behind him I can see a Kayapo boy watching, startled at the behavior of this angry stranger with a face the color of blood. *Who here is "civilized"?* I ask myself. *Is it us with our steel instruments and stressed-out schedules? Or is it these Indians with their war clubs, lip plugs, and drug-induced shamanistic rituals?* This little episode of pushing, shoving, and screaming is probably as incomprehensible to this young boy as some of the Kayapo "war cries" that we witnessed yesterday back in the Civic Center. I imagine that it must only confirm the stereotypes of the white man that have become a part of the folklore of his world. Such tales are passed from village to village and from generation to generation: that the white man drinks too much, that he is greedy and violent, that he is the one who does not know how to live by a civilized code of conduct. In a weird way I am thankful for little dramas like this one. They allow me to take a step back and look beyond my own culture. For a few seconds I can, through the boy's eyes, get a glimpse of our world. And a scary place it must be.

Suddenly the boy's head snaps to the side and his eyes lock on a group of still photographers who have just abandoned a cluster of Indians like a school of sharks suddenly departing from a feeding frenzy. The journalists move in the direction of an approaching mob—mostly Indians—who are surging in from the front gates, a tassel of blond hair bouncing among them, a sign perhaps that Sting has arrived.

The scene quickly descends into bedlam. Payakan is out in front of the pack accompanied by a half dozen Kayapo who are using war clubs like crowbars to push their way through the crowd of adoring groupies and anxious photojournalists. A short white woman with a French accent and bright red lines painted across her face is closely following the group, shouting Sting's name and holding an autograph book in her hand. I stand my ground against the wave of bodies that rises up around me. When I am at its center I start to backpedal, slowly keeping pace with the momentum of the mob. In spite of the pushing and shoving, I am able to get a good twenty-second shot of this frenetic scene. The image works in that it is immediately comprehensible to an international audience: the rock star arrives in the Amazon and encounters the same chaos and clamor he is confronted with on world tours. But I will need other images if I want to put together a report. So I circle the perimeter of the mob in the hope of rejoining the crews lined up in front of the larger thatched hut.

As I sprint around the side I glance to my left and spot the Wolf in deep conversation with a beautiful dark-haired Brazilian woman, her back against a tree and my trusted soundman leaning close to her. Unfortunately for me, the Wolf is exactly where I left him and the cables he had gone to straighten out remain lying by his side—somehow more confused than ever—in a tangle of branches and leaves.

I whistle a few times, trying to get his attention. Then, unable to break away from the crowd, I call out urgently for the tripod. I am embarrassed by the shrillness of my voice; it sounds like the last panicked plea of a drowning man. Beside me I can see the Kayapo boy staring up, his eyes confused and questioning, an unfortunate confirmation that I too have joined the demonic and incomprensible world of the other, crimson-faced white man.

"Wolf, I need the tripod!" I call out again in a tone intended to be less strident.

Ever so slowly he glances in my direction, blinking to acknowledge my request but careful not to break his composure or allow his friend to move away from the tree. I can tell by the tilt of his head and his sleepy-eyed expression that he is at a critical juncture in one of his delicate negotiations. I have heard various versions of this routine on different trips to the Amazon: "Where will you be later?" "Do you live with your parents?" "Do you want to have dinner with me and my friends?"

I can feel my anger at the Wolf swelling as the mob of journalists surges forward, crowding the already limited space we have to cover this event. Without a tripod I will have to do it handheld, which will make the shoot a backbreaking task. I caution myself not to react too angrily to the ways of the Wolf. This is the manner in which things get done in Brazil, the way in which life unfolds; to question it is to go against the rhythm of the culture. The gringo option, an in-your-face confrontation, would be absolute suicide. I've learned that in the past. Brazilians simply shut down when faced with hostile Americans who believe that angry rages in tropical cultures can get them what they want. Besides, I tell myself, there is probably a logic to what the Wolf is doing; I just can't see it. There have been countless times on other trips when his Don Juan antics have paid off in the long run. This woman probably works for Varig airlines and will be a key contact when we try to leave without a reservation.

"Okay, can we get started please," says a young Indian man in Western dress, his accent revealing a perfect command of American English. Immediately he repeats his instructions in Portuguese in hopes of settling the anxious crowd. His name is Jorge Terena, and he has received a college education in the States funded by the American missionaries who worked among his people, the Terenas, when he was a young boy.

Sting has now positioned himself in the circle of cameras. He looks nervous as he glances about, head tilted, scanning the crowd. He has a blond ponytail, blue eyes, and strikingly hand-some features mitigated by a sharp, pointy nose. He is wearing an earth-color combination of green pants and boots and a red and green patterned shirt. This eco-conscious fashion fusion allows the rock star to blend in with his indigenous entourage yet distinguish himself from the motley array of brightly colored anthropologists, journalists, and Indian wanna-bes who have descended upon him. The rumor floating among the journalists is that Sting is here to announce the formation of a foundation to help save the rain forest. And, not surprisingly, he is doing it in collaboration with Raoni, who has just appeared by his side and set off another flurry of photos. The elderly Kayapo leader, conspicuously absent from the early part of Payakan's confer-ence, has now managed to steal the limelight from his nephew. Payakan might be able to muster the support of environmental-ists and politicians, but Raoni has come up with a rock star, a figure from the world of the new whites who has the power to raise millions of dollars while consistently attracting the atten-tion of the international press. In the last few days there has been talk of internal dissension between these two Kayapo leaders. But here, at least for those of us on the outside, they appear to be getting along.

As Jorge Terena tries to settle the crowd, Sting takes a few moments to pose for the press. But he appears ill at ease in this setting. It's as if the serious environmentalist within him is uncomfortable inhabiting the body of the rock legend. Perhaps this is the trade-off whenever fame is used to proselytize for a cause. There is a confusing set of signals being sent that, in this case, seem to confuse even the sender.

Sting's collaborator in the foundation project, the filmmaker Jean Pierre Dutilleux, quiets the crowd. Sting whispers some-thing to Raoni, laughs to himself, and takes a step forward to meet the press.

"I spent a day yesterday with some Kayapo in the jungle and realized that I was in Paradise," says Sting. "That I was in the Garden of Eden." He pauses, takes another nervous breath, and continues.

"If that culture is destroyed, then the world loses something that is invaluable," he says. "I also think that by saving the Indians, you save the rain forest. They are the gardeners of the forest. So we have to protect them to protect the forest."

Sting waits while Terena translates and there is another round of photos. Click: there's Sting with his arm around Raoni. More clicks and a flurry of flashes: Sting, Dutilleux, and Raoni standing and talking.

"What is it you are trying to do?" shouts an English reporter from behind me.

"I am here to speak for my own people," Sting quickly shouts out so as to avoid being deluged by more questions. "We want to help save the rain forest. We want to try and declare a huge National Park in the center of the Amazon. We need funds to do it. We need a few million dollars. I'm confident we can raise it with Raoni's help."

Sting's statements are again translated into Portuguese as he, Raoni, and Dutilleux, arms draped around one another, stand together for another round of photo opportunities. All of these images have been set against the picturesque background of the largest of the Indians' thatched huts. It gives the scene "local color" and provides a high point in an expertly orchestrated press junket. In spite of his initial anxiousness Sting now seems content with the attention of the press.

The Wolf finally arrives with the tripod. "Getting through that crowd was really difficult," he says.

"What was her name?"

"Who?"

I look up at him for a moment as I fix the tripod. "Mario, my friend. Please show me some respect."

"Yes. This is true. Respect is important," he says. He pauses as if to reflect on this concept, on the girl, or both. "Angela is her name," he says finally.

"I am happy for you," I say, then laugh as I lock the camera in and return to my shot.

The rock star rambles on for another fifteen minutes, giving details of his plans to establish boundaries around the part of Kayapo land known as Mekragnoti territory. He has recorded an "appeal," he says, in seven languages. A worldwide tour has been planned with Raoni to get the message out. He peppers his statements with assurances that his new foundation will be working "with" Brazilians, that this is "a Brazilian initiative," that it won't be like "North Americans trying to tell the Brazilians what to do."

Sting is proving himself to be a savvy diplomat. These declarations are aimed at many of the journalists here, particularly the Brazilians, who are suspicious of the Englishman's intentions. The legacy of outsiders interested in the Amazon triggers immediate feelings of xenophobia: Teddy Roosevelt raised eyebrows when he arrived here in 1913 and Henry Ford received a similar reception in 1926. The Midwestern megacapitalist had indeed come to exploit the Amazon's rubber trees, while the rough-riding naturalist claimed he was simply interested in writing about the region's flora and fauna. More recently, in 1967, the American billionaire Daniel Ludwig shocked Brazilians when, during the military dictatorship, he bought a section of the Amazon forest the size of Austria. He then spent tens of millions of dollars over two decades on an ambitious project to harvest lumber from rapid-growth trees imported from Asia. Rumors quickly began to circulate that the entire operation was actually a covert U.S. military base. The project eventually collapsed and Ludwig left the Amazon. Sting, now playing the humble rock star, says he doesn't want to exploit it but only "save it." Yet the Brazilian journalists want to know exactly what that means. In spite of his disclaimer, Sting's plans could easily be interpreted as imperialistic, just another European or American telling the Brazilians what they should be doing with their country. Even if he is well intentioned (and the jury is still out) his proposal—and it is a bold one—treads on sensitive ground for Brazil, a country beset by pressing economic woes to which, some feel, the Amazon's untapped wealth holds the solution.

"It's a Brazilian problem to be solved by Brazilians," Sting repeats in the final moments of the press conference. "I just want to help the Brazilians solve their problems."

When the speeches are done, a group of Kayapo begin performing a traditional dance in honor of Sting. They line up in single file, forming a snakelike pattern consisting of about thirty men. Suddenly they break into one of the ceremonial Kayapo songs. As they sing the line advances, the men lurching forward, shuffling one foot in front of the other, their backs bent and slightly arched. Their movements are powerful and dramatic. But within two minutes this beautiful ritual is aborted: the crush of cameramen has made it impossible for the Kayapo to complete the dance's intricate pattern. Leaving the crowd, the Wolf and I linger on the outskirts of the village, hoping to grab a few more shots before heading back to the Hotel Americana. I then spot a cluster of photographers at the far end of the encampment. We wander over in that direction. I always find the peripheral scenes most telling at such events, so it is not surprising that we have stumbled upon the most fascinating moment of the day.

The group of photojournalists is surrounding a Kayapo woman—her face painted red—who is holding a young boy. The pose is strikingly like that of a Madonna and Child. Enriching the iconography of the scene, she also holds a machete raised defiantly—a gesture calling to mind images of left-wing revolutionaries from the 1960s: Che riding into Havana on the top of a truck, a heavily armed Black Panther on the steps of a government building. The photographers standing in front of her are calling out instructions, telling her to raise the machete a little higher or tilt it slightly this way or that. Payakan, who has been standing off to the side, begins to insert himself into this scene, working with the journalists to make certain they are able to get the exact pose they desire. He takes the woman gently by the elbow and turns her to face the sun. He suggests that she lift the child up a little higher. I walk about the scene grabbing close-ups of the woman, long shots and profiles of the photographers, and every shot possible of Payakan as he works his mise-en-scene. The Wolf, following behind me with boom pole extended, is doing an excellent job, careful not to allow any shadows to fall across the images I am gathering. When Payakan steps back, the cameras fire away at their creation perfected with his collaboration: an archetypal New Age icon, an Amazon Woman for a new era. She—or the image they created of her—is part caring mother, part fearless warrior ready and poised in the new global fight to save the rain forest. But what she really represents is a resurrected icon, a descendant of the original Amazon. This mythological figure of a "man-killing" warrior who seduces and then murders her male opponents was made famous by Herodotus in the fifth century B.C., recounted by Virgil in the first century B.C., and then transported to Brazil by the Spanish explorer Francisco de Orellana in 1541. It was Orellana who applied the misnomer to a group of Tapuya Indians with whom he fought during his four-thousand-mile expedition up what was thenceforth called the Amazon River. He referred to the Tapuya as Amazons because, he noted, the women fought side by side with the men. Today's reappearance of the woman-warrior image attests to the residual power of ancient myths.

Certainly there is an innocent side to this impromptu photo opportunity. Many of my colleagues did not get a shot of the woman with the machete in the Civic Center, the defining image of the Altamira Encounter, so they are now trying to save their jobs by capturing an approximation. Payakan is only trying to help by acting as a cultural interlocutor, a position he has become accustomed to over the last two decades. Before he arrived, this poor woman was surrounded by a pack of overeager journalists shouting instructions in Portuguese, a language probably incomprehensible to her. Payakan has simply interceded, translated, and made some suggestions of his own.

As the Wolf and I move about this scene, it becomes clear to me why I have been feeling an odd disconnectedness ever since I got to Altamira. Something is haywire. To participate in such photographic encounters is like entering a strange dimension of time and space, a state of being both real and unreal. For me these illusory moments have come to define my experience at Altamira. I find myself increasingly drawn to documenting images of my fellow photographers and filmmakers who in turn are grappling with their perceptions of the Indians, churning out these approximations in a mad rush to circulate them to an unsuspecting outside world. It's no wonder that I am often asked, "Are there still really Amazon women in the Amazon?"

Images such as this Madonna with Machete will simply add to the long list of cloudy perceptions that have come to dominate the middle ground between our two worlds.

For the photographers "capturing" this scene it is not important who the Amazon Woman really is. She is only a token as fake as wooden cigar-store Indians, celluloid savages, the noble profiles on nickels, and the potent indigenous symbols borrowed by athletic teams in my part of the world. But what makes this scene fascinating is that Payakan is colluding in the fabrication of the images of his people. He is in fact seducing the media while they in turn are seducing his people: this is a complex, double-edged deal that even the desperate Dr. Faust would have taken time to consider.

Perhaps this is the only way that mass movements can be organized for change, by galvanizing a shared sense of *communitas* through the creation of attractive and identifiable images. Perhaps I should relax and let myself get swept up in the euphoric flow. Isn't that what happened in the sixties? People underwent spontaneous transformations and got in touch with another way of life. Here the Kayapo's efforts do appear to be paying off. They've clearly won the support of the international press, which will make the World Bank think twice about granting the Brazilian government a loan for the Kararaó hydroelectric project. No indigenous group has ever been able to galvanize so much support for one of its causes; this is a truly historic event. Yet somehow as I document the scene I can't escape the feeling that such moments are going to come back and haunt us all someday: Payakan, the journalists, and all those who have made "saving the rain forests" their cause of the day.

The uneasy feeling—the disconnectedness—is reinforced as I focus in close-up on one of the last images of the day. As I look through the lens I am struck by something I didn't notice before. It is the face of the young Kayapo child cradled in his mother's arm as they remain standing in front of the photographers. The expression on his face is one of absolute horror. It appears no one has asked him if he wants to participate in the insanity surrounding him. I steady myself and focus in on his face, and I wonder what will become of this new generation of Kayapo.

_____

On my last night in Altamira I leave the Wolf sleeping at the hotel and walk to the Posto Telefônico, a building with a bank of phones for domestic and international calls. I want to contact Patricia Monte-Môr, my friend and researcher in Rio, and also my office in New York, so that I can begin laying the groundwork for selling a story on the Altamira Encounter. If I can ship my tapes back to the States in two days, the story will still be fresh. Any longer and I will probably be beaten by the competition.

I ask directions from an old man with a stubby beard, pushing a dilapidated wooden cart filled with cardboard and pieces of metal.

"*Onde fica a telefônica?*"—Where is the telephone bureau?—I manage to say in another of my pathetic attempts to pronounce this beautiful language.

"*Direto,*" he assures me with a crooked smile as he points down the street. "*Tudo direto.*" Straight ahead.

At this time of night the only illumination on the town's back streets is the bluish light emanating from television sets which spills out from the doors and windows of one-story houses. The old man turns back to his cart and walks on, mumbling to himself so low I can't make out what he is saying. As I pass by a few of the houses I hear the quiet calls of young girls in darkened doorways. "Pssst, pssst," they whisper. "*Gato, vem aqui.*" Cat, come here—playful, seductive advances like these are common in backwater towns. The occasional gringo passing through can represent a ticket out for a desperate young woman or a profitable evening for the professional hooker.

I remind myself not to get involved with either one. Not again. On one of my first trips to the Amazon I spent a wild evening at a nightclub in the backstreets of Belém. My friend Thomas and I had met three young women who were beautiful and fun. We bought them drinks. I spoke my broken Portuguese. We danced and joked all night. It was very casual and friendly, simply a group of young people out having some fun.

Then the negotiations began: How much were we going to pay for sleeping with them tonight? Which motel were we going to take them to? Who was going to pay for the taxi home? I was caught off guard, feeling like the naive gringo. I had not realized that I had been carousing with a group of professional hookers; that had never entered my mind. I had been around the world and back. I thought I could spot a prostitute in any city. But here prostitution is not as cold a transaction as what takes place in cities like New York and London and Paris where street-smart pros working the sidewalks negotiate their deals in a matter of seconds. Here it works differently. There is more seduction involved.

Now as I continue down this side street I hear footsteps behind me, slow and deliberate: stiletto heels on the cobblestones. As I come near the pool of light from the Posto Telefônico I turn and face the person who has been following me: a beautiful dark-haired girl in her early twenties with a curvaceous body packed tightly into a low-cut, silky black dress.

"*Eu quero ser tua mulher*"—I want to be your woman—she says, quickly stepping in front of me as I start towards the stairs of the white brick building. From the corner of my eye I can see two men and a woman talking on the top step. They stop and stare. Up close the smell of her perfume is strong and sweet, as if its power has been enhanced by this dense humid air.

"*Eu não quero,*" I say—I don't want to.

"*Não quero dinheiro.*" I don't want money.

"*Não, obrigado.*" No, thank you.

I move to step around her but she grabs my wrist, clamping down hard, her fingernails cutting into my skin. "*Não quero dinheiro,*" she repeats.

"*Entendo mas não quero.*" I understand, but I am not interested.

Pulling my hand free, I walk up the steps of the Posto Telefônico. Her strength caught me off guard, the experience confusing yet erotic in a way which also caught me by surprise. As I enter the crowded building I decide to call a woman I started seeing just before leaving on this trip. It's been a while since I thought about my home and those parts of my life I left behind. Looking back I can see Ms. High Heels standing in the shadows, her body swaying precariously as she tries to balance in those stilettos on the rocky street. I think about this thing called seduction and how it seems to be so much a part of the fabric of life here. It manages to infuse almost every human interaction—including the reckless economic expansion of the frontier: the bartering, the exchanges, the "courtship" of the missionaries, the interviews of the journalists, the photographic moments, the "teams of attraction." In a land where people want so much and have so little, seduction is a force to be reckoned with.

13

Documentation

journal entry
New York City
1990

Some facts I need to remember:

—from 1985 to 1990 under the Presidency of José Sarney
inflation in the Brazilian economy rose from 200 percent a year
to 2,000 percent a year. 66 percent of all Brazilians are
classified as poor.
—in 1988 two hundred and forty thousand cases of malaria were
reported in the state of Roraima. That number represents 20
percent of the state's population.
—900,000 Indians live in all of Amazonia.
—the number of Indians in Brazil is 220,000 or .2 percent of the
country's population.

In 1988 DNPM geologists at the Belem residency, who have more regular contact with garimpos and garimpeiros than any other formal-sector mining professionals, estimated 1987 garimpo production at around 120 metric tons of gold.... Historically, this level of production matches and even surpasses the great nineteenth-century gold rushes. California from 1848 to 1856 produced an average of 80 tons of gold annually, while the Klondyke produced a total of 42 tons between 1896 and 1900.

—David Cleary,
Anatomy of the Amazon Gold Rush (1990)

"You know gold ain't like stone in a riverbed. It don't cry out to be picked up. You got to know how to recognize it. And finding it ain't all. Not by a long shot. You got to know how to tickle it so she'll come out laughing."

—Walter Huston, in the film
The Treasure of the Sierra Madre (1948)

In 1939, Lucy Young, a member of the Wintu tribe of northern California, told a local historian her life story. . . . Mrs. Young describes her family's terrible experiences during the gold rush itself. The gold rushers and homesteaders who flooded into California then were responsible for murdering over fifty thousand Native Americans between 1848 and 1870 alone.

—*Native American Testimony*,
Peter Nabokov, ed. (1991)

Our Lord in his goodness guide me that I may find this gold.

—Christopher Columbus, December 23, 1492

We are exterminating the Indian and doing so in the worst possible way—by convincing ourselves that we are great humanists, extending over the Indians wings of protection. . . . This is how you can interpret all the humanity we have been imposing on the Indian.

—Orlando Villas Bôas

If you can persuade yourself that people who stand in your way are savages, you can rationalize gunning them down and forcing them to adapt to your purposes.

—David Maybury-Lewis, "Societies on the Brink,"
Harvard Magazine, 1977

The conquest of the earth, which mostly means the taking it away from those who have a different complexion or slightly flatter noses than ourselves, is not a pretty thing when you look into it too much. What redeems it is the idea only. An idea at the back of it; not a sentimental pretence but an idea; and an unsentimental belief in the idea—something you can set up, and bow down before, and offer a sacrifice to. . . .

—Joseph Conrad,
Heart of Darkness (1902)

"I am honored to be your guest here, and you have treated me kindly," I answer. "I believe that the forest is yours. But the white man has no real home. He is lost in a world that he doesn't understand. He has ceased to communicate with the spirits of the earth and the forest, the river and the air. So he is alone.

"Unhappy, he searches for happiness, and when he sees happiness in others, he become angry and wants to destroy it because inside he is empty. I am not a politician, I am only a singer, but many people listen to me. I promise you that whenever I can speak on your behalf, I will do so. I shall tell your story to whomever I can because you are the protectors of the forest, and if the forest dies, so does the earth. Even a white man can understand this."

Raoni looks content.

—Sting, quoted in "Primal Sting," *Vogue*, 1988

The Indian . . . stands free and unconstrained in Nature, is her inhabitant and not her guest, and wears her easily and gracefully. But civilized man has the habits of the house. His house is a prison.

—Henry David Thoreau, *Journal*, April 26, 1841

Their innocence is as great as Adam's.

—Pedro Alvares Cabral, "discoverer" of Brazil, 1500

Virtuous principals, ideological purity, willingness to die heroically for cherished ideals are no more than white fantasies. Indigenist activists who cultivate such an image do not seem to realize that by demanding it of the Indians they are, in fact, creating a perfection model of the honorable, incorruptible Westerner. The

contrast between the martyr Indian and the sold-out Indian is a facsimile of the contrast between the honest white and the corrupt white.
—Alcida Ramos,
"The Hyperreal Indian," *Critique of Anthropology* (1994)

This is what happens when the white man destroys. This was a palm tree rich in fruits. . . . The smoke . . . it's going up in the air to be carried to who knows what other people. . . . We've been considered criminals by the government of our country. We took a trip to Washington at the beginning of this year to help the government of Brazil to preserve our forests. Instead of thanking us, the government accuses us of being criminals. This is the kind of deforestation that is committed by the white man.

And this is another way that white men destroy. This is a mine.
—Paulinho Payakan, commentary to slide show,
in Elaine Dewar, *Cloak of Green* (1995)

The nakedness of the inhabitants seemed to be protected by the grassy velvetiness of the outside walls and the fringe of palm trees: when the natives slipped out of their huts, it was as if they were divesting themselves of giant ostrich-feather wraps. . . . It was as if an entire civilization were conspiring in a single, passionate affection for the shapes, substances and colours of life.
—Claude Lévi-Strauss,
Tristes Tropiques (1955)

They have been fashioned very little by the human mind, and are still very close to their original naturalness. The laws of nature still rule them, very little corrupted by ours. . . . I am sorry that Lycurgus and Plato did not know of them; for it seems to me that what we actually see in these nations surpasses not only all the pictures in which the poets have idealized the golden age and all their inventions in imagining a happy state of man . . . there is no sort of traffic, no knowledge of political superiority, no custom of servitude, no riches or poverty, no contracts, no succession, no partitions, no occupations but leisure ones, no care for any but common kinship, no clothes, no agriculture, no metal, no use of wine or wheat. The very words that signify lying, treachery, dissimulation, avarice, envy, belittling, pardon—unheard of. How far from this perfection would he find the republic that he imagined: *Men fresh sprung from the gods*.

—Michel de Montaigne,
"Of Cannibals," *Essays* (1578–80)

It is thus extremely naive to look for ethnology among the Savages or in some Third World—it is here, everywhere, in the metropolis, among the whites, in a world completely catalogued and analysed and then *artificially revived as though real*, in a world of simulation: of the hallucination of truth, of blackmail by the real, of the murder and historical (hysterical) retrospection of every symbolic form—a murder whose first victims were, noblesse oblige, the Savages, but which for a long time now has been extended to all Western societies.

—Jean Baudrillard,
The Process of Simulation (1983)

At the end of 1989, the deputy Helio Campos, renowned for his hatred of the Indians, indulged in obvious scaremongering, which seemed designed to influence military officers in the security forces. He said that the Yanomami and other Indian groups practiced a type of 'tribal socialism,' and that to create large reserves for them on the country's border could be 'the first step towards dismembering these areas from the rest of the country.' He thus proposed that no Indian reserves should be created within 150 kilometers of the frontier and that all Indians living within this zone should be relocated elsewhere in Brazil. Anthropologists and others in Brazil immediately denounced this scheme as 'premeditated genocide' and it was eventually dropped.

—Sue Branford and Oriel Glock,
The Last Frontier: Fighting Over Land in the Amazon (1985)

The white men in the East are like birds. They are hatching out their eggs every year and there is not enough room in the East and they must go elsewhere; and they come west, as you have seen them coming for the last few years. And they are still coming, and will come until they overrun all of this country: and you can't prevent it. . . . Everything is decided in Washington by the majority, and these people come out west and see that the Indians have a big body of land they are not using, and they say, "We want that land."

> —General George Crook,
> during treaty hearings regarding the
> Great Sioux Reservation, 1889

This is a promise that I can strongly make: we are going to create a policy of integrating the Indian population into the Brazilian society as rapidly as possible. . . . We think that the ideals of preserving the Indian population within its own "habitat" are very beautiful but unrealistic.

> —Mauricio Rangel Reis, Brazil's minister of the interior, 1974

While Mr. Reagan said in Moscow that he was willing to hear the Indians out, he also said: "Maybe we made a mistake. Maybe we should not have humored them in wanting to stay in that kind of primitive life style. Maybe we should have said: 'No, come join us. Be citizens along with the rest of us.' "

> —Julie Johnson, *New York Times*, Dec. 13, 1988

The Navahos, squaws, and children ran in all directions and were shot and bayoneted. . . . I then marched out to the east side of the post; there I saw a soldier murdering two little children and a woman. . . . After the massacre there were no more Indians to be seen about the post with the exception of a few squaws, favorites of the officers. The commanding officer endeavored to make peace again with the Navahos by sending some of the favorite squaws to talk with the chiefs; but the only satisfaction the squaws received was a good flogging.

> —Captain Nicholas Hodt, 1861, quoted in Dee Brown,
> *Bury My Heart at Wounded Knee* (1970)

journal entry
Rio de Janeiro
August 1988

Questions to be asked of the Yanomami:
—Who is getting sick? Has anything happened to the women?
Have they been shot? Have they tried to protect themselves?
Why haven't they retreated? Are they selling game? Are their
gardens being raided?

But when we reached the waters off Spain, around two hundred of these Indians died, I believe because of the unaccustomed air, which is colder than theirs. We cast them into the sea. . . . We disembarked all the slaves, half of whom were sick.

—Christopher Columbus

It will be found, by the united testimony of all that this disease [gonorrhea brought by whites], more than all other diseases, and perhaps more than all other causes, is the active agent of destruction of the Indian race.

Senator James R. Doolittle, "Condition of Indian Tribes," U.S.
Congressional Report, 1867

Most Indian tribes "never had a word for Devil until Columbus landed," [Mary Louise Defender-Wilson, a Northern Sioux] said. "We have many words to describe a bear. But it wasn't until Columbus arrived that he brought the Devil."

—*New York Times*, December 13, 1988

One group is coming to Plinio's village just north of here in a few days. They said they were interested and wanted to hear more about God. One village, Bocalahudumteri, did not receive them well at all. They indicated to Roberto that the foreigners were actually the spirits of dead yanomama that had come back again. Bruce Hartman was formerly a yanomama that was shot with an arrow and God rubbed his flesh in some mysterious manner and he came back to life again. I am also a spirit. They say it is quite obvious because I don't have any

hair on my forehead. Francisco, too, is a spirit. This is quite evident to them because his teeth are loose. (They have never seen anyone with false teeth.) Roberto was telling me how Francisco had eaten a banana and dropped the peeling on the ground. One of the Indians called a small boy and said, "Throw this spirit's banana peeling away."
—Keith Wardlaw, in the New Tribes Mission journal,
Brown Gold, 1968

In the Amazon, a rubber boom that began in the mid-nineteenth century sent thousands of people up previously uncharted rivers in search of the native rubber tree. . . . When Indians refused to surrender to gradual assimilation, they were targeted for more rapid extermination by grim killers known as *bugreiros*. On one occasion, a German ethnologist, Gustav von Koenigswald, reported that a *bugreiro* "poisoned with strychnine the pools of drinking water of a Kaingang village . . . causing the deaths of some two thousand Indians of all ages." At different times, *bugreiros* organized for the exclusive purpose of hunting Indians.
—Alan Riding, review of John Hemming's *Amazon Frontier*,
New York Times Book Review, January 31, 1988

Mr. Reagan also drew criticism from some Indian groups for saying in the Soviet Union that a large number of American Indians had become "very wealthy" because the reservations were an oil-producing land. "And you can get very rich pumping oil," Mr. Reagan had said, speaking at Moscow State University.

Today the President, asked if he regretted having mentioned the American Indians' "primitive life style," replied: "I don't recall saying that."
—Julie Johnson, *New York Times*, December 13, 1988

This country was a lot better off when the Indians were running it.
—Vine Deloria, Jr., *New York Times Magazine*, March 3, 1970

The Wish to Be an Indian
If only I were an Indian, instantly alert, and on a racing horse, leaning against the wind.

—Franz Kafka

journal entry
Blue Mountain Lake, New York
1990

Conquest becomes a necessity because the mechanisms of
exchange of the indigenous society are too complex, too time-
consuming to co-exist with the agenda of the outsider. That's why
we have always believed that they must learn our ways and
succumb to our desires.

What the Europeans sought on the coast was, above all, sea-otter pelts. Between 1785 and 1825, some 330 recorded vessels revisited the coast. . . . Sea-otter skins were obtained, at first, in return for iron and tobacco, molasses and muskets. The native American traders were mostly "chiefs" who mobilized their followers and personal contacts to deliver the otter skins, and whose power grew concomitantly with the development of trade.

—Eric R. Wolf, *Europe and the People Without History* (1982)

They . . . brought us parrots and balls of cotton and spears and many other things, which they exchanged for the glass beads and hawk's bells. They willingly traded everything they owned. . . . They were well built, with good bodies and handsome features. . . . They do not bear arms, and do not know them, for I showed them a sword, they took it by the edge and cut themselves out of ignorance. They have no iron. Their spears are made of cane. . . . They would make fine servants.

—Christopher Columbus, *Log*, 1492

We shall . . . show how our facts contribute to a general theory of obligation. . . . One gives away what is in reality a part of one's nature and substance, while to receive something is to receive a part of someone's spiritual essence. . . . Whatever it is, food, possession, women, children or ritual, it retains a magical and religious hold over the recipient. The thing given is not inert. It is alive and often personified.

—Marcel Mauss, *The Gift* (1925)

Diverse peoples adjust their differences through what amounts to a process of creative, and often expedient misunderstandings. People try to persuade others who are different from themselves by appealing to what they perceive to be the values and practices of those others. They often misinterpret and distort both the values and the practices of those they deal with, but from these misunderstandings arise new meanings and through them new practices—the shared meanings and practices of the middle ground.

> —Richard White, *The Middle Ground: Indians, Empires and Republics in the Great Lakes Region, 1650–1815* (1991)

When there is an invasion of Indian territory—and usually it is an illegal one—the Indian for me is really a victim of the non-Indian. But from the moment that the Indian attacks he become the cruel Indian, the one who doesn't deserve anything, right? So what I am saying is for them to continue being victims—that is the best policy for the Indian—to avoid aggression.

> —one Senhor Sigfrido, Brazilian Indian Agency employee, to Waiapi Indians complaining of gold miners on their land, 1989

se•duce (si-doos) *v.* . . . . 1. to persuade (especially into wrongdoing) by offering temptations, *was seduced into betraying his country*. 2. to tempt (a person) into sexual intercourse.

> —*Oxford American Dictionary*

Natives were sold to buy wine, oil, vinegar, salt pork, items of clothing, a horse, or whatever else the butcher and his men imagined they might need. A man would be invited to choose from among fifty or a hundred young girls the one he most fancied, and she would then be handed over in exchange for an *arroba* of wine or oil or vinegar, or for a side of pork.

> —Bartolomé de Las Casas,
> *A Short Account of the Destruction of the West Indies* (1559, published 1875)

The Scythians could not understand what was happening and were at a loss to know where the marauders had come from, as their dress, speech, and nationality were strange to them. . . . The Amazons used to scatter and go off to some little distance in ones and twos to ease themselves, and the Scythians when they noticed this followed suit; until one of them, coming upon an Amazon girl all by herself, began to make advances to her. She nothing loth, gave him what he wanted. . . . The young man then left her and told the others what had happened, and on the next day took a friend to the same spot, where he found his Amazon waiting for him and another one with her. Having learnt of their success, the rest of the young Scythians soon succeeded in getting the Amazons to submit to their wishes.

—Herodotus, "The Amazons," *Histories*, c. 446 B.C.

Did you sleep with any of the Indian women?
    —question repeatedly asked of the author by men and women
        in North America, Europe, and Brazil

ex•ot•ic (ig-zot-ik) *adj.* 1. (of plants, words, or fashions) introduced from abroad, not native. 2. striking and attractive through being colorful or unusual. **ex•ot´i•cal•ly** *adv.* **ex•ot•ic•cism** (ig-zot-ĭ-siz-ĕm) *n.* **exotic dancer**, a striptease dancer.

—*Oxford American Dictionary*

> *Lo, the poor Indian! whose untutor'd mind*
> *Sees God in clouds, or hears him in the wind:*
> *His soul proud Science never taught to stray*
> *Far as the solar walk or milky way;*
> *Yet simple Nature to his hope has giv'n,*
> *Behind the cloud-topp'd hill, an humbler heav'n.*
> —Alexander Pope, *An Essay on Man*, 1733–4

It is my wish that nothing My Lord the King, my daughter the Princess, and my son the Prince may do, or allow to be done, shall bring any harm to the Indians living either on islands or terra firma, to either their persons or property. Indeed, they shall see to it that these peoples are treated in a just and kindly fashion.

—Queen Isabella of Spain (1451–1504),
last will and testament

The violence in the countryside is, in its essence, the result of an unjust agrarian structure that, besides generating tensions and deaths for possession and use of the land, constitutes the heart of the problem of accelerating urban growth.

> —Antonio Cabrera, Brazil's minister of agriculture
> and agrarian reform, June 17, 1991

Fifty peasant squatters were rounded up from various estates and from the villages of Monte Sato and Parauna, Pará state, and detained by military police on one of the estates without judicial warrant. Some of the peasants, including children, were bound with rope, many beaten with rifle butts and sticks, two women were raped, and an attempt was made to rape a twelve-year-old girl; all were threatened with summary execution, some forced to eat human and animal excrement, thorns, and lighted cigarettes; some had bottles forced down their throats, and others were subjected to additional degrading and cruel treatment.

> —Human Rights Watch, *The Struggle for Land in Brazil* (1992)

Scholars agree that Indians were a particular target when the army broke the peasant revolt in El Salvador in 1932. Some 30,000 people are believed to have been killed, many of them indigenous. The great majority of the Indians who survived abandoned their communities and traditional dress to avoid summary execution, and from then on no longer spoke indigenous languages in public.

> —Amnesty International, *The Americas: Human Rights*
> *Violations Against Indigenous Peoples* (1992)

The causes which the Almighty originates, when in their appointed time He wills that one race of men—as in races of lower animals—shall disappear off the face of the earth and give place to another race, and so on, in the great cycle traced out by Himself, which may be seen, but has reasons too deep to be fathomed by us. The races of the mammoths and mastodons, and the great sloths, came and passed away: the red man of America is passing away.

> —General James Carleton, "Condition of Indian Tribes,"
> U.S. Congressional Report, 1867

I am of the opinion that an area as rich as this—with gold, diamonds, and uranium—cannot afford the luxury of conserving a half a dozen Indian tribes who are holding back the development of Brazil.

—General Fernando Ramos Pereira, March 1975

journal entry
Brasilia
September 1993

The Attorney General's office in Brasilia has tried on three occasions to prosecute cases of genocide resulting from violence against indigenous populations over the last ten years, all of them taking place in remote parts of the Amazon. To date no case has ever been successfully prosecuted. What is more unbelievable is that there has never been a successfully prosecuted case of genocide involving any Indian population anywhere in the Western Hemisphere.

I read an article today where the French filmmaker Jean Rouch refers to the camera as a "thief of reflections."

I am eye. I am a mechanical eye. I, a machine, am showing you a world the likes of which only I can see.

—Dziga Vertov, Russian documentary film pioneer, 1922

14

Just after dawn we drive out to the city's tiny airport in Father John's beat-up yellow Volkswagen, passing Brazilian workers on their way to two-dollar-a-day jobs in Boa Vista's shops and restaurants. Through his open window comes a steady gust of warm air pushing back the priest's shoulder-length salt-and-pepper hair. There is no black shirt and white collar for this Church emissary; traditional priestly garb is now donned only for formal Catholic services. He is one of a new generation of "liberation theologians," Catholic clergy who have allied themselves with the poor and dispossessed and, in the process, rejected certain traditions of the Church that they believe distance them from their flock. Padre Giovanni Saffirio, or Father John as I call him, is a quirky but shrewd Italian cleric who is quickly revealing himself to be Catholicism's answer to James Bond. Today's task of frontier espionage is to smuggle us past the military guard at the airport and get us on one of the Church's planes into Yanomami territory.

"It is a bea-u-ti-ful day, isn't it, Geoffrey," says the good Father, his English delivered in a thick Italian accent overlaid by an American intonation acquired studying anthropology at the University of Pennsylvania several years ago. As we talk he slams his fist on the steering wheel, using each of his impassioned gestures to punctuate a point in the conversation. Today's theme is his interpretation of ethics in a frontier region dominated by politics and miners whom he calls "corrupt, tyrranical, and villainous criminals."

"Boa Vista, ha!" shouts this wild-eyed priest over the sound of his old VW rattling down the highway. "This city is the armpit of the world! I hate this place for what it represents."

"So why do you stay here?"

"This is a good question." He pauses, his head bobbing as he contemplates his response. "Because somebody has to fight back. No? Somebody has to help these poor Yanomami."

"John, to be honest, I think there's a part of you that enjoys all this."

"Yes. This is true. I love to break the law," he says, smiling. "Not in the United States, a country that has protected me and where there is respect for the law, but here in Brazil where no one follows the law." *Boom!* Another hand crashes down on the steering wheel. "When you break the law like we are doing. This is a good thing. This I know you understand. Otherwise you wouldn't be here. No?"

"I'm here to cover a story."

"Yes, I know how you journalists respond. 'I am objective, only interested in facts.' You think I have not heard this kind of answer before?"

"I'm sure you have."

"Yes. I've heard it all before," he says, his face suddenly serious. "Don't forget I am a priest. I am the one who takes the confession. There is nothing I don't know about people. Even you, Mr. Geoffrey."

Boom! Again Father John crashes his hand down on the steering wheel and then begins to laugh to himself.

As we drive on I think about what he calls "breaking the law" and what I choose to call "getting the story." From my perspective we are only doing what forty-five thousand gold miners have been doing for the past two years: flying into an area that has been declared by the military a "national security zone" and remains off limits to any outsiders including journalists, aid agencies, and medical relief organizations. Yet, as Father John and I are both aware, the presence of the military has become more pervasive since I first ventured into the gold camps four months ago. They still give the miners free rein, but covert travel in the region—particularly for foreigners—has become more precarious. Several of my colleagues who have recently attempted to smuggle themselves into Yanomami territory have run into trouble. Some have been apprehended by local officials and their equipment has been seized. Others have been robbed at gunpoint by miners and pilots who entrap them by pretending to act as friendly escorts into the area. Gaining entry today will necessitate getting past the military checkpoint at the runway entrance so we can grab a short flight to a village known as Wakathautheri. This settlement of seventy Yanomami sits next to the Catrimani River and the jungle outpost of Father John's group of missionaries known as the Consolatas, an Italian order of Catholics established in Turin at the turn of the century.

Unlike my past three assignments in the Amazon, this trip I will make without the incorrigible Wolf. In spite of all my complaining I will miss him dearly. "Can't go," he told me over the phone when I called three weeks ago from New York. "My girlfriend is having trouble with me. A *lot* of trouble!" he added. There was then a long pause and a sigh. "Too much time out of Rio. My life is becoming difficult. You understand. No?"

The Wolf seeking to mend his ways? This didn't make sense to me. Yet I understood what he was saying. He was being polite. He'd probably had enough of traipsing about the Amazon with a wide-eyed gringo. The "trouble" he really wanted to avoid was the kind I could get him into: trouble with the miners, trouble with the military, trouble he didn't need in a country making its first tentative steps towards democratic rule. I'll probably never know the truth about his "trouble" in Rio but, one way or the other, I'll miss him. His all-night carousing didn't always produce the best results (sometimes there was no sound on the tape), but the Wolf was always entertaining and always there when I needed him to back me up. He had been the right choice for the roughneck gold camps with their castaway characters. We had more than a few tricky moments there, and I know we wouldn't have gotten through them had it not been for the "old shoe."

Vincent, my new soundman, is a character cast in a very

different mold: he's a native of São Paolo as opposed to Rio, his behavior more confined and internalized than that of crazy Mario. "If you are in an Indian community," he told me today, "the most important thing is to be yourself. Don't try to be anything else. That will never work." For twenty years Vicent has roamed the Amazon working as a photographer, indigenous rights activist, and most recently an excellent ethnographic filmmaker. His sly grin, green eyes, and wavy brown hair give him the look of a *malandro*, or scoundrel. But he is an individual with a serious past. In the late seventies, he was jailed for aiding the Frano Indians during a period of sporadic conflicts with the government. That action could have easily placed him in the ranks of the "disappeared" of Brazil, those thousands of people who just vanished after being arrested during the military's dictatorship. His years of working with various indigenous communities will undoubtedly make him more at ease with the Indians and, I hope, help us to break through some of the cultural barriers I confronted at the Paapiú airstrip. Without a doubt, I'll miss Mario. But I know Vicent is the better choice for this particular assignment.

We switch cars outside the airport and pack our things into a dented brown pickup truck also owned by the Church. This last-minute crime-novel maneuver adds another layer of tension and intrigue to our venture. And Father John seems to thrive on each and every one. Over the last few days our meetings in Boa Vista have always been held after dark in small out-of-the-way cafes where the good Father personally knew the proprietors: "friends of the Church." Specific details of the trip—even in these trusted locales—were always delivered in a hushed voice followed by an over-the-shoulder glance. He and his fellow Church emissaries have had their share of death threats. Father John doesn't want to take unnecessary chances.

"Don't talk about this trip to anyone," he warned two nights ago when he dropped me at my hotel. "No one can be trusted here."

Early this morning he instructed us to pack our cameras, tapes, and batteries into nondescript bags. The occasional jokes that leavened our conversations over the last few days have become less frequent as the day progressed. We've agreed that if anyone questions us we will say that we are French doctors working with the Consolata missionaries.

When we arrive at the airport checkpoint, the military guard—a disheveled young boy of nineteen with an M-16 dangling from his shoulder—stops the truck. As he glances about the vehicle Father John mumbles a few words of greeting and a brief explanation of our destination. He is nervous, a little frantic; clumsy in his actions in a way that reminds me of Peter Sellers doing Inspector Clouseau. In my conversations with him I've come to learn that this bumbling-clergyman routine is something Father John has consciously cultivated in Boa Vista, a protective cover that works to his advantage in his encounters with the citizenry, many of whom would like to see him and his fellow "communist priests" expelled from the community. And once again it works: the soldier waves us through with a smile. Score one for Father 007. So much for Brazil's National Security Zone. Another victory in Father John's furtive little war.

It is a quick hop to the missionaries' outpost, one hour in a Cessna 206, this time with seats and safety belts—first-class accommodations compared to the gutted gold miners' Cessnas that the Wolf and I flew just a few months back. Father John has assured us that the pilot is "another friend," someone who can be trusted not to tell the gold miners or the military that two filmmakers entered Yanomami territory today. His immediate superior, the bishop Dom Aldo, is accompanying us on this journey. This is not an overnight stay for the bishop; he'll be returning when the plane flies back this afternoon. This is just a "meet and greet" with the local Indians, to see for himself how their life has changed since the miners have occupied their lands.

Dom Aldo is a tall and affable man in his late sixties with silver gray hair, a broad nose, and weary but intelligent eyes, the kind that can pass judgment on you in a quick flicker. He's also got an eerie distanced quality I am having trouble pinpointing. I've never been close to a bishop before. I didn't know what to expect. But there is something a little discomforting about his presence: he seems too "collected." That's the only way I can describe it. Perhaps my unease is exaggerated by the claustrophobic quarters of this tiny aircraft and the bumpiness of our flight. I assume his elevated position in the Catholic hierarchy has put him in closer touch with God and therefore given him a more otherworldly comportment. Maybe, as one assured of his place in the afterlife, he feels more comfortable up here in the heavens bouncing about in these violent wind pockets.

As for me, I am not certain what awaits me in the world beyond. I haven't thought about it much. It is this world that preoccupies my thoughts, particularly when I get this high up in the clouds. Usually I think about what it would be like to suddenly experience engine failure and crash into the forest. Maybe such thoughts are a reflection of my godless upbringing. My current state of existential being operates in a terrain that could best be described as "suspended judgment": I push ahead full speed through life certain that spiritual redemption awaits me but troubled by the knowledge that I can't clearly decipher the passing signposts. In recent years I have let myself be guided more by circumstance than by the hand of God. I find a kind of solace in not really knowing where I am going and what will happen when I get there. Getting to my next immediate destination is my prime concern. My ultimate end is another story, once again sidetracked by the preoccupations of today's pressing assignment.

After an hour's flight we touch down on a soft grassy track cut from the rain forest and still damp from yesterday's heavy rains. As the plane jogs down the runway I look through the murky plastic window and can see a dozen Yanomami men and women standing about like statues waiting to inspect us, the new arrivals, envoys from the white man's world. The landing of a plane in isolated Indian communities is always a special event complete with its own rituals of reception acted out by adults and children alike. The men and women who have emerged from the forest to witness our arrival are now following us to the far end of the airstrip near the six small buildings that make up the Consolata mission complex. As we turn around at the end of the runway the pilot revs the engine one last time, which sends a powerful blast of air sweeping over a group of children; their ecstatic laughter reminds me of great nights with childhood friends caught in a wind tunnel at a local fair.

Stepping down from the small plane, I catch myself staring at the Yanomami who now congregate around us. The Bishop pats a few Indians on the head, shakes hands with a priest, and strides off in the direction of the group of small wooden houses at the end of the airstrip.

Once again I am struck by what I still find odd about the Indians' appearance: their nudity, the small, thin sticks that have been inserted into the chins of the women, the bowl-shaped hairdos and penis strings of the men. The Indians in turn stare at me, a reminder that I am as much an oddity to them as they are to me: too many clothes, too much strange facial hair, and, I can only imagine, too much of an astonished expression on my face. I've reentered terra incognita, an alien if still recognizable land populated by a people vastly different from my own, a people about whom I know so little.

After lunch in the mission house the bishop suggests we pass out *bolachas*, or cookies, to approximately thirty Indians who have gathered in the patches of shade surrounding the mission complex. I hesitate. Vicent refuses outright. In principle, he is contemptuous of missionaries and feels compromised by the bishop's request. However, Dom Aldo is insistent and goes off to get the packages from the plane.

I am troubled by the patronizing nature of this gesture, fearful that it will initiate a strained dynamic of exchange between the Yanomami and myself that will only lead to further problems in the days to come. But I need to remember that the Consolatas have agreed to put us up and act as our translators. We will also require their help in the coming days. Diplomacy is once again required. I think about what happened with Sabastião at Paapiú, about my reckless pride, the problems it caused us, and the pleas of Mario to be more flexible. So when the bishop returns, he and I pass out the cookies. Vicent takes a breather under a nearby tree.

As we dole out the little round vanilla wafers I am having doubts about playing the diplomat. Perhaps I have become an unconscious dupe in a ritual act of Christian proselytizing: the cookie substituting for the Eucharist, the appetite of the Indians a means of gaining access to their souls. *Am I paranoid?* I ask myself as I hand out the little *bolacha* to grown men and women as well as children. The relationship between religious emissaries and Indians is by no means a simple one. For most of the missionaries in the Amazon, particularly the Protestants, the objective is to "break" the culture of the Indians. But Father John has assured me that the Consolatas are a new breed of evangelist. "We are not interested in proselyting anymore," he told me in Boa Vista. "We respect their way of life. Their beliefs. We know that God is talking to them, so we don't try to change them."

I'd like to believe him but I don't know enough about their "mission" to feel comfortable just yet. Besides, among these people every action takes on a complicated dimension, including this paternalistic act of bestowing *bolacha*. Therein lies the problem. The simplest, most well-intentioned gesture can easily backfire, subverting your mission (be it journalistic or religious), even threatening your life.

"Don't play games with fire, don't talk alone with women on the path, and don't leave the day or the day after someone is sick," the anthropologist Ken Taylor told me when I consulted him about entering Yanomami territory. "If you do the first, they will think that you are practicing sorcery, the second, that you are trying to steal their women, and the third, that you are responsible for afflicting that person with the ailment and are then trying to escape," he said. "These are simple things but they can save your life."

Thinking about Ken's warnings, I start to become nervous about my new role as a novitiate. What would happen if one of these Indians fell ill tonight? They'd come looking for me, but the cool and collected bishop would be safely ensconced in his prelate's chambers back in Boa Vista. Of course he isn't worried about what he is doing. I'm the one who would suffer the repercussions.

journal entry
6/1/89

Here are a few things I need to remember:

It is the Yanomami tradition for a village to separate after it reaches 75 people. It seems that this pattern is changing as a result of contact with the gold miners. Villages are afraid to split up, fearful that if they splinter off in small numbers they'll become too vulnerable to attacks by bands of miners.

Women go into the forest by themselves to have children beginning at twelve and thirteen years of age. They are assisted by their mothers and grandmothers the first time around. They have the children on their own after that.

I saw a Tapir today, something that looks like a pig with a long curling nose. Supposedly it can swim.

The Padre tells me we are one and a half degrees above the equator. No wonder it's so unbelievably hot.

We are lucky to have arrived here when we did, catching a clear day at the start of the rainy season. Showers will come more frequently now, followed by torrential downpours, thick walls of precipitation that come rumbling through the forest sweeping over you in a matter of seconds. It makes everything difficult; filming, eating, even walking become laborious, painstaking chores. Nothing stays dry. Life in the village is also restricted: less visitation, less hunting, and a general reduction in activity as people seek the shelter of the maloca to avoid the heavy sheets of rain that can last for days at a stretch. I did consider postponing this return to the forest—my back has been giving out, contracting into spasms after only a few hours of shooting—but if we had waited another two weeks there is no way I would have been able to get into this part of Yanomami territory. It will soon be closed off for several months. Rainstorms, short ones, are blowing through every day. The airstrip is slowly dissolving into one large, grassy swamp. It is uncertain whether we will be able to fly out as planned. And still this story remains unresolved. No one to date has brought back any images or concrete evidence that, as they're saying in the cities, a malaria epidemic is raging in the forest. Miners claim the rumors are circulated by the missionaries, and call them fanatical alarmists. The Consolatas respond by accusing the prospectors of genocide. Gold and God emerge once again as catalytic forces in the conquest of the Americas.

After dispensing the last of his cookies, the bishop pats a few more Indians on the head, climbs into his plane, and flies back to Boa Vista. As we stand on the airstrip watching the little Cessna disappear in the distance, our new host, the resident priest Padre Guilherme, apprises us of the current "plight" of the Indians. He is a short, intense man in his late thirties, a chain smoker with blond hair, thick black glasses, and the hard, wiry body of a middleweight boxer. He doesn't really speak but hurls words at you in a rapid-fire staccato that I have come to associate with a certain type of impassioned advocate. In listening to his assessment of the miners' recent incursions, I find myself missing the flamboyant sensationalized accusations of Father John. Guilherme's account is a drier, more rhetorical analysis of the culture shock, violent threats, and, he says, increase in disease that have accompanied the miners' recent penetrations into this part of Yanomami territory. He is probably a more reliable source than his fellow clergyman but still one whose accounts will need to be double-checked. He and John do share a characteristic that I am beginning to believe is common to all Italian clerics in the Amazon: a wild-eyed look that seems to proclaim that they will do whatever is necessary to carry out God's agenda.

As we walk the soggy airstrip towards the six small buildings that comprise the Consolata mission, Guilherme describes the gold rush in this area as if he were talking about an approaching army.

"The sounds of the gold miners' boats passing on the river will make the hunters stop dead in their tracks," he says. "You should see them twisting their heads as they try to gauge the distance by the sound of the echo in the forest."

He stops for a moment to light another cigarette, the third or fourth—I'm losing count—that he has smoked in the last half hour.

"How have the miners been getting in here?" I ask.

"They've been gaining entry by truck on the abandoned portion of the Northern Perimeter Highway that ends just over there," he says, thrusting his arm in the direction of a cluster of trees at the far end of the airstrip. I can't see any signs of a roadway but I know from my map that it is supposed to be very close. "It was constructed in the 1970s and shut down within a few years. The Indians were dying from measles and tuberculosis brought in by the highway workers." He pauses for a moment as he weighs what he is about to say next. "There was also a big problem with syphilis and gonorrhea."

"Who is letting them through now?" Vicent asks. "The military or the Indian Agency?"

"The highway checkpoint is controlled by the Indian Agency," he says as he draws on the remaining inch of his hand-rolled cigarette. "They are the ones letting them through. Just last week a Czechoslovakian anthropologist tried to go undercover with a group of gold miners but he was pulled from the truck." Guilherme takes another drag on the cigarette pinched between fingers stained yellow by the tobacco. "They just sent him back to Boa Vista and let the miners on through. That's the Indian Agency that is supposed to be protecting the Indians."

Guilherme drops his cigarette and crushes it into the dirt with his foot. When he looks up he simply stares at us, looking first at Vicent and then at me. We lock eyes for a fragment of a second and I can see him squinting from beyond those big black glasses. He appears to be carrying out a personal ritual of assessment before committing to take us on a tour of the mission.

"So, what is it you want to see?" he says.

I ask him to introduce us to the people of Wakathautheri and we head off in the direction of their village, which sits only fifty yards from the Church's complex.

Similar to the one at Paapiú, this maloca is a large enclosed thatched structure. Ducking through the small opening that serves as a doorway, I can immediately tell that this village is in what anthropologists call a situation of controlled contact between cultures. It is completely different from the chaos I witnessed at Paapiú. These people have obviously been living in a state of peaceful semi-isolation with the missionaries for quite some time. Undoubtedly there have been problems between the Consolatas and the Yanomami, but these Indians don't show any of the trauma that overwhelmed the villagers at Paapiú. On the contrary, there is a semblance of relaxed order to the living environment. Groups of families gather around individual hearths that line the perimeter of this cylindrical structure, while some children are laughing and playing games in the center of the maloca. Three women at three separate fires are cooking in blackened metal pots. But most of the adults are just sitting about in hammocks, taking a break from the bitter heat that has arrived with the clear weather.

Speaking to various villagers, I begin to detect an underlying tension seeping through the conversations. As Guilherme has told us, the nearby presence of a group of miners had become an unnerving fact of life for these villagers.

One man cleaning a turtle for dinner waves for us to come over to him. He calls himself Machadão—roughly, Big Ax. His command of Portuguese consists of a rough mix of nouns thrust up against an occasional verb. It sounds a lot like the way I speak Portuguese. I would guess—by the number of his children and the wrinkles around his eyes—that he is in his mid- to late thirties. I'll ask the priest about that later. Missionaries often get fanatical about recording the births and deaths of villagers, which provides them with important statistical barometers for evaluating the success of their "mission"—and also a means of occupying their time.

"A lot of gold miners come over here. Now I am afraid," Machadão says.

"Why?"

He rips out a large piece of turtle intestine and tosses it to the side. I hope that it is not going to be part of the evening's meal. Father John had mentioned that, on occasion, we might be eating with the Indians.

"Too much coughing sickness," he says in answer to Vicent's question. "Gold miners have a lot of the coughing sickness."

"Do you have coughing sickness now?" Vicent asks.

"Yes, I am afraid," he says. "And with my father. In his time we had much."

Guilherme, who has been playing with Machadão's children, waits for him to finish and then adds his own thoughts. "The leaders here, like that man over there named Carrera"—he points across the maloca, fixing his glasses as they slide down his nose—"are now sending extra men with the women to the gardens because they are worried that the gold miners are going to steal their women."

He translates briefly what he is saying for Machadão, who continues to watch us as he goes about the bloody task of extracting and unraveling the organs and lengthy intestines from the shell of what must have been a giant turtle. Placing a hand on Machadão's shoulder, he continues.

"This man knows what it is like to suffer from his encounters with the white man. In the 1950s his people—they were from another village—they came in contact with a group of rubber tappers in the forest. Soon after, everyone came down with pneumonia. He lost his first wife and most of his family. Only Machadão—" He stops for a moment and asks him a question, then continues. "Yes. Only Machadão, his mother, and his brother survived."

I jot a few notes in my journal, reminders of scenes to shoot, some background on this villager's life, questions to ask in the coming days. As I write I can see Machadão staring at me. Although theirs is an illiterate society, we've been told his oldest son has started taking classes at the mission school. I look up and catch his eye. He gestures with his head to the paper, smiles, and lets forth a high-pitched cackle. He then returns to the work of extracting bits of meats from the turtle, still chuckling to himself. I like this guy. He could become the focus of our work here, his story a way of personalizing what has been happening to these people.

Leaving Machadão, we continue to move in a circle around this large communal structure, going from family to family, introducing ourselves and explaining that we will be filming them over the next few days. Already I can see that access to the Yanomami will be much easier at Catrimani than at Paapiú. But while photographers, anthropologists, and some journalists have been to this area before, the presence of a camera is still rather unique to them. I won't film today. I want to be careful about the way I introduce the camera into their daily lives.

As we greet the various families sitting in clusters of hammocks, Padre Guilherme explains that within the current worldview of these Yanomami outsiders like ourselves fall into a different category than the gold miners. The whites here at Mission Catrimani, he tells us, have been appropriated by the Yanomami. Since Vincent and I are with the missionaries we fall into the category of "their whites," whites owned by these villagers, not to be shared by other communities. We are perceived differently from the gold miners. Those whites want to take their land. And us? We give them cookies.

journal entry
Wakathautheri Village
6/3/89

Today we met Machadão. He comes from the group Waka. Machadão is his Portuguese name, his Yanomami name is never spoken, a custom to ensure protection of the spirit. He is also a shaman, an intellectual in his community, someone responsible for the relationship of his village to the spiritual world and, since the arrival of the miners, with this world.

A rapport was struck up between us right away that probably has more to do with inexplicable, non-translatable, aspects of our personalities than anything else. It can be seen in the pauses between exchanges in conversations. The body relaxes, no longer trying to overcompensate with gestures for the inadequacies of speech. It's in moments like these that nonverbal signals of trust are exchanged. I also look to the eyes when I work with cultures whose languages I don't speak. I search for a quality, a connection. I saw it in his eyes. I think he saw it in mine. I'd like to do an interview with him for our documentary, something that could also be used in some spin-off news reports. Maybe he is someone who could tell us the full story about what is happening here. Maybe though I am deceiving myself. Maybe that's what happened to Padre Calleri?

In Boa Vista Father John told me that the Consolata missionaries had attempted to establish ongoing contact with the Yanomami as far back as 1952. Over a period of thirteen years they sent priests on sporadic missions up various rivers in futile attempts to lure the Indians from the forest. Although the Yanomami in this region had been contacted by the Indian Protection Service in the 1940s, it wasn't until Padre Giovanni Calleri became part of the contact expeditions that the Consolatas began to show some success. This robust Italian priest entered the forest with a head of steam and an unbending will. He worked too hard, often pushing himself from dawn to dusk, frequently going without meals and ignoring the complaints of colleagues who wanted to stop and take a break. In October of 1965, after two weeks of traveling by canoe through Yanomami territory, Father Calleri and Father Bindo Mendelosi landed on the banks of the Catrimani River, claiming it as the site of their Catholic mission. There they set out immediately to contact the Indians by the practice of *atração* or attraction.

This technique, perfected by Brazil's Indian Protection Service under the tutelage of Colonel Rondon, consisted of using objects to lure Indians from the forest. Teams of men known as *frentes da atração*, attraction fronts, spent months at a time in the forest. The objects they brought with them were knives and machetes but also glass beads in bright colors and mirrors. They were usually left hanging from trees strategically placed on Indian paths or at the entrance of an uncontacted village. Steel products were the most prized possessions. They could revolutionize an indigenous community almost overnight. A metal ax in the hands of a Yanomami will cut through a tree six times faster than a stone ax. Knives and machetes perform similar miracles in clearing forests and constructing houses.

It was precisely a miracle that Father Calleri must have thought he was witnessing on the banks of the Catrimani River. Within three days of his arrival a group of Yanomami came to visit. According to Father John, Calleri bestowed upon them more "gifts" of machetes, axes, and "mirrors for the women." This began what the Consolata missionaries referred to as *namoro*, their courtship of the Yanomami. After a few days this initial group of Indians disappeared into the forest, returning two weeks later with a dozen other villagers. There on the opposite bank of the Catrimani River these Yanomami set up a temporary village and garden. In just a few short weeks Father Calleri had succeeded where his fellow missionaries had failed. The Yanomami had been attracted, courted, and finally seduced into maintaining an ongoing contact with the Consolatas. "Before the white men arrived," a Yanomami shaman at Wakathautheri told me, "we sharpened the points of our arrows with rodents' teeth, we cut up our game with bamboo, that's how we lived until we first encountered the whites." As a result of these contacts—first with the Indian Protection Service and later with the missionaries—the Indians had a new time frame introduced into their worldview: events were dated with reference to the introduction of material goods from outside the forest. Their culture had changed, forever.

Meeting the whites transformed not only the Indians' understanding of the outside world but also their relationship with the network of 350 communities scattered throughout this corner of Brazil. Padre Calleri eventually learned that one reason for his success in luring the Yanomami from the forest was that their society was predisposed to the exchange of goods. Such exchanges were, and continue to be, a vital part of the fabric of their culture. When one Yanomami community goes to visit another, gifts of metal objects and ceremonial food are lavished upon the visitors. Such ritual exchanges obligate the visiting community to reciprocate at a later date by hosting a similar feast in their village. These traditional interchanges are part of the way in which alliances between communities are formed. They also open the way for personal relationships to develop, for young people to meet and marry. They are a kind of social adhesive that binds together Yanomami culture.

When Padre Calleri arrived here he probably thought he and his colleagues had stumbled into a missionaries' paradise. Their gifts of manufactured metal objects were extremely popular. Within the first three years of contact, the village opposite the river grew to be five times its original size.

The Indians who relocated there solidified the trading relationship with the priests while excluding other groups who were competing to gain access to these benevolent white men and their seemingly endless supply of valuable goods. This was the beginning of what Father Guilherme called "being appropriated" by the Indians. They weren't stupid. They had their own agenda which came from their culture. They wanted to control for themselves this vital link to trade goods. That was their stake in the creation of this new middle ground. It was an investment, a way of propelling their society into the realm of manufactured objects while bypassing the laborious and painstaking phase of industrialization. When you look at it from their perspective, it was a pretty good deal.

What the good Padre Calleri did not know at the time was that his success with the Yanomami would also ensure his downfall. In October of 1968 this Italian cleric, owing to the breakthroughs he had made with the Yanomami, was asked by the Indian Agency—then under the control of the military—to help make contact with a group of hostile Indians known as the Waimiri-Atroari. They had been killing dozens of highway workers who were involved in a project to connect the port city of Manaus with the frontier town of Boa Vista by a roadway called BR-174. This was in the early stages of the dream scheme to open up the Amazon and the government was determined to push through the project in spite of the violent attacks by the much feared Waimiri-Atroari. Brimming with confidence from his courtship of the Yanomami, Father Calleri accepted the mission to make contact and pacify this unregenerate tribe. Using a small boat specially fortified with protective walls, he went upriver into their territory. After this initial trip he reported that it would take six months to safely make inroads into the hostile society. But the local military commander rejected Calleri's evaluation. Ignoring the historical evidence of the need for a protracted attraction process, the officer convinced Calleri to enter the territory on foot via the roadway that had been partially constructed. "To this day we don't know why Calleri accepted to do such a thing," Father John told me.

In October of 1968 the obstinate cleric and a team of six men and two women flew in a military transport plane to the end of the roadway. There Calleri led his party on foot into the forest, perhaps confident that his experience among the Yanomami had provided him with the key to pacifying the Waimiri-Atroari. On October 31, 1968, he radioed back to a group of nuns at their mission in Manaus. He told them: "Pray for us because if we don't succeed arrows will start flying." They were never heard from again. Fearing the worst, the nuns contacted the local military commander. Two weeks later a team of soldiers discovered Calleri and the others in the forest. They had been bludgeoned and shot at close range with the long deadly arrows of the Waimiri-Atroari, their bloated bodies left to rot in the harsh equatorial heat.

The military response was to close off the area. For several years the project was abandoned. Then in 1974 SUDAM, the government highway department, resumed work on BR-174, this time in conjunction with FUNAI, the newly established Indian Agency. FUNAI started using a more aggressive approach to the courtship process. On a weekly basis they flew over villages in helicopters dropping gifts of machetes, beads, and mirrors. They also set up "posts of attraction" along the rivers. But the Waimiri-Atroari were fiercely resistant. In the first months of 1974 they launched four attacks, killing fifteen Indian Agency employees and highway workers. Then, in December of that year, four more government workers were killed, including the local director of the Indian Agency's pacification effort. Eventually, and at considerable expense, the Waimiri-Atroari were subdued, but not before their population had been reduced from two thousand to three hundred. The roadway, completed in 1976, is often flooded and can only be used at certain times of the year.

The "tragedy of Father Calleri," as Father John refers to it, is that he learned his most important lesson too late. The rules and logic of one society of Indians do not apply to another. The Waimiri-Atroari were not the same people as the Yanomami. There are more than 170 different indigenous groups living in the rain forest north of the Amazon River. Each has its own specific historical relationships with outsiders. Unlike the Yanomami who had been avoiding outside contact for five centuries, the Waimiri-Atroari had a history of violent antagonisms with whites throughout the nineteenth and twentieth centuries. When Calleri's expedition of eight soul-seekers arrived in their territory, the Waimiri-Atroari probably found them indistinguishable from the bands of whites who had destroyed their forests and murdered their relatives in centuries past. Calleri walked straight into an incipient ambush, blinded by the belief that God was on his side. He was not the first white person nor would he be the last to suffer such a fate: reckless hubris seems endemic to whites on the frontier, regardless of whether they are missionaries or gold miners or journalists.

As Father John Saffirio said in speaking of his late predecessor, "It is very dangerous to be a fearless man."

15

journal entry
Mission Catrimani
6/5

Pedro, a local villager leader, says he gave two hundred
bunches of bananas to the gold miners three months ago and
now he is still waiting for payment. He has two wives: one in
Jundia and one here in Catrimani. His father was killed by
Brazilian rubber tappers when he was four. After lunch he
told us the myth of the origin of white people. He and his
friend Joaquim laughed the entire time especially when they
did their imitations of the way white people talk.

The political roles are complicated here. José, Carrera,
and Pedro are tuxawas who are the village leaders separate
from the shamans who oversee the spiritual life of the
communities. A few years ago Carrera hit his brother, Luis (a
tuxawa) with a machete in a fight over the division of meat.
The son of Luis, José, is now a tuxawa and holds Carrera
responsible for the death of his father. The communities
have been splitting up along these divisions. Family members
and friends from one side have set up a separate village on
the other side of the airstrip not far from here. We might go
over there tomorrow. I wonder if that will cause any
problems with the group we are staying with now?

These days Mission Catrimani is administered by both Father Guilherme and Sister Florence. We met her briefly upon our arrival with the bishop, but she spent the majority of the afternoon separate from us, caring for a few of the Indians at the mission's small medical clinic. Florence, who is also a nurse, is a tall, stocky black woman with enormous hands. She appears to be in her mid-forties. Originally from Guyana, she speaks Portuguese, broken English, and fluent Yanoman. I have already started to think of her as the Amazon's equivalent of Mother Teresa—a dedicated woman of the Church who spends endless hours caring for these inhabitants of the forest. Guilherme, on the other hand, I would describe as Father Workaholic. In the course of a two-hour period his schedule will include fixing the mission generator, instructing Indians on the use of the motorboat, and teaching a class in Portuguese to the children. These tasks are accomplished with the utmost efficiency, the wheels of discipline and progress spinning forward at a rapid clip. In their combined efforts at this outpost for Christ, these missionaries over the last decade seem to have gained the trust of the Indians. And the Yanomami, in turn, have made a lasting impression on the Church emissaries.

"I like the Yanomami, I like to serve the Yanomami and, I would even say, I adore the Yanomami," says Father Guilherme towards the end of an interview we are conducting with him under the shade of a tree on the mission grounds. "I learned their language. I learned to appreciate everything that is theirs and, in this way, I would even say that if I could be born again, I would be born a Yanomami."

When I hear that phrase I shut off the camera for a moment because I can't believe it. To be certain, I lean across to Vincent and ask him to translate the final part of the interview.

"Yes," he says. "He wants to be reborn a Yanomami."

I look back at Guilherme, who is smiling, his body trembling slightly from his constant nicotine infusions. The interview up to now has not been all that unusual, but, knowing these priests, I had expected a guilt-ridden revision of the history of Catholics and Indians in Brazil in which his generation has emerged to make amends for his predecessors. During this past "any Indian who converted to Christianity was a dead Indian," he had told us just a few minutes ago. Now they have opted for "a new form of evangelization. We are here to serve the Indians."

Something, however, is becoming apparent here that Father Calleri would never have expected: Guilherme seems to have been seduced by the very Indians originally seduced by his predecessors. The tables are turning. This priest is dangerously close to "going native." He is, in a way, a benevolent version of Joseph Conrad's Kurtz, the crazed explorer who disappears upriver in Africa in *Heart of Darkness*. Whereas for this missionary the desire to become one with another culture is an attractive fantasy, Conrad's Kurtz is portrayed as living a nightmare where "his—let us say—nerves went wrong, and caused him to preside at certain midnight dances ending with unspeakable rites." Interestingly enough, Kurtz, like Guilherme, had been sent into the jungle with a mission. He was there to write a report for the "International Society for the Suppression of Savage Customs."

journal entry
Mission Catrimani
6/3/89

Got woken in the middle of the night by the most insane raving and chanting I have ever heard in my life. It was the wild child from the village, a boy who looks like he's sixteen but could be thirty. A man but possibly an animal. He is the one who rants and raves during the day walking through the village unwashed, unkempt and whacked out. When we flew into the village he positioned himself under the wing of the plane and sat, squatting and mumbling to himself. Today we started to call him "Pierrot le Fou" after the character in the Godard film.

Last night he stayed in front of our door spinning in circles and screaming the most bizarre primal chant. There is a guttural noise that emerges from his throat that sounds as if his lungs were being torn from his chest with each utterance. He is not a shaman, so there were no justifying ritual associations for his behavior. Vincent and I nervously joked about who was going to go outside and calm him down. Eventually the priest came with a plate of food which did the trick. It seems he gets out of control from time to time and a little nourishment is the best tranquilizer.

I guess it is only by day that Father Guilherme flirts with the idea of becoming an Indian because at night he retreats into the world of the white man. The meals I have shared with the missionaries so far reflect the uneasy and ambiguous relationship that Westerners have with the cultures of the forest. Each night at the Consolata mission the traditions of our world are enacted: Sister Florence does the cooking as well as the dishes, while the Father reads the paper with his coffee after the meal. A BBC radio program runs continuously in the background, drowning out the soft sounds of the forest nighttime.

Throughout the evening various Yanomami men, women, and children pass by, peering through the screen doors and windows, silent silhouettes with their faces distorted as they press up against the wire mesh. Occasionally they will stand there asking for *bolacha, bolacha,* but most of the time they are just staring. You get the impression that your meal is open to the public—that you are part of a stage play revealing how people from outside the forest eat and pass their time. This, of course, is natural to the Yanomami. Theirs is a communal existence. They all consume their food together and sleep in one vast lodging. What are not natural to them are the doors, the screens, the privacy that is enforced here at the mission. Who, they ask, are this man and this woman who spend so much time alone together, who work together, who cook and eat together, yet are not husband and wife? These alien beings have entered their space, their forest, their world, even speak their language—and yet here at the mission, less than a two-minute walk from their village of Wakathautheri, a vastly different set of customs prevails.

Of course, the missionaries are from another culture, one that must be respected even though it has been transported here. The house is not a communal structure. Meals are eaten at a table. Tobacco is smoked, not chewed. And if a Yanomami tries to enter the room, a quick word from Sister Florence sends him away.

The message is clear: the missionaries want to be close to the Indians but a line has to be drawn. The intermingling of cultures is fine as long as it is on the terms of the missionaries. They control the supply of manufactured products, so they make the rules. A balance of power has been struck, less overtly manipulative than the gold miners' but equally clear. That is what bothered me on that first day with Dom Aldo. I can see that now.

Perhaps Sister Florence and Father Guilherme are trying to avoid the fatal mistake made by their predecessor Father Calleri. They are taking nothing for granted, delineating strict limits while keeping in check their own curiosities about the world of the Indians. It is as if they are afraid of going over the line, crossing the blurred boundaries of this now familiar but still alien culture. They are attracted but afraid, two common preconditions of many forms of seduction.

In my experience the fear is shared by most outsiders who enter the territory of the Indians. Be they gold miners or missionaries or anthropologists, they warn themselves: keep one foot always in "your" world, don't allow yourself to be completely overwhelmed by the Indians, don't go too far into their terrain. Getting back might become very difficult. Perhaps this is why Father Guilherme would welcome a second life when he could cross over into their world without hesitation—could start with a clean slate, free of the baggage of his culture, unconstrained by the precedents of his ancestors. Perhaps also he knows that in that other life there could never be someone who would come for him—another priest perhaps—as Marlow had come for Kurtz, trying:

> to break the spell—the heavy, mute spell of the wilderness—
> that seemed to draw him to its pitiless breast by the awakening of forgotten and brutal instincts, by the memory of
> gratified and monstrous passions. This alone, I was convinced, had driven him out to the edge of the forest, to the
> bush, towards the gleam of fires, the throb of drums, the
> drone of weird incantations; this alone had beguiled his
> unlawful soul beyond the bounds of permitted aspirations.

16

In the morning we travel with Machadão, chopping our way through the forest in search of a tapir—three and a half hours nonstop through brown, murky swamps, then rivers and soggy paths covered with slippery wet grass, an obstacle course of protruding roots, sharp branches, and fallen trees. Machadão sets the pace, dexterously moving across the terrain, barefoot and wearing nothing but the traditional penis string—the small piece of twine the Yanomami ties around his foreskin and then pulls back around his waist. It hurts just to look at it, yet it also makes perfect sense for their lifestyle. My rain-soaked clothes are extremely cumbersome, making this work even more grueling. I guess I continue to wear them out of habit. I too am not ready to go native.

To cross rivers we have to march waist-deep through strong currents, our equipment held above our heads. We then have to run full speed down narrow, slippery trails in search of game. Already we must have traveled twelve miles. This is easily the most difficult work I've done in the Amazon. Occasionally I am able to grab shots of Machadão as he tiptoes his way through the forest in search of the cunning tapir, a long-nosed beast that somewhat resembles a pig and yet can swim across a river in a matter of seconds. But the weight of the camera seems to be increasing as the humidity sucks away at my energy.

Throughout this trip the Yanomami have been making fun

of Vincent and me, cackling and chanting as we white men stumble through the forest trying to keep up. Our native escorts are following an elaborate system of paths that would have been imperceptible to me in this dense web of vines, trees, and swamp. I can only assume that all the joking is intended to urge us on in the sardonic manner that I am quickly learning is the basis for Yanomami humor, one that finds in the failings of others the basis for comedic relief.

Occasionally we are lucky enough to find footing on a muddy path, but it usually isn't long before we are back waist-deep in the cold, murky waters that seem to dominate this region, an ecological necessity for rain forest preservation but a severe hindrance for hunters or for any filmmakers attempting to accompany them. Miraculously, however, the equipment doesn't get wet and Vincent and I find the energy to keep up.

When we reach a stretch of dry path I take a moment to pull out my still camera for a snapshot of myself. As I push down on the shutter I can imagine the image that will be developed upon my return to New York. I have seen myself in other photos brought back from the Amazon: bearded and beaten and rain-soaked, a vacant, vaguely puzzled look in my eye, as if my soul had been taken from me and replaced—in the split second of a shutter—by something I don't really understand. Upon first viewing, I usually find these snapshots disturbing—a glimpse into a part of myself that I'm seeking but afraid to come to terms with. Usually I toss them into a back drawer in my studio, forgetting almost immediately that I have taken them. Then, months later, they resurface and I am compelled to witness again my own private ritual of self-documentation reminding me that I am drawn to this region because of the sense of escape it provides. But now no sooner have I taken this self-portrait than I have lost sight of Machadão, who has disappeared around a bend in the path. So I step once more waist-deep into the swamp, the Yanomami cackling behind me as I trip over another root in this endless expanse of brown water and thick, clinging muck.

In order to survive as a Yanomami you must be able to hunt, and Machadão is one of the best in Wakathautheri. He has the reputation of being a deadly marksman. The rifle he carries belongs not to him but to the missionaries, a precious item from our world loaned to the hunters on a case-by-case basis. Of the dozen men on this trip, the majority carry bows and arrows. Most of them are dressed in bathing suits also obtained from the missionaries. Only a few wear the traditional penis string sported by Machadão. The quest here is for meat—*nagi*—the preferred source of protein in their culture. A man's honor is tied to his ability to provide it for his family. And Machadão appears to be feeling the demands of his role. When we met him this morning he was nervous and edgy.

"Many days," he told us. "It is many days that my children have not had meat." The Yanomami numerical system does not go beyond two. By my calculation he meant to tell us that it's been four days since they've eaten meat.

"And today, Machadão?" Vincent asked.

"Today I will kill a tapir," he responded with a big smile.

Machadão's wife and children have been subsisting on fruit found in the forest and vegetables from their garden. But, he tells us, they've been asking for *nagi*. The tapir we are trailing was wounded by Machadão the day before but escaped from him just after nightfall.

Accompanying Machadão on this hunt has given me a new sense of respect for these people. This is difficult, exhausting work: survival in this forest means a constant cycle of hunting, foraging, and planting. Most Yanomami villages are semi-nomadic. They move on average every two years, seeking out new gardens and unexploited hunting grounds. When the people of Machadão's village decided to settle next to the missionaries, they broke this traditional cycle, forcing them to travel farther into the forest in search of wild game. And now the arrival of the miners is exacerbating the problem. Local prospectors have been competing with the Indians for wild game, causing severe reductions in an already scarce resource.

After four hours on the trail we finally catch up with the wounded tapir at the edge of a river. Everyone now stops and listens; the hunters' eyes dart about the forest in search of their prey. I glance away from Machadão for a moment to power up the camera. When I look back he has disappeared into the thick wall of vines and trees that surrounds us. I charge off in the direction where I believe he has gone, which is into a dense area of trees and vines. After just fifteen yards I collide into a bee's nest, providing my Yanomami companions with still more comic relief: the white man swirling in circles, swatting the bees as he slips and slides, trying to maintain his footing on the soft floor of muddy leaves, his cumbersome clothes caught in the thorny branches of an adjacent tree, cursing to himself in a series of angry expletives, which, to them, must sound like the dying shrieks of a bludgeoned pig.

Minutes later we all sit huddled together in the pouring rain, the Yanomami smacking away flies with their machetes, occasionally looking up at me and laughing as my head swells to the size of a melon from the bee stings. We are waiting to see if Machadão returns. In the interim, Vincent and I use our ponchos to try to protect the equipment. I think of the shots I was able to get, wondering whether there will be enough to put a sequence together.

After a while it is obvious Machadão is not coming back, so we head home, single-file, on what I estimate will be a two-hour trek. The jocular banter that accompanied us on the earlier part of our journey has disappeared. Everyone is overcome with exhaustion. For now there is only the steady sound of rain hitting the leaves of the forest.

An hour after our return, I see Machadão quickly enter the village and dart into the maloca. There's no sign of the tapir. No meat for his wife and children tonight.

journal entry
Mission Catrimani
6/4

There is a kind of exchange going on here. During the day I move about throughout their village staring at them through the lens of my camera. At night, I put down the camera and they stare at me, coming to my window and looking in one by one, as if Vincent and I are on display for them.

Tonight Machadão and his family came to visit. This is

the third day he has failed in the hunt. I gave them my
camping kit. Was that the token gift of the guilty white
liberal or simply an attempt to reciprocate in a manner
consistent with their culture? Fact is that he's done a lot for
me in the last few days. He deserves it.

I've been reading some books about the Yanomami in the
missionaries' library. The anthropologists refer to their
funerary rites as "endocannibalism." It's a form of
cannibalism. *Endo* as opposed to *exto* means they eat their
own people rather than others. They don't actually eat the
bodies, but they consume the ashes of the pulverized bones
after the deceased has been cremated. It is done only in the
case of children. When adults die, their ashes are buried near
the families' fireplace in the communal lodging. The whole
ritual is said to make certain that the spirit has some place to
go, so that he or she is not lingering about.

17

In the late afternoon of the next day we do an interview with Machadão outside the maloca. Although the tapir continues to elude him, he is in better spirits today. His wife's brother brought back three turtles from a forage in the forest. It's enough meat to keep the family satisfied at least temporarily. As we set up our equipment, the warm light of the afternoon falls across the forest giving the flora a rich green hue. Above the line of trees in the background I can see the sky, bright blue and streaked with thin white clouds. Most of the villagers are inside the maloca at this time of day, resting and preparing their meals. Occasionally a child appears at the doorway, makes a face, and darts back inside. Machadão has his face and body painted with a bright orange vegetable dye, a preparation not (I trust) for the cameras but perhaps to complement his positive change in mood. "Tomorrow I will go kill the tapir," he says as he raises both arms to mimic the shooting of a rifle.

I have spent three months planning this trip with a view to getting an interview with one or more Yanomami in their own language—thereby, perhaps, illuminating the still impenetrable terrain of their culture, which has remained hidden from the world since the start of the gold rush. Now over the last several days I have observed Machadão closely, trying to determine how he would come across on camera, whether he would be relaxed and forthright in his opinions, whether he could speak about his people from an informed perspective. I am being careful because I know I'll have only one chance for an in-depth interview with one of these Indians. I have very little battery power and I can't keep bothering Father Guilherme to serve as our translator. I've considered approaching other villagers but they don't seem as engaging as Machadão. As a shaman, he is one of the intellectual leaders in the community and it shows in his grasp of Yanomami history and cosmology.

I also thought it would be interesting to interview a woman. But now I realize that to do so would mean crossing a barrier even more formidable: not only of culture but of gender. The problem I face in this community is not so much fear; it's getting them to take the interview (and me) seriously. Lately when I have inquired of the village women about a particular custom or practice, they simply laugh in my face, then deflect any further questions with requests for tobacco and pots and pans, or jokes at our expense.

"You two are both horribly ugly," a woman told Vincent and me yesterday afternoon as we were hanging our laundry outside the little wooden shack where we sleep. "You must be brothers," she added, her body trembling with laughter at the thought that two such horrible-looking creatures could have emerged from the same womb.

This tiny, acerbic comic with sagging breasts, short bangs, and a funny twisted smile was an older Yanomami woman, probably in her late forties but looking sixty. Father Guilherme had pointed her out to us the other day as an example of a female who had two husbands, an anomaly within the Yanomami's male-biased culture. But I guess her unique marital status qualified her—at least in her own opinion—as an expert on men.

"We're not brothers," Vincent told her.

"Well, I am still sorry for you both, because no woman would marry ugly men like you."

"Vincent has a wife," I informed her with the help of Father Guilherme's translation. "But you are right, I'm not married."

"His wife must be old and blind!" she cried out. "And the children must look like rodents!" More laughter, then she pointed to me. "And as for you, I don't think you will have much luck finding a wife."

This was typical of the way our conversations with Yanomami women unfold. They poke fun at us, taunt us with machetes, make suggestive remarks about the lens on my camera, and in general joke at our expense. But they never answer a question seriously. Perhaps if I'd traveled here with a female sound recordist it would have been easier. I've seen women connect across cultures in other parts of the world, and I am certain a female collaborator would have facilitated my access to the women here. However, any woman who accompanied me would be taking a chance with her life and I didn't want that responsibility. There were lots of rumors of Indian women being abducted and raped by miners. The nature of this job was crazy enough. I didn't want someone's safety being unduly jeopardized. It had become clear on my first trip that the miners' camps were violent, very macho locales. When I decided to come here with Vincent, I knew that it would limit my ability to work with the women. But one thing I did not foresee was becoming the brunt of jokes for an entire female population.

This morning I asked Father Guilherme to join us and translate my questions into Yanoman so that Machadão could respond in his own language with maximum fluency. We have agreed that Father Guilherme will give me abridged versions of Machadão's responses. Unless I have any follow-up questions, we'll simply go on down the list of queries I have scribbled on a scrap of paper. I am hoping to touch on a variety of subjects ranging from Machadão's personal history to how shamans perceive the white man and his diseases.

As I set up the shot I ask Father Guilherme to explain to Machadão how we are going to conduct the interview. He points to the camera and the boom pole, explaining the function of each instrument. Machadão follows all this very intently, occasionally laughing as he makes jokes about the way we fuss over the cables and battery bag. At the last minute I decide to add a wide angle to my lens. The shot I have planned is calculated to complement his style: the frame is now

expanded slightly to allow Machadão to use his arms in the
expressive manner he is accustomed to. From what I have seen
so far, Yanomami oral tradition seems to entail one individual
speaking the parts of different characters in whatever story is
being recounted. This traditional oratory is a little more the-
atrical than normal conversation as the narrator takes on the
intonations of all the characters in the tale. But most important
from my perspective, there will be no setups here, no attempts
to position the Indian in accordance with my preconceived
image—at least none that I am conscious of. I see my role as
facilitating the possibility of real dialogue in a debate that has
been dominated by the miners. My camera will act as an electronic mirror seizing Machadão's voice and image and then,
after editing the raw footage, reflecting them back to the world
in the context of documentaries and news reports. For the last
two years the miners have been manipulating the media
through their press conferences. Their images are the dominant
images, the images of the dominant culture. But now a member
of the Yanomami—in his own village and in his own language—will have the opportunity to express his people's
opinion on the changes that have come to them as a result of
this gold rush.

> Over here in this direction is where I lived. I lived there
> while traveling from the Rio Demini. It is close to that river
> that my mother made her home and my father was killed by
> warriors from another village who captured my mother and
> brought her to the lower stream of the river where we are
> now, on the Rio Catrimani. It is on the rapids of the
> Piranteira where my new father had his home and he
> eventually moved from there. He traveled from one garden
> to another, then he moved again and settled in another area.
> He finally set up his home on the Rio Pacu. It is there that I
> grew up.
> In the early days, there were no whites. We did not have
> any encounters with them. We did not eat our game animals
> with salt. We drank its cooking juices with nothing to add to
> the taste. It wasn't until a very long time that my father first

met the whites. It was when I became older. He saw white
people near here where we were living. We did not know the
whites at that time. Our hands were empty. We had no
manufactured objects. This is how we lived until we first
encountered them.

The whites had arrived here to collect latex. They visited
our community and we returned their visit. It was then that
my father caught the flu and he eventually died from it. Most
of the generation that I called "father" died from it. That is
why I decided to come here to live. We at our village had
been visiting with Village Wakathautheri for many years.
They had initiated the relationship with us and we then
visited each other many times. And later, when my wife was
dead, the village headman Carrera called me over and
proposed that I take a new spouse. He said to me: "Take a
woman from among us! Without a wife you can't help but
suffer from want!" He then said to me: "You must be
desperate! Take a new wife and settle yourself here."

My youngest brother remained on the Rio Pacu, as well as
my mother, but I no longer had a father and that is why I
left. That is why I abandoned my community and came to
live here. Later, Chagas, my brother-in-law, asked me to go
back there but I didn't accept. I told him: "I will not go back
to the place where my father and then my wife died from
disease!" He said to me: "Come back to the community that
is yours!" That is what my brother-in-law Chagas said to me,
but I did not accept his words. I told him: "You will live on
this site without me because I have abandoned it and I will
not go back! I have really settled myself here at
Wakathautheri!" I said to him for emphasis: "I will live here
indefinitely! My gardens and my children are numerous!
And you will have to stay there and live without me!" Only
my young brother lives there at this time. It is not far. He
comes to visit here often.

Many other people also died. There were large numbers of
the men who I had called "father" but they are all dead now.
There were no medicines back then. I had much sadness and
anger because of all those people who died. These problems

occurred because of a white man called Nonato who wanted
to take one of our women. He asked incessantly for a
woman. He said: "Give me a woman. I must have a woman. I
want to have sex with a woman." When the whites speak in
that fashion I have fear that they will make sorcery with fire
and release the fume of the coughs. I am afraid because it is
this type of anger which could provoke them to cause a new
epidemic of flu. It is when they become angry like that that
the epidemics arrive.

And now we have many gold miners here and they are
living very close. I say to them: "We are not able to go up
the river. Why do you not go back to where you live?" But
they respond: "You cannot stop us from entering this
territory. We are only passing through." This is how they lie
to me.

I tell them: "You are killing all our wild game. Do not
come downstream where we are living." But in spite of my
words, many of them have come to where we live now. They
say to me: "We will not obey someone who is so young. We
will stop coming here only if an old person tells us. You,
however, are too young. We will not obey someone so
young. And once we have left, others, who won't have heard
of you, they will continue to come." But I responded to
them: "You have to stop coming here! There at Paapiú you
destroyed the forest and many Yanomami are in the process
of dying! Who else is going to arrive here? This is what I
want to know!"

I am afraid this is what will happen to us too. This is what
I have been thinking about these days. But they have not
responded to me. At Paapiú they killed the fish in the rivers
and the Yanomami have gone hungry. This is a shame
because the Yanomami at Paapiú are dying. The numbers of
gold miners have become very large. And now very few
Yanomami are still living at Paapiú. I said to the gold miners:
"Don't do the same thing to my territory that you did at
Paapiú!" But they don't respond to me because I am young.
"If you come here without causing any damage, if some of

you don't do anything but pass through here then I will be happy." This is what I said to them.

Then the gold miners responded to me: "If you speak like that, if you refuse to allow us to enter your territory, we will kill you. Don't say anything." This is why I have fear. We can only protest a little bit. They say to us: "The old people did not refuse us entry on this territory. The old people do not speak against us." Then, and this is the truth, they said: "If you, the young, if you speak, we will not listen. If the old speak, maybe we will listen."

This is what they said: "The old people want the manufactured goods that we bring." But I say to the old people: "Do not ask for the goods. The gold miners will only lie to you. They do not have friendly intentions. When there are enough of them, they are going to kill us. They are very ferocious. They have already killed the Yanomami at Paapiú." This is what I say but no one listens.

The old people are hesitant to show their hostility at encounters with the gold miners. This is because they do not know the language of the whites. We do not understand it. We do not understand each bit of their language when they speak to us. The gold miners also ask for women incessantly. And this is bad. I tell them: "Father Guilherme who lives here, he gives us sufficient numbers of things already." I tell them: "I will not approach the other whites." Then they say to me: "Okay, okay. Stay in the forest, there where you live." But another gold miner, far from here, he said to me: "This territory belongs to me also. This forest is also mine. A little of the forest belongs to me. The rest, downstream, you can keep for yourself."

These are the lies that they tell me. And I respond to them: "No, I will not give a little of the forest. This is where I hunt and where I search for game and where I fish. It is also here where at night I light up the river with a flashlight to shoot the fish with my arrows." This is what I have told the gold miners. At Paapiú they destroyed everything. They ruined the earth by digging huge holes in the ground. If they had not done this maybe I could have become friends with them. But they have destroyed all the land and that is bad. If they continue destroying the land then I don't want anything to do with them. I said to the gold miners: "This is my forest and it is I who live here."

The whites, after they have built this road, their numbers have become very large and that has made me angry. If some of them who entered here were content to simply pass by that would be okay. I would be satisfied with that arrangement. As for me I do not want to make friends with them. But if there are other whites, different whites, who want to live here with us maybe I would be friends with them but only if they were like Father Guilherme.

Machadão continues for another hour presenting his vision of the gold rush. Most of it is comprehensible to me, but clearly a more intimate knowledge of the complex fabric of Yanomami cosmology is required. As Father Guilherme translates, I often find myself at a loss for a follow-up to Machadão's responses. Towards the end of the interview, when we start asking some questions about shamanism, he says:

Do you know the evil spirits, Omamari? Do you know the supernatural image of the evil spirits? The spirits that live in the waterfalls, those whose call is "hahahahaaa." They live in the rapids. They have big beards. Like the beard of a white person. Their beards are like this. They dance in the morning. "Hoou reke reke reke!" It's like this that the Omamari spirits talk. They seize the Yanomami and hold them captive here. When they are like an iguana, they carry the Yanomami captured in their mouths.

Machadão is offering me a glimpse at his cosmological vision, but my understanding is limited by the layers of culture that distinguish his society from ours. Yet his comments do recall things I've read in various anthropological texts. For example, the idea that whites "make sorcery with fire and release the fume of the coughs."

The French anthropologist Bruce Albert, who has written

extensively on this subject, says the Yanomami traditionally believed that epidemics were passed into the body of the victim by the fumes of smoke emanating from fires. The perpetrator—a neighboring enemy or local rival—would initiate this act of sorcery by placing magic plants in the fire and then directing the *xawara*, the malevolent fumes, towards the intended victim. But since contact with outsiders, the Yanomami began to reevaluate the way in which these diseases were being transmitted. The trading of metal objects—the gifts of attraction—also started to have an ambiguous significance as the arrival of missionaries and Indian Agency employees gave way to anthropologists and then highway workers and frontier explorers. Missionaries and anthropologists maintained a pacific relationship with the Yanomami. But many rubber tappers, highway workers, and now gold miners competed with the Indians not just for the forest but for wild game and, at times, for women. The encounters between these two groups were often tense and their contacts, with no medical supervision, frequently brought the onset of new and deadly epidemics. During this period Yanomami shamans like Machadão began to theorize that it was the smell emanating from metal objects (particularly objects bestowed upon them by adversarial whites) that was responsible for the transmission of the white man's disease. In their view of the world this theory made sense. They were learning from experience, processing their historical encounters with different whites and correlating them with the onset of new diseases. Such a shamanistic interpretation did not meet the scientific rigors of Western medicine but it provided their people with a cautionary metaphor regarding the consequences of greed for a society who should be satisfied with who they are and what they have. With the fervor of a street-corner Isaiah, Machadão was simply trying to warn his peers of the potential dangers of making deals with the Devil.

journal entry
Wakathautheri Village
6/5

I realized today that I will need two scenes: some shots of families relaxing in hammocks would be good followed by some scenes of women and children fetching water or cutting wood. I also need to explore the forest and I have to remember that there is where the significance of life lies for the Indians. "Urihi" is what the Yanomami call it. It is a place inhabited by supernatural spirits but one which they are also dependent upon for their sustenance. One Indian today gave us a partial list of what they hunt. It included tapirs, two-toed sloths, mazama deer, nine-banded armadillos, three-toed sloths, agouti, squirrels, small caimans, giant anteaters, silky anteaters, macaws and monkeys of which there are several variations including howlers, spiders, white monkeys and capuchin monkeys.

I also learned today that a woman died recently during a festival at the village of Demini. The Indians here at Catrimani and the Indians at Jundia have decided with the help of a Shaman, that another village is responsible, and they are planning an attack against that village. I wonder if they have any intentions of going after the gold miners living down river. Perhaps they already have.

18

"In May I made fifty tests for malaria and thirty-one were positive," says Florence, wiping sweat from her brow as she shuffles about her tiny one-room clinic looking for a needle to give another injection to another Indian in search of more of the white man's medicine. "This was only in the month of May." She pushes down on the hypodermic, thrusting the needle into the arm of an old woman who flinches, cringes, and then lets out a squeaky little sigh. "This is truly the year of malaria."

Florence yanks the hypodermic from the woman's arm with a suddenness that catches me off guard. I step backwards, bumping against a rack of blood samples sitting on a small wooden table. Hearing the sound of the test tubes rattling, I freeze and watch as Florence's head whips around. There's silence for a moment but no breaking glass. Vincent has managed to catch the bottles before they fell. He is now pushing them back, near where she left them, intact on a corner of the table. Florence shoots me a quick nervous glance followed by a smile—a sign, I take it, that I can continue working but that I should proceed with caution, that I shouldn't forget that the fate of whole villages is dependent on the work being done within the confines of this one tiny room.

Along the blue wooden walls of the clinic, old shelves are stacked with an odd assortment of medicines. Another half dozen test tubes sit on a desk to my right—more blood samples to determine if the Indians who visited the clinic today have malaria and, if so, what strain. This clinic is so small that Vicent has moved outside to record sound from the front porch. His boom pole is dropped in through the doorway, carefully positioned to stay out of the way of my shot. But even more than the cramped space, it is the light that is making my work difficult. The harsh sun coming in through the door contrasts sharply with the dark shadows of the clinic's interior. For ten minutes I've come up with nothing but overexposed shots as I have tried to capture Florence's routine of taking blood samples, interviewing Indians, and giving injections. I'm feeling frustrated and claustrophobic, the technological equivalent of a bull in a china shop. My attempts at fluid handheld camera work are proving almost impossible.

An older Yanomami man shuffles into the room, and Florence stands with a hypodermic needle in her hand, her back to me, preparing to take another sample of blood. He's one of the shamans from a neighboring village, a wizened old character with a couple of long gray chin whiskers and baggy bloodshot eyes. Just a few minutes ago he sat outside on the porch bench passing his hands over his arms and chest, letting forth a few feeble chants—attempts (I am assuming) to rid himself of malaria with a traditional cure. Now Vincent sticks his head through the window and raises his eyebrows in the direction of the nurse and the old shaman; he knows a good shot when he sees one. I shake my head, trying to convey my frustration. *Can't roll. No shot. Going to let this one pass.* His eyes widen in feigned disbelief, a not-so-subtle critique that only adds to my concern. I need images like this one—a traditional shaman seeking the aid of Western medicine—to tell the full story of the complex ways in which these two worlds interact. Florence, detecting the problems we are having, asks the shaman to take a step backwards, allowing me to get my shot. He winces and groans as the long thin needle pierces his flesh.

"*Eyyup*," Florence calls out and another Yanomami woman enters the room with a baby that can barely stand on its own and a child of perhaps three. The old shaman shuffles out rubbing his arm.

Florence is now seated behind her small wooden desk diligently making another entry in the clinic's log. She has just asked the old man a number of questions about his medical history, giving us time to take a break. I've been able to collect my thoughts, allowing me to approach this next scene a little differently—to "work the space," as my colleagues say. I've decided to use the cramped environment and its bad lighting to tell the story. These limitations can shape the pictures and the camera moves, the angles, adding another dimension to the images I am trying to capture—all of this a delicate balancing act between getting the shot and imposing on the subject. I flip the start switch on my camera and take a step forward, framing Florence behind her desk as she makes another entry in her log book. She exchanges a few words with the young woman who has just entered. Up close this mother of two looks to be no more than eighteen and is probably much younger. I have been told by the missionaries that it is not uncommon for a Yanomami girl to be married at eleven or twelve years of age and be bearing children soon after her first menstruation. Still she looks incredibly young to have borne two children.

Florence scribbles into the notebooks what I assume is the case history of the young woman. She is, as usual, focused and intense. To me she is paying little attention, barely glancing up, a sign that she's finally getting used to the presence of the camera. The young Yanomami woman looks pallid and unsteady, rocking back and forth as she mumbles responses in Yanomany to Florence's occasional queries. The children, their eyes rolling, stare up at the strange white man before them. One of them is tugging at the legs of my pants. I see Vincent lean in through the door and gently pull the child away, allowing me to concentrate on the work at hand.

"And what about this woman, Florence, what do you think she has?" I ask as I pan the camera to the young mother, trying to find a way to add context to the scene.

Florence's high-pitched voice with its Caribbean lilt comes in on cue: "I think she has malaria because her husband had malaria, her two children had malaria, and since yesterday she has fever and chills." The words "fever and chills" punctuate the end of my shot as the final frame settles on the young woman, her body shaking, her face twisted into contortions of pain, two thin legs pulled together and bent to the side as she tries to fight off another attack of the chills.

I've finally gotten the kind of image I've been searching for since I arrived here. It is ambiguous and unexpected: no hint of preconceived icons. It manages both to document this world and to conform to the rhythms of life here, an image not stolen but bartered. These people are aware of why we are here and have agreed to participate in this process of documentation. Like any visitor to the village, I will leave gifts of pots and pans and machetes. Their acceptance of my presence as one of the "friendly whites" has given me license to enter their world and to shape it through my images. There is always manipulation involved in this work, it's inevitable. Our images are just surface reality. They can never reflect the full experience of their personalities or their culture, nor can they fully capture the pain they might be suffering. Photographers are at best visual intermediaries to the world at large who must be able to fluctuate between detachment and involvement. The photographer who shot the famous photo of the napalmed girl in Vietnam is a perfect case in point. He got his shot, then took her in his van to the hospital. Arguably, that shot contributed substantially to our understanding of war and of that war in particular. For me, it is the unreal perspective of the lens that allows me to film things I would not normally be able to witness with my own eyes. I care about this woman, but she is still a subject who must be considered in terms of light, composition, and storytelling. These aesthetic considerations distance me from her world. I need to be able to summon that detachment in order to do my job. I need to focus on the end result: the images that are taken and the side of the story that needs to be told, that I have chosen to tell. I don't second guess the importance of that part of the work, otherwise I wouldn't be here.

In a search for another angle I take a quick step to my left. With my back to the doorway it is easier to take advantage of the bright rays of light kicking in from outside. As I drop to my knees I glance from behind the black-and-white viewfinder of my camera to take a look at my subject in the colors of the real world. The girl's skin is bright yellow. The liver's deadly bile must have already hit her bloodstream; jaundice has set in. Suddenly her body relaxes and she lets out a sigh. Then just as quickly she seizes up again, racked by chills, a bizarre sight considering that the temperature must be hovering around a hundred and four degrees.

Having subjected this young woman to enough of the camera's scrutiny, I pan back to Florence, who is preparing to take a sample of her blood. "What are the range of health problems that you have here?" I ask her as I try to prepare a follow-up question.

"It's the worst problem here, one after another—when you finish something, something else starts," says Florence, struggling with her English. "Maybe the Indians have malaria; when I treat the malaria there appears a cough, then comes bronchitis and if I don't treat that then comes pneumonia."

Florence tells the woman to stand, grabs her finger, cleans it with an alcohol swab, and then pricks it with a pin, letting the blood flow onto a glass slide to be tested later. This procedure is done in one quick, efficient move repeated by Florence a dozen times throughout the day as she tries to cope with this sudden wave of Indians who have descended upon the mission's clinic. According to her statistics for the previous month, she treated three cases of pneumonia, eight cases of bronchitis, and thirty-one cases of malaria, seventeen of which proved to be falciparum, the most lethal strain. These numbers don't include the half dozen Indians who are waiting to be seen outside or the other ten or fifteen who have come and gone in the last few days. And these Yanomami are the lucky ones. They live near a clinic; they have access to a trained nurse and medicines. The few Brazilian Indian Agency outposts in this area suffer from a lack of trained medical personnel and supplies, the latter commonly looted by gold miners seeking remedies for their various ailments, particularly malaria. Before coming here I spoke to other missionaries and anthropologists who recounted rumors among the Indians of more remote villages being hit by waves of malaria. If they are true, then this society of nine thousand could be in trouble.

Malaria is a disease that can destabilize a group in a matter of weeks, a fact well documented in case studies of smaller societies succumbing to sudden epidemics. At its onset the routine tasks of hunting and gardening can become too arduous for villagers. People spend days trying to recuperate in the hammocks, food is therefore in short supply, and malnutrition sets in. One by one the villagers begin to die off. It's the old people and children who go first, the ones whose immune systems have the least resistance.

Diagnosing malaria is relatively simple. Withstanding the disease is another story. The gold miners I've met in the Amazon describe the initial symptoms as a sudden loss of appetite and pounding headaches that feel as if "someone is taking an ax to the back of your skull." Waves of fever interspersed with chills can last for several hours and attack the body over the course of three or four days. Then the face goes pale, the fingers turn white, and the nails become blue. Taking a look at the young Yanomami mother talking to Florence, I see that she has all these symptoms. But there are two more stages that this girl may yet be spared. One is characterized by dry heat and burning skin with the body's urine turning strange colors. And then there is stage three: the killer. That's when the body is drenched in sweat and the urine turns into a thick blood-red liquid. The victim naturally panics. These are signs that the untreated illness has attacked the spleen and the liver, enlarging them, blowing them out of shape, shutting down their vital functions. Then anemia develops, making the victims susceptible to other epidemic strains circulating through their communities. Malaria can also go right for the brain, invading the cerebral tissues, driving people crazy. "Jungle fever," "hill fever," "marsh fever"—you remember those black-and-white movies from the forties and fifties. All those people in pith helmets with mosquito netting draped on cots in the background. Odds are if you are in an infested area long enough, you are going to get nailed by an Anopheles mosquito carrying with it the deadly infection. In the few days since we have arrived I have learned that swatting bugs is a way of life. Throughout the day I find myself constantly wiping splotches of blood off my hands, residue of the dozen mosquitoes I will have killed in the course of a half hour. The Indians have come up with a clever counterattack: they use the flat side of a machete, swinging it swiftly about the body in an efficient rotating motion to kill the pestilent creatures as they land on their bare skin. But even their technique is not proof against the hordes of insects that descend upon us daily. The Indians' bodies are exposed as ours are not. I've seen entire Yanomami backs that resemble one massive mosquito bite. Up close there is an endless series of dots connected to each other in an island of puffy, swelling, reddened skin. Even in spite of my "modern" precautions—bug sprays, mosquito-netted hammocks, long-sleeved shirts—I too am covered with bites. There isn't an inch of exposed skin that has not been attacked. My neck and face are an inflamed and itchy mess. Yet so far I am lucky. I am not showing any symptoms. No ax to the back of the head.

At this time in Brazil the controversy about malaria in Yanomami territory has become a tricky political game of placing the blame: did the miners bring it into the Indians' land, or was malaria endemic to their communities? At the center of the debate is that bloodsucking little creature the Anopheles mosquito, which, usually in late afternoon, injects a "causative organism" known as a plasmodium from the blood of an infected person into the blood of the unsuspecting victim. This insect is an intermediary—an "agent of transmission," as epidemiologists say—between those who have it and those who don't. But also germane to the debate are historical precedents about disease and the indigenous populations of the Western Hemisphere, precedents the gold miners and local politicians are conveniently ignoring.

Since the arrival of Columbus epidemics have been the number-one killer of New World natives. Certainly the conquistadores raped, plundered, and pillaged. And, yes, tens of thousands of Indians were killed in North America during armed fights across that continent. But the most devastating killer has always been simple disease: the common cold, measles, and smallpox. These epidemics have the ability to destroy once-isolated Indian societies, groups that had no prior contact with the infections. The genetic makeup of their people does not provide them with a set of antibodies predisposed to attack the various viral, bacterial, and protozoal agents that come with the carriers of new diseases. Measles erupted in massive outbreaks among indigenous populations in Mexico and Peru between 1531 and 1539, then in Canada in 1635, then in the Amazon in 1745, and in Tierra del Fuego in 1884. Contemporary historians refer to the Spanish conquest of the Americas as the period of Great Dying. During the first one hundred years of the conquistadores' campaign there were fourteen major epidemics in the Americas. After Pedro Cabral, in the name of the Portuguese crown, "discovered" Brazil in 1500, epidemics regularly accompanied the explorers of the Amazon and the frontiersmen and pioneers who colonized the rest of the country. The historical records of Jesuit missionaries in Brazil are filled with horrific accounts of native deaths from diseases imported from Europe and Africa. In the 1550s eight thousand Indians died in the area surrounding the French colony in Rio de Janeiro. One priest estimated in the mid-1580s that of the sixty thousand Indians baptized in Bahia between 1559 and 1583, only three hundred survived. Baffled by the devastation that unwittingly accompanied the arrival of Western Europeans, this cleric wrote "the numbers of people who died here in Bahia in the past twenty years seems unbelievable. No one ever imagined that so many people could ever be expended, far less in so short a time." Such sporadic, deadly epidemics continued over five centuries, striking isolated Indian societies whenever they came in contact with European colonizers. By the time I started working in Brazil in the late 1980s the Indian population, which had been four million strong in 1500, was now hovering at just over 220,000 people.

And among Indian societies throughout the Amazon, death by disease was still the number-one concern.

Epidemiologists say that malaria came to the Western Hemisphere from Africa with the arrival of Columbus and the subsequent voyages of other European explorers and slave ships. Over the last five centuries it has worked its way through the Americas in a pattern of epidemics usually accompanied by several facilitating factors. Foremost among them is the creation of large cleared areas of tropical forest and pools of stagnant water that serve as breeding grounds for the lethal Anopheles mosquito. These are common sights when flying over Yanomami territory today: hundreds of large gold pits filled with water stand out like massive blemishes in what would otherwise be lush green forest. The pits are mined, but abandoned as the prospectors move on in search of other gold deposits. The construction of a hundred new airstrips by gold prospectors in just two years has also drastically multiplied the potential breeding areas for the Anopheles.

However, this is not a one-dimensional story. Placing the blame is more complicated. The Yanomami might also unknowingly be contributing to their own demise. Many villages, attracted by the prospect of trading goods, have in recent years started moving nearer to rivers, placing their people in closer contact with groups of outsiders as well as pools of stagnant water, thereby increasing the possibility of infection. The risk of epidemic has been further enhanced when, with the machetes obtained by trading, they have begun to clear larger plots for villages and gardens. These in turn become expanded breeding grounds for the mosquitos.

While these details might suggest a shared responsibility for the way malaria spreads, its onset per se in Yanomami territory can only be blamed on a government in Brasília that has been unwilling or unable to stop the influx of forty-five thousand miners. These men who have descended upon the Indians' territory are wildcat prospectors acting beyond the supervision of any corporation, paying little heed to medical precaution. Many of them are recent immigrants from the infamous Serra Pelada gold rush where malaria ran rampant over a period of several years. Others come from various gold rush towns in Brazil where the World Health Organization is predicting that malaria will strike as many as one million people in the next year.

What does the historical record show? When the gold rush began in 1987 the government doctors who had worked in this area stated there had not been any malaria reported in Yanomami territory in more than a decade. The last series of small outbreaks dated back to the middle of the 1970s when highway workers entered the Indians' forest during the construction of the Northern Perimeter Highway. There were earlier recorded incidents, usually linked to the arrival of Western Europeans. But there has never been any medical or historical proof to substantiate the miners' claim that malaria has always been in the forest. In fact, most of the medical research done to date—at least what I could find—has contradicted their claims. One expert I spoke to was an epidemiolgoist at Yale University by the name of Dr. Frank Black, a cautious scientist with a soft voice, a man who, he told me, didn't trust journalists. He refused to be interviewed on camera and would talk to me only on the phone. His answers were guarded, evasive. Several years ago he had done work among the Yanomami and several other indigenous groups in the Amazon. He didn't want to get involved in what to him was a political issue. Like many academics who work in the rain forest, he perhaps feared having his research visa refused the next time he applied. But I didn't really need Dr. Black's on-camera assessment, because a careful look at his research reveals significant patterns in the spread of diseases such as malaria through isolated indigenous communities. In a dense medical tract entitled "Evidence for Persistence of Infectious Agents in Isolated Human Populations," Dr. Black and several collaborators document how diseases, after killing off large numbers of indigenous inhabitants, will run their course in small communities and eventually disappear. I'll call it, for lack of a professional term, the "burn-out factor." This is what appears to have happened in the remote Yanomami communities bordering the Northern Perimeter Highway in the 1970s. A disease arrived, it killed off a number of members of the communities living near the roads, and eventually it burned itself out without spreading to other communities. What distinguishes the outbreaks of the 1970s from the ones occurring today is not only the numbers of people entering the forest (there were fewer than a hundred highway workers as opposed to forty-five thousand miners) but the extent to which these prospectors have been penetrating previously isolated communities distant from any roadway or missionary outpost. As Black and his colleagues conclude from their survey of several previously isolated Indian societies in the Amazon, "it has been clear that many infectious agents do not persist in small communities but must be reintroduced from larger populations *at the onset of every epidemic.*" At the rate of two hundred miners arriving daily, the possibility of reintroduction here in Yanomami territory is extremely high.

Sister Florence ushers in a middle-aged woman with three small pieces of wood sticking from her chin, and I scramble to get the last of my shots before losing the afternoon light.

"Where do you think the Indians get these diseases?" I ask Florence as she searches for another clean slide for a blood sample.

"Well, these Indians are from the village of Jundia. And they say the gold miners pass by their villages all the time and then they catch colds, pneumonia, and the other diseases."

Florence herself looks unsteady as she rocks back on the balls of her feet, wiping more sweat from her brow. She has been working since first light and she'll probably continue well into the night. I am beginning to feel guilty about pestering her with these questions after such a long day. I turn off the camera and set it down in a corner of the room. Outside, Vincent is stepping into the mission yard to take a breather.

"How are you feeling, Florence?"

"I'm not certain," she responds. "I think I might have come down with something."

"Like what?"

"Like malaria."

"Are you sure?"

"Yes," she said. "I have not tested my blood but I know too well the symptoms."

At this point the older shaman, still standing by the doorway, asks a question of Florence in Yanoman. As they begin to talk I join Vincent in the mission yard to discuss our plans for flying out this afternoon. A minute later Florence calls me over.

"This man is going to do some shamanism," she says.

"On who?" I say.

"On me. When I told him I was sick he offered to help me."

"You believe in shamanism, Florence?"

"Yes."

"Forgive me. But I don't understand. How you can you believe—"

"—in shamanism?" she says.

"Yes."

"I have seen what they can do. A shaman tells me a baby is sick and goin' to die then that baby dies. There is nothing I can do. He tells me the baby goin' to get well, the baby gets well." She flashes that crazy smile of hers.

"But you also take their cure?"

"They take my medicine and I take theirs."

"You're not supposed to believe in this type of thing."

"But I do," she says.

"Can I film it?"

"Certainly. But hurry on now," she says to Vincent and me. "He is going to do it right now in the temporary house for the Indians." She begins to walk away and then calls out over her shoulder. "We will meet over there. I need to get a drink of water."

A few minutes later we enter the little maloca as the shaman begins his preparations for his curing ceremony. Florence, in her long blue nun's habit, sits beside her naked healer, quiet and patient. Squatting on the ground the shaman unfolds a leaf and begins snorting the hallucinogenic powder *yakōana* into his nostrils. It is a dark green powder derived from the dried bark of a *virola* tree. Taken like snuff, it is considered by the shamans to be a critical step in contacting the *hekura*, tiny but powerful beings who live in the spirit world and control many of the events in the lives of the Yanomami. As the drug takes effect the shaman begins a slow, rhythmic chant, shaking his head occasionally to fight off what I imagine are psychedelic explosions detonating inside the recesses of his brain. After a few minutes of these chants, he rises and begins circling the nun, his melodic incantations now more guttural, his gestures and facial expressions more exaggerated. He appears to have left us and entered another universe. "*Aaaaa—rrrreeeee*" goes the beginning of the chant and then everything else becomes incomprehensible as he communicates with the *hekura*.

At first I keep at a distance with the camera, grabbing mostly wide shots and a few close-ups of his feet as he shuffles about attempting to attract the *hekura* spirit. I am self-conscious about intruding on this sacred ritual, but very quickly I realize that he has little concern for my presence. He is off in the Yanomami cosmos, his entire attention focused on Florence and his interactions with "those whose call is *hahahahaaa*," as Machadão referred to them the other day. It is also common that these rituals are performed in public spaces as villagers go about their daily life. Also, I made a point of telling him before we started that he could stop me if I got in his way.

After about twenty minutes the pace of his chanting quickens and the tone of his voice becomes yet more guttural as if he has summoned up some force from deep within himself. Suddenly he squats beside Florence, grabs her head with both hands, and bursts into a long, high-pitched chant to the spirits. He rakes his fingers over her face and down along her legs, extracting the evil spirits that have invaded her body. Reaching her feet, he cups his hands, lets out an agonized shriek, and rises, extending his arms above his head, unclasping his hands, releasing the spirits back into this world. For the next hour the old shaman alternates between dances and chanting, as he summons the help of the *hekura*. Each of these rites seems more intense than the one before it. Then suddenly it is over. For the first time in two hours I can hear the forest—and faintly, in the distance, the sound of an approaching plane.

Florence steps outside. Vincent and I follow her with the camera rolling. I don't want to miss this moment.

"How do you feel now?" I ask.

"Well, better, the headache is gone," she says. "Maybe it is psychological but I do feel better." As she finishes her sentence the shaman walks past us smiling serenely, something I find hard to believe in a man who has just danced about in a drug-induced frenzy for the past two hours. Somehow I expected him to be collapsed in a corner of the maloca. But then I remember that, like the nurse, he is a trained professional. He has gone through years of apprenticeship to become a shaman. Such tasks are second nature; the side effects are part of the job.

The old shaman, like the other villagers, heads off to the airstrip. We follow them, grabbing our clothing bags and extra equipment on the way.

The pilot is anxious and wants to leave quickly. There are reports of a storm heading in our direction. We say goodbye to the missionaries and the dozen Yanomami who have come down to the runway to see the plane. As we board the aircraft I can see Pierrot le Fou circling in the background near the forest perimeter, talking to himself and clutching his chest.

The plane accelerates down the runway, avoiding several large puddles on the grassy track, picking up speed, then lifting. As we rise above the mission complex I catch a glimpse of a young Yanomami women fetching a bucket of water at the well. She looks up and waves as we soar past her, a wide grin stretching across her face. Then there's just a blur of trees. It all seems to happen in slow motion as the pilot banks due west, lifting us farther above the forest, the cabin humming from the plane's engine, my mind trying to absorb all that I have seen and heard in these last few days.

19

When I wasn't in the Amazon or off on assignment in another part of the world, home was New York City, a rambling Upper West Side apartment on the top floor of a six-story building. On my first days back from a trip to the forest I was always driven crazy by the intolerable city noise outside my window: the empty trucks bouncing along Amsterdam Avenue, my neighbors screaming to friends down on the street, car alarms, ice cream vendors, a plane roaring overhead, and the constant wail of small children—all these sounds intermingled in a nonstop cascade of urban clatter broken occasionally by a flurry of gunshots from another *engagement* in my neighborhood's burgeoning drug war. Then, and only then, there would be a moment of silence followed by screams, slammed doors, and hysterical cries for help.

My neighborhood was called Manhattan Valley, at one time an enclave of Irish and German immigrants but recently it had become home to a five-million-dollar-a-year cocaine trade run by Dominican youths and operating within a three-block radius of my home. The individual dealers used pseudonyms like Chick, Popcorn, Macho, and Joey Tell. They were members of gangs who called themselves the Latin Kings, Purple Top Crew, and Young Talented Children. From my living room window I could look down on the corner of 107th Street and Amsterdam Avenue where they congregated throughout the night, draped over cars and plastic milk crates, stashing their wares between plantains on the vegetable stands as they tried to seduce young girls from the block in front of Pedro's All-Night Market II. This was a community the *New York Times* had cited as the neighborhood with the highest rate of homicide in Manhattan: a free-fire zone where greedy dealers blew each other away in lethal competition for the most profitable street corners in the area. One sick but imaginative thug carried a semiautomatic pistol with an infrared beam that he flashed on the chests of rivals and residents just to let them know that, with one little squeeze of the trigger, their life could be ended. Among the dealers' clientele were desperate urban lowlifes, Hispanic hookers, and "jarhead" New Jersey frat boys, all of them negotiating the street in hopes of scoring enough crack to propel them through the night. These legions of addicts—there could be as many as two thousand each evening—entered the neighborhood with downtrodden, paranoid expressions, their clothes soiled and unkempt from days on a binge. Then minutes after they made their connection, they exited the block electrified, their body parts all ajostle like some hyped-up half-time band leader gone berserk without the rhythmic solace of his baton.

I came to learn that crack or crank or rock—the name seemed to change every time another chemical was added to the addictive concoction—was an indiscriminate drug. Those who fall prey come from all walks of life. Tourists, many of them Japanese, would stumble into this neighborhood looking for some pharmaceutical thrills to enhance their exotic excursions to urban America. I considered warning them about the violent characters they were dealing with, but I always hesitated. I didn't want to become one of the victims of this violent turf war. Corpses on street corners were already a common enough sight. Often in the days following a murder impromptu memorials would pop up in the form of graffiti epitaphs on the sides of buildings or candlelight altars erected in the empty shells of abandoned telephone booths. Messing with the clientele was simply not allowed, an unspoken rule in the uneasy relationship between the community (mostly decent working-class immigrant families) and the dealers (their sons, cousins, and childhood friends).

"Blues out," the peddlers would whisper to me as I entered my building after a long night of editing in my downtown studio. "I got red top if you want it," they would add if their first offer didn't elicit any response.

Not surprisingly, it was the young dealers, those new to the neighborhood and eager to establish an identity, who hassled me the most. Their bosses, smarter and more aware of the local street politics, would often intercede if their "boys" got too aggressive in pushing their wares. "Sorry," they would tell me, a hand placed on my shoulder, signifying our bond as inhabitants of the same tough terrain. "He don't know you live here."

When I asked a young cop one afternoon what his precinct was doing about the problem, he answered the question with a question: he asked me if I had "ever thought about moving out of the neighborhood." This is what it was like in the late 1980s on the forgotten fringe of New York in a neighborhood that had been passed by in the wave of gentrification then sweeping Manhattan. No one cared about us, not even those who had been designated to protect us. Yet this was what I called home, a place to return to between trips to the forest and assignments to Moscow or Tokyo or Costa Rica, a rent-controlled way station for an itinerant freelance journalist unable to spend a lot of money on an apartment where he didn't spend a lot of time. Ironically, it was part of an urban frontier, a terrain not very different from the lawless region I had left behind in Brazil.

But although I was far from the Amazon, its inhabitants— the region's lowland Indians—seemed to be ever present. The impact of the Chico Mendes assassination and the Altamira Gathering had set the stage for a sudden explosion of the Save the Rain Forest movement in North America, Latin America, and Europe. Images and incarnations of Indians were everywhere. There were the Body Shop Indians whose life-size posters adorned the display tables of that chain's cosmetics stores, there were Sting's Indians who appeared with the rock star in layouts in *Vogue* and *Paris Match*, and there were my Indians, the Indians I had photographed in Brazil who now swished by me each day on television monitors as I edited documentaries and news reports for broadcast around the world. And then there were the real Indians: indigenous Amazonian leaders who traveled to New York in search of support for their people.

There were also Indians who weren't Indians but dressed themselves and painted their faces in tribal styles. These were people—almost always middle-class white Americans and a few expatriate Brazilians, also middle-class—who were on a sincere if misguided quest to connect with the indigenous traditions of this hemisphere. They chose facial paint, native dress, and, very often, natural hallucinogenic drugs as their entrée into what they believed to be the consciousness of lowland Indian culture. They were not the first to attempt to span the abyss that separated European and indigenous culture. In the 1960s the hallucinogen peyote combined with a thorough reading of the works of Carlos Castañeda had provided a psychedelic link between the hippie counterculture and the "native experience." But in the 1980s it was the mind-expanding drink ayahuesca that was the drug of choice. This powerful concoction was created by Brazilian Indian societies and appropriated by rubber tappers who in turn passed it on to visitors who smuggled it into the Untied States or consumed it clandestinely during informal eco-tours of the rain forest. These were the days before the Save the Rain Forest movement had become a part of a new era of green marketing and before it was embraced (some would say co-opted) by institutions like the United Nations. It was never a formalized, card-carrying organization but rather an emergent state of global consciousness that informally linked a loose ensemble of international human rights organizations, environmental groups, savvy activist academics, eco-enlightened politicians, concerned celebrities, "green" corporations, and students. A belated passenger on this bandwagon was the mainstream media which slowly began to discover that the public at large were concerned about the future of their planet. In 1989 environmentalism was definitely "in" and a seemingly endless parade of New Age Jeremiahs (mostly academics) appeared on radio and television and in print with their dire proclamations of an impending environmental holocaust. "We have a decade left to solve the problem of the destruction of tropical forests" was their common refrain in the late eighties. "The deleterious consequences of the greenhouse effect will be upon us any moment if we don't do something." Sun-block sales were suddenly soaring, recycling became a household ritual, cosmetics companies scrambled to release products from the forest, and many of us found ourselves eating foods whose ingredients had been derived from the forest and whose profits were purportedly being returned in part to the Amazon's indigenous communities. During this era the consciousness of the world had definitely taken a significant turn and, if the growing number of children's books on the rain forest was any indication, the impact would be seen for generations to come. Indians were being depicted as central figures in the push to preserve the planet: "the gardeners of the forest" is what Sting had called them, people who could turn us down the path of ecological salvation if we just listened to what they had to say.

"Turn on *Donahue*," a voice screamed from my phone early one afternoon just a day after my return from a trip to the Brazilian Amazon. My friend hung up before I could reply. I dropped the laundry I had been folding and turned on the TV. There before me was Raoni seated on a studio stage with a fellow Kayapo leader named Meguron. Also in attendance were the rock star Sting, Jean-Pierre Dutilleux, and the ecologist Tom Lovejoy from the Smithsonian Institution. In brisk cutaway shots the show's host, Phil Donahue, was seen working his studio audience. In his overly earnest, slightly acerbic way, he focused his listener's attention on what was being referred to with ceremonial flair as the current crisis of the day: the destruction of the world's tropical rain forests. One potential solution was offered by the bow-tied environmentalist Tom Lovejoy, who explained his "Debt for Nature" initiative whereby the U.S. and other creditor nations could cancel portions of Brazil's crushing debt if they would just agree to designate large areas of their tropical rain forest as forest preserves. Donahue listened intently to Lovejoy's proposal, then turned his attention to Sting and his collaborator the filmmaker-activist Jean-Pierre Dutilleux.

"Uh, does it bother you," Donahue said to Dutilleux, "that we have to use someone with the power and influence of Sting to get on television in the daytime in America?" He paused in mock reflectiveness. "Do you have any idea the chances of a talk show speaking to these issues given the realities of our competitive game right now? How does that make you feel?"

"We've been struggling for this for over twenty years," responded Dutilleux. "I, myself, have been trying to do this for sixteen years. This is the way it works today."

A curious phrase, I thought to myself: *the way it works today*. I thought about how Dutilleux and Sting had gotten to this point in their campaign. Since Altamira they had taken the rain forest issue and given it extensive international exposure in Europe and North America. Their strategy had been to publicize the plight of the Amazon's indigenous peoples by accessing the global institutions of popular culture. In print, radio, and television they simplified the struggle of rain forest Indians by capitalizing on identifiable icons that people like those in Donahue's audience could recognize. Not only did Sting talk about Kayapo territory as a "Garden of Eden" but he and Dutilleux published a glossy book of photographs called *Jungle Stories* in which the rock star often appeared with the Indians seminaked and adorned with Kayapo body paint. This popularizing approach unnerved the anthropologists and die-hard activists who ran such indigenous rights organizations as Survival International in London and Cultural Survival in Boston. To these established activists Sting and Dutilleux represented a dangerous influence on the Save the Rain Forest movement. Their steamrolling attempts to popularize the Indians' struggle were perceived as dangerously close to trivializing a serious cause. These organizations tolerated the efforts of Sting and Dutilleux but they wouldn't lend their names. So in the months following Altamira, Dutilleux and Sting and the rock star's wife, Trudie Styler, set up their own organization, which they called the Rainforest Foundation. As part of their awareness campaign they made public appearances or held concerts in London,

Paris, Madrid, and Rome. Accompanied by Raoni they met with François Mitterrand and his wife, the king and queen of Spain, and Pope John Paul II. The English pop star was at the height of his popularity and Dutilleux, a one-time rock promoter, was maximizing Sting's clout to send a message to people whom the more established groups had been unable or unwilling to reach. These were the people who bought Sting's records, went to his concerts, and were moved by his popular lyrical messages regarding spiritual redemption and a sentimental concern for the fate of the planet. As I watched *Donahue* it was apparent that the Rainforest Foundation had indeed found a way to mainstream a cause that for years had been languishing in obscurity.

"We are far away from the rain forest. What can *we* do to help?" asked a young man in his twenties with the shag haircut of a rocker.

I had been waiting for that one. It's the question most commonly asked at any discussion of the rain forest in the United States. These were people for whom political action has not been a part of life, yet they had within them the kernels of altruism essential for any large-scale social movement. Their souls were ripe for conversion. These were the people Sting and Dutilleux had been intent on reaching. So with the patience and sensitivity of the schoolteacher he once was, the rock star adeptly addressed the young man's concerns.

"This area controls our climate, controls our ability to grow food," said Sting, gesturing emphatically, his hands positioned carefully within the frame of the camera. It was obvious when he spoke that the English rocker was the most polished of those assembled onstage, the one who was in complete control of his telegenic presence, a person for whom all this is second nature. "I think we have to realize it's our problem because we are part of the problem so we have to be part of the solution."

As Sting continued speaking, the camera cut away to the studio audience. The group was mostly white, mostly women, overlit by overzealous technicians presenting us viewers with images of a blow-dried people living in a world without shadows, a land where texture had been replaced by video brilliance, so bright it's unreal. In this world, sound bites replace conversation as part of a chess-game quest to get points across and become part of that culture of the glowing blue box that now dominates most American living rooms, an electronic social space that seems irreversibly part of the fabric of our lives, our postmodern community complete with its own rules, language, heroes, and rituals. Whether we like it or not, television has become our way of spinning myths, the place where we as a culture seek explanations as well as cathartic resolutions. As Dutilleux reminded us, *this is the way it works today*. But what are the consequences? I asked myself as I watched this display of contemporary ritual with its own assortment of ceremonies, icons, and taboos.

Sting as pop star had mastered the art of media manipulation and for this current crusade he had assembled a powerhouse team of indigenous activists and environmentalists. Each individual on stage including Raoni had delivered a sound bite addressing a different dimension of the rain forest issue, the points cleverly orchestrated, building in crescendo to the inevitable big pitch delivered by the band leader himself.

"First of all," Sting said in response to the what-can-we-do question, "I would like everyone to send a little money to the Rainforest Foundation. I think we have a plan that is very concrete. It is not a dream."

The camera cut back to the young man who asked the question. He was nodding. He got the point. Send money. Another mainstream convert for Sting's newfound cause.

The rock star then lectured the audience for a few more minutes about the importance of individual empowerment and the growing need for the consumer to influence corporations to change their ways. This was an act he had polished since Altamira. He no longer faltered in his delivery or displayed that nail-biting nervousness that made you wonder if he really believed what he was saying. He was much clearer about his intentions, more in command of the complexities of the issue.

Donahue interjected his own story about meeting the recently deceased Chico Mendes two years earlier at a Better World Society dinner, an awards benefit for good causes sponsored by the TV magnate Ted Turner. Phil's moment of confessional participation signaled to us that we were well into the cathartic I-wanna-testify part of this daytime television ritual, the part that has been co-opted from our nation's more animated churches or the twelve-step programs of AA, COA, NA, and the like. It is the moment when we as Americans can speak up and be heard, when we can testify in a manner that previously has been the exclusive domain of organized religion. Here, like a preacher's aside at a Sunday morning service, Donahue's personal account served to motivate us all to step forward in imitation of him, our pastoral televisionary. The underlying message was simple. He was moved by Chico's death and we should be too. This was not TV evangelism, but neither was it journalism. It was a new institution, part church revival and part town meeting, a postmodern ceremony that was as much about ritual participation as it was about issues—no different, ironically, from those fireside village rites I have witnessed a half dozen times among lowland Indian societies in the Amazon. There, sequestered in the clearings of that dark green tropical forest, chiefs or shamans or village leaders hold court on the issues before the tribe, the fire's glow contributing its own evocative mood and texture to the event, distinguishing it from both day and night, making it special, giving such a moment an almost sacred dimension. Those assembled (usually men) chime in with respectful additions to the speaker's comments or they voice encouragement for the points he is making. Among the Waiapi Indians, to repeat the last phrase of what has been said is the way to signal support for the position being espoused. In America on daytime television, it is to stand up and make a statement, to declare your opinion before millions of unseen, anonymous others. And yet even in the remote indigenous cultures of the Amazon, the focus of the ritual almost always comes back to the most important and respected member of the community, just as the lens of the talk-show camera never strays far from the host.

The appearance of Raoni and Meguron on *Donahue* wasn't the first time forest peoples had made network television. And Sting wasn't the only "celeb" out there working for the preservation of the fragile Amazon. Jerry Garcia and the Grateful Dead had held a rain forest benefit concert at Madison Square Garden, and Madonna had hosted a concert–fashion show called "Don't Bungle the Jungle." Saving the rain forest was now not only topical, it was hip, and Hollywood was quick to catch on. Members of the motion picture and television community had established two groups, ECO and EMA, both dedicated to the promotion of rain forest issues in film and television productions. In Europe, Danielle Mitterrand, the wife of the French president, had made saving *la forêt tropicale* a top priority, while her husband had infuriated Brazilians with his suggestion that the Amazon could be protected *from Brazil* by establishing "limitations" to the country's sovereignty over the region. England's Prince Charles got involved in the cause when he publicly condemned the gold rush in Yanomami territory.

And then came the movie deals. Robert Redford, a longstanding environmentalist, was developing his own story about Chico Mendes based on a *Vanity Fair* article that had been sold by its author to Redford's company for $200,000. Word of this deal quickly traveled south, infuriating local rubber tappers, who saw it as another gross example of North American imperialism. According to the Brazilian rumor mill, the author had not offered a cent of the $200,000 either to Mendes's Rubber Tappers Union or to his penniless survivors. When the magazine writer attempted to do a follow-up story, he was unceremoniously escorted out of town by Mendes's dirt-poor compatriots. This sad saga of big bucks, good intentions, and ill-conceived deal making didn't get any better when Chico's widow got involved in the movie morass by selling the rights to her husband's story to a Brazilian producer who promised he would make the definitive Brazilian film on Chico's life. The Brazilian filmmaker at "J. R. Pictures" quickly turned around and sold the story to the Hollywood mega-producing team of Peter Guber and Jon Peters, two L.A. heavyweights who made an occasional film of social relevance but were known primarily for such box-office fluff as *Flashdance, D.C. Cab, Who's That Girl?* and *Caddyshack II.* And the machine whirred on. In the pages of *Variety* the names of Hoffman and Pacino were put forward as possible stars to play Chico, while in Brazil the news of the

Chico Mendes movie-rights fiasco—and the deceptive role that a Brazilian company played in it—was a front-page story.

All of this only reconfirmed a nagging anxiety I had about the rain forest cause: that it would ignite the short fuse always smoldering below the surface of encounters between Brazilians and Americans. It also made me think of a story, both surreal and foreboding, that I had heard at the time of Chico's assassination. Within hours of the arrest by the police of Darly Alves da Silva, a woman named Francesca cut her own throat with a kitchen knife on the property of the Fazenda Paraná where she had been carrying on an affair with Darly. The local media attributed her suicide to her fears that her imprisoned lover would punish her because she had been speaking to the police investigating Chico's murder. But a friend of hers, Margarete da Sena, claimed that Darly's mistress had taken her own life because she had been told by the police that "North American ecologists were going to drop an atomic bomb on Fazenda Paraná."

The bomb never dropped but Hollywood deals continued to get made. The American producer Saul Zaentz hired Brazil's preeminent *auteur* Hector Babenco to direct a film adaptation of Peter Mathiessen's *At Play in the Fields of the Lord*. Other movies in the works included *Medicine Man*, *Amazon*, and an adaptation of Payakan's life to be directed by *Blade Runner* director Ridley Scott.

Nor did the Chico Mendes feeding frenzy end with the deals made by Robert Redford and Guber/Peters. More than a year after Chico's death even unglamorous characters like myself continued to be approached by big-name producers, actors, and screenwriters looking to angle their way into a story about his life. But I wasn't about to get involved. Beyond the ethical issue of profiting from a subject's death, there was the practical consideration of being involved in any sort of deal struck over Mendes's body. Such a deal would not only have corrupted my soul but also have tarnished my image in Brazil so irrevocably as to make any future work in that country impossible. Dropping into impoverished frontier communities with a fifty-thousand-dollar camera and a rented car necessitates establishing a bond of trust not only with your subjects but with the intermediaries—missionaries, anthropologists, activists—all of whom form critical, often lifesaving links in a precarious chain that on dozen of occasions got me from New York to Rio to small villages in the interior of the country. These contacts are putting their reputations on the line for *your* story. They're the ones who have made a particular community their life's work. And they are the ones who, long after you're safely back in the States, will catch hell—or bullets—for the muckraking that pays your rent and makes your reputation. I wasn't about to jeopardize the alliances I had forged in the last two years simply to get involved in the slippery world of Hollywood deal making.

"Quiet down, everyone," said a spry woman with a Southern accent from a small stage one night in Manhattan. She was Turner Broadcasting's producer of films from the Amazon and part of a core group of activists and academics who were accompanying Payakan on his tour through the United States. As the microphone caught a little reverberation, the crowd settled into a gentle murmur.

"I want to introduce you to Payakan, chief of the Amazon's Indians," she said to her audience. As she welcomed him on stage, the crowd broke into a raucous round of applause peppered with a few strangely inappropriate war cries.

"This is the man who is trying to save the rain forest, and I want you to help him by buying some of these items," said the TBS producer.

The last time I had seen her was at Altamira, where she stood in the Indians' temporary village adorned in Kayapo facial paint posing for a friend taking her picture. At one hotel rooftop gathering during this time she was so elated by the apparent success of the conference that she let out a war cry and then proceeded to kiss Payakan up and down his arm in front of a dozen journalists and environmentalists. By then she had already produced a number of documentaries on this "Amazonian chief" which were essentially vehicles to place him at the center of a global movement for environmental change. Her work had been instrumental in his winning one of Ted Turner's Better World Society Awards for his contribution to environmental preservation. And now rumor had it that she was developing Payakan's life into an animated series for children.

Payakan was becoming bigger than life and this woman was presiding over his transformation. Yet here in the dimly lit club Payakan seemed to have lost the wit and charm that he displayed in Altamira as well as in the documentary films TBS had made on his life. He looked ill at ease in this strange atmosphere, pushing ahead only because he felt it would eventually help his people. The remarks he delivered were rather perfunctory clichés about the need to help the Indians so that they could help us. Then Payakan's filmmaker friend returned to the stage and began to auction bits and pieces of Kayapo regalia.

As the lights came up on the audience, I scanned the crowd. There before me was the avant-garde of a new generation of environmentalists, a legion of scraggly haired kids in their twenties wearing tie-dyed T-shirts, hippie paraphernalia, long skirts, jeans, and baggy khaki shorts. There were also clusters of older people in their thirties and forties. The men, an inordinate number of whom seemed to have ponytails, were dressed in power ties, suits, and suspenders. The women wore skirts with matching jackets, the buttons of their blouses undone a little more than at the office, their feet comfortably sheathed in running shoes after a day on Wall Street and or in Midtown.

As the television-producer-turned-auctioneer cajoled the crowd to up their bids for the traditional headdresses—"Don't you people care about saving the rain forest!" she suddenly screamed, and "Now come on let's s-e-e-e-e some hands!"—I started thinking about her phrase *chief of the Amazon's Indians*. It could be said that Payakan was a chief, although the word has no equivalent in the Kayapo language. The term *chief* is in fact used by the Kayapo and many other of the Amazon's Indians only when speaking to whites. It is our term imposed on their cultures. This shortcut reference to leadership roles is a dangerous misnomer, because it implies a uniform hierarchial structure that in fact does not exist. Yet its malapropos assignation to Indian cultures in this hemisphere is part of the distorted way we have come to perceive them. Hack Hollywood screenwriters have played their part. So have popular figures of speech—"Indian givers," cowboys and Indians (we all know who the bad guys are), "Indian (false) summer," "the only good Indian ..."—and Indians as sports symbols, including the Atlanta Braves baseball team (owned by Ted Turner) whose fans' "tomahawk chop" has caused consternation among countless native Americans.

Ironically, we have historically identified as "chiefs" those who acted as point person in the early encounters between their peers and the white man's world. At times leaders in their communities, just as often they are not. But their liaisons with whites give them power and status because they are conduits of products ranging from steel swords to liquor. When I first arrived in the Yanomami village of Wakathantheri it had recently been overrun by gold miners who won over one of the local leaders. This was during a period when the Consolatas had been expelled as part of a government effort to clear the area of foreigners. After the missionaries were reinstated, the miners' influence on the village *tuxawa* named Carrera remained evident. While most of the villagers continued to live with a minimum of clothing, Carrera now wore a brightly colored tropical shirt, a pair of pants, a captain's hat, and what appeared to be a doorman's jacket that vaguely suggested military rank. He had been singled out by the miners in a society where decentralized group decision making was the way of life. Carrera's new status exacerbated long dormant tensions within the community. The village splintered into two factions shortly after the departure of the gold miners. Carrera's rival Pedro, a traditional *tuxawa* who didn't care for the miners, had picked up and formed his own community not far from Wakathautheri, at the other end of the mission airstrip. Although Carrera had benefited in the short term from his new role, when the miners left he lost his base of power.

As I watched Payakan on stage, I wondered how his life would be changed by his contact with these outsiders, the people who referred to him as "chief of the Amazon's Indians."

The title was not just a distortion but a lie. However, the movement to save the rain forest was in full swing. The headdresses needed to be sold. And no one seemed to be considering the consequences.

20

By the year 1990 those remote, difficult-to-pronounce places the Wolf and I had visited in Yanomami territory—Baiano Formiga, Wakathautheri, Paapiú—were appearing in thick bold print on front pages of major newspapers and magazines. The *New York Times*, *Time*, the *Washington Post*, *Le Monde*, and the *Times* of London had suddenly shifted their attention from Chico Mendes and Sting to the malaria epidemic on Yanomami lands. The initial cases I had documented the previous year had now blown into a widespread epidemic working its way from village to village, wreaking havoc on a rapidly dwindling population of nine thousand endangered Indians.

The story broke when the miners, suddenly reversing their stance that malaria didn't exist, tried to position themselves as the Indians' saviors by flying planeloads of the stricken and dying into the frontier town of Boa Vista. There had been growing criticism of their occupation of Yanomami lands and this last-ditch maneuver was intended to deflect criticism onto the Brazilian Indian Agency FUNAI, the branch of government, presently debt-ridden, that had been charged with the Indians' health care. For years the miners had been decrying the ineptitude of the Indian Agency, proclaiming themselves the most responsible force on the frontier and contending that their legions of wildcat miners were doing a better job of caring for the Yanomami than the disorganized and underfunded bands of FUNAI employees scattered through the forest. "Incompetents," "jackasses," and "clowns" were some of the common epithets I overheard in bars and mining pits when I inquired about this government agency in conversations with miners. When the Cessnas bearing Indians began arriving in Boa Vista, the miners felt they had concocted a flawless plan to strike a severe blow to the credibility of FUNAI. They transported the Yanomami, emaciated and feverish, to a small, run-down, understaffed Indian Agency outpost called Casa dos Indios on the outskirts of town. This wretched halfway house, a circular, prisonlike building for visiting indigenous populations, was quickly overflowing with three hundred disease-ridden Yanomami, most of them collapsed into filthy hammocks, flinching and writhing from the lethal effects of late-stage malaria. Still the miners flew more planeloads of Indians into Boa Vista.

But this bold move, consistent with their entire operation in the forest, backfired almost immediately. What the miners had forgotten was that the world would accept their version of the truth only as long as they controlled the flow of information in and out of the forest. Once the Indians were in the city, the story was up for grabs. Anyone could tell it.

The press went to work. Pitiful shots of feverish and debilitated Yanomami looking jaundiced and confused under the glaring lights of local news cameras began circulating on Brazilian television. They posed a frightful contrast to the sterotypical images of robust and contented Indians living in a pristine forest, a virtual Eden. The plight of the Yanomami became an international cause célèbre when these crude and horrific images were broadcast across Europe and North America. Within a few short days Boa Vista's tiny airport was packed with foreign journalists paying big bucks to commandeer Cessnas, hoping to get a few shots of the dead and dying. As the ever astute renegade José Altino had predicted, "the international press" had proven to be his biggest obstacle.

This sudden explosion of concern for the Yanomami forced Brazil's newly elected president, Fernando Collor de Mello to finally allow international medical teams—accompanied by anthropologists—to enter the Indians' territory. One of the first was Bruce Albert, a tall blond Frenchman who had the cool comportment of a Jean-Paul Belmondo. Albert was not only an expert on Yanomami society (his dissertation focused on the Yanomami's intepretation of disease, funerals, and warfare rituals) but he was one of the few people in the outside world who was fluent in their complex language. As a French national brought up in North Africa and married to a Japanese woman, Albert was also accustomed to straddling multiple cultures. He had also worked among the Yanomam for two decades. Now working temporarily under the auspices of Brazil's ministry of health, the French anthropologist traveled for three months through thirty villages documenting the extent of the deaths in a cryptic culture that forbade survivors from mentioning the names of the deceased. Attuned to the intricacies of Yanomami ways, he ingeniously came up with various methods to circumvent their traditional taboos. He would ask the survivors a series of circuitous questions about each person's fate but that did not force them to openly declare that the person had died. "This man is not living here and he is not living in any other village, is that correct?" was the typical line of questioning Albert would use to confirm a death while respecting Yanomami tradition. "He is not living with the priests and he has not left the forest to live with the white men?" he would add, making sure that he was covering all his bases. Albert's unique skills made him one of the few people who could interpret what had been happening to the Yanomami. And the final tabulations were horrifying.

In the past three years fifteen hundred Indians, or twenty percent of the tribe, had been wiped out by malaria and other infectious diseases introduced—the medical reports asserted—only recently by the invasion of forty-five thousand Brazilian gold miners. In many Yanomami villages up to eighty percent of the inhabitants were suffering from various stages of malaria as well as the anemia and malnutrition that commonly accompanies it. Albert and the medical teams he collaborated with began treating the Indians who showed early symptoms of the disease and whose blood samples had tested positive.

Helicopters were requisitioned from the military to transport those in danger of dying.

Two out of every ten people succumbed for eight out of ten infected—imagine the impact the epidemic had on their communities. What would happen if eight out of every ten people in Manchester, England, or Portland, Oregon, were struck down by a deadly epidemic? Think of them bedridden and convulsive, debilitated by raging fevers as deadly parasites ate away at their brains and livers. This indiscriminate disease affects everyone, so it is just a matter of time before the key leaders— the priests or preachers, the doctors, the local farmers, the town's police—are all infected. Within a matter of weeks, the entire community is a shambles: food is almost impossible to obtain, the rotting bodies of the dead pile up. The family unit crumbles. What makes matters worse is that you may know there is a cure, but it is controlled by the same people who gave you this strange disease, those who live beyond the edge of the world. Sympathetic members of their group—missionaries, a few health administrators—have access to the cure but you are too weak to make the two-to-three-week walk to reach them. You can only wait, and die a slow, tormented death.

"They gave us rice and wheat but then we got sick," a Yanomami man told a *Time* magazine reporter when asked about the impact of the gold miners on their society. "They pretended to be our friends," he continued, "but they are killing us."

21

Davi Kopenawa also had malaria when I met him at JFK airport in April of 1990. He came off the plane smiling but sluggish and dizzy from the effects of a high fever. In stature typical of a Yanomami man, Davi was around five foot four, probably in his mid-thirties, with a roundish face and Western variation of the bowl-shaped haircut customary among his people. His general demeanor was low-key and jocular, yet his eyes were always working the room. This guy wasn't missing a thing.

Davi was accompanied by a thin, intense woman with short brown hair named Claudia Andujar, a human rights activist who had spent most of her life living and working in Brazil. While Claudia was said to be in her late fifties, there was the air of a teenager about her. She had a sprightly walk and a girlish laugh that belied her tragic youth: her father, a Hungarian Jew, had died in a Nazi concentration camp during World War II. Claudia had been brought up by her mother, a Swiss national. She lived in New York as a young woman, then moved to Brazil, where she started working with the Yanomami in the early 1970s taking photographs as part of freelance assignments for magazines. I had always admired her beautiful black-and-white shots. Her work transcended most photojournalists' attempts to record life in indigenous societies. Each shot seemed to bring with it a sense of Yanomami culture and an intimate understanding of their lives. In the last decade Claudia had given up photography and spent most of her time working around the clock as head of the Committee for the Creation of the Yanomami Park, or CCPY, an organization of scholars and activists campaigning for the demarcation of Yanomami lands.

Davi and Claudia's trip to the United States had a twofold agenda: to obtain emergency medical funds for the malaria epidemic and simultaneously to seize the momentum of the Save the Rain Forest movement to force the Brazilian government to recognize Yanomami lands. But their first task in the United States was to tackle the matter of lost baggage. Davi had hoped to bring a few Yanomami bows and arrows to the States as presents, but they were seized by the Pan Am flight crew when he boarded his plane in São Paulo. Now, in New York, Claudia conferred with Pan Am's baggage representatives about the missing items as Davi and I sat together on molded plastic chairs bolted to the floor of the airport lobby.

"*A primeira vez que você tem malária?*"—This is the first time you have malaria?—I asked Davi, hesitantly testing out my Portuguese as we sat pondering one of Calder's enormous but elegant metal sculptures suspended above us.

"No, the tenth time," he responded.

"*Tem muita malária agora na sua aldeia?*" Do you have a lot at this time in your village?

"*Sim, agora tem muita.*" Yes, a lot at this time. "Many of the older generation died from it," he added in Portuguese as he leaned over to take a deep breath. Then a nervous smile inched its way into the corners of his mouth as he winced and let forth a sigh of pain—the malaria was working its way through his body. The drugs—a combination of chloroquin and prima quim—given to him by a doctor yesterday in São Paulo had yet to kick in. He sighed again and took a second look up at Calder's sculpture.

Claudia returned empty-handed. Pan Am was going to get in touch with us in the next few days. Welcome to America.

We drove into Manhattan from JFK on the Long Island Expressway, passing endless rows of two-story houses in Queens as the black barren branches of city trees zippered by in silhouette. It was a bitterly cold day. Winter had yet to give way to spring in New York. Fortunately someone (I assume Claudia) had been wise enough to give Davi a heavy jacket.

"*Por que todas as árvores estão mortas?*"—Why are all the trees dead?—Davi asked as he peered through the rear windows of my little rent-a-car.

"The trees here change during the year," Claudia told him. "They sleep during the winter and come out again in the spring."

Davi had made one trip to France and one to England, both in the full bloom of late spring, but this was his first exposure to the colder seasons in the Northern Hemisphere.

"*E o Kenny, onde fica ele?*" And Kenny, where is he?

"*Momentinho,*" Claudia said and turned to me. "Do you know Ken Good? The anthropologist who ran off with the Yanomami woman." As she spoke I could detect traces of an Eastern European accent in Claudia's English. It gave her speech a melodiousness, as if the words were filtered through the soft rounded chamber of a wooden flute.

"I've spoken to him on the phone," I said.

"Davi wants to meet him."

"Okay."

"I think that would be good," she said. "He's been asking about him since he arrived yesterday from Boa Vista."

I glanced in the rearview mirror and caught Davi checking my reaction in the reflection as Claudia translated our conversation. Kenneth Good was an American anthropologist who had broken the ethnographer's taboo by marrying a Yanomami girl, a member of a village where he had been conducting his field research. Their liaison had caused problems not only in the anthropological community but with the Yanomami and the Venezuelan government as well. Because of their troubles they left Yanomami territory and settled in the United States. At present Ken was teaching at a local college in New Jersey and his wife, Yarima, was adapting to her new role as a suburban housewife.

As we drove I thought about what I had read in different anthropology texts about women in Yanomami society and

what I had seen in the villages and been told by my anthropologist friends in Brazil. Women were a very important part
of that culture, to be certain. But to what extent they affected
larger Yanomami society was a matter of heated debate in academic circles. Some experts like the American anthropologist
Napoleon Chagnon have claimed that women represented a
scarce resource that created intense intervillage conflicts and
even warfare. This theory has been vehemently challenged by
many of Chagnon's colleagues in Brazil and abroad. They
have countered that contact with white society and the
importation of guns and material objects have actually done
much more to escalate conflicts within Yanomami communities by disrupting the traditional balance of power and age-old
traditions for conflict resolution. Most anthropologists who
have studied the Yanomami acknowledge that the occasional
abduction of women is a part of their culture of warfare. For
this reason women usually go in groups on forays into the
forest, often accompanied by a male member of the village.
This practice is common among many lowland Indian societies. Whether violence against women is much more prevalent in Yanomami society than it is in Western European
culture is the real point of contention in this debate—a point
yet to be proven either way in any kind of objective statistical
analysis.

What was obvious to me driving in from the airport was that
when Ken Good plucked a Yanomami woman out of the
Venezuelan rain forest, it not only sent tremors throughout
Yanomami culture and the academic community, it resonated
deeply within the psyche of my new guest in the backseat.

"Ken lives with his wife not far from here," I said as we
descended into the momentary darkness of an underpass. "Just
across the river from Manhattan. We can give him a call
tomorrow."

Claudia translated as Davi sat motionless, taking in her
words, his eyes locked on the passing sidewalk, searching, I
imagined, for "Kenny," the errant anthropologist roaming
North America with his young Yanomami spouse.

No one spoke again until we crossed the Triboro Bridge, the

image of the Manhattan skyline fluttering by us between suspension pylons like film in a projector suddenly gone out of control.

"*Nova Iorque*. New York," said Davi as he stared out the side window.

I unloaded their bags and hustled Davi and Claudia into my apartment building, dodging a few addicts, their heads snapping back and forth, still flush from a blast of crack. Across the street I saw the early warning signs of every New Yorker's nightmare: workers were setting up jackhammers. They looked like they were going to be staying awhile. In the elevator I considered explaining to Davi and Claudia about the drug-dealing dynamics of the neighborhood but I decided to wait for a more appropriate time. *I'll let them rest—if they can—after the overnight flight. That should provide Davi with enough time to orient himself.* At least that is what I thought.

In the afternoon Claudia slept in the back bedroom, the quietest place in the apartment, while Davi and I sat in my kitchen drinking fruit juice and eating ham sandwiches. The jackhammers droned on endlessly just beyond my window. Davi said he wanted to see pictures of American Indians, so I pulled several books down off my shelf. The first I opened was Dee Brown's *Bury My Heart at Wounded Knee*, a historical overview of the Indian experience in North America. As I turned the pages I read aloud the captions of the photographs, giving rough translations where I could. The majority of the images were portraits typical of the era: men and women, their backs arched uncomfortably (obviously at the photographer's request), staring forward, their eyes locked on the lens of the camera. Some wore the clothes of the white man, while others were adorned in ceremonial dress. All of them, however, seemed to fascinate Davi. The photos, many from the nineteenth-century archives of the Smithsonian Institution, seemed to reflect more about the persons who took them (and perhaps the technology available) than they did about the subjects. These were Indians abstracted from their environment, objects for the perusal of white culture. The photos did not reveal how they had happened to end up in front of the camera. The nineteenth-century photographer Edward Curtis is said to have paid his subjects to sit for him. But

I also wondered what these native men and women thought of the process, and what the white photographers imagined they were accomplishing in creating such lifeless depictions. True, they were working within the technological limits of their medium, but that did not require that their subjects be *taken from the context of their lives*. Even when the images of this era show Native Americans at home, in their villages, it is almost always in set-up poses, adorned in ceremonial dress, very rarely in the customary outfits of daily life. If there was one unifying element to these photos it seemed to be the testament of the subjects' blank stares: the no-win realization that their world was disappearing before them and that there was little or nothing they could do about it.

I've always had mixed feelings about the photographers of this period. I find their images lifeless and controlling in a way that suggests they were practicing the same techniques of manipulation as were being practiced by their pioneer contemporaries. Yet these men with cameras, like Edward Curtis, Eugene Dixon, and the dozens of others who roamed the West at the turn of the century, took great personal risks to give us today the only visual records we have of this time. Was I not doing in Brazil what they had done in the American West? Tagging along on the coattails of gold miners and cattle ranchers, documenting a disappearing culture along a vanishing frontier. Like my predecessors I was taking images from the perspective of the dominant society. Neither they nor I had much comprehension of the complex cultures we were encountering. "The whites told only one side. Told it to please themselves. Told much that is not true," reads a quote from Yellow Wolf of the Nez Percés at the beginning of one chapter. "Only his own best deeds, only the worst deeds of the Indians, has the white man told."

"Qual é o nome dele?"—What is his name?—Davi asked, pointing to a photograph of an Indian man in native dress and braids.

"Kicking Bird," I said, hoping that Davi wouldn't ask me to come up with a translation for that one.

"Kick-ing Bi-rd," he repeated, his English already sounding

better than my Portuguese. He then took a moment to study the stoic face of the black-and-white image.

"*O povo?*" The people?

"Kiowas," I say.

"Ki-o-was," he repeats.

"*Tem muito?*" Are there many?

"*Antes, sim. Agora, não.*" Before, yes. Now, no.

I turned the pages and landed upon the profile shot of a striking, bold-faced Indian man in a feathered headdress. He looked like the archetype that adorned the Indian-head nickels I had grown up with. Davi pointed to the man's photo, then looked at me as I wondered what happened to all those silver nickels.

"Two Moon," I told him.

"Two . . ."

I chimed in. "Mooo . . ."

"Mooonnnn," he said, completing the phrase.

"Which people?" he asked.

"Cheyenne."

"*Tem muito agora?*" Are there many of them now?

"Before, yes. Now, no."

I turned the pages again and this time was presented with an image entitled "Big Foot in death" photographed at the Wounded Knee battlefield. In a snow-covered field a large Indian man, wrapped in layers of the white man's clothes, lies on the ground, his lifeless body frozen and contorted, fingers twisted, his back forming a strange arch, and his eyes—barely visible in this black-and-white print—staring off into the distant sky. This is almost the only photo in the book not shot in a studio. It is also the most shocking. Davi takes more time with it than the others.

"*Qual é o nome dele?*"

"*Pé Grande.* Big Foot," I said, pleased that my scant Portuguese vocabulary would allow me to come up with this translation.

"*Morto?*" Dead?

"*Sim.*"

"*Por que?*" Why?

That's a good question, I thought to myself. Then I took a moment to look at the book.

In the closing chapter of *Bury My Heart at Wounded Knee*, historian Dee Brown focuses in precise detail on the events leading up to the death of Big Foot on a blustery cold day in late December of 1890. The U.S. War Department had recently issued orders for his arrest and imprisonment. He was one of several indigenous leaders charged with being "fomenters of disturbances." The government campaign was intended to prevent Native Americans from practicing the Ghost Dance, an outlawed activity of a Christian-based millennial cult—pacifist in nature—which was attracting great numbers of converts among the survivors of the army's brutal Indian campaigns of the post–Civil War years. Members of the cult were commonly friends and families of victims of the campaigns—in the case of Big Foot's group mostly "widows"—who had come to believe that with the return of the Messiah, an Indian Messiah, they would see restored to them their life as it once had been, on a new earth, "where only Indians would live" and where they could be reunited with the ghosts of their ancestors.

One of the Ghost Dance faith's key proselytizers was a man named Kicking Bear, who traveled among various Sioux communities spreading the word of this new religion. The Messiah had appeared, Kicking Bear told them, and had said that "God made the earth, and then sent the Christ to earth to teach the people, but white men had treated him badly, leaving scars on his body, and so he had gone back to heaven. Now he had returned to earth as an Indian, and he was to renew everything as it used to be and make it better." Native dancing and singing would prepare Indians for the approaching day when God would lift them into the air and a new earth would be created and the buffalo replenished.

The message fell on receptive ears. One leader named Short Bull led a band of three thousand converts into the Dakota Badlands where they danced in the bitter cold snow from dawn until dusk driven by the belief that their efforts would summon the Messiah. But the U.S. government—receiving panicked reports from the region's Indian agents—was not pleased by the newest activity of these unruly people. One Indian Agency official on a Sioux reservation sent an urgent telegraph to Washington saying "Indians are dancing in the snow and are wild and crazy. . . . We need protection and we need it now." The War Department responded by calling for the immediate prohibition of Ghost Dancing and the imprisonment of those practicing it. Sitting Bull was on this list; so was the Minneconjou Indian leader Big Foot. When Major Whitside of the Seventh U.S. Cavalry encountered Big Foot and his Ghost Dancers, they were en route to the Pine Ridge reservation. He instructed them to set up camp on Wounded Knee Creek. The old Minneconjou leader, hemorrhaging from a severe case of pneumonia, complied with Whitside's order. Whitside called for the company's doctor to attend Big Foot and then ordered a portable heater installed in the old man's tent overnight. In the evening Major Whitside's troops camped on a hill overlooking the creek, setting up their Hotchkiss machine guns with the barrels trained on the Minneconjou encampment. In the morning, in accordance with their orders from the War Department, the cavalry called for the Indians to turn over their arms. Most complied, but after an extensive search two Indians refused to give up their weapons. One man named Black Coyote clung to his Winchester rifle, claiming that he had obtained it at great personal expense. When a scuffle started, the first rounds of gunfire occurred. Who fired the first shot is still contested to this day but the outcome is well documented. As Dee Brown relates it:

> In the first seconds of violence, the firings of carbines was deafening, filling the air with powder smoke. Among the dying who lay sprawled on the frozen ground was Big Foot. Then there was a brief lull in the rattle of arms, with small groups of Indians and soldiers grappling at close quarters, using knives, clubs, and pistols. As few of the Indians had arms, they soon had to flee, and then the big Hotchkiss guns on the hill opened up on them, firing almost a shell a second,

raking the Indian camp, shredding the tepees with flying
shrapnel, killing men, women, and children.

"Massacre," I told Davi, putting down the book. I wasn't
about to try to explain the sequence of events that led to the
killing: my Portuguese just wasn't up to it. I wondered who had
taken that shot of Big Foot in the snow. And how long the
body had lain there frozen. And what the other photographs
were like that had been taken that day.

"*Quantos indios mortos?*"—How many Indians were killed?—
Davi asked.

"*Trezentos*." Three hundred.

"*E brancos?*" And the whites?

"*Vinte e cinco*." Twenty-five.

In the evening Davi, Claudia, and I went for a meal at the
Embarrada Restaurant on Amsterdam Avenue, a simple, clean
Dominican establishment with lots of Formica and bright fluorescent lights. In the corner a jukebox blared salsa as a small
contingent of waitresses spun about the room in tight jeans and
low-cut blouses sharing gossip with neighborhood patrons as
they shuttled orders to the steamy backroom kitchen. To get
into the restaurant we had to circle around a cluster of young
dealers in Timberland jackets and work boots doling out tiny
glass vials of blue-top crack in exchange for tightly rolled bills
proffered by two anxious young addicts—long-haired, gaunt-
looking suburban white boys. Once seated in the restaurant we
ordered rice, beans, and chicken as I contemplated how to
explain the presence of the dealers and addicts who, particularly in the evenings, were an inescapable presence in this
neighborhood. Handing the menus back to the waitress, Davi
cut me off before I could begin speaking.

"We don't take drugs," he said, using Claudia as an interpreter to make certain he was being completely understood.
"We inhale the *yakõana* powder so that we can go visiting other
places with the forest spirits."

The waitress brought a bowl of white rice and the black
beans Davi had ordered for a starter.

"These drugs the people take here are destroying people, not giving them knowledge," he said as he lowered his spoon toward the steaming dark beans. "We take our *yakōana* to understand the world, not to kill ourselves. It is not a drug." He smiled, then swung a huge helping of beans into his mouth.

Claudia, who had lived in New York, had obviously spoken to Davi about the trafficking of drugs on the block, relieving me of the sensitive role of cultural interlocutor. Davi's perspective on our "drug problem" was, interestingly enough, derived from a culture in which for the shamans—the spiritual leaders—the consumption of the hallucinogenic *yakōana* was an essential element in their belief system. Davi himself was a shaman's apprentice who had, over the last year, diligently taken part in numerous *yakōana* sessions in a quest for further knowledge about the Indians' complex spiritual world. *Yakōana*, a dark hallucinogenic substance derived from the bark of virola trees, provides for the Yanomami a means of contacting the tiny humanoid spirits known as *hekura* who live inside the chests of shamans or hide out in the tall trees or dark, dank crevices of the Amazon forest.

In his classic *Yanomanö, The Fierce People*, Chagnon wrote at length about the apprentice or "novice":

> An older man or older men instruct the novice in the attributes, habits, songs, and fancies of the *hekura* spirits. During the period of fasting, the novice must also be sexually continent, for the hekura are said to dislike sex and regard it as filthy. Novices attempt to attract particular hekura into their chests, a process that takes a long time and much patience, for the hekura are somewhat coy and fickle, apt to leave and abandon their human host. The interior of a shaman's body is a veritable cosmos of rivers, streams, mountains, and forests where the hekura can swell in comfort and happiness. Only the more accomplished shamans have many hekura inside their bodies, and even then they must strive to keep them happy and contented. Once you are on good terms with your hekura, you can engage in sex without having your spirits abandon you.

"You people have faxes and telephones," Davi told me later that night as we sat in my apartment. "But we have something better. Our shamanic spirits. Through them we can communicate to other Indians in the Amazon." He gestured widely with his hands. "This is how we know what is happening to our relatives in other parts of the forest."

Since he was a child Davi had been widely exposed to "modern culture," so I found it hard to comprehend that in this day and age he could still believe that he visited other Amazonian societies simply by taking the hallucinogenic *yakōana* shot blowgun-style into his nostrils by fellow shamans. He was not a "Stone Age Indian," as the North American press loved to call the Yanomami. He had been brought up around the New Tribes missionaries and as an adult had been working for the Indian Agency as their contact in the village of Demeni. He had anthropologists as friends, and had traveled to São Paulo, London, Paris, and now New York—which made him as cosmopolitan as me or many of my friends. I thought that when Davi was saying these things, it was certainly a front, you could even say a barrier, a way of protecting himself from the white man, of assuring himself that he was from another world and planned on staying there. Perhaps this stance had been necessary for him to fend off those who throughout his life had been interested in changing his ways: missionaries, Indian Agency officials, misguided anthropologists, even those well-intentioned liberal activists who wanted him to be a mouthpiece for their particular agendas. His culture, Yanomami culture, had suffered tremendously in recent years but its shamans, men like Davi and Machadão, still considered it as strong and compelling and vibrant as it had been in the days of their fathers. Shamanism was the spiritual backbone of their culture, it was a core belief that distinguished them from us.

As I spoke more with Davi in the following days, I realized that these "wild ideas of his" simply reflected the way he looked at the world—that he was just expressing the frame of reference of his culture, a culture in which the assertion "I possess the truth" is a common refrain in day-to-day discussions. What distinguished this apprentice shaman, with his *hekura* spirits and transcendental visitations, from the Second-Coming fervor of the Ghost Dancers was that Davi's beliefs retained all the central tenets of traditional Yanomami cosmology. The Ghost Dancers, on the other hand, had embraced a fusion of their own traditional beliefs and an apocalyptic construct derived from Judeo-Christian tenets foisted upon them by frontier missionaries. They had departed from the spiritual bedrock of their culture and they were lost. The way Davi expressed his vision and the way the Ghost Dancers came to express theirs represented two radically different attempts at adjusting to two very different contact experiences. Although Davi's people had suffered tremendous hardship, they still managed to retain strong roots in their own culture, transformed slightly to accommodate the existence of outsiders. The messianic beliefs of Big Foot and the other Ghost Dancers, however, were a last-ditch attempt by a defeated people to free themselves from the domination, dependence, and devastation that had overtaken them in the nineteenth-century American West. Resistance, treaties, adaptation—all were alternatives that had failed the Ghost Dancers. Their culture and way of life had been destroyed. Awaiting an Indian Messiah was their only remaining option. The Yanomami, however, still retained enough of their culture to preserve their world.

Davi's current path—cultural affirmation combined with political resistance—had been part of his way of life for several decades. His experiences as a child had prepared him for the leadership role he came to play during the gold rush. He had grown up in the forest surrounded by milk-skinned evangelical American missionaries.

The ones who had settled in his community of Demini in the early 1960s were members of the New Tribes Mission, a Protestant group currently based in Florida but, at the time of their members' first sojourns in Yanomami lands, headquartered in Woodsworth, Wisconsin. The New Tribes international headquarters documented the proselytizing efforts of their hundreds of missionaries, in Davi's community and in other backwater parts of the Third World, in a missionary journal with the dubious title *Brown Gold*. This low-budget eight-by-ten-inch periodical resembled a cross between the Jehovah's Witnesses publication *Watchtower* and the mercenary magazine *Soldier of Fortune*. It featured black-and-white snapshots and the rambling prose of its Christian crusaders working among the Yanomami "savages" and "witch doctors." The titles of the articles bristled with apocalyptic and militaristic jargon. One day I called the resource department at the New Tribes headquarters in Sanford, Florida. I asked a pleasant woman named Theresa how they had come up with the title *Brown Gold*. "Well, there's gold gold, and black gold, which is oil," she said, then paused. "But brown gold, that's for tribal peoples; that's what we are after, because we're searching for souls."

According to the back issues of *Brown Gold*, their missionaries were in Yanomami territory so that "the word of the Lord may have free course" and so that God could "do a mighty work in the hearts of these Indians." I had discovered *Brown Gold* in a library in New York when I was helping the anthropologist Bruce Albert with research for a book he was doing in collaboration with Davi on his experiences growing up in Yanomami territory. In one account a missionary wife, a Mrs. Bruce Hartman, sent in a dispatch about the experiences of her husband in contacting a new group of Indians who had suddenly showed up at their outpost:

> Before the Indians left Bruce had several good opportunities
> to talk to two of the men who had shown the most interest.
> They both made decisions or professions of faith, as near as
> Bruce could tell, but he still isn't really sure that they
> understand and believe enough to be actually saved. Only
> God knows at this point but, with prayer and further
> teaching, time will tell. God knows their hearts although it is
> very hard for us to know whether they have actually been
> born again.

In another entry submitted by missionaries, a reference to Davi crops up in a description of activities in his village:

Davi still has his problems but continues to show some growth and is doing well in his reading.

And an account also written in the 1960s by a New Tribes missionary named Keith Wardlaw shares some of his experiences working with the unregenerate Indians:

We meet each morning about 6:15 a.m. for prayer preceded by about five minutes of instruction in some Christian truth pertinent to their needs. Yesterday, it concerned taking a wife, disciplining children, and abstaining from committing adultery.

The propagation of this "Christian truth" among a people whose most common expression was "I possess the truth" was not an easy task. The back issues of *Brown Gold* are filled with frustrated accounts by doubt-ridden missionaries who are never really certain if in fact they have converted a few new believers or whether the Indians returned to their heathen existence of tobacco chewing, polygamy, shamanism, endocannibalism, and all the other little cultural idiosyncrasies that the missionaries deemed sinful. In an article entitled "Satan Counter-attack," one group of missionaries wrote about their efforts to win over the souls of the heathens in an area known as Toototobi, the region where Davi was born. Ironically, it was the positive disposition of the Indians—something one would assume they should be happy about—that they saw as an obstacle to be overcome:

Good times and an abundance of food, plus a number of other sneaky factors, seem to be detrimental to the growth of the Church and the propagation of the Gospel of Christ. Spiritual sluggishness, unthankfulness, and a rejection of our wonderful God and Savior are the principal earmarks of this hour on the Toototobi.

When I first traveled to Boa Vista in 1988 to do research for my documentary on gold mining on Indian lands, the New Tribes missionaries were still an active presence in Yanomami territory. From the Hotel Tropical, I tried for two days to set up an interview by calling the New Tribes office and asking to speak to one of the Americans on the staff. But the timing couldn't have been worse. A climate of heightened xenophobia had recently descended over Boa Vista. The priests and nuns of the Consolata mission had just recently been expelled from Yanomami lands on the pretense that they were foreign saboteurs. The New Tribes Mission—as foreigners also based in this sensitive border area—obviously didn't want to jeopardize their crusade by speaking to a potentially troublesome North American filmmaker. There were long, uncomfortable silences on the other end of the line when I tried to explain that I simply wanted to do an informal off-camera interview on their work with the Yanomami. In subsequent calls, I heard "they're in a meeting," "he just stepped out," "can he call you back?" No return phone call. So I decided to make an unannounced visit to their headquarters in Boa Vista.

I entered the cool shade of a dimly lit office on the ground floor of a small house situated on a quiet back street in the residential section of town. This was the New Tribes Mission Home. From the backyard next door I could hear the piercing, playful screams and laughter of children. Behind a small wooden desk sat a young Brazilian man with short-cropped dark hair. He spoke English with an American accent—a crusader, I assumed, who had been sent north to Florida for a season or two to perfect his language skills and get some first-hand exposure to the center of operations.

"Hi," I said. "I'm here to see . . . Paul." Paul, a Biblical name, seemed like a logical choice for one of their American staff members.

"Paul?" he asked, standing suddenly and looking attentive. A *good sign*, I thought.

"Yes. He's American. One of the program supervisors." I started searching through some papers as if I was looking for something I had written down. "I'm sorry," I added, "I am terrible with names."

"You probably mean Bob."

"Yes, that's right, Bob. Is he here?"

"Do you have an appointment?"

"No, but he is expecting me," I said, assuring myself that this wasn't exactly a lie. Someone had probably told him about my phone calls. Maybe it would have been more accurate to say "anticipating" me, but the young man was already off and down the hallway. Stopping him now would only confuse things; at least, that's how I justified this journalistic intrusion.

Within a few minutes I was shown into a larger office, where I met Bob, who didn't look as if he was too busy or had just led a prayer group or had just rushed in from an urgent meeting on soul saving. In fact this little man with a dour smile and a madras shirt looked bored and a little sleepy. I introduced myself, and said I had only a few questions and would very much appreciate his time for a brief background interview. Neither he nor I acknowledged that he and his staff had ignored my calls over the last few days or that I had lied my way into his office. It was all very polite and formal. Very *norte-americano*.

Bob started off our conversation by acknowledging that he was one of the organization's supervisors—a position that, he took great pains to point out, he "shared" with his Brazilian counterparts.

"Do you think the presence of tens of thousands of gold miners on Indian lands is affecting the Yanomami in your area?"

"The boys don't really worry about this type of thing, Mr. O'Connor."

Okay, I thought. *The boys?* "You mean the people in the village where you have a mission?"

"Yes, you see they are happy with the way things are right now." He paused a moment and looked directly into my eyes. "Have you been speaking with the Catholics?"

He means the competition. "Yes."

"Well, we don't really believe in the kind of position they are taking. We're not civil libertarians."

He means, I'm thinking, *liberation theologists*.

"And as I said, the boys are quite content the way things are."

There it was again. *The boys.* He seemed oblivious to the patronizing tone of his comments. I asked him a few more background questions about their mission and how long it had been in existence, interjecting a couple of lighthearted comments about the difficulty of keeping track of the National League standings or finding "Colonel Sanders" in such a remote part of the world—these intended to be icebreakers. Yet my informal asides elicited no response from stoic Bob except for a deep inhalation, a not so subtle hint that I should think about finishing up. Perhaps my questions had been too direct, or maybe he saw me scribble *boys* and *madras shirt* into my little reporter's notebook.

As our conversation progressed I found myself wanting to know about Bob and where he got his image of Indian men as boys, how he and his fellow crusaders came up with terms like "witch doctor" and "savages." These characterizations had very little to do with the Yanomami I had known, yet for the last three decades Bob and his Christian crusaders had taken it upon themselves to transport such misconceptions into the forest, along with the multifarious accoutrements of a missionary life including Bibles, toothbrushes, camping stoves, pots, pans, machetes, and shotguns as well as (and for me the most disconcerting item of all) a film projector. From what I understood from a back issue of *Brown Gold*, the projector was used to show films to the Yanomami. "Bruce Hartman has used his little projector here very effectively. The story of Noah and the ark was a real blessing the other night, and four people indicated that they wanted to accept the Lord the following day." As I worked my way towards the final question, I found myself trying to picture Bob out there in the forest. *Would he be wearing a pith helmet?* I wondered. *Who would be working the projector? Did they show other movies?* I guess I thought visualizing Bob in that context would provide some understanding about who he was and why he chose to do what he did. I wondered if he had the same thoughts about me. Most likely he didn't care.

I concluded our talk by asking if there was any possibility I could visit his area when I returned to do some filming next January. "That wouldn't be a possibility right now," I was told as he stood. "It is our policy that only mission personnel are allowed in the area." I really wanted to know more about the specific tactical maneuvers involved in defending oneself (or one's adopted tribe) from a counterattack by Satan. I thought about staying a few more minutes to try and convince Bob to let me enter the mission. But his body language and avoidance of eye contact told me to save my breath.

The history of the New Tribes Mission in Yanomami territory dates back to 1954. The first wide-eyed North American proselytizers to enter Davi's region based themselves at an Indian Agency outpost called Ajuricaba. The anthropologist Bruce Albert estimates that the first contact of New Tribes missionaries with Davi's group occurred on the Toototobi River in 1958 in a place called Marakana. But the first prolonged visit of the evangelical group was in 1960 for a one-month period. Then in 1963 a triumvirate of New Tribesmen—James McNight, Keith Wardlaw, and Bruce Hartman—established a permanent mission on Yanomami lands and moved in with their families.

The *Brown Gold* articles of this era, written primarily by the Wardlaws and the Hartmans using the nom de plume "The Toototobi Gang," carry titles like "Trouble at Toototobi" and "Change of Heart." In a curious entry entitled "On Another Planet" written in 1968, Mrs. Bruce Hartman reconstructs her husband's recent experiences among the Yanomami, beginning the article with an excerpt from one of his letters from the field: "I draw a blank every time I think of writing a general letter or an article. I feel like I have been on another planet for about a year doing things that no one else would understand anyway."

The reader learns from Mrs. Hartman's account that a measles epidemic had broken out and "three different groups were exposed." Approximately one hundred thirty cases were reported from which—"counting babies"—there were twenty deaths. In the bottom left-hand corner of the page there is a photograph of one of the missionaries, a Mr. Jon Enns, with a smile on his face, his large white meaty arms thrown over the shoulders of two scantily clad Yanomami companions (both men). In the background a few other Indians stand wearing an odd assortment of skirts and pants, the details of their faces indistinguishable in the severe shadows of the harsh afternoon light. The photo, we are informed, is from 1964—a good three years before the outbreak of the measles epidemic. The caption written by Mrs. Hartman reads: "No doubt some of them have already passed on to a Christless eternity. How many more?" The article takes great pains to recount the tireless efforts of the missionaries who "worked day and night over a period of weeks" to nurse the Indians back to health. Mrs. Hartman writes at one point that "we know that God never makes a mistake and now that the crisis is passed we can see how the Lord is working in hearts through the things that have happened."

What isn't mentioned is something the anthropologist Bruce Albert discovered in the course of his research: that the missionaries themselves were responsible for the sickness and death that decimated the community. Measles and malaria are epidemics that are transported into isolated indigenous communities; the "carrier" in this case was a daughter of the missionaries. Davi's mother was one of the victims. Perhaps "God never makes a mistake," but in this case someone had conveniently left an important detail out of Mrs. Hartman's letter home. *Is this omission of fact a sinful act?* I thought after I read the article. *How about the inability to recognize responsibility for one's actions?*

There was something surreal, almost kitsch, about the attitudes of these missionaries towards the Indians. I thought again about what the woman at New Tribes headquarters had said about the title *Brown Gold*: "that's for tribal peoples, that's what we are after because we're searching for souls," and about the way Bob referred to the Yanomami as "boys." Showing a Biblical film on Noah and the ark to a group of Yanomami in the rain forest was also an act I found strange in its arrogant assertion of one cultural belief system over another. These little details and others reminded me of the way Milan Kundera described life in Communist Czechoslovakia and what he calls "the aesthetics of kitsch," those "images, metaphors, and vocabulary" that become part of an operative system in a totalitarian world, a system that never questions itself or the duplicity of its failed agendas. It is an aesthetic that simply imposes itself as a given, as the way things are and should be. I detected an ideologically driven kitsch aesthetic in the New Tribes, with their Noah film and their insulting titles such as *Brown Gold*. Kundera was writing about Communist kitsch (May Day parades, slogans, symbols) but, as he points out, it applies to all "faiths, religious and political." As he says:

> Since the days of the French Revolution, one half of Europe has been referred to as the left, the other half as the right. Yet to define one or the other by means of the theoretical principles it professes is all but impossible. And no wonder: political movements rest not so much on rational attitudes as on the fantasies, images, words, and archetypes that come together to make up this or that *political kitsch*.

I had seen a lot of kitsch during the Save the Rain Forest movement: missionary kitsch, miner kitsch, environmentalist kitsch, celebrity kitsch, and, yes, journalistic kitsch, all of it swept up in its own hubris as the image of the Indians was being made over (as, at times, were the Indians themselves) by self-described well-intentioned whites who, in one way or another, had all been involved in the transformation of the world's last remote indigenous cultures.

"Essa é a casa dos missionários?"—Is this the house of the missionaries?—Davi asked me one morning standing in front of the imposing edifice of St. John the Divine on Manhattan's Upper West Side. I had decided to take him around the neighborhood for a little tour. It was a gray Sunday. Sharp, cold gusts of wind shot up the concrete corridor of Amsterdam Avenue. Small groups of Japanese and Italians wandered about with long colorful scarves wrapped around their faces. Occasionally they stopped and gazed up at the towering gothic columns of the cathedral which had turned black with city smut. Most of the tourists, however, simply knocked off a few quick family snapshots and then headed into the church interior. Working the crowd was a homeless man, a paper cup extended, with a downtrodden countenance.

"Yes. I believe they have missionaries," I said in answer to Davi's question.

"But is this the house of the Padres or of the New Tribes?"

"Neither."

He looked at me, puzzled.

"They are Episcopalian, closer to New Tribes than to the Catholic priests in some ways. But different." *Where do you start when you try to explain the numbers of different religions and sects that exist outside the forest?*

We entered the church and stood overwhelmed just inside the portals.

"In my dreams I have traveled to places like this," said Davi as we walked by the various altars that line the sides of the cathedral. I pointed to the tomb of William Thomas Manning, the Episcopal Church's tenth bishop; a funeral effigy was molded in concrete on the lid of the tomb.

"A dead man's body is inside there," I say.

"I understand. But what are they going to do with it?"

"They leave it there."

"But where does the spirit go?"

Where, indeed?

Negotiating subway turnstiles or crossing streets with Davi was one thing, but I wasn't prepared to answer questions like this one. I had tried to make his visit to New York enjoyable, as any host would. On his first day here he told me he liked a certain fruit drink with a picture of a tropical bird on the label, so I made certain there was plenty of *suco do tucano* or "juice of the toucan" around the house. I had considered putting up a hammock in the guest room, but he seemed comfortable using the bed. For the most part his stay went very smoothly, but sometimes his simple requests would have more complicated dimensions.

In one such instance, to my surprise, Davi asked where he could get some hair gel. *Hair gel?* I thought. *Why does this guy who lives in the rain forest need hair gel?* He had seen me using some earlier that day in my bathroom. He now wanted to get a tube to bring back with him to his village. I was perplexed. I was also uncomfortable to think that I would be the one responsible for introducing a new coiffed look to the Yanomami, transforming a once unaffected people with bowl-shaped hairdos into a culture of stylish hipsters. I had seen my role as trying to protect these people, helping them preserve their traditional way of life, not introducing them to the newest trends in hair care. Yet, as I would come to learn, Davi's request made perfect sense from his perspective. The gel, he pointed out, would be useful in ceremonial life, particularly feasts. In preparation for such events the Yanomami adorn their hair with small tufts of white pigeon feathers, traditionally held in place by a friend's or family member's saliva applied to the wearer's head. The interest in acquiring hair gel signaled a smart adaptation of the white man's (in this case, my) cosmetic accoutrements.

Davi was no fool. To selectively assimilate what he could use from us was a key part of his strategy for survival, learned over the years. He had been taught by the missionaries to read, but rejected their religion. As one of the few literate Yanomami also fluent in Portuguese, he had emerged as the sole person from his society who could speak in public forums about what was happening to them. He was now a key player in the fight to refute the gold miners' contentions that they were helping the Indians. Part political activist and part shaman, Davi was uniquely qualified to present the positions of his people. Without him, they would have no credible voice in the outside world. In spite of my initial reservations, Davi was indeed shrewd enough to decide for himself whether or not he should have hair gel. He was simply *appropriating* another product from our world. I was not *imposing* it on him. That, I felt, was an important distinction.

Of course, each step Davi took into our world brought with it the potential for problems in regard to his traditional life back in the forest. He told me that this trip abroad, and the others he had taken, were tasks he did not enjoy. His wife complained bitterly about his absence. When he returned to his village after his journeys he would bring presents for his family, which created jealousies and rivalries with others members of his community. He was perceived by some Yanomami as trying to maintain exclusive access to the white man's manufactured goods. Often it would take months for him to extricate himself from such complex social contretemps. Yet the response he received in the Untied States assured him he had done the right thing in traveling here. People were listening. The plight of the Yanomami people was being recognized in the international arena.

In the course of the next three weeks Davi appeared on NBC's *Today* show and the CBS *Evening News*, and he was profiled in the *New York Times*. He lectured at the Museum of Natural History with former governor Bruce Babbitt, met with the head of the United Nations Human Rights Commission, then traveled to Washington, where he spoke before a packed press conference of Beltway journalists and had meetings with several influential senators and congressmen.

In between Davi's various engagements we made two trips to the home of "Kenny" and his wife, Yarima, in a quiet suburban community located in northern New Jersey. On the first visit Davi was extremely anxious about what he would find. He had heard the stories of the courtship of Kenny and Yarima through the chain of gossip passing from village to village in the forest—"the Yanomami grapevine" Claudia called it. I wondered how the accounts Davi heard in the forest compared to the graphic and brutal version Good gave in his book *Into the Heart*, which documents his perplexed romance with his Yanomami bride. In this account he describes the way he became involved with his Yanomami wife (they were "betrothed" when she was twelve years old) and the circumstances under which he had left the forest with her. I assumed that Davi's version was different. I don't think it had the tone of romance that permeates Good's popular nonfiction account, subtitled *One Man's Pursuit of Love and Knowledge Among the Yanomama*. Davi made it clear to Claudia and me that he disapproved of their union.

In one part of Ken Good's book he describes how he had left Yarima in the rain forest for several weeks after one of his extended stays in her village. It was December of 1987 and he needed to extend his research visa. By this time Yarima had already been given to him as a wife and their marriage had been consummated. Yet upon arriving in the Venezuelan frontier town of Puerto Ayacucho, he started to have trouble with the local Indian Agency officials. They had heard about his liaison with Yarima and some other exaggerated tales about his purported exploitation of the "Yanomama," as they are called in Venezuela. After four months of tense negotiations he eventually got a three-month extension on his research permit and headed back to the village of Yarima's father, where he had left her so that she would be "safer." But Good—even though he had spent more than two years living among the Yanomami—had miscalculated the grave consequences of his extended absence. Not long after he had left the forest the village men began circulating stories that Ken had been killed, which, according to the version Yarima eventually recounted to her husband, is when her trouble began:

> "After everyone thought you were dead, they started to come
> for me. . . . When I went out to the forest to gather they
> came for me. When I went out to bathe they came. They
> never left me alone. My father could not help me. He tried
> to stop them, but there were too many. Sometimes one
> would take me. Sometimes two at the same time. Sometimes
> three. . . . At night they dragged me out of my hammock.
> During the day they dragged me into the forest. They never
> left me alone."

Not only was she raped repeatedly but, in a fight with one of her assailants, a part of Yarima's earlobe was torn, which bled profusely even after crude attempts by some Yanomami women to stitch it together with thread. In his published account Good claims he had no option but to leave the forest and take his wife with him. In his mind she would no longer be safe when he was not there, and the only choice was for them to relocate to the United States, where he would be able to earn a living for them and their child. What Good never seemed to consider was his own complicity in this tragic episode. Among the academic community the case rekindled debate about sexual violence in Yanomami culture. Was Ken's involvement with Yarima the catalyst for such brutal acts, or were rapes a part of everyday life for all Yanomami women? The occasional abduction of Yanomami females during village raiding is a well-documented part of their history. But Yarima's story seemed unusually violent. I couldn't help but wonder what would have happened to Yarima had she been married to a Yanomami man. Would her bond have been respected differently? Would the husband have been separated from his wife for such extensive periods of time? Maybe Ken Good had taken too much for granted. Perhaps he had been mistaken in thinking he had transcended the cultural differences that separated their world from ours. He had embraced their world, but had they actually embraced him? Maybe, as with the late Father Calleri, Ken Good's own hubris had gotten in his way.

Eventually Ken, Yarima, and their child settled in New Jersey, where he had found a teaching position at Jersey City State College. Soon their exotic love affair began to attract national attention, and *People* magazine did an article on them. Then their story was optioned for a movie by Columbia Pictures. The book deal came next. But while living in a small American town might have been the only option for Ken and his family, it also seemed to be an incredible (maybe unbearable) sacrifice for his wife. Their living room was littered with dozens of videotapes that Ken had recorded of life in Yarima's village. She watched these, he told us, throughout the day in order to fight off the intense nostalgia that had beset her since she had left her community. Yarima had also recently gotten a frightfully bad "perm," possibly an attempt to conform to our society's standards for female appearance but one that, in my eyes at least, only seemed to underscore her distance from such standards and from the culture she sorely missed. Yarima was a beautiful woman, and the photographs I had seen of her in traditional dress posed a harsh contrast to the sullen housewife she had become. All this aside, Ken was a caring father and an excellent husband. His love for his wife and children seemed abundant and genuine. In spite of my own misgivings about an anthropologist or any outsider getting so intimately involved with an indigenous culture, my heart went out to someone trying to make a relationship work against incredible odds. Still I couldn't help but think this kind of cultural transgression was going to have serious consequences.

As I thought about this issue, I came up with my own theory as to why Kenny had become an obsession for Davi. This young shaman's life had been devoted to halting the white man's attempts to appropriate all the things of his world. The missionaries who had come to save his people's souls had taken his mother's life. Kenny had taken a woman and thereby denied some Yanomami man a wife. The miners, if the efforts of the Collor government are not successful, will eventually overrun every last inch of his people's territory, raping the land in their quest for precious metals. Davi's people would then have nothing left; their ecological and cultural base would be destroyed; like Big Foot and the Minneconjou a century earlier, the Yanomami could potentially find themselves in a clearing one day performing their own millennial Ghost Dance in a desperate quest for some form of salvation.

After three weeks in the States, Davi returned to Brazil, exhausted but anxious to see his family. He left, however, content with the reception he had received in the United States and the outpouring of concern he had encountered for the plight of his people. Just weeks after his return, Brazil's newly elected president Fernando Collor de Mello arrived in Washington for a series of informal meetings with American businessmen and then-President George Bush. This trip was intended to signal a new era for Brazil. Collor was not resisting U.S. political and financial advice; he was openly seeking it. In recent years there had been a lot of tension on Wall Street and in Washington regarding Brazil's outstanding debt payments. Collor wanted to begin his new presidency with a clean slate and on good terms. But what he didn't realize was that he had arrived in America in the wake of Davi Kopenawa. Everywhere he went Brazil's new president was confronted with questions about the Yanomami tragedy and the ongoing presence of tens of thousands of gold miners on Indian lands. Collor was surprised and embarrassed. When he returned home he immediately ordered the federal police to evict the gold prospectors from Yanomami territory. The army was then instructed to blow up the one hundred airstrips upon which the miners had depended for their invasion. After a three-year hiatus, the Yanomami could once again reclaim their lands as their own and Davi could return to his traditional life as a shaman's apprentice.

In 1993 Yarima, Kenny, and their children returned to her native village in the Yanomama section of Venezuela. They wanted the children to see traditional life, and Yarima wanted to visit her friends and her family. To help pay for the journey Kenny had agreed to take along a documentary team that was interested in recording this latest chapter in their extraordinary romance. When they arrived in the village, Yarima learned that her mother had died. She was devastated. But eventually she came to terms with her grief and returned to the United States with Ken and the children. A month later they made a second trip to Yanomama territory to participate in a census study funded by the Venezuelan government. This time Yarima decided to stay. After days of heated discussions, Ken felt he had no choice but to leave her in the forest. Someone had to get back to the children in the States. Three months later he returned to the jungle with his youngest child to see if he could convince her to return to life in the United States. This time he had more luck. She went downriver with him in a canoe, urged on, Ken says, by her brothers. But at a jungle airstrip near a missionary outpost, she suddenly disappeared into the forest, leaving their youngest child alone on the edge of the runway. It seemed no amount of videotape could replace the experience of actually living in the forest. Yarima wanted the real thing. Ken waited by the airstrip, the plane arrived, and he boarded it with their child and headed back to the United States. According to recent news reports, Yarima currently lives in her native village. She has remarried and has given birth to another child. Ken remains in New Jersey, where he divides his time between raising the children, teaching anthropology, and seeking a buyer for the movie rights to this new chapter of their troubled tale. When the documentary segment on their first trip was eventually broadcast, there was no mention of the dissolution of their relationship, even though it had happened within weeks of the first trip. Maybe that part of the story was too complicated, too real. Maybe it was too easy to go with the kitchified account.

Whenever I hear updated stories about Kenny and Yarima, I think about the way Davi used to react when he returned home from seeing them in New Jersey or at conferences in New York. He was usually sulky and depressed and would go directly to his room. There for the rest of the night he would play cassette recordings of Yanomami shaman chants that he had obtained from Yarima. I remember on his last day in New York we stood on a crowded street amidst the converted residential loft buildings of Soho. The warm weather had finally arrived and New Yorkers were out in the streets embracing the beautiful evening with its deep blue sky. Two lovely young women in flowered dresses strolled by, leaving behind a strong scent of perfume.

"Geoffrey," Davi began, then paused, letting me know that a question was coming. "Why is it that Kenny had to go into the forest and take a Yanomami woman when there are so many women that are already here?"

As if on cue a group of three women came out of a restaurant and walked by Davi and me.

"I am not certain," I told him. And I wasn't.

22

This sleepy town of Rio Maria is strangely quiet even in midday. The air is wet with humidity. Somewhere down the street, out of sight, I can hear a dog wailing and whimpering, someone—some psychopath—beating the life out of it with a blunt object: *whack, slap, whack.* As I pull my camera from the car, a tall, dark-skinned man with a face the shape of a brick steps directly in front of me. The old wooden door to Father Ricardo's enclosed compound rests slightly ajar, just as I left it, only a few short steps away. *Who's the guy?*

It is April of 1992, and my soundman, Vincent, and I are about to follow Father Ricardo Rezende to a local hospital where a peasant squatter called José Fininho has just arrived, his body pierced by bullets, another casualty in the ongoing land conflicts in the southern part of the state of Pará. This scene will be part of a follow-up story on the good father, who, just like five years ago, continues to be plagued by death threats and assassination attempts as a result of his work as a human rights activist. Today he intends on making an initial inquiry into the circumstances of this most recent shooting in the region's violent land war. It seems José Fininho received three bullet wounds when he was apprehended early this morning by the military police. The area of conflict, Lote Sete or Lot 7, is part of a large estate that has been occupied for several months by a group of four hundred *posseiros*, peasant squatters.

"*Onde fica a casa do padre?*"—Where is the house of the priest?—says the man with the bricklike face, his breath heavy with garlic. He then takes another step forward. This confrontation has caught me off guard. *Why is he standing so close to me?* My eyes wander down to his hip where I see beneath his T-shirt a large handgun, the pistol grip bulging beneath the fabric. I feel myself go weak-kneed while my Portuguese—poor, but recently getting better—disintegrates into *desequilibrado* or "unbalanced," the only word that springs to mind but one I don't think I'll be sharing with this character, who, I take it, is here to put a bullet in Ricardo. *Will he shoot me on my way inside? I shouldn't have left the door open.* I try to muster some neutral answer to his question in Portuguese while I simultaneously consider running off down the street leaving Vincent and Father Ricardo to fend for themselves. *If I ran would I be a coward? Would this man really kill me?* The truth is that it is only the threat of death that I find attractive in situations like these. Not the real thing. I only want to be close to it, not a part of it. To feel the adrenaline rush of knowing I had been there and gotten away. The exhilaration when the threat passes, when the fear paralyzing my body suddenly subsides, confirming in that very moment that *yes I am alive.* I am ashamed to say that I never expected this flirtation to go so far. I'm not supposed to die here. That was never the intention. I'm the voyeur, not the victim.

"*Eu . . . não sabe . . . o padre.*"—"I . . . don't know . . . the priest"—I say, the words falling out of my mouth in awkward clusters as I step quickly around his large frame and head for the door, my back already tensing to receive an explosive blast of metal bits. I make it into the small compound, close the door behind me, and slip the old metal latch against the rusted bolt.

For the moment I feel safe in the cool shade of the trees and the tall walls of the compound. There's something gothic about this place: the sad countryside town, the cloistered cleric, the murderer with a weapon roaming the streets, the illusion of sanctuary created by the high walls of this little home. It all feels like part of a dark tale from the Middle Ages. *Move away from the door,* I tell myself.

"There is someone with a gun outside," I say to Ricardo as I cross the yard into his house. My Portuguese has failed me completely, so I resort to French, the language in which Ricardo and I share the greatest fluency.

He mumbles a few words to his bodyguard. The man slowly rises and leaves the room, his hand gently touching his small holster, checking to make certain that he's armed. This is done discreetly, probably at the priest's instructions. Ricardo has already told us he feels uncomfortable about having a plain-clothes bodyguard assigned to him by the military police. He objects, he says, to being singled out while so many others are under constant threat of death.

"Tu veux un café, Geoffrey?"—Do you want a coffee, Geoffrey?—Ricardo says calmly as if this happens every day. It probably does. He hands me a *cafezinho* and as I grab it I realize I am drenched in sweat, soaked through by the fear and the humidity. No sooner have I taken a sip than I can hear two people approaching, the heavy sound of their feet scraping against the pebbles in the courtyard. Boots, military issue.

"C'est lui que tu as vu dans la rue?"—Is it him that you saw in the street?—says Ricardo.

I turn to look over my shoulder. "Yes."

"It is the changing of the guard, the military police," says Ricardo. "He is here for me."

Here for you, but not to kill you.

A wave of laughter passes through the room. Ricardo, always the compassionate priest, puts his hand on my shoulder in a show of empathy, yet he too is having a good laugh.

Usually I can keep fear in check. I do this by preoccupying my mind with a wide range of preparations and precautions—gringo delusions that make me believe I am in control of the situation. But this confused encounter, however ridiculous it might seem, has allowed me to enter the psychological space the good Father occupies daily—to see through my own panic-stricken eyes the manner in which his life unfolds, never knowing from where your assassin will finally appear, whether you will have a chance to look at his face before he takes you out, whether that image will be the last thing you see in your pitifully curtailed life.

As the laughing dies down, the two military policemen enter the kitchen to complete the formalities of turning over the shift. I take a moment to go to the bathroom and collect my thoughts. *How could this have happened? How could things have gotten so confusing so fast?* I run cool water to calm myself and I realize that my former defenses—gringo naivete, hubris, a foolish but stubborn belief in my own immortality—have broken down and I am left, like those who live here, completely vulnerable to terror. I look in the mirror: my face is pale and gaunt, my eyes bloodshot. I'm wired. Too much stress, too many long days on the road. *Why am I doing this to myself?*

In southern Pará nothing is as it seems. I learned that before but now, several years later, it is more apparent than ever. This place is a paradise for a paranoid, where the most minor accident or sudden illness can be easily construed as an assassination attempt: the man emerging from the shadows your killer, the accusations of the town mayor part of an organized slander campaign, the new cook in the local restaurant plotting to poison you. All events resulting in death are suspect because shootings, kidnappings, and murders are never successfully prosecuted in the courts. They are never confirmed or refuted. They exist in a strange state of limbo where they feed the imagination. It was only in the 1980s that a justice system was put in place here and it is a sham. The files of cases constantly disappear, detainees are arbitrarily released, judges' lives are often threatened. Justice is decided by intimidation, and assassination practiced with impunity. It is as if the victims never existed, forgotten in public record, remembered only by people like Father Ricardo Rezende who have worked tirelessly for decades to make certain that with each death there are photos taken, facts documented, testimonies submitted, and pressure—however futile—levied on this chaotic, inept, and, some would say, corrupt justice system.

In the last two decades, more than five hundred peasants, human rights activists, and community leaders have been selectively assassinated in the state of Pará. And for every death there are usually a half dozen unsuccessful attempts against others who remain, and another dozen threats forcing still others to flee. These days Padre Ricardo refers to the telephone as an "instrument of terror" because of the frequency of death-threat phone calls. They come at any hour of the day or night. Sometimes the voice on the other end will simply ask for the "dead man." At other times the message is more elaborate and sinister, the caller reveling in the power of his violent intent, increasing the frequency of the calls to heighten the tension, occasionally bringing friends or girlfriends on the line to participate in the ritual.

One such call, to a local activist and Socialist Party candidate named João Bernardo:

"What's the address of Sebastião, that agitator on the city council?" the caller asks.

"I don't know," says João Bernardo. He has already received four suspicious calls.

"What's his telephone number?"

"I don't know that either."

"You know it. He will die, just like you. You're not involved in land problems, but you agitate a lot around here."

"Here? Where?"

"In Rio Maria. I'm going to kill you."

"Why?"

"Never mind. You're going to die."

João Bernardo left Rio Maria shortly after this call. Others, however, have chosen to stay on. There is another man in town who has received so many death threats that his friends jokingly refer to him as "A.D." for Already Dead. Often Father Ricardo's phone will suddenly go on the blink. He can only receive calls but can't call out. He finds that suspicious, but there is nothing he can do about it. This is southern Pará, a region where the phone company and the court system are equally inefficient and unreliable. Is it part of a plot? That is left up to the imagination.

As I was driving to Rio Maria this morning, I thought about Ricardo's best friend, a man named Father Josimo Tavares, who was shot in the back of the head several years ago while walking into the offices of the Pastoral Land Commission. Just two weeks before he had escaped an attempt on his life when his assassin—possibly the same man who eventually killed him, but perhaps not—riddled his car with bullets, none of which happened to hit him. The man ultimately convicted of his murder didn't know he had killed a priest. "If I had known he was a priest I wouldn't have done it," said Geraldo Rodrigues, his killer. "I am a Catholic," he added from his jail cell. Tavores's assassin was the only man to be successfully prosecuted for a politically motivated murder in this region. Yet he managed on two occasions to escape from prison. The frequency with which accused murderers awaiting trial "escape" from "notoriously lax jails" has become the focus of criticism by human rights groups. But no one knows exactly how they happen, whether bribes or political pressure are involved. Rodrigues, after his second escape in 1990, was recaptured in 1991 and is now serving a sentence of eighteen years and six months.

This story on Padre Ricardo is just one of a series of news pieces I will be doing in the Amazon in 1992 prior to the United Nations Earth Summit. There have been six attempts on his life since he first started doing human rights work in southern Pará in the 1980s. Recently there was a drive-by shooting that strafed the outside of his compound. The threats have become so serious that he now has a twenty-four-hour armed bodyguard assigned by a state judge. His new home of Rio Maria is even more violent than Conceição do Araguaia where I filmed him five years ago. Friends are urging him to leave the area until the death threats subside. Like Chico Mendes, he insists on staying. He doesn't want to give in to the tactics of intimidation.

My report will consist of five days of filming, a look at the work of Father Ricardo and a slice of life on the *posseiros*, those without land who attempt to possess it. The United Nations international conference has intensified environmentalists' concerns about the farming practices of both the large-scale cattle ranchers known as *fazendeiros* and the peasant farmers who work the smaller plots. Ecologists are claiming that the Amazon's soil is weak in nutrients, that the practice of slash-

and-burn agriculture depletes the soil and sends unwanted carbon dioxide into the earth's atmosphere while irreplaceable plants and trees—"the lungs of the world"—are consumed in flames. In recent years environmental concerns have come to dominate the headlines and newscasts. The "greenhouse effect" is being anxiously watched. Holes in the ozone layer have been documented. Planet Earth is in trouble. That's the message being sent from the Northern Hemisphere to the South as we approach the Earth Summit—the UN Conference on the Environment and Development. But many people here in Brazil consider these apocalyptic warnings part of a one-sided, even imperialistic, message: the John Does of this world can have their two cars and air-conditioned homes but the José da Silvas below the equator have got to change their ways.

Driving here from the airport in Maraba, I pulled off the road when I saw smoke billowing up out of a nearby canopy of forest. *Good burning shots*, I thought to myself as I banked up a hill on a dusty road and found an old peasant, a small child by his side, torching a small plot of land. He was no different from the thousands of other peasants I have met on my trips here, just one of the millions who roam this forest with their clusters of ten children and straggly-haired, wafer-thin wives. The young boy standing next to him, presumably his son, looked to be about ten years old. He had no shoes and was dressed only in torn pants and a dirty white shirt. He was sleepy-eyed, sickly, malnourished; perhaps that had stunted his growth. I fired up my camera and walked over to where they were standing, my soundman, Vincent, trailing behind. The peasant, startled by all the attention, just stood with the torch burning in his hand looking at me.

"Can I take some pictures of you while you work?" I said.

The man listened to my question as if he were a defendant awaiting a judge's sentencing. He had serious and worried eyes. He shot a quick glance at Vincent, then looked back at me. "If you take pictures of me doing this," he said, "then they will see what I am doing on the television in America and they will try to stop me from working my land."

The old man pulled off his straw hat. I watched as his bushy eyebrows pushed up into the worry lines of his sweaty forehead like the bellows of an old accordion.

"How am I going to feed my children then?" he said. "Can you tell me that?"

I stood there for a moment speechless, the gringo caught off guard.

"*Entendo,*" I said finally. Then I trotted back to my air-conditioned car, put away my expensive camera, and drove on to Rio Maria, another concerned citizen brought up short by the paradoxes inherent in the North-South dynamic of our fragile world.

"*A vida è complicada,*" Vincent mused as he turned the radio dials searching for some decent music. Life is complicated.

In Rio Maria one of the Amazon's most high-profile human rights cases occurred just over a year ago in 1991 when a mayoral candidate and the president of the Rural Workers Union, Expedito Ribeiro da Souza, was shot dead on a Saturday night returning home from his union headquarters. The streets, as always, were dark, the lampposts few and far between, their dim yellow light providing only the most minimal illumination. Earlier in the evening Expedito had been watching the news on a friend's television, then he proceeded to the union office to take care of some paperwork. Walking home alone he took his usual route, the sound of the cicadas dominating the air of the town's quiet streets. As he neared his home a boy named Francisco passed him on a bicycle. A few seconds later a man dressed in blue jeans, a white shirt, and a simple gray hat stepped out from the shadows. He first shot Expedito in the back and then, once he fell, the gunman came closer and fired another two shots at point-blank range into his head. Within minutes Expedito's daughter, who had heard the gunshots, arrived. After taking in the bloody scene, she ran home crying out, "Mother, they killed my father! They wanted to shut the mouth of an honorable man." The body was left on the street until someone with a camera arrived to document the murder. This became part of the evidence that Father Ricardo collected. Expedito's wife heard the shots but she never left the house. She said she knew her husband's day had come. The death threats had been going on for too long. She was not surprised that the assassins finally made good on their threats.

Expedito left his widow with ten children and a large batch of unpublished poems. The following day she received another call from a threatening stranger. The man informed her that Padre Ricardo would be the next person to die. In spite of pleas from friends and colleagues he once again refused to leave town. That afternoon he officiated at Expedito's funeral.

I was told before arriving here that Expedito's death had become a kind of obsession for the priest. The two had been close friends. They shared a love of politics and verse. Father Ricardo was determined to see justice served and he was conducting his own personal investigation into the assassination. What struck me about him when I arrived in Rio Maria was the dramatic transformation of his physical appearance: his curly black hair was now gray and receding, his once cherubic features had become furrowed by severe creases across his forehead and along the sides of his face. On the left side of his head just above the hairline stretched a scar from a questionable hit-and-run accident with a truck that had left Ricardo immobilized and near death for several months. Though his coworkers remained suspicious, no one had been able to prove anything about the circumstances of the crash. But perhaps more troubling was the death of Father Ricardo's spiritual mentor, an Irishman by the name of Joseph Hanrahan. Bishop José as he was called by the Brazilians, died suddenly from what was commonly believed to be stomach cancer. No official diagnosis, however, was made, and no autopsy conducted. Ricardo hasn't ruled out the possibility that the Bishop could have been poisoned by a local cattle rancher.

Of course such conjectures can never be included in an official human rights document. There are no hard facts to substantiate them. But they all contribute to a precarious psychological landscape. And very often in southern Pará old suspicions resurface years later when new facts filter in from a *pistoleiro*'s jilted lover or a cattle rancher's former maid. People like this frequently show up at the priest's door. Some are guilt-ridden, others just vengeful. In their testimonies to Father

Ricardo they provide detailed accounts of a murder witnessed, a conversation overheard, or a secret carelessly revealed. These unsolicited "testimonies" usually arrive too late for the pathetic courts to take any action, but they become part of the landscape of threat and suspicion. As Ricardo has said, "The practice of terror carries with it a message. It not only deforms the body of the victim but it works to terrorize those that remain alive." Truth here, like everything else, travels on slow and bumpy roads.

We hop out of the truck and enter a small frontier hospital, to be immediately confronted by two military policemen. Father Ricardo negotiates our way past them, allowing us to enter the room of José Moura a/k/a José Fininho, the young peasant who was wounded early this morning. Fininho means "thin man" and it is a fitting moniker. The guy is a human toothpick. He lies on a bed with a handkerchief covering his eyes. Various parts of his body are wrapped in bandages.

"José Fininho?" the priest whispers. "My name is Padre Ricardo. I want to speak to you if you feel up to it."

José Fininho raises his right hand, pulling away the handkerchief and then the white bedsheet. His actions are slow and deliberate. It's as if we are watching Lazarus come to life. The young man has dark brown hair, a thick mustache, and a perfectly round head. His eyes are red and watery. He's maybe twenty-five years old.

"Are you here to give me my last rites, Father?" the peasant asks in a soft, sleepy whisper.

"No. We are only here for a visit."

"I need to tell you something, Father," he says. "I became a Protestant this morning. A minister has promised to get me food. I am sorry."

"That's all right, José Fininho."

"I hope you understand."

"I do."

"There is nothing to eat here in this hospital. He promised me his people would bring me some food."

"I understand."

Suddenly Ricardo turns to his bodyguard who entered the room with us, the giant I mistook for a *pistoleiro* this morning. In a swift Jekyll-and-Hyde moment his voice and demeanor change from the caring compassionate priest to the hard-line human rights activist.

"A moment alone please," he says, punctuating his request with a raised eyebrow—a signal, I take it, that this is one of those times when the priest wants—must have—his privacy.

"Understood, Padre," groans the military policeman as he walks dead-eyed—*this guy never blinks*—out of the room.

Although Ricardo is accompanied by military bodyguards twenty-four hours a day, he doesn't trust them. He believes that some members of the local military police—the very militia group assigned to protect him—have been participating in the violence in this region. Ironically, the ranks of the local militia have swollen in the last nine months, increasing from just five to more than one hundred. Evidence that the government is trying to exert more control over this volatile frontier? Not if you believe Father Ricardo. He contends that many of the military police are moonlighting as hired gunmen for local ranchers, bolstering their negligible salaries with fees paid for murders on the side. In this region there are many *agências de pistolagem* or "rent-a-killer agencies" with names like the Sheik's Clique, Snake-Killer, or the Colonel's Mafia. The killing of a labor leader can bring approximately six hundred dollars, while a priest—a more problematic target in this Catholic society—might earn an assassin the equivalent of two thousand dollars. The going rate for elected officials is four thousand. No bad for a day's work, particularly in a region where the average wage is thirty dollars a month.

Once the guard has left the room, Father Ricardo helps José Fininho to sit up in bed, tilting him carefully as if he were an old clay pot about to spring a leak.

"They shot him in the back of the head and the bullet came out here," says Father Ricardo. "In the front," he adds, pointing to the stitches on the bridge of the young man's nose. There are other gunshot wounds on his chest and rib cage covered only by bold splotches of mercurochrome and held together by a crude assortment of stitches.

"*Você tem muita sorte, José Fininho*"—You are very lucky, José Fininho—says the priest to the Thin Man, who manages to smile despite his injuries. He seems more alert now and perhaps relieved that the priest isn't here to give him his last rites. As I step around José Fininho to get a better shot I almost kick over a large bowl filled with blood and mucus, the drainage from his head wound which now sits on the floor by his bed. A sudden wave of nausea seizes me, a sensation I am able to shake by focusing on my work; the tiny black-and-white images dancing before my eyes conveniently separate me from the unpleasant moment. From this angle I can get an image of Ricardo pointing to the back and front of José Fininho's head. The bullet hole is now clearly identifiable: a round red dot the size of a coin marks the spot where the bullet entered the base of his neck before shooting through his mouth and exiting his nose. Some God—Protestant? Catholic? anyway, some force beyond us all—was clearly looking out for this guy. No one wounded like this should be alive and sitting up in bed talking about it.

I drop to my knees to get close-ups of the other wounds. Here I can see the full extent of his injuries: his hand wrapped in blood-soaked bandages is missing two fingers, while his left breast has been ripped apart by a second bullet, the wound left exposed to the air. I am so close now I can smell the mercurochrome coming off his wound.

After I grab these shots Vincent interrupts me momentarily. He is worried about the sound in the room. The tile walls are creating the effect of an echo chamber. Even the most clear-cut pitch is lost in the space's wild reverberation. To help him, I agree to move the camera closer to the subject, allowing him to position the microphone better.

"Now tell me what happened this morning," says Padre Ricardo as he pulls out a pen and paper.

"One day a gunman came," says José Fininho, "and he identified himself as a Department of Justice official and he told us he would give us only one thousand hectares [2,500 acres] of land. I told him"—José Fininho pauses momentarily, his small brown eyes flicking about as he checks his thoughts—"I told him that we needed three thousand hectares because we were too many families."

"And then what did he tell you?"

"He said okay. Then he came back with two other gunmen and killed one of the peasants who were occupying the land."

"And then two of the gunmen were killed twenty days after the peasant was killed?" asks Ricardo.

"Yes."

"Was it on the *fazenda*?"

"Yes."

The-man-who-got-shot-through-the-back-of-the-head-and-lived-to-tell -about-it reminds me of many of the people I have come to know in the Amazon. They could be characters from a García Márquez novel. Their stories are not one-dimensional tales of woe. They contain ironic moments of comedy and grace, as well as occasional bits of absurd human behavior, all of it offering surprising revelations about what we have come to call the human condition. Vincent and Ricardo and I have just experienced such a moment when José Fininho told us how the bullet passed through his head and came out his nose. He said it was all over before he realized what had happened. We all laughed when he finished his tale—including the victim. Perhaps it was the twisted grin he used to punctuate the story or our own sense of relief that this didn't happen to us. But the laughter, and the release it brought, was undeniable: it ricocheted off the tile walls and spilled into the hallways.

I continue to be reminded of García Márquez, particularly his *Chronicle of a Death Foretold*. It could apply not only to José Fininho but to any number of people in this region, including Father Ricardo. I have always been struck by Márquez's descriptions of the way death creates an aura around those whom it encircles. In some ways his fiction contains more insights into what takes place here than the countless human rights reports that get dispatched from this region. Perhaps this explains why Ricardo has taken to writing poetry, verse being the only way he can comprehend (and cope with) the terror he witnesses here. Maybe it's his way of retaining a sense of truth denied each day by the courts and public officials. I read one of his poems recently and jotted down an excerpt in my journal:

> *On that last night of agony*
> *Fifteen leagues I rowed,*
> *Watched over by the moon,*
> *Pursued by the waters;*
> *I drew from them my comfort,*
> *From love my senselessness;*
> *I buried in the past*
> *That night of agony.*
> *When the rod is broken,*
> *The fish will go free*
> *In the clearest waters,*
> *In the River of Hope.*

While Ricardo, the union leaders, and the *posseiros* have, through their activism, "taken on" the world in Rio Maria, many of the poor in this community have rejected it outright. They are the mystics and millennialists, splinter groups of the Catholic Church, desperate pilgrims who go on crusades through the rain forest in a last-ditch quest for salvation. Some are searching for a mythic "white flag" that will bring them release from this world. Others seek a Heaven on Earth that they believe exists deep in the forest's interior. They are, they say, fleeing the towns and cities because the Araguaia River that runs through this region is about to boil over, an act of God sure to kill all those who have not joined their crusade. These little ragtag sects go by such names as Mary of the Beach or the Society of the Divine Father. They travel in small bands through the jungle, clutching rosaries and praying under the forest's canopy, occasionally trespassing on Indian reserves, most of them fixated on some forgotten saint, too poor to emigrate someplace else, too tired to return to the chaos and violence that awaits them as peons or *posseiros*. Their actions, their beliefs seem crazy, but I wonder. Perhaps their fantastic imaginings have allowed them to see southern Pará for what it might really be: hell on earth.

―――――――

According to his account, José Fininho was shot early this morning trying to escape from his simple peasant lodging. Before dawn the police had surrounded his mud hut, telling him Hollywood-style to come out unarmed with his hands in the air. But it seems José Fininho had his own movie playing in his head, one that starred James Cagney. First he huddled against a far wall trying to calm his common-law wife and her two children. Then, certain that he was going to be killed, he burst out the front door with gun in hand and was met immediately by a phalanx of militia and local police who laid into him with a series of gun blasts. Somehow he managed to run fifty yards before collapsing against a tree at the edge of the forest, bleeding and in shock. As he was dragged away by the military police, he says he recognized two *pistoleiros* from a local cattle ranch among those who had shot him. He adds that it took nine hours to bring him back to the town of Xinguara where the hospital is located. Along the way he coughed up blood and tried to ease the pain of his mangled hand by wrapping it in a dirty blood-soaked shirt. Before being brought to the hospital for treatment he was interrogated by the police—a procedure, Father Ricardo points out, that is a flagrant abuse of a prisoner's rights.

The priest is diligently writing down José Fininho's testimony in a pocket-sized notebook, occasionally stopping to clarify a detail or get the correct spelling of a name. This is part of his job with the Pastoral Land Commission, a Church organization that documents human rights abuses and provides legal representation for clients with legitimate cases. But I am having some problems with José Fininho's account, and I think Father Ricardo is, as well. The facts aren't adding up. And there is something in the man's eyes. He's not just scared, he's hiding something.

We bring him some food and then leave him in his room as I gather the last images I'll need to make this scene work: details of the nurses at their station, a shot taken from the hallway of him lying in the bed, a couple more close-ups of the wounds:

"money-shots" that will help me sell this story in North America and in Europe.

According to José Fininho's directions, we will need to travel six hours by truck and two hours on foot in order to reach his squatters' community located in the area called Lot 7 on the São José estate, a section of rain forest currently occupied by four hundred *posseiros*. Vincent is not happy. He groans like an old cow when I ask him to get detailed directions from José Fininho. Lot 7 is one of the most contested areas in the region, the site of numerous evictions and not infrequent acts of violence. But if I am going to accurately document this story then I will need to go there. I want to look into the circumstances of José Fininho's shooting, and I need to show the people who represent one side of this land conflict. I need to film in a squatters' camp, interview the people occupying the land, and see them at work. I don't want my report to be simply another sensationalized account, indistinguishable from hundreds of others, of terrorism and murder in a lawless Latin American country. With what I gather in the next few days I hope at least to delineate the factors that lead up to conflicts between *posseiros* and *fazendeiros*, the weak and the powerful, so that viewers can understand how this dispute this morning was resolved as it was, with a man like José ending up in the hospital. These are not random acts. They are part of a culture, a historical trajectory, and larger political forces.

According to José Fininho there is no place to stay over at Lot 7, so we will have to set out in the early morning and return the same day. This will entail at least twenty hours of driving, hiking, and filming in a region that has seen considerable violence in the last several months.

As we are leaving, José Fininho asks Padre Ricardo if we might bring his common-law wife back when we return from this occupied territory. I agree, then grab one more shot of the military guards stationed outside the hospital: two men in fatigues, rifles at their sides, standing guard over a prisoner whom their comrades nearly killed this morning. In a land where you can't trust appearances, I wonder what this little scene really means. And why, if his testimony is true, were there *pistoleiros* with the military guard when José Fininho was arrested?

At two in the morning we wake and drive down to an oil-slicked Esso station on the main road in Xinguara. There we find, loitering among the gas pumps, a half dozen short, dark-haired, somewhat desperate-looking men waiting to rent out their trucks (mostly Japanese) for transport jobs in the area. We negotiate with one *motorista* named Nilton and agree to hire him and his Toyota truck, a sturdy little pale green model, for the day: One hundred fifty dollars plus gas and expenses. With José Fininho's jumbled directions to guide us, we head off into the countryside at first light. For hours we travel crude one-lane roads, bouncing about in the vehicle's cabin like passengers on some whirling bumper car. We cut through patches of thick uncut forest and happen on occasional clusters of cattle. Mostly, however, the terrain is dominated by endless stretches of pasture—some green, some faded by the sun into rough textures of brown and yellow, all of it cordoned off by miles of cruelly constructed barb wire fences broken now and again by a signpost with *fazenda* names like Green Brazil or Big Valley. I'm constantly rolling my window up and down, dodging clouds of dust as I try to protect my equipment from the ever-present yellow silt that lingers in the air, leaving you cotton-mouthed right after a large gulp of water.

After a few hours we pass through a makeshift wooden toll booth signifying that we are leaving one estate and entering the next. In this region the *fazendas* are the size of nations. One estate named Pedro Dotto has four million acres, an area nearly as big as the country of El Salvador. Another, owned by Mario Jorge Moraes, has two and a half million acres, comparable in size to Jamaica. Often in this region the toll posts are manned by the owner's most trusted employees, who in turn are watched over by gunmen with side arms lingering about in the distance. It is common knowledge that inside a *fazenda* anyone—even former felons—can carry a gun. No permit is needed, a situation human rights groups have deemed a "recipe for violence."

Slavery, although formally abolished in 1898, is not an

uncommon practice in places like this. Last year alone, Father Ricardo Rezende's Pastoral Land Commission documented 620 people who had been held captive and forced to work in southern Pará. The men and women, usually from out of state, are hired and transported to this region by labor contractors known as *gatos*, "cats." The workers are lured to the *fazendas* with promises of large salaries for work cutting down the forest. They can spend up to three days in covered trucks in order to arrive at their "jobs," often paying for their own meager allotments of food. Once they are relocated deep in the confines of these mammoth estates they are forced into debt peonage, very often in malaria-infested areas of the forest. Many have been threatened at gunpoint if they complain, or chased by *pistoleiros* into the forest if they attempt to leave. While some have escaped, others are brought back, never to be heard from again. These tales contribute to the rumors that on these lands there are numerous unmarked graves where the disgruntled are disposed of. In the nearby municipality of Ourilandia do Norte two *fazendas*, Santana do Indaia and Santo Antônio do Indaia, were recently visited by Brazil's secretary of labor and the military police. The owners had enslaved more than one hundred workers for a period of three months. The evidence was right at hand, the crime punishable by imprisonment. Yet in spite of the presence of the secretary of labor no arrests were made. No one was charged with a crime of any kind. That's the way it works here.

"The laws exist here in this region," a cattle rancher named Geraldo Tosta told us yesterday, "but they don't work." Tosta, a lawyer, described himself to us as politically "moderate," someone trying to find solutions to the problems in the region. Clean-shaven and dressed casually in slacks and a rugby shirt, he is part of a new generation of smooth-talking ranchers who have realized that the confrontational hardball tactics of the UDR, or Rural Democratic Union, aren't winning them any points in the eyes of the Brazilian press. According to local human rights activists Tosta is not someone who enslaves or kills workers, yet that didn't stop him from blaming the victims and apologizing for the perpetrators. As the head of the newly formed Rural Landowners Union, his job is to protect the interests of his cattle ranching constituents. It's a job he takes seriously. The Brazilian worker, as far as Tosta is concerned, is "lazy and apathetic," and for this reason he says agrarian reform will "never work." With his wife goading him on just off camera, he told us that the "large landowners, acting within their rights, were justified in using this alternative way of doings things." He then went on to say that someday he hoped *fazendeiros* would "stop using force." But that day had yet to come.

After several hours the dirt road ends abruptly before a cluster of bushes. To the left can be seen a small rocky footpath that conforms with José Fininho's description. We unload our equipment and set off on this trail which goes straight into the mountains. After about a half hour we pass several small peasant cottages whose withered and suspicious occupants answer our questions in a broken Portuguese that doesn't sound like any language I've ever heard. Were it not for Vincent I would be completely lost here. He is expert at navigating the Amazon's backwoods. This is an environment where he comes into his own. Somehow he has managed to make sense of José Fininho's cryptic directions which consist of vague phrases like "go left at the big wooden stump" or "cross three little rivers and one big one and then turn left again" or "when you see Jaimundo's old burnt house you will know you will have two more hours." Vincent has spent a lot of time in this region, first living as a teenager with the Kraho Indians, then researching and writing a book about the Araguaia *guerrilha* revolts that occurred here in the 1970s. As we climb the mountain he converses easily with the peasant men and women who speak in a clipped dialect shouted out above the sounds of yapping dogs. We never actually see these people fully exposed, just their tiny heads popping over bushes and out of doorways, probably a self-protective reflex in light of the recent troubles. Even though Vincent is Brazilian, we are still outsiders in this backwoods community. We carry strange gear and, being urbanites, we lack the weatherbeaten look common among these people who spend their lives laboring in the sun. "*É perto*"—it is close— they always add after we ask some specific question about the directions. This is a refrain I have come to learn has no meaning. It exists more as a gesture of encouragement. The peasants have been saying *é perto* for the last two hours as we have stumbled up the mountain following a treacherous path that more closely resembles a dry riverbed.

Finally, in the searing heat of the Amazon's midday, we arrive in a sunbaked village inhabited only by children and women. There are some donkeys tied up at the end of the street but otherwise the town—a cluster of six thatched houses with yellow mud walls—is deserted. This must be Lot 7. I wander about the village trying to figure out why it is so empty. I leave Vincent at a small bar and dry goods store to converse with the local women. On my way out I catch a glimpse of an old man who sits in a chair by an adjacent doorway. He stares straight ahead, his eyes never blinking, a group of flies swirling about his face. If it weren't for the fresh froth at the corners of his mouth I would have mistaken him for dead. He is, however, the only male over ten years of age I have seen so far.

"There is no one here who knows José Fininho," Vicent says when I return from my little scouting trip.

"Come on."

"*Ninguém*, nobody, *nada, personne.*"

"This is Lot Seven?"

"Yes, Chefe," he says, flashing me a forced grin.

I look at the emaciated peasant women sitting and standing in the cool shade of this little hut, their black and blond hair greasy and streaked with gray, their skin wrinkled beyond their years, the history of this region written in their tired faces. All of them are clad in dirty T-shirts and skirts; some carry a piece of worn and filthy cloth which they use to wipe the sweat from their brow or wave about to chase away the flies. Many of them have crooked gap-toothed smiles. Others simply stare straight ahead, their mouths locked in a grimace, avoiding contact with my eyes or perhaps simply lost in thought. There is, however, one woman who seems less distant than the rest of the group. She has meaty, strong arms and a broad face. Her name is Flora, she is the owner of this little store. She is the only person in the room who will look us in the eye.

"*Este aqui é Lote Sete?*"—This is Lot 7?—I ask Flora. "*Lote Sete?*" I repeat as I point to the ground.

I admonish myself immediately for doing again the one thing I've always promised myself I wouldn't do: resorting to hand gestures to supplement my badly pronounced Portuguese. I suddenly envision myself as resembling a lone lost tourist in Europe trying to navigate his way out of a back street in Rome or Paris, an amiable guy with a someone-help-me smile. The problem is that we don't have much time here. We will soon have to get back down the mountain. As I scan the room, however, I can see a few heads begin to nod up and down. Signs of confirmation. But it is still only Flora who looks directly at us.

"*Vocês me entendem quando eu falo português?*"—Do you understand me when I speak Portuguese?—I ask the ladies, this time my hands safely thrust into my pockets.

"*Sim,*" says a woman in the front followed by a few other feeble, almost inaudible, grunts which, in my desperation, I take for signs of affirmation. Then in the back of the room a tiny little mouse of a woman with one eye and a shrill voice says *não*, at which point the rest of the group breaks out laughing. Vincent lowers his head, shaking it left and right, making sure I know, if I don't already, that he is *esmagado*, overwhelmed, by the ridiculousness of my attempt to engage these women in conversation. But at least now the mood has lightened. There are a few smiles in the room. I notice Flora has a silver tooth.

"And you say they don't know José Fininho?" I ask.

"No," Vincent says. He makes a clicking noise with his teeth, then nods his head and kicks the dust. Sitting on his wooden stool, he leans over like some heroin junkie about to go down on his last nod into oblivion.

"Strange they don't know him," I say to myself as I look to Vincent for a reaction. He, however, is clearly withdrawing from me. Perhaps it is the absurdity of being stuck up here with a hand-gesturing gringo or maybe it is just the oppressive afternoon heat. I decide not to push him. We're both proud men. The worst type, some say. Better to be a diplomat.

"I also think it is strange," Vincent says finally.

An opening. "Have you asked anyone else?"

"A couple of the women outside." He finally looks me in the eye. "They are all the same. Nobody knows anything."

I take a walk out on the dry clay street and survey the town. The sun now seems softer and warmer in color, its angle against the mud shacks adding texture to what a short while ago had resembled a shadowless lunar landscape. A group of five children are playing in a patch of sun. In the background two stocky mules are tied to a wooden post. I take a quick shot of the street, then another one focusing in on the children before I walk back inside. A few of the women have taken the opportunity to duck out in my absence. Those that remain, I guess, are the curious few and Flora, the proprietor who has no other choice.

"Why do you think they are not talking to us?" I ask Vincent. In my absence he has purchased a soda from Flora and is drinking it. She must bring them up here by donkey. "Did you explain to them what we are trying to do?"

"No."

"What do you mean?" I ask, unable to disguise my irritation. Vincent and I discussed our strategy on the way up the hill. We decided that as soon as we got to the village we would explain to whoever was there that we were journalists doing a story about human rights abuses in this area.

"I told them we were lawyers sent by the priest," he says, then pauses. He looks at the women in the room. "I said that we were here to do an investigation and collect their testimony."

I look at Flora who is the only one in the room who seems to be trying to follow our conversation.

"You did what?"

"I thought this way they would talk to us."

"Don't you think it is obvious that we are not lawyers?" I say.

I look back at Flora who seems attuned to every word. She glances away. She is smart. She can interpret behavior. She doesn't need languages.

"These people aren't stupid," I add, immediately wishing that the words could somehow be sucked back into my mouth.

Gringo arrogance, as I have learned in the past, is a mortal sin in Brazil, a nation that has lived too long in the shadow of the United States. I try another tack.

"Why don't you start by asking Flora if she thinks we are lawyers?"

Vicent just stares at me, then takes another sip of soda.

"Okay," I say. "I'll ask her. *Flora, um momento*—"

"*Flora!*" Vicent cuts in before I can get started. "*Você pensa que nós somos advogados?*"

She stares at him for a moment, then looks at me.

"No." Her response hangs in the air for several seconds, followed by a flurry of old women's laughter, hoarse and breathless.

"What did you think when we first came to this town?"

"A young boy came running to the village shortly before you arrived. He said the military police were returning."

"So you thought we were the military police?"

"Yes."

"So what about now?"

"I don't think so," she says, wiping the back of her hand across the bridge of her nose. "You have these cameras and you are traveling with this American." She pauses a second, considering what she is about to say. "And now you are fighting with each other like a couple of women. I don't think you are military police."

The other women in the room again break into laughter when she delivers this jibe.

"So what do you think we are doing here?"

"I don't know. Why don't you tell us?"

"We are journalists," he begins, then goes on to explain (finally) why we have come and what we want to do. For me this part of the process is perhaps the most rewarding: to see people engaged and, to use that overused word, empowered by someone recognizing that they too *should* have a voice in any public debate on the conditions of their lives, that the realm of television is not solely the domain of the politicians or city people, that they too can share the airwaves. Probably no one is more aware than they that they have been forgotten, that as the poorest of the poor, they have fallen between the cracks of government policies that only give them lip-service alternatives with each of the changing administrations. Former president Sarney promised to find plots of land for 1.4 million people but settled only 115,000 during his administration. The current president Collor is promising to distribute parcels of land to 500,000 but no one here believes him. That's why they have taken to the mountains and appropriated the land for themselves. These uncultivated plots—once they've occupied them for a five-year period—can legally be considered theirs. And that's where the *pistoleiros* come in. They push the people off the land before, and even after, they have had the opportunity to make a legal claim. Violence has become endemic to the region. Just last year the minister of agriculture, Antônio Cabrera, said that "the violence in the countryside is, in its essence, the result of an unjust agrarian structure." In speaking about land conflicts on a recent trip to Brazil, Pope John Paul II warned that "all private property carries a social mortgage." Radical words from a traditionally conservative papacy, but it has been his priests and nuns who have been dying on the front lines here. As far as I can tell, the Protestants have yet to make their way to this remote mountaintop. These people, like the majority of Brazilians, are still Catholics.

When Vincent finishes explaining our presence Flora turns to a young boy standing by the door. *"Vai buscar Anita"*—Go get Anita—she says. Then she turns to us.

"She is José Fininho's woman. She is the one who was there. The only one who can tell you what *really* happened."

Flora then goes on to tell us that the men of the village went off to hide in the bush when they heard of our approach. She sends another young boy to tell them they can return. Minutes later, a small, wiry woman with curly black hair and knobby elbows arrives in the village almost out of breath. She looks to be in her early twenties and is dressed in sneakers, an orange blouse, and a black miniskirt. This is Anita, José Fininho's common-law wife. If her clothing is any indication, she has spent most of her life in towns. How she ended up with José Fininho is another story.

Anita leads us out of the village, and we arrive at a crudely constructed mud hut with a thatched roof sitting oddly alone in a forest clearing as if it had just dropped down from the heavens. This is the home she has shared with José Fininho and her two children from a prior relationship. In her squeaky voice she reenacts the shootout for us, providing background details that José Fininho left out. It turns out he is a thief who has been stealing cattle from the owners of the São José estate. José's rustling put him at odds not only with the landowner but also with the other squatters of Lot 7, four hundred impoverished men and women. For a while José Fininho lived among the other peasants, but then he was banished to this stretch of woods by the legitimate *posseiros* who were attempting to legally claim plots of land. The *posseiros* believed José Fininho's criminal activities would only bring trouble. And they were right. One day the landowner sent a gunman to look for the stolen property as well as the culprit who was taking it. José Fininho saw the man enter the village and he killed him before he had a chance to inquire about the missing cattle. The Thin Man, showing considerable strength, disposed of the body in a nearby ravine. When the landowner sent a second man, José Fininho killed him as well. Why he lingered in the community isn't clear. What *is* clear here is that José Fininho has tried to take advantage of not just the people of this community but the good Father Rezende and me, the gringo journalist.

"He is not a good man," old José Maria tells us later in the day. "José Fininho is trouble, only trouble."

José Maria is one of a dozen men who have now returned to the village, having received word from Flora that it is safe to come out of hiding. He tells us that he has been roaming about this region for decades trying to secure arable plots in between jobs as a peon on local *fazendas*. While José Fininho might be a charlatan, most of the people in this community seem to be legitimately occupying the land, working it in accordance with Brazilian law, hoping one day to claim it as their own.

"The large landowners have everything, am I right?" José Maria says. The words pop from his mouth like marbles spurting in a pinball machine. "They grabbed the land just like we are grabbing it. But they have money so they can put up fences. They make holes and then fortify the area around it. But we pass under the fences and go into the forest."

In less than two hours we work our way around the village interviewing other peasants, filming people at work, taking occasional breaks to quench our thirst or answer the questions of those who have just returned to the community. As night descends on the mountain, we decide to make our way home.

Anita has collected a few bits of clothing and personal possessions, stuffing them into a small bundle. She expects to be with José Fininho for a while. She has arranged for her children to be looked after by her mother. But five minutes down the path she suddenly asks us to wait a moment. As she stands there in the moon's milky blue light her frail body appears to be shaking.

"I am not coming with you."

"Are you sure?" says Vincent.

"Yes."

"Why?"

"I don't know why I am going."

"What do you want us to tell him?"

"I don't know. We lived together but I don't love him. You decide."

And with that she disappears into the night.

———————

The following day in Rio Maria we meet Orlando Canuto, a big-eared, razor-thin guy with sad eyes that tell you he's seen it all, too much, more than you'd ever want to imagine. Maybe that explains why at twenty-six he's got the dejected walk of a man in his eighties. Life has been sucked out of him. When I hear his story I understand why.

We've arranged to meet him at his one-story clapboard house on one of the town's side streets. Finishing his coffee, Orlando steps out onto his front porch followed by his twenty-four-hour guard, a policeman recently assigned by a federal judge. With their added weight I can feel the floorboards bend under my feet and I struggle to keep the frame line steady and composed. Their steps produce a faint, hollow echo as they lumber down the porch steps and into the federal policeman's blue pickup truck. For me filming is difficult today. Yesterday's venture has taken its toll. My legs are stiff and sore, my mind groggy from lack of sleep. I adjust the camera's focus ring as I follow them down the steps. Then I quickly change positions to catch them entering the car. I grab a few extra shots of them getting seated, closing the doors, starting the engine. Although this type of coverage has become second nature, I feel as if someone has attached sandbags to my legs. But I've managed to film one really good image, one I know I'll use. It's a zoom out from the federal policeman's gun to Orlando seated in the front seat, his eyes flashing left and right as he scans the street. This is a guy who can't hide his fear. His face tells you he is terrified of dying.

At the modest one-story union headquarters in Rio Maria, Orlando gives us a tour of what I can only describe as their Wall of Ill-Fated Fame.

"This is Raimundo Ferreira Lima," he says, pointing to a photo of a stern man with glasses whose image, unlike most of the portraits, sits behind a glass frame. "He was a trade unionist killed in Conceição do Araguaia. 1980.

"There, also, is the president of the union in Tomé-Açu," he says as he points to a political poster with the photo of a baby-faced man in his thirties. "Benezinno. He was assassinated on July fourth, 1984."

As he shuffles over to other photos, he continues reciting names of victims of assassinations, including Expedito and Father Josimo. Finally he comes to a painting of an older man with glasses, a mustache, and black hair. For the first time there is a flash of emotion in his voice, a little life coming to the surface, stuck there in the quiver of his throat.

"This is my father, João Canuto, the first president of the union, this union. He was killed in 'eighty-five—December eighteenth, 1985."

In a small enclosed back room we set up for a more elaborate interview. Orlando seems uncomfortable on his feet. I sit him down by a window, taking advantage of a technique practiced since the days of Vermeer: soft light spills in from the side, fading off into the background shadows. Once seated, Orlando is more relaxed. He then gives us some background on what happened to his father, João Canuto de Oliveira.

In the mid-1980s João became the first president of the union as well as a mayoral candidate in Rio Maria. He was known as a tenacious peasant organizer who had successfully orchestrated several occupations of contested areas of rain forest. It was common knowledge that he was held in bitter contempt by landowners in the region. At the time of his death in December of 1985 he had been representing forty-five families who were in a dispute with the *fazendeiro* of the Canaã estate. These *posseiros* had already been evicted from the land three times. The most recent eviction was in October, when sixty military police accompanied by gunmen forced them from their occupied lands. João Canuto, his son tells us, was an outspoken and confrontational man. He believed the town's mayor, Adilson Larangeira, was secretly acting as a intermediary between the landowners, the *pistoleiros*, and the military police. João went to the local press with his story, which is when the real trouble began. Suddenly the death threats increased and João, fearing for his life, traveled to the state and federal capitals to ask government officials for protection. He refused, however, to back down or leave the area.

Then in mid-December five armed men appeared in front of the union headquarters in a truck owned by the Canaã estate. Accompanied by the trade union's lawyer, João went to the local police station and registered an official complaint against the Canaã estate. One week later he was gunned down while walking home. His killers shot him fourteen times at point-blank range just outside the town cemetery. No one considered the circumstances of his death excessive. Not in this town. Not in comparison to the one hundred forty pieces of lead that were fired into the body of Belchior Martins Costa, a peasant and local activist who had been killed in Rio Maria three years earlier.

Orlando and his brothers were teenagers at the time of their father's death. They didn't much care for politics. They followed their father's case and watched as a familiar pattern unfolded: several arrests were made, the police investigations were never completed, the detainees were eventually released. The boys grew up, married, and started their own families. Orlando eventually moved out of the area to the state of Goiás. In 1990 pressure from Amnesty International resulted in a reopening of João Canuto's case. That is when Orlando's life changed. His brothers, Paulo and José, who weren't involved in politics, started to receive death threats. Then one day Orlando and his brother-in-law Carlos Cabral, a union activist, were picked up by the police in connection with the killing of a man Orlando refers to as "a *pistoleiro* from a local ranch." Hearing of their arrest, Father Ricardo quickly intervened, and, lacking any plausible evidence, Orlando and Carlos were released. Orlando then went to see his mother before he went back to his wife in Goiânia. And "then it happened."

"What?" asks Vincent.

Orlando pauses for a moment, his slack and motionless body leaning against the windowsill. His voice, as always, is a monotone. His eyes dart left and right as if bombarded by the images of a flashback.

"They came to the house and said that they were from the federal police. They arrested us. They put handcuffs on me, with my hands behind. Paulo and José were handcuffed together. They pushed me into the car, then my brothers. They said that we were going to Maraba. During the trip they kept asking, 'How many have you killed?' We answered, 'None.' They asked if we were part of the invasion in Redenção. We said no. 'Yes, you were,' they kept saying. I told them that I had already been arrested on that charge and that I proved in court that I had nothing to do with it.

"They were carrying a machine gun, a 7.65, and three .38s. We left Rio Maria and passed through Xinguara. Before Sapucaia the car got stuck. A wheel had slipped through between two planks of the bridge. They put me outside and forced my two brothers, who each had one hand free, to lift and push the car. We then continued on the road. We passed through Sapucaia. Then when we were near the entrance of the Pontão

Ranch, one of them said, 'Let's go in here to piss.' I knew then that they were going to kill us. Then and there. They got out of the car and pulled my brothers out. I was the last one out of the car. Someone punched me hard on the head, then the driver shot me. The bullet passed through my belly and hit my wrist. At that moment I didn't feel pain. I threw myself against him and then against the other one who was getting ready to shoot me. I ran across the road and bumped into a barbwire fence. I fell over the fence and into the pasture. The bullets passed over me. If I hadn't fallen, I would have been shot. I got up, ran a little more, and fell down again. It's hard to get up when your hands are fastened behind your back so I decided to stay very still in the grass. Not moving at all. I then heard a lot of shots. Two of the men were coming through the fence looking for me. But they closed the circle in the wrong place, leaving me outside of it. I noticed the woods just ahead of me and I ran into the old brush. It's almost forest. I could hear them start the engine of the car and leave. I stayed in the woods a long time. I was afraid they were going to come back again. At eleven-thirty I went to a house near the crossroads. I asked someone to go to the road and get a ride for me because I couldn't raise my arms. They were handcuffed behind my back. The people were scared, so they wouldn't do it. But they offered to cut the chain, freeing my hands. It was midnight. I went out on foot in the direction of Xinguara, through the woods, afraid that the men would catch me. I was thirsty but afraid to drink, in case I might hemorrhage. Eventually, I made it to a gas station in Sapucaia where I hid until my friend Seu Rafael came and got me and brought me to Xinguara."

"And your brothers?"

"Both killed. Shots to the head. Their bodies left on the side of the road."

A year later Orlando's brother-in-law Carlos—he was acting president of the union after Expedito's assassination—was shot in the leg returning home from a meeting with Father Ricardo and some local activists. The gunman had fired three times, the first two bullets passing over his head. The *pistoleiro* had been hiding behind a wall in the town cemetery, the same cemetery in front of which João Canuto had been killed six years earlier. Two years after his brothers' death and seven years after his father's, there have still not been any convictions in the Canuto family murders, their cases "lost" in the disorganized bureaucracy of Rio Maria's court system.

—————

In the afternoon we visit one more time with José Fininho before heading back to the airport at Maraba. This time we slip past the guards with very little problem. We give him some food and explain to him that his wife decided not to come with us. "She couldn't leave the children," Vicent tells him. He takes this news in silence. His eyes, watery, drift off to some spot in the ceiling. He knows we are lying.

"I'm sorry but I can't sit up today," he says after a long pause. "I don't have the strength."

"Can we ask you just one more question?" Vincent asks.

"Certainly."

"You said the other day you were afraid for your life. Do you still feel that way?"

"Yes."

"Why?"

"I am concerned about being sent to Belém and being murdered on the way, in an arrangement made with one of the large landowners." For a second his eyes wander back to the ceiling. "That's common here." He turns and looks at us again. "I was lucky to have the civil police around, which prevented my murder. If they were not around, I would have been killed."

He pauses for a moment and looks to the doorway to see if anyone is listening.

"If I was left solely under the jurisdiction of the military police or the hired gunmen, I would be dead now." His head begins to nod and his eyes water as he bites his lower lip. It is sad to watch a man realizing he will be facing death alone.

Driving from Xinguara to Rio Maria, I watch as a light rain washes over the green fields and I ponder the sociological phenomenon that calls himself José Fininho: cattle thief, gunslinger, con artist. He had killed two men, frontier style, who probably would have killed him had they been given the chance. His wife had left him. He knew no one in town (the Protestants hadn't shown up for two days). Father Ricardo's Pastoral Land Commission refused to take on his case because of his criminal actions. He was in trouble and alone, his fate now solely in the hands of a highly suspect "justice" system. His fatal mistake in his downward spiral apparently was that he acted alone for much of his life. The Thin Man alienated anyone who could have come to his aid at a time like this including—as we saw—his wife. A man alone on the frontier is a man in trouble. José Fininho seems aware of that now.

Before leaving Rio Maria I go by to see a plaque in the middle of town that has recently been the focus of contention between the local mayor and the families of eight activists assassinated in the last decade. Father Ricardo told me part of the story and it piqued my interest. It seems just five months ago the Nobel Peace Prize winner Adolfo Pérez Esquivel visited Rio Maria. As someone who had attained international acclaim because of his work on behalf of Argentina's "disappeared," he wanted to show his concern about the violence that terrorized this region. Father Ricardo got permission from the town to hold a reception for the esteemed visitor and unveil a simple three-by-five-foot plaque commemorating the occasion. It read "On this day, December 4, 1991, in the presence of the Nobel Prize laureate Adolfo Pérez Esquivel, we pay homage to the martyrs of the land in Rio Maria." Drink and food were served, the press arrived, the Nobel laureate said a few words and then continued his tour of Brazil. The next day the mayor, Sebastião Emidio de Almeida, and several of his friends went to the site of the memorial and started digging up the plaque. When local journalists arrived on the scene, Mayor Emidio kicked one of the photographers while his cronies threatened and scuffled with the others. Eventually, Emidio and his men succeeded in removing the plaque and they carried it back to the town hall. Word of the confrontation quickly got back to Señor Esquivel, who sent a harsh letter of protest to Mayor Emidio. Fearing an embarrassing international incident, Emidio agreed to replace the plaque. But he rewrote the text.

"I'm not going to tell you what he replaced it with," said Ricardo. "Go see for yourself. It is just down the street."

So here I stand in front of "a gesture of peace" that only added to the insane havoc of this little frontier community. The mayor's version reads: "On this day, December 4, 1991, we pay homage to the winner of the Nobel Prize for Peace 1980, Adolfo Pérez Esquivel, and we thank him for his visit for Peace to our municipality." No mention of those who had died in land conflicts, those "martyrs" Esquivel's visit commemorated. This is the way life unfolds in southern Pará, a land where slavery still exists, where murderers go free, and where the quest for the truth brings with it a price tag of bloodshed.

> *Death will arrive one day;*
> *Only the hour is uncertain.*
> *Often it comes by surprise*
> *And like a bolt from the blue.*
> —Expedito Ribeiro da Souza
> (assassinated 2/2/1991, Rio Maria)

23

Rio de Janeiro, 1992

We've just passed through two roadblocks flashing our press credentials to bored guards in ill-fitting brown uniforms, probably employees of some obscure branch of the Rio de Janeiro police. Driving through the city earlier today we saw dozens of soldiers standing on street corners with machine guns dangling from shoulder straps. Some of them hassled us when we took their picture but the majority of them simply stood there, lockjawed, in statuesque military poses. Tucked away on strategically chosen side roads there were also tanks and armed personnel carriers filled with combat-ready troops. According to my Brazilian friends who were here at the time, this whole scene is eerily reminiscent of the 1964 military coup d'état. But in 1992 the abundance of soldiers in the streets of Rio simply reflects heightened security measures in anticipation of the United Nations Conference on Environment and Development—the Earth Summit. The city, a shell of what it was during its heyday in the 1960s, has also undergone a rapid cosmetic transformation in recent weeks: ambitious highway projects have been completed and new sidewalks put in place, dilapidated buildings have been refurbished, and water once again flows from turn-of-the-century fountains.

Increased security measures might explain the two roadblocks we just passed through, but we've now hit a third one, which appears to be a little different. Three guards with bizarre churlish grins step into the road flagging down our car. They are dressed in baggy blue jeans and shiny synthetic shirts, their hair crudely chopped. One of them pokes his head into the back window demanding cigarettes from my soundman Chris. Another pushes his face up against the front windshield, his bulbous nose and lips pressed flush against the glass, distorting the look of an already strangely contorted countenance. The third man, ignoring me in the driver's seat, thrusts his head into my window and addresses himself to our Brazilian production assistant Maria who sits next to me. *Why did I stop the car?* I ask myself.

"What is your name?" he says to her, his breath stale with nicotine, a little bubble of white froth forming on the edge of his mouth.

"Maria," she says with a small defensive smile.

The man whose face was pinned to the windshield is now off to the left of the road, arms extended, elbows bent, doing a little dance on the grassy edge, some odd version of *Fiddler on the Roof.*

"What's going on here?" I say to Maria.

She pauses a little too long. "I don't know," she says as her suitor suddenly laughs and looks at me.

"Whoa-whoa, big fella," I hear someone say in the backseat. In my review mirror I can see that the third "guard" (I'm beginning to have questions about their status) is rifling the pockets of my soundman Chris for cigarettes. A few fall to the ground, but the man catches one and lights it instantly with a match pulled from his shirt pocket.

"I think it is time to go," says Maria.

"Com licença"—With your permission—I say to the man standing by our window as I slowly put my hands on his chest, easing him away from the vehicle. He backs off with quick steps, looking like Charlie Chaplin spinning in reverse in a silent film. The cigarette thief now puffs away as he moves about our car taking photographs of us with an imaginary camera. I throw the vehicle into first gear and accelerate quickly down the dirt roadway, passing a large complex resem-

bling a religious retreat. On the front lawn are more people in ill-fitting clothes, standing about like discarded mannequins, some talking to themselves, others simply staring off into the distance.

"Check out those guys," says Chris, glued to the rear window. Looking back in the rearview mirror I see our three guards crouched by the roadside collecting the cigarettes that fell from our car.

"Is this what I think it is?" I say to Maria.

"The state psychiatric hospital," she says.

As we round the next corner we finally arrive at our intended destination: the Karioca Village, a cluster of three large thatched communal houses, recently constructed, nestled on a ridge of green mountains. This is the outskirts of Rio, an hour's drive from the high rises and beaches of Ipanema and Copacabana as well as the mountainside shantytowns the Brazilians call *favelas*. The Karioca Village is to be the site of the World Conference of Indigenous Peoples, an alternative meeting of native leaders from across the planet scheduled—strategically—one week prior to the start of the official UN conference. We were told earlier in the day by one of the Karioca Conference *representantes* that they expect sixteen hundred journalists and four hundred indigenous leaders. Already the place is packed with camera-toting foreigners spouting forth in a dozen languages. "It's a media zoo," I say to Chris as we unload our equipment from the car. "Roger that, Captain," he responds.

Chris Caris is a sinewy, short-haired, Marlboro-smoking son of Greek immigrants who was brought up in Washington, D.C. His most salient character traits are a love of quasi-military jargon and a predilection for abbreviations—part of his zealous, can-do attitude that has made him an excellent collaborator in the world of shoestring documentaries. He calls himself "C. C." and me "G. O." and has already started calling Rio de Janeiro "R. J." C. C. is here working as my soundman to take a break from his normal job as the production coordinator of our New York office. When we arrived yesterday he insisted on taking a taxi ride by the shoreline, his head swiveling left and right as he whistled "The Girl from Ipanema," another gringo in a tropical paradise, his head full of illusions created by the strange bits and pieces of Brazilian culture that through time have managed to sift up to North America: Carmen Miranda in black-and-white films, the bodies of murdered street kids on CNN, the beach with its girls in "dental floss" bikinis, and finally Carnaval: "the biggest and *wildest* fucking party in the world," as a young American tourist once described it to me on an overnight flight to Rio.

Never in the history of the world has there been so large a gathering of indigenous peoples. There are Sarawaks from Malaysia, Hill People from Pakistan, Apaches and Onondaga people from North America, Sumi people from the Nordic countries, Aborigines from Australia, Maoris from New Zealand, and dozens of other "forgotten peoples," as they've been called in the popular press, including a wide spectrum of indigenous societies from Brazil. There are those who have arrived here in the clothing of the Western world but most of these leaders are in traditional dress. Some are wearing flowing grass tongas, tall elaborately woven headdresses, brightly colored cotton skirts, shorts, and shirts, ornate necklaces, beads, earrings, and nose rings. They are here holding symposiums on the "struggles" of their communities, and occasionally giving impromptu press conferences to international journalists looking for a little background color prior to the start of the UN conference.

"We are here to speak about the problems of the villages and to tell the other Indians to continue fighting together," said Davi Kopenawa to a group of journalists earlier in the day. "Because if we don't unite, the whites are going to go on dominating our lives and our work."

Davi, whom I haven't seen in two years, has become a veteran of the movement, someone with wide recognition in the international arena, someone the press seeks out, an acknowledged spokesperson for the Yanomami people. And he has got something to talk about. Not only did President Collor drive the gold miners out of Yanomami territory two years ago but just two days before the start of the Karioca Conference his government completed the demarcation of Davi's people's land, thereby officially recognizing their traditional territory.

But as with any of the large conferences I have attended in recent years, there are early warning signs of problems to come. For every indigenous leader here there seem to be at least two or three photographers colliding, cursing, tripping, and shoving, all of them trying to get the best angle, the most intimate exposure. The scene is similar to Altamira, but more extreme: there is more hysteria, more tension. Given the current climate of interest in tropical forests, images of indigenous people are hot-ticket items. These photographers seem to be particularly interested in Brazilian Indians whose elaborate ritual outfits have attracted the largest hordes of image gatherers.

As the day draws to a close I notice a handful of errant psychiatric patients from the local hospital appearing in the crowd of photographers. Among them are the "guards" who confronted us earlier in the day. The patients stand alone, catching the action as their heads pan back and forth, very often engaged in lively conversations with themselves. Somehow they manage to blend into the insanity that has come to dominate this event, and they go unnoticed.

There has been a great deal of tension in Brazil leading up to Earth Summit '92, much of it traceable back to the Woodstock of Amazonia, the Altamira Conference in 1989. That crystallizing event galvanized a generation of Brazilian and international citizens increasingly concerned about the future of the environment. Among their ranks were legions of schoolchildren, journalists, ecologists, college kids, and politicians. All of these groups have in their own way been trying to stop "the threat to our tropical forests." This seemingly innocent phrase triggers a wave of xenophobic fear in the hearts of Brazilian nationalists. The American senator Robert Kasten— one of a new generation of "green" politicians—declared shortly after the death of Chico Mendes that, regarding Brazil's rain forests, "We need them and we use them—so they're our rain forests too." While those of us in Europe and North America see ourselves as expressing concerns, within Brazil such sentiments are perceived as threats. And the government has been quick to react.

"It is the greatest international pressure that Brazil has lived through in the whole of its history," Brazil's foreign secretary Paolo Tarso Flecha de Lima said in 1989 just one month after the Altamira Conference. The environment secretary Fernando Mesquita—a man booed off the stage in Altamira—was more direct: "There is a real danger of foreign occupation of the Amazon. We are seeing a concerted international effort to hold back development in Brazil."

In 1990 the former president José Sarney—a politician well known for his close ties to the military—took a strongly defensive posture vis-a-vis his adversaries from abroad and what he termed their "international greed." He began lashing out at his foreign critics while reasserting Brazil's control over the region. Environmentalism, Sarney said, was a "Trojan horse" hiding other interests, and statistics on rain forest destruction part of a "campaign of scientific falsehoods." In his speeches he began to use the age-old Brazilian battle cry *"Amazônia é nossa"*—The Amazon is ours. Addressing the high command of the armed forces, he said that "now more than ever" the military had a "mission": defend the Amazon. In 1991 the Brazilian Congress also took action. They began an investigation of a purported foreign plot to "planetize" the Amazon, to quote the country's justice minister Jarbas Passarinho. The message being sent back to the international community was clear: Brazil's politicians— and average citizens—didn't want anyone telling them what to do with their country. It was bad enough that the nation was hostage to North American banks with $121 billion of debt—a legacy of the military dictatorship that had appointed Sarney as part of its transition government. Compromise proposals like Tom Lovejoy's "Debt for Nature" were out of the question as far as Sarney was concerned. "We accept international aid but we don't accept conditions," was how he put it.

But President Sarney's bid to rouse nationalist sentiments could not resuscitate his ailing political career. He was part of the old guard. In 1985 the Archdiocese of São Paolo published *Brasil: Nunca Mais (Brazil: Never Again)*, a thorough documentation of the thousands of people who disappeared and were tortured during the two decades of military dictatorship. In later years, a great deal of public rage was vented against the former dictators and their henchmen who had been given unconditional amnesties as part of their agreement to return the country to democratic rule. Now the electorate wanted to distance itself from the past. With the 1990 election, the nation's citizens ushered in a man who came to symbolize the arrival of a new generation: Fernando Collor de Mello, the country's first democratically elected executive official in twenty-six years. Collor was a young, flamboyant *politico* with the slicked-back hair and Teflon manner that defined high-powered players in the 1980s, a man who spoke six languages, wore designer suits, and came from one of the most powerful families in Brazil's Northeast.

Once in office Collor took special care to distinguish himself from his predecessor. Unlike Sarney, he has been sensitive to international concerns, more accommodating to the wishes of *estrangeiros*, foreigners. His quick response to the barrage of questions about the Yanomami after his visit to Washington was just the beginning of a campaign to give Brazil a greener image. Since he took power, he has completely reshaped the country's agenda on environmental concerns. He not only kicked forty-five thousand gold miners out of Yanomami territory and demarcated their lands, but his administration also pushed through the initial paperwork to recognize Kayapo territory. Collor also enticed the UN to hold the Earth Summit in Rio and he appointed a vocal government critic as the country's environment secretary.

But while the new president was scoring points in the international arena, tensions were building at home. Conservative politicians and frontier developers were depicting Indians as obstacles to development, pawns of gringo environmentalists in an international conspiracy to limit the growth of the Brazilian economy. Outspoken Brazilian congressmen believed the indigenous societies' retention of their extensive traditional homelands was holding Brazil back, trapping the country in the Third World. "Civilizing" them or "integrating" them were recommended as the optimal solutions to the Indian question. In 1990 the frontier politician Gilberto Mestrinho, governor of

Amazonas, the largest state in the Amazon Basin, said, "Behind the environmental movement there are economic interests who fear that the economic development of the Amazon would risk investments made in other parts of the world." His recent campaign for reelection included hyperbolic promises to provide every peasant with a chain saw and promote the hunting of endangered species. "In Canada and the United States people use chain saws. Why do our people have to go back to axes?" he asked a North American reporter in Rio. But while Mestrinho and others lambasted international environmentalists, in the run-up to the UN conference Collor's new government was attempting to take a tough stance on environmental issues. It had recently levied million-dollar fines on the illegal activities of two mining companies and a lumber concern in the Amazon, assertive actions that contrasted sharply with the laissez-faire attitudes of the Sarney government. These actions, praised in Europe and North America, were referred to as "absurd exhibitionism" by nationalist critics like Governor Mestrinho.

But it wasn't only the frontier politicians who were outraged by Collor's actions. Shortly before the Earth Summit there was a wave of anti-interventionist journalism in the Brazilian press, much of it critical of the recent role that Indians and the international community had come to play in determining the future of the country's Amazon Basin. Paulo Francis, a popular columnist and TV commentator, wrote a scathing critique of Collor as someone who "gives land in abundance" to the Indians, a people, he said, who "weren't even of use as slaves." The preeminent Brazilian newsmagazine *Veja* warned in the week prior to the summit that "it's time to correct the mistakes of foreigners who talk about Indians, burning, and Amazonia." These nationalist sentiments were echoed by frontier fortune-seekers in the Amazon Basin. In the northeastern state of Amapá, just a month before the start of the summit, I spoke with Antonio Feijáo, president of a local miners' organization that has been vying with Indian groups for the mineral rights to their land. Feigão was also a protégé and ally of José Altino

Machado. "For us, if the indigenous areas continue growing, then they will eventually connect," he told me outside a gold store in the state capitol of Macapá. "So then we are concerned that the UN and the First World countries will intervene here in order to create a state, that is a geographic area and a people, which will be used as a device to create a new nation. And then we will be left with a separate enclave such as there is in South Africa as in the case of Swaziland."

In this current climate of heightened xenophobia Brazil's Indians were increasingly being cast as worthless social drones, the naive dupes of international environmentalists. Gilson Machado, a conservative congressman, wrote during this period: "The image of the Indian using feathers, living naked and useless, and sleeping in grass huts, really belongs in Westerns from the beginning of this century.... We should take advantage of Rio-92 and the lessons of the experiences of more advanced peoples so that we can have above all *Ecology with Development*. And as for the Brazilian Indian, all of us who love our land and our people would like to have him properly integrated to true civilization, as in developed nations. We should never agree to see him *eternally dressed in a tanga*."

This image of the Indian as a pawn and token of a larger international plot was, however, very different from another image that was circulating outside of Brazil and within certain liberal cliques in Rio and São Paulo. To these groups the Indian was not an obstacle to development but a saintly, often child-like, being who was also key in the movement to save the environment—someone who could make the world a better place for a new generation of New Age, sympathetic, ecologically concerned citizens. This 1992-model Nobel Savage was an elaboration on the version that had appeared at Altamira in 1989. The Save the Rain Forest movement had taken on momentum in the intervening years, accelerating the resuscitation of an icon of Western European culture that had lain dormant for several decades.

As repackaged by the environmentally concerned, this new sentimentalized token of eco-consciousness emerged in a wide variety of media incarnations in the weeks prior to the summit. In a Brazilian documentary series on Indians of the Xingú Park, the on-camera commentator told viewers: "The world of the Indian is like a dream. The encounter with the Indian is like a submersion into another time and space, a departure from our civilization, a return to innocence." Championing the cause of the Kayapo, Anita Roddick, founder of the Body Shop Corporation, described Paulinho Payakan as "a new Gandhi"—a characterization, considering its prior application to Chico Mendes, that was now bordering on cliché. She went on to provide the Kayapo leader with a plane while setting up a Brazil nut processing plant in his village of A'ukre. Kayapo products and jewelry were now regular fixtures in her stores, part of the Trade-Not-Aid project she had devised with her husband and partner Gordon. In the weeks prior to the Earth Summit life-size photos of smiling Kayapo also added an exotic element to Body Shop displays in Europe, Canada, and the United States. Brazilian television commercials, even more blatant in their appropriation of the Indian, used images of indigenous peoples as trendy icons in a product pitch. In one Lee advertisement a young white man encounters a group of semiclothed, potentially threatening natives in the forest. He takes off his jeans, trades them for a bow and arrow, and walks off smiling and victorious with the Indian weapons in hand. The tag line: "It's not Lee that is different. It is the others that are the same."

However one views these popularized images—exploitation? cultural appropriation?—they received minor play in comparison to one depiction that turned the noble savage into a virtual deity. This was a cover story in the U.S. publication *Parade* magazine which appeared in April of 1992. The article was part of a public relations effort tied to the broadcast of a rain forest documentary on American television. The magazine's cover carried a color photograph of Paulinho Payakan in extreme close-up wearing ceremonial paint and looking directly into the camera, staring at us, confronting our world with his vision. The story was entitled "The Man Who Could Save the World." The noble savage as ecological redeemer had now reached Christlike proportions. "I Fight for Our Future" read

the subtitle accompanying a photograph of Payakan at Altamira, followed by another line that read: "It's a battle Chief
Payakan began for the survival of his people, but what's at stake
is the survival of us all." The opening paragraph was strangely
reminiscent of the prologue to a Disney story:

> Several years ago, a young Kayapo Indian named Paulinho
> Payakan left his village in the Amazon rain forest of Brazil in
> order to save it. He ventured to the outside world, warning
> that if the forest disappears, his people will die. Today he is
> still standing against the forces of destruction as time runs
> out. At stake is far more than the fate of a remote Kayapo
> village. . . .

This depiction of Payakan contrasted sharply with the man I
had come to know over the years. Just prior to the release of this
article I had seen him in New York, where he was speaking at a
conference. He seemed anxious and depressed, but he was
someone who had a reputation for violent mood swings. When I
asked about his participation at the upcoming Earth Summit, he
said he was uncertain if he was going to attend the UN event.
He was beginning to question the point of all these trips to
North America and Europe. He didn't know what they'd
amounted to. The confident, charismatic leader who at one time
had been at the forefront of the Save the Rain Forest movement
seemed, in just three short years, to have become one of its most
embittered refugees. He said he was tired of hearing "promises"
to help his people—promises that were never fulfilled. On this
trip to New York, Payakan seemed much more intent on
escaping our world than on saving it. But that was not a story to
interest *Parade*. These current concerns of Payakan were
probably too real, too specific, too complicated. What the media
at this time wants is a kind of truth that approximates fiction in
its blending of fantasy and reality to propagate a cause. The
Parade article was simply part of a groundswell of attention concerning Amazonia which, it appears, was reaching its apex at
the Earth Summit. Environmentalists in Europe and the United
States and, with increasing frequency, "green capitalists" and

media organizations were in need of heroes around which to focus their causes and campaigns. The bigger the heroes, the better the exposure.

———

Brazilians are world-renowned for their Carnavals: raucous, Dionysian four-day celebrations that revolve around the parades of samba schools in minute, shimmering, sensuous costumes whose occupants dance through the boulevards of the country's towns and cities immersing themselves in bacchanalian excess just before the arrival of the Catholic Lent. It is a ritual without sanctions, without rules, a time of unlimited possibilities. Carnaval, Brazilians say, helps them to recharge their batteries. The residual effect of this annual event is deeply embedded in the Brazilian psyche. It can manifest itself throughout the year: a party, a soccer match, or some simple celebration can suddenly become transformed into frenzied, cathartic ritual at a moment's notice. That is what has happened on the fourth day of the Karioca Conference: the place has started to get out of control. It has became Carnavalesque.

News stories on the conference have been running on Brazilian television all week. But it must have crossed a threshold because today there is a surge in the number of tourists stopping by to get a look at the plethora of indigenous peoples. Middle-class *mamães* and *papais* with kids in tow are arriving in the village, cameras dangling from their necks, their heads glued to video recorders. All of them seem to be searching for tourist trophies: an Indian necklace or flute purchased for a few cruzeiros, perhaps even a photograph of *la família* with one of *os indios*. As C. C. and I take a break from filming, we watch Brazilian fathers flagging down passing conference participants in traditional dress, mostly Brazilian Indians. Politely they ask the men or women to pose with their wife and children. *"Por favor,"* one man says. "It would make them so happy." If the Indian accepts—which in most cases they do—the father invariably lines everyone up with the Indian in the middle of the shot. And there before us is a sociological centerpiece of Brazilian culture: an indigenous icon captured in a photographic moment, the troubled totem of a conflicted culture, a recognizable but very distant cousin. Watching this scene unfold only reconfirms what has become obvious in recent days: that the Indian in Brazil has become an object of contemplation—to some a relic of a distant past, to others the Achilles' heel of a faltering national economy.

Among today's new wave of Carnaval characters is a strange cadre of rear-guard gate-crashers. Some of them dress as Indians. Others call themselves Indians. But neither of these two groups are, in fact, Indians. They are whites who have decided to cross over into the world of the indigenous people, a world "of exoticism and fascination," according to one such aficionado. In this group is Loretta Bartel, a gangly woman in her late twenties with long, bleached blond hair. She is dressed in a cowhide bikini top and an ankle-length leopard-skin skirt. Her face is adorned with two large diagonal swaths of red and blue paint. The intention, I assume, is to approximate indigenous facial paint, but it makes her look more like a walk-on character from a *Star Trek* episode than a legitimate participant in a conference of global indigenous leaders. Originally from Yugoslavia, she has in recent years made Brazil her home. C. C. and I have approached her in the midst of her publicity efforts for the dance group she manages, called Indio Olegui, whom we filmed earlier in the day.

We introduce ourselves, explaining that we are covering this event for a documentary for U.S. television. She hands me a press release for her group. Yes, she says, she would be delighted to answer a few questions.

"Could you tell us why you are dressed the way you are dressed today?"

"I am dressed like this for very personal reasons."

"And?"

She shakes her head no. This is sacred ground, I suppose. I glance down at the opening line of the press release. It reads "Let me invite you to a thrilling journey to a past we all share." I try another tack.

"When do you think white people first became interested in the life of the Indians?"

"It started when white women were first kidnapped by the Indians," she says as she pushes her hair back and adjusts the straps of her rawhide bikini top.

"How is that?"

"The European women arrived here and the Indians kidnapped them. Then they took them to their tribes. Then the white men's leaders would send soldiers to bring back the women. But they arrived there and saw how happy the women were, that they didn't want to come back. This is the way miscegenation began."

Okay.

"What do you think lies in store for the future of Indian people?"

"Indian man is strong. Indian man knows what he wants. Indian man has survived all these terrible things for the last five hundred years. He is strong and he will survive."

"Right. Okay, let me ask you another question."

"I am sorry, I have to go with these other journalists," she says, gesturing to a cluster of photographers anxious to do another photo session with their exotic subject. "Please come and see us perform this afternoon."

C. C. and I spend the next several hours filming indigenous leaders in different workshop settings, trying to capture aspects not covered earlier in the week. Later in the day we look for Loretta and her group but they seem to have disappeared. One conference organizer tells us they were asked to leave. In the tradition of Buffalo Bill, I assume Loretta has taken her show on the road.

The next day we encounter "Tall Strong" seated among a group of journalists diligently taking down his every word in notepads. "If you add up the Cherokee people in Oklahoma and the Cherokee in Taos, you probably have well over eight million people," he says. "Because my tribe alone, Atoyak, which is the name of a river in Texas, has about four million people."

In the center of Tall Strong's circle, one lone television camera is focused on him. Next to the cameraman is a slender woman in a flowing white cotton dress, large oval glasses, and a white turban. She is holding a clipboard and occasionally leans over to whisper directions to the cameraman. Tall Strong continues.

"You cannot see an Indian killing just for the fun of it. An Indian does not kill a beast if he doesn't need to. But that doesn't mean that Indians do not raise cattle. An Indian won't kill a tree if he does not need to extract it from the soil."

Tall Strong doesn't converse, he makes pronouncements. His every word is uttered as if it is about to be etched in stone. His hair is short, brown, parted on the side. He is dressed in a light brown three-piece suit with a pale blue tie. It's the look in his eye that is unsettling. It's glazed over in a way I have come to associate with American Jesus freaks and TV infomercial hucksters: an empty look, as if the human spirit has been vaporized from his body and replaced by some synthetic substitute. A tabloid print reporter would have a field day covering the Lorettas and Tall Strongs of the conference. I can imagine the headline: ALIENS INVADE BODIES OF WHITES WHO BECOME INDIANS.

We move about the periphery grabbing various shots of this alien Indian interacting with reporters. At one point he stops his lecture and pulls out both his Brazilian and Cherokee passports. Tall Strong, he tells us, is his Indian name. His Brazilian name is Reinaldo Livio. The proof of his dual identity is in his documents. A German photographer fires off shots of Tall Strong in various poses: Tall Strong smiling, Tall Strong serious, Tall Strong with passports extended before him. Part white man and part Indian, Tall Strong, we are being asked to believe, is a living example of someone who has actually crossed over and *become* an Indian. Why am I so skeptical when all these other journalists seem to be accepting his words at face value? Isn't it possible that he has done what others before him have not been able to do? Could it be that Father Calleri or even Sting could have learned from his experiences? What can Tall Strong tell us?

As I move closer for a better angle of Tall Strong with the photographers, someone grabs my arm, then steps in front of the camera. It is the woman in the white turban, her face "fish-eyed" by the distorted perspective of my wide-angle lens. By her accent I can tell she is from North America.

"You cannot film this man!"

"Excuse me?"

"I said you are not permitted to film this man."

"Okay." I continue filming.

"I have exclusive rights to his life. This press conference was arranged by us for our film," she says as she grabs hold of my arm again, ruining my shot.

I stop and stare at her.

"We are the only ones who can film him."

"I'm sorry, but that's not possible."

"No. I'm sorry."

"Listen, you are in a public space. Look around, there are a dozen other journalists here. I can do whatever I want."

"Sorry. No other television cameras." She steps in front of my lens again. Tall Strong, in the midst of his press conference, glances at us from the corner of his eye.

"Can I ask who you are?"

"I'm not telling you that."

"Okay," I say. "Listen. You find someone from the Conference to tell me to stop doing what I am doing, and until then I am going to continue filming this event." I pause. "Okay?"

"You have no right . . ." she says, her jowls trembling with rage. She stares at me for a moment, silent, her eyes blinking rapidly. Then she turns and disappears into the crowd, leaving me and the reporters with Tall Strong.

By this time I have heard a good deal of Tall Strong's official biography as presented to the press, none of whom seem to doubt that this man is in fact a Cherokee Indian. He is, he says, also "a Tupi Indian from Brazil" by virtue of his one-eighth Indian ancestry. He was born and raised in Brazil but then came to the United States, where he lived for ten years in New York. There he met a Cherokee Indian who "understood that I was an Indian" and introduced him to the Cherokee people, who issued him a passport and made him a "Cherokee citizen."

"Can you explain for us your official status here?" I ask Tall Strong after we pull him away from the other reporters.

"In this particular event, okay. I am a guest lecturer here to talk about the Cherokee nation, our history, and the way we face the indigenous cause nowadays."

"Do you think that, as someone brought up in white society, you can really understand indigenous people?"

"There are several misconceptions about the way the white man is interfering with the indigenous cause," says Tall Strong as he clears his throat, his eyes now scanning left and right. "You are going to find, studying a little bit of history, that in several occasions, the ones who were fighting for the human rights most bravely were not Indians at all."

"Really?"

"Yes. It is proven. In history."

"But what are the qualities that you have that distinguish you and allow you to enter that society?"

"It took me some time to understand what it takes to become an Indian and what it takes to fight for the Indians, but it's so damn simple, it's so easy that I've surprised myself," he says, suddenly elated. "And I've asked myself, Why in the world didn't I jump in this boat before?" At this point Tall Strong laughs to himself and flashes a smile. A photographer behind me takes his picture.

"And what is that simple answer?" I ask, waiting for my photo colleague to move on.

"The simple answer?"

"Yes," I say. "I'd like to know what it is."

"Willingness, that's all. If you want to play tennis and if you want to be the best, what do you do? You learn how to play it and then you get on the tennis court and you play it. And then you can become the best." He smiles again. Eyes no longer flashing. He's concentrated. On a roll. This is what he came here to do. To "use the media today," as he put it.

"But if you sit down and just watch, you are never going to learn. If you want to swim. It is the same thing. Anything in life happens to be the same. Fighting for the Indians is no different at all."

"Anything else you would like to say?" I ask, noticing that his agent/producer has returned, lingering in the background, her image caught in the corner of my frame, once again ruining my shot. I step to the right, adjusting the angle to make certain she is out of frameline.

"No. I think I have said enough," he says.

"Roger that" says C. C. as Tall Strong walks away.

For the rest of the afternoon I keep thinking about Tall Strong's concept of "willingness," his tennis metaphor, and the regret he now feels for not "jumping in the boat before." In the five years I have been covering Brazil, I have met a good number of people who have tried in various ways to cross into the world of the Indians. There have been gold miners and missionaries who lived with them, anthropologists who spent their lives studying them, and activists, rock stars, and filmmakers who have spent countless hours toiling away in apparently sincere efforts to understand and support their causes. In both Brazil and the United States I have met many people like Loretta and Tall Strong, individuals who appear at such events adorned in facial paint or Indian regalia claiming to have some distant link to an indigenous heritage, all of them speaking on the Indian's behalf without questioning the irony and potential pitfalls of inhabiting another culture so very distant from their own. Is it possible Tall Strong has succeeded where others have failed? Has he found a way to transport himself unmolested through that tricky middle ground that exists between their world and ours? *Yes*, I think. *Maybe I have been too hard on Tall Strong.* But then I run into Oren Lyons, one of the elders of the Onondaga people, a group of North American Indians currently living on a reservation in upstate New York.

"What do you make of this guy Tall Strong?" I ask.

"We questioned him and he said he was from the Salagas Nation in Texas," says Oren, a veteran of North American Indian activism. "And we said 'How many people do you represent?' And he said there were one hundred in one group, two hundred in another group, and three million in Texas." Oren pauses for a moment, then gives the camera an exaggerated roll of the eyes. "I mean, it made us suspicious because there's maybe one-point-eight million Indians in the United States, maybe the same in Canada." Oren looks into the camera, shakes his head, laughs, and walks off with several other North American Indians.

Later in the day we get a few more establishing shots of the conference grounds and some interviews with various participants. In the course of filming I notice in the midst of the crowd several more patients from the psychiatric hospital. They are jittery and nervous and among them I recognize, once again, two of the culprits from the roadblock. As before, they are puffing frantically on cigarettes and talking to themselves. But today there is something different about them. Their faces have been painted in broad strokes of red ochre stretching from the center of the forehead down to the tip of the nose. Maybe they too have crossed over the line and become Indians. That wouldn't surprise me. At this point nothing would.

24

"Where's Payakan?" I was often asked by journalists and environmentalists as the Karioca Conference drew to a close. "He should be here," they would say as they walked off, dejected, into the crowds. The big event, the Earth Summit, was just two days away. More than one hundred of the world's leaders would soon be deciding on the environmental and developmental policy of the United Nations for the coming decade. Payakan represented the voice of the disenfranchised, a *symbol* of ecological alternatives, one person whose international recognition would be critical in drawing attention to the fact that indigenous people were being excluded from casting a vote in the official UN decision making.

That Payakan's absence posed a dilemma for environmentalists was easy to understand. For those who had followed the Save the Rain Forest movement for the last several years, it was difficult to imagine an event of this magnitude without him. He was the person environmentalists wanted to see confronting world leaders just as he had confronted the Brazilian government in the past. He was a hero, a fixture in their imaginations. His absence created a strange anxiety in Rio. It was as if you were at the local cinema watching *Rocky VI* without Sylvester Stallone in the lead. Something was missing. It just wasn't the same movie.

The impact of Payakan's efforts was inestimable. Over the

last few years he had been the central catalyst for a series of unprecedented ecological victories in Brazil—and in the process had become a shining example not only for domestic and international environmentalists but for countless other indigenous societies in the Western Hemisphere. This was the man who helped to block the construction of dams at Altamira, who led a successful effort to halt nuclear waste disposal on Kayapo lands, who outwitted the judicial system by shrewdly combating charges of defamation, who campaigned domestically and internationally for the rights of the Yanomami Indians, who helped Raoni to set up the demarcation of Kayapo lands, who created the beginnings of a pan-Indian alliance in Brazil, and who forged an unprecedented, ecologically sustainable economic partnership with the Body Shop Corporation, the first of a new generation of green capitalist corporations that was reaching out to the "peoples of the forest." In recognition of such efforts Ted Turner had recently presented him with a Better World Society Award at New York's Waldorf Astoria, where he had his picture taken with Jimmy Carter—an image (with Payakan in a yellow feather headdress) that received gratifying international circulation, especially in the Brazilian press. And in 1992 the United Nations awarded him its prestigious Global 500 for his work in environmental preservation. So, yes, he is a big draw.

The problem is that so far Payakan isn't anywhere to be seen. He's not even in Rio. At least, not in the flesh. On the opening day of the Summit his image does appear in living color on every street-corner kiosk in town. Brazil's most popular newsmagazine, *Veja*, is running a glossy cover photograph of Payakan similar in style to the one that appeared recently in *Parade* magazine.

This time, however, a different message is being relayed. The article is entitled "The Savage," and its cover headline reads: "The symbolic leader of ecological purity tortures and rapes a white student, and then flees to his tribe." Overnight, the Man Who Would Save the World has suddenly been transformed from an environmentalist hero into a violent, diabolical monster. "It is a story to make your skin crawl," write *Veja*'s journalists Laurentino Gomes and Paulo Silber, "documented in the testimonies of five witnesses recorded in an inquiry conducted by the chief of police and in the work of a medical team from the hospital in the city of Redenção."

"I don't believe this for a second!" says an American television journalist as she glances through the article, snapping through its pages like an anxious client in a hair salon. She is surrounded by other international journalists and environmentalists who have congregated at a week-long conference running parallel to the Earth Summit and calling itself the Earth Parliament. This is another of the events where Payakan had been expected. He is on the Earth Parliament's board of advisors, a longtime friend of its organizer Darel Posey, and listed as one of their key speakers.

According to the report in *Veja*, not only has Payakan committed a brutal rape, but he *and* his wife, Irekran, are being charged with acts of "cannibalism" and attempted murder. The article is running with the subtitle "An Explosion of Savage Instinct." Its contents provide lurid, sensationalist descriptions of a purported attack by Payakan and his wife against a "white virgin" named Sylvia Letícia Ferreira. Letícia, as she is known in town, is an eighteen-year-old high school student, a neighbor of Payakan in a frontier community located near Kayapo territory. *Veja* calls Letícia a "Friend of the Indians," a babysitter who on occasion looked after the three young children of Payakan and his wife. "He raped her," the journalists write, "with the help of his wife, Irekran, and in front of his eldest daughter, Maial, five years old." The car in which this brutal and "cannibalistic" act took place is a tiny white Chevette which, according to the *Veja* reporters, looked "as if an animal had bled inside it."

As I glance through the article there are a number of aspects of the reporting that I find disturbing. Most of the prosecutor's accusations are presented as established fact. Nowhere does the story mention that the alleged incident took place in a town in southern Pará notorious for its long history of vendetta, trumped-up charges, and manufactured evidence.

"It's a plot, a conspiracy," the American television journalist tells me when I ask her what she thinks happened. "They've been trying to get to him for years. They killed Chico and they couldn't kill Payakan. So they did this."

The *Veja* story is only the beginning of what appears to be a media blitz. Later that afternoon TV Manchete, the country's second largest television network, runs an interview with the state of Pará's chief of police, Brivaldo Soares.

"He said his wife was to blame for the incident because she was jealous," says Chief Soares, surrounded by a group of journalists, their microphones anxiously bobbing within inches of his face.

"Both took part in the rape, then?" asks one of the reporters.
"Yes."

"Did they force her to take off her clothes?"

"Both used violence to take off her clothes. She didn't want that. He admitted she didn't want that."

Throughout the country, reports such as this one dominate the print and television news. With Payakan secluded in his village, most of the accounts focus on interviews with local Redenção officials or the family of Letícia Ferreira. The Kayapo attending the Earth Summit—including Raoni—give only guarded responses to the leading questions of Brazilian and international reporters.

Then just two days after the initial *Veja* article, TV Globo—Brazil's number-one television network—broadcasts an interview with Payakan from his village of A'ukre. After a long day of covering the events of the Summit, I watch the newscast at the home of Patricia Monte-môr and José Ignacio Parente, friends and colleagues who have provided invaluable help in every story I have done in Brazil. On camera Payakan looks nervous and disoriented. Behind him I can see his lawyer, José Carlos Castro, pacing in the background, the same attorney who represented him in 1988 when he was accused of defaming the nation of Brazil after his trip to the World Bank. In a relatively fluent but still problematic Portuguese, Payakan speaks to the reporter from TV Globo who remains off camera.

"It really happened. We drinking. I drinking, my wife drinking, the girl called Letícia drinking, and the people accompanying, drinking. Everything happened because of the drinking. Now, I'm not afraid or hiding here."

There is complete silence in the living room as we all react to what Payakan has just said. "I can't believe he said that," says Patricia. I couldn't believe it as well. Was this in fact an on-camera confession, the last act of a fallen hero? It appeared to all of us to be a confession. But then, as I watch, I realize we never heard the question that prompted the response. His answer could in fact be interpreted in several different ways. He did say, "It really happened." But *what* really happened?

It is becoming a question increasingly difficult to answer in Brazil. This story—packaged with its bizarre imagery of savages, virgins, cannibals, and demons—is hard to believe and almost impossible to decipher. It's symptomatic of an increasing problem I am having covering stories here. The more I know, the less certain I am of what I am seeing. Somehow in the beginning, in those early years in Yanomami territory, the dimensions of the conflicts between indigenous people and Western European cultures seemed much simpler, more black and white: Indians and gold miners were fighting over land. People were dying. In spite of the miners' denials there were definite historical precedents for the potential impact of contact diseases. And there was the undeniable proof of the bodies of the sick and the dying. That story made sense in a very tangible way. But this story is different. The exaggerated tale of the "savage" Payakan has gone beyond the dimensions of credible journalism. We now seem to be operating on the level of myth, ritual, and ceremony. Perhaps this new dimension of the story is the inevitable result of the hype and hyperbole of recent years, part of the confusing middle ground that results when our worlds become intimately intertwined in collaborative ventures as simple as harvesting Brazil nuts or as complex as saving the rain forest.

It is the choreography of this breaking news event that first alerted me to the fact that this story has entered a different plane of reality. What I find most troublesome is the way news of the purported rape appeared on the opening day of the Summit, and how the layout and writing of the *Veja* article seems to have been self-consciously created as a counterweight to the *Parade* story.

Who is there to blame for the mess that Payakan now finds himself in? I have asked myself repeatedly over these last few days. Is this the story of an Indian who has gone too far into our world and actually lost his mind? Is it, as the American television journalist suggested, part of some sinister plot conceived in southern Pará and then acted out in collaboration with vindictive media people in Rio? Is *Veja* perhaps right? Is Payakan really a savage? Have I been deceiving myself every time I refer to him simply as "a Brazilian indigenous leader concerned with the environment"? Perhaps this entire story is simply the inevitable result of overinflating the status of a leader—the killing-our-heroes complex resurfacing once again, from Joan of Arc through Gandhi, JFK, Malcolm X, Martin Luther King—and now Payakan?

Whether or not Payakan and his wife are innocent or guilty doesn't explain the severity of this attack in the press and its strange dialectical relationship to the previous press coverage, which had recently approached the level of idol worship. The responsibility for this part of the story, I am beginning to believe, is on all of us who have at one time or another followed or participated in Payakan's rise to fame: environmentalists, journalists, gold miners, anthropologists, loggers, politicians, eco-groupies, rock stars, green capitalists, and—yes—even Payakan himself. Over a period of four years we've all been actors in one way or another in an elaborate, and inevitably destructive, modern ceremony that has brought about his ritual downfall, a ceremony as complex and significant as any currently being acted out in those secluded forest villages lying north of the Amazon River. We, of course, can't see our own rituals taking place because we've come to believe we are divorced from this part of the "primitive world." We live in different times. We consume culture; it doesn't consume us. That's what makes us different from them—the savages, be they noble or violent—those who have not yet entered our civilized modern era—the ones who have yet to be acculturated, miscegenated, saved, protected, preserved. We like to think that we operate in a universe separate from those people steeped in their primitive rituals, a people who ironically have baffled the conquering white man for the past five hundred years. Indians in the Western Hemisphere represent the ultimate "other" in a multicultural society. The ones we've yet to figure out, but whose culture we often appropriate. The ones whose way of life, we tell ourselves, is so vastly different from our own. The savages.

But I have come to believe that we are not so distant from these people as we like to believe, or, as that lone soldier in the New World once wrote, *We are all savages*. I've come to accept the fact that our own lives are steeped in our own dense layers of ritual, myth, and ceremony. We call them sports, politics, the arts, and journalism, but they are part of our ritual expression, our attempts to establish a place for ourselves in this world, to maintain an equilibrium and make sense of the tragedies and mysteries of the human condition. Try as we might to deny it, human beings are ritual beings. We can approximate a dispassionate objectivity but we can never attain it: our stories and our beliefs get in the way. The stories we tell attempt to make sense of our lives, yet they also reflect our collective desires and dreams in our particular moment in history. The Indians' belief systems and ours have evolved over the centuries with different totems, different rituals, and different spiritual leaders or gods. When they become intertwined there is often confusion. We have no common ground for understanding. There is only the precarious middle ground with its patchwork of compromises and ad hoc agreements, surface attempts to bridge the gap between our worlds. When it fails us, we find ourselves at cross-purposes and our peoples in conflict.

As the Payakan "scandal" unfolds, I become increasingly convinced that the UN's Earth Summit is part of a ritual of conflict resolution for the Northern and Southern Hemispheres. In this modern-day ritual, the Indian societies of Brazil are caught at the center of a ceremonial dispute between the hemispheres. The site of this ritual event is Rio de Janeiro, which, like a coliseum in ancient Rome or an African village square, functions as a "decisive meeting place," to use the term of anthropologists. It is the setting of an extraordinary event, a place that by its very nature is separate from the normal rhythms and circumstances of quotidian life. What prompts this ritual is the sense of impending ecological doom that has descended on the nations of the world in recent years. In attendance are the international heads of state—Bush, Castro, Mitterrand, and a hundred others—all there with their political underlings to participate in the formal ceremony of government decision making. But the ceremony participants I am referring to are those multitudes of others who have made the pilgrimage to Rio. There are seven thousand international journalists, tens of thousands of environmentalists, indigenous people from across the planet, the Dalai Lama, and a cast of international celebrities including Shirley MacLaine, Jane Fonda, and Bianca Jagger, as well as several American presidential candidates. This pilgrimage is equal in size to anything witnessed in medieval Europe. And as with those ancient events, these ritual participants have arrived with high expectations, hoping to contribute to a global discussion about our shared ecological destiny.

This ceremony follows a period of rapid change that has disturbed the equilibrium between Brazil and the countries of North America and Western Europe. Power has shifted, and the roles and status of many key players have changed. The environmentalists now have the momentum and want to add to their recent advances. This movement in the press, in politics, and in global environmental policy threatens the economic and political interests of those who want to see the old equilibrium restored, to see a return to the status quo of disenfranchised Indians and unrestrained environmental destruction. On the one hand there are frontier developers and politicians who have the support of conservative and increasingly nationalistic federal legislators and journalists. On the other hand there is an unprecedented alliance of Brazilian and international environmental and human rights groups working with indigenous leaders who have won the support of international politicians, foundations, and celebrities. In the middle are the Indians whose "image" is tied to the preoccupations and agendas of these two dissenting groups from the dominant societies of Brazil, Europe, and North America. These groups, in spite of what they profess, are ultimately in conflict over who the Indian *should* be. Their stated cases represent a desire—or, in some cases, a fantasy—rather than an evaluation that takes into consideration the specific culture of these people and their historical relationship with Western Europeans living beyond the forest. The Indians, with the help of their international "friends," suddenly have achieved a new sense of power. Environmental groups are enjoying previously unavailable access to politicians and world leaders. The Brazilian government, in turn, is experiencing unprecedented international pressure to remedy its lack of environmental safeguards and its neglectful treatment of its indigenous peoples. Frontier entrepreneurs and large landowners—long accustomed to the laissez-faire feudal conditions of the Amazon Basin—are also not adjusting well to the sudden demand for justice and democratic rights on the part of Indians, rubber tappers, and *posseiros*—all the so-called "peoples of the forest." This jarring and sudden sequence of changes, just four years after Chico Mendes's assassination, has hit a threshold, a crisis point, and our societies through the institutions of the media are searching for some form of resolution or, you could even say, ritual sacrifice.

The question of who the Indian is (and in turn what image he projects) has once again become a preoccupation of the white man's world, almost an obsession. In recent years these two opposing camps—through the media, through the courts, through the channels of legislatures in Brazil and throughout the world—have essentially been involved in a ritual dialogue. At the center of that dialogue is Paulinho Payakan, someone who is both a participant in that discussion and a symbol of dispute for the opposing sides. As he has emerged in the *Parade* and *Veja* articles, Payakan is not an actual person but only an image of what these opposing groups feel the Indian should be. Certainly the reporting on who he is and what he does contains factual elements, but it is also infused with allegorical distortions and conscious omissions. Emerging at a certain moment in history this symbolic Payakan—through the ritualizing process of the media—can no longer just be a Kayapo indigenous leader who, because of his intelligence and his language skills, has become an intermediary with the world of the white man. That is not possible during these times of heightened environmental concerns. Payakan's destiny (in which he is a willing participant) has been to become swept up in the aspirations and frustrations both of those who seek to preserve the rain forest and of those who want to exploit its natural resources. Drawing on clichéd notions from history, these groups have sanctified him and demonized him in accordance with their opposing agendas. He is no longer just Paulinho (his Brazilian name) or Krebenoti (his Kayapo name). Rather he has become, depending on who is looking at him, the Man Who Would Save the World or a "savage cannibal." He is bigger than life, the stuff of Hollywood movies, and part of a debate that has been taking place for five hundred years, one in which the opposing moral and ethical forces of the Western European world have sought repeatedly to define and determine the destiny of the Indian. These are the same forces that have been at odds since Las Casas first made his scathing critique of Columbus's desire to *subjugate them all and make them do whatever we want.* They have become part of the allegory we have been replaying from one decade to the next, from one century to the next—an allegory that continues to reappear as the numbers of Indians slowly dwindle. Our "modern world" is, in fact, no different from the "old world." We've been fooling ourselves. We in fact have been unable to break free from the same cycle of wild presumptions that have led to tragic misunderstandings, a cycle started when Columbus arrived on the shores of the Americas and came face-to-face with those strange imponderable people he mistakenly called Indians, a people at once frightening and fascinating, a culture neither he nor we have ever understood.

Who then are the masters of this modern-day ceremony? Who are our contemporary equivalents of the shamans, the village priests, and the elders who control and orchestrate those "primitive rituals"? It is, I believe, "my people" who play this role: that select caste of journalists, filmmakers, and photographers who have dropped in and out of this story in the course of four years. Certainly it is society at large that provides us with our preconceptions of who the indigenous people are. But we are what the anthropologist Victor Turner refers to as its "ritual authors." With our pens, laptops, and pictures we take reality and transform it to fit our belief system. In this sense our articles, news clips, and films are like magic mirrors reflecting back to the world our vision of who the Indian is. In Rio we bestowed upon Payakan—through the image we created of him—a ritual aura (one horrific, the other beatific) separating him from the norms of life, giving him a grandiose, mythic dimension. And over the years Payakan—urged on by his friends in the movement—participated in this process of ritualization as well. He often dressed up for the white man by putting on the ceremonial paint and the headdress of brightly colored feathers, giving us the exotic image he knew we desired. In his speeches he distorted his depiction of his people, leaving out important facts that didn't fit the agenda of the Save the Rain Forest movement. This role had come naturally to Payakan. It had been part of his upbringing, part of the middle ground the Kayapo had worked out with the white men. Through the stories we wrote, the films we made, the pictures we took, we shaped him into a hero for some, a scapegoat for others, but always someone bigger than life, someone beyond the ordinary. That is why in the *Veja* and *Parade* cover photos he has an expressionless face. We need a blank canvas upon which to impose our own illusions. A smile would have told us too much. It would have robbed us of the opportunity to project onto him who we want him to be, what we need him to represent.

Just two months before the start of the Summit I had an experience that has helped me to understand the way in which images have come to play a role in the story of Payakan. I was up north in the state of Amapá visiting an indigenous village leader by the name of Wai-Wai. Three years earlier I had first filmed him and his people for a documentary I had done called *At the Edge of Conquest*. During that period I did not have much money, so the editing process was protracted. I would work out a rough version of the documentary over a period of a few months, then stop, search for foundation funding, and begin again a few months later. As it turned out I finished the film just four months before I returned to see Wai-Wai in the frontier town of Macapá. I arrived there hoping to do a follow-up story prior to the start of the Earth Summit. All this time I had been carrying images of him in my head—images that I had shot, selected, and edited into the context of a half-hour documentary. The completed film I believed was a sympathetic but still accurate depiction of the problems he and his people, the Waiampi, were facing in protecting their land from outside incursions. Yet I would come to realize it was still simply *my* story of their lives.

Although I had not seen Wai-Wai in three years, I arrived in Macapá certain that I knew him intimately by virtue of the film I had made. But when we finally met, I was shocked and disappointed. He was much smaller in stature than I had come to imagine him. In the setting of this frontier town he also seemed out of place, clumsy and pathetic. He had worn ill-fitting Western clothes into the city which, in the context of our society, gave him a clownish demeanor. His Portuguese was rough and, I remember thinking, "childish"—a word I had often heard used by the miners when talking about the Indians. That night I remember having trouble sleeping, disturbed by the thought that I too had inadvertently become a dupe of the Save the Rain Forest movement. How could a serious journalist think this way? Perhaps Wai-Wai was not the man I thought he was? Perhaps I had made a dreadful mistake? Perhaps I had *imagined* him?

The next day was April 19, the Day of the Indian in Brazil. To my surprise and delight I saw another Wai-Wai on that day, a person much closer to the one I had gotten to know over the years. He was dressed in his traditional clothes and seemed much more comfortable. He was also speaking through an interpreter in his native language, providing a clarity to our conversation that had been lacking the day before. Perhaps most important, on this day I was also seeing him through the camera. The composed shots and camera angles took him out of the ambiance of this chaotic frontier town and placed him in the context of a defined story, one that allowed me to see him through my perspective, my vision of who the Indian was. He now existed in the confines of a familiar allegory: a David and Goliath tale of a village leader combating a mighty political machine. He was the victim, the underdog, someone the liberal fringe of the white world could sympathize with. I had made my choice as to the way in which I wanted to see him. It was my truth, one that existed in opposition to the frontier entrepreneurs in this region who wanted the Waiapi integrated into Brazilian society and their lands given over for mineral exploration. On that day in Macapá I recognized that I too had been holding up my own mirror reflecting my vision of the Indian back to the world at large. My documentary image of Wai-Wai had become part of "a hall of mirrors" contributing to the ritual dialogue about who the Indian really is, a dialogue we impose on them, a dialogue that seems to have culminated in the vilification of Payakan during the Earth Summit.

25

Pedro Martinez Barros used to brag that he was the one who broke the story of the Payakan scandal to the magazine *Veja*. He was a local politician and a mayoral candidate in the town of Redenção where the incident occurred. He had been running on an anti-Indian platform in a community embittered by the recent decision of the Collor government to pursue legal recognition as Kayapo territory of an area containing the most sought-after mineral deposits and mahogany reserves in the state of Pará. The proposed demarcation, still to be ratified by the Brazilian government, would give five thousand Indians control of ten thousand square miles of pristine forest, an area encompassing four percent of the land in the state and equivalent in size to the country of Belgium. Local residents were enraged, and Pedro Martinez hoped to convert their rage into a successful mayoral campaign.

"It was a very opportune moment," he said of the publication of the *Veja* story on Payakan. "It came right in the middle of Eco '92. It ruined the Earth Summit. And it ruined the Indians, you must understand, because it had just come out in a magazine in the United States that Payakan was a 'man who could save the world.' "

Pedro Martinez, it turned out, was also the uncle of Letícia Ferreira, the alleged victim. His pivotal role in this convoluted and absurd story is one bizarre element in a plot thicker, more surreal than any García Márquez novel. And much darker. Yet although this part of the story contains conspiratorial elements, it is not a simple conspiracy. I would call it a witch hunt in which certain catalytic elements—economic tensions, heightened xenophobia, and intense anti-Indian sentiments—came together in one historical moment of shared hysteria. Its perpetrators were journalists, frontier politicians, corrupt police officials, and the desperate citizens of a local frontier town who were unified by the threat posed to them by an economically and politically empowered Kayapo and one of its preeminent leaders, Paulinho Payakan.

I never made it to Redenção but a journalist friend of mine did. Scott Wallace spent a month in this community in southern Pará in order to follow Payakan's story after the conclusion of the Earth Summit. I returned to the States to start editing news reports I had gathered in Rio. I knew, however, that someday I'd be forced to put together the pieces of this troubling puzzle, particularly since I wanted to make a documentary on the larger question of the indigenous rights struggle in Brazil. That day came several months later when I decided to include Payakan's story in my documentary. So I got together with Scott in New York and he told me what he had discovered in Redenção, a town that ironically translates as Redemption.

Scott had met Pedro Martinez at his house in town about a month after the story first broke in *Veja*. Letícia's uncle was a thin man of medium build with a mustache and short-cropped dark hair. "I was the one responsible for the immediate dissemination of the information," he said. He then gave Scott a breakdown of his plans to have the country's Indian Statute changed. He made it clear that he wanted Indians to be like "common citizens," without any special privileges. "If the laws are not changed, they are going to end up owning the whole city," he told Wallace.

By the time Scott contacted Pedro Martinez no one was denying that some kind of violent altercation had occurred that Sunday night in the countryside near Redenção and that it involved Letícia Ferreira, Payakan, and his wife, Irekran. But the Kayapo leader's newly appointed lawyer had begun to publicly criticize what he called distortions in the media. He claimed his Indian client did not understand the Portuguese word for rape, *estupro*, when he was interviewed by the reporters for TV Globo. He had, the lawyer said, understood it to mean "attack." His client was willing to admit that an assault had taken place and that Letícia had suffered injuries. The extent of these injuries, however, was still subject to debate. Payakan declared to the press and in initial court hearings that he was not the one who had attacked Letícia. It was, he said, Irekran who had gone after Letícia in a jealous rage. In early court testimony he described how Irekran had inserted her hands into the vagina of Letícia as an act of revenge after she had caught him and Leticia "flirting." He later told a local paper that "your alcoholic drinks can affect any human's head—Indian, non-Indian, rich, poor. We were drinking, including the girl drank a lot. We used forty-eight bottles of beer. A lot of drinking shifted the head." When Irekran took the witness stand she admitted only that "with my fingernails I clawed at her with all my strength." Referring to Letícia's claims that she lost her virginity when she was raped by Payakan, Irekran looked Letícia in the eye during her court testimony and said, "I want her to look me in the face and tell me she was a virgin." All these details were reported extensively in the Brazilian press. The story captured the nation's imagination, competing in its lurid subject matter with the most popular of Brazil's television soap operas.

Before and during the trial the person who spoke publicly on Letícia's behalf was her father, Waldemir Ferreira, the brother-in-law of Pedro Martinez. In his conversations with Wallace and other journalists he made no pretense regarding his feelings about Payakan. A "filthy and lying Indian" is how he referred to him. "He says he's an ecologist. A barbaric criminal, that's what he is," he said on another occasion. As for the Kayapo people: "For me Indians are not fit to live in Christian society. They should stay on their reserves among their own kind." Ferreira's sentiments were supported by a number of townspeople who staged a protest shortly after the alleged rape had occurred. "An Indian's place is in the village, a rapist's place is in the jail" read one of their banners which was paraded through town. In one of two interviews Wallace conducted with him, Ferreira claimed he did not learn of the Sunday-night incident until the following Tuesday when his son, Luis, arrived with the news at his two-hundred-acre ranch located thirty-one miles outside Redenção. He told Wallace he went immediately to his brother-in-law's house in town, arriving there late Tuesday night.

"Payakan owes me a big favor," Pedro Martinez said, "because I asked him [Waldemir] what he wanted to do and he said he wanted to kill him. I wouldn't let him do it, so we went to the authorities."

Also assembled in Martinez's home that Tuesday night were a group of politically active local citizens including Manoel Franco, a lawyer and special advisor to Jader Barbalho, the governor of the state of Pará and an outspoken opponent of the plans for the Kayapo demarcation. After discussing the various options available to the Ferreira family, Pedro and Manoel Franco took Waldemir to the home of the town judge that same night. There they arranged for Letícia to appear in court the next day. It was also agreed Manoel Franco would represent the Ferreira family in a $300,000 civil suit against Payakan.

As Wallace points out, what is puzzling about the chronology of these events is that the father, Waldemir, went directly to his brother-in-law's house without stopping at the hospital to see his daughter, a young woman who had supposedly been the victim of a rape, attempted murder, and acts of cannibalism. "I was nervous," he told Wallace in explaining the apparent inconsistency of his actions. "I didn't know what to do."

For Wallace, however, the timing of this gathering as well as the father's apparent indifference to his daughter's well-being raised serious questions about the nature of the charges against Payakan. That nighttime meeting could have been the beginning of a well-constructed conspiracy—or it could equally have been the coincidental intersection of some local members of the anti-Indian lobby. He decided to investigate further by checking the "facts" of the *Veja* article against the statements of people he encountered in Redenção.

One of the key players in the case against Payakan was José Barbosa da Souza, the local police chief. According to *Veja*, Barbosa found the vehicle in question, the white Chevette, "abandoned" in a local gas station two days after the alleged rape. "It was covered with blood from the floor to the ceiling," he was quoted as saying, "as though an animal had bled to death inside." *Veja* also reported that it was Helio Ribeiro de Lima, Payakan's housekeeper, who came to Letícia's aid when he heard her anguished cries for help. It was Ribeiro who said he had seen Payakan holding a piece of wire against Letícia's neck in an attempt to strangle her, an accusation that, with Letícia's testimony, was considered crucial evidence in the attempted-murder charge facing Payakan. The alleged strangulation was described by *Veja* as part of a "demonic ritual." Barbosa was quoted as saying: "The examinations confirm that there was violence and acts of cannibalism that were beyond our imaginations." Yet a month after the *Veja* cover story Wallace met Barbosa in Redenção, where he heard a different version of these events. Barbosa told him that he had never located the car during the investigation. Wallace pushed further.

"Then what about your quote in *Veja*?" the American journalist asked.

"I never saw the car," Barbosa responded.

Chief of Police Barbosa might not have been able to find the car but, with a little investigative work, Wallace did. Following a tip given to him by a young Kayapo in Redenção, he traced the car to Amelton Lopes, known in town by the nickname Borguinho. The Chevette, which had a gray plush interior, came into Borguinho's possession directly from Payakan within seventy-two hours of the incident, a day after *Veja* said that Barbosa had found it soaked with blood "from the floor to the ceiling." Payakan, Borguinho said, had owed him a lot of money. The Chevette was partial payment on their long-standing debt. "The car was in normal condition without any blood or anything," Borguinho said. "And it had not been washed." Wallace, a veteran of bloody wars in Central America, inspected the vehicle but couldn't find any traces of the cannibalistic carnage described by *Veja*. "Not a spot of blood," he told me.

Although Letícia's testimony was extensively quoted in the Brazilian newsmagazine, the authors of the article never questioned the veracity of her allegations and only occasionally used the word "alleged." They did, however, display a great deal of journalistic panache, embellishing the story with gory details straight from the pages of a tawdry gothic novel. "She was biting me all over my body while he was attempting to strangle me," Letícia supposedly testified to Barbosa in the police report regarding the attack by Irekran and Payakan. According to the magazine's writers, three different Redenção doctors had found "wounds spread all over Letícia's body, signs of brutal beatings to the face, the tips of her breasts lacerated by bites." Chief Barbosa was quoted as saying, "It is the most barbaric case I have seen in the ten years of my career in police work." But subsequent medical evaluations requested by the state's prosecuting attorney, Lucia Bueno, clearly refuted the assertions of *Veja*, Letícia, and Barbosa. According to doctors at the Institute of Legal Medicine, Letícia had suffered only "scrapes" and "bruises." Her breasts, they stated, had not been lacerated or bitten. On the question of an attempted strangulation, the same medical examiners concluded that the testimony of Barbosa's key witness, Payakan's housekeeper Helio Lima, could not in fact be true. Lima had been quoted in *Veja* as saying that he had seen Payakan standing with a piece of wire in his hands trying to strangle Letícia. Yet the medical examiners found no sign whatsoever of "strangulation." Helio, a former gold prospector, was a young man in his twenties with short, curly hair and, according to Wallace, blue eyes—one of which wandered off to the side as the result of a birth defect. Not only was his vision impaired, but when he "witnessed" the strangulation he was standing approximately one hundred feet away from Payakan in pitch dark, on a road with no streetlights, and with only the dim beam of a dime-store flashlight to cast any illumination on the distant altercation. When Wallace questioned Helio's brother Edelsen several weeks after the incident, the North American reporter was told that "Helio never saw

Payakan strangle Letícia," that the story had been fabricated. A local farmer named José Raimundo Batista, who came to Letícia's aid that night, also contradicted Helio's testimony. Letícia, he said, had run to his house naked from the waist down. But she suffered only from minor injuries. There were no signs of the bloody carnage described by *Veja*. In the week following the alleged rape, Wallace learned that it was Letícia's parents who convinced Helio to talk to *Veja*. Helio also accompanied Letícia to the courthouse on Wednesday morning, where they both gave their testimonies to the judge. When Wallace tried to interview him a month after the incident, he was told by family members that Helio had gone "into hiding" for fear of reprisals by the Indians.

The state's case against Payakan took almost two years to come to a resolution. There were requests on the part of the defense for a change of venue and a great deal of debate as to whether Payakan and his wife were "emancipated" Indians and therefore fully accountable to the Brazilian courts for their actions. But there was also a serious, unexpected problem facing the prosecution. Lucia Bueno, the state's prosecuting attorney, was having trouble amassing a credible case of material evidence against Payakan. It turned out that Chief of Police Barbosa—*Veja*'s key source and the person who compiled the initial police report—had been arrested one year into Payakan's court case and jailed for being the ringleader of a local gang of bandits. Barbosa and his accomplices had been highjacking trucks and buses in the vicinity of Redenção and robbing the vehicles and their passengers of all valuables. After Barbosa's conviction, the public defender, Rosa C. Rodrigues, moved that the case against Payakan be dropped owing to the "incompetence" of Chief Barbosa. This setback caused further delays.

But the case was eventually tried. The verdict—almost two years after the date of the *Veja* article—came from the presiding judge Elder Lisboa Correa da Costa who, as is customary in Brazil, heard the case without a jury. "There is not enough proof, either material or in terms of witnesses, to confirm that Payakan had raped the student," Judge Correa told reporters. The charges against Irekran were more complicated. According to the judge, "there were evidences of serious bodily assaults against the teen" perpetrated by Payakan's wife. Yet, in accordance with Brazilian law, Irekran was considered a ward of the state, someone who cannot be subject to the codes of Western law. "Because she is free from punishment," Judge Correa said, "she cannot be taken to court."

And what, you might be wondering, ever happened to Sylvia Letícia Ferreira? She married a twenty-one-year-old farmer by the name of Roberto Afonso Cruz one year into the trial against Payakan. Roberto was an agricultural worker and, it turned out, a small-town thug who moonlighted as a thief in one of Pará's most notorious carjacking gangs. While married to Letícia he managed to commit a murder and get captured. He was sent off to jail for nineteen years on convictions of of auto theft and homicide. Several months after the Payakan verdict, Letícia herself was arrested for attempting to help her husband escape from jail. According to the local police she had brought her imprisoned husband "escape tools" (a drill bit and six small saws) sequestered in the false bottom of a thermos. "It isn't true," she told the new chief of police, Aldo Gomez de Castro, who had replaced the now imprisoned Barbosa. "The thermos which I brought was not this one," she was quoted as saying to him at the time of her arrest. Chief Gomez locked her up in a tiny six-by-three-foot cell with just a hammock in which to sleep. "This is a dirty frame-up," Letícia screamed to reporters who had congregated outside her jail cell in Redenção. "My husband is honest. I know our imprisonment is directly linked to Payakan. I am going to request a meeting with the Federal Police in Belém so that that case can be reopened," she said. She was eventually convicted of plotting and attempting to facilitate the escape of her husband. In one of her last public statements a desperate Letícia told a Brazilian journalist, "Just as Payakan raped me, now he is entrapping me."

Her words had little impact. By 1993 Letícia had lost all credibility in the eyes of the Brazilian press; she was but a pathetic footnote to a forgotten tale. But the press had not finished with the fallen hero Paulinho Payakan.

26

The 1992 *Veja* account of Payakan's purported rape, attempted murder, and cannibalistic violence against Letícia Ferreira was only the beginning of his problems with the press. In a series of investigative reports triggered by the accusations, the world at large slowly came to realize that some Kayapo had been involved in gold mining and mahogany contracts while their people were being championed as saviors of the forest. The most shocking revelation of all was that the movement's preeminent hero, Paulinho Payakan, was deeply involved in the sale of endangered mahogany trees to frontier loggers. Suddenly the man who had been branded as both a savage and savior was now depicted by conservatives and liberals alike as an avaricious huckster, someone who had been deceiving not just his foes on the frontier, but his allies in the international environmental movement as well.

Reports critical of the Kayapo's entrepreneurial activities began appearing in high-profile publications shortly after the rape allegations. The initial *Veja* article featured photographs of Payakan sitting in a new car and eating in a plush restaurant with his wife and children. While he was not directly linked to logging activities, a sidebar to that same article described the Kayapo as the "richest Indians" in the country with an income from logging totaling sixty million dollars since 1989. In subsequent articles, *Veja*'s journalists attacked environmentalists—

particularly those from North America—asserting that they suffered from "green blindness" because they did not immediately accept Payakan's guilt in the Ferreira case. In one story entitled "Gigolos of the Amazon," they stated that Payakan's rape charges resulted in millions of dollars of financial loss for "a category of shrewd people who exploit Payakan and other indigenous groups." Among the ranks of these exploitative gigolos, the magazine included "Indian Agency employees, businessmen, professional ecologists, and anthropologists." Over the next two years, more articles and news reports on Kayapo mahogany deals circulated in Brazil and abroad, most of which depicted these former heroes as sellouts and villains.

Prior to these press revelations, only a dozen or so anthropologists, environmentalists, and journalists had been aware of the full extent of Kayapo contracts with frontier entrepreneurs. For the majority of knowledgeable insiders, awareness of the Indians' deal making was limited to a gold contract negotiated by Payakan in 1985. The mining agreement, created under the supervision of the Indian Agency, gave the Kayapo five percent of profits stemming from gold sites located near the villages of Gorotire and Kikretum. Finalized under the threat of a full-scale gold rush, this stopgap measure was intended to be in effect for only two years. But Brazilian prospectors managed to remain in Kayapo territory beyond their deadline, allowing the Indians to eventually increase their revenue shares to thirteen percent by 1991.

While the Kayapo gold contracts of the 1980s had been openly discussed in the public sector, the mahogany contracts—particularly those negotiated by Payakan—had been hidden from the world at large. But in the years following the rape scandal, links between Payakan and the logging community in Rendenção were exposed. During this era frontier loggers and miners became acutely aware that pots, pans, and machetes were no longer sufficient to seduce the Kayapo. The Indians wanted more and got more because they knew they had what the frontier capitalists wanted. The Kayapos' negotiating successes introduced the Indians to an entirely new dimension of middle-ground deal making. By the early 1990s, most villages had received gifts of satellite dishes, Brazilian-style houses, or other expensive modern conveniences from frontier entrepreneurs in exchange for the right to exploit natural resources. And Payakan, in spite of his popular image as selfless crusader, also appeared to be benefiting from such exchanges. The little white Chevette he had been driving in Rendenção was reportedly registered in the name of a logger by the name of Osmar Ferreira, a local businessman with no family ties to Letícia. His *chacra* or bungalow—the scene of the alleged crime—was also owned by Ferreira. In 1993, a young Kayapo by the name of Mokuka, a self-professed "employee" of Payakan, gave a detailed description of the young leader's business activities to the American anthropologist Terence Turner. According to Mokuka's account, Payakan's dealings with Ferreira dated back to 1990, when an agreement was worked out for the logging of mahogany trees near the villages of Gorotire and A'ukre. Payakan's income from mahogany extraction during this period was, according to Mokuka, approximately twenty thousand dollars per month. "Payakan made contracts for A'ukre and Gorotire," Mokuka told Turner, "then he asked me to go in the forest and account for the wood taken out. I took two Indians with me and we did the work for him." While Payakan was selling endangered mahogany reserves to frontier loggers, he also negotiated a contract with the Body Shop Corporation to process Brazil nuts for a new line of hair care products. The English company's "Trade Not Aid" arrangement increased his personal revenues and provided surplus cash and medical services for his community. In spite of the reported success of this ecologically sustainable project, in 1992 Payakan once again negotiated contracts with Osmar Ferreira. He sent other Kayapo to supervise and sign manifests accounting for the number of mahogany trees removed from Kayapo lands. "Payakan said go ahead," Mokuka explained to Turner. "He did it so people wouldn't see him earning money." By 1992 Payakan's income as a key Kayapo middle man had earned him a modest home in Rendenção, a bungalow in the country, two cars, an airplane, and a new set of important allies. When former Chief of Police Barbosa tried to apprehend Payakan for the alleged rape of Letícia, it was the logger Ferreira—intent on protecting his investment—who warned Payakan of his impending arrest.

Payakan, however, was not the only Kayapo actively engaged in carving out a capitalistic niche along the Amazon's frontier. There were probably a dozen other leaders, as well as a new generation of young Turks, who were involved in contractual relations with miners and loggers. Many of them had no direct links to the familial lineages, which for centuries defined leadership structure in Kayapo communities. Their new sense of power resulted from their rudimentary understanding of Portuguese and a basic grasp of arithmetic. They provided a critical link in negotiations with the outside world and, as enterprising intermediaries, these young businessmen quickly gained strong footholds in village life. They provided their fellow Kayapo with badly needed medicines and educational opportunities and unprecedented access to consumer goods from the outside world. They were popular, generous when necessary, and their influence in the villages quickly grew. Older leaders were pushed aside and a power struggle ensued.

The most fanatical of these new free-market converts was Tutu Pombo, a man in his mid-sixties who was considered to be the founding father of Kayapo capitalism. He hailed from the village of Kikretum and was known popularly in the region as "Colonel Pombo." A corpulent and rambunctious villager, the Colonel was often seen at public protests wearing a distinctive multicolored headdress resembling a shower cap plumed with red and blue parakeet feathers. Among international photographers and journalists, his innate sense of vaudevillian theatrics made him a favorite subject of those in search of local color. Many of us at the time naively considered Pombo to be the frontier equivalent of a circus buffoon. We later discovered that he had been a pivotal figure in Kayapo history. Almost single-handedly, he had opened the floodgates for the mining and mahogany deals that transformed Kayapo society in the late 1980s and early 1990s.

As a young child, Tutu Pombo had been the sole survivor of the massacre of his family by a violent band of frontier pioneers. Adopted and raised by Brazilians, he learned fluent Portuguese at an early age. When he returned to Kayapo territory as a young man, his language skills and his basic understanding of mathematics attracted the attention of local Indian Agency officials. Although he had no familial ties to the traditional Kayapo power structure, he was given the title of "chief" and designated as the village's intermediary for encounters with the outside world. But contrary to the expectations of the Indian Agency, Pombo exploited his new position to broker deals with frontier nut gatherers, miners, and loggers, who in the 1950s and 1960s were anxious to exploit the untapped resources of Kayapo territory. Over the course of four decades, he developed his ventures into a profitable business that, according to the Brazilian press, made him one of the richest men in the country. When the Payakan scandal broke in 1992, Pombo's high-profile status made him the first to be scrutinized by investigative journalists. News reporters in Brazil estimated his combined annual income to be approximately four million dollars, an astounding figure given that most Kayapo still survived by subsistence activities such as hunting, fishing, and the gathering of food from the forest. When Pombo died in 1994, his estate included several cars, three ranches, a hotel, and an airplane, which, with characteristic flare, included a rendering of his profile on the side of the fuselage. Local frontier doctors attributed his death to modern ailments: stress and hypertension, as well as an unhealthy appetite for chocolate and sweets.

journal entry
Megragnotti territory
10/26/92

We were dropped down in a clearing this morning near the border with Bau, the Kayapo area adjacent to Megragnotti. Low forest here, dense with small thin trees much like those of New England. Last night I sat in the Kayapo village of Pukanu watching television. The families were spread out in the village square as if awaiting a display of fireworks. The Brazilian television show *Fantastico* did a review of the week's events: images of the Bush-Clinton presidential

debate, anti-ethnic protesters in Germany, the lifting of a
space shuttle, all passing by this forest culture that has lived
in relative isolation for hundreds of years.

I first entered Kayapo lands in 1992 to do a story on the successful realization of Raoni's two-decade campaign: Megragnotti territory, an area of tropical forest the size of Switzerland,
was finally being demarcated. The Rainforest Foundation,
which Raoni had established with the rock star Sting, was
supervising as well as funding the complicated task of establishing boundaries in this dense tropical forest. For several
months, teams of workers armed with chain saws had been
traipsing behind topographers through the rain forest carving
out a six-meter swathe where no natural boundaries had ever
existed. They placed markers and signs along the way, warnings
to any trespassers that they were entering Indian lands.

During my one-week stay in Kayapo territory, the village of
Pukanu became my base of operations. In this community of
two hundred villagers, a dozen large houses made from branches
and dried leaves circled the perimeter. In the center of the village was a flat, dusty square, a site for ceremonial dancing, and a
men's hut, which served as a meeting place for village discussions. While the architectural design of the village conveyed
the appearance of a traditional society, the community was
actually swept up in a cultural tidal wave. Empty Coke bottles
littered the square. A satellite dish sat prominently in front of a
traditional thatched hut. In the men's house, clusters of young
boys and girls spent their days transfixed before a television set,
watching soccer games, soap operas, and an endless array of
commercials. Over the last two decades, Protestant American
missionaries had infiltrated the community and were diligently
translating the Bible into the Kayapo language while providing
medical care for the villages. The Body Shop Corporation had
also carved out a niche for itself by establishing a Brazil nut processing plant on the outskirts of the village. Just upriver gold
miners operated a mining site that was contaminating the villagers' drinking water with high levels of toxic mercury. Vene-

real disease, contracted by young men at frontier bordellos, was infecting their female partners in the community, and posed a serious health hazard for the Indians.

The changes taking place in Pukanu were confusing, and often contradictory. In my few short days there, I searched for some kind of context to understand the logjam of cultural forces subverting this community. I had learned enough about Kayapo history to know that these people had consistently defied the pigeonhole classifications of white society. Simple, and by now tired, concepts like "culture shock" and "alienation" couldn't begin to describe the diverse forces tearing at the fabric of their culture. However, while environmentalists, anthropologists, and other sympathetic whites pondered the problem, individuals within the community were attempting to solve, or at least alleviate, it. Throughout this era, Raoni and several other traditional leaders had been actively lobbying to end logging and mining activities on Kayapo lands. His village of Cachoeira-Mentuktire and a second village, Kapot-Roykore, were calling for a return to a more moderate means of contact with the outside world, one devoid of the rampant consumerism that had arrived in this era of frontier deal making. As I got to know some community leaders in Pukanu, I discovered that in spite of the conspicuous signs of consumerism, many of these villagers were bitterly divided over their current situation. "Television is just to see what the white man is doing in the cities," an older leader named Puketheri told us one afternoon. "But bicycles and motorcycles, these things; the people buy them, but I don't like them. I just think about medicines, about getting medicines to help my people, and about getting guns and ammunition to help us to hunt."

I visited village medical clinics and local frontier schools to see firsthand the way surplus cash had been used effectively by the Indians to support social services abandoned by the Brazilian government. But the cash also had less admirable uses: expensive flights to the city to pick up cases of Coca-Cola, cookies, and alcohol, and to allow young men to go whoring. The Indians I met were becoming increasingly dependent on Brazilian foodstuffs like rice, beans, and meat purchased in the cities and consumed in place of their traditional foods attained by hunting, gathering, and slash-and-burn agriculture. Puketheri and a number of traditional leaders were now preoccupied by the precarious future of their people. "The elders have been talking about things long passed in the time of our grandparents. They talk about it all the time and I am also talking about it so that we don't lose it," said Puketheri on one of my last days in the village. "But the young boy who is born into this world today is quickly affected by the ways of the whites. He doesn't know anything else. He just goes about without direction. That is why I continue talking about our culture, so that the Indians will hold onto it."

Between 1992 and 1994 Kayapo commercial activities were the focus of numerous shortsighted press reports in which rain forest experts—many of them former allies of the Indians—declared their critical assessments of recent Kayapo entrepreneurial activities. Shortly after Payakan's rape accusations, the head of a British human rights group claimed that the charges could be attributable to his recent economic activities. He went on to say that "in our opinion, the projects that the Body Shop has run with Payakan are at least in part responsible, in that the company has put him in a position of considerable wealth and power." In 1994, *The Wall Street Journal* ran an article with the title "Kayapo Indians Lose Their 'Green' Image" followed by the subtitle "Former Heroes of Amazon Succumb to Lure of Profit." What these critics failed to recognize, however, was that Payakan and his fellow Indian entrepreneurs were simply doing what the Kayapo had always done: they were trying to get the best deal they could from the white people they encountered. In recent years, social services to their communities had severely diminished while their land was pillaged by outsiders. The time-consuming and exhausting task of safeguarding boundaries had become too much for the Indians. Why shouldn't they profit from their natural resources while pursuing other money-making ventures, such as the sale of Brazil nut oil? The Kayapo sold tracts of rain forest while championing the cause of saving it. From their perspective, this was consistent with their own indigenous *real politick*, developed over the last two centuries and modified to fit the changing conditions of a local frontier society and, more recently, the international community. If a rock star wanted to tour the world with them, if a green corporation wanted to use them as figureheads, if the Pope or the Sierra Club wanted to give them a special commendation, that was just fine. They were willing to play along just as they always had. That was how they had brokered relationships with outsiders in the past. It was consistent with their worldview. From our perspective, they were guilty of questionable ethical behavior. But we in the Western world were also responsible for the outcome of this embarrassing scenario. In our rush to save the tropical forests of Brazil, we embraced the Kayapo as one monolithic entity rather than the fractionalized and complex society they are. The tragic flaw in our plan was that we imposed our vision on them, arrogantly assuming that it complemented the vision they had of themselves. We were deceived, but we also deceived ourselves. Ironically, Sting, a person frequently criticized for his naivete during this era, was one of the few people to admit to his own complicity during this period. "At first it seemed very simple: Let's stop chopping down the rain forest and support these people," Sting told me in a 1993 interview. "But the complexity of the issue, when you take into consideration the whole of Brazil and the Brazilian economy, the poor people of Brazil, and the Indians' needs themselves vis-à-vis the forest, it is much less simple than I originally thought." I interviewed Sting in a New York rehearsal studio the day before one of his annual Carnegie Hall concerts to raise funds for the Rainforest Foundation. "It's really been a learning process," he said as his technicians secured instruments for the next session. "And I've realized that a miracle is not going to happen. What happens is process, long, hard, *boring* process which eventually, I hope, pays off. I mean all we can really hope to do is slow down the process of destruction until people come to their senses."

"Process" did prove to be a deciding factor in changing the course of Kayapo culture in the early 1990s. In fact it was two processes, one from within their communities and one from outside, which reversed the disastrous trends of their troubled society in the mid-1990s. In January of 1994, Brazil's federal prosecutor threatened to enforce constitutional decrees prohibiting the extraction of wood and minerals from Indian lands. Simultaneously, in various Kayapo communities, years of reckless environmental exploitation had taken their toll. There was a sudden increase in problematic pregnancies and a small but significant rise in the number of birth defects that, medical experts believed, could be attributed to the toxic runoff of mercury from local mines. Malaria, which found a breeding ground in stagnant pools of water left by hydraulic mining, was also on the rise. Leaders like Raoni, who for years had been arguing against logging and mining activities, began to gain new support among villages long associated with logging and mining activities. Pukanu closed down its gold operations in 1993. In 1994, a small but significant revolt took place in Gorotire. Young warriors rose up against Kayapo entrepreneurs and evicted three thousand Brazilian gold prospectors at a mining site known as Santido. In December of 1994, federal officials from Brazil's environmental and Indian agencies capitalized on the Indians' initiatives and called a meeting of Kayapo leaders in the nation's capitol. The outcome of this landmark encounter was that the Kayapo agreed to respect constitutional decrees prohibiting mining and logging activities on Indian lands. In January of 1995, federal police—acting on the agreement worked out in Brasilia—entered Kayapo territory, shut down all logging operations, and seized illegally cut trees. In the wake of these radical changes, various villages established intercommunity associations to pursue eco-tourism and a pilot project for "sustained-growth mahogany harvesting." Once again the Kayapo were redefining the middle ground between their world and ours. A new era was in the making. But unlike the earlier idealistic proclamations of the late 1980s, no one was now making grandiose claims about the Kayapos' future. Perhaps our world had finally learned an important lesson. The Kayapo had defied us before. They could easily do it again.

27

"In the early morning the jaguars come out onto the roadway. They look for small animals to eat," says Father John, shouting over the medley of squeaks and rattles coming from our Toyota truck. "This highway was a terrible thing when it was built, but we use it now." We hit a pothole and momentarily rise off our seats as the Toyota veers to the right heading towards a ditch on the side of the road. Father John thrusts his body against the steering wheel, twisting it to the left and straightening the vehicle before we slip off into the forest. "The cost of driving is much less than a plane," the priest adds without missing a beat. "But the ride," he pauses, "it is not so smooth."

I'm headed back into Yanomami territory, to Mission Catrimani to be exact, traveling with my old friend, the crazed Italian cleric. We are driving through dense green tunnels made from overhanging branches as the vehicle propels us farther into the forest, down a roadway which will not arrive at any specific destination, but will simply end because the money ran out. The dictators became weary of their dreams, the forest was far more impenetrable than the planners had imagined, the Indians' immune systems too fragile, and the protests of human rights activists too loud and too far reaching to hide the atrocities that took place in the names of "development," "progress," and "civilization." BR-210, as this roadway is known, is one of the forgotten highways of General Medici's failed plan to penetrate the heart of Amazonia. Like hundreds of miles of abandoned arteries in the forest, this little highway sits in a state of semi-completion. Each year its neglected dirt track becomes increasingly eroded by the constant rains while the forest creeps in threatening to devour it. Today, BR-210 is used almost exclusively by missionaries, Indian Agency employees, the military, and the occasional curious anthropologist.

As the sound of the vehicle drones on, the forest—dense, moist, and green—flashes by on both sides, a soothing hypnotic blur. Occasionally we drive into an area of open savanna, where we are blinded momentarily by the harsh white light of the late Amazonian morning. Then, within seconds, we are delivered back under the shade of the forest's thick canopy with its pleasant, gentle coolness. Bouncing about in the Toyota with me and Father John is my soundman, Francisco Lattorre, a dark-haired, thick-bearded native of Uruguay, who has traveled with me from the States. Every five minutes, he and the priest break into off-key Italian renditions of World War II resistance songs. Their singing is a valiant effort to keep the overworked cleric awake so that we don't drive off into one of the brackish swamps running along the roadway's perimeter. Every hour or so, we stop to get a shot of the mountains or to film a sequence of the truck passing through the forest. Then the humidity soaks its way through our clothes while mosquitoes home in on unprotected parts of our bodies. I've noticed over the course of this trip that Father John has lost his enthusiasm for such endeavors. The days of "Father 007" seem long gone. Maybe that is because it seems his side won. The Yanomami got their forest. It's been demarcated. Most of the miners were kicked out. He even raised enough money to build a hospital for the Indians in Boa Vista. Weariness, however, has taken over. He's looking forward to a new assignment in Toronto: coffee shops, bookstores, and cosmopolitan conversations. He is "happy," he says, "to be leaving this armpit."

We pass two Yanomami communities, Yawori and Rohahipi-itheri, which border the roadway. The inhabitants resemble Holocaust survivors. Gaunt, sickly looking, and dressed only in rags. Their houses are dilapidated. The village grounds are in complete disarray. When we get out of the truck, a number of the Indians surround us. A man asks me to give him my watch, then asks for my silver bracelet, and, finally, a metal necklace (a warning for a penicillin allergy) that I wear on trips abroad. "I need these things," I tell him in Portuguese, only to be met by a blank stare. The man eventually wanders off to inspect the truck. He'll probably be asking for that as well.

Father John unloads a bag of mangos in the roadway, and a large crowd of Indians form around us. There is pushing and yelling as the villagers fight among themselves for the fruit. "There are no older leaders here," the priest comments as he stands watching the Indians jostle for mangos. "No one to give them any direction. That generation died from disease when the Indians came in contact with the highway workers in the 1970s." Here I can see what the term *cultural destruction* really means: no leaders, no rules, no order. Desperation is the dominant social force in the community. I wonder if these people will ever be able to regain what they once had.

Back in the truck, I make a shot list for what we will be filming in the coming days and I think about this, my tenth trip. I came back out of professional obligation, but also compelled by my personal curiosity. I want to see for myself what has happened to Father Guilherme, Machadão, and the other inhabitants of the village of Wakathautheri. I want to see if the world's attention actually made a difference, to see if the sacrifices I made were worth it: the long, difficult journeys, the negotiations, the arguments, the late-night editing sessions, the humiliating pitches to indifferent news editors, the lost weekends, the travel-torn romances, and the continuing obsession that this forest has nurtured within me. If you listen to those who edit the news, freelancers like myself have returned to square one. "No one cares anymore about the Amazon," has become a common refrain in 1995. The Earth Summit in 1992 served as the official end of the story. The United Nations intervened. World leaders took charge. The message was clear: the media can move on to another story. And move on it did. To Central Europe, with its bullet-strafed buildings, bombed-

out squares, and a people caught in the cross-fire of ethnic violence. Those who remained working in Amazonia were, for the
most part, the ones who had been there from the beginning,
along with a few recent converts: the agronomists, the botanists, the anthropologists, the Indian Agency employees, a
handful of journalists, and a dedicated group of Brazilian and
international human rights activists, who for years have toiled
away to make a difference for the people inhabiting these lands.

journal entry
Boa Vista
5/16/95

I read a couple of items in the newspaper about the state of
justice in the Amazon. In the first, it turns out one of the
murderers of the Canuto brothers was, as Father Ricardo
suspected, a former military policeman. The judge gave him
fifty years. Then in the case of Expedito, there were also
some convictions: a *pistoleiro* and a rancher were sentenced
to 24 and 21 years in prison. Their appeals have been
denied.

The other item was about the assassins of Chico Mendes.
The father Darly managed to escape, but was recaptured and
sent to a Federal penitentiary in Brasilia. The son, who also
escaped, was later apprehended in southern Pará.

It also turns out that José Fininho, the thin man, was found
shot to death in Xinguora after he supposedly "escaped" from
jail. Whether he died as a result of an "arrangement," as he
had prophesied, is unclear. According to Father Ricardo, no
one is investigating the circumstances of Fininho's death. No
one seems to care.

I am calling this my last trip here because the "angles" to this
story are no longer readily apparent. The answers I am now
looking for cannot be found by way of simple documentation.
Maybe I saw too much. Or not enough. Maybe I am afraid to
admit that no matter how long I stay here, I will never be able to
understand this region, that I failed to shed any light on the

forces at work here. But I am not the first to face such a dilemma. Impenetrable, enigmatic, indecipherable: those are just a few of the words that explorers and chroniclers have used over hundreds of years in their attempts to describe this region and its inhabitants. Maybe this is my last trip because weariness has overwhelmed me as well and I just don't want to admit it. Maybe it's time to lift myself from the Amazon's couch and get on with my life. Whatever the case, I've returned here because I feel a need for closure, and that seems to be enough of a justification.

journal entry
5/17/95

Passed through two villages contacted by highway workers in the 1970s. According to Father John, someone was killed there two months ago. An Indian Agency employee named Edevilson shot a Yanomami man named Juliao in a dispute over the sale and transport of twenty bags of bananas. Edevilson told the Yanomami that he didn't have diesel to make the trip back to Boa Vista. The Indians threatened him with "kirima," a ritual threat—the Yanomami version of a macho display of bravado. "Only a threat," reiterated the priest as he told us the story. The Indian agent responded with kicks and punches, then his gun went off. An accident, he claimed. When Edevilson drove away, the Indians shot at his jeep with bows and arrows. He hasn't returned since. The Indian Agency post remains vacant. The people are desperate. The tension here reminds me of the havoc at Paapiú. Depressing.

"We are almost there," says Father John in his lilting Italian accent. "Another few minutes," he adds, then mumbles something incomprehensible about this part of the roadway. I'm now getting concerned about losing the light, as I was hoping to do more filming today. The highway ends abruptly and we turn onto a smaller roadway leading us onto the grassy landing strip of Mission Catrimani. Various clusters of Indians emerge from the little settlements bordering the airstrip. They are splinter groups from the village of Wakathautheri. Undoubtedly they've heard the sound of our vehicle and have come to check out the new arrivals. A woman with a child at her breast and two sticks protruding from her chin steps forward from an overgrown path of tall grass and walks out onto the runway. A small girl follows her and stands by her mother's side resting her head against her thigh. An old man, farther back, wearing only a penis string, stands by the forest's edge holding a bow and arrow in one hand and scratching his leg with the other.

Seeing these people, I feel that old sensation brought on when two vastly different worlds are suddenly juxtaposed. Each of us awestruck by the other. All action seems to slow down as we each try to comprehend the existence of the other, someone so vastly different from that world we call our own.

"There he is," says Father John pointing straight ahead. Through the smudged windshield I can just make out a group of Indians standing outside one of the mission's wooden buildings. Among them is Machadão, the village shaman I met on my first trip here, as well as Pedro, an older shaman who lives in one of the neighboring settlements. With them is Father Guilherme, cigarette in hand, dressed in a striped shirt, white shorts, and sandals. He has retained the stocky look of a prizefighter, but the years have also given him more gray and a receding hairline. "Guilherme has changed," Father John said on the ride in. "He is no longer a priest. He's become a Yanomami." Stepping from the truck I shake hands with Guilherme then clumsily with Machadão and Pedro. I let the camera roll, hoping to use this moment in the film I am currently making.

Machadão appears to be much smaller and thinner than I remember him. But what has not changed is that intelligent energy in his eyes, constantly scanning, absorbing what you say, never missing a gesture or intonation. He begins speaking to Pedro in Yanoman, then lets forth a wild laugh.

"He remembers you from before," says Father John smiling. "He says that you came here with a camera but with another man."

The next morning I survey the mission grounds: more order,

more buildings, less tension. The impending sense of disaster which permeated this community during the gold rush also seems to have dissipated. There is a new medical clinic, a new school-house, a full-time cook, two full-time nurses, and a second priest to assist in teaching and administrating the mission. The Indians have recently destroyed the old maloca adjacent to the mission, and are constructing a new one about a twenty-minute walk from here. Machadão, Father John told me, has left the communal structure of the village and set up his own little hut for his wife and nine children. "We asked them to move their community further away. It was too close," Father Guilherme said. He paused before adding, "For our relationship." The tentative seduction begun by Father Calleri some three decades ago has evolved into something more permanent. A strong bond now exists between the missionaries and the Indians. But the courtship is over. The Indians have acknowledged that the missionaries are a permanent fixture in the forest, and that their lives, particularly those of their children, will never be the same.

Life has improved dramatically for the Indians since 1989, and these missionaries have contributed to the changes. Forty-five thousand gold miners have been evicted from Yanomami territory and there is now an international effort to eradicate malaria and bring medical care to sick Indians in distant villages. Funded in part by the World Health Organization, this program is coordinated by Brazil's National Foundation for Health and unites the work of its own personnel with that of doctors and nurses sent here under the auspices of the Committee for the Creation of the Yanomami Park, Medicines du Monde, Medicines sans Frontier, and various Protestant and Catholic missions based throughout Yanomami territory. It was the domestic and international public outcry which brought the medical relief and millions of dollars of aid that has come with it. Dedicated teams of doctors and nurses have managed to quell the tide of epidemics, but there are still serious problems in the region. In some Yanomami communities, particularly in the state of Amazonas, malaria infects eighty percent of the population. More than half of those infected suffer from its most lethal strain, falciparum. Since 1989, these Indians have lost twenty-one percent of their population to infectious diseases introduced by outsiders. Fortunately, the majority of deaths came at the height of the gold rush and the numbers have dwindled in recent years. For the moment, the Yanomami have avoided becoming another statistic in Brazil's long list of disappearing cultures. But all this international attention has raised suspicions among local politicians. The mayor of a frontier town bordering Yanomami territory stated recently that "Too much benevolence is suspicious."

Although my limited budget will permit me only a few days here, I don't want to start filming too quickly. I'd like for the villagers here to get to know me once again. I'd also like a better understanding of the changes that have taken place before I start asking questions. So I keep the camera under wraps, and wander about the village eating mangos and talking with passersby. Earlier I met up again with the daughter of Carrera, the village leader, and, just as she had done three years ago, she threatened me with a machete. She then said something and broke into laughter as she put away the long, sharp blade. I had no idea what it was she said, but I wouldn't be surprised if was another crack about my resemblance to a rodent.

In the afternoon, Francisco and I set up for an interview with Father Guilherme in the shade of a large tree adjacent to the priests' lodging, a wooden one-level structure painted a rich dark blue. Six years earlier, Guilherme had told me that "If I were to be born again, I would like to be reborn a Yanomami." At the time his comment struck me as odd but innocent. In the intervening years, however, I've learned to mistrust the all-embracing sentiments of outsiders swept up by a desire to help the Indians. The naive and unbridled idealization of the Indian was the double-edged sword of the rain forest movement. Its catalytic energy inspired the public outcry which helped resolve the Yanomami crisis, yet its need for perfect icons created a dangerous dilemma for groups such as the Kayapo who could never live up to the unrealistic expectations of admiring whites. I am now suspicious of anyone who professes a special identification with the Indian. I mistrust their all-encompassing enthusiasm that turns people into kitsch objects and denies them the possibility of ambiguity and imperfection. No one can live up to those ideals, and no one should be subjected to them. So now more than ever, I am interested in seeing if Guilherme's beliefs have in any way been tempered by the changing times.

"I'd never be a good Yanomami," he says when I refer to his earlier comment. "I've realized I cannot be a good one, but I try to be a very good friend of the Yanomami," he adds. "I'm trying to understand all the positive aspects of their culture and, with benevolent eyes, I try to forgive the negative aspects of their culture. So my commitment to these people, considering the passion I have for them, is to try to guarantee their survival."

We stop for a minute waiting for the light to change. Harsh beams of the midday sun have been breaking through the foliage, ruining my shot. I've gotten tired of trying to reposition Guilherme under bits of shade so this time we decide to just sit patiently for the angle of the sun to change. As we wait, I think about this priest and the sixteen years he has spent working with these people. He speaks their language, knows their culture intimately, and is considered by most villagers to be their "true friend." Those are not easy accomplishments. Though he has managed to immerse himself in their lives, he is probably right. He will never become an Indian, not in this life and probably not in the next. But to me, his devotion appears to be saintlike and I wonder if his church will ever recognize his efforts. Too far from Rome, too controversial, and, I conclude, not enough of a self-promoter. "The children that are growing up here are like my sons," he tells me as we conclude the interview. "I could die for them; maybe if the situation arose, I could even kill to defend them." The priest pauses for a second and adjusts his black, thick-rimmed glasses, perhaps feeling the weight of his commandment-breaking last statement. "This is because I feel for these people as if they were my own, as if I belonged to them, as if I was adopted by them. We are connected in that we suffer the same problems, the same hardships of existing in such a difficult environment. All this becomes a challenge to strengthen my will to stay here and work with them."

The next morning Father Guilherme tells me there will be a meeting with the adults and adolescents of Wakathautheri. Upon "their approval," he says, it will be determined whether I can film in the village. This sudden introduction of formal protocol has taken me a little bit by surprise. On my last trip here I simply approached Carrerra, the village leader, and presented him with gifts of machetes, fishhooks, and knives. I explained my intentions and agreed to leave more gifts for the community when I departed. He contemplated my request, asked how long I would be staying, and then granted me permission to film. It was simple. I had done what any outsider would have done. That, I gathered, was the problem as far as the missionaries were concerned. In past years the miners had done exactly the same thing. They gave gifts of food, machetes, and clothing in exchange for the right to mine the Indians' lands. It now seems that the missionaries are intent on abolishing the means of seduction that they and others had used to access and manipulate this culture. They're trying to replace it with a new, more democratic procedure based on group decision making rather than the desire and traditional power of one individual.

The meeting takes place in a one-room schoolhouse recently constructed, Guilherme tells us, in order "to prepare the people to defend themselves." Those attending are mostly men, but there are a few adolescent girls and older women. The priest introduces Francisco and I in the Yanoman language and stands off to the side to act as a translator when necessary. Carrera is the first to speak and his tone is surprisingly confrontational.

Por que voce está aqui? "Why did you come here?" he says.

Eu estou aqui porque. . . . "I am here," I say, "because I want to make a film to show my people how the Yanomami live today, after the gold rush."

E o outro filme, o que voce fes come ele? "What did you do with the other pictures that you took here?" asks a young man who is maybe sixteen years old.

O outro filme. . . . "The other film. . . ." I respond. "That one I showed it in on television in America and in Ireland, Britain, Austria, Spain, Australia, and many countries in South America."

Father Guilherme interrupts at that point. He explains that

Davi Kopenawa, who lives in an adjacent village, stayed at my house when he first came to America. He is well known among these villagers, respected for the way he campaigned internationally in defense of their people. The atmosphere changes. The Indians appear to relax. The tone and direction of the questions begins to change. How long will I stay? Do I know Bruce (Bruce Albert, the French anthropologist)? Do I have a woman? How many children do I have? Who is my friend Francisco? Where is the other man (Vincent) whom I was with on the last trip?

I answer each of their questions as best I can. When my Portuguese falters, Francisco jumps in with a quick translation. After about twenty minutes everyone appears satisfied. None of the women have spoken. There are only silence and blank faces.

Tudo bem! "Okay," says Father Guilherme suddenly. He and Carrera exchange a few words in Yanoman. Rising from their chairs, Machadão, Carrera, and the older men exit the room with the adolescents and women following. The priest turns to me and lights a cigarette. He looks content. "You can film," he says. "Begin anytime." No one had spoken about the fishhooks, machetes, and knives we have brought as presents for the community. At Father John's request, I gave them to Father Guilherme when we arrived. He placed them in a storage room adjacent to the radio shack to distribute or dispose of as he so desires. When will the Indians see them? After we leave, I guess. Maybe never. I don't ask. I am a guest and this is their terrain.

After this formal encounter in the schoolhouse, I better understand Guilherme's cryptic statement about preparing the Indians to "defend themselves." Recent events have necessitated public forums like this one. On July 23, 1993, near Haximu, a remote village near Brazil's border with Venezuela, fourteen Indians were murdered by Brazilian miners in an incident that the federal prosecutor is classifying as an act of genocide. Among the victims were three adolescent girls and seven children ranging in age from eight years to one year of age. In the first reports of this incident, the exact details were shrouded by language and cultural barriers. Initially seventy Yanomami were reported to have been killed. Then within a few days the number was reduced to thirty. Some articles claimed the miners killed the Indians as an act of protest against a recent government eviction of prospectors from the area. Another report stated that the killings were prompted by revenge, that Brazilian miners were seeking to punish the Yanomami because they had served as scouts for the Venezuelan military tracking gold prospectors who had crossed into Venezuelan territory. However, the most realistic assessment of the massacre stressed the fact that problems have occurred whenever whites have attempted to barter for the Indians' resources.

The anthropologist Bruce Albert happened to be in the region when the killings took place. He conducted extensive interviews with the survivors, visited the site of the massacre, and collaborated with the federal prosecutor's office in the earliest stages of the investigation. From the testimonies of the survivors, Albert learned that the Yanomami of Haximu had been involved in an ongoing series of exchanges with prospectors over a period of several months. Following in the footsteps of missionaries and Indian agents, the miners had given the Indians gifts of hammocks, guns, and ammunition in exchange for permission to work in the area. A balance of power had been struck. The terms of this informal agreement, as far as the Indians were concerned, appeared to be clear: the miners were a steady source of material goods for the Indians just as missionaries and Indian agents had been for other communities in the past. But the miners had another vision of this relationship. Their perception of the balance of power was based on their experiences in the gold rush. They were prepared to entertain some of the Indians' requests, but they felt free to arbitrarily dismiss and ignore others. The prospectors acted as if they were still part of a conquering army. They had forgotten that times had changed and now they were outnumbered.

The wildcat prospectors working in this border region had been part of a clandestine group of two thousand men who had managed to remain in Yanomami territory after the 1992 demarcation which had officially made their presence illegal. Working in small bands of ten and twenty, these men no longer commanded the presence of the legions of miners who had swept through these forests in the late 1980s. Not only were they outmanned but—because they had been giving guns as gifts—they had armed a people who were their potential adversaries. Initially they appeased the Indians with gifts, but over time they refused to honor their promises of machetes, guns, and ammunition. Then the ecological damage caused by the miners' presence began to take its toll. The local rivers became brown and filthy from the runoff of hydraulic mining and game animals became increasingly scarce. The people of Haximu began demanding greater compensation for these hardships. The miners responded with more false promises or simply gave the Indians less than they had originally agreed upon. Conflicts arose. The equilibrium between the two groups shifted. The Indians' relationship was transformed from one of dependency to one of independence and open hostility. Then the violence started.

In early July a young Yanomami *tuxawa* (leader) named Kerrero accompanied by another Indian named Davi arrived at a miner's encampment threatening a Brazilian prospector with a shotgun after an argument about an unfulfilled promise of some trade goods. Kerrero fired his shotgun at the man, but there were no injuries. The miner fled into the forest and the Indians destroyed the encampment. Then on July 15, 1993, six Yanomami men, at the request of their village elders, went to another miner's encampment on the Rio Tabocca to lay claim to food, goods, and a gun that they had been promised by a prospector in exchange for the right to continue working in the region. But the miners had been expecting them. They lured the Indians into the forest and killed four of them. Two young men managed to escape. One hid in the forest while the other fled back to the village. The survivor informed the community of what had happened. Village leaders, concerned about the spirits of the dead, sent the young man back to the site of the murders with several other villagers. The bodies of the victims, which had been buried by the miners, were exhumed and cremated. The Yanomami then pulverized the carbonized bones and, according to custom, buried them next to the domestic fires of their families. In the case of children, custom dictates that the ashes be mixed with a banana gruel and consumed by the parents. Consuming the ashes of the deceased assures that the spirits can return to the "world of the dead" located at the back of the sky. If the spirits are not treated in this fashion, they are believed to roam between the world of the dead and our world, causing prolonged bouts of melancholy in the living, a state considered to be worse than death itself.

According to Yanomami tradition, revenge for the dead must be exacted by taking the lives of the perpetrators. So several days later, a group of Indians attacked the miner's encampment killing one prospector and wounding another. The Indians bludgeoned the head of the dead man with machetes, shot his body full of arrows, then stole ammunition and a shotgun from the encampment. In response, various bands of miners in the area organized a vigilante group of fifteen men to retaliate. Over a period of two weeks, the group armed themselves with shotguns and pistols and traveled to Haximu. But when they arrived at the remote village, it was deserted. Frustrated, they burned the maloca to the ground, and set off into the forest in search of the Indians. During this same period, a group of Haximu warriors—still intent on exacting revenge—conducted a second raid against another mining site, wounding one prospector and scaring several others into the forest.

The next battle in this jungle war occurred on July 23, when the vigilante band of miners encircled a temporary village inhabited by the people of Haximu. Most of the men had gone to the neighboring community of Makayu for a festival commemorating the dead. They had left the others unprotected believing that, according to their code of honor, women and children would not be vulnerable to attack during times of warfare. The miners, however, lived by a different code. They surrounded the village and opened fire. Nineteen Indians were there when the shooting began. Five managed to escape. Twelve people were killed instantly. Among the dead were three adolescent girls, six children, and a one-year-old baby. After several minutes of gunfire, the prospectors—according to the testimonies of survivors who hid in the village—completed their work with knives and machetes. Most of the Indians' bodies were desecrated beyond recognition. A young girl suffered severe head wounds and died several days after the attack.

Almost one month later, the prospectors heard on the radio that news of the massacre had reached the outside world. They immediately fled their encampments and returned to Boa Vista. Some were arrested by the federal police. Others managed to escape into hiding in the nearby states of Acre and Amazonas. By this time the Indians had recovered the bodies of the dead and carried out their ceremonial preparations. They burned the corpses and placed the ashes in a gourd sealed with honey, careful to follow the proscribed traditions for containing the spirits of the dead. The final ceremony of ingesting and burying the ashes had yet to take place when Bruce Albert accompanied the federal police to the site of the massacre. What for the Yanomami was considered a sacred and life-preserving act became for the federal prosecutor's office a seemingly unsurpassable obstacle in their attempt to build a case. There were no bodies. No material evidence. Although two of the prospector's cooks and two miners had identified two suspects, the local judge in Boa Vista released those accused within weeks of the murders on grounds that there was not sufficient evidence to hold them in custody. When I did a follow-up story on the massacre in early September of 1993, I interviewed Aurelio Rios, a young federal prosecutor in Brasilia who had been assigned to the case. In spite of the release of two suspects, Rios seemed determined to exact justice for the killings. He was classifying the incident as genocide. If successful, this would be the first proven case involving indigenous people in the Americas. "What proof was there that six million Jews died in German gas chambers during the reign of the Nazis?" he asked rhetorically during an interview in his office in Brasilia late one afternoon. "There were no bodies . . . no records. There was only testimony from the survivors who witnessed what had happened." A successful prosecution of the Haximu case, he said, was a matter "of adapting the law to this other reality."

On December 19, 1996, five Brazilian gold miners were convicted in a federal court of murder and genocide in the 1993 killings of the thirteen Yanomami Indians from the village of Haximu. Each of the miners received sentences of twenty years in prison. To date, only one of the convicted felons, a man by the name of Joao Neto, has been apprehended.

"**M**y ancestors who transformed themselves into whites and who were carried away by the floods, it is their land that you inhabit now," Machadão tells me outside the small maloca he has constructed for his wife and children. "Our land is still here. It stops itself here," he says pointing off into the forest to his right. "It is for that reason I do not want the gold miners to try and take from us our land. The gold miners think that we are infants and that we are ignorant. They say to themselves 'I am going to give them objects and I am going to take their land.' This is how they attempt to deceive us, but we are adults. It is only them who take us for children. They think 'The Yanomami are ignorant, we want to take their land,' and that is why they give us presents while lying to us."

It is the morning of our last day here. After a brief but torrential downpour, we have begun interviewing Machadão, the man who over the years has become not only a key informant, but someone I have come to consider a friend, my trusted link to the world of the Yanomami.

"What are your concerns for the future?" I ask Machadão as Guilherme diligently translates my question into Yanoman.

"You the whites, you must stop the gold miners from coming into our lands. This is what I think. I am not friends with the whites except for the Father who lives here with us. It is us who let him live here. He cures us with his medicines. We are friends with him. The gold miners do not possess the medicines. They do not do anything but make us sick and we die."

"There are many whites in the cities who say that the Yanomami should become like them," I say to Machadão. "They say that many of you are already like the whites. What do you think of this idea?"

"The whites stare at the Yanomami because they do not recognize them. The Yanomami appear to them to be a very different people. After having looked and stared, the whites ask themselves, 'Who are these people who act like this?' Then they say that they are like us, that they want to be our friends.

They think that and for that reason they stare at us so as to be our friends. But only the trusted whites are our true friends and that is the way it should be. The gold miners make believe as if they are our friends, but they are not. They are bad. They are only pretending to be friends. They tell us lies. They are pretending. The trusted whites who come to visit us see our festivals and say 'Oh look, this is who the Yanomami are and what they are doing is good.' These people are our true friends."

Interviewing Machadão makes me think about all the changes that have taken place here since the gold rush. I feel good about the work I have done, believing that in a small way I have contributed to the preservation of this culture. At midday a plane lands for a brief stop at the Catrimani Mission runway. Davi Kopenawa is among the passengers. We drink some small cups of cafezinho and talk about his work and the films I have made in recent years. It's been three years since I have seen him, and he has continued to travel extensively in North America and Europe. Today he is on his way to a regional conference of indigenous leaders in a trip paid for by the missionaries. Towards the end of our talk, Davi tells me he appreciates the fact that I have made several films about Indians in the forest. He says he has met many people in the United States and Europe who have seen them. The films, he says, make it easier to explain to people what the Yanomami have been going through in these past years. I walk down to the runway with him and watch as his plane banks west over the forest and heads towards Boa Vista. I walk back to the mission with a renewed sense of satisfaction in my work. I feel more accepted by these people, more relaxed, less the critical outside observer. Three young hunters pass me by with turtles strapped to their backs, and next to the mission medical clinic, a young woman is knocking mangos out of a tree with a long stick. She smiles as I pass and a mango falls to the ground. I begin to toy with the idea of what it would be like to spend several years living among these Indians as Guilherme and Father John have done. The idea is alluring, but carries with it a vague and burdensome feeling. *Is it fatigue or the weight of self-deception?*

In the afternoon, I return to Machadão's maloca to get some final shots which I will need to complete my film. When we arrive, we are told by his oldest son that he is inside the little maloca. When I enter the dark and smoky confines of his home, I squat and take a moment to let my eyes adjust to the light. Then before me appears a primordial image. Machadão sits in his hammock finishing his midday meal. His wife and three small children sit scattered about in various small hammocks holding round gourds of some kind of milky plantain broth. A gray smoke lingers everywhere, and I can taste its ashen fumes. Machadão looks content, rested, and a little surprised to see me.

Posso filmar um pouco com voces depois que voce terminar sua comida. "Can we film a little with you after you finish with your food?"

Certo. "Certainly," he says with a big smile. *Depois.* "After."

Respectful of his privacy, I rejoin Francisco outside in the muddy courtyard and await the arrival of my friend. Ten minutes go by. I check on him again. He has finished eating, but he remains in the dark, in his hammock, relaxed and still smiling. I give a halfhearted wave which he acknowledges with an awkward lifting of his hand. *What now?*

I decide not to press further with my request and return once again to the muddy clearing in front of his hut where Francisco and I make small talk and throw stones at trees in the forest. Five minutes later, Machadão still has not come out. An old woman passes by and I get a shot of her as she wobbles bowlegged down a slippery path towards the new communal village. "Look at that," says Francisco pointing to a parakeet nestled amidst the branches of a nearby tree. I turn and in that instant I hear a twig break. Looking back I see Machadão exit the little hut, bow and arrow in hand. As he leaps nimbly into the forest he glances over his shoulder, and then disappears behind a wall of tropical flora. I stand there stunned. He was simply waiting until I turned my back to escape into the forest.

"Should we go after him?" asks Francisco.

I'm struck dumb by Machadão's vanishing act. Not only have I missed the opportunity to get a sequence I desperately need, but Machadão—with whom I shared a mutual trust, or so I let myself believe—has deceived me.

Francisco and I gather our equipment and head off down the

path back to the mission outpost. We pass the Indians' large communal village and wave to a few Yanomami putting the finishing touches on the roof of the maloca. A few of the men laugh at us. Others smile and wave. As I walk, I consider what has just happened. Deceit was not the issue here. Survival was. Machadão needs to hunt in order to feed his family. My needs, my intentions, they're part of my world—the white man's priorities. That's just the way it is. Conflicting agendas of disparate worlds. An old story. As old as that first encounter between whites and Indians on the shores of the Caribbean. No one has ever been able to get around it. Not even me.

ACKNOWLEDGMENTS

This book could not have been written without the generous help of colleagues, friends, and untold strangers I encountered during a decade of traveling and working in the Brazilian Amazon. I am particularly grateful to Chris Caris at Realis Pictures in New York and to Patricia Monte-Môr and José Ignacio Parente of Interior Productions in Rio de Janeiro, three great collaborators as well as trusted friends who were always there when I needed them.

Alcida Ramos at the University of Brasilia, Terence Turner at the University of Chicago, and Bruce Albert at ORSTOM in Paris provided critical insights during the research and editing stages of this work. Many ideas drawn from their books and articles were adapted by me into this work in my own eclectic distillations. In particular I was influenced by Alcida Ramos's "The Hypereal Indian" and "From Eden to Limbo: The Construction of Indigenism in Brazil," Terence Turner's "Representing, Resisting, Rethinking: Historical Transformations of Kayapo Culture and Anthropological Analysis," and Bruce Albert's "La Fumée du Métal: Histoire du contact chez les Yanomami (Brésil)."

Although this book is based almost exclusively on my personal experiences, I relied on several books for background information, including John Hemming's *Amazon Frontier*, Ricardo Rezende's *Rio Maria*, Eric R. Wolf's *Europe and the People Without*

History, Andrew Revkin's *The Burning Season*, Napoleon Chagnon's *The Fierce People*, Shelton Davis's *Victims of the Miracle*, Sue Branford and Oreil Glock's *The Last Frontier*, Victor Turner's *The Anthropology of Performance*, the Instituto Socioambiental's *Povos Indígenas No Brasil 1991/1995*, as well as various articles including Beth A. Conklin and Laura R. Graham's "The Shifting Middle Ground," Cecilia McCallum's "The Veja Payakan," and Scott Wallace's "Rape and Politics in the Rain Forest." The Ford Foundation kindly provided financial support for the task of putting words to paper, and the Blue Mountain Center provided the environment for its initial genesis.

I had the good fortune of working with Rosemary Ahern, a caring and extremely talented editor whose insights and comments allowed me to create a work that grew beyond my expectations. Larry Schoen and Madeleine Cousineau Adriance read portions of the manuscript and provided many helpful comments and suggestions. Special thanks to Cristina Miranda at Realis Pictures for her excellent research, Sandra Martin, my agent, for walking into my studio several years ago and asking me if I had ever thought about writing a book, Ann Marlowe, for her excellent copy editing and thorough fact-checking, and Kari Paschall at Dutton. Thanks also to Mario Lo Boa, Vincent Carelli, Tito Rosenberg, Maria Byington, Biorn Maybury-Lewis, Dominique Gallois, and Francisco Latorre for hard work and friendship in the field. Finally I am indebted to the Consolata Missionaries, the Rainforest Foundation, Miranda Smith, Stephen Schwartzman, Ken Taylor, Anthony Anderson, Andrea Taylor, David Maybury-Lewis, Davi Kopenawa, Machadão Yanomami, Puketheri Kayapo, Cultural Survival, Survival International, the Brazil Network, the Committee for the Creation of the Yanomami Park, Insituto Socioambiental, Centro do Trabalho Indigenista, the villages of Wakathautheri and Pukanu, and the untold other gold miners, peasants, anthropologists, and indigenous people of Amazonia who generously shared with me their hearts and homes during this long journey. *Um grande abraço*.

INDEX